Also by Ilka Tampke

Skin

SONGWOMAN

ILKA TAMPKE

HODDER

First published in Great Britain in 2018 by Hodder & Stoughton
An Hachette UK company

This paperback edition published in 2019

1

A CIP catalogue record for this title is available from the British Library

Paperback ISBN 9781473616493

Typeset in Garamond Premier Pro

Printed and bound in Great Britain by Clays Ltd, Elcograf S.p.A.

Hodder & Stoughton policy is to use papers that are natural, renewable and
recyclable products and made from wood grown in sustainable forests.
The logging and manufacturing processes are expected to conform to the
environmental regulations of the country of origin.

Hodder & Stoughton Ltd
Carmelite House
50 Victoria Embankment
London EC4Y 0DZ

www.hodder.co.uk

For Mum and May, who helped me find the elusive lake.

ALBION
47AD

CARVETTI

STENWIC

PARISI

BRIGANTES

MÔN

DECEANGLI

ERYR MOUNTAINS

CORITANI

ORDOVICES

CORNOVII

ICENI

DEMETAE

DOBUNNI

CATUVELLAUNI

TRINOVANITES

LLANMELIN
SILURES

RIVER
HABERN

CAMULODUNUM

ATREBATES

REGNI

CANTII

BELGAE

PORT OF DUBRIS

DUMNONII

DUROTRIGES

PORT OF BONONIA

ROMAN BRITAIN

FREE TRIBES

I'm a craftsman, I'm a radiant singer;
I'm as hard as steel, I'm a wizard, I'm a sage, I'm a craftsman;
I'm a serpent, I am desire, I eat voraciously,
I'm not a stunned poet, I don't falter.

From 'The Haven of Poets'
The Book of Taliesin

1

Memory

All of the earth is made by a song.
Each river, each stone, a different note.
Those who sing are the Mothers and we worship them.

The Singing was before time, before seasons,
but in every generation, there is one woman who can remember it.
I am that woman.
I am the one who carries creation.

THE MOTHER'S whiskers quivered. Her ears flicked forward then back, though neither Neha nor I made the slightest rustle as we crouched behind the cover of sedge.

She was a mountain hare, tough and fatless, but would give our sunken bellies something to suck on. If we could catch her. She loped one length closer to the three leverets grazing near their nest. They were only days old. But what little meat covered their bones would at least be tender.

Neha whimpered as she stared at our prey. I knew how she felt. Slowly I raised my weapon. I was no trained slingswoman but a year's hungry practice had given me fair confidence I would make this mark. Neha took her silent command. I sensed her haunches tighten as she readied to strike.

I drew a plum-sized stone back into the plaited gut, stretched it taut, aimed, then released. It hit the hare's shoulder, stunning her just long enough for Neha to pounce and break her neck with one swift crunch. The leverets scattered. I did not pursue them. The mother would be meat enough for several days, accompanied by ground elder shoots if the weather was still kind enough to coax them up.

The carcass flopped against my thigh as we walked back to our cavern, my mouth flooding at the thought of meat juices sizzling over the fire. I paused at a branch in the trackway that I did not immediately recognise. The turns and dips of the mountainside were less familiar since autumn had begun to strip the forest of leaves. But where my senses became unsure, Neha's never did, and we soon reached the crag of mossy rock set in the hillside that was our home, our doorway a fissure in the stone, hidden between ferns.

Inside, I dropped the hare on the ground and squatted at the hearth to kindle the embers cooled by the chill morning. Neha watched me, eager for the spoils of our hunt.

The flames surged, brightening the walls of folded limestone that had sheltered us through every season, puckered and pale, unmarked by human hand, except for the row of grooves I had scratched near the head of our sleeping place to mark the setting of each day.

Our dwelling place was not without comfort. There was height enough to clear the smoke, yet it was not so cavernous that I could not seal most of the crevices with clumps of moss against the drafts. Our bed was dried grasses covered with the pelt of a sow that wolves had killed and abandoned half eaten, leaving me with a bristly bedskin. The short sword beside it and the sling and knife at my waist were my only possessions.

The grooves above my bed numbered almost five hundred. Five hundred nights slept in this Mothers' place, this wild place.

Five hundred days since I had seen another human face. Or perhaps I should say another face of living flesh, for there were always faces in the knots of the oak trunks and the crags of the cliffs; ghosts of my tribe that had followed me, asking why I had abandoned them. Why I had not kept them safe.

I grabbed the hare and stood up, lurching with the light-headedness of hunger. I was thin, but my limbs were roped with muscle from the daily descent to the river. There was food enough for one who had learned to distinguish the edible from the poisonous of the forest fruits. We had fed on small quarry, berries and roots that lay dormant beneath the snow, but, in truth, I had chosen to eat little. For I was full to sickening with what I had seen, with what I had done.

Once I had been frightened to sleep alone. Now I could scarcely remember the shape or smell of another body, let alone imagine one lying beside me. Now I would rejoice to know only that fear.

I stepped back out through the cave's opening. An autumn shower had left droplets on every twig and blade. A wind stirred, loosening leaves to the ground. The forest was in flux.

I breathed the wet air. This was my place now. I had been condemned to it. It had not forgiven me, but it had chosen to let me live. There was no one I could harm here and nothing that could harm me. My breath was the howling winds and my skin was the mist that held to the mountainside. I was this forest place.

I walked a short distance, then pulled my knife from my belt, lifted the hare, and sliced its underside from throat to anus, holding it at arm's length while the innards splashed to the ground. Neha looked to me, cocking her head, and I nodded my permission for her to eat. The meat would strengthen us both and we would need it.

With the coming of winter, it was time to come down from the mountain. It was time to rejoin my kind. I was strong enough now, I hoped. I had eaten directly of the Mothers' meat and drunk of their rivers' water. I knew this country as a woman knows her own body, her own skin.

I needed to know it thus, because I was its protector.

I knew that when I returned to the world of the tribes, the hounds of change would be feasting on their own hunt spoils, threatening new laws, new knowledge, new language that called this land their own. I had been one year in a place where the soldiers could not touch me. Now I had to return to see what they had done.

Crouching on my haunches, I slit the hare's neck and began working the pelt free from its shoulders. As well as the innards, Neha would eat the skin, the feet and the head. The muscles were mine. I hooked a thick hank of hair behind my shoulder. My curls were now so matted and strewn with grass seeds that no combing or washing would ever release them. I wore my hair thus because I was in mourning.

But my grief could continue no longer.

I had a title to bear. I had a war to win.

✠

My calves ached from walking. It had taken four days to be free of the mountains, and another three to convince those I'd met on the farm roads that I was not a scout for Plautius, the Roman Governor who also sought the war chief Caradog.

It was an iron miner, his clothing as frayed as my own, who told me, in an accent so broad I could barely understand it, that I was very near to the township of Llanmelin, but that the war chief had not been seen there for nine parts of the year.

Nine parts. The time our poets said it took to travel to the hidden world, Annwyn, and back. I smiled my thanks. In western Albion, as yet unclaimed by Rome, the ways of the tribes were unchanged. I knew these ways, I had trained in them, and I reminded myself, as I walked towards Llanmelin, that I could expect to find much that was bound in riddles.

Through dense woodland, I heard the settlement before I saw it: lowing cattle, striking hammers, children screeching in play. Beyond the next turn it stood before me: Llanmelin, tribal centre of the mighty Silures, one of the last free tribes. If this was where Caradog had taken refuge, he had chosen cleverly, for I had not seen the hill town until I stood almost at its gates. Two human heads stared blankly from wooden stakes, flanking the entrance path. Their ash grey faces were clean-shaven, belonging to Rome or her fighters and not long dead. Neha sniffed at the dried blood that had dribbled down the stakes. I called her back. They were not worthy even to feed our animals.

I passed between them and began the ascent to the gate. Builders were at work on the ramparts, digging a second ditch, their picks ringing as they hit the limestone bed. Llanmelin was strengthening its defences.

'Halt there!' A gate guard dropped from his platform to block my path. He was taller and fairer-skinned than the dark, compact men working the walls, and he questioned me with a gaze so direct I could scarcely meet it. 'What is your purpose?' he asked. 'We have scant spare grain for beggars here.'

I knew I looked like a fringe-woman. I had washed my dress in the river stones, but the fabric was in rags, and my cloak was spattered with mud from my journey. 'I am no wanderer. My home was Caer Cad of the Durotriges and I come seeking Caradog of the Catuvellauni.'

The guard looked suspicious. 'He commands many more than the Catuvellauni now.'

'Is he within?'

'Why do you seek him?'

'I would speak to him directly—'

'Speak to me or you will not pass a step closer.'

Who was this tribesman to command a knowledge-bearer, albeit one who stank of bat piss? 'Do you threaten a high journeywoman?' I said, drawing back my shoulders. There had been no time before the attack for my teachers to pierce my forehead with the dark patterns that would mark me as a journeywoman, a woman of learning. But the sword that hung at my belt spoke of my position. I put my hand to its hilt.

He frowned as he read the shapes carved into the bone. Then I startled as he broke into laughter.

'What amuses you, tribesman?' This guard was beginning to grind at my patience.

'The Mothers' mischief,' he said, smiling. 'They give me a priestess wrapped as a fringe-wretch.'

'They give *you* nothing,' I said. 'Who is chieftain here?'

'Hefin commands Llanmelin—' the guard leaned towards me '— but he, in turn, is commanded by Caradog.' He straightened back to his full height as I stared at him, galled by his loose tongue. 'Be sure to bathe before you see him,' he added. 'He prefers his visitors more sweetly scented.'

'I will bathe,' I said, furious. 'And *you* can be sure that I will speak to Caradog of his guard's disrespect.'

With this he laughed even harder and stepped aside for me to pass. 'He will be delighted to hear it.'

Inside the gate, a surge of sorrow and relief broke my stride at the sight of the township spread before me—the first I had entered since I left Caer Cad.

My wild-fed limbs, so tireless in the forest, began to shake as Neha and I walked past the grain stores, the clustered roundhouses, the goat pens, and ale huts with their rich odours of rotting barley. Everywhere there were people, tending, crafting, kneeling at querns. Conscious of my dishevelment, I passed them quickly.

'Behind the forge huts,' answered one of the women when I asked where I would find the chieftain's hall.

Only when I saw the vast building—more than a hundred paces in circumference, its walls as thick as an oak trunk, its roof a mighty cone of silver thatch reaching almost to the ground—did I truly know I was returned to a place of the tribes.

Hefin's stable yards were crowded with ponies. Caradog must have been persuasive to have gained the alliance of such a prosperous king. I knew he had ridden the breadth of Albion since the Romans came, gathering fighters to join his war band, enticing those who opposed Empire rule wherever their leaders did not. It was said that his warriors wore tartans from every clan of Albion. But the Silures were the first whole tribe who had knelt at his sword.

To the east of the chieftain's hall was the cook hut, marked by a white hide nailed over the doorway. I glanced at my blackened nails and turned towards it. The guard was right; I could not stand before a man such as Caradog until I had bathed.

I struck the bell and a servant appeared through the doorskins, her face falling in disgust at the sight of me. 'I am no dirt-dweller,' I said quickly, emotion rising in my chest. 'I come from deer country, though I am skin to the dog.' The words tumbled out as the servant's frown blurred before me. 'I am a high journeywoman but I have wild-dwelled for fifteen moons. And—' my legs swayed, '—my tribe are all dead.' I fell to my knees.

I do not know for how many hours they tended me in the cook hut. I was washed then given a linen under-robe and a dress of rust-coloured wool, simple clothing that was soft and clean against my skin. I ate a porridge of wheat and sheep's milk as a servant rubbed fat into my blistered feet. Another took up a bone comb and began running it through the ends of my hair, but I bade her stop. I was not yet ready to relinquish my loss. So she bound the tangled mats into one thick clump at the nape of my neck and picked out what burrs she could loosen without combing.

When I was almost ready, a noblewoman came through the doorskins and sat beside me at the fire. Her shawl was the hue of the sky and her hair was spirit pale, bound in intricate braids. 'You seek Caradog?' she asked in an eastern accent.

'Ay.'

'With what purpose?'

I looked at her. 'To win this war.'

'How?' She sat perfectly still. Her eyes were as blue as her shawl.

'I don't yet know.'

She frowned.

'But I bear a knowledge possessed by no other.'

'Of what?'

I paused. Had my story been so easily forgotten? Had it even reached these tribelands? 'Of the Mothers.'

She stared, appraising me, then nodded. 'War has tested our bonds to the Mothers,' she said. 'If you can rekindle them, then I, for one, will welcome you. But know this—' Her voice was soft. 'Caradog is a man of many weathers. He could deliver us or destroy us. Learn to predict him and you will bring us to firm ground.'

'Why are you telling me this?'

'Because I want my home to be safe again.'

I gazed at her as she spoke. An excess of silver ringed her wrists and swung from her earlobes. She was as luminous as the moon. 'I have lived under sky for more than a year,' I said. 'There is no storm that can frighten me.'

'Good then.' She smiled. I had not seen a woman more gracious.

'Are you journey-trained?' I asked, though she bore no mark.

'No.' She laughed. 'My name is Euvrain. I am Caradog's wife.'

I was mute with surprise.

She pulled one of the bands from her wrist and held it forth in her palm. 'You should wear some metal when you meet him.'

I walked through the late-day sun to the chieftain's hall, where Hefin and Caradog awaited me.

With their servant's announcement, I stepped through the inner doorskins. A fire smouldered at the centre of the hall, surrounded by several rings of benches carved with patterns of oak sprigs. Facing the doorway, in the strong place, sat a warrior. He was silver-bearded, though solid as a bull. 'Come forward,' he called. He could only be Hefin, for Caradog was surely a younger man. A bald-headed journeyman sat at his west, tracking my entrance with hooded eyes. He wore the bone-hued robe of an elder and clutched a staff, despite not being in ceremony.

Only when I neared the fire, did I notice another figure at the hall's periphery. He had his back to the room, pouring ale into a bronze cup. Was it him? There was something I recognised in the span of his shoulders, the height. As he turned, I stifled a yelp. It was the guard who had stopped me at the gate.

'Welcome, journeywoman,' he said, walking into the firelight. 'I am Caradog, son of Belinus.' He handed me the tribal cup with the same proud smile with which he had met me. Only now, at least, it accorded with his true position. Resistance leader. War Chief. The man whom Rome could not defeat.

I watched him above the rim of the cup as I drank. His eyes were shaped as if he had just heard a joke or was brewing to make one. A silver neck-ring marked him as royal, yet otherwise he wore no embellishment over the warrior's shirt I had met him in. He needed none.

'I have slain one hundred Roman soldiers at the Medway and many hundreds since,' he continued. 'I am enemy of Claudius, once prince of the Catuvellauni, now defender of all free tribes.'

'I call him Horse-end,' cut in Hefin, 'because of the amount of shit that comes out of his mouth.'

Caradog laughed. 'This is my faithful host, Hefin, and his journeyman, Prydd.'

I bowed, swallowing a smile. All warriors proclaimed themselves, but this man was as sure as the sun. 'I am Ailia of the Durotriges, skin to the dog, and enemy of Rome.'

'Fret not about Rome,' said Caradog. 'They will be gone by next spring.'

I half-laughed. 'How?'

'Because I will remove them. With the help of this war god, Hefin, of course. These are our tribelands. They will remain with us.'

He spoke as if there were truly no doubt. As if over fifteen kings had not already submitted to Claudius, by will or force. As if he were not the only man from eastern Albion who still fought them. 'How can you be so certain?' I asked.

'Because the Mothers will it. Because I will not rest until it is done.'

It was dazzling. I had never seen such self-belief, a spirit so sound, so impermeable, that it shone like polished metal. Silently, I praised the Mothers. They had given us someone who could protect us. I could swear allegiance to this man. I could commit to him my knowledge.

I felt the heat of his appraisal as he took back the cup.

'Ailia?' said Prydd the journeyman. 'Did you say this was your name?' His voice was unusually high-pitched.

'Yes.'

'Is your township Caer Cad?' Though I was of his kind, a knowledge-bearer, Prydd offered no kinship in his tone.

'Ay, though it now lies as ash.' I paused, suddenly hesitant to confess my status. 'I am thought to be—'

'I know who you are.' Prydd turned to Caradog. 'She is no mere journeywoman,' he said. 'Her story has travelled to the edges of Albion, although the journeymen have kept it well-hidden, lest it fall onto Roman ears.' His mouth twitched beneath a sparse moustache. 'She is Kendra of Albion.'

No one had yet bade me sit. I stood, unmoving, wondering what configuration of my story had survived and spread. Did it condemn me?

'This bud?' said Hefin. 'She is scarcely ripe!'

'Years do not determine it,' said Prydd.

Caradog stared at me. 'Why was I not told of her?'

'Why were none of us told of her?' said Hefin.

'We believed her dead. Slaughtered with Caer Cad,' said Prydd. 'She has been unseen for more than a year.' He looked at me. 'Where did you hide the Kendra's torch when it was so needed?'

I had not expected the accusation, as pointed as a whittled stick. 'I...I have lived wild in the mountains, and sat in solitude, in contemplation...'

It was common for journeypeople to take seclusion in untouched places. It had been my retribution, my strengthening. It had never occurred to me to see cowardice in it. I glanced at Caradog. What would he see?

'You lived a year alone in the forest?' asked Caradog. 'And hunted alone?'

'I had my dogess.' I wished Neha were beside me now, but she had not been permitted to enter the hall.

His brows lifted. 'Would that I had one warrior so skilled.'

'Would that I had a spear to show you one,' said Hefin and both men laughed.

'The Kendra is Mother-chosen,' said Prydd over their laughter. 'None may withhold her, not even the earthly woman who bears her title.' He looked at me. 'Your knowledge belongs not to you, but to the tribes.'

'And so here she is, wiseman!' said Caradog, before I could answer the reprimand. 'Are we not honoured to receive her in these tribelands?'

Something altered in Prydd's expression, as if he had turned a tarnished coin and found its other side gleaming. 'Indeed we are honoured,' he said.

'Why have you come to Tir Silures?' asked Hefin. 'We can scarcely keep our own journeymen here. They are always trotting off to Môn on the smallest spin of the stars...'

'To offer my aid to Caradog's war.'

'*Horse-end's* war?' said Hefin. 'Who do you think provides the men? And the weapons?'

'What aid do you propose?' asked Caradog, ignoring him. 'With respect, journeywoman, the Kendra is a figurehead, albeit a powerful one. I would be honoured to fight in your name, but this does not require you to stand at my side.'

I frowned. 'I bear the voice of the Mothers—'

'A long-grown oak bears the voice of the Mothers,' said Caradog, 'yet is of little use in crafting battle strategy.'

I flinched at the rudeness. Yet his question was valid. 'I can augur...and I have visioned for battle...' My answer wavered. I had been prepared to defend my actions. I had not been prepared to defend the Kendra's purpose. This had never been questioned.

Caradog shrugged. 'I have augurers already, but another would do no harm...'

'I think not,' said Prydd. 'That you are returned will hearten our warriors. But you will need to be taken to Môn and held in sanctuary.'

I met his stare. Most of our learning places had been destroyed by the Romans. The island of Môn was the last training place for the journeypeople. I had long hoped to go there. But not now. 'I have no wish to go to Môn—'

'You cannot stay here with the man the Romans pursue above all others,' said Prydd.

'Let her stay,' said Caradog. 'I am curious to learn of her talents.'

Prydd frowned. 'It invites danger, War Chief. To her and to yourself. She will serve us best from the safety of the Isle.'

I bristled. They were speaking of me as if I were a prize mare at market. As if I were not the Kendra of Albion. In Caer Cad I had been acknowledged as the voice of the Mothers, Albion's highest knowledge-bearer. Perhaps they knew, after all, what I had done, how utterly I had betrayed my tribe. Was this why they dishonoured me? But nothing had been spoken, no questions asked. 'I do not wish to be held in safety,' I told Prydd. 'I do not wish to be sheltered from this war. I am ready to stand in danger.'

'Then you shall.' Caradog was fastening his cloak. 'I like you,' he said. 'There's a place for you here.'

Hefin chuckled.

Prydd was silent.

'I didn't know war chiefs served as gate-keepers now,' I said to Caradog as we walked through the vestibule to the outer doorway.

'I do as I ask my fighters to do,' he said. 'How else can I expect their loyalty?'

'I only observe that it is not typical.'

'This war won't be won by doing what is typical.'

We stepped outside. Daylight revealed faint lines in his face, betraying the strain of three years of war. Though he was not especially fine featured, I saw now the evidence of royal breeding—the even bones, straight nose, strong jaw. His expression was one of shrewd intelligence, a sense of constant reckoning mixed with a little mirth. His skin was pale, his hair the colour of dark rust. His eyes were guarded by a heavy brow, their hue, in the last of the sunlight, a shade between grey and green, a melancholy, hybrid colour of neither sky nor earth. There was nothing in his outward form that claimed his authority, rather, it was his certainty, an inner sovereignty, that rendered him magnificent.

I stood, unspeaking. Perhaps it was that I had not been with any human kin for so many seasons, but I was unsettled by him, reminded of another, whom I wished to forget.

Hefin and Prydd emerged behind us. 'We will feast at sunset to welcome our guest,' said Hefin. 'Caradog, will you show her to her hut?'

'I must leave that to you, chieftain,' he answered. 'I have scarcely spoken with my men at camp today.'

'I can escort her,' said Prydd. 'And show her the township.'

I nodded my agreement. I did not crave time with him, but I was curious to see more of the settlement.

Caradog strode away.

Prydd led me down a street of densely built houses, until we stood before Llanmelin's temple. He seemed to take much pride in it. 'See its bell?' he said. 'The bronze contains gold shipped from Erin.'

Like all journey-temples, its walls were not round, but straight, aligned to the angles of the solstice, and built of timber instead of daub to keep the sky and its weather close. From each of the posts that marked the outer ambulatory hung a rag of lamb, piglet, or dog in various stages of decay: gifts for the sun to be borne by the crows. A cool wind carried the familiar scent.

Prydd led me back to the southern entrance, where we climbed a ladder to the viewing platform behind the wall. To the east were endless crop fields and pastures seamed with dark hedges of gorse. A vein of water glittered on the horizon.

'It is the river Habren,' said Prydd, following my eye. 'Near to the point where it meets the sea.'

'So close...' I murmured, surprised. Though I had travelled a much longer, land-bound route, this thin snake of ocean was all that lay between these tribelands and mine. For all my life it had borne boats carrying tin, iron and slate between the Silures and the Durotriges, but now this watery threshold marked the edge of the Empire. Beyond it, the Romans stood in wait. Were any of them staring, as I was now, upon the silver boundary?

I followed Prydd as he walked northwards along the wall. Halfway to the next platform he stopped. 'That is Caradog's war band.'

Past a border of forest, a cluster of tents and timber huts sprawled over several paddocks, fires smoking between them. Carts ringed the camp, livestock tethered to every pole and axle. It was twice the size of the township, and far more densley populated.

I stared in wonder. Moment by moment, the enormity of Caradog's task revealed itself. He did not creep alone through Albion's war lands; he moved an army of thousands—men, their wives, elders, children, horses and cattle. And he needed to keep them hidden. Again, I marvelled at his power to convince Hefin to shelter this army. 'Does the war chief camp among them?' I asked.

'No,' Prydd said. 'He sleeps in Hefin's finest guest hut.'

We stood in silence, watching the movements of the camp.

'Kendra—'

I turned back to him. From this too-close vantage I could see the blue spiral mark pierced into his forehead and the flaking skin on his bald crown. I felt an urge to step backwards but the narrow walkway did not allow it.

'We must cloak your arrival in some secrecy,' he said, glancing at the boundary guard who stood at the next platform. 'The Romans know it is the journeypeople who steer the resistance against them. If Plautius were to learn that our highest knowledge-bearer walks among us once more, he would hunt you like a solstice sow.'

'But the tribes need to know that the Mothers have returned their Kendra—'

'We must manage the knowledge. We cannot pour such a strong ale in too large a quantity. We must distribute it artfully, where it will do the most good.'

I said nothing. I had been one year forest-hidden. Without doubt, Prydd knew the weather of tribal politics better than I.

He looked at me. 'You are young.'

'Eighteen summers.'

'How far had you progressed in your training when you were made Kendra?'

'Not far,' I admitted. 'I came late to the poems and the Mothers claimed me quickly. But I've known medicine plants since babehood.'

Prydd's face revealed nothing. 'You will need further training,' he said. 'With an elder. If you will not go to Môn then I must teach you.'

'As you wish.' I would do what was needed in order to stay.

I felt his stare linger as I turned my gaze back to the camp.

'You are bold to travel without kin or companion,' he said.

'You know my story. I have none to travel with.'

'I know the finality, but not the pattern by which it unfolded.'

I shivered as the wind stole through my dress. It seemed that the full story of Caer Cad's slaughter had not reached greater Albion, and I was grateful. It had taken a year and a season for me to accept that I had acted in truth. I could not be sure others would make the same judgement. 'When I am better rested I will tell you.'

'I shall await it.'

As I stared at the camp, busy with people preparing for the evening, I knew a loneliness I had not once felt in my mountain seclusion. 'Perhaps you would take me to my hut now?' I asked. 'So I might ready myself for the feast.'

'Of course.'

We descended the ladder and he led me to the northern quarter of the township, where a small hut stood apart from the larger houses nearby. Its thatch was fresh and thick, and a ewe skull stared down from the lintel.

Prydd stopped at the door.

'With whom will I share such a close dwelling?' I asked.

'With no one.'

I looked at him in surprise. 'I am to live alone?'

'One of your stature cannot dwell among the throng of the tribe. You must be held apart.'

My heart dipped. I had held myself apart for the last sixteen moons. I wanted to bring my knowledge closer to the tribespeople, not further away. 'I had hoped to live with journey-kin.'

'The Kendra lives alone.' His tone was sharp, lacking in respect.

If it was not because of my story, then I needed to know why. 'Do you doubt me, journeyman? Do you think I am not who I claim to be?'

'Why should I doubt you? All of Albion awaits you, yet you have come to me.'

'I have come to Caradog.'

He stared at me. 'Caradog was not easily welcomed here, where the chieftain's family has ruled since iron was first dug. It is I who have cleared his path.'

'He appears to me a man who strikes his own path...'

'Caradog relies on the journeymen's favour to succeed in this war. As do all.'

I frowned. This was not the way of the journeypeople with whom I had been raised. Prydd knew the meaning and power of the Kendra better than any. Yet I seemed to conjure neither reverence nor joy in him. My title was not long-gotten and had borne a heavy blow. It would not serve me to make an opponent here so soon. I nodded my acceptance.

Prydd rattled aside the door screen, then put a veined arm across the entrance as I went to pass. 'One more word, Kendra—?' his voice was low.

I hungered to be free of him. 'Yes.'

'You are young and little-trained and I would not see you fail.'

I met his eye.

'You have knowledge of the Mothers greater than any other, but that does not mean you understand the workings of the tribes.'

'I do not pretend to—'

He held up his hand to quieten me. 'War has changed this land,' he said. 'The Kendra's title is precious, but it is no longer all powerful.'

✝

I sat cross-legged by the fire, churning from Prydd's words. In the months I had spent alone on the mountain, I had questioned many times whether I was worthy to bear the title I'd been given. I had never imagined that the title itself could be questioned.

Kendra. Highest knowledge-bearer. None could command me, for I was Mother-chosen, the bridge between the tribes and their creators. How could Prydd deny this power?

I reached for a log from the basket and placed it on the fire. My hut was oven-warm. Like all our dwellings, it was windowless, a perfect circle on the ground. Its walls sang with the spiralling red and black patterns of our totems. A narrow box bed stood against the western wall, piled thick with lambskins and woollen blankets. On the eastern side stood a set of low shelves, furnished with two bowls, a water jug and my old clothes, neatly folded. A servant must have brought them from the cook hut.

This was my home now.

Staring at the flames, I reached into the yoke of my dress and pressed my fingertips to the scar on my chest. The crescent-shaped keloid had grown since it was cut, spreading like a dark red tuber across my skin.

It was ugly, always itchy, and painful to touch, but this scar had been made by the Mothers' knife and I wore it proudly. This was the wound that marked me as Kendra. I closed my eyes, remembering the moment they had opened my skin to let their song enter me. It felt like a dream now, or a conjuring of trance. But the scar beneath my fingers was real.

Neha stretched on the floor beside me, needing only my presence to be at peace.

Prydd had said that the power of the Kendra's title had lessened in the war.

I needed to restore it.

It was true that I was not long-trained. I had not yet given my years to memorising the laws and histories that were held in chants and imparted, over lifetimes, from the wise to the initiates. But my scar bore testament to one moment of transcendence, in which I had stood witness to the Mothers' singing. To bear this memory was my Kendra's task. And now, as Rome tore the bonds we held with this country, was it not more important than ever that the soul of our land was remembered?

Outside the robins called to the last of the daylight. I stood up, faced the doorway, and performed the series of bows and arches to acknowledge the sun's farewell. Then I sat down to chant, running my fingers over my knotted belt to count the cycles.

I stroked Neha's head when I had finished and she looked up, panting from the fire's heat. Her face was oddly coloured, halved into night and day, one eye brown and the other pale blue. One saw this world, and the other beyond.

A bell rang in the distance, signalling the commencement of the feast. I re-tied the yoke of my dress over my scar. Now I would stand before the township. By the grace of the Mothers, it seemed that none here knew the story of my past. This was my gift. My second chance.

I did not doubt my title. But Prydd was right. I knew little of how the tribes had changed since I had been hidden. I needed a teacher. If it had to be Prydd, then I would embrace him.

Caradog had called the Kendra a figurehead. I knew I could be more. I knew I could help the tribes to survive the war. I just needed to know how. I had failed once, as Kendra, and barely endured it. I could not fail again.

✢

'To your liking?' asked Caradog, pork juices streaming down his chin.

I nodded. The meat was tender and seasoned with sorrel. I bit a strip from the joint on my hook and washed it down with a sip of barley ale. It was good to feast again, to taste the long-stewed flavours of my childhood and drink the sweet, brewed waters I had so long forgone.

The hall was crowded and hot with a raging fire. I had been seated between Caradog and Hefin in the centre circle, closest to the meat, an honoured position. The journeymen and the clan heads of greater Llanmelin made up the rest of the inner ring, while the lesser warriors and their families were seated behind. I glanced at Prydd who ate silently across the fire. He had bowed deeply when I entered the hall, displaying a far greater reverence than when we had been alone.

I turned back to Caradog. He had stiffened his hair with lime-water and wore a thick gold neck-ring with a wren's head on each terminal. There was no mistaking him as anything other than a leader of the tribes now. He spoke to me attentively, in the correct manner of host to honoured guest, but I saw that he was aware of every movement in the room.

Euvrain sat on his other side, her posture proud, breathtaking in a green tartan threaded with silver. Though she faced away from her husband, her head thrown back in laughter at someone else's joke, her hand rested lightly on his thigh. There could be no more fitting match for Caradog.

I pressed him to speak of the Roman campaign. It had been almost four summers since Claudius's army arrived on our shores. In the first few months eleven tribes had submitted, lured by the false prize of a peaceful alliance. But for those who had not, submission had been demanded anyway and not peacefully. The governor Plautius now controlled the southern and eastern tribes. The north and the west remained free. Rome was far more established than I had imagined.

Caradog described how the summer had been spent making small, but relentless, attacks on the Roman camps, burning their fort walls, emptying their grain stores, blocking their supply routes, diverting their water channels, destroying their carts as well as killing soldiers wherever they moved in small numbers through the forests. 'I have not made myself a friend of Plautius,' he said, laughing, 'and he hunts me because of it.'

I learned he had been barely half a year in Llanmelin, drawn here by the fervour of the western warriors who remained staunch in their hatred of Claudius, unlike the eastern chiefs who had been too long softened by the luxuries of Roman trade. It was good to speak of war again after so many months without fresh news. 'So what is Rome's boundary?' I asked. 'Where does Plautius stand at this moment?'

'A day's ride away on the banks of the Habren,' said Caradog. 'But he will come no further.'

'Because the season is over?' I asked. None fought past the onset of winter.

Caradog shook his head. 'Because he has met the edge of his war.'

Hefin and a few other chiefs had quieted to hear our conversation.

'He knows I am within these tribelands, but he cannot reach me. The paths are too steep and tribesmen too brutal. I return every scout he sends, tied to his horse and missing his head. We are guarded by the mountains and the currents of the Habren. The Mothers themselves stand watch for us here.'

Others were listening now.

'Does he retreat then for the winter?' I asked, too curious to be shy at the audience.

'He has pulled some men back,' said Caradog. 'But he does not leave the front unguarded.'

'They have levelled the Sun Road,' said Prydd, 'and laid it with stone. They call it the Fossa. This is the line they hold.'

'So it cannot be walked,' I murmured.

The Sun Road was one of our oldest story roads. It ran south to north, bisecting the line of the winter solstice through several tribelands. Journeypeople from all of Albion walked it each winter to remember the songs embedded in the rise and fall of its path. It was as if Rome knew the exact places to cut, to ensure we bled.

'Neither walked nor crossed,' said Caradog. 'Plautius has been building his twig forts to guard it. Over fifty at last count—'

'But the fool cannot man them!' said Hefin.

'Indeed not,' said Caradog. 'The legions have been pulled back to the east to hold peace in the captured territories over winter. Plautius has left only the auxilia to guard the front line—' He paused, eyes dancing, as if to give me time to imagine what he might next reveal.

'Go on,' I urged.

The hall was now quiet, all were listening to the war chief.

'The Sun Road is long and Plautius must spread his men thin to hold it. There are feeble numbers at each fort: one-fifty, two hundred at most. Often far less.' He paused again. 'His line is weaker than thread.'

'So...will you attack next season?' I asked. 'And claim back the road, at least?'

'I am planning an attack,' he said, 'but not only to claim the road.'

'What then?' My voice was low.

Despite all eyes upon us, his own did not leave my face. 'All of Albion.'

The warriors began to chant and call.

'How?' I asked over them.

Caradog stilled the men so he could continue. 'It is not just the front that is weakly defended,' he said. 'The province has grown so rapidly that the legions are stretched to control it. I have message lines to the eastern tribes, even those who have long since signed treaties. Many chiefs have pledged their allegiance to Claudius, yet their warrior oaths remain with me. They are weary of enslavement and they are ready to act.'

I listened, amazed. The tribes had always fought for themselves. Had this man begun to bring them to one mind?

'When I attack the Sun Road from the west,' said Caradog, 'the tribes of the east will take up their weapons against the legions.'

'The Romans will be torn in two...' I whispered.

'Yes,' said Caradog. 'If they come forward to meet our attack, they will lose the east. And if they defend their provinces, they will lose their line. Either way, we will gain ground and they will be weakened.

They will learn that Albion cannot be subdued.'

'And you have brought the tribes to agreement on this?' I marvelled. No other had done so in this, or any, war.

'Enough of them,' said Caradog. 'I have the Iceni, the Coritani...'

These were powerful tribes, and among the first to have submitted to Claudius. Caradog had the power of a magician if he had seduced their alliance.

'But surely,' I continued, 'Plautius will replenish his numbers before the next season?'

'He will,' said Caradog, leaning forward. 'But we do not wait until next season.' He paused, eyes on mine. 'We attack this winter.'

'But that is madness,' I gasped. None fought in the cold, when snow obscured the landscape and nights demanded heavy tents. 'Forgive me...I did not expect a campaign in winter—'

'Just as Rome will not expect it,' said Caradog.

'Why should we not launch in the cold?' said Euvrain, slipping her arm through her husband's. 'We are hardy to it, and they are not.'

Caradog kissed her and the warriors called and stamped.

I took a long sip of ale and felt its warmth spread in my tightened belly. I had missed its numbing pleasure. It was a bold plan. And had I not come in search of a bold plan? Caradog followed only his own rules. Perhaps this was his strength.

'And there is a greater reason for a winter attack,' he said over the din.

'Is this not a matter for council, War Chief?' said Prydd quietly.

'Bah! Let the warriors hear it. It will stir them.' He sipped his ale, wiped the froth from his beard and turned to the gathering. 'Plautius finishes his term as governor this month and Claudius sends a fresh man to rule the province. Ostorius Scapula.'

I watched him, impressed. He must have spies and messengers in every corner of Albion.

'They will make the exchange in winter when they believe the campaigning is quiet,' he announced. 'The new man will know nothing of Albion's forests, nor weather, nor the ways of the tribes. He will be weak-footed. He will not expect an attack so late in the season.' He turned back to me. Despite the bleariness of ale, his eyes burned. 'This is when we will strike.'

His audience cheered, but the plan unsettled me. 'Surely you do not propose open battle?' I asked. 'I have seen the Romans fight. They abandon their souls—'

'Kendra, I too have seen the Romans fight!' said Caradog, laughing. 'It is a costumed dance they repeat without variation. They fight like cocks, but have the minds of sheep.' He paused as a servant replenished his horn. 'We of Albion fight with our own mind. Our only costume is the night and the forest.' His eyes glittered as he stared at me. 'No, journeywoman, we will not meet them on the field. We will not allow them their preening battle dance. We will use stealth, and slaughter them as they rest. And they will learn that they can advance no further.' His voice filled the breadth of the hall.

I saw now the flame that had entranced this tribe, one of the fiercest in all Albion.

'Tell us why we fight!' cried a warrior from the outer circle. The men were drunk, lusting for a war cry.

Caradog did not hesitate. He rose, drawing himself to full height until it seemed that his spiked hair nearly touched the roof beams. 'We are sovereign to these tribelands,' he began. 'Our ancestors' bones are crumbled in the soil we farm. Our mothers' blood runs in our rivers. We will not bow to another sovereign power on this land. We are this land's descendants. We are formed by it, and only we can rule it.'

Among the roar of the audience, Euvrain caught my eye and smiled.

'And now I am certain that the Mothers bless our battle plan—' Caradog pulled me by my wrist to stand, '—because the Kendra has come to us.' He bent to kiss my hand, then looked up at me with a wild mischief in his eye, before grasping me around the waist and lifting me high above his head, spinning me around as he sounded a war shriek, quickly echoed by the warriors. 'We cannot lose!' he shouted over the noise. 'The Mothers are with us. We cannot lose!'

I gasped as he spun me too close to the fire, then he loosed his grip and I slid, laughing, to the ground with a thud.

The room returned to laughter and conversation.

I sat down, my waist bruised where he had held it. Despite the high spirits, unease stirred in me. I had seen the devastation of war. Should we not wait and see the nature of this new governor before we act? Learn of his limits? His goals? I sipped my ale. I was sitting beside the greatest war leader Albion had ever known. Who was I to question him?

Some hours later, when the joints were sucked clean, Caradog called for his Songman. I drew a skin over my legs, readying myself for the pleasure of music. I wondered why the Songman had not feasted among us, nor regaled us throughout our meal.

The figure that emerged from the room's periphery, bearing a rhythm staff, was no taller than a child. As he moved into the firelight, my breath caught, and I saw why he had kept himself hidden. This was a journeyman of ill-favoured formation. His skull was misshapen, as though collapsed on one side, and his left eye swam in a sunken cavity. An eruption of bone seemed to bulge at the back of his head, exposed by a scantness of tufted hair. His face was one of the most wretchedly-forged I had ever witnessed.

If Caradog noticed my shock he did not acknowledge it. 'His name is Rhain,' he whispered in my ear. 'He is the finest Songman in Albion.'

I sipped my ale and watched him walk once around the hearth's circumference. Despite his formation, his posture was graceful and he walked proudly. He was beautifully dressed in the embroidered cloak of a chieftain's poet and silver bells tinkled around his hips. Usually one so cruelly wrought as this would shunned by their tribe, or given back to the Mothers by death. It must have been Caradog who ensured otherwise.

A place was made on the inner bench and Rhain stood ready, facing his war chief.

'For whom do you sing?' called Caradog, making the familiar preamble to song.

'I sing for Caradog, son of Belinus, prince of the Catuvellauni, mighty warrior of the Medway, slayer of Romans, protector of Albion, father of warriors yet to be born. I sing more beautifully, more powerfully, than any poet.'

I felt my eyes widen. His voice was as strong as flame. He spoke with authority. As if he bore no imperfection. How did one so flawed learn such grace?

Glancing at me, he lifted his staff, then closed his eyes as he prepared himself.

The hall fell quiet.

Of what would he sing? The role of the Songman was three-fold: to praise his chieftain, to mock our enemies, to revive the great warriors of the past by invoking their voices. Always the words were riddled to draw the audience beyond their surface.

He began to pound the earth with his staff, setting the pulse that would sustain his story.

Then he started to sing.

Even the beauty of his speech had given me no warning of what I now heard.

What was this sound that came from his chest? How did he

create, with only breath and the tissues through which it passed, something so powerful? It was his soul unsheathed. His voice was bone and muscle, a serpent, birthed in his belly and formed with his tongue.

The audience listened, enthralled, as the serpent wove through the silent hall.

> *I sing of a maiden who leaps to bright Annwyn*
> *As strong as a salmon, as swift as a hound.*

> *I sing of a maiden whose chest has been opened,*
> *Whose breast is a vessel that runs with the song.*

I smiled. A Kendra's story. I glanced at Caradog. Had he commanded his Songman to sing one of these ancient stories in my honour? He stared straight ahead, entranced by his poet. It seemed that the Songman's choice had been his own.

> *I sing of an army who spread like a bloodstain,*
> *Who run like the soulless, un-kept by the song.*

> *I sing of a maiden who sees not the danger,*
> *Whose eyes wear a skin, though her spirit: not yet.*

I sipped my ale. It was not only the words that told the story. There was meaning in his rhythms, his sound-shapes, his very bearing. The riddle was bewildering, yet somehow familiar.

> *I sing of a stag who buries the maiden,*
> *In Annwyn's dark chamber she finds the sky's light.*

I sing of a maiden who soars as a raven,
Who sees the land's headless and knows they are lost.

My fingers tightened around my cup with the horror of recognition. This was not just a Kendra's story, timeless and oft-sung. This was *my* story.

I sing of a she-dog, voiceless and buried,
Who howls to her warriors to lay down their swords.

I sat unmoving, rigid with fear. Was this to be my exposing? The poets were tasked to pour scorn as well as to praise. Their judgements were revered. Would Rhain condemn me with this song?

He went on singing verse after verse. Each told, with greater clarity, the story of what I had done in Caer Cad. Yet, as I glanced around me, it was not condemnation I saw in the faces of the audience, but rapture. Did they not hear the hidden meaning? Were they too caught in the thrall of his voice?

No, it was not this. Although Rhain's poem bore witness to the harm I had caused, it was not the deeper truth of what he sang. As I listened, I began to hear another story finding its shape.

I sing of a Kendra who walks through the bleeding,
Their dying breaths knitting to weave her a skin.

I sing of a Kendra, so beloved by the Mothers
That they would slay thousands to bring her to song.

I sing of a Kendra reborn of the mountain,
Whose wound pours the song from which Albion drinks.

My eyes ached with tears. His song did not betray me. It took my failing and forged it into something beautiful. It spoke of the purity of my intent. It was my story, but he had created something greater.

I did not know how Rhain had come to learn my history. There were so few living who knew it. He must have heard, in the winds of Albion, what even Prydd had not. It did not matter now. He had chosen to protect me and I would not question it.

There was no sound other than the low moan of the wind outside the hall and the voice within. Rhain's craft was a rope that lashed us together.

I stared at him. He was nothing but beguiling now, despite the oddness of his bones. What was his own story that he should wield such tools of enchantment? There were many singers in Albion, one at least for each chief and many beyond, but his was a skill above all others.

I wanted to learn it.

The song finished and Rhain bowed as the guests stamped and cried their appreciation.

I closed my eyes in a silent prayer of thanks to the Mothers. For I would not train with Prydd. I would ask this man Rhain if he would be my teacher, if he would share this gift.

If I could wield song in this way, perhaps I would be worthy of the praise he had offered.

If I could wield song in this way, I would not be a figurehead, a title. I would be a shaper of souls.

2

Annwyn

We call our land Albion, *meaning* light,
or that which can be seen.

Within it is the unseen.
We call this Annwyn.
It is place and not place.
It is another way of knowing.

LLEU. THE sky's gleaming warrior. He who lives, dies, and lives
again. The sun.

At his first light, I walked to the temple to offer libation. As
highest ranked journeywoman, it was my duty to acknowledge Lleu's
rebirth each day on behalf of the tribe.

I pushed aside the speckled mare-skin that covered the doorway
and stepped in.

The temple was larger than that of Caer Cad. Four separate fires
marked the directions, each guarded by sheep skulls and smoking
herb pots.

Opposite the entrance, aligned to the light of the midwinter
dawn, was an oak box, waist height, fitted with a bolted lid. On the
outside was a skin of sheeted silver hammered into intricate patterns.

Inside were bones, blood, flesh and viscera; slain offerings seeping into the earth below.

This was the belly of the temple: the altar. I stood before it, a square of sky visible above me through an opening in the roof. Were it not for this vent, the stench would be so overwhelming that none could sit in chant for the hours that our worship required.

I lowered my head to begin, and breathed in the aroma of putrefying flesh mingled with nettle and thyme smoke. This pungent soup was the smell of our reverence. I had missed it.

⁂

'Can you sharpen this and restore the blade?' I asked, holding forth my bronze sword.

The smith took the weapon and examined it. He traced his blackened fingers along the blade-edge and over the carved bone hilt. 'A good piece.'

I had not used my Kendra's sword in battle since I had last met Roman soldiers. It was not the journeypeople's role to fight, yet I had learnt it in my training, and I wished to be prepared should I be called to use my weapon now.

The smith laid it down on the workbench between us. 'It will take me some time. Come back this afternoon—'

'I'll wait now...if you will permit it.'

He looked up. 'As you wish.'

I nodded and picked up a rod of black, unforged metal. It was cold and heavy in my palm. Iron. The Mothers' blood, congealed and hardened. Drawn from the earth to form our wheels, hinges, tools and knives. I rubbed my thumb over its gritty surface. It had none of the magic of bronze, but a different, more stable, power.

'There's a bench outside.' The smith motioned towards the back door. 'One of my students is working there. He'll keep you company.'

The back of the smith's hut faced the western wall, above which sharp-edged rain clouds shone silver in the autumn sun.

'Lleu's greetings,' said a voice from behind me.

I turned to see Caradog seated on a bench, a bronze disc wedged between his knees.

'And to you.'

He frowned. 'Do you seek me?'

'Oh no...I await my sword.'

He stared at me for a moment, then turned back to his work. In one hand was a puncturing tool, in the other a smith's mallet. A set of measuring points lay on the bench.

'What do you craft?'

'A plate for my shield. Could you steady it?'

I moved the measuring points aside to sit down, and took hold of the disc.

Caradog had embossed a circle border, and was beginning a pattern of triskeles within it. He took up the measuring points and marked out the centre of the final spiral.

I watched his large hands with surprise. I had never known a warrior to have learnt this craft, let alone one who commanded a war band. The arts of the pattern-smith required long training and a knowledge of sacred angles that was closely guarded. 'How have you learned this?' I asked.

'I threatened to cut off my first teacher's thumb if she didn't tell me. I had my axe raised and her hand on the block before she would spill.'

'I—'

'I am joking!' he said. 'I had a teacher who cared more for a hungry mind than an initiated one. Besides, I came close to pursuing the journeyman's path, but I was too brilliant a swordsman.' He shrugged.

I laughed. 'I, too, have known such teachers. Without them I would not be Kendra.'

Caradog looked up from his work. 'My Songman tells me you came late to skin?'

'Yes.' It was still tender to speak of it. Skin was our kinship to the land and the Mothers who formed it. The disgrace of skinlessness was not easily cast off.

Caradog looked back to his bronze. 'How long were you without it?'

'Seventeen years.' It was a long time to have lived in shame. How would he judge it? How freely did his mind roam beyond the confines of our laws?

'I am impressed,' he said. 'It takes strength to survive without a totem.'

I nodded, my shoulders softening. 'What is yours?'

'I am skin to the wren.'

I smiled. Elusive. Cunning. King of birds. I stared at the place where his beard became sparse, at a tiny blemish, part-healed, on his cheek.

'Can you hold at the top?'

I changed my grip. With a steady tapping, he formed one tentacle of the swirling triskele. There were many meanings in the shape: the turning of the sun, the cycling of the seasons, the interweaving of future and past. The proportions echoed the structures of oak leaves, mistleberries, and the solstice angles of Lleu himself, but only those trained in measurement knew what they were.

He had a gift for this craft. 'Why do you do this?' I asked. 'Is there an abundance of spare time when you are leader of the free tribes?'

His eyes creased at the corners when he smiled. 'Because it settles me,' he said. 'And I like the smell of the metal.'

I smiled. 'It has no smell.'

He lifted the plate.

I leaned forward and breathed in the coppery bronze. There was a faint mineral scent of wet earth and flesh.

'Some say metal is all we fight for.'

'More than that, surely?'

'Is it not all? For Rome, it is the fuel of their Empire.'

'And for us?' I asked.

'For us it is something else.' He looked at me. 'But you don't need me to tell you what we fight for.'

I met his gaze. 'I would like to know what *you* fight for?'

'I fight because I am good at it.'

He reached over me to pick up a measuring tool and I flinched at his touch. I saw him notice and my face grew hot. A silence stretched between us.

Finally he said, 'Kendra, if you wish to aid me, I will put you on my war council. It is small as I do not desire the word of many advisors. But you should know something of me if you wish to be in my service.'

I frowned. 'What do you wish me to know?'

'There are two things I despise above all others. The first will be easy to guess. It is the enemy of every warrior. Or should be.'

'Disloyalty,' I said.

'Yes. I value little more than the commitment of a man to his chief and his tribe. And—' he glanced sideways at me, '—to his wife.'

I stared at the town wall, my face smouldering with humiliation. He had seen me flare in response to him and he was warning me off. He had no need, no right, to do so. My heart was claimed, bound. No warrior, no touch, would ever turn me. 'I share your contempt,' I said.

'Good then.' He resumed tapping the shield plate.

'What is the second thing?'

'What?'

'What is the second thing you despise?'

'Oh.' He paused. 'Boredom.'

I thought for a moment. 'Those two aversions may fall into conflict.'

He smiled. 'They do...always.'

Our quietness was shattered by shouts, then a woman's scream.

Caradog met my eye and set down the bronze.

As we hurried through the winding streets, more and more voices took up the wailing. Others had heard it, and were hastening towards Hefin's courtyard, from where the cries were rising.

'He is cut!'

'They've taken his tongue!'

Caradog pushed through the dense crowd that had gathered in the courtyard and I followed.

At the centre of the throng, braced by Prydd on one side and Hefin on the other, was a knave of no more than fifteen summers. His eyes were wide with terror, his jaw and tunic black with dried blood. He convulsed in a cough and a fresh, red stream trickled from his mouth.

'Was it by Roman hand?' Caradog asked.

The youth nodded.

The women cried and keened.

'Who is he?' I gasped.

'He is one of Hefin's messengers,' said Prydd. 'He was sent to bear news of your arrival to the other chieftains—at Caradog's command, but against mine. He left at dawn this morning.'

I reeled in horror. 'But how did they find him?'

'Scouts,' said Caradog. 'They take the tongues of our messengers whenever they find them, but this is the first attack since midsummer.' He looked to Hefin. 'Plautius is still roaming.'

'At least we know he didn't spill,' said Hefin. 'Else they wouldn't have torn his tongue.'

'Or he already had,' said Caradog.

The messenger began to pale and sway. 'Give him air!' I commanded. I tore a strip from my under-robe and made a wad for him to bite, to stem the bleeding. 'Make way,' I said, 'I need to take him to the healing hut.'

'Our healers will tend him,' said Prydd. 'It is not your task.'

'I have knowledge of medicine,' I answered. 'And he has taken this wound on my behalf. I will heal him.'

Prydd frowned. I had no wish to further arouse his disfavour, but I knew that I had the best knowledge to tend this wound.

The messenger fell against me as I took Prydd's place in holding him upright. My heart lurched as I realised I could heal him but never restore him. By this act, the Romans inflicted an injury worse than death. The tongue was speech, our humanity.

'Make way,' I called again, as Hefin and I walked him forward.

Caradog gripped my wrist. 'Leave him.'

'Please, War Chief. He won't survive without—'

'What purpose is his survival? They have taken his soul.' In a practised movement, he took hold of the injured man, cradling him in one arm and drawing his knife with the other.

A scream of protest rang out from the crowd.

The messenger's head fell back against Caradog's chest, his throat exposed. He was too weak from blood loss to struggle.

Caradog kissed him, then killed him and laid him on the ground. 'I will not have the mark of Rome's evil in my presence,' he said when he had risen.

The watching township stood in silence.

Prydd stood before me as the crowd dispersed. 'This is not well,' he said. He turned to Caradog. 'I hope my counsel will not go unheeded again.'

Caradog nodded.

After I had helped carry the messenger's body to his house for washing, and given his mother a tea of sun wort to still her shaking, I set out towards Caradog's camp in search of Rhain, who had not been present at the death.

My mind turned the event as I walked through the ramparts. Prydd had been angered by the killing. I feared he would see me as its omen and convince Caradog so. And what should I make of the war chief? He had revealed thoughtfulness at the smith's hut. Now I saw that he could not be predicted.

I glanced skyward as I wove through the woodland bordering the camp. The clouds had darkened, threatening rain. Neha kept pace with my hastened stride.

The camp was a warren of tents and huts. Draped across their openings were tartans of almost every tribe, from the Catuvellauni at our land's far edge, to the Dobunni, to our immediate east.

The camp-dwellers were sitting around fires, or resting on the backs of carts. A strange stillness hung over the makeshift town. These people were homeless. They had torn themselves from their tribelands, rather than remain on soil ruled by Rome. They nodded and greeted me as I passed them, but there was a paralysis, a sense of suspension in the idleness that could not be filled with tending their fields or grinding their wheat. They were surviving on Hefin's surplus grain, and I wondered what Caradog intended for the winter when this ran low. A young woman, suckling a babe, told me that Caradog's Songman often took to the wild apple grove at the camp's south edge.

The path into the grove was a tunnel of gnarled branches and blackberry bushes, its air syrupy with the rot of fallen apples. Neha found Rhain beneath a still-laden tree, head bowed in chant. He looked up at my footsteps.

I was startled anew by the contours of his face. The flesh of his left cheek seemed to pull backwards, twisting his features and exposing too much of his eye's white orb. He looked like a being in transformation, like a journeyman caught between realms, half-bent to animal form and trapped partway in the transition. But his brown eyes were steady.

'Join me,' he said, petting Neha, who was sniffing at his harp propped against the trunk. 'She can smell the fat on the strings.'

I sat down on the grassy root bed. 'Are you composing a war song?' I asked. 'For the winter's attack?'

'Not a war song,' he said. 'A cauldron song.'

I nodded. These were beloved stories among the tribes, tales of magical vessels that provided ever-replenishing nourishment and could restore beheaded warriors to life. We needed their hopefulness now.

'Your song last night...' I began. 'How did you learn of...the story?'

Rhain laughed. 'Poetic inspiration.'

'I am in earnest.'

'As am I.'

I smiled. Of course he would not reveal himself. He was a journeyman after all. 'How did you come to song?' I asked.

'When you look like a boiled turnip you must find another pathway to beauty.'

I spluttered with laughter. 'But how have you...?' My words faded.

'...endured with such a disfigurement?' he finished for me.

I nodded.

He held my gaze for a moment, then turned his back to me and loosened his shirt, letting it fall from his shoulders. His back was broad and handsomely shaped, but the skin that covered it was as puckered and crimson as raspberries.

I recognised the scarring of fire. 'How?' I whispered.

He re-fastened his shirt. 'On Caradog's initiation day,' he said. 'Two other newly-made warriors—drunk as suckling piglets—wished to cleanse my impurities with flame. One held me, as the other brought his torch to my skin. Caradog found us. He sent them both to Annwyn.'

'Slayed them?'

'Ay. His father was furious. The honour price for two fresh warriors was not low, and Belinus hated to part with his cattle. But none touched me after that.' Rhain chuckled. 'In return, I pledged Caradog my voice.'

I frowned. It was right and honourable for Caradog to have protected this gentle man, but was slaughter required? Was it this morning?

Rhain read my pause. 'He kills readily when he believes it fair. It is both strength and weakness.'

I stared at the knotted tree roots. 'He stilled a man too quickly this morn.'

'Yes, I have heard,' said Rhain. 'Night and day.'

I frowned. 'What say you?'

'Night and day is what he sees. He knows no mingled light of dawn or evening. Others must tell him of this.' He glanced at me. 'But he listens to few others.'

'He listens to you.' I realised I envied him this.

'Ay,' agreed Rhain. 'He is soothed by my song.'

'More than that. Your song guides him.'

'Perhaps,' he said, 'I have led him once or twice through the gloaming.'

We sat unspeaking. The air had grown heavy with the promise of rain.

'Journeyman,' I ventured. My heart began to beat faster. 'I am Kendra, but I am not long-trained in the knowledge of the tribes.' I paused. 'Will you be my teacher in the craft of song?'

His gaze was direct. 'I know of no Kendra who has trained as Songwoman,' he said. 'It is too arduous, too tedious. It is not thought to be the most powerful use of her gift.'

'And yet I believe that it is.'

He began to laugh.

'What is amusing?'

His eyes shone. 'You are a riddle. A journeywoman who rose without skin. A Kendra who would be Songwoman.'

'But will you teach me?'

'It is certain that I might.' His fine hand ran over the bells attached to his belt. 'Why do you want to learn song?'

'Because I...I bear the Kendra's knowledge, but not the voice to make it heard.'

He smiled. How quickly his disfigurement receded once his spirit emerged. 'Some will not want you to learn this craft. They will fear the power in it.'

'Yes,' I said. Prydd. There would be others.

His eyes shone. 'What form will you take when they come in pursuit?'

My mind sparked. 'I will transform myself into a hare.'

'And if they transform to a hound?'

'Then I will become a fish.'

He could not hide his delight. 'And if they transform to an otter?'

'Then I will become a bird.'

'And if they then become a hawk?'

'Then I will fly into a grain store and transform myself to a grain of corn.'

Rhain laughed and laughed. 'None will find you there and your knowledge will be safe.'

Cold droplets of rain began to spit on my cheek. How I had missed the play of journey-law, the axle on which our knowledge turned, the dance with what was hidden. I had tasted it in my short Kendra's training. I wanted to feast on it. 'I ask you again, Rhain the Songman: will you teach me?'

'Be warned,' he said, 'it will madden you...and you will grow tired of my company...'

'I will endure it.'

'Then ask the hairless one,' he said. 'With his approval I will teach you. Without it, I will not. I have no wish to provoke the man who wields the staff of Môn in this tribe.'

I grabbed his small, cold hand and pressed it to my lips. 'I will make Prydd approve it.'

By the time I reached the outskirts of the township, the rain was steady. I made a hood of my shawl.

The men who had been digging the new rampart were trailing back to the township, crowding the path so that I did not at first notice a tiny, barefooted girl, crouched at the road's edge. Neha nosed her as she whimpered with cold.

'Tidings, small one,' I said, squatting before her. 'Where is your Mam?'

She looked up with the black-brown eyes so common to this tribe. She was no older than five summers at most, with the wizened features and scabbed lips of the poorly fed.

I hooked a wet tendril behind her ear. She was not one of Caradog's followers; she was too untended. She was a fringe-child, daughter of those who lived in rough huts beyond the walls of the township, shunned by the tribe for a crime, or disfigurement, or for being without skin.

I looked around, but there were none who appeared to be searching for a child. 'Come.' I helped her to her feet then lifted her into my arms. 'I will feed you, then we will find your Mam.'

She clung to my neck as I continued up the steep path. I had not held a human body so close since I had left my township. I had forgotten the sweetness of it, though this one trembled in my grasp. 'Are you skin to the mountain sheep?' I whispered, panting with my cargo. Most of Llanmelin bore this totem.

'Unskinned,' she bleated, close to my ear.

I tightened my grip.

In the warmth of my hut, I pulled off her sodden dress, wrapped her in a blanket and gave her a cup of the broth I had set on the fire this morning. She began eating with a hound's hunger.

I hung her dress on the firedog and sat beside her.

We did not speak as I watched her eat. Her gaze darted around the room. Damp, black hair stuck to her neck. Unskinned, she could hope for neither marriage nor admittance to learning. It took little skill in prophecy to see that her future was ended before it had begun. It angered me that she should be so condemned for the ill-fortune of her birth. But these were the laws of skin. And I, as Kendra, was their highest custodian.

She nodded frantically when I offered another ladleful of broth.

'Shall I sing you a song?' I asked, unsure of how to settle her.

Her dark eyes widened. 'Ay.'

Watching the flames, I sang her a lullaby that my suck mother had sung to me.

She listened, barely moving, and when it was finished, she looked at me so hopefully for another, that I began to sing her one of the songs I had learnt in my training. It was a forming song about the creation of a mountain not far from my home, and the trees and birds found on its slopes. Such songs were for the journeypeople, not intended for the ears of a half-born child. She would never be taught them. What harm could it do for her to know a taste of their magic and beauty?

Partway through the song I heard a movement at my door screen. I paused, but hearing nothing further, I lifted my voice again.

With sudden force, the screen was shunted aside and Prydd stepped inside. His expression was controlled, but I felt his fury. 'Kendra—' he bowed hastily, scarcely honouring rank. 'Perhaps you have not yet learnt of this, but you cannot sing the journeysongs to a skinless child. She should not be within the township, least of all in your hut. She is impure.' He took the girl's hand and pulled her firmly to standing. The blanket fell from her shoulders, exposing her twig limbs and her sheer, veined skin: the very image of purity.

Prydd stepped back, as if fearful of her nakedness.

'I was merely feeding her,' I said, tugging her still-damp dress back over her head. 'The song was only a comfort.'

'Journey-songs are not intended as a comfort.'

I looked up at him. 'Forgive me, journeyman, I thought that was exactly what they were.'

I stood to face him.

His voice strained to contain his displeasure. 'Please return her to the fringe huts,' he said, 'and do not bring her past the town's threshold again.'

Without speaking, the little girl reached for my hand.

'When you return, come directly to the temple,' he continued. 'I will begin your instruction this day.'

There was no purpose now in asking if I may learn instead with the Songman. Especially as song was the very craft I had now transgressed. 'Yes, journeyman.'

He turned and left.

I finished dressing the child, combed her damp hair, then took her hand and walked out the door.

'What is your name?' I asked, as we passed the smith huts. The rain had subsided and we could walk at her pace.

'Manacca.'

I smiled. 'In my old township, I cared for a child called Manacca.'

'Is she still there?' she asked.

'No.'

'Where is she now?'

'Annwyn,' I answered.

'What is Annwyn?'

I stopped and stared at her. Could she know so little? I looked around, then stooped and said softly, 'Annwyn is the hidden world, the place of the Mothers, where souls live after their body has died.'

'Is it far?' she asked in wonder.

'It is all around us, but we cannot see it.'

Manacca looked up and down the street, eyes wide in alarm.

'Don't worry,' I smiled, taking hold of her shoulders. 'It is a beautiful place—the trees are always heavy with apples...' I leaned forward and whispered in her grubby ear, '*I have been there.*'

'How?'

I was deep in journey-law now. What should I say? By ritual? By rapture? Both were true. But she would never know either. 'By looking beyond,' I answered. 'Watch carefully, and you may glimpse it.'

'Will I go there?'

'Not soon, if Caradog can help it.'

We walked through the northern gate and I asked Manacca to show me where she lived. She led me past the lowest rampart and looped west to the lowlands beside the hillfort. There were fewer fringe huts here than there had been in Caer Cad. But as I watched her run into the jumbled nest of stick huts and tents, and smelt the fetid streamlet that trickled from its midst, I wondered why there should be any at all.

As I strode back to meet Prydd my anger grew. Why was I

forced to withhold truth from an innocent child? The Mothers had not withheld it from me. What was Prydd's purpose in wishing to distribute my Kendra's knowledge *artfully*? Would it not strengthen us? Especially now, when we were under such threat from our enemy, and so many tribes had already relinquished their rituals. Was now not the very time to allow the few tribes who still remained free to drink as freely as possible from learning's deep cauldron?

My questions fell away when I entered the temple. Prydd was seated on the first bench before the altar. Beside him sat Caradog. The silence rang with the echoes of their discussion.

'The journeyman tells me that you are stirring trouble,' said Caradog, as I walked forward. His tone was sharp, but his eyes hid a trace of a smile.

'Hardly that.' I looked at Prydd. 'The girl is returned to her swine yard as instructed. Her hunger and ignorance are ensured.' I sat on a stool to face them both.

Caradog said, 'You do not desire to go to Môn—'

'I am no use in Môn.'

Caradog nodded. 'If you wish to remain here, then you must play a role.'

I frowned. 'We have already discussed that I will sit on your council.'

'I think we can make further use of your Kendra's grace.'

'How?' I asked with suspicion.

'The attack we will make this winter is outside the time that is sanctioned for war.' Caradog paused. 'To ensure its success, we must make an offering to the Mothers of great value.'

I knew from his voice that he did not mean a calf or a lamb or even a dog. Offerings of human kin had been outlawed in the Roman-ruled townships, and were rarely made in the free tribes. I had not seen such a rite since I was a child. They were terrifying and dangerous if wrongly done, yet they bound the tribes to the Mothers more powerfully than any other ritual.

'Do you wish me to augur for the best day for an offering?' I asked.

'No.' Caradog paused. 'I want you to make it.'

My eyes closed. 'Not I...'

'Who better to perform this most sacred rite than the Kendra?' said Prydd.

I stared at him. This was not Caradog's idea, it was his.

'I cannot,' I said. 'I have never performed it, nor learned its arts.'

'I will teach you,' said Prydd.

He does not think I will do it, I thought. *He thinks I will ask, instead, to be taken to Môn.* I looked to Caradog. Did he not see the hidden motive?

'I understand your aversion,' said Caradog. 'It takes stomach to put iron into flesh.'

'I have the stomach.'

'Then you accept?'

'Are you certain it is needed?'

'Yes,' said Caradog. 'My men are already beginning to turn on each other. This morning a parry went far beyond practice and one of my best fighters was cut.'

'I will attend him—'

'—he is well. But the offering is needed to settle them.'

I knew he was right. With one ritual act of killing, the offering would appease the hunger for violence that might otherwise erupt between tribesmen in the days before war. The blood of a calf did it well. The blood of a tribesman would do it better. But I had never slayed a tribesman. I had only killed once, and my victim had been a Roman. In truth, I knew not whether I had the stomach.

'If it is done by the Kendra's hand,' urged Prydd, 'our fighters will be all the more blessed.'

'Kendra?' Caradog beat his fingers rapidly on his long thigh. He was tiring of this discussion. 'Will you do it?'

I took a deep breath. Had I not come to lend my Kendra's glimmer to this war chief? I met his eye. 'Who will I give?'

Caradog looked to Prydd.

'One who is...marked by the Mothers,' said Prydd, trying to cloak his surprise at my acceptance.

I nodded. Offerings were selected from among those at the thresholds: criminals, the misshapen, those at the cusp between childhood and adulthood.

'Your Songman is an obvious choice,' said Prydd to Caradog. 'And his voice would honour the Mothers.'

'No!' I gasped. 'He...he is needed in other ways...' Heart pounding, I looked to Caradog.

'Not Rhain,' he murmured.

Prydd frowned. 'Then I will search for one equally distinctive,' he said.

I exhaled in relief. Prydd influenced Caradog, but did not control him.

'Good,' said Caradog. 'Then we are finished here.'

They both stood.

'Were we not beginning instruction this night?' I asked Prydd.

'Tomorrow,' he said, walking to the door. 'Await me at the eastern gate, at Lleu's last hour.' He was gone before I could query it.

Caradog hesitated. 'I am expected by my wife for bread...'

'Of course.' Did he think I would detain him?

'Ailia—' It was the first time he had called me by name.

I met his gaze. Now it held no humour. 'I cannot afford any disturbance in the township as I ready for the attack. You must comply with

48

my head journeyman. You cannot defy him or cause him further annoyance. Only then may you remain and assist me.'

I was speechless. Was I a child to be so chastised?

He bowed swiftly, then strode past me to exit the temple.

I turned back to the altar. Things were askew. I commanded a knowledge above all others in Albion, yet I did not command the respect of this war chief.

Evening drew near but I could not yet bear to go back to my hut. Once more, I headed for the northern gate, seeking a quiet place by the river Castroggi where I might sit with the Mothers.

As I passed Hefin's guest houses, I saw Euvrain standing outside the largest of them, calling to two fair-haired children fighting with wooden swords in the courtyard. She held the doorskins open as the girl and boy tore inside. The room within looked bright and welcoming. I hastened my pace so that she would not see me.

The northern path was deserted. I passed the fringes and headed to the wetlands, where the earth became soft under my step. A timber causeway had been built over ground too porous to walk upon. This was a boundary place, neither land nor water, but a merging of both. Annwyn felt close. On the horizon, mountains rose into cloud.

I had only been two days returned to the world of the tribes. Already the clarity I had gained in the forest was fading. I was determined to retain it. I would not repeat the mistakes I had made. I would perform the offering. I would meet whatever was asked of me.

Neha bounded ahead as we stepped down from the causeway, wending between pools and tussocks of nettle to reach the river. Here, the Castroggi was barely more than a stream. I sat at its babbling edge. The low sun cast a gauze light across the marshlands, and the small pools glowed like liquid metal. I pulled the knotted cord from my pouch and let it rest in my lap. Each nodule recalled a poem of praise to the Mothers.

As always, the chanting of their names brought them close and I welcomed their breath in the wind on my skin. But it was not just the Mothers whose nearness I sought. My heart called out to another being. One who had always found me by water. One that I had loved not only as spirit but as flesh.

'Taliesin?' I murmured the name into the river haze. The missing of him was a stone in my chest. I had not known his presence since I had failed him.

Neha barked and I looked for what had roused her. But it was only a heron, stalking at the water's edge.

I turned to observe the rising moon. The time of Winter's Eve drew near, the festival to mark the transition from one year to the next. This was a night of change, of disorder, where the spirits of Annwyn could roam, once more, among the living.

On this night, I prayed, I would see Taliesin.

✝

'Stop here,' said Prydd.

We had reached the boundary of forest.

I had met him at the gate at sunfall, as he had commanded, and he had bidden me follow him, by torchlight, to Llanmelin's north, where fields gave way to the untamed places.

'Are you frightened?' he asked, nodding to the darkness before us.

'No.' I had lived alone in the forest. I knew its laws.

He slipped into the trees, leaving me to follow.

No daylight remained. Our torches made shifting figures of the silver birch trunks. The path was narrow and soft underfoot, the air teeming with the scent of rotting leaves.

We were making an ascent. Prydd moved quickly for a man of his summers and several times I lost sight of his pale cloak. Finally we reached a clearing, circled by a ring of oaks. Prydd stopped at its threshold and took hold of my wrist.

This was a nemeton, a grove for worship and teaching, wherein only the initiated were permitted to stand. A boulder formed an altar within the clearing, and the torchlight revealed its thick mantle of blood.

'Are you frightened?' Prydd asked again.

I told him I was not. But this time it was a lie. Faces loomed in the knots of the trunks. He had not permitted Neha to accompany us from Llanmelin and I felt unguarded without her.

With a grip that belied his age, he held me at the boundary, murmuring skin chants to protect me from the spirits that swirled within. Had he forgotten Kendra law? Did he not know I had drawn closer to these spirits than any other?

He led me into the grove, my arms pimpling in the sudden cold. 'Sit,' he said. Several fallen logs were arranged as benches. Prydd knelt to kindle a flame in the stone-rimmed fireplace in front of the altar. He pulled out a small jar of mead from his leather sack and poured a libation. Then he sat before me, silhouetted by the fire behind him. After some time he said, 'Tell me the spine of our law.'

'Flesh dies, but the soul endures,' I said, unsure of why he asked for this most basic truth. Any farmhand could repeat it.

'And?' he said, prompting the second utterance of the couplet.

'Most things remain hidden,' I said slowly. 'What is unseen is always greater.' Why did he test me on the simplest of our laws?

'Correct.' He paused. 'This is why our knowledge must be hidden.'

I rubbed my fingertips on the course wool of my skirt. Was this another chastisement for singing to Manacca?

'And the deeper purpose of the journeypeople?' he went on.

'To honour the Mothers...to seek the wisdom of Annwyn.'

'Not this.' He paused. 'We command the unseen.'

I frowned. 'We seek it. We cannot command that which is greater.'

'Yet it is our art to show that we do. The tribespeople look to us to control the forces that terrify them. Time. Death. War. Our tool is the sacrifice.' His face was concealed by darkness, his voice emerging from a pool of shadow. 'You, Kendra, possess an unseen force,' he continued. 'You are a cauldron that holds the pure will of the Mothers.'

I dipped my head briefly at his acknowledgement.

'How wasteful is the cauldron that boils over untended, spilling its contents over the ground for only the dogs to drink.'

The fire crackled in the silence, as if sounding its agreement.

'Let us begin.' Prydd began to sing in tuneless drone, summoning the teaching he was about to give.

At first I almost giggled; his high, scraping voice held so little resonance.

But then I saw, as he prayed, something of the grace that long-learning bestowed. Prydd's goal was as mine: to preserve our sovereignty, to preserve our law, and he had done much to achieve it. For the first time, I saw that I could learn from this man. My hands softened in my lap as I listened. He did not despise me. He wanted to ensure I tore no holes in the fabric of his power.

He had ceased his chant. 'How great is your knowledge of death-craft?'

'Poor,' I answered, 'I am better practised at healing than killing.'

'The first lesson is that death must not come too quickly,' he said. 'The moments between the infliction of the wound, and the death that arises from it, are the most potent. He who is offered must be held at that brink for as long as possible.'

'But...' I stared in horror, 'it will cause immense suffering.'

'This brink is the gate into Annwyn, Kendra. It honours him. And you.'

I half laughed in shock. 'How does such cruelty honour me?'

'You cut the passage to the hidden world,' he said. 'You determine how long it is held open.' There was a tremble of excitement in his voice. 'For that moment, you command the unseen.'

I wanted to heed his greater training, but I could not endure it. 'Journeyman,' I said. 'Only the Mothers command the unseen.'

'Perhaps,' he answered, 'but the people must see that you command it. This is how you are powerful.'

I flushed hot with confusion. Was this the journeyperson's art? To conjure an appearance of power? A faint itching in my scar protested the idea. I would not be made powerful by artifice. My knowledge of the Mothers was true. It needed no design or embellishment. My brief moment of faith in him dissolved into the grove air. This was not knowledge. This was wile. I would not lead in this way.

'Do you understand, Kendra?' said Prydd.

I went to argue, but as I opened my mouth, I remembered Caradog's warning. This man held Caradog's trust. I had to gain his. 'I understand.'

'Good,' he said. 'Then let us begin learning the chants that will precede the offering.' He pulled out a linen bundle from his sack, unwrapped it, and placed on the ground a set of twelve metal rods of different lengths and thicknesses, each incised with intricate patterns. Even in the firelight, I recognised the varying lustres of bronze, iron and silver. Learning rods, one the most gruelling methods of teaching I had ever endured.

I exhaled deeply, already fighting fatigue; this would be a long night.

Dawn broke through the forest. Our fire had dwindled. Prydd gathered the rods strewn between us. One by one, through the hours of darkness, he had picked up each rod, handed it to me, and sung one of the chants that I needed to memorise in order to perform the offering. As I listened to the words and repeated them, I observed the size, shape and colour of the rod, as well as the number and spacing of the ridges gouged along its length. In the future, I could remind myself of any of the chants afresh by picking up the rod that was its analogue.

Prydd had tested me night-long, handing me one rod then another in various orders, quietly correcting me when my recitations faltered. It would require many more nights of grove-teaching to ensure I could recall them without hesitation or error.

I looked up with weary eyes at the forest. Lleu's light fell in muted shafts through the trees. The grove was peaceful in the early sun, and I saw that it had only been the movement of flame that had given the trees faces.

I helped Prydd wind a leather band around his tools. My hand slipped as I was tying the knot and the rods clattered to the ground.

Prydd cursed with irritation, and continued to grunt as I handed them back to him in turn. Was it only exhaustion or had something else caused his annoyance? Had I not been diligent in my attention to his teaching? I could not risk him speaking ill of me to Caradog.

'Prydd?' I ventured. 'Have I displeased you this night?'

'No, you learn well,' he said. 'The words come swiftly to your command. But I fear that what is too easily gained, will be too easily given.'

I stifled my protest. 'I regret my poor judgement with the fringe girl,' I began. 'I was beguiled by the innocence of a lost child.'

'A Kendra should not be easily beguiled.'

As I helped him tie the rods for a second time, I saw my chance. 'Perhaps it would improve me to learn something of song law...My art in that branch is not strong. Sometimes I am not sure when I am, or am not, permitted to proclaim a poem...'

'I am no Songman,' he said wearily. 'My branch is law.'

'Which is a higher branch...is it not?'

He muttered his agreement as he fastened his sack across his shoulder.

'Perhaps I would be more worthy of your teaching if I first strengthened my knowledge of song.'

He looked at me with reddened eyes. 'If it would benefit you to learn when to remain silent.'

'Do you esteem the talents of Rhain?'

'Of course. He is Albion's finest poet.'

I waited. I knew it must come from him or he would not approve it.

'I will speak with Rhain and see if he would be prepared to take on another twig.'

He turned his back and did not see me smile.

My whole body ached with exhaustion as I walked back to my hut. I was eager to speak to Rhain, but I needed to sleep first.

When I pushed open my door screen there was a small figure crouched at my hearth. Manacca looked up at me with eyes as round as moons.

'What are you doing?' I said, closing the door. 'Are you hungry?'

She nodded.

I scooped us each a bowl of porridge and loosened it with sheep's milk from a full jug that had been left on my table.

'You cannot stay here,' I said as we ate, although it was greatly comforting to sit with another at my hearth.

She finished her food and giggled as Neha licked the scrapings from the bowl. She was poorly clothed and in great need of a wash. But I was too tired to sew or bathe her now. I could not stay awake any longer. Yawning, I rose and walked to my bed. 'I have to sleep now,' I told her. 'You must return to your hut.'

I took off my cloak and dress, leaving my under-robe, then lifted the blankets and lay down on the sheepskin that covered the straw. When I turned around, she was standing beside the bed. I stared at her, too weary to chastise her. I had told Prydd I would be resting. No one else would be seeking me. Surely no one would know if she stayed for an hour or two?

I wriggled sideways and held open the blankets.

In an instant she was in the bed, her knobbly back against my belly. Despite her grubbiness, she smelt of grass and warm bread. I drew her close.

'I have seen it,' she whispered.

'...seen what?' I murmured. I was halfway to sleep. Had she even spoken?

'The place of many apples.'

'Good...good,' I breathed, too adrift to grasp her meaning.

She squirmed deeper into my embrace. We slept through the rest of the day and into the night.

⊹

'Messenger arrives!'

I heard the guard's shout as I drank milk by my fire. I had awoken at dawn, alone. Manacca must have left during the night. I drained my cup, pulled on my cloak and went outside to hear what news had arrived so early in the day. The sky rang with the distant sword strikes of warriors at practice on the flatlands. Preparations for combat had begun.

A throng of townspeople had gathered in Hefin's courtyard. At their centre was a chestnut stallion, its fur clumped with sweat. The messenger beside it was breathless.

Hefin ordered his servant to bring him ale.

Caradog strode into the courtyard, high-coloured from training. 'Your origin?' he asked when the rider had drunk.

'Tir Cantii,' he said, still panting. 'I bring knowledge from the eastern chiefs...'

There were murmurs in the crowd. The messengers rode day-long, passing their whispered words to fresh riders when their horses fatigued, so that their intelligence may be more swiftly borne. This message had travelled the breadth of Albion.

'Plautius has ceased his term. Ostorius Scapula, the new governor, has reached our shores.'

The townspeople gasped.

'This is sooner than expected,' said Caradog.

'What is known of him?' said Hefin. 'What breed of gut worm is he?'

'There are stories of his violence,' said the messenger. 'He invited the chiefs of Camulodunum to feast on his first evening. The heads of the three who refused him provided table decoration for those who accepted.'

I saw Caradog's jaw tighten.

The messenger paused to drink again. 'The Roman criers say that Scapula will deliver the last of free Albion to the hands of the Empire, that he will subdue the tribes that his predecessor could not.'

Wind whipped hair across Caradog's face. 'He sounds like an enemy who is worthy of my fight.'

'Do we prepare, Horse-end?' asked Hefin.

Caradog turned to him. 'Send riders to the free tribes today. We will launch as soon as they are gathered. We must strike before Scapula has a chance to learn this land.'

'The warriors will come quickly,' said Hefin. 'They are rotten for a fight, as we are.'

'And the offering must be made sooner, also,' said Prydd,

who had appeared beside Caradog.

'Yes,' said Caradog. 'Augur for the day, journeyman.'

'No augury is required. The festival of Winter's Eve is upcoming. We will offer then.'

Caradog turned to me. Although I had not stepped forward, he knew exactly where I was in the crowd. 'Kendra, prepare. You will make the offering on Winter's Eve.'

Seven nights hence.

'May I speak with you, War Chief?'

I had followed him to the temple, where he had come to pour libation for the hastened attack.

'Yes, but I will not stay long,' he said. 'I am keen to send out the riders.'

I sat beside him on the bench. Now that conflict drew imminent, I needed to speak truthfully. There could be no discord between us as we launched into war. He wished me to yield unquestioningly to Prydd, but I could not.

'I have commenced learning with your journeyman, in preparation for the offering.' I paused. 'But there is something in his method that...disturbs me.'

Caradog's eyebrows arched. 'What is it?'

'I am not sure if his reverence is...true.'

His expression fought a smile. 'Are you accusing one of Albion's longest-trained journeymen of falsehood?'

I ignored the mockery. 'His teachings do not...accord with my knowledge of Annwyn.'

Caradog snorted, impatient. 'Prydd is so esteemed a knowledge-bearer that initiates come from farthermost Gaul to train with him. He has allowed me to take leadership here; it would otherwise be impossible. He has been a loyal servant to the tribes.'

'But is he loyal to the Mothers?'

'Ailia...' He frowned, all humour gone. 'I do not seek advice from those of weak faith in my judgement.'

'Please call me by my title.'

'Forgive me, Kendra.' He rose. 'I have a war band to arrange.'

'Forgive *me*, War Chief,' I said. 'But if your war band does not fight with the Mothers, it will fail.'

His face filled with sudden anger. 'Who are you to tell me this? Since when does a girl of no known history advise Albion's greatest war chief?'

My heart thudded with the insult. 'A Roman would show me more reverence than you just did. I am the Kendra. I have come to help you. Why do you disregard me?'

'Because none can help me!' His voice was raised. 'Do you not see that I stand alone in this task?'

'But you do not. What of Hefin, and all the chiefs who have aligned?'

'Ay, but each of them bears his own small piece of Albion. I alone see the greater shape.'

I watched as he sat down again. His calf-skin shirt fell open to his chest and the scent of fresh sweat rose from his skin. He commanded more of the free tribes than any other. I had never considered the cost of such power. 'It is a heavy vessel,' I said softly. 'Why do you choose to bear it?'

He stared at me again, as if appraising my readiness for what he might say. Then he spoke slowly, all mockery gone. 'Albion is a land of many tribes. We have warred with each other over our boundaries. But it is the same Mothers' blood that brims at our wells.' He met my eye. 'We could be one force under one high king.'

'You...?' I murmured.

'Perhaps,' he said. 'I have already done much to bring the western tribes to one mind for this attack. If I could unite all of Albion, it would be undefeatable.'

His voice. His gaze. The pulse in his throat as he spoke. If any could fulfil such a vision it would be him. But was there too much pride in it? 'What of the chiefs' independence?' I asked. 'A love of freedom is also something that the tribes share.'

'I do not wish them to be puppets, for then they would be as mindless as the Roman soldiers. But they must see that unless there is some relinquishing of tribehood, they are subject to the greatest thief of freedom we will ever know.'

'Rome.'

'She does not come here to conquer one tribe. She wants Albion whole and we must fight her whole. Power must be met with power.'

I stared at the flames before the altar. Must we become like our enemies to defeat them? I knew Caradog did not mean this. We all mocked the servile obedience of the enemy's soldiers. Yet none could deny what it had achieved.

I looked back at him. 'Why do you not return east to build such a kingdom?' I asked. 'That is your home. The eastern tribes hold the greatest wealth in Albion. You have already said that their allegiance to Rome is weak—'

'It is not my home,' he interrupted. 'And I do not agree that the greatest wealth is held in the east. I have found a richness here without equal.'

'In metal?'

'Not only this. These are not the gentle hills of the east. This country is harsh and its people are strong. They know how to fight. The eastern kings rolled over like dogs when Claudius came. The mountain chiefs will not roll. Nor will I.'

'What of your own tribe?' I asked. 'Do you bear it no loyalty?'

60

'I have no tribe. My loyalty is to greater Albion and to the Mothers who feed her.'

I took a sharp breath of recognition. We were the same.

'And the Mothers are close here,' he continued. 'Perhaps closer than anywhere I have yet stood. Do you not feel it too, Ailia?'

'Yes,' I said. 'I do.'

'This is the true heart of Albion. This is where I will birth my kingdom.' He shifted on the bench. His beast of a body never seemed to be still for too long. Soon he would rise and leave.

I knew not whether his vision was attainable or if it would buckle under its own ambition. But I saw that it was rightly intended and that his love for the Mothers was fierce. 'You say none can help you,' I ventured. 'But I can.'

'How?' Now he was still.

'It is not only you who has a duty to greater Albion. I, too, must serve many tribes. I am tasked to carry the Mothers' knowledge for all who worship them. Can we not stand together and share this weight?'

He smiled, then said with kindness, 'You are intriguing, and your Kendra's title is a beautiful ornament upon my war, but your power is to inspirit, not to advise. You know nothing of war-craft. You cannot share my burden.'

My face was aflame. What forces had robbed his faith? 'Do you forget the Kendra's strength?' I cried. 'I stand as a bridge to the greatest power you will ever know. The Mothers are within me. Use me. Speak with them through me. Know that they have come to you, because your war is true.'

There was no hope for me if I could not make him see. Hurriedly, I loosened the ties of my dress. 'I have stood face to face with the Mothers and watched them birth the land for which we now fight. See these scars?' I wriggled my dress down my shoulders so he could see the red welts. 'This is where their creation song entered me.'

He startled at the violence in my chest, then lifted his eyes to my face.

'Will you touch the scars, War Chief?' I whispered. 'Some have said that they hear the Mothers' voices in them.'

Slowly, Caradog raised his hand.

My heart was crashing under the scars. Was their song still in me? Would he hear it? His fingers drew closer. I realised how much I wanted his hand on my skin.

'Journeywoman!' Prydd's voice cut through the temple air, sharp as an arrow.

Caradog withdrew his hand, and I was untouched.

I fastened my dress as Prydd walked forward. 'I have spoken to the Songman,' he said, showing no reaction to what he had witnessed. 'He wishes to see you. He awaits in the fruit grove beside the war camp where, I believe, you have previously met him.'

A crow moaned and wheeled through the pale grey sky as I hurried from the temple. Pausing to watch its flight, I yearned for the wild places and the spirits within them who cared nothing for my title. Rhain will teach me, I reassured myself. Rhain will give me the words, the tools, to give voice to my knowledge.

⊹

'Greetings Songman.' Neha and I emerged from the bushes surrounding the grove.

Rhain sat beneath the same tree, as still as a carving. 'How persuasive you are,' he said when I was beside him. 'I did not predict the hairless one would approve you.'

I unwrapped my basket without responding. Did no one imagine me capable of anything? I pulled out a loaf of fresh-roasted bread that

I had collected from Hefin's kitchen, tore it in two and handed him the larger piece, still steaming.

We ate in silence. I had taken no food since yesterday morning and was stupid with hunger. My thoughts quietened with each mouthful of the fragrant bread.

'Are you settled in your new home?' Rhain asked.

'The hut is comfortable.'

'I mean the township. All of us.'

I was grateful he should ask it. Yet I found myself too overwhelmed to answer. By the torch of his question, I saw how wearied I was by being observed and assessed, by having to account for myself with every word, every gesture, by being unknown and, most exhaustingly, by being doubted. The role of Kendra was one of service to the tribes-people. What purpose was the title, if they did not esteem it? Neha stood close, grunting softly as I fondled the loose skin of her belly.

'You are weeping...' said Rhain.

'I am only tired,' I answered. 'Prydd has been grove-training me for the offering.'

'He gives you great trust...'

'In the one task I did not desire.' I brushed breadcrumbs onto the ground.

'Do you fear the offering, Kendra?'

He was impossible to lie to. 'Yes.'

'We all do,' he said. 'That's why it is powerful.'

I glanced at him. The sun had emerged and late-clinging leaves cast speckled shadows across his face. He looked more of the other-world than ever.

'What do you fear in it?' he asked.

'The suffering.'

'But Caradog says you know medicine...'

'I do.'

'Then use it.'

'I am not permitted. Prydd has said that—'

'Are you not a journeywoman? Hide it.'

I met his eye in surprise, then smiled. I felt myself growing yet fonder of this man.

'Make the offering in service to the tribespeople,' he continued. 'It allows them to glimpse Annwyn. None of us can touch the Mothers as you have done.'

I stared at him. I could use my knowledge of plants to dull the pain of a dying man, but I knew no remedy for the impotence that seemed to have beset my title. 'Then why is the Kendra so poorly respected in these tribelands?' I felt shame at the plea in my voice.

Rhain took breath. I saw the muscles of his cheek tighten. When he turned to me his eyes were hardened with despair. 'Because war has changed all,' he said. 'We are fighting for our land and we are losing. Those who lead us are holding to whatever is most easily grasped: the fight, the coinage to fund it. In their fear, they are forgetting what is harder to see...'

He spoke of what was embedded in the land: the vast root bed of knowledge, yielding fruit when it was fertilised with ritual, withering when it was not, the very thing I was tasked to tend. 'But if this is not remembered,' I said, 'what then do we fight for?'

Rhain nodded. 'Whether or not we retain our sovereignty, the war begins to tear us from what is true.'

The grove was alight with darting wrens, drawn by the insects hovering near the fruit.

'What shall I do, Songman?'

'I will not presume to advise she who has stood at creation,' he said gently.

I nodded, grateful that he, at least, acknowledged my memory.

He picked up his water skin and unplugged the stop.

'May I?' I asked when he had drunk. My own skin was empty.

He handed me the flaccid bag. 'I like it stronger than most,' he warned.

I took a thirsty sip then almost spat out the liquid. Many mixed a little spirit with their water, especially where it was not freshly drawn, but this was undiluted ale, dark and potent. How did he withstand a day's worth of such powerful refreshment? Something in the way he stared unwaveringly at the bramble as I gave him back the bladder urged me not to question him.

'When shall we begin the lessons of song?' I asked.

'Now,' he said. 'If you are not too tired.'

'Not at all,' I said, turning to face him.

'The first lesson is short,' he said. 'It pertains to the three aspects that make a poem strong. The first is its meaning. The second is its beauty. The third is the most important and difficult to teach. It is always the last thing to be attained...'

'What is it?' I was not in a mood for riddles.

Rhain paused, then said softly, 'The poet's authority.'

I half-laughed. 'I am Kendra. Surely authority is what I already possess?'

'It is not the appearance of authority that the poem requires,' he said. 'It is true sovereignty of the voice.'

I frowned. 'But is this not what you will teach me, Songman?'

'I can teach you the stories that will create meaning,' he said. 'I can teach you the word-craft and intonation to bring your poems beauty.' He paused, wrapping his fingers around his staff. 'But the boldness, the authority of the Songwoman, must be yours alone.'

⁜

Caradog sent out riders, through forest trackways where enemy scouts would never be met, to carry the news that an attack was now imminent and that whoever opposed Rome should join him by the next dark moon.

Prydd had measured the stars. Winter's Eve was in six nights. The war band would ride for Tir Dobunni three dawns after that.

The first band of warriors emerged from the northwest mountains only a day after the message was sent, late-morning sun glinting from their shields as they rode towards the ramparts. Euvrain and I stood beside Caradog as he met them at the gateway. I saw the thankfulness in his face as they knelt before him to make their vows. There was humility in his ambition, after all. He knew that he could not do it alone.

For six days the bands trailed in, broadening Caradog's camp until it was an ocean of tents, carts and horses. Fighters from the Decleangli and Ordovices came from the north, the Silures to our west. Never had I seen such numbers of warriors.

By day they trained their weapon skills and by night they drank ale and demanded stories by their fires. Caradog walked among them constantly. He was not a leader to rule from the chieftain's hut, but parried with them, learning their strengths that he might place them well in battle, and sat at their fires, praising their courage and the greatness of their ancestors. 'This is the strongest fighting band Albion has ever known,' he told them in turn. 'This is the band that will turn the war.'

I saw the ties of loyalty it wove.

Caradog often asked me to accompany him as he walked through the camp, announcing that the Mothers had blessed this war by returning the Kendra. But beyond these displays, he spoke little to me, and did not linger beside me when we returned to the township.

No matter how early I rose to walk to the temple, Caradog was always standing on the northern platform, looking out towards the mountains in the chill autumn dawn. Although over forty chieftains had joined us, there were still many others who had not. They sent back messages that they would not move on an enemy who was yet to threaten their territory. But we all knew it was because Caradog did not yet have their trust.

In the meetings of the council one name arose more often and with more argument than any other. Cartimandua. Queen of the Brigantes. It was her war vows that Caradog desired above anyone else's. Yet she had been one of the first to swear allegiance to Rome.

'Why does he care so greatly for the alliance of this queen?' I asked Prydd on a foggy dusk as we headed for the forest grove. 'He does not pursue the other traitor chiefs...'

Prydd looked at me with the faint disdain that told me I had asked, again, of something I should already have known. 'There are strong ties between Caradog and Cartimandua. She was raised in his father's house,' he said. 'She is his sister by fosterage and his cousin by blood.'

I nodded and walked on. Despite my distrust of Prydd, I had learned much by his instruction as we prepared for Winter's Eve. I had not raised my concerns with Caradog again. I needed to wait until I had the war chief's respect. I needed to prove my authority.

But there were no hours in the day for further lessons with Rhain. Instead I gathered late-growing yarrow and brewed the tinctures that would ensure the tribesman I offered would journey to Annwyn without fear or pain. I practised the chants Prydd taught me in the grove, tracing my fingers down the metal rods he had given me to remind me of which words came next. And I sharpened my Kendra's blade that it would do its work quickly and with accuracy.

✝

The day of Winter's Eve dawned cold and windy.

Outside, cattle bellowed as they were drawn down from their

summer pastures into their winter pens. Today commenced the blood month, when the oldest and weakest of the herds were culled, beginning with the beasts we would eat this night.

I prepared alone in my hut, fasting and observing silence throughout the day. As dusk drew near, Prydd came to my door to accompany me to the temple. We passed the slaughter yard, where two of Hefin's women were butchering the day's kill. Neha lapped at the blood that pooled on the path. Already the scent of death was beginning to dissolve the boundaries between our world and Annwyn. The year was readying to turn.

Rhain and the journeymen were gathered in the temple. In long fur cloaks and horned head-pieces they looked half-animal, hybrid beings that straddled the realms, which tonight they were.

None more so than I.

Prydd handed me a leather cloak of black-green feathers, ceremonial dress, designed for splendour, not ease. It hung heavy across my shoulders and the spikes of the quill ends dug into my neck. I would wear this for the procession, then shed it for the offering when I would need to move freely.

From a basket on the floor, Prydd pulled out a silver circlet upon which the upper part of a dog's skull was mounted. 'It was made for this night.' He placed it on my head, grunting as he adjusted the band. 'Groom your hair, Kendra. These knots are unfitting.'

I said nothing. My hair bore testament to whom I had lost, to Taliesin. I would not alter it until I had seen him.

When Prydd was satisfied with my costume, he met my eye. 'Albion looks to Caradog to free us from our enemy,' he said. 'Tonight he looks to you to sanctify his war.'

I held Prydd's stare. Was he willing me to fail?

He was right. My competence tonight would cast the seed of a successful attack. If my hand trembled, if my cut to the throat was ragged, not only would I show myself unworthy, but I would endanger the war. Beneath my cloak, sweat beaded on my back and chest. I straightened my shoulders. I could not let him see that I was terrified.

At Prydd's instruction, the journeymen took up the rattles and belled staffs that would summon the Mothers and signal to the township that the procession had begun. I adjusted my sword belt, hooked a string of bells around my neck, and took my place at the head of the line. With three strikes of his staff on the ground, Prydd started the chant and we proceeded from the temple.

The clouds were aglow as Lleu neared the edge of the sky. Our path was lined with tribespeople. Their eyes widened as we approached in our dazzling adornment. For a moment, I swelled in their awe. We, the journeypeople, were something other as we moved steadily forward: a many-headed beast that moaned in strong, low unison. I had known little chance to stand before my own people in ritual before I had condemned myself to the forest. I sensed, now, for the first time, an inkling of the glamour, to which Prydd gave such importance.

Then a sweet, familiar face caught my eye in the crowd, and, as quickly as it came, the sensation receded. Manacca would be forbidden to attend the offering. No glamour could obscure her lack. I held her bright gaze as I passed her, smiling to reassure her that it was still I beneath the black halo of feathers, the gaping skull.

The crowds thickened as we neared the northern gateway. I felt myself to be part of a giant turning wheel. War had torn me into pieces that one year in solitude had barely made whole. Now war was coming again and I was called to bless it and perform the acts that would ensure its success.

My belly curdled with a wave of fear.

I trusted Caradog. I trusted the Mothers.

I prayed that I could trust myself.

3

Night is Day

Nothing exists but by its opposite.
Where force is untempered, it cannot endure.

THE DUSK was windless, the moon almost new.

The lake held the sky in a quivering likeness, a perfect surface for the ritual we would enact. Fires blazed along the shore, mirrored in the water, calling the Mothers close, that they would clearly see how much they were loved.

We had proceeded almost an hour along the Castroggi path to arrive here, a remote inland lake, surrounded by woodland and bordered by peat.

I had asked not to be told his name. He was dark-haired and beard-less—fourteen or fifteen summers—a part-trained warrior. We were giving the Mothers a fighter we could scarcely afford to lose, trusting that they would repay us manyfold in strength and victory. He had been chosen because he was still in his threshold time, shoulders and chest only freshly swollen under a child's skin.

He had been readied and washed before my arrival. As he kissed my hand, I forced a tiny square of moist bread into his mouth. His black eyes looked up, alight with fear. I gave him the smallest nod and prayed that the wolfsbane would work its magic swiftly.

Now we both waited.

The people of the war camp and greater Llanmelin stood in a shifting silence behind me, mothers hushing their young. A gradual slope rising from the bank allowed all a clear view.

Caradog, Euvrain, and their children stood at the front, flanked by Hefin and Rhain. Prydd and his assistants laid out tools in front of the gathering.

The lesser journeymen grew silent. For many hours they had stood at the water's edge chanting and drumming as the crowds gathered in. The steady rise of sound had brought all present to readiness, to the precipice of Annwyn.

Slowly, despite my terror, I began to drink in the nourishing communion, the dissolving of separate skins that only came with ritual. There was purpose to this act. It made us thankful. It joined us. One death to sustain the living.

'Begin,' said Prydd.

The boy's eyes rolled, half-closed, as two journeymen braced his arms. The wolfsbane had taken effect. He would endure three deaths: one for our ancestors, one for us, and one for our children. I was to perform the second and most important death: for our sovereignty.

Already my hands trembled too much. I could not risk inaccuracy. Quickly, as Prydd was positioning the boy, I turned to the lake, pulled a tiny bronze vial from my belt pouch, and sucked its contents into my mouth. Within moments, my heartbeat slowed and my hands grew still. I turned back to the kneeling boy.

Two figures appeared at my side to remove my headpiece and

feathered cloak. Only a thin layer of linen now screened me from the chill air.

Prydd handed me a woollen bandage. 'Close his sight.'

I crouched before the boy. For a moment, he roused and his eyes found mine. As I tied the bandage around his head, I felt the soft heat of his temples. He whimpered. I pressed my lips to his cheek, then stepped aside. It was time for the first death.

A journeyman came forward bearing an iron axe.

Prydd sang in a tuneless drone. *Mothers hear us. Bear witness to our reverence. Open the gates to Annwyn and stretch out your arms to us.*

At the conclusion of these words, the journeyman raised the axe high, then swung its blunt stub to the back of the young man's head. With a dull crack he fell to the ground.

The two journeymen on either side lifted him back upright, while I stepped forward, grasping my sword. My heart was a frenzy of motion, though I felt its pounding as if from a distance. I knelt before the youth and gently lifted his chin. His head lolled—was he conscious?

Was I?

'Brother,' I began. The word sounded muffled as I uttered it. I did not feel like one who could make speech.

This night we alter your form that you become sacred. Your death is a knife that parts the realms, an opening by which we might glimpse our creators.

I felt myself beginning to sway. I drew breath and carried on.

Your death is our awakening.

Your death is our reverence.

Our lives are a debt to the Mothers.

Your death repays it.

I continued to recite the dedications that I had learnt at Prydd's instruction to protect a soul that would soon be cast from its earthly vessel. With each verse, my legs seemed to grow weaker until I was struggling to hold myself upright. Had I drunk too much of the medicine? I had never calculated quantities in error before. Prydd was behind me, his voice urgent in my ear, bidding me make the cut.

I inhaled and reeled with the sudden intensity of smells that flooded my nostrils: the shit that had fallen from the boy as he was struck, his sweat, his fear, so pungent I could open my mouth and taste them on my tongue. This was not *my* body. These were not *my* senses. I was knowing through another form.

I buckled forward, grasping hold of the boy to keep myself upright. My sight found no clarity, no detail, just the shape and heat of the body to which I clung.

I could not push myself back to kneeling; my legs, my arms were as soft as water. With my next breath, my limbs had entirely dissolved and I was only muscle and spine. Slowly, I began to wind my length around the boy's warm torso, squeezing his hips, his belly, his chest— how loudly his heartbeat drummed through my body—until my nose was at his throat.

'For Lleu's sake, Ailia...now!' Prydd growled under his breath.

I heard the sound, but I knew only the desire of the adder. My tongue flickered, searching the rhythm of my prey's pulse. I found it. I drew back my head and struck, plunging my teeth into tender sinew. Blood erupted, fragrant over my skin as I tightened around him.

There was no more fear. Just the need to draw his warmth into my hungry body.

The boy crumpled. I felt hands pulling me off him. I twisted and writhed, angry to be pulled from my prey, but the journeymen had taken him to the bank's edge and left me lying alone on the ground. I lifted my head, now heavy as a woman's, and watched as they laid him in the shallow water.

They held him upright, exposing his wound for all to see. It was a perfect opening: wide and deep enough to promise certain death, shallow enough to permit a last few enduring moments of life. A gate to the Mothers.

The black sky shivered. We were with our creators.

The journeymen began a low, keening chant, quickly joined by the crowd. There were no words, only sound that flowed from each tribesperson into the wound. By this sound, the boy would carry our voices back to the Singing.

When the initial violence of twitching had ceased, the journeymen released the boy and submerged him in the water. For some time there was still breath and movement. At last the bubbles ceased rising from the cut at his throat. The water was opaque with blood and stirred mud. He was not given the final rites to free his soul from his body, but instead was weighted with stones so that his spirit could not escape back to Llanmelin, but would remain here at the brink of Annwyn, for as long as the Mothers chose to preserve him.

The lake was still and shallow here, its bed swampy. Floating islands of moss formed blankets over much of its surface. Fish did not thrive in this air-deprived water, but death would endure here. Death was sustained here.

I lay my head back down, comforted by the firm ground. I sensed Rhain crouching beside me. 'Is it done?' I whispered.

'Yes.' He helped me to my feet.

My dress stuck to me, wet with blood. I had scarcely any strength in my legs. It was as if they were newly grown and never used. The serpent's keen sense still lingered in me and I could smell Rhain's skin, the oil of his scalp, the woody scent of his relief.

'You did it beautifully,' he said.

Caradog's voice spoke behind me, 'Well done, Kendra.'

I spun to face him and reeled with the force of his smell: iron, salt, and the fierce animal odour of his sex. I gripped Rhain's forearm, as the limbless adder threatened to possess me once more. This was the scent of Caradog's power. But beneath its raw strength, I could smell something else: tender and intricate, like a freshly-crushed acorn or milk just-soured with a drop of apple vinegar. It was the scent of self-doubt.

I stared at him, unable to speak. I could smell his fear, that which no one saw.

'What's wrong with her?' said Caradog to Rhain as I leaned heavily against him.

'She's exhausted from the rite,' said Rhain. 'I'll attend to her.'

'Bring her to me when she is steady,' he said. 'I want the chiefs to share in what she has done this night.' He met my eye before he turned away. In his gaze was a different regard.

✣

The darkness was complete now. The crowd dispersed quietly by torch-light onto the forest path. Some were already taking long draughts of the wormwood mead that would open their sight to the spirits of Winter's Eve, hoping for a glimpse of those they had lost.

I stood at the bank, Neha at my feet, while Prydd and the lesser journeymen collected the instruments. I felt at peace with what I had done. Later, in the township, there would be fires, meat and dancing throughout the night. Never did the tribes rejoice in their living more fiercely than when they had witnessed a gift.

'Mead, Kendra?' Rhain held forth his bladder.

I drank thirstily. The strong water spread through my limbs, melding with the wolfsbane that lingered in my blood.

'Shall I walk back with you?' he asked.

'I will stay a little longer.'

'Then I will stay also. You should not be unguarded on Winter's Eve.'

'Thank you, Songman. But I would prefer to be alone.'

The last of the crowd were leaving the shore.

Rhain nodded and kissed me farewell.

I watched as he and the journeymen disappeared into the trees, then turned back to the lake. Now that my Kendra's work had been completed, I hoped to make my own claim on this night's sacred promise.

Following the lake edge, I walked north of the boy's silt grave, until I reached a section of shore obstructed by willows. Slipping between their branches, I found myself in a chamber edged by a grove of watery trees. Mist from the lake met the drifting fronds.

In such a place, perhaps, I would see him.

I wore only my blood-soaked dress. I unbelted my sword and tore off the string of bells that marked me as Kendra.

Unmetalled, I stood at the water's brink, staring across the black surface. Would he come? I felt half-formed for the wanting of it. 'Taliesin,' I whispered, shivering. 'Are you there?'

The lake was silent. Distant shouts from the celebration and the pulse of a drum drifted down from Llanmelin. Neha sniffed, indifferent, at the shoreline.

I prayed to the Mothers. Had I not made reparation for at least some of my mistakes? Had I not honoured them with my every thought, every gesture, since those mistakes were made? 'Taliesin, come,' I murmured.

I hung my head under the weight of stillness that met my prayer.

Neha growled, alert to a sound in the forest behind me.

Was it him? I listened intently. Neha barked and I hushed her to quietness.

A faint crunch of footsteps in the distance, louder as they approached.

'Taliesin?' I called through the mist.

The footsteps drew closer.

'Praise the Mothers,' I murmured, my heart galloping.

The footsteps stopped just beyond the screen of the willow.

'Reveal yourself.' My whispered voice trembled. 'Stand before me, my love.'

The fronds rustled as he pushed between them.

For one exquisite moment it was Taliesin in the darkness, before Caradog's powerful scent told me otherwise. 'What are you doing?' I spluttered in shock. 'Why are you here?' Disappointment robbed me of my graces.

'I saw that you did not return with the journeymen...' He paused. 'You seemed unsteady after the rite...I was unsure of your safety.'

'My safety? I can survive the forest better than any. Have I not proven that, at least?'

He stood unmoving. The thin moon's light was smothered by the grove and I could not see his expression. 'Even the most powerful warrior can fall if the wound is well-placed,' he said.

My heart softened. I knew that he bore his leadership heavily and now I was among those whom he believed he must protect. 'Be free of duty to me,' I told him. 'Now you have made me slay a tribesman, there is little left for me to fear.'

'Who is Taliesin?'

I flinched at the word on his lips. I had told no one in Albion of his name.

'He is...' How should I have answered? Who *was* this man, this Taliesin, whose memory would not release me? He was someone I had loved to the limits of my being. But he was lost to me. And I had not yet understood it.

'Just a teacher I lost in the slaughter of Cad,' I answered. 'I thought I might have glimpsed him this night.'

'Perhaps I should become a teacher,' he said. 'If they call forth such affection.'

I said nothing, gathering my bells and sword.

He walked to the bank and dropped to a crouch. 'Shall I wait for you?' he asked. 'Is your business here finished?'

'Do as you please.'

'Then it pleases me that you sit with me.'

The mead and wolfsbane had ebbed from my veins, leaving my mouth dry and my forehead aching. I had hoped to speak with Caradog again, but tonight I had little appetite for it. 'For a moment only, as I am tired.'

I squatted beside him and looked over the lake. The moon's bright lip seemed to smirk from the water.

'Three days from now we will have struck,' he said.

How different he was from the one I had loved. Caradog was not wounded. His spirit sailed forth unquestioningly, its certainty unbreached. And yet there had been that scent, that fear. I could still catch a trace of it when he moved his head close: soft, faintly curdled, like the scent of a child. He was not unbreachable. But it was only through the adder's senses that I had seen it. 'Why do you do it?' I asked him. 'Why do you fight on when so many others have accepted defeat?

He looked at me, his eyes catching the moon's thin light. 'Because I was born for this war.'

I startled at the claim. 'Do you admit no doubt?' I asked. 'No fear?'

'Of course there is fear. If I did not stand with fear, I would be no war chief.'

'Is it death that frightens you?'

'No,' he paused. 'I fear the loss of our sovereignty.'

78

'And yet you would ask chiefs to relinquish their sovereignty to you...in country that is not your own.' These were not the lands of his ancestors. He held no blood claim to them.

He chuckled. 'I will earn sovereignty by defending it. This war is the Mothers' test to prove I am worthy of ruling the breadth of their country.'

I stared in disbelief. He spoke as if he were the earth, and the tribespeople, the Romans, and the Mothers were the stars that circled it. 'Surely you do not suggest that the Mothers *summon* the Romans? Against their own people?'

'I do not say it freely, Ailia, but I trust you to hear it. The Mothers determine who rules their land. They are powerful enough to repel this army if they so choose. They allow this war to test our bonds to these tribelands. To test me. No other has the command to lead Albion to victory.'

I shook my head. 'Nor the ambition.'

'Is ambition not needed? The Roman Empire has claimed more land than any before it—Aegyptus, Africa, Anatolia...it would take years to walk its span. If I can defeat this army, I am defeating the greatest power in the world.'

And then, with perfect clarity, I saw the shape of the fear that I had smelled so distinctly. His fear was not of this war. His fear was what he would be without it. I felt a power in the knowing of it. There was a frailty in him, as in any soul. One that even he was not aware of.

His features were hidden in the darkness, but his voice was clear and close. 'What of you, Ailia?' he said. 'Why have you come to fight with me? Are *you* not afraid?'

I stroked Neha's back. What held me to this war? Like Caradog, I was steered by the Mothers. But I knew they were victims of this war, as much as its makers. They needed protection. I knew that what was most powerful, was also most fragile. Rome knew this too, and this was why she must be fought.

But beneath all this, there was another reason. For most of my life I had been without skin, untethered and unformed. Even with skin, even as the Kendra, I still had no home, no belonging. Caradog and I were the same. The war told us who we were.

✢

A shadow of confusion passed over Euvrain's face as Caradog and I entered the feast hall. 'Forgive our lateness, noblewoman,' I said, sitting beside her. 'I knew deep trance during the rite and I remained at the lake until it passed. Caradog lingered to ensure my safe return.'

Euvrain smiled. 'He is as much shepherd as warrior.' She sipped her mead. 'Are you restored now?'

'Yes,' I said. 'A little tired.'

'Exhausted I am sure.' She placed her hand on top of mine. It was as cool as water. She wore no cloak and her blue dress was pinned to reveal the swell of her shoulder. 'What did you speak of as you returned?' she asked, drawing her hand back to her lap.

I paused. Like Rhain, she compelled my truthfulness. 'We spoke of his motivations for war.'

'Oh?' She frowned. 'He told you of Togidumnus?'

'No...' I knew that Caradog's oldest brother had been killed in the Medway battle, only days after Rome's arrival, but nothing more.

'It would have surprised me if he did. He speaks little of his family...' She lowered her voice. 'But it is much of why he fights.'

'To avenge the death?'

'Yes.' Her face was turned so that I alone might hear her words. The scent of nut oil rose from her throat. 'And to prove himself worthy of surviving what his brother did not.'

'Who doubts it?' I asked.

'None living.' Euvrain leaned yet closer. 'But Belinus, his father, would have wished Caradog killed in his brother's place.'

I drew back. 'That cannot be true.'

'Why not?' She looked at me. A dark outline of ground stone made her blue eyes luminous. 'Does a whelping bitch not condemn the weakest of her pups to perish?'

'But Caradog is no weak pup.'

'No,' she agreed, laughing. 'He is certainly no longer that.'

I glanced at Caradog, speaking with Hefin on the opposite side of the fire. What flaw could his father have seen? Even the fragilities I had scented did not weaken him, but provided a grit, an alloy, to the metal of his nature that only increased its lustre. I turned back to his wife. 'Why have you told me this?'

'Because I trust you. And the better you know him, the better you will serve his war.'

'Then tell me more.'

She smiled. 'Spin with me tomorrow, if you are free.'

'I will be free.'

Someone was striking a spoon against an ale-pot.

'Hear me speak!' Prydd was struggling to raise his shrill voice over the gathering. The guests grew silent. 'I wish to honour the Kendra. This night she has performed the offering with the power and grace of the Mothers.'

The feasters murmured their agreement.

'It was no easy task to train her,' he continued. 'But it appears that my efforts have been well-rewarded.'

I bowed in response to his words. He did not will me to fail. He sought my success as testament to his design. If I allowed him to think it was, he would continue to strengthen me.

'Well said, journeyman!' said Caradog. 'A noble acknowledgement and rightly made. I hope she brings us such power as we fight in Tir Dobunni.'

Prydd stared at him. 'Do you take the Kendra into enemy territory?'

'Of course,' said Caradog. 'In my own war band.'

As I worked at my table the next morning, measuring ointment into jars to take to Tir Dobunni, my thoughts twitched with memories of the killing, of Caradog's scent.

A tap on my door screen roused me from my task.

'Euvrain?' I called.

But it was Rhain who slipped into my hut, quiet as a deer, and sat at my fire. His face looked drawn.

'What is amiss?' I asked. 'And why did you not sing last night?' I had not even seen him at the feast.

'I was taken unwell as I returned to the township.'

'With what symptoms? I will treat you...'

He shook his head. 'It has passed with the dawn.'

Like all illnesses caught from the ale-pot, I thought. 'Then what brings you, Songman?'

'To know how you fare after the rite,' he said. 'I saw how far you drifted to Annwyn. I know what such a journey can cost.'

He was right. The offering had emptied me, yet I was glad that I had known animal form. The Mothers were still within me. I still held the power of change. I stared at my jars, unsure what to make known.

'What is it?' Rhain said, reading my quietness.

'I...I knew change in the ritual.'

Rhain smiled. 'As you should. Why so stern? What form found you?'

'Serpent.'

Rhain's smile dropped away.

'What's wrong?' I asked, cursing the scantness of my training.

He rubbed his eyes in agitation. 'Do not tell the hairless man. He is already fearful...'

'What, Rhain?' I said. 'What does it mean?'

'The serpent is too powerful for most. It holds the very essence of journey-law. For the adder is not reborn by death, but many times within its own lifetime...'

'...by the shedding of its skin,' I murmured.

'Ay,' said Rhain. 'Only the strongest can command the serpent.'

☩

The smiths' fires roared as I passed them on the way to the saddler to collect my new bridle. Caradog had ordered more spears and arrows to be made for the war bands. There was no need for helmets or other battle ornaments. Our work would be done before we were seen on any battle field.

As I stopped to watch one of the smiths at work, I felt a tug at my skirt. She must have seen me pass by the north gate and run in after me. 'You can't come in here, youngling,' I told her gently. 'You know the journeyman has forbidden it.' And it was I who would pay if he saw us, I thought.

Manacca nodded, crestfallen, and turned away.

I grabbed her small, filthy hand. 'Watch the forge with me for a moment. It is pretty to see the iron glow.'

The smith was making a snaffle ring for a bit. He took a thin bar of iron, set it in the coals, and pumped the bellows. Manacca and I stared as the bar grew red, then orange. When it was almost white, the smith pulled it out and hammered it thinner, working deftly to turn it before it hardened. The strikes rang like a musical beat, the hum of the furnace a steady accompaniment. When its colour had faded he thrust the bar back into the coals. This time, it was hammered even thinner, and, just as it was almost too cool, the smith lifted it from the anvil in two pincers and bent it swiftly, fluidly, into its perfect, curled shape.

I stared, enthralled. There was no template, no measurement. He forged in the moment, by some grace, some instinct, in his hands. I glanced at the pieces that hung from his hut roof. Each was uniquely shaped. How many years of training had bestowed on him this skill?

He caught Manacca's eye and smiled. Then he plunged the iron into a bucket with a mighty hiss. He examined the cooled snaffle, then shook his head. 'Too narrow,' he said, holding it toward Manacca. 'You can have it if you want.'

I farewelled her outside the north gate, where we could not be seen. 'I won't be back for a little while,' I said, kissing her cheek.

'Where are you going?'

'I am going with the war chief...to fight the Romans in Tir Dobunni.'

'For cattle?'

I laughed. 'Not cattle.'

'Then what?'

I crouched before her. She was starved of even the most basic knowledge. 'We are fighting for our land, Manacca. The Romans want to claim it.'

'But Hefin is chief of this land...'

'The Emperor wants to be chief.'

'Will he live here, if he is chief?' she gasped, eyes round.

'No. He lives in Rome.'

'How can he be chief if he is not here?'

I wiped a smear of ash from her forehead. 'I don't know.' I wished

I could bring her back to my hut and comb out the lice that teemed in her scalp.

She clutched the snaffle bit, thoughtful. 'Will we win the fight, Aya?' she asked. 'Are we stronger?'

'We have to be.'

'But what if we are not?' By Lleu, she had the persistence of a mule.

'Then we must learn to love the taste of turnips. For our apple trees will not yield fruit if we are not sovereign.'

Manacca gripped my hand as I stood to leave. 'Are you scared?'

'Yes.'

✛

Dawn broke cold on the day of the attack. Frost crunched underfoot as I walked behind the tents to squat. 'Go on!' I shooed Neha, who sniffed at my stream. She trotted off to join the war hounds.

Forested slopes rose on both sides of the camp. We had departed yesterday morning and ridden day-long on mountainous paths, reaching the Habren an hour before sunset. Caradog had cast a silver sword into the fast-running water, before the way-finders had searched a shallow part of the river where the horses could cross, then led us another hour in dusk to reach this hidden clearing.

A rustle in the leaves made me jump to my feet, but it was only a badger trundling through hawkweed. We were in the Cuda Forest, only half a day's ride to the Dobunni border, where we would launch our attack. We were close to our enemy, beyond the protection of the river's boundary. I had barely slept.

Caradog was awake, warming his hands and joking with the chiefs gathered at his fire. I nodded a wordless greeting and crouched at the fire-edge.

'Sleep well, Kendra?' asked Caradog.

'As well as any might sleep before meeting their enemy.'

'I sleep as a babe, on the eve of battle,' he said. 'I don't want to waste what might be my last night.'

'Then why spend it sleeping?' said one of the chiefs, and the men laughed.

Caradog began speaking to them of the route we would take to the Sun Road, scarcely glancing at me.

I had been sure that the offering would have heightened his esteem of me. But since that night, when I had glimpsed what lay within him, he had shown even greater reluctance to hear my council, barely speaking to me during the days of war preparation. I had spun twice with Euvrain at her invitation and she told me what I was already learning for myself: that his moods were as capricious as the solstice tides and just as impossible to turn.

'Is this what his father protested in him?' I had asked, as we spun at her fire.

'This, and the fact that Caradog would see no compromise in the dealings with Rome.' Euvrain smiled. 'In that matter he is entirely constant.' She leaned forward to correct the line of my wool.

'Do they weary you?' I asked, setting my spindle beside me. 'His tempers?'

'At times. But once you have his loyalty, it is as certain as sunrise.'

He had offered me no such certainty. But it was me he had chosen to accompany his personal war band and bless it for battle, while Prydd had been sent with another.

'Thank you,' I said as a servant handed me a bowl of steaming porridge.

Amidst the laughter, there was a heightened alertness in the warriors. Slowly they dispersed to sharpen their weapons and pace through their sword strokes in preparation for tonight's attack.

Caradog had split his fighters into five bands of over a thousand men. Each band had taken a different path from Llanmelin, with a different target at its end. But tonight, when the star of the hunter reached its apex, the bands would move all at once. Five of the Roman outposts would be burned and their soldiers slaughtered. The grain fields, store huts and bridges that supplied the camps would be destroyed as well.

I had questioned this when Caradog announced it at the council, for these actions would injure the Dobunni tribespeople as well as the Romans.

'They forfeited my loyalty when they knelt before Claudius,' he had said. 'We will protect them if they join with us. Otherwise they are my enemy.'

Night and day.

We had already been joined last night by Dobunni resistors who were ready to fight with us against their Roman captors. Other messages had come from the Durotriges, whose chiefs pledged to move northward with their spears, into the tail of Tir Dobunni, while we tore at its belly. There were insurrections planned and promised by warriors in the Iceni to our east and the Coritani to our north.

I glanced at Caradog, now standing alone at the fire.

All across Albion was an invisible web of hope and rebellion, the war chief poised at its centre, alert to any tug or movement on its strands. Yet there was one space, one branch where his thread had found no purchase.

Even now he stared northward, as if Cartimandua may emerge from the forest at any moment.

I scraped the last of my porridge and stood up beside him. 'She is not sending men, War Chief,' I said. 'We will defeat them without her.'

He turned to me. 'When the Roman army lies butchered across

the fields of Tir Dobunni,' he said, 'then she will come to my hearth. Then she will honour me as war chief.'

'Turn to those who honour you now,' I whispered.

'Do you seek to command me yet again?'

'I seek to help you.'

'I will ask for what help I need.'

Caradog was intuitive as an animal. He must know that I had seen his fear. How could I tell him that I honoured him despite it? Because of it? 'You have my loyalty, Caradog,' I said.

He nodded, without expression, and walked to his tent.

The soldier stood at the northwest corner of the viewing platform, behind spiked palisades. His face held a faraway expression as he stared into the Dobunni night. Was he thinking of the bread he would eat when he finished his shift, or was he remembering his wife's sun-coloured shoulders in the warmlands of Italia?

I looked at the sky. Fifty of us crouched behind a hedge of gorse, hidden by darkness. Despite the cold of early winter, the men were bare-chested, the warmth of their muscles releasing the foul cabbage stench of the woad on their skin.

The rest of our war band was positioned in clusters of warriors surrounding the fort.

Caradog's best slingsman had his first stone poised. I stood beside him. My task was to tell Caradog when the hunter's star had reached its crest. Prydd had taught me the calculation using cord and the horizon.

'It is time,' I whispered to Caradog, pocketing the cord. I looked to the fort, inhaling sharply as a second soldier appeared on the platform. The scouts had told us explicitly that by night the forts were guarded by only one.

'I cannot hit two at once,' whispered the slingsman in panic.

'We need a second slingsman,' said Caradog. 'Hefin? Patuix? Who is confident?'

It was at least forty paces, with a keen gradient, but I had shot more difficult targets when I was forest living. 'I am,' I said.

'You?' hissed Caradog. He had never seen me wield a weapon.

My sling still hung beside my sword on my belt. I knew the skill was still sharp in my fingers. 'Let me try.'

'Go then!' he said.

The slingsman passed me a river stone, heavy and smooth as an egg in my palm.

'Prepare,' said Caradog.

'Shall I take the closer one?' I whispered to my companion as the warriors made space around us.

'Yes,' he answered. 'He is taller and easier to hit.'

I circled my shoulder to loosen its movement, then positioned the stone in the cradle of the sling, jiggling it to sense its weight.

The wind carried the voices of the guards and their clipped Latin tongue. The first of them looked suddenly in our direction, frowned, then turned away.

'Begin,' said Caradog.

I could barely breathe for my thundering heart. I set my eye to the soldier's chest. I had not trained to the warrior's mind. I could only imagine that he was a buck and my belly was empty.

We began to spin the slings in full circles. My pulse grew steady with the motion. The slings hummed softly in perfect alignment as the bands of leather sliced through the air. We increased our speed, summoning the force that would make the stones kill.

My buck looked up.

'Now,' whispered Caradog.

My eyes were welded to the buck's breast. At the apex of our next arc, we opened our grasp and let the stones fly.

Both soldiers crumpled behind the points of the palisades. The Mothers were with us.

Caradog gave the whistled signal and several hundred fighters surged forward from the darkness, throwing hooks and ropes over the palisades, and pouring like water over the walls, in silence.

I stood at the base of the fortress as a tide of bodies rushed past me, whispering prayers to the Mothers to strengthen our fighters. I would not follow. The Kendra must be preserved.

Within moments, the clashes of swords and howls of injury rang out from the fort. Now I could lift my voice in curses to the enemy. I screeched and ululated into the smoking sky, but my cries felt empty when I could not see whom I condemned.

The last of the tribesmen were over the wall. Their ropes hung free, awaiting their departure. I felt outcast, useless, hiding my flesh while my people risked theirs. I could stand here no longer.

I ran, grabbed a rope and hauled myself up, struggling over the palisades and onto the platform behind it. Below me was killing as I had never seen it. Fire, smoke, bodies, shit. And blood, so much blood the ground was dark with it.

The Romans had been sleeping. Many must have been slain before they had even awoken. The rest now fought, without armour or strategy, clumsy with shock.

Many tribesmen were shooting arrows from the platform, while others wielded spears and swords on the ground. Caradog was among them, attacking a thick-set soldier with the fervour and skill that I had often heard praised, but never had seen. I stared, entranced, as he blocked and stabbed, eyes blazing, skin shining with sweat, his movement precise, yet utterly free.

He bellowed as he impaled the soldier through the chest, alive with the exhilaration of granting his body the task for which it was born. And there was no question now, as I watched him pull his sword from his opponent's sternum, then turn to another, that he was born for this war. I saw now what it must cost him to fight by stealth. For he was a warrior.

Hefin and Caeden fought at his flank, protecting his back with equal fire. This was not the order and discipline of the Roman army. This was the soul of the tribes brought to flesh, iron and motion, the animal turmoil that channelled the Mothers. This was pure spirit. And Caradog was at its shining head.

As if called by my gaze, he looked up and saw me. 'Get back!' he roared, scowling, before he lunged again, immersed in the battle.

I was not supposed to fight. But, by the Mothers, I wanted to. I had no stones to throw from the platform, but I had my sword. It had killed a Roman soldier once before. It could do so again. I dropped down from the platform, skidding in blood pooled on the dirt.

A man shouted in Latin behind me and I spun to face him, drawing my sword. He was young, soft-lipped and his eyes were full of fear. I faltered—he was a son, a brother—then I raised my weapon; these were our tribelands and they would stay free.

The force of each strike shuddered through my bones. Mothers, what had I done? I was in no practice. I swung wildly, desperately. This was not like any fight I had known in my training. I was not seeking to be artful, nor outwit my opponent. I was seeking to kill. The purpose awakened my skill.

I was not deft, but I screamed with the fury of the Mothers and the soldier was scared. With three swipes, I knocked his sword from his hand. With the fourth I buried my blade between his ribs, until I felt it hit bone at the back of his body. He met my eye, cursing my people to eternal suffering, as he sank to the ground.

I withdrew my blade and wiped it clean on his night tunic.

Through the roar of burning, I heard Caradog shouting. 'Rise Ailia! To your rear!'

I spun to face another, his short sword raised and his face confused, horrified to meet a woman in the ambush. I lunged at him while he reckoned it. All my days I had worshipped life. Now I was determined to leave this fortress a tomb.

We fought on. Without planning or equipment, the Romans could not organise themselves into formation, and it fell to each soldier to command his own fight, sword against sword, body against body. It was combat that demanded brazen courage over strategy and, in this, our warriors were far superior. Gradually the enemy began to fall.

I was not the only woman in Caradog's war band, there were at least nine or ten from the northern tribes: fierce, well-muscled women, who must have distinguished themselves in training and given their chiefs no reason to withhold them from the war. I saw how they disoriented the enemy, how the Romans faltered with the shock of bare breasts and a smooth-cheeked face, regretting their delay once the blade had been put through their throat.

Our fighters began to shriek with elation as it became clear that no Roman soldiers would remain. As the contest quieted, I saw Caradog slip into the doorway of a hut. It was the largest of the soldiers' barracks, the commander's tent. I followed him in.

The commander was slain, slumped at a table.

Caradog spun, sword raised, at the sound of my entry. 'Ailia!' he exhaled. 'Are you harmed?'

'No.'

'You did not tell me you could use a sword,' he called over his shoulder as he strode to the table.

'I did not think it would be needed.'

'It's always needed.' Caradog lifted the commander's head by the hair and began to saw through the neck.

I glanced at a pale, stiff sheet of fabric spread on the table, its ends wound around a cylinder of wood. It was covered in row upon row of tiny black shapes made with the finest brush. As Caradog continued his hasty surgery, I moved forward to examine it. These were Roman letters. I had seen them on coins from the east and on the jars and boxes that had come to Caer Cad by trade. I had heard of the messages that were entrusted to sheets of stretched calfskin, but I had never seen one nor gazed upon its patterns. It was said that the Romans no longer held their stories in song. These insectile marks were their knowledge. I traced my fingers over the symbols. What did they mean?

Caradog grunted with the labour of his task. I looked up. The throat gaped open, but the blade had lodged in the spine.

'Here,' I said, taking hold of his sword. I had treated many injuries of the back and I knew how the nodes of a spine locked together. 'You must cut through this cleft between the bones—' With a firm jerk and a wiggle of the blade, I had the commander's head free in my hand as the body fell heavily to the floor.

Caradog roared with laughter and crushed his lips against my cheek. 'Mighty woman,' he murmured, his breath warm on my skin, 'is there nothing you cannot do?'

I stared at his face, speckled with blood-spray. His eyes shone with the rapture of killing. What was this praise?

Shouts and burning timber roared outside the barrack. Inside it was silent.

Caradog lifted his hand and touched my face.

For the briefest moment, it felt possible—certain—that I would step forward and lay my cheek against his chest, imprinting my skin with his sweat and dye.

Instead I turned and walked to the entrance.

I leaned on the doorway, reeling with desire. I had not hungered for a man since I had lain with Taliesin. The fierceness of it shocked me. Yet I was dizzy with killing. I was not of clear senses.

I turned to see him setting a torch to the bed and then to the table.

When he was satisfied they had caught, he walked to the door and pushed past me without further word.

As I watched the flames consuming the room, I saw the sheet of letters flare bright, then perish into ash. Where, I wondered as I backed away from the surging heat, was their knowledge now?

The war band gathered to take count of themselves and replenish with water. There was no time to celebrate our victory. 'Do not rest too long,' said Caradog, passing his bladder to the warrior beside him. 'We must go to the settlements and finish our task. The Dobunni were the first tribe to submit to Claudius. Remember this when they cry for you to spare their grain.'

And so we continued through the night, destroying the store huts, smashing the structures they had built to passage water, burning fields, and roping the best horses. The townspeople took up arms and some were slain in the fight, but Caradog had not come to slaughter men of the tribes. Our purpose was to incur as much damage as possible to property that lay within Roman territory, so that repairs would bleed out the governor's purse.

I no longer used my sword, but chanted the rites of whomever had met their death. Throughout the rampage, Caradog called to the Dobunni to shun their new Roman lord, to bring a tent to his war camp and move forth with his band.

At dawn we rode back to our camp, leaving a network of scouts. We sat exhausted by fires as the morning became golden, drinking ale and eating strips of smoked beef. Within hours, riders bore news from camps to the north and south of us along the Sun Road that the other four attacks had been successful. The forts were destroyed, thousands of Roman soldiers had been slain, and the tribespeople of the Dobunni had not risen to defend them.

Today we would rest. Tomorrow we would move our camp

forward. We would continue the attack on Roman-held territory for as long as it took Scapula to mobilise his wintering legions. And when he did, it would leave at least one region within the rear of his province unguarded, giving the eastern chiefs their chance to act. Whatever Scapula did now, Rome's position would be weakened.

Caradog was right, I thought, as I sipped my ale, and watched the bruised and muddy fighters sprawled and laughing. We could defeat them. We could free our tribelands.

4

Two halves of Sovereignty

Warriors seek victory.
Journeypeople seek knowledge.
The pull between them holds the land firm.

I SPENT THE rest of the day in my tent, tending wounds and binding limbs with strips of linen. My own back and shoulders had never ached so deeply. Killing asked much of the body.

By sunset we had packed the carts for tomorrow's march. Caradog spoke to the men of his plan to continue until the first sighting of a legion. Under no circumstances would we engage in field battle with the Roman army, for this would hand them certain victory. Our triumph would be to erode them by stealth.

At dawn, I heard the thud of hooves. Blurry with sleep, I stumbled from my tent as Caradog and the other chiefs emerged.

The messenger dismounted swiftly and bowed to Caradog. 'I carry news from Anwas's camp, now disbanded,' she said, panting. 'There are reprisals.'

Anwas was a chief of the Ordovices, a steady and cool-headed warrior, to whom Caradog had entrusted the command of the northernmost band.

'Which legion has marched against us?' asked Caradog. 'And by whom is it led?'

'It is Scapula himself who leads the force, but it is not one of the legions.'

'Then what?' said Caradog. 'Who comes?'

'A small force of auxilia, entirely on horseback.'

'Cavalry?' questioned Hefin. It was not typical of Romans to fight with horses.

'You say a small force,' said Caradog. 'Therefore easily defeated?'

She shook her head. 'They are no horsemen of this world,' she said. 'Their skin is blacker than night and their horses run with unearthly speed.' Her eyes were bright with fear. 'I spoke to one who had seen them. He said their agility is inhuman. They ride without reins and cast spears with both hands.'

'I know of these riders,' said Caradog. 'They are not of the otherworld. They come from the desert lands near Carthage. They are the Empire's most deadly cavalry, but they have never been posted in Albion.'

'So Scapula has brought them with him,' I said.

Caradog nodded. 'How many of my band are lost?'

'Anwas commanded them to retreat, but the riders were too swift. There are few survivors.'

'And Anwas?' asked Caradog.

The rider paused. 'He is fixed to a cross of wood, by means of iron nails through the wrists and feet, and the cross is stood upright as a tree.'

Caradog closed his eyes. We knew of this method of execution, reserved by the Romans for their most despised enemies, a warning that others might see. 'It has been but a day,' said Caradog.

'This governor is quick to act,' said the rider. 'He drove the horses without rest once he had learned of our attack. And he rides southward this day in search of further camps.'

I looked around at the chiefs, each grappling with our first taste of our new enemy leader. Brutal. Decisive. Our warriors were skilled on horseback, but Scapula must have known by our ambush that we had come prepared only for foot combat and would be no match for a force of cavalry. He forced us to retreat, yet left the eastern tribes firmly held by the legions.

I stared at our war chief. How would he respond? How would he salvage the will of his war band?

His face was still. He drew breath and straightened. If he was unsure he hid it well. 'Scapula must feel great concern to have led the dark riders out himself.'

'He states that his highest priority is to remove *Caratacus*,' said the rider.

'Is that what they call me?' Caradog said, half-smiling. '*Caratacus*?'

'That and more!' said the rider.

The chiefs laughed.

'So now we retreat as intended,' said Caradog, turning to his fighters. 'And as we leave, we know that we have achieved a great victory.' He met every eye in turn. 'We have taken back the reins of this war. We have shown that Rome cannot hold us with their line, nor can they advance beyond it.'

The chiefs murmured their agreement.

'I have Scapula, Governor of Britain, moving to Albion's drum,' he continued. 'I play the music of this war. And he is forced to dance.'

There was more laughter.

I exhaled with relief. Caradog had turned Scapula's retaliation to a mark of honour.

'We shall return to the mountains and grow our war band in numbers and strength. We have horses and men from the Dobunni. These will serve us well as we prepare for our next attack. Now, pack the horses. We are going home.'

Anwas's camp was no more than day's ride away. We had to leave immediately.

Caradog sent riders to the remaining camps with messages to retreat and we prepared our departure. Though he joked with the warriors as we rolled our tents and loaded our saddles, I caught glimpses of him when he thought himself unwatched. His expression held no trace of humour.

A heavy rain set in as we rode. The Habren swelled and we had to search for a shallower ford than the one we had used on our first crossing. Water muddied the ground and loosened stones, slowing the mountain ascent and forcing us to take longer paths. The two-day journey would take at least four.

'Horse-end!' shouted Hefin as we crested the first mountain late in the day. 'Look to the east.'

Caradog called us to stop. We had reached a vantage from which we could see our war camp in the valley below. It was swarming with men in the bronze helmets of the Roman auxilia, searching the remains of our brief settlement.

'See how easily we evade them?' called Caradog. 'Even their fastest black wolves cannot catch this hare.'

An overhanging branch dripped steadily on my neck as I watched them prodding at our abandoned hearths and circling the clearing.

'Warm your hands on our fires!' shouted Caradog into the valley. 'For that is all you will touch of us.'

His fighters cheered. In that moment, we were unassailable, protected by the river, the forest, and the mountain itself. Scapula had taken some of us, but he would take no more. And our leader still stood at our front with the head of the fort commander knocking against his stallion's shoulder. 'Ride on!' he cried.

I glanced backwards as we set off. A lone figure stood at the camp's edge staring towards us. Even from this distance I saw the fury in his stance and I knew it was Scapula.

⁜

Caradog did not speak to me alone that day, nor any days of the journey home. At the evening fires he praised my fighting and was as friendly with me as with any other. But no more so. And he would not approach if I stood alone by a spring nor seek my council on where next to steer this chariot of war.

I saw now the pattern of him, how he bore himself to me then hastened to re-armour, as if he feared I would injure whatever flesh he had exposed. But I had no wish to exploit his weakness. I wanted to help him win this war.

I silenced my frustrations, but as I rode the drizzling forest tracks, I could not rid myself of the memory of his mouth on my cheekbone. There was no meaning in it. It was merely Caradog's way: impulsive, unbridled. He was a bonfire of a man and I would be mistaken to think that his heat blazed for me above any other. There would be no surer way to diminish my power.

We rode into Llanmelin in the late afternoon. The townspeople lined the entrance path, casting petals and grains of barley and wheat over us as we approached the gateway. Caradog held his sword above his head and shouted 'Your people are victorious! The Silures are undefeated!'

The crowd cheered, but I flinched at his words. It was right that our war chief paint a shining image of our success. But the truth beneath was a knot. We had not even begun to untangle it.

The smell of roasting meat and damp fur filled Hefin's hall. Caradog had arranged for a feast on the night of our return, as payment to the chiefs who had fought under his command.

The spits dripped with sizzling pork and mutton, and the servants' arms strained under platters of walnuts, dried plums, cheeses, and loaves. The spread was too extravagant for a chief whose war camp had swelled with numbers far greater than what Llanmelin's grain stores could feed over winter. But Caradog was right to provide it, for only feasting could affirm the bond between chief and warrior and restore the order that killing had unsettled.

After wheat cakes glistening with honey had been served, Caradog called for his Songman. All chattering ebbed as Rhain walked to the fire.

For the second time, I watched him take his place at the centre of the hall. For the second time, my breath caught at the disruption of his face in the flame light.

He stood unmoving, letting the silence wait for his bidding. Then he parted his lips and summoned the ancestor in whose name he would sing.

I shivered to my marrow with the strength of his authority.

'Sing the battle of Tir Cantii,' cried a woman from the audience, when he had finished his invocation.

'Sing Cun's rampage of Tir Dumnoni!' shouted another.

Rhain shook his head. 'Tonight I sing Caradog's attack on Tir Dobunni.'

There were murmurs of surprise. It was an honour to hear a new song, freshly-conjured. But there was also apprehension. He would sing of our attack, but how would he describe it? The Songmen alone had the power to judge their chief's nobility, to praise or to satirise.

They were granted this freedom, for without it, their praise would carry no weight.

I looked at the war chief. He sat straight and unsmiling.

But if Caradog had feared Rhain's judgement, he needn't have. For the song that poured from Rhain's chest described, in spinning rhythms and weaving language, a warrior chief so mighty, so luminous, that no one could shield their eyes from his light.

The song did not shy from his errors or failures. It spoke of the retribution that had come too soon, and of Caradog's hopes, not yet fulfilled. But Rhain drew forth, with intricate precision, his courage, his nobility—all interwoven with older stories of other great chiefs, stories that echoed Caradog's own.

Though his stature was small, the muscles in Rhain's arm were thick and strong from pounding the staff. He drove the song forward with a ceaseless rhythm. Sweat poured from his face. He worked as hard as any smith.

I looked around at the audience, enraptured by every word. I saw the song soothe the warriors, and affirm all that bound us to this land. But then, as I watched this strange-shaped man continue to sing, I began to see a purpose that was yet greater.

The true spirit of the war chief was captured in this song. Rhain would sing it tomorrow, on the next moon, and many more times. While this song was sung, the war chief would live. The song made Caradog immortal.

I took a deep draught of the strong ale and stared, transfixed, at my teacher. This was his power: to determine what endured. He had crafted and memorised this song in the few hours since we had returned. I hungered more than ever to know his craft, to devote myself to it.

I still did not know my role in this war. I was still fighting to have my Kendra's voice heard. I ran my palms through the dense deer fur on which I sat. Was it possible, I wondered, that now, with our land under threat, it was not the Kendra's power that was most needed, but the Songwoman's?

⊹

Early the next morning I went to seek Rhain. The township was quiet, still slumbering after the feast. Only journeypeople and farmers had business with the dawn.

I could not find him at the temple nor in his hut. It was Neha who barked up at the eastern platform to signal she had caught his scent. I climbed the ladder and found him slumped against the wall.

He turned to me, his face crumpled with sleep. 'Greetings, Kendra.'

'Have you been here all night?' I asked, sitting beside him.

'Perhaps,' he murmured. He brought his water bladder up to his lips and tipped it high.

'You must have frozen.'

He shook his head. 'I barely feel the cold.'

He smelled sour and fleshy, in need of a soaping, yet I felt no urge to draw away.

'Are you glad to be home?' he asked.

I shared his bleak smile. This was neither his home nor mine, but now home to both of us.

'I am glad to be returned to your teaching.'

'Is that why you have tracked me here to my nest?'

'Yes—but if it is too early...'

'No, no...' He propped himself higher against the wall and drank again from his water skin, before holding it out to me. 'Something from the Mothers?' he offered. The tang from the bladder's opening told me it was not water he drank. I shook my head and he hooked the pouch back on his belt. 'The craft of the Songwoman has two parts, two powers,' he said, without prelude.

I drew my cloak tighter and waited, surprised. I had thought we might return to the grove or temple. But I would learn here if he wished it.

'The first is well known, nine tenths of our art.'

'Voice,' I said.

'Not voice,' he said. 'Memory. You have learnt poems already in your training to journey-law, but these are mere droplets compared to what will come. As Songwoman, your memory will become a cauldron whose depth is without limit.'

I nodded. The Songmen knew hundreds, thousands of poems: battles, histories, magical tales, summoned from a vast inner pool at a moment's notice.

He rubbed his eyes. 'I will teach you to remember when I do not have such a headache.'

'Of course,' I assured him. 'And the second part?'

Rhain drank again. 'To understand the second part, you must go to the craft huts and watch the smiths.'

I laughed. 'Why this?'

'Because there you will see the metal being shaped.'

I frowned in confusion.

'Forging!' he said. 'The making of a new vessel, a new sword...'

'Yes, I know the craft,' I said, 'but not the relevance.'

'Memory is a strong art, but the greater skill of the poet is forging.'

'As you showed last night...' I whispered, beginning to understand.

'Yes.' He nodded. 'Metal and song. Both drawn from the land. Both wrought by fire.'

'What is the fire that forges song?' I asked, warming to the correspondence.

'Inspiration!' he said. 'The Songwoman is not only one who can recall the poems at will, but one who can soften the metal of the stories and find new ways to shape them, new lustres in their meaning. This is her purpose.'

I stared at my hands, grazed from fighting. Rhain's poem last night would preserve Caradog's spirit as a sword never could. Here was a craft that offered hope. 'When can I begin to learn it?'

'Hoo! Not for some time. First you mine the ore. Then you learn to forge.'

'How long, Songman?'

'You will be quick to learn the poems and how they are structured,' he said. 'But I cannot predict when you will gain the authority to create them.'

Inwardly I groaned.

Fine beetle trails in the platform we sat on reminded me of what I had seen in the Roman hut. 'Can you write letters?' I asked him. I knew many journeypeople learned Greek and Latin.

'Of course,' he answered. 'I was raised on the fringe of the Empire. I know Latin letters, but I do not practise them. Writing will make your songcraft weak.'

'How?' I asked, suprised.

'Because it steals your memory.'

Slowly, I nodded.

'This is the sickness of the Romans. They cannot remember.'

I helped Rhain descend the ladder. We were both expected in the Great Hall after libation to meet with the war council. As we walked I asked him why he kept mead in his bladder, not water.

'Against the cold,' he answered.

'But I thought you did not feel it?'

He tapped the bladder. 'And this is why.'

✢

We huddled on the inner circle of benches in the Great Hall, stamping our feet and cradling cupfuls of warm ale from a pot on the fire.

Caradog sat, as always, in the strong place facing the doorway, his fists balled on spread knees, speaking with pride of the attack. Scapula's swift reprisal had shocked us all, yet Caradog saw only the glory in his war band. He was unbreakable as the greenest timber.

The council murmured their approval as he spoke.

'But I have thought long on our journey home,' he continued. 'It is clear to me that we cannot drive Rome from Albion unless we meet her army and defeat it in open battle.'

'War Chief,' said Prydd in surprise. 'We have, for years, sought to avoid this.'

'Because we did not think we would succeed in it. But I saw a spirit of fighting in Tir Dobunni, more powerful than I have seen in any combat.' He looked to Hefin. 'There is power in this soil that grows strong fighters. My own men have strengthened here. I believe we are ready.'

Hefin sat tall in Caradog's praise. 'I agree with you, Horse-end,' he said. 'We need to settle this. These dog skirmishes are like picking a scab.'

A few other warriors muttered in agreement but I was astonished. This went against everything we knew. 'Stealth has long been your success in this war,' I said. 'What has turned you, War Chief?'

'I am hungry to end this,' he said. 'We all are. This war is draining both our grain stores and our spirits. Now is the time to act.'

The council were listening, nodding.

'But,' he continued, 'we cannot do this unless we have numbers.'

'The Brigantes,' murmured Prydd.

'Yes,' said Caradog. 'We cannot defeat Rome without the Brigantes. I have decided to go to Cartimandua and speak to her myself.'

'Are you sure that is wise?' said Prydd slowly. 'She is in treaty—'

'She is kin, journeyman,' said Caradog. 'When I stand before her, she will not put a treaty with Rome above the bonds of blood.'

Prydd frowned, clearly unwilling to favour a plan that was not of his design.

'Which route would you take?' Hefin asked. 'The Cornovii paths will be thick with Romans.'

'That is fine knot work!' said Caradog, waving the question away. 'You and the way-finders determine the best route, and I will ensure that I ride it.'

'Through Tir Deceangli would be the safest route,' said Hefin.

Caradog nodded, enlivened by the plan. 'It would also give me opportunity to meet with the Deceangli chiefs after their loss at Tir Dobunni, and make firm our union.'

Once again, Caradog had described his intention as unquestionable. Yet it was far from this. I had heard much of the great tribequeen, Cartimandua. She was feared throughout the tribes for her ruthlessness. And she was a friend to Rome. She had already made her choice.

'How can you be sure that your cousin will join you when she has refused you already?' I asked.

'I cannot be sure she will join me,' Caradog answered. 'But if I don't go, I can be sure that she will not.'

'But what of the danger?' I said. 'To present at her hall will expose you to great risk of capture...'

I looked to Prydd. Would he not speak out against such a gamble?

Caradog paused before answering. 'Do you think me so unpersuasive, Kendra?'

'No...I do not, I—'

'War Chief?' Rhain's voice was quiet. 'If you are resolved to this plan, I might know a way to convince Cartimandua to turn back to you.'

All eyes fell upon him. Rhain rarely spoke at council, attending only to verify questions of history. 'We must establish, beyond question, your rightful bond to these tribelands,' he said. 'Beyond the immediate jurisdiction of a war chief.'

'A fine suggestion, but how?' asked Caradog.

Rhain stared at me. 'Here sits, among us, the living embodiment of our sovereign spirits. The Kendra has stood with the Mothers. She carries the soul of the land.'

I waited, unbreathing. What did he mean by the acknowledgement?

Rhain held my gaze. 'Our kings are made through their bond with the land.'

I gasped. 'You do not suggest that I...?'

Rhain nodded. 'Marry the war chief.'

Hefin roared with laughter.

'This is no occasion for humour,' said Prydd.

'I have a wife, Songman,' said Caradog.

'Ah, but I speak of sacred marriage,' said Rhain. 'A marriage between land and king. If Ailia chose you as husband, then you would be a king chosen by the land and wedded to the land. Cartimandua would not refuse such a king.'

I stared, speechless. His idea echoed one of the oldest rituals of the tribes, whereby a king's true sovereignty was affirmed by his ritual marriage to the Mothers. They would be summoned, in the form of a wild-caught mare or other forest beast, brought to him, wedded to him, then slaughtered and boiled in a broth that he, alone, would drink before spilling the rest upon the ground. It was one of Albion's most beloved ceremonies, for it ensured the land grew fertile by the seed of the chosen king. But in all my knowledge, it was always a beast who stood as surrogate for the Mothers, not a mortal woman. Not I.

I looked to Prydd. To marry Caradog would give me great prominence. Surely he would oppose it. He leaned back, his eyes fixed on the war chief. His expression revealed nothing, but I sensed the whirr of reckoning behind his gaze. 'I see a certain sense in it,' he said at last. 'It would greatly enhance Caradog's standing, and establish beyond question his bond to these tribelands.'

'Yes,' said Rhain.

'I'll kneel to King Horse-end,' said Hefin. 'But what of the chiefs to the north? They may not be so ready to bend to another sovereign.'

'When they learn that he is king by marriage to the Kendra, they will kneel,' said Prydd. His eyes began to shine with quiet excitement. 'You would need strong counsel in such a role, Caradog. I am prepared to provide it.'

I swallowed a surge of fury. How quickly he turned the mirror to brighten his face. Did none think to ask my view? And what of Euvrain? Did she have no say in it? 'Surely the Kendra is not permitted to marry a...warrior?' I stammered.

'It is not typical,' said Prydd. 'But there is no law against it.'

'This is nonsense,' said Caradog, laughing. 'I will not divorce Euvrain.'

'There is no need to,' said Rhain. 'This is sacred marriage. You would lie together only once in ritual. You would not dedicate a hearth together.'

'It will deliver a powerful message if you travel to Tir Brigantes as king and Kendra, War Chief,' said Prydd. 'It will convince Cartimandua that she breaches sacred vows by maintaining her alliance to Claudius. I am certain Euvrain will bless this marriage in honour of her tribelands.'

'She would bless it more readily if it were only to a mare,' chuckled Hefin.

'Kendra?' Rhain asked, noticing my silence. 'What is your view of it?'

'I would not ask this of Euvrain.'

'I am asking you.'

My thoughts spun. To marry Caradog would give me inarguable authority in this war. My Kendra's voice would be less easily ignored. But even if Euvrain blessed it, I could not marry him. I was bound to another. My promise to Taliesin was the last thread that linked us. Even if he was lost to me, I would not betray him. 'I do not wish to marry the war chief.'

Prydd frowned. 'You are Kendra. Your duty is to your role, not to your wishes.'

I drew my cloak tighter around my shoulders. I knew he was right.

'You cannot delay, Horse-end,' said Hefin, 'if you want to go north before the mountains are impassable with snow.'

Prydd looked to Caradog then to me. 'I will give you each two days to consider this proposal and give me your answer.'

'I do not need time to consider,' said Caradog. 'If Euvrain will bless it, then I will join with the Kendra in sacred marriage.'

Prydd smiled. 'And you, Kendra?'

'I will give my answer in two days as you have requested.'

'I cannot marry Caradog!' I said to Rhain, as soon as I had drawn the door closed behind us.

'You do not wish to?' he said, as he sat on the bench by my fire.

'It is not that.' I could not sit. I paced the small circumference of my hut, rubbing my wrists as if they still bore the tight-wound strips of linen rag that had bound me to Taliesin. 'I am betrothed to another.'

Rhain looked up. 'Who?'

I forced myself to sit beside him. Other than revealing his name to Caradog at Winter's Eve, I had not spoken of Taliesin since I had fled from my homeland. Here, Taliesin might never have existed. I needed to speak of him. I needed to remember him before I lost him entirely.

I placed a log of spruce into the fire and watched its sap bubble. 'He is called Taliesin,' I began. 'He is a knowledge-bearer of great wisdom.'

Rhain shook his head. 'I have not heard his name.'

'Nor could you have,' I said. 'He does not walk the ground of Albion, though he craves to return. I met him here fleetingly, when he was permitted to journey, but I did not truly know him until I stood deep in the realm of the Mothers.'

Rhain looked at me with a frown of confusion. 'So he was a vision to you?'

'No. He was not vision...I knew him as flesh...He dwelt with the Mothers, and dwells there still.'

Rhain paused, then said, 'No man might dwell with the Mothers.'

'I know this! He is trapped there...' My voice was shrill with the panic of being disbelieved. 'He yearned to return here, Songman. I was given a weapon by the Mothers to cut a passage that he might pass back...But there was a geas on the sword, a prohibition, and I breached it, Rhain. I failed to free him.'

Rhain stared at me for a long time without speaking. By now I could read the expressions that lived in his strangely-cast face. It was like a secret language. One that I shared, perhaps, only with Caradog. In this moment it revealed a bemused fascination. 'Do you tell me that the Mothers lured you close with a man who was beguiling yet bound, gave you means to free him, then set magic about the instrument that it would fail?'

'Yes,' I said softly. 'You have understood it.'

Rhain gave a long and musical laugh.

'Why does it amuse you?'

'Because the Mothers are so wonderfully cruel. I could make a song of it,' he said, smiling. 'And so I will.'

'I see no humour in it.'

'Then look deeper!'

I could not bear his brazen delight. I turned away, fixing my gaze on the hard earth of my floor.

'Do not be tormented, Ailia,' he continued. 'Don't you see? This is the Mothers' way. They have played with you...to test your strength! You have been entrapped in the most artful web of conjuring I have yet heard of.'

I looked back at him, fighting the ache of tears. 'You are mistaken, Rhain...'

He smiled again, this time more kindly. 'The Mothers are capricious. You know this better than any. In their realm, night is day. Little is as it appears. It is both wonderful and terrible. But we cannot grasp onto it, nor anything that comes from it. This man, this Taliesin, is no more enduring than flakes of snow in a fire.'

I felt the air grow thin. 'It is not as you describe,' I said. 'I knew him as firmest flesh. The Mothers would not—'

'The Mothers taunt us for their sport, and yet we must honour them with our every breath. Do not bind yourself to the memory of this man. Show the Mothers that you can withstand their games. And then they will strengthen you.'

I shook my head and whispered, 'He is real.'

'He is a conjuring,' said Rhain. 'It is testament to your strength of vision that you knew him so powerfully.'

I wiped away the tears I could not stem, then rose to pour some fresh water. My hand shook as I lifted the jug.

'Are you well?' asked Rhain as I gave him a cup, my hand still trembling.

I nodded and told him we would speak of it no further.

Every word Rhain had spoken was true and I had already known it. I just could not bear to hear it.

As evening fell, I went to the Castroggi. The sky was leaden, Lleu faint on the horizon, already defeated by the coming winter. The river was running high and fast with the rains, the air moist with the boundary spirits, who surged at the seams between earth and water.

I sat on a hillock, soft with comfrey. I had come to farewell Taliesin. But the rush of the river was too noisy. He would not hear me. I rested my head on my knees and let the cold spray prickle my neck. There was no need to farewell what did not exist.

My fingers found their way into the yoke of my dress and touched the warmth of my scars. What of the Mothers' song I had heard? Was it, like Taliesin, merely a manifestation of trance? No. War was forcing these questions, tearing us all from knowledge that had been undoubted since this land was first sung.

I looked up. A lone sheep had wandered from its paddock and was standing among the reeds on the opposite bank. I smiled at its startled expression and stood up.

I had no choice but to follow what was real and firm-edged before me. I was Kendra in the eyes of the tribes, whether or not I understood her purpose. I had been asked to marry a strong yet imperfect man to make him a king. And within all this, I was apprentice to Albion's finest Songman. He was no vision, no trance. To sing a sweet note into a dark night was a power that could not be questioned.

Tomorrow I would speak with Euvrain. For the choice to marry Caradog was not mine. It was hers.

✝

The call of a rider summoned us to Hefin's hall early the next morning.

'I bring news of the east,' said the messenger when the council had gathered. 'Scapula is disarming the captured tribes.'

Caradog flinched. 'Which tribes?'

'All those he suspects held sympathies with the Dobunni attack. And those he fears may turn to your leadership, War Chief—the Iceni, the Coritani—'

'Those tribes did not ride with us,' said Caradog. 'He cannot disarm warriors who have taken no action against him.'

'After the attacks at Tir Dobunni, he fears action. He seeks to crush any suspected disloyalty to Rome, before it takes hold.'

Caradog laughed in disbelief. 'What fool commander is he? These tribes are under treaty to him. He will incite the warriors by this, not subdue them.'

'Ay. There is great unrest. The disarmaments are violent. They are killing those who do not yield their weapons and burning houses wherever they suspect hidden metals.'

Caradog stared at the flames.

No other Roman commander had disarmed peaceful tribes. To strip the men of their weapons stole their history, their lineage, their humanity. Without command of metal, we were nothing more than slaves.

'Might as well tear off their balls,' said Hefin.

'This is in breach of the treaties.' said Prydd.

'This governor cares not for the honouring of treaties,' said the rider.

'He wants the tribes impotent,' said Caradog, looking up. 'So they cannot rise when he moves into the west.'

The rider nodded. 'This is the view of Aedic of the Iceni and many eastern chiefs,' he said. 'Scapula has commenced rebuilding the forts on the Sun Road, and has sent greater numbers to defend them.'

Caradog inhaled. 'And has he stated his intentions in the west?'

The rider paused. 'He proclaims that he will not rest until he has the head of *Caratacus*.'

Caradog nodded, then suddenly seemed deeply weary. He was always enlivened by talk of the enemy. What now sapped him? Had the suggestion of marriage caused unrest at his hearth?

'Will we go to the east, War Chief?' I ventured.

'No. There is no purpose in taking action until I hold the Brigantes within my war band.'

His certainty surprised me. 'And what of the deaths in the meanwhile?' I said. 'These tribes are bearing the retribution for our action. Do we not owe them our aid?'

'We owe nothing to tribes who are under treaty to Rome.'

'Yet you have ties among them—' I pressed, '—for which they are now being punished.'

'Kendra,' chided Prydd.

Caradog stared at me. 'My loyalty is to those who have never doubted me.'

I heeded the rebuke and said nothing more.

'So what now then, Horse-end?' said Hefin.

'I will hasten for Tir Brigantes,' said Caradog. 'As soon as I learn whether or not I am to wed the Kendra.'

Only when we were walking out into the cold morning, headed to the cook house for bread, did I notice that Caradog had remained in the hall. 'I shall join you shortly,' I said to Hefin. I returned to the vestibule and peered through the inner doorskins.

He sat at the fire, his gaze cast downward. Alone in the vastness of the feast hall, he looked half his size.

'Caradog?' I called.

'Do not await me,' he said, looking up. 'I will not remain long...'

His voice, usually so resonant, was as thick as felt.

I walked to the fire and sat down on the bench beside him. 'Is something amiss?'

'No,' he said. 'I was simply thinking on the message...' His explanation trailed away. 'Go to the kitchen. I will join you shortly.'

I touched his forearm that held his sword on his lap. 'War Chief—'

He flinched at my touch. 'Don't call me that.'

I paused, confused. 'Is that not what you are?'

He did not answer. Agitation brimmed at his skin. Was this the dark weather of which Euvrain had spoken?

'What ails you?' I asked. 'Don't tell me you are well when I see, clear as Lleu, that you are not.'

'Let me be.' His voice was harsh.

'As you wish,' I said. 'I will not cajole you.'

'Thank you.'

I felt his shoulders rise and fall with heavy breaths.

The fire sputtered, needing fuel, feeble against the strong cold.

After many moments of silence, he spoke to the floor. 'The attack was wasted,' he murmured, almost inaudibly. 'It was reckless, poorly conceived. I moved with haste.'

I stared at him in shock. 'But we fought well,' I said slowly. 'We destroyed their camps, we drew the border. We named the terms of war. You have said all of this.'

'I have incited Scapula to even greater cruelty. I have gained no ground—'

'What is this alteration in you?' I said. 'Why are you saying such things?'

Still he did not lift his gaze. 'Because I am as lacking in judgement as my opponents claim me to be,' he said through a tightened jaw. 'Because I cannot achieve what I have hoped.' His breath trembled, yet he forced the words. 'Because I have led men falsely, for my ambition.'

I was mute with amazement. I had scented the doubt that lay

116

within him. I had never imagined that it would find such a voice. This was another man. But who possessed him? 'These are not your words,' I said. 'None of those things are true.'

'They are true!' he flared. He threw the sword clattering to the stones around the fireplace. 'Give it to Caeden or Hefin,' he muttered, 'that it might serve the tribes through a better man.'

'And who should lead us then?'

He snorted. 'My father thought I lacked the temperament to lead. That I was too hasty, too bold...'

This was the voice that possessed him. How could he deny its authority? 'Yet now you lead,' I said quietly. 'There is no other.'

At last he turned to face me. 'The fight is unwinnable and it is only my vanity that compels me to lead it.'

His gaze challenged me to deny it. But I could not. There were fragments of truth in what he said. And yet, somehow, despite his wretchedness, he was more powerful for seeing it.

His shirt was unfastened, his throat pale beneath his beard. Now I saw the payment he made for his assuredness, for being the man strong enough to lead Albion against Rome. He paid with a spirit that suffered despair. It was an ailment that he could never confess, for none would kneel to a war chief whose doubts could flay him so mercilessly. But he could confess it to me. For Taliesin had borne this sickness and I had seen the precious light that its darkness could yield, as stars were revealed by the night. 'War Chief, you do not truly believe all that you have said. It is the voice of an ailment. You are spirit-ill. It alters your judgement and worsens in winter. It can pass. It *will* pass.'

'Leave me, Kendra.' He stared at the fire. 'I regret that I have spoken.'

'I will not leave you,' I whispered.

He turned, once more, to look at me. '*You* have seen it,' he said. 'You have seen my weakness.'

'I have seen your fear,' I confessed. 'But you have said yourself that you would be no war chief if you did not stand before fear.'

He stared at me as if seeing me for the first time. 'You see my fear, yet you do not doubt me.'

'No, War Chief. I do not doubt you.'

Still he stared. 'Who are you, Kendra? You possess the mystery of Annwyn.'

I almost laughed. 'Because I have stood within Annwyn.'

'You have, haven't you...?' Did he see, only now, that I was not as any other woman, that there was a story in the title I bore?

'I have heard the Mothers sing,' I said. 'I have seen what you fight for.'

'Do you wish to marry me?' he asked, holding my gaze.

I startled at the question. I had been asked to marry him as an act of duty. But as he stared at me, his eyes soft beneath a deep frown, it did not feel as if he were asking me as the Kendra.

'I will answer tomorrow.'

I returned to my hut and set a full pot of water over the fire, then searched out a piece of tallow and a strong bone comb from the baskets on my shelf. With the wash bowl wedged between by thighs I laboured for several hours, untangling the clumps of my hair until the water turned black with dirt.

Once the comb could pass through without snagging, I knelt and bent my head near the fire. Steam rose from my hair, and with it, the last memories of Taliesin. When I lifted my face, my hair fell in waves, soft as mist, over my shoulders.

Euvrain was spooning porridge into her children's bowls as I took a seat at her hearth that evening. Caradog was at the war camp. Without asking, she handed me a bowl of the thick grain, fragrant with broth.

Their house was finely provided and lavish with decoration. Even the earthen bowl in my hand was beautifully painted in the patterns of the Catuvellauni, Euvrain's tribe.

I ate hungrily, smiling between mouthfuls at the children who tugged at my belt pouch and asked in their eastern accents what was inside it. They were both fair, like their mother, but the elder, a girl, had Caradog's intent stare and brimming liveliness.

Euvrain shooed them away and sat beside me. Despite the sweat that beaded her forehead from standing over the cookpot, she was calm as polished stone. 'Your hair becomes you.'

'I must have washed three cups of mountain dirt into the bucket.'

Euvrain smiled. 'You will answer the council tomorrow, will you not?'

I nodded.

'So then,' she said quietly, 'are we to share a husband?'

'I will not make the marriage with Caradog,' I said, 'if you do not bless it. Some marriages are more than the laws that bind them, and if yours is such a marriage, then I would not betray it...'

'You are kind to think of it.'

'I know what it is to love.'

'Do you?' She gazed at me, then folded her hands in her lap and straightened her shoulders. 'I have told you before that my husband is a man of turbulent tempers. If a marriage to the Kendra will anchor him, then I can only welcome it.'

I thought of the bleakness that had imprisoned Caradog this morning. In marrying me, Caradog would be chosen king by the very ground he would rule. But I did not imagine it would console him when the ground of his own soul began to crumble. I glanced at the woman beside me. 'I am sure that none could steady him any better than you.'

She took my hand. Her skin was cool. I felt a rush of comfort.

How I missed a woman's touch and sisterhood.

'Marry him with my blessing,' she said. 'Help him win this war so we can go home.'

There was burst of movement through the doorskins, then a howl of pain as her boy tripped on the entrance stone and fell on his hands. In a moment, Euvrain had gone to him, scooped him up and brought him back to the fire, where she cradled him as she kissed his grazed palms.

My numbed heart was awoken by the sight of it. It was not only the warriors, but tribespeople like her who were the strength of this resistance, nourishing their child kin, even as they had been torn from their homelands and did not know if they would ever return.

I met Euvrain's stare over her son's shaking shoulder. I knew why she blessed my marriage to Caradog. She believed it would hasten what she desired above all else: an end to this war.

'Let this bring us close,' I whispered. 'Let this bind us. We are united in our desire.'

She released her son from her lap with a kiss on his cheek, and turned to me. 'Would you like me to dress your hair?'

I gasped with the honour. 'Very much.'

She walked to a set of shelves and returned with a basket full of combs, braiding sticks, ribbons and oils.

Standing behind me, she began to segment my hair. I closed my eyes as her fingertips brushed against the nape of my neck.

'I ask but one thing,' she said.

'It will be granted,' I murmured, languid with the strokes of her comb.

'Marry him, strengthen the tribelands...but do not allow yourself to love him.'

My eyes opened. 'Euvrain, there is no danger...'

'Ensure it remains so,' she said steadily. 'Otherwise, you will betray not only me, but all of Albion, for the fate of the war cannot rest on the eddies of love.'

I said nothing more. She had no cause for concern. Taliesin was gone. I would not love another. My heart beat now only in service to the Mothers.

When she had combed and divided my hair, Euvrain began weaving the braids. They were firm and tight and foreign to my scalp. Yet even the sharp tugs could not mar the pleasure of being tended.

The children were asleep in their beds when Euvrain touched my shoulder to tell me she was finished. I lifted my hand and felt the rows of smooth coils that wound around my head and snaked down my shoulders in green-ribboned tendrils.

'Thank you,' I said, standing to face her.

Her eyes widened and she smiled. 'I have fashioned a queen.'

I laughed. 'This queen is weary. I will sleep before I take our decision to Prydd.'

✢

Caradog was behind the smith's hut, bent over a bronze cup with his punching tool poised, and did not seem to hear me as I approached the next morning.

'War Chief—'

He looked up, radiant with the pleasure of his hand-work. Then he frowned. 'You have dressed your hair.'

'Your wife has.'

'For what purpose?'

'Because...' I paused. I had dressed my hair because I was no longer mourning someone I loved. 'Because I will accept you in sacred marriage.' I felt a wild embarrassment, as if this were my own desire and not a command I had been given.

He set down his metalwork and I sat beside him.

'This is a gift to Albion,' he said.

I nodded.

'And to me. You are gifting me sovereignty.' He took my hand and pressed it to his lips.

I closed my eyes against the warm current that shot through my blood. I knew that he did not yearn for me, nor I for him. It was just the parts of me that Taliesin had injured, searching indiscriminately for comfort. I drew back my hand and placed it in my lap, before glancing at his face. He looked tired, but the anguish of yesterday morning seemed to have lifted. 'I wish to ask you, War Chief, are you—?'

'Do not ask about yesterday morning,' he said, felling my question. 'You should not have pursued me.'

'I did not *pursue* you, I—'

'Besides, there is no question to be answered. The temper is nothing more than some strange breed of drunkenness. It passes in time. I cannot shed it by will.'

'But what is the ale that produces the...impairment?'

He seemed to flinch at the word. 'None. It is merely the pestering of a wrongful spirit.'

'But War Chief—' I ventured, although it was clear he had no wish to discuss it. 'Sometimes there is meaning in such a spirit.'

'There is no meaning,' he insisted. 'When it comes upon me, I seek solitude until it is defeated.'

I heard the battle in it. 'I can treat you, with herbs—'

'No.' His voice was sharp. 'I don't need herbs.' He looked at me. 'Do not speak of it to others—not Hefin or Prydd. And do not speak of it to me again.'

I nodded. I was not welcome at the hearth of his struggle. 'I won't.'

But I did not believe his despair was simply a drunkenness or a crafty spirit that descended unbidden. I believed that it arose, just as it had in Taliesin, from a mind that knew great depths. It was part of his strength.

I had seen, in his darkness, the glimmer of questions that needed to be asked. Could we win this war? Was it worth the cost to us all? They were precious questions and I wished we could bring them into the light.

⊹

Prydd was alone in the journey-hut, awaiting my arrival at the highsun hour we had arranged. 'Very pleasing,' he said, staring at my hair as I entered the room. 'Far more the likeness of the Kendra now.'

I wanted to remind him that I *was* the Kendra, whether or not I held the likeness of her, but I murmured my thanks and took a seat by the fire.

'Ale?'

I shook my head. 'I come only to give you my answer.'

'Good then.' He sat beside me, pleased to dispense with the flourishes of statecraft when there was no audience to admire them.

When I told him my decision, his lips drew back in a rare smile. 'Thank you, Kendra.'

His warmth took me aback. In his relief that I had done his bidding, he was almost affectionate. 'This will seduce the loyalty of the tribes. Few will deny a king who is Mother-chosen.'

I nodded, yet felt disturbed. The tribes were worthy of truth, not merely seduction.

Prydd lifted his hand and placed it on top of my head. 'You are doing a great service.' He met my eye. 'You are doing the will of the Mothers.'

I dipped free of his touch. He may have known statecraft better than I, but he had no place giving voice to the Mothers. This, at least, was where I had greater claim. 'When will the marriage take place?'

'As soon as possible. Midwinter, if we can make the journey in time.'

'The journey?'

'To Môn,' he said, frowning. 'This is where you will wed.'

I saw the art in it. To wed on the holy isle of Môn would cloak the union in great glamour, and would embed the marriage in Albion's law. I did not wish to sour his good temper, but was I always to be commanded like a trained dog? 'Journeyman,' I said. 'If my Kendra's title is to be put to this use, I would be grateful if my counsel was sought in the design.'

Prydd raised his eyebrows. 'As you wish,' he said at last. 'You are the Kendra. I may not command you...'

'In truth, you may not.' My boldness surprised me.

He stared at me then he gave a quiet chuckle. 'I see what has occurred,' he said.

'What amuses you?' I asked with irritation.

'It seems, perhaps, that in your innocence,' he said, 'you have misunderstood the nature of the Kendra's power.'

My belly tightened. 'I understand the Kendra's power.'

'Then you would know that it is just as a babe's: beguiling, enchanting, hope-giving. The babe calls forth the strength of others, but she, herself, has no actual strength. She is dependent on those who act in her thrall.' Now his laughter was gone. He stood. 'Do not mistake the power of a babe for that of grown men.'

I was locked in his gaze. There was so much to say against him, but this small, hairless man had rendered me silent as surely as if he had cut out my tongue. Was he correct? Was this my only power—a bright star to which pilgrims might orient their path, but lacking the heat of the sun or the pull of the moon? Now I saw why he had been so willing to bestow on me the title of Caradog's wife—he saw it as nothing more than the king's embellishment. I reeled from his words.

'Forgive me, Kendra, I must to the temple.' He walked to the doorway and unhooked his cloak.

Still I could not speak. A hollowness yawned in my chest, as though I had been gutted. I gazed at the flames, barely noticing Prydd bow and slip out through the doorskins. Where were my words, my knowledge? Why did they abandon me now?

Gradually, as breath hissed hot through my nostrils, an anger kindled.

Speech was the Mothers' tool. Robbed of it, I was indeed no stronger than a wordless babe. Prydd had taken my voice. He had taken my authority.

I stood and pushed my new braids behind my shoulders. There would be no trust now, no hope of a bond of any kind between us. Prydd was an enemy to my purpose.

With Neha at my heels I made for the fringes where it did not take long to find Manacca, playing with a pup outside the northern gate. She ran to my embrace.

'Would you like to see where the Mothers live?' I whispered into her matted hair.

All the way to the Castroggi, she clutched my fingers, babbling without breath about the dark spirits she had seen among the fringe tents on the night of Winter's Eve, and squealing with horror and delight when I told her how many Romans I had slain in Tir Dobunni.

On the same bank where I had farewelled Taliesin, I bade her sit beside me and drew her fledgling's shoulders beneath my own cloak.

I gave her a thick strip of smoked mutton I had stuffed into my belt pouch and watched her eat hungrily. Then, as winter sun sparkled on the river, I taught her of the first lesson of journey-law: nothing endures but by death.

I told her that her body will perish, but that her soul, like the sun, is indestructible.

It was simple law, known by instinct to anyone in the tribes, for it was embedded in our daily libation, our festivals, our all. But to hear it spoken with the precise words that named it clearly, gave it sharpness for a skinless girl who had never been taught.

She frowned and fiddled with a stalk of nettle near her feet. 'Does it mean I will never die?'

I squeezed her tiny bare calf, warm and hairless. 'This will die, the part you can see. The part you cannot see, the part inside—' I touched my palm to her chest, '—will live forever.'

'Why?'

'Why what?'

'Why does my leg have to die?'

I smiled. 'So it can walk in Annwyn for a while and come back a little faster!'

She looked up at me, her brown eyes curious. It pleased me to see them grow wide, then darken with the weight of knowledge. She reached up and fondled one of my new braids. 'Pretty,' she murmured.

'Shall I do yours later?' I asked.

Manacca nodded.

I chose to teach this skinless child. She would be transformed by my teaching. Reborn.

Prydd would not silence me.

5

Winter Solstice

We fear the longest night.
Yet if we attend the darkness, the sun will return.
As every soul also rises from the night of its death.

As I stirred the next morning, floating in the sweet waters between dream and waking, I was again a kitchen servant, basking on a riverbank with a lover whose face I could not see. But then, at a rooster's gargling call, I was once more alone, I was the Kendra, and the warmth beside me was no lover's but Neha's.

I rose and looked through the doorskins to observe the hour. Rhain expected me at his hut after libation. I had found him in the apple grove yesterday afternoon and asked that we continue our lessons in haste, that I might glean as much as I could before departing to Môn.

I splashed my face with unheated water and rubbed a little calf's fat on my cheeks to protect them from the cold.

The sky was winter heavy. Rhain led me on a familiar path along the Castroggi, but as we approached the forest, he took a fainter trail that clung close to the bank and entered the woodland on stonier ground. His gait was swift and we had climbed almost an hour before we reached a turn in the river where he called me to a stop.

I had not walked this part of the forest. The ground was steep, the river tumbling between limestone boulders. Sprawling oak boughs formed a canopy overhead, entrapping the moisture released by the water's churn. In such wetness every surface pulsed with growth, every stone and log was vivid with moss, beech ferns, spleenwort and lichen. We had entered a threshold. We were close to Annwyn.

I crouched at the bank to drink. I could reach out my fingers over the water and touch the hand of the Mothers in the fine mist spray. Here, deep in the land, I knew no doubt. My Kendra's knowledge was as true as the cold water in my cupped palms. Why was it not so when I walked among the tribes?

I watched Neha, sniffing furiously at the river's edge, scenting otters or trout.

Rhain sat on a stone beside me and drank from his water skin. 'You are troubled,' he said.

I glanced at him. 'It is only Prydd,' I answered. 'It matters not what I do. He awards no true authority to my title.'

Rhain nodded. 'Authority cannot be gifted,' he said. 'It must be claimed.'

I sighed with exasperation. 'How do I claim it?'

He shrugged. 'Be the serpent. Shed a skin.'

I groaned and Rhain laughed. 'We will begin. What is the first part of song?' he asked.

'Memory,' I said.

He nodded. 'And there are many ways to make it strong. From the beads that we carry to the patterns on our staffs. But the most powerful way to remember is through the land itself.' He stood and began walking upstream towards a ledge of limestone, over which the river flowed.

I jumped up to follow.

Standing close to the stone, he placed his hands on its surface, motioning me to do the same. 'See its shape, its colour. Feel its temperature.'

His breath was warm and unscented by ale. I was glad that for teaching he safeguarded his fine wits. I pressed my palms against the cold rock.

'I am going to teach you some of Caradog's history. It will be a praise story of warriors and their wisepeople, the battles they have fought and the territories they have gained. To this stone you will entrust the first verse. Then we will walk back, and to each boulder or trunk or bend in the river you will assign one other verse. When we are home you will know the story.'

I nodded, still unspeaking. I had learnt short poems of leaf and berry lore, but I had never learned a sequence of an hour's duration.

'We will walk this path many times over many days until you render each verse at each place without prompting. Then, without coming here, you will recall these places and walk them in your mind, as you have done in body, and you will remember. When this is done we will begin again with another poem.' He looked at me. 'You will need strong foot wraps.'

I laughed.

'But hear this,' he said, now serious. 'Once you make this bond between poem and earth, then you are bound to this place. The land will hold the poem for you, but you must come back to renew your memory and to honour the bond.' He placed his palms over mine and pressed them firmly against the stone. 'For as the land gives you the song, so too must you give it the song.'

He stood close, his hands warm over my numb fingers.

Pilgrimages binding words to the land were walked by journey-people throughout all of Albion—I saw yet another layer Rome's swords had cut.

'If we lose this land,' I murmured, 'there will be no more places by which we will remember.'

Rhain nodded, holding my gaze. 'This is what we fight for.'

I smiled. 'Caradog says it is the metal.'

He shrugged. 'Song. Metal. They are the same. Rome would steal one and destroy the other.'

I took a deep breath of the watery air. 'Speak then,' I said. 'Give me the story.'

He laughed, then inhaled and began to incant the history poem that told of Caradog's brave ancestors, their branches of lineage, the territories they had ruled.

I closed my eyes to listen. The ribbon of his voice held both lightness and grit. In the pull of these opposites, the story spun.

'Now you,' he said when he had finished.

Hesitantly, I repeated what I could of the first verse. Rhain chuckled, corrected me and bade me do it once more, then a third time. By the fourth time I spoke it without error and looked at him for praise.

'The words are correct,' he said. 'But you are dancing only on their surface: the names, the places, the happenings. You need to bring forth what is within the words.'

I looked him. 'But it is a simple praise poem, Songman.'

'The first glance tells of one thing. Deeper scrutiny reveals another.' He leaned closer. 'It is your *authority* that will release the meaning of the poem.' He was beaming.

I frowned, frustrated by his incessant playfulness, his inscrutability.

'Laugh!' he commanded, and at that, I did.

Immediately the flow of breath in my laughter released the coils of effort that had drawn taut within me. I started reciting again, letting my thoughts flow over the shape of the words, seeking the qualities that lived within the ancestral names: courage, nobility, a deep love of the land. As I spoke, this time fluidly and freely, I began to sense another truth emerging from the poem, a rhythm that was familiar to me, for I had sung it with the Mothers.

I felt the cold, granular stone beneath my palms and how it entwined with the words I spoke, as if they were one thing. My poem was just a different utterance of the same source that had wrought this rock. I gasped, delighted, with the force of it.

Then Rhain smiled as he saw me understand. 'Do it again.'

☩

The days grew shorter.

Over the weeks before we left for Môn, I walked daily with Rhain into the forests to embed his poems in the trunks, springs, caves and stones. I stood for hours of recitation, my nose streaming with cold, my cloak soaking with river spray, until my memory held songs of a number that surprised even Rhain.

Once I had walked the poem's forest path and knew it perfectly, he taught me how to use devices to ignite my memory within the walls of the temple: a staff scored with lines, a pouch of stones, a string of bronze bells. With a glance at these tools, I could call forth histories of kings, warrior lineages, and the laws that bound them, as well as savage, dizzying stories of men wrought to animals, murderous giants, women made of flowers: stories of revenge, honour, love, trickery and, above all else, our kinship with this moist, black earth.

There was nourishment in the songs. My memory grew as lean and muscular as the legs that walked it. I learned how the web of language was spun and used it to entrap the succulent new words and pairings that Rhain taught me every day. I learned how breath and posture could render character and marvelled as Rhain conjured heartbroken maidens and enraged kings with only his face and voice.

He was pleased with my learning, yet burst into laughter when I suggested, at the successful completion of a most difficult piece, that I might be ready to forge a song of my own. 'Your memory of the poems is without flaw,' he said, as his laughter subsided, 'and your inflection in telling them is as artful as any I have taught.' He took a sip from his ale cup and closed his eyes with the pleasure of it. 'But when you speak, I still hear deference.'

'To what?' I asked.

'Indeed...to what?' He grinned at me. 'The time must come when you are the only authority.'

+

Scapula continued his disarmaments. There were further messages from the east that whole townships had been burnt in the search for weapons, that the Roman soldiers were relishing the chance to unleash their fists on the people, who over four years had submitted in body but never in spirit.

Several chiefs called for Caradog's aid, claiming treaties had been broken and must be avenged. He sent messages back that he was gathering an army of sufficient greatness to restore Albion to the tribes if they would only wait. But we all knew they were warrior chiefs, and they would act as they determined, just as he would in their place.

We learned more of Scapula. He invoked the meaning of his name—'sharpened spade'—in his pledge to dig the war chief from this soil. His speeches were relayed to us in full: he would not rest until the head of the resistance—the man he called Caratacus—had been severed from the body of Albion.

Rhain took great pleasure in satirising him as crowing rooster, making us all roar with laughter with his strutting and preening. We mocked his pride, but beneath our ridicule we were beginning to understand that Scapula was as powerful an enemy as Caradog would ever meet and we would need our greatest courage to defeat him.

The grain stores ran low and Caradog was forced to go to a neighbouring chieftain to purchase more wheat. He would not allow Hefin to relinquish any cattle, but bore the cost of feeding his war camp from his own herds and metals. He walked among his men daily, renewing his promise that he would deliver them their sovereignty. He spoke jubilantly to his warriors of his betrothal to me, describing the yet stronger bonds he would forge with the tribes once he was king. He kissed my fingers as we stood at the camp fires. But outside of our duties, we barely spoke. Once or twice, I noticed him bearing the dark cast I had seen after the news of disarmaments, but whenever it came he took pains to hide it. I settled to the fact that ours was an association of tribecraft, and that friendship would play little part in it.

I took Manacca food and sat with her by the stream whenever there were spare hours and I could evade Prydd's gaze. Her sweet spirit and eagerness to learn were a comfort, but it pained me that I could not bring her openly to the temple.

Lying alone in my Kendra's hut each evening, I was brutally lonely, as rootless and kinless as I had ever been. But as I drew Neha close beneath the blankets, I told myself that this must not matter now. I had my songs, my teacher, and the business of war. These were enough. My purpose was not to know closeness to another soul. I lived for the tribes now, for all of Albion.

As the day of our departure drew near, Caradog had an armband wrought for Cartimandua. Its many silver strands were twisted into a thick rope, and its terminals wrought into the heads of a horse and a wren. Although he had charged the silversmiths to make the gift, the final and most detailed etching he completed himself. I knew as I watched him toil over the work, making himself humble before the craft, how much it meant that she would come to him.

✛

We had allowed three quarter moons to reach the island of Môn by midwinter.

The travel band was small: Caradog, myself, Rhain and Prydd as well as a lesser journeyman, Caradog's first warrior and two servants to attend us. Hefin would remain with his tribe. Euvrain had requested to join us, but Caradog had counselled her against it and I was relieved that she would not be there when I was made wife to her husband.

Our journey was blessed by low winds and dry skies, and we made good time, even as the mountains grew steeper and the paths less known.

Caradog rode with a hawk's gaze, constantly appraising the rivers and cliffs for where strong defences could be made and safe war camps struck should the war ever drive us further north. He spoke little by day, but among the farmers that hosted us by night he was good-humoured and curious about which crops had grown well and the merits of their breeds of sheep.

As we drew further northward, we reached country like none I had seen before. Forests gave way to windswept, stony slopes and vast, ice-clad mountains reared on every side of us. These were the mountains of Eryr, named for the eagles that soared at their crests.

I rode beside Rhain, staring up at the jagged peaks dissolving into cloud. There was no soil or woodland to soften the Mothers' temper.

They did not whisper here. They bellowed. I smiled at the thought of Rome imagining that they might claim this ground. 'If these are Môn's guardians, then she should fear no intrusion,' I said to Rhain.

The slow terrain forced us to make camp wherever we could not bridge the distance between one settlement and the next. I savoured these wild nights when the sky's milk emerged in startling brightness. As we sat by a small campfire and Rhain sang into the black sky, I knew a kinship with this ground that knew no breach. And when I joined him in song, our voices in the darkness were a peace and purpose that even a Kendra's duty could not equal.

Caradog said little on these evenings, but took pleasure in our song, surprised at first that I had knowledge of the craft. Often I sensed him sleepless while the others snored, but if he saw me rise to pass water or lay fuel on the fire, he did not acknowledge our shared wakefulness. By day, also, he would kick his mare forward if I tried to ride abreast of him. I was patient at first, then angry. I was giving him all I had to this marriage, this war. The least he could do was speak to me.

Two days before midwinter, on a clear afternoon, we reached the north coast. Before us, over a wide stretch of churning tidewater, the island of Môn rose out of the ocean. Its treed shores swirled with mists, making it hard to see where water ended and earth began. This isle was of Albion and yet not of Albion. It was our last remaining training place, a threshold place, possessing all the power and risk of ground that spanned two worlds.

It was here that the journeypeople returned every year to renew their vows. It was here that the advisors to the most powerful chiefs in Albion determined where funds were best spent in the ongoing resistance. It was here that shipments of gold flowed into Albion from Erin across the western sea, ensuring Môn was as fertile in coin as it was in soil and knowledge. All our other learning places, including my own, had been claimed by the legions. Now there was only Môn, Albion's soul, its deep, singing heart. It stood at the farthermost edge of the world, so remote, so well-hidden, that Rome would never reach it.

After a night's rest we walked down onto the muddy beach, where the ferrymen stood by their carved longboats, awaiting passengers. I sat frontmost in the vessel, as Neha trembled at my feet, refusing to sit and floundering to her keep footing as the ferryman pushed us out. Our passage was slow and rough in the surging winter currents.

The tide was low as we pulled into the shallows and we had to walk over the black, stony sandflats to reach the bank.

I waited beside Caradog and Rhain as our attendants procured horses and a guide to take us to the settlement of Cerrig. Môn was not large, easily traversed in a full day's journey. We would reach our destination by late afternoon, if we rode at good pace.

The vast sky and glittering ocean on the western horizon cast the whole isle in a searing brightness that made my eyes stream. After a lifetime of low cloud and dappled forests, I felt immersed in light.

The streets of the settlement gave way to vast fields of winter wheat. Môn's soil was renowned for its fecundity, yielding crops far in excess of its needs. There were clan tartans from the breadth of Albion among the field workers, for Môn was a sanctuary, a refuge, for those who had fled the Roman occupation. Between the small settlements and farmhouses along the road were huddles of tents and wagons. Several times over the day, Caradog called us to stop, dismounted and spoke to these displaced people. It was clear that Môn had sufficient grain to absorb such homelessness, yet still I was unsettled by the extent of it. Western Albion relied on this island to supply wheat to those tribelands whose crops had failed, and demand had increased since farmers had been pulled into war bands. Môn was Albion's grain store, but even she was not limitless.

Fields subsided to woodlands. These were the learning forests and the groves nested within them were among the most sacred in all of Albion. I felt a body hunger to kneel at their shrines.

The day drew late. My back ached from the saddle. At last our guide announced that we would ride only one more hill before we reached our destination. I strained to glimpse Cerrig's sacred lake as we crested the peak, but it was so hidden by the blaze of sun on the ocean, that we were almost at its edge before I saw it.

Lake Cerrig. Albion's holiest water, place of pilgrimage for the journeypeople. Its bed lay dense with offerings of gold, bronze and silver from every corner of Albion and the Gaulish lands beyond. Even as we arrived it was thronged with song-walkers, murmuring their chants and casting in metal. No place in Albion was closer to Annwyn.

Prydd dismounted and walked up a rocky rise that bordered the lake. From its edge, he cast an iron knife into the water. I slipped from my horse to offer my own greeting to the Mothers. No sooner had my feet touched the ground than I felt their song in the tremor of my legs. I closed my eyes against the roll of emotion that threatened to engulf me. This island place would heal me. It would make me strong.

Caradog stared at me as I remounted. Had he seen how I softened at the brink of the Mothers' realm? His face held an expression I could not read.

We arrived at a settlement of round houses and craft huts noisy with penned goats and sheep. There were no ramparts here, for there was no fighting. Neha bounded to join three other hounds that had been thrown the scraps of a carcass. I watched her with surprise for she was usually wary of other dogs.

As we dismounted, three journeymen strode towards us, their robes billowing behind them.

'Greetings Prydd,' said the first and eldest of them, kissing his journeybrother. He turned to me. 'This must be she.'

'Yes,' said Prydd, his voice thick with false pride. 'Our Kendra.'

'Welcome.' The elder kissed my fingers and pressed his forehead to the back of my hand. 'I am Sulien, head journeyman of Môn,' he said as he straightened.

His hair and beard were grey as ash and I could see his smile was well-worn in his face. He motioned forward one of his companions who handed me a bronze cup filled with ale.

All three bowed as I drank the strong liquid.

'It has taken far too long for you to come to us,' Sulien said as he took the cup.

'Not too late, I pray,' I said.

'Perhaps just in time.' He passed the cup to Caradog. 'We received riders two days ago...'

'With what message?' said Caradog.

'The Iceni have risen,' said Sulien. 'They no longer tolerate the disarmaments. Chiefs from the Coritani have made a war bond with them and they are gathering at the edges of Tir Iceni to prepare for battle.'

'It is too soon!' said Caradog. 'Does Scapula call back his men from the Sun Road to meet them?'

'No, War Chief. He prepares his legions. He leaves the auxilia in place along the Sun Road to watch over the west.'

Caradog smiled. 'He is no fool.'

We spoke no further for it was not correct to conduct statecraft before meat and bread had been taken.

Sulien walked beside me as we went to the guest huts, querying my training and my history with the lively curiosity of a true journeyman. 'Does it please you so far, our precious isle?' he asked.

'Very much,' I said. I loved this place: the light, the lake, the endless glinting freedom of the ocean. But this was not all. This was a place unbound to any tribe. It belonged to the Mothers. It belonged to everyone and no one. This was why it could be home to the homeless. Why, perhaps, it could be home to me.

⊹

I sat beside Caradog as the fire burned low in the guest hut.

The rest of our party were asleep behind woollen curtains that screened the beds.

Caradog was sleepless, preoccupied by the evening's discussion with Sulien and the other journeypeople. He had asked the elders whether he should take his fighters to join the Iceni, despite his displeasure at their timing. 'If I do not go to them now,' he had said, 'I cannot hope for their friendship when I require it.'

But the elders had been clear. 'Leave the eastern tribes. They are lost to us,' said Sulien. 'Our purpose now is to protect Môn and the tribelands around it, the mountain country. Let this be your kingdom. Give the Iceni to Rome.'

Caradog had yielded to this wisdom but I saw now how it pained him. He was born of the east. The Iceni and the Coritani were tribes that bordered his homeland. But he could not defy the elders of Môn. In exchange for his protection, his tireless fight, they gave him grain and weapons and metals for trade. They paid for his war.

I looked at him in the flickering light. He gave himself willingly to fight for our freedom, but he was not free. He had been bought as all things are bought. As my own Kendra's title had been bought by a far simpler contentment.

I stared at my hands, calloused from the reins. As a child, I had known many things to be pure and bestowed without cost: the sweetness of a wild grown apple, the icy thrill of spring's first river bath, our belonging to the land we stood on. But the Romans had robbed us of this innocence. Now there was nothing untouched or unquestioned.

'Tomorrow night, we will be wed.'

I looked up. It was the first time Caradog had made mention of our betrothal since we had left Llanmelin. 'I thought you had forgotten...'

He ignored my jibe. 'You are Kendra of Albion—'

'So I am called...' I ventured, wondering what he meant by stating it.

'You have been asked by the journeymen to name me as high king.' He paused. 'It is not them, but I, who asks you now... do you think I am worthy to be king?'

I stared at him. He was not asking me as Kendra. He was asking for *my* judgement, *my* authority. He had never done so before. What should I say? He was flawed. Prideful. But he had a love of Albion that I had never known and he had the courage to defend it.

'Yes,' I whispered.

Without words, he reached for my hand.

I looked down at the worn leather plait that circled his wrist, his marriage band. This was the marriage he had made by choice. Beside it was a much newer band, by which he was betrothed to me.

I closed my eyes and pulled my hand away. I had to silence the stirrings of my heart before it was too late. My task was Albion's protection. If I loved again, as I had loved Taliesin, it would destroy me.

✣

The next day commenced the final preparations for the solstice and the marriage ceremony.

Midwinter was the fulcrum of the year. Caradog and I would be wed in the belly of the year's longest night, so that when Lleu rose in the east—if our rituals had been strong enough to turn him back—we would know that the marriage had been blessed, that the king was true.

Many chieftans and their families had already arrived, on the advice of their journeymen, ready to forswear their territories to a greater power—one they believed the Mothers had chosen, one they believed would protect them: a sacred king.

All day I was fasted, washed, and sung over in the temple by the journeypeople. Now, many hours after sunset, I stood on the stony rise before the lake with a flaming bonfire next to me.

A gathering of many hundreds of people rimmed the lower shore, huddling around lesser fires and jostling for a better vantage. Sulien, Prydd and a throng of other journeypeople milled around me, readying the cups and oil for ritual. Beside me was a mighty archway wrought of leafless branches of apple and oak, and woven with sprigs of our holiest winter fruit: the translucent, moon-pale berries of the mistle.

Standing within the arch, obscured from my sight by the sprays of mistle, was Caradog. I could not see him, but I knew he was unclothed, so that all could be certain he bore no imperfection.

I wore only a white, horse-skin cloak over my own nakedness and a garland of mistle in my hair. Mare's blood had been painted across my cheeks and breasts, as well as sitting heavy in my churning belly. My flesh and the land were as one. Tonight Caradog would be joined to both.

A steady drum beat and a journeyman's chant lapped against my skin.

Sulien stepped forward and quieted them both. The crowd hushed. The ritual was beginning.

'Check that he is unblemished, Kendra,' Sulien commanded

in a voice that carried far over the lake.

I walked to the archway and turned to face Caradog, hiding my shock at the force of his nakedness. He was paler-skinned, less haired than I had imagined him to be, but somehow, unrobed and unmetalled, adorned only by the light of the torches, he looked more noble, more commanding, *more of a king*, than I had ever seen him.

I placed my palms on his chest. I could not meet his eye.

Perhaps it was that I had neither eaten nor drunk all day, but I felt suddenly unsteady as I stood before him. I was not prepared for him to be so beautiful.

He saw me falter and took hold of my arm to brace me.

In accordance with my instruction, I ran my hands over the length and breath of his body. His chest muscles twitched as I brushed them with my fingers and his skin pimpled in the cold. I felt his strong arms and his powerful legs, as firm and straight as carved wood. His penis hung long and soft, its crown of curls stirring in the wind. I checked his back, his buttocks, the sole of each foot. I had not touched a man's skin since I'd lain with Taliesin. I stood upright. 'He is perfect,' I said in a voice thin with desire.

'Then robe him and stand by his side,' said Sulien, handing me a heavy cloak.

I fastened the pin at his throat, yet still I could not meet his eye. As I stepped into the archway, my nostrils flooded with the scent of oak sap and Caradog's sweat.

Sulien was speaking. 'We gather under the gaze of the Mothers of Môn, first spirits of Albion, to bind the Kendra to her chosen consort. By this marriage, he will be sovereign to the land she carries.' Sulien walked to stand in front of both of us. 'Caradog of the Catuvellauni, son of Belinus, skin to the wren, will you honour the three duties of a king?'

'Name me the duties,' said Caradog, with the clear diction of ritual speech. Nerves, if he had them, did not disturb his voice.

'Will you bestow grain and ale on the farmers with generosity?'

'I will.'

'Will you lead the warriors in battle with courage?'

'I will.'

'Will you serve the Mothers and the journeypeople who uphold their knowledge with reverence?'

'Yes.' He glanced toward me. 'All this, I promise to do.'

The gathering was silent, waiting.

Sulien turned to me. 'Kendra of Albion, skin to the dog, you bear knowledge in origin. Your flesh is Albion. Your breath is Annwyn. Your voice is our Mothers' song in perpetual renewal.'

He handed me a pair of deep bronze spoons, one within the other, and another journeyman filled it with a dark, slippery liquid. 'With this holy oil, blood of the Mothers, anoint the high king of Albion, sovereign protector of all that you uphold.'

I turned to Caradog. He held out his broad hands in the shape of a cup.

I slid the bottom spoon out, and a small piercing in the upper spoon allowed a thin stream of oil to fall onto his palms. I spoke in a clear voice, though my body still trembled. 'Let your hands be anointed.'

I lifted the spoons and poured onto his chest. 'Let your breast be anointed.'

Lastly he lowered himself to one knee and I poured a smooth trickle onto the topmost part of his head. He looked up. A copper-coloured rivulet ran down the side of his face.

I felt a moment's panic. Was this, in truth, the will of the Mothers? Did I have this authority? Was I enough to make him king?

Sulien proclaimed, 'He is anointed. Stand.'

The crowd roared as Caradog stood and I felt the great wash of hope that this marriage gave them. This marriage would turn the war. It would bring Cartimandua to Caradog's command. My breath steadied. *This* was enough, this image of our union. What lay within it did not matter.

Sulien took the spoons and said to me, 'You have chosen this man as king. Let me now bind him to you as husband so none may deny the truth of his rule.' He turned to Caradog. 'Make your promise.'

Caradog and I took hold of each other's wrists. Ours were to be as any other marriage vows of the tribes: simple and plainly spoken. But unlike other vows, these would be spoken by our titles and not by the hearts that lay beneath them. Caradog began with words I had heard for all the summers of my life.

I fixed my eyes firmly to our hands as he spoke.

You are the pure love of the moon,
you are the pure love of the sun, the dew, and the rain,

I tightened my grip on his forearms. These words were too sharp, too wanted. I could not admit them.

You cannot possess me, for I am sovereign to myself,
You cannot command me, for I am free.
Yet freely and willingly, I pledge you the first bite of my meat.
I pledge you the first sip from my cup.
From this day, it will be only your name I cry in the night,

I was not prepared for my response to his words of love. They were as spears piercing whatever covering had grown over my longing. His promises were spoken in the service of statecraft, of war. Yet my heart drank them in like a thirsty child.

This is not Taliesin, I said silently to myself, forcing my ears to shun his voice. *You do not love this man.*

I shivered in a sudden breeze. Through the roar of my thoughts I was barely aware of Caradog finishing and Sulien commanding me to begin. With my mouth dry, I stepped dutifully through the same words of promise. But as I neared the end of the verse, I could no longer stem the tremor that rose in my voice, nor the meaning that spilt from the poem;

> *You are blood of my blood.*
> *Bone of my bone.*
> *I will cherish and honour you through this life*
> *and into the next.*
> *By Lleu's faithful course, may you follow me.*
> *By the power of the Mothers, may you love me.*
> *As I love you.*

At the uttering of the words, they were true.

I was making a marriage to a man I had no business to love beyond the surface of ritual, and yet, as I stood here in the dark of winter on our most sacred shore, grasping his wrists before half the tribal heads of western Albion, I realised that I did love him. As much as I had ever loved. For it was a love of hope.

I could not hold the realisation within my own form. Emotion rose in my throat. The adder's shape stirred within me.

'Bow to the King!' cried Sulien to the gathering. 'Bow to the King and his Kendra. May they bring grain to our fields, milk to our cattle, fruit to our trees and victory to our battles.'

As the crowd roared and dropped to their knees, I allowed myself, for the first time, to look directly at my husband's face. With the strike of his stare, all resistance to the serpent fell away. Light distorted and sound grew distant. Only his face was clear.

'Embrace!' called Sulien from somewhere behind me. 'Let them see your union.'

Caradog stepped closer and the force of his scent robbed me of all other senses.

My legs swayed. He drew me firm against his chest.

I heard then, with the serpent's instinct coursing through me, the will of the Mothers. They called for our joining, not in likeness, but in truth. They called for our love.

I did not wish this to be true, but it was.

Our love would strengthen the tribes. Our love would sustain the land.

Prydd's angry whisper roused me. 'Set him a prohibition, Kendra.'

'A geas...' I murmured, tumbling back to an awareness of the gathering.

'Ay,' hissed Prydd. 'Otherwise he is too great, too wayward.'

I released Caradog and looked to Sulien. I had not prepared a geas, though I knew, of course, it was essential to kingship. Without a prohibition, a king's power was too unbridled. Sulien nodded. I had to create one.

I stared at my husband. He needed no geas. He was already firmly restrained by the iron rings of self-questioning. What should I say?

Prydd stood close, hastening me with increasing annoyance. As it had done before, his displeasure began to blur my thoughts and steal my words. I grasped for what was close in my mind. 'I bid that...' I stuttered, '...for fear of your death, you shall never consume the flesh of an adder.'

Caradog's brows lifted with bemusement. 'It should not trouble me to keep such a geas.'

'It is not enough,' said Prydd, scowling. 'Set a stronger geas.'

With the serpent's awareness still alive within me, I saw something in Prydd that I had not yet seen. He was frightened. Despite his desire to see the war chief triumph, he was frightened of Caradog's power, that it might swell beyond his control.

No sooner had I seen this than my voice grew clear.

'No,' I answered. 'It is enough.'

The bonfires had been kept. All had eaten of a mighty feast. We had drunk the mistle's milk, as potent as the seed of men.

Now it was midnight. The darkest moment. The air in the tent was hot and close. The mare-hide walls admitted no firelight. It was here that our marriage would be made irrevocable.

I sat naked on a buck-pelt spread over thick straw.

Journeypeople encircled the tent outside, chanting, beating their staffs on the ground, shaking their rattles. They were readying Caradog to enter.

Beyond them, the gathering stood witness. I sensed the hope in their ululations, their stamping feet. This joining would save them. When the true king ruled, the land was strong.

I anchored my heartbeat to the pulse of the chant.

At last the tent's opening was held apart. For a moment, Caradog was silhouetted against the blaze of the fires. All around me was voice, rhythm, fire and intention, all converging to change man to king.

The door skins fell closed behind him as he entered, leaving only darkness between us.

I heard him lower himself to his knees and shed his cloak. Outside, the journeypeople lifted their chant.

I feared my ribs would crack with the violence of my heart.

This was the man I loved. Did he feel as I did? Had he heard the Mothers' cry as I had?

I sensed him come close. He was kneeling before me, only a thin channel of air between us.

'Tidings,' he whispered. Was there a tremor in his breath?

'And to you.'

He paused, unmoving. 'Is this your desire? For if it is not, I shall not force it.'

I lifted my face and found his lips. He tasted of mead and mistle, his mouth warm and hungry.

I brought my palms to his chest to feel his body for a second time. This time, free of the gaze of the crowd, I touched him slowly, tracing the curve of his muscles, the hollows of his throat, the corrugations of his ribs. I squeezed his lean waist, his strong buttocks, seeking to know the shape and texture of every part of him. 'Yes,' I breathed over his most tender skin, 'this is my desire.'

I lay back onto the deer pelt as he positioned himself above me.

Outside, the journeymen kept their steady pounding, calling and rattling, hungry to know that the land had received its king.

It was too dark to see his face. I could only smell him: leather, dried blood, and the ocean salt that infused his skin. He had the scent of a king, but within it, the deeper, ruptured smell of a man.

I parted my legs and lifted my hips.

He groaned as he pierced me.

Wordless with pleasure, I yielded to his rhythm.

The tent opened, and a torch was held briefly within so that the journeymen could know the joining had taken place.

There was no shame. It was not Caradog and me now; we were greater things.

Our bodies beat an immortal pulse. I was making him king.

With each slow thrust he claimed his authority.

Then, gripping the span of his shoulders, I rolled him onto his back and swung myself atop him to claim my own.

He moaned an urgent cry that hastened me.

The drums and chants beat ever louder around us. Within and without me was an eruption of rhythm.

My muscles quickened. I held still, I did not wish it to end, but the pleasure was too great, it knew its own momentum.

Caradog pushed upwards and I shuddered with an explosion of heat and light so powerful that it rendered me into a simpler form of spine and muscle. Now I did not resist the serpent, but let it come, strong and powerful, through my body, writhing and twisting, as Caradog spasmed with his own release.

Our bodies spiralled, awash with sweat.

The entwining of our forms was a new creation.

A new birth.

A new king.

†

A voice whispered through the opening of the tent. 'Awaken, Kendra. One hour until rise.'

'Thank you,' I murmured. 'We will come.'

The journeyman hung a torch from the door pole and withdrew.

We must have slept for several hours while the gathering celebrated through the night. Now we had to ready ourselves for the final and most important moment of the ceremony. I turned to my husband, still sleeping.

For this moment he was mine, his face gentle. I studied the ridge of his cheekbone, the raised vein on his forehead and the first faint silvering at his temple. Within this fragile parcel of flesh lay a spirit strong enough to hold back an empire.

His eyes flickered beneath closed lids. What worlds was he visiting? What armies was he slaying? He exhaled and shifted in his sleep.

I dipped my face closer and drank in the brine tang that lingered on his skin. He had shown me, this night, that he felt the same need for me as I for him.

I thought of Euvrain with anguish. Would she relinquish him? Could we ask it of her? She had said that the war must not fall to the eddies of love. But what if love were the very force that the war demanded?

I stretched against him, resting my cheek on his shoulder.

'Tidings, queen,' he murmured, hoarse from the celebration.

I propped on my elbow to look at him. 'Tidings.' Would we be shy of each other?

He frowned through bloodshot eyes. 'What hour is it? I must arise—'

'An hour until dawn. There is time.'

He sat up. 'I need to prepare, find my metals...'

Would he leave so quickly? 'Caradog—'

He turned to face me, stared for a few moments, then leaned forward to kiss my mouth. Our limbs coiled and our hunger surged, but he broke from the embrace to sit, straight-backed.

'What is it?' I asked.

He faced the doorway and would not meet my eye. 'I have promised Euvrain that I would lie with you once to make the marriage and not again.'

I stared at his broad, freckled back. 'That cannot be *your* wish?'

'She has stood beside me as I have dragged her, through mud and snow, from one side of Albion to the other. Her wishes are mine.'

'I, too, care for the wishes of Euvrain. But here, in this tent, can you not speak of the desires that are yours alone?'

Still he would not face me. 'I desire you,' he said coldly, 'as any man would desire a woman of your beauty and power. But I have my greatest task ahead and I cannot be drawn from it.'

I stared at him in shock. It was not possible. He loved me. I had heard it when he cried my name. Why did he deny it now?

The scent of sea mist closed in through the tent's leather walls.

'Are these Euvrain's words, War Chief? Did she warn you, as she did me?'

Now he turned to look at me. His gaze was guarded. 'In one hour I will be crowned high king. My task is to build a war band strong enough to defeat Rome. I must be free and clear-minded to do this. And I cannot betray my wife. She is beloved by my warriors. And by me.'

My voice was thin, my heart buckling. 'So this marriage is nothing more than the making of your kingship.'

'As has always been discussed.' He frowned, and said in a tone that felt more cruel for its kindness, 'Did you expect otherwise?'

I had expected nothing. Least of all to realise that I loved this man with the fierceness of the sun.

I had thought I heard the land itself cry out for our joining. Perhaps I had misheard.

I stared at my hands, resting on my bare thighs. The same drowning sadness I had known with Taliesin began to rise within me. I had misjudged Caradog. He knew no love for me. He feared that I would burden him. Two nights ago, he had asked me if I chose him truly. I had confused his intention. It was only my choice—not me—he wanted.

He was reaching for his cloak.

'Is it still your wish that I come to the Brigantes with you?'

'Of course. The chiefs will want to see the Kendra and her chosen king. And Cartimandua will like you, I am sure of it.' He slipped through the doorway.

I shook my head, inwardly cursing as I sat alone. How foolish I had been to imagine the Mothers would grant me Caradog. They had granted me pardon for my betrayal. I could hope for no more.

Cerrig's streets were ablaze with torches as we walked to the temple for the dawn ceremony. The lake fires still burned, the people were all awake. The longest night required a diligent vigil. There were no more drums, nor voices. We had made our prayers. Now we would see if Lleu had heard them.

We entered the temple. Caradog sat in the strong place, his oak stool not a hair's width to the east or to the west of the stakes that marked the angle of the sun's solstice rise.

I stood behind him, holding a bronze crown that Sulien had handed me.

The journeypeople ringed us in a tight circle, leaving only a gap for the light to enter. Behind them the townspeople and guests crammed into the temple, gathering outside when the space had been filled.

Then Sulien bade us be silent.

Through the temple doorway we could see a paleness on the horizon, a thin glow that told us Lleu had not been defeated, that he rose again from the year's strongest darkness, that summer would return.

The back of Caradog's head brushed against my chest as he straightened.

Now that Lleu had been glimpsed, a single voiced chant unspooled into the faint light. It was Sulien's sweet, certain voice that began to regather the torn threads that flailed within me. Here, in ceremony, I could find strength. Caradog did not love me, but his goal for our tribelands was also my own. In this way—if no other—we were of one mind, one heart.

The sky had brightened from red to salmon. Soon Lleu would appear. Sulien bade me to ready the crown. I raised my hands and held the bronze circlet above Caradog's head.

Now the other journeymen joined Sulien in chant. The horizon was aflame.

I lowered the crown to the war king's head just as the sun crested over the fields, slowly, irrefutably, painting him golden.

6

The Unseen

The Mothers hate what is obvious and love what is hidden.

I WALKED TO the lake and splashed my face with cold water. The revellers had returned to the settlement, or dispersed to their tents for some sleep. Other than a bittern stirring the surface, I was alone.

As I crouched at the water's edge, I heard a choked cry emerge from a bank of sedge behind me. It was a muffled hybrid of whimpering and singing, an ailing sound. I pushed through the bushes to find a shallow trench. There, lying in the mud, ale horn in hand, and wailing senselessly in praise of the marriage rites, was Rhain.

'You're drunk,' I chastised, as I pulled him upright, brushing grit from his robe. He was limp, heavy and utterly useless. 'You daft creature! Don't you know we ride in a few hours hence?'

'Mount me now!' he shouted, his speech slurred. His sour breath turned my head. 'Let me know you, at least, if I can know no other.'

'Hush!' I hissed. 'You are beyond senseless.' Somehow I managed to drag him into the marriage tent, where I gave him water and tried to settle him. Between bouts of song-wailing, his gaze focused on my face. 'Ailia?' he breathed, as if I were a marvel to him. 'Is it you?'

'Hush—' I urged, fearful that he would be discovered in this improper place. 'Yes, it is I.'

'Tell me what occurred in here!' he demanded. 'How flies the wren in the arts of the bed?'

'What?' I said, shaking my head. 'Why do you speak so leeringly of Caradog?'

'Why?' he repeated, giggling stupidly. 'Why should I not? Do you think you alone deserve to taste the sweetbreads of marriage?' He laughed again as his head lolled to his chest.

I paused as his blurred words slowly found their meaning. He was so misshapen that I had never imagined he might know the hungers and desires of any man. But of course he must. We were flesh until we ceased to breathe.

'Oh Rhain.'

He lifted his eyes to mine and I recognised in them the immense sadness that mirrored my own. I felt a wave of compassion. The tribes placed such value on our bodies' perfection. We were fined for every expansion of our belts, our chiefs replaced if they became maimed or blemished. Rhain stood little hope of finding a wife. And yet any woman would be blessed to be loved by so deep a mind, so full a soul.

'Is it me you wish for?' I asked.

'Nay, not you.'

We sat in silence. I would not ask him to declare himself. As I hoped I would not have to declare myself.

'Come, dear teacher,' I said, smoothing the bed. 'Sleep off your ale in my tent and then prepare a new song to teach me as we make our ride. We both need the sweet milk of a poem to fill us this day.'

My head swirled with the tides of our human yearnings as I packed my saddle bags in the guest hut. Despite my sadness at Rhain's suffering, it gave me comfort to have seen it. If a Songman as powerful as he still knew unmet affection, then perhaps my own longing would not be a barrier to my strength.

At highsun, we gathered in the hall of Cerrig to discuss the safest route to Tir Brigantes. The journeymen were bleary-eyed from the rivers of ale drunk at the marriage feast, but Caradog was adamant that we not delay our departure by even one day. Even dressed in a simple shirt and woollen cloak, his new kingship was palpable.

'Certainly, you cannot go in your own guise,' said Sulien. He had been one of the few to show restraint at the ale tap, and it repaid him now in clear wits. 'If Roman scouts find anyone with the likeness of the war king on the roads, you'll be in leg-rings before you can slice their shaven throats.'

'Then bring a farmer's shirt and a sack of barley to give me purpose,' said Caradog. He smiled at Rhain. When his temper was bright, the whole war was sport to him.

Sulien was seated beside me. 'You must alter yourself also, Kendra,' he said. 'Scapula is brutal against the journeypeople. His soldiers are instructed to dispatch anyone found on pilgrimage in treaty lands. I have lost three brothers at the border of Tir Brigantes.'

'That is murder,' I said.

'That is fear,' said Sulien. 'They know that it is we who are their strongest enemy.'

'What of the Brigantes?' I asked. 'Do you still hold ties to their journeypeople?'

'Some,' he said. 'The Roman soldiers are noisy and ignorant of the forests. It is easy to evade them. My bonds to the Brigantes have weakened, but not yet died.' He stared at my forehead. 'You are unmarked?'

'Yes.' I held back my hair to reveal my bare forehead. 'I have completed no branch of learning.'

'Thanks be for that,' he said, 'so you might travel as a peasant's wife.'

Our greatest disguise would be the smallness of our party. None would expect the leader of free Albion to travel unattended.

That Rhain would come with us was never questioned, despite that he would give us away to any who knew that the war king's poet was strange-formed. For what hope did Caradog have of turning the heart of the great queen, Cartimandua, without the magical voice of his Songman?

'What shall be my disguise?' asked Prydd, whose hairless scalp revealed the mark of the initiated all too clearly.

Sulien smiled. 'Your disguise shall be your return to Tir Silures. For even if we could hide your marks, your journeymen's graces are impossible to obscure.'

It was true. While Caradog's sword-built shoulders could easily be attributed to a farmer's labour, Prydd's stooped and delicate bones could belong to none but a journeyman, and even then only one who practised the branch of law or judgement, not surgery, measurement, or astrology, which required arm strength and fortitude for long walking.

Prydd must have been angry beneath his wordless nod. Yet he had no choice but to defer to his knowledge-elder, who glanced at me after making his pronouncement.

Sulien met the world with light humour, but I saw how sharply he perceived the textures of statecraft. He must have sensed it would aid me to be free of Prydd's fettering gaze, and he was right. Perhaps, with Prydd gone, alone with Caradog and with Rhain my teacher, I could at last find a Kendra's voice that would not be silenced.

✣

An hour later, Sulien, Prydd and several other journeymen stood at the edge of Cerrig to bid us farewell. Our horses pawed at the path, ready to move. They had arrived carrying riders of nobility and learning. Now we were as peasants, in rough-woven wool, our throats and wrists unadorned by metal. Only my sword and sling, bound firm, as always, to my leather belt, betrayed any falsehood in my likeness to a farm-woman. These were as vital to me as the body that bore them.

Sulien spoke to Caradog. 'I have sent messengers to the Deceangli chiefs that Môn acknowledges you as high king,' he said. 'I expect they will acknowledge you in accordance with our advice. But whether the same will be said of the Brigantes chiefs—and of Cartimandua—that is in your hands alone.'

Caradog glanced at me. 'And my wife's.'

Prydd stepped forward. 'The journeymen have made you king,' he said to Caradog. 'But make no mistake—your power is increased, not absolute. You must consolidate the tribes and you must secure our sovereignty. Otherwise your kingship will fail.'

Caradog frowned. 'I shall not fail.'

'No, you shall not,' said Sulien, kissing his cheek. 'And please do not wait too long to end this war.' He nodded toward the fields that held the homeless. 'We will not have enough grain to feed this number for another winter.'

'It will be soon,' said Caradog. 'Is there any further news from the Iceni?'

'None yet,' said Sulien. 'Though I'm sure there will be battle before you reach Cartimandua. And if the Iceni are successful against Scapula, then she will be forced to consider your approach even more carefully.'

And if they are not? I thought. I called Neha to my side as I mounted my mare, but she had crept behind Sulien's robe skirt and would not come.

'What is this?' I murmured as she continued to refuse me. I dismounted and crouched beside her, fondling her soft white ear. 'Do you wish to stay, dogess?' Never, without purpose, had she failed to attend me.

'Perhaps she would remain to ensure you return,' said Sulien.

I stared into her eyes of blue and brown. Day and night. 'Perhaps you are right,' I marvelled, laughing. She licked my face, but would not follow.

'Leave the hound, Kendra!' called Caradog. 'Or we will miss the last ferries.'

'She is accustomed to sleeping fireside,' I whispered to Sulien, 'and she is no easy friend of other dogs.'

'I'll watch her,' said Sulien.

We passed our first night in a farmhouse on the mainland, leaving before light the next morning. It would take at least twenty dawns to ride to Stenwic, from where Cartimandua ruled her tribe.

Our first week was spent in the territory of the Ordovices, where we were met with welcome. Rhain sang Caradog's praise songs as we rode into the stony, mountain-bound settlements, and forged stories of his rise to kingship around the fires by night.

These misty tribelands were untouched by Rome. The lurching black mountains and the deep lakes between them had known only the tribe's law and the eerie grey cast of the Mothers' light. The presence of Rome felt unimaginable here, and the chiefs were not fearful to commit their fighters to Caradog's war.

When we passed the border stone into Tir Deceangli, Caradog had to toil harder to solicit war-bonds from the chiefs. Many held strong friendships and marriage ties with the petty chiefs of south-west Tir Brigantes and were reluctant to betray them, despite their hatred of Rome.

Caradog was skilled with persuasion. He convinced many of them that the Brigantes and its fighters would soon be within his command, proclaiming how the Kendra, herself, had deemed him worthy. Above all he spoke of how we were bound to this land by law and by love. How our wounds were the land's wounds, how our capture was the land's slavery, how he could protect them from both.

One by one, even the chiefs who had refused to join him in the attack on the Sun Road laid their swords at his feet.

I was always at his side as he walked through the settlements, offering my Kendra's blessings to the winter calves and new-born children, watching the tribespeople's eyes well as they kissed the hand of the woman who had heard the Mothers' song.

By day, it was a perfect union.

But nights revealed a different truth. In the quietness of the guesthuts the war king and I barely spoke. This time it was not he who drew away, but I. For I had no strength to permit myself small sips of what I longed to drink in great, spilling drafts.

Each wakeful night I prayed for my heart to release him.

Each morning reminded me I still adored this tireless, headstrong creature, who did not shy from the world's trouble but plunged into it with all the reckless courage of a stallion descending a sheer cliff to evade capture.

Caradog joked with Rhain in easy laughter, while I rested in silence, hollowed by a man who had lain with me just once, but enough to set a torch to a bonfire of hunger that now burned from inside.

In the larger townships I wandered the fringes, drawn to the unskinned people who dwelled there. It was in these untended places, where dark eyes stared up at me from bodies too poorly-fed to be useful to farmers, that I felt my Kendra's blessings might carry some power. I brought them bread, which I shared at their fires, and spoke to them of the war, of which they knew almost nothing.

Caradog called me back whenever he found me at such places. He felt it tarnished his nobility for his wife to drag her skirts through the mud and shit of the fringes, even if it were only a farm-woman's dress and not the Kendra's cloak that she wore.

But I felt at peace among those without skin. I had been one of them and did not see them as something other. Although I had skin now, and a title, I still recognised myself in their struggle for place and purpose. I felt needed among them. Far more than when I sat around the council fires with the chiefs and listened, unspeaking, to the negotiations of weapons and warriors that Caradog was so fond of, and about which he rarely asked for my view.

He desired my esteem, seeking it often as we rode out from one township to another, demanding that I reflect on how persuasively he had spoken, how impressed the chiefs were with his generosity and bearing. But I knew that I had no real influence upon him. He did not yet seek my guidance. He did not yet heed my authority. He did not love me.

Perhaps Prydd had been right. It seemed that my Kendra's title was valued for its glamour and little more.

But there *was* more. My only hope could be to show it by song.

I learned Rhain's poems. One, then another, then another, in every hour that we rode through mizzling winter rain. There was no time to stop and re-walk the mountain paths and rivers we were passing in our travels, so I picked up pebbles, feathers, acorns and fallen coins from the roadway whenever we stopped to replenish our water skins, fastened them to the cord that I carried in my pouch, and used their shapes and textures to index my knowledge.

I gorged on Rhain's teaching until I felt heavy with memory. He was always pleased to begin a new cycle of history, a myth of Annwyn, or a song that mapped the route we rode and ensured I could ride it again alone. Although I could not alter the words of the poems, I poured into them my love for Caradog, my devotion to the Mothers, and Rhain praised my voice for its depth and richness.

As we neared the border of Tir Brigantes, where we would have to cease our singing, I asked him, for a second time, whether I might be permitted to forge a song.

'Not yet,' he said with a maddening smile.

'Why not?' cried Caradog, who often rode close as I sang. 'I would like to hear it!'

'You must wait, War King,' Rhain said.

'For what?'

'For sovereignty.'

Caradog smiled, thinking, of course, that Rhain spoke of our land.

Only I knew he spoke of my sovereignty of voice.

As we rode into the last Deceangli settlement, the chieftain warned us that Roman scouts had learnt of our journey. 'There were soldiers here two dawns ago,' he said, as we dismounted. 'They were looking for three travellers, one with a disfigured face.'

Caradog stared at him. 'How have they discovered this?'

'We are thick with scouts,' said the chieftain. 'Rome does not leave such a precious border unwatched.'

'I cannot go on with you,' said Rhain.

'Caradog needs you to sing,' I said. 'I will return, then at least you will be two and not three. If you hood Rhain's face, I am sure you will be safe.'

Caradog looked at us both. 'You will remain with me, Kendra. Rhain will return to Llanmelin.' He would hear no argument.

I wept as I farewelled Rhain an hour later.

'Shed a skin,' he said as he kissed my cheek.

Caradog and I passed into territory bound by treaty to the Emperor Claudius. The Brigantes, by size and numbers, were Albion's largest tribe, prosperous with lead, coal and hides, and revered for the fierceness of their warriors.

The country was harsh, defended by mountains and fast-flowing rivers. As we rode northward into its core, forests gave way to vast, desolate moorlands, where mists clung like shrouds, and sheep fossicked for scant growth amidst stones and snow. We passed few grain fields—wheat grew poorly here—and yet there was a dark strength in this land, an unyielding wildness. How strange, I thought, as our horses stooped to drink from a part-frozen stream, that it was one of the first of the tribelands that Rome had tamed.

Sulien had given us the names of chiefs who would be certain to welcome us. We found food, ale and shelter readily enough, but no chief would make war vows to Caradog until he could evidence the friendship of their mighty queen. Even those professing great sympathy with Caradog's war and hatred of Rome would not betray vows made to Cartimandua. 'Bring us sign of her alliance to you,' said one, pushing silver coins into Caradog's saddle pouch as we prepared to depart, 'and our swords are yours.'

The first thing amiss was the position of the entrance. Stenwic's gates faced the west. Our townships were always entered from the east, in alignment with Lleu's midsummer rise. But we could afford no query that may alert the guards we were anything other than farmers wishing to see the queen about our tithes.

As we walked through the courtyard to Cartimandua's hall, a watchman with bulging eyes and curling horns followed our every step. His face was wrought of hammered bronze and stared out from the front panel of the most ornate war chariot I had ever seen. This queen possessed wealth. I saw it in the strong and gleaming horses that whinnied in the yard behind the chariot. I saw it in the gold-inlaid doors of the hall, and the waist-high bronze pots that stood beside them.

In the immense size of the hall and the row of young horse skulls that lined its lintel, this royal courtyard displayed all the mystery and earth-hewn grandeur of the tribes, yet there was another power on show here. Something more flagrant, something that exalted the hand of its makers, its bearers, in ways our tribecrafts did not—the presence of Rome.

Caradog had sent a trusted rider from last night's township to convey our arrival secretly to the tribequeen. A servant admitted us into the hall, and instructed us to await Cartimandua's attendance. This also, was unusual. We would not normally enter a leader's hall in the absence of the host.

We took our seats around a robust fire, leaving free the strong place. Caradog stretched and loosened his cloak. I looked around. The tall walls were skirted with shields as dazzlingly ornate as the chariot outside. From smoking pots poured a spicy, almost oily scent, unfamiliar to my nostrils.

Into this foreign and dizzying theatre strode a red-robed figure so tall, so awesome, that were I not certain I sat in Albion, I would have sworn was a creature of the Mothers' realm.

'My brother! My dog!' Her voice boomed like a lowing heifer. 'You brew trouble like an ale-smith! And you have the hide of a bullock walking into my township—how do you know there are not five legionaries waiting beyond the door? I could fulfil Scapula's dearest wish with just one word to a rider...'

Caradog rose, smiling. 'But then you would be denied the pleasure of watching what trouble I am yet to cause.'

She roared with laughter and they embraced warmly as kin.

'Brother,' she repeated more softly, clasping his shoulders as she looked at his face. 'Last time I saw you, you had barely a sprout on your chest, yet now you are sought by the Emperor himself. And as handsome as a cockerel!' She laughed again, then her eyes fell to me. 'And who is this? Wait—do not tell!' she said, clapping her palms. 'I have heard of this trinket from the few remaining journeymen bold enough to attend me—this is she who is Mother-chosen, Albion's last Kendra!'

'Last?' I questioned, although we had not yet greeted. I suspected she would forgive my directness.

She frowned through her smile. 'Do you believe that Claudius will permit any such an idol to stand once he has laid claim to this isle?' She cocked her head when I did not answer. 'If you do you are a fool. The wheel has turned, Kendra, as surely as spring follows winter.'

I turned to Caradog. Would he permit such disrespect, even from someone who had chosen to step outside of the Mothers' reach?

But he was smiling, enjoying the spectacle of our encounter.

'The Romans will pull journey-law from our soil as our farmers pull the dead roots before new seeds are sown,' she continued. 'When my grandchildren are grey, the tale of the last Kendra will be a pretty fire-story, nothing more.' Cartimandua walked towards me and grabbed my hand. 'But *I* will still kiss your fingers, journeywoman, for it is no faint soul that might rise to the Kendra.' She squashed her soft lips against the back of my hand.

Staggered, I could not speak.

'I greet you,' she said, rising to kiss my cheek. 'I am Cartimandua, daughter of Trintovan. Skin to the horse.' Beneath the thick, lily scent of her perfume, she emitted an animal pungency. She may have marked the treaty in Claudius's tent, but her spirit rose up from the earth of the tribes.

I told her my name and bowed to her skin.

She sat down in the strong place with all the ease and bearing of

164

one who had been born to rule. She was not fresh—perhaps five and twenty summers—but she was poised at the very crest of her succulence, like fruit softened just beyond perfect ripeness, its flesh only sweeter for the first musky traces of decay.

She wore a dress of blood red, its plainness serving only to highlight the weight of metal and gemstones that hung from her ears and throat. Her forehead was high, her hair dark as cherrywood and her black eyes both shrewd and merry.

I stared at her in all her shimmering, muscular heft. This woman, more than any other being I had yet encountered, possessed authority.

I wanted to lie at her feet and drink from the cup of her.

Cartimandua called her servant from the doorway and bade him pour wine into cups made of glass.

'Do you like my gift?' said Caradog, accepting his wine. The armband lay on the bench between them.

'Breathtaking,' said Cartimandua. 'To what do I owe the honour of such an offering?'

'To kinship,' said Caradog.

The tribequeen smiled and slid the band over her wrist beside several others. 'Where is that sorry wretch of a Songman you always dragged around with you?'

'Too precious to bring into these fallen lands.'

Cartimandua laughed and motioned to me. 'And she is not?'

'She is strong enough.'

'Is his voice as sweet as I remember?'

'Sweeter than any croaking Brigantes frog, I'll wager!' said Caradog.

Cartimandua chuckled again. Firelight flickered on her skin as we sipped the dark wine. 'Riders tell me that the elders at Môn have crowned you high king.'

'True,' said Caradog. 'And I come to you, sister, to ask you to acknowledge my title. And to promise your warriors to my war.'

I stifled a gasp. Could he not have dressed his intention in even the lightest of cloaks?

Cartimandua stared at him for a long time, unsmiling. 'What is your purpose in this war?' she asked.

'Our sovereignty,' he answered without pause. 'The tribes of Albion were not born to be slaves.'

Gold bracelets tinkled as Cartimandua stretched out her arms. 'Do I appear as a slave to you?' She placed her hands back in her lap. 'It seems that *you* are the ones dressed as workers in fields.' She glanced at my threadbare dress.

'It is but a costume,' I said.

Ignoring me, she turned to Caradog. 'I confess it surprises me,' she said, 'that you fight so desperately to be free of Rome. Were you not raised with all the privilege and comfort that came from their trade ships? I was there, Caradog. You could have made a fine Roman prince. You would have led a powerful life, and yet you lead a war against them. What turned you?'

'*I* did not turn.' For the first time she had roused him. 'My father was Rome's servant. He thought he could hold them back with tin or slaves or dogs. But I knew, even as a boy, that they would come for more whenever they chose—'

'It was your actions that called them forth!' Cartimandua said, herself now angered.

'And it will be my actions that banish them.'

Cartimandua breathed deeply, air hissing through narrowed nostrils. 'You are fuelled by pride,' she said. 'Your father—my uncle—was the mightiest of kings. Even now I model myself on his judgement.' She sipped her wine. 'But he shunned your views on the Empire, so now you oppose him against all reason.'

'How little you know me and yet we were so close,' said Caradog.

'I know you yet. You would be sovereign to tribelands that are not your own. Tell me, what difference should I see between your desires and Rome's?'

My body stiffened. The cascading whinny of a horse in the stable yard was loud in the silence.

Caradog sat motionless. If her words had breached him, he did not reveal it. 'She,' he said, turning to me. '*She* is the difference. The Mothers have chosen me through their Kendra, and she is my testament.'

Cartimandua stared at me. 'What does she say then?'

My heartbeat quickened. What could I say to reroute this torrent of a woman? My only choice was the truth. 'We are born of this land. We are its kin.'

Her eyes narrowed and I saw the sharpness of her mind behind her splendour.

'And this, my dear ones, is exactly the heart of it. Rome offers kinship through ties that are beyond land, beyond birth.'

'Bondage?' asked Caradog with a smirk.

'Citizenship,' said Cartimandua, savouring the word. 'You can be made citizen of Rome without ever having set foot in the city. It is kinship unfettered by birth or land. It can grow without limit. The whole world could be granted citizenship of Rome without ever once sighting its walls. Does such power not intrigue you, Kendra? Brother? Do you not wish to dive in and bathe in it?'

I looked at Caradog. I knew such power did enthral him. But he said only, 'Are you such a citizen, sister?'

'Of course!' she said. 'It is bestowed to all who sign client treaties. And who wish it.'

'So you relinquish your kinship to these lands?' I said in disbelief.

'Not at all. I am bound to two places at once!' She laughed again.

'Do not look so shocked. Such things are possible in the modern world.'

My thoughts spun. She spoke of an idea I had no understanding of, and yet had I not lived much of my life without knowledge of my birthplace? Did I not now live far from my home? Did not Caradog? What tied us to land we were not born to?

An answer stirred deep in my breast. But I could not yet hear it clearly.

Suddenly Cartimandua exhaled with a heavy breath and turned back to Caradog. 'Brother,' she said, softening. 'I hate the fucking Roman maggots with all the juice in my body. They are guileless, soul-less, dogs' arseholes of men. But if we want to hold power in the tribes, then we must walk at their side. They have harnessed the gods of war to their armies, Caradog, and they will not be stopped.'

I glanced at my husband. Did she not know such words would only incite him? What strange power did she wield that he now remained so silent?

'You claim that you are high king, and this your sovereign queen—' she nodded towards me. 'Well *I* am sovereign to this land. I seek no other ruler. And I will lie with whomever will strengthen my rule. Claudius is my chosen consort.'

Caradog tightened his grasp of his cup. 'This cannot be the will of your tribe—'

'Certainly for some of them it is not. My people are as various and changeable as seasons,' Cartimandua answered. 'It is a delicate dance I lead in binding them together, yet nothing is more important to me than keeping the Brigantes whole and within my command. You, of all people, must comprehend such a goal.'

'Yet I do not pursue it by courting the violence of Rome.'

'Caradog! You are like the last pup to open its eyes. Rome brings us peace! Before I made terms with Claudius, the petty tribes of the

Brigantes were ever at the brink of war. Now there is stability in my tribe.'

This, at least, was true. We had witnessed the loyalty of her chiefs.

'So, my answer is no,' she continued. 'I will not bow to you. I will not give you men.'

Caradog sipped his wine without expression. 'How does it feel to know no love of Albion?' he asked.

Cartimandua was unflinching at the insult. 'Perhaps in my allegiance to Rome, I show a love of Albion greater than your own. Perhaps we must become as they are to preserve what we are.'

'I pray that I will never be loved with such disloyalty,' said Caradog.

My own thoughts were beginning to swim. *Was* there love of the tribes beneath the surface of her betrayal?

'I love you as I have always loved you,' said Cartimandua. 'You have flame in your breast equal to no other tribesman's. You are a strong king—' she leaned towards him, 'but Rome is stronger.' She sat back, filling her wide, jewelled chest with a long breath.

Caradog straightened also, no less commanding for his absence of metal.

Cartimandua could not dent him. 'I accept that you are now a willing subject to your captors,' he said. 'But there are still some chiefs in treaty-held Albion who will yet rise against Scapula. Aedic of the Iceni is mounting a rebellion.'

'Oh, you have not heard?' she said. 'The Iceni are savagely defeated several days ago. They took up arms in the mountains of Coritania. But they were trapped within their own fortifications as the legion came, and were almost all slain. Scapula has installed Prasutagus as king and he rules with his second wife Boudicca. Aedic asked also for help from me, but I did not supply him.'

I startled as she gave another throaty laugh. 'Tell me what lies beneath *that* costume, my wise Kendra!'

Despite our lack of agreement, Cartimandua was eager to show Caradog her home, gifted by Plautius in honour of their treaty.

When she led us through the gateway in a high stone wall, I stopped in shock.

Here, deep in the Mother-sung moorlands of northern Albion, stood a most startling testament to Roman ambition. Two snarling carved beasts, as large as bulls, stood sentry at a mighty doorway, each resting a clawed paw on a moon-shaped orb. Fur flowed from their stone heads, like rays of the sun.

Scores of white columns, like sapless trees, fronted a dwelling so absurdly wide it might house a whole clan without any feeling the heat of the centre fire.

Strangest of all was a collection of painted urns that lined the path along which we walked. From each sprouted a youngling tree of a species I had never seen, with foliage as sparse and silver as an old man's head. By what class of plant-law did a tree grow from a vessel? For what purpose were they arranged so?

I remained quiet as Cartimandua led us into the puzzle-like passageways within the house and past square-cornered walls that seemed to shun any alignment to the solstice. I observed politely as she explained how the bronze dog heads in the bathing room spurted fire-warmed water with the pull of a lever, and the names of the unseasonably lush blossoms that grew within the very walls of the building.

But when Cartimandua took us into the room that held her shrine, and I saw a row of small clay figures in an exact human shape, I could no longer contain myself. I burst out laughing.

Even Cartimandua was forced to smile and shrug. 'Such is the worship of those who see themselves as gods,' she said.

'What are they?' I asked, picking up a white stone statue, carved into the perfect likeness of a robed young woman.

'They are the Mothers, rendered by Roman craftsmen.'

I snorted. The rendering was entirely obvious, there was nothing to decode, to unknot, nothing to lead the mind's eye to what lay beneath the surface. Were the Romans so unseeing, that they must force our spirits into their own image to know them?

We walked back to the interior garden within and stood by a pool dug into the floor where the Mothers had not intended it. Everywhere I looked, there was a bending of nature as if I were in a dream, or a festival of inversion where the fool was queen, and the queen made subject. Everywhere was gleaming stone, glass tiles, and polished metal, all in honour of nothing more than human glory and conquerors' pride. I sat on a bench and accepted a cup of elder wine from a servant.

If this was the Romans' grandeur, then I saw only their weakness. They sought to make their greatness visible.

But what was truly powerful would always be hidden.

✠

'Do you think you can turn her?' I whispered as I washed my face at a basin in the guest hut.

There was scarcely time for us to speak before Caradog and I were expected back at the hall to take bread and meat with the Stenwic council. Cartimandua had warned us, as we left her, that the gathering would be neither lavish nor well-attended, or else the Roman procurator might hear that she had hosted a feast and he would demand to know which visiting chief had sat at her fire. But she had sent a servant woman to our hut, bearing an armful of dresses and neckpieces I was bidden to choose from for the evening.

Her foster-brother was delivered no fine clothing.

'No,' he answered as he rested on his bed. 'Even as a child, she wanted the brightest jewel, and the most tender joint at the feasts.

I have always known that she thirsted for greatness. I did not know how rotten she would become with its attainment.'

'Was she always so...' I searched for the word, '...ferocious?'

He smiled. 'Yes, but she has been enflamed since I last saw her. She is made volatile, like any wild creature, by the bars of its cage.' He lay back on the bed with a groan.

I dried my face and sat beside him. 'Are you so surprised by her answer?'

'Yes...no.' He rubbed his eyes. We were both weary from travel. 'I am surprised she would allow the Iceni to fall unaided. Their alliance has stood since before I was born. I am surprised that the infection of *Romanitas* runs so deep in her.' He spat the word, so often quoted from the governor's speeches, that described the mindstate, the very consciousness, that the Empire sought to spread. 'We were foolish to have come,' he said.

'No we weren't,' I answered. 'Do you not always claim that we must know our enemy?'

'Surely she is not yet that.'

I did not answer. He stretched out beside me. 'Does she dissuade you from your purpose?' I asked softly.

'If I faltered at every barrier, Ailia, I would have long ago been sent to Annwyn. She thinks the Empire is unstoppable, yet four legions cannot catch the single man they seek above any other. My purpose is unwavering.'

'What of her...citizenship?'

He scoffed. 'Honey to coat the sourness of enslavement. She can suck it. We will win this war through our bonds with our land.'

But what were these bonds? I wondered, startling myself with the question. Of what were they formed that whole nations may be so free of them? I stood and picked up a dark blue robe from the pile laid over the bench.

'What does your Kendra's wisdom say of our Cartimandua?' he asked.

I turned to him, curious. He had not sought my counsel since we had sat at the fire at Môn. 'It takes no wisdom to see she is your sister. I like her.'

'I knew you would. Do you agree with her?'

'Of course not,' I answered. 'Albion is my soul. Your war has my loyalty.'

His gaze lingered on my face. This journey, if nothing else, had bridged us. 'We will leave tomorrow, Ailia. There is no purpose in remaining here.'

I nodded and held another dress against my chest. It was a deep berry-red, threaded with gold. If I put it on, I would have never worn anything finer.

'Do not choose that one,' he said, tilting his head.

'Why not? I think it the nicest. Don't you?'

'I do,' he said, sitting upright and undoing his cloak. 'But if you wear it, I may not keep my promise to Euvrain.'

My face filled with a furious heat.

He pulled off his shirt to wash and I turned away.

'Does it offend you to look upon me?' he asked.

'No,' I said—his candour had made me bold—'but, if I did, I may not keep my promise to Euvrain.'

By her standards, Cartimandua's feast may have been humble, but the herb-flavoured meats and peppery oils were finer than any I had tasted.

Venutius, her husband, sat at her side, listening closely but speaking little. She had proudly told us that this fair, thin-faced man had been next in line to the Carvetti throne when their royal marriage was agreed, but it was clear that whatever authority he had within his birth tribe was lost to Cartimandua's now.

A sparse cohort of councillors ringed the fire, including two journeymen who were not robed or metalled as wisepeople, but bore the small blue spiral on their brows by which I knew them.

'Are you not forbidden to remain here?' I had whispered to the younger of them as we were seated.

'I am her physician, and my elder is her augur. When the legionaries come to collect the taxes, she calls us servants and bids us kneel before her to assure Rome we are subdued.'

'Yet she consults you still?' I said, frowning.

'Always.'

There was another man present, barely more than a youth, though impressively built, who sprawled on a cushioned bench on Cartimandua's other side.

'Who is he?' I asked my neighbour, through the hum of talk.

'Vellocatus. The king's armour-bearer.'

'Why does the queen seat her husband's servant at her left hand like a consort?'

The journeyman smiled. 'Why does the queen do as she does?'

I lifted my bowl to receive a spoonful of the fragrant sauce. We ate using small bronze spoons instead of meat hooks. They made me clumsy, as I was accustomed to sopping stew with bread. I noticed Caradog was at ease with the tool.

He argued with his cousin over the number of weapons that she might supply to his war and under what terms. She was more generous than I had expected.

'You shall have rod silver and as many spears as may be convincingly disguised as trade,' she said. 'But in payment for these you will not speak to my chiefs. You will not further factionalise my territories.' There was colour in her cheeks. Perhaps she feared Caradog more than she revealed. 'It has been no small effort to bring the Brigantes to one alliance. I will kill any chiefs who betray it at your incitation. You will have their deaths on your hands.'

'Wife—' said Venutius, by way of pulling reins on the threat.

'Hush!' she snapped with a sourness I had not yet heard. 'It was not you who persuaded the chiefs to swear. You have not the arts for it.'

Venutius stared blankly at the fire, then called for more wine.

'Your insistence on loyalty is one that I share,' replied Caradog to Cartimandua. 'I gratefully accept your metals and will honour your sovereignty over your people.'

'Then let us drink to your war,' said Cartimandua, smiling and raising her cup. 'Win it if you can—the moon may yet defeat the sun—but do not ask me again if I will join you. We are the Brigantes and we stand alone.'

Cups were filled, drained and filled again. Dried fruits were served that looked like pig turds and tasted like sunlight. Cartimandua told stable yard jokes she could barely finish for her own howling laughter, and she and Caradog competed to recall the greatest mischief they had caused as children in Camulodunum.

I saw the affection that flowed between them. Caradog was not mistaken to have come. Their bond was true. It was easy to see why he had believed it would be enough. And though it had not been, he now laughed at her hearth. She needed no journeywoman. She was a magician of her own kind.

I sipped my wine and wondered what she made of me. Was I babe-like in her eyes, as I was in Prydd's? An entrancing innocent? As I watched her in all her lavish sureness, I asked myself whether I *had* failed to see something she saw: a deeper merit in Rome's intrusion.

Then I recalled her home, her indifference to Lleu, and I knew it was she who had lost her grasp of something true. Something subtle and generative, humming quietly at the core of everything. I closed my eyes that I might try to hear it. The land's voice, the Mothers' voice.

She was staring at me when I opened my eyes.

Venutius whispered, frowning, into her ear. Despite Cartimandua's belittlement of him, at least he had the pleasure of her bedskins each night.

But as the evening drew late, and the wine bore us partway to Annwyn, it was not Venutius, but the armour-bearer on her other side, whom Cartimandua began to loll against, while her husband stared grimly ahead.

'Agh, I must go to bed!' she said, sitting upright.

'I am not tired,' said Venutius.

'I was not thinking of sleep,' she drawled. Her glazed eyes fell to me. 'What of you, Ailia? Surely your title affords you the pick of the warriors? You have this one, at least, in your thrall.' She motioned Caradog.

Caradog smiled. 'Ours is a ritual marriage.'

'Perhaps in title!' She roared with laughter. 'A blind man could see that she is as ready for you as a mare in season. Why, I grow wet just watching the pair of you. Venutius, ready yourself—if you can. I will need someone tonight.'

Heat seared in my face until I feared I would blister with it.

Caradog, for once, was silenced.

Never had I been so aware of Caradog's breath as I lay beside him. Despite the empty pallet between us, I felt as though I could hear the coursing of blood through his veins. Did he sleep? My belly churned with the reckoning of it. He had said nothing as we had returned to our guest hut and I, too, had been silent with humiliation. I rolled onto my back and stared up at the bunches of sorrel hanging from the roof beams. Euvrain had been right in her warning. There was no space in war for the turmoil of desire.

Sleepless, I swung my feet to the floor and slipped outside. Stenwic was bright under a clear half moon. I wandered across the courtyard, relishing the cold air on my skin. Something moved in the corner of my vision and I stopped still. 'Who is there?' I said.

'Who asks?' The growling voice was Cartimandua's.

'It is I, Ailia.'

She emerged from the darkness, clasping a bearskin around her bare shoulders. 'Why are you wandering? Do you need a servant?'

'No...I can't sleep.' My heart thudded. 'What of you?'

She chuckled. 'I had a preference for a different bed, but I'm in no rush. Speak with me a moment.' She grabbed my hand and led me to a bench in front of the stables. A sand-coloured hound sniffed at our feet, making me miss Neha intensely. I smoothed my under-robe over my legs.

Cartimandua sat close, her broad thigh against mine. 'Why do you not sleep?' she asked. 'Are my guest huts uncomfortable?'

'Oh no. The bed is...most restful.'

The scent of her unwashed skin was overwhelming. The silence grew tight as a drum between us. She picked up my hand, turned it over, and circled her thumb in my palm with the lightest of pressure.

I did not pull away.

'Listen,' she said in a lowered voice. 'I have long since lost trust in the journeymen and have turned instead to my own judgement.' Her fingers tightened. 'But I see in you the true fire of journey-law. You do not seek power, and yet it burns within you.' Her eyes glittered wetly in the darkness. 'So I say this...' She leaned forward. 'Close your ears to the journeymen who would command you. Make no mistake, they are as self-seeking and power-hungry as any Roman general. You are a journeywoman in possession of your own mind. Use it.' Now she pressed her thumb deep into the bone and muscle of my hand.

'Why are you telling me this?' I gasped.

'Because I would see strength thrive.'

'Then give Caradog your armies and he will thrive.'

'No, it is you who are stronger. Caradog sees by only one light. You see by many torches and your vision is greater.'

My breath was shallow, barely filling my chest. I was light-headed with her words, her scent.

'Have you made a lover of the king yet?'

'Only once...for the marriage.'

'And not again?'

'No. He does not...wish it.'

Her laughter tore through the stillness of the night. 'Then you must change him, journeywoman. It is not merely pleasure and fat babes that the bedskins beget. There is nobility in desire. It is the whirling of all life. The light of Lleu is between you. Do not douse it. Feed it. It will make strong his kingship. And it will make strong the tribes.'

I stared at her. It was as if the Mothers were speaking. 'I have sworn to his wife—'

Again she laughed. 'And who is she to stem the force of the Kendra's desire?'

'She is of true nobility...'

'And you are not?' She shook her head. 'Do not erode yourself with doubt. Fight against the Romans if you choose, but swear to me that you will never take up a sword against yourself.'

'I will not,' I murmured.

'Swear it, Ailia! Promise me this.' Her face was close, her breath hot.

'I swear to you.'

She kissed me. Wine and fig flavoured her mouth. 'You are sweet as nectar,' she murmured, her lips at my neck. 'Will you join with me and Vellocatus, if Caradog will not sate your hunger? Stupid beast.'

My senses swam. Who was this shaman who invited me to her bed? Who authored her story exactly as she pleased? Blood surged through my body but I pulled myself free. I desired her, but I did not trust her. 'I shall not join you, though I don't doubt there would be pleasure in it.'

'I did not see you as one who would shy from pleasure.'

'There are pleasures I seek.'

Cartimandua smiled. 'I am certain of it.'

I rose from the bench.

'When do you leave?' she asked.

'With Lleu's rise.' I looked to faint light on the eastern horizon. 'I must return to my bed.' I walked a few steps then turned back to face her. 'Thank you,' I said.

'What for?'

'For what you have given me.'

Caradog snored softly from across the room. I would speak differently to him as we rode tomorrow. I would question his thoughts and insist he heard mine. I would demand respect as his advisor. Cartimandua was right. I was useless to this war if I fought another against myself.

As for her other council—Caradog rolled over in his bedskins and now faced me, his sleeping face lit by the low fire—it prodded a yearning too raw to touch, and I could not allow myself to think of it.

Steam billowed from our horses' nostrils as we readied them to depart. Cartimandua stood, wrapped in a grey woollen blanket, waiting to bid us farewell. Her face looked pouched and weary in the dawn light. Venutius stood beside her, taut as a cart-spring.

Cartimandua embraced me with a whispered reminder to honour my promise and an invitation to return, then she turned to Caradog.

Her red-rimmed eyes were hard as iron. 'I love you, foster-brother,' she said to him. 'You are kin. I wish you and your war all the strength of the Mothers. But if you come here again I will hand you to the Romans.'

7

The Role of the Songman

The poets craft kings as smiths craft metal.

THE SKY was heavy as we rode. Caradog did not speak. I puzzled, yet again, at the swing of his temper. He might be silent as stone in one hour, then rival a gaggle of servant women at spring wash in the next. What was it now that fuelled his quietness?

'What say you of Cartimandua's threat, Caradog?' I finally asked, kicking my mare forward to breast his.

'She betrays us all,' he answered. 'And I hate her all the more because I cannot help but love her.'

I smiled. 'There is always love within hate.'

'Not for the Romans,' he snapped. 'My hate for them is pure.'

'In one sense,' I said.

'And in another?'

'You surely admire them,' I said carefully. 'Is it not their greatness that will make your defeat of them all the more splendid?'

He turned to me. 'Do you think I welcome this invasion?'

'You have said yourself that the Mothers seek to test your bonds to these tribelands, to secure your kingship...'

'That does not mean that I pursue my position above the lives of my people.'

'No! I did not mean...' I had gone too far.

He stared at me. 'You think my purpose is impure?' His voice was cold.

'Caradog, I do not.' Why did I push him when I had seen that he was already disturbed?

'Then do not imply that I am treacherous. You were not able to help me sway Cartimandua. Do not now begin to doubt me, or you will have no value by my side.'

I stiffened. 'Are you not strong enough to withstand my doubt? Then you are weaker than I thought.'

Our argument ceased at the sound of galloping behind us. Caradog placed his hand to the hilt of his farmer's knife as the rider drew closer.

But it was no Roman soldier who wrenched his mount to a halt before us.

'Venutius!' said Caradog. 'Why have you followed?'

'Quickly,' he urged, as he dropped from his horse. 'I am here under great deception—' This was barely the same man we had just fare-welled. His cheeks were flushed and his eyes alight. He tethered the horses then led us several paces into the forest, where we were hidden from view.

'It is not as Cartimandua has described,' he said in an urgent whisper. 'She says the Brigantes chiefs are united against Rome, but they are not...' He paused. '*I* am not.'

'Speak on,' said Caradog.

'Many chiefs are angered by her failure to help the Iceni. Our ties with them were strong, and she has severed them. She betrays our alliances in order to keep peace with Rome.'

Caradog frowned. 'Why do you tell me this now, tribesman?'

'So you know that you have friendship here,' he said. 'Cartimandua will not yield to you, but there are many of the Brigantes who will. There are chiefs in the north—my homeland—who are ready to strike against Rome.'

'Are you saying they will revolt?' I said.

'Not yet. But soon. When the moment is right.' He stared at Caradog. 'When the commander is right. Cartimandua stands on the back of the Roman army. But she is giddy with her own rise. There will be a moment of weakness. In the meantime, you must strengthen your ties among the Brigantes. I will tell you the chiefs and townships to which you must ride. I have sent messengers by the lesser routes to tell them you are coming. Be sure that you see them all. Lay your message lines. Open the pathways that they may supply weapons, and later, men.'

Caradog stared at Venutius for a few moments then drew him into a forceful embrace. Venutius returned it and I saw the spirit that must have once caught the great Cartimandua's eye. I had thought him castrated, but he was not.

'This is our land,' he said, standing back. 'We are with you, Caradog.'

The war king nodded. 'Who commands those who would rise?'

Venutius frowned. 'I do. By great stealth. I learned much in my time in the Empire's forces and I learn much in Cartimandua's bed.'

I could not help but ask, 'Do you know no love of your wife?'

'I have loved her. But I love Albion more.'

'Go to your men in the north,' said Caradog. 'Tell them to stand ready for my word.'

'I will,' said Venutius. 'Listen now as I tell you the names of the settlements you must pass.'

'You listen, Ailia,' said Caradog. 'You are better memory-trained than I.'

When I had heard him, Venutius kissed my hand and bade us farewell. 'Wait a few moments after I leave, that none may say they saw us speaking.'

'Brother,' called Caradog when Venutius had walked several paces. Venutius turned.

'May the Mothers be with you.'

Emotion flickered in his face. 'You will always find haven here.'

'Did I not tell you, War King?' I said, when Venutius had disappeared. 'The Mothers find a voice to assure you that your war is right and true.'

Caradog met my eye. 'Yet you have said it is not.'

Caradog showed little gladness of Venutius's pledge, but rather, with every turn of the woodland pathway, fell more deeply into a dark temper, until I feared that no chief would believe that so miserable a man could be Caradog, the famous war king who would deliver us our freedom. For the first time since leaving Llanmelin, I looked forward to returning him back to the woman who could weather him, for I began to grow weary of his moods.

In the late afternoon, we came to a trickling spring. Small stones ringed around it, forming a shrine to the Mothers. 'I need to fill my skin,' I said.

I dismounted and filled my pouch, then sat on a log by the stream to drink. Caradog sat beside me. His finely-muscled neck, bare of its torc, looked pale and soft emerging from his farmer's shirt. I fought an urge to press my mouth to its skin. 'What ails you?' I asked gently. 'We heard good news this day, and you have mourned it ever since.'

184

'Nothing ails me. I am well.'

My patience cracked. 'As Lleu is my witness, Caradog, I will not ride another pace with you unless you tell me what is wrong. Are you not pleased for Venutius's alliance?'

'Of course I am pleased,' he said. 'But it condemns us to yet more waiting, more secrecy. Forgive me if I had hoped to raise a more glorious war band.'

'Glory does not mean strength—'

'But men do!' he flared. 'For every follower I may have among the Brigantes, Cartimandua will have three. If she joined me, we would win this war. But I failed to convince her, and so did you.'

I swallowed the barb. 'Your sister observed her own wisdom as we must observe ours.'

'Yet ours sees me travelling by stealth, creeping under rocks like a spider.'

'By the Mothers, Caradog, what did you intend?'

'I have fought for five seasons in darkness. I intended to return with a war band strong enough to fight in the light.'

I looked out. Late sun turned the birch trunks bronze against the grey sky. 'Do you think you are stronger if you are better seen?'

'Yes, Ailia.' He looked at me. 'I tire of hiding.'

I thought of my promise to Cartimandua. 'And yet to be hidden is our greatest power. We are named for it...Night People, Secret People...We are the unseen. This is our strength.'

'It is *your* strength Kendra, the journeywoman's strength—'

'It is the strength of us all.' A certainty was unfurling within me. Something I had heard many times, but never fully possessed. 'You are a craftsman, Caradog, you know that your designs are full of riddles, their meaning for us alone. And Rhain does not commit his poems to Latin letters that any fool may know them, but protects them in land and memory. Something too easily seen has no power.'

'This is pretty, Ailia, but it has nothing to do with war—'

'Yes it does.' I was surprised at the sureness in my voice. 'You want to fight in the Roman way, Caradog, where your strength is on show. But the reason you have succeeded above all others is that you have fought in the way of the tribes. We are tricksters, conjurers, shifters of form. And so too must your war be a riddle to the Romans, a seduction, a trick.'

Caradog was silent.

My fingers had gone to the scars on my chest, tracing their familiar bulge through the fabric of my dress. 'The answer is not in greater numbers. The answer is in protecting what is hidden. Venutius has promised you men. But the bonds must be secret. If Scapula learns of the ties you made with the Brigantes, your power will be gone. What is unseen is always greater.'

Caradog gave a soft chuckle. 'You make even my weakness sound like a poem.'

His smile was heavy with regret. At last I realised this was no sour temper. This was the affliction that changed him as night changes day. How had I not seen it sooner? 'War King,' I ventured. 'Your illness returns—'

'I said I am well!' His mare startled at the force in his voice.

He drank from his water-pouch. Torment strained at his skin.

I was about to speak when he took a sharp breath and threw his bladder to the ground with a strength that split its seam. 'I do not wish you to see me in this way!'

'Then show me something else!' I cried, unnerved by his violence. 'Show me what wound lies within, that I might help you heal it!'

He stared at me.

A crow's call fell through the sky.

'If I speak, then no other can know what I say.'

'I see no other, do you?'

186

'Aedic was one of the fiercest chiefs Albion has ever known,' he said. 'And when she was made queen, Cartimandua was a mighty and loyal tribeswoman. If souls such as these are kneeling to Rome, then how can I hope to escape it? Am I so much stronger than these?'

'You are.' It was not comfort. It was the truth. 'You must fight this doubt.'

His eyes briefly closed then he looked to the ground. 'I cannot,' he said. 'I am unafraid of Rome's most brutal soldiers, yet I am powerless against this...despair.' He met my eye. 'Do the Mothers punish me with this suffering, Kendra? For this war? Am I so mistaken in it? Do they want Rome's great temples on this land, and I cannot see it?'

Never had he revealed to me such frailty. Only with his question laid bare between us, did I realise how truly I believed that he was Mother-chosen. He was flawed, turbulent, proud and rash. But all this converged to a greater purpose. Even his sorrow brought a necessary tenderness to what might otherwise be too hard.

I reached for the fist that was balled on his thigh and gently opened his fingers.

He grasped my hand with a swordsman's strength.

'Caradog, I can help you. I can give you the plants and treatments that will strengthen your spirit, but more than this, I can see this part of you and tell you it is well. You are imperfect. You are as stupid as you are brilliant and as ass-headed as you are noble. But you are not mistaken, and you are strong enough to win this war.'

Then Caradog, war king of Albion, wept in my arms.

✢

The hour was late. We needed to remount and continue riding if we wanted to beat the darkness.

I released Caradog and walked a short distance into the forest to piss. Just as I squatted behind a clump of bracken, I heard horses approaching. I peered through the tangle of bracken, then sank back down behind my cover, chest pounding, as my skirts soaked in my own water.

The riders were Roman auxilia.

Should I stay hidden? Caradog stood to greet them. He carried only a simple peasant's knife. I had a journey-sword, but it would reveal me if they discovered it. I could hide it beneath the bushes and approach without it, but then I would be unarmed, for my sling was useless in hand combat.

'State your business!' said one of the soldiers to Caradog in the language of the Empire.

Caradog spoke perfect Latin. Please Mothers, would he remember not to use it? No farmer would have ever known that droning tongue. 'I travel to the borderland,' he answered in our own language, impersonating a northern accent, stammering slightly as if he were only guessing at their question.

I exhaled silently in relief.

'For what purpose?' The second soldier knew our language. His accent was Gaulish, I guessed, and I hated him all the more that he wore his conqueror's clothes.

'I bring this horse and its saddle as a gift to my wife's family.'

'And where is your wife?' asked the soldier.

'She awaits at our farmhouse near Stenwic.'

I crouched, frozen. He did not wish me to appear.

'It is a fine horse,' said the first soldier, stepping his mount closer to my young grey mare. 'Far finer than a farmer's horse.'

'I would not gift a nag to my family.'

The soldier stared at him. 'What would you give the soldiers of Claudius?'

'Their dues,' said my husband.

Be careful, I begged, *do not provoke them.*

The soldier dismounted, followed by his companion.

Caradog straightened. He was a head taller than each of them, with the powerful shoulders of a swordsman. He had no limp, no blisters, no callouses from the plough. His back was not bent and his skin shone, well-fatted and rosy from the abundant meat of the nobleman's cauldron. He was no more a farmer than I was the Emperor's wife.

'Men have told us the dog, Caratacus, rides through these roads in disguise with his sorceress-bitch,' said the first soldier stepping closer.

My breath went still.

'Tell me, farmer, have you seen such figures in your travels southward?'

'I could not be sure,' he answered. 'Though surely the leader of the free tribes would not be so stupid as to ride through country under treaty to Claudius?'

Hush, Caradog, I willed him as I stared through the branches. *Do not stir agitation.*

'He is exactly so stupid,' said the soldier, 'He squanders half the fighting men of Albion in fruitless battle. Why would he not also risk squandering himself?'

'Well then how would I know him?' said Caradog, as if taking pleasure in the game. 'Is he handsome? Strong?'

'Ugly as a snake's arsehole,' said the soldier. 'But tall, even among his own kind.'

The soldier drew and raised his sword until its tip was parallel with Caradog's forehead.

Even from this distance I smelt the fight hunger that rose from Caradog's skin. 'Then it seems,' he said slowly, 'that with neither skill nor strategy, you have stumbled upon your prize.'

My heart stopped.

In an instant, both soldiers had raised swords and shields. 'Be still!' shouted one. 'You are captured, enemy.' He began to laugh. 'What favour it will buy us to bring Scapula your head!'

'He will want to meet me alive, surely?' said Caradog.

My chest hammered. He goaded them.

'Of course. You will whimper for your life before him, then he will take you to Claudius in chains and let him strangle you in the forum.'

With swords poised, they manoeuvred to surround him.

Still Caradog did not draw his knife. What was his intent? Surely his despair did not compel him to submit?

Both soldiers stood half-facing my direction. If I moved now, they would see me straight away.

'Come then,' said Caradog, stepping backwards and turning slightly. 'Claim your prize.'

I saw now his purpose. He was positioning them that I might rise unseen.

The soldiers edged towards him, turning their backs to me as they tracked Caradog's movement.

Caradog glanced fleetingly in my direction and I saw the almost imperceptible shift of his head that told me which one he wanted me to take.

I searched the ground near my feet, praying for a stone and finding none. But there was a small chunk of black ironwood that was heavy enough. Silently, I unhooked my sling, loading the missile and rising to stand in one deft motion. I began to swing.

Caradog met my eye and nodded.

'Mothers curse you!' My target turned at my scream. I released the stone, sending the first soldier to his knees as Caradog seized the second from behind, breaking both his arms and pressing his farmer's knife to his throat.

I ran forward. The soldier I had hit was pierced at his shoulder but not dangerously. 'Shall I kill him?'

'No,' said Caradog, releasing his soldier to the ground and starting to strip him. 'Let them know shame to have let the war king escape. Let them be forced to confess it.' He wanted to humiliate them, to humiliate Scapula.

We stripped them naked and tied them face-to-face on either side of a birch trunk, using rope from our packs. Caradog gagged them, then broke off two low-hanging branches of spiky spruce.

'What are you doing?' I hissed, keen to make our escape.

'Leaving my standard in the conquered land.'

The soldiers both moaned in pain as he stuffed one branch firmly into each of their arses.

'Enjoy claiming your prize from Scapula,' he told them as we mounted to ride. 'Please tell him that he can pursue me until his balls swing at his knees and I will never whimper before him. Tell him that as I have stated it.'

I smiled as we rode on. His melancholy had not dulled his tongue.

Scapula would now know that we had been in Tir Brigantes. It was dangerous to remain here, but Caradog was determined that we meet with all Venutius's sworn resistors, even if it meant a more winding route through enemy land.

Over several weeks of deep winter, we followed a pathway of chieftains and chieftainesses who opposed the alliance their queen had made with the Empire and were ready to act against her. They were furious that she had sent no fighters in support of the Iceni. 'Our ties to the Iceni are old and deep,' said many, 'yet she betrays them to please Rome.'

These were different leaders from those we had met on our approach to Stenwic. They did not fear Cartimandua. They had tolerated her flirtation with Claudius only for so long as their own independence

was retained. But now the brutal war on the Iceni—and the disarmaments that had triggered it—showed that the Romans could turn on
even a sworn ally at any moment. Cartimandua had lied, they said,
as we gathered in their halls. This was no friendship between equal
powers. This was theft of land. The coals of hatred were beginning to
glow.

'Be ready for my word,' said Caradog, grasping the wrists of every
one of them. 'I will be back within this fighting season and we will
claim the Brigantes back.'

Slowly, farm by farm, settlement by settlement, we built an iron
chain of agreement that ran the length of Tir Brigantes, reaching
from the border townships to Venutius's chamber and beyond. This
chain would be our message pathway, where news of our war would
be borne by riders, or, where the terrain was too slow, by billows of
smoke, or an echo of horn or voice across a valley.

By day at the council fires, Caradog was ablaze with battle-spirit,
but by night in the guests' huts he was often subdued, and I knew that
the darkness had not yet fully lifted, that he was still unresolved to the
shape of this war.

'When we return I will prepare you a tonic,' I said, as I climbed
into my bedskins after an evening when he had been especially quiet.

It was our final night in Brigantes territory. Tomorrow we
would pass back into Tir Deceangli and, soon after, into Tir Silures.
I looked forward to seeing Rhain and Manacca, and returning to
songcraft. But I would miss these nights when the war king was mine
alone.

'Sing to me,' he said as he stared up at the bay leaves hanging from
the beams. He had asked often for my songs as we had journeyed, and
I had willingly given them. Since we had left Stenwic he had begun
to seek my counsel, to trust my judgement, but never did he listen so
attentively as when I sang.

I sang a lament for a long-ago war, where two serpents, one white, one red, writhed in a battle for a magical mountain. The serpents were the kings who fought for the land, and the mountain was all of Albion.

'Your voice is why I fight,' Caradog said when I was silent.

Then call me to your bed, I thought, hating my need.

But he did not this night, as he had not any other.

We arrived at Llanmelin as the first lamb spilled from its mother's belly. Spring would soon return. The townspeople laid down their tools to line the road and cast grain over their high king and his sovereign queen as we rode in.

Euvrain greeted her husband when we had dismounted in Hefin's courtyard. I looked away as Caradog held her against his chest. His long embrace and murmured words must have left no doubt that he had kept his promise.

'You were missed,' whispered Rhain as he kissed my cheek.

'As were you.'

We walked towards the hall where Hefin and Prydd awaited.

'You are changed, Kendra,' Rhain said, turning to me.

'Exhaustion is all, I am sure.'

'Nay, nay,' he said, 'You are renewed.'

I shook my head and smiled at his words.

᛭

'Has the journey borne fruit?' said Prydd to me across the hall fire. 'Did your Kendra's allure persuade Cartimandua?'

'She would be no tribal queen if she were swayed by mere allure,' said Caradog.

Prydd frowned. 'So the Brigantes have not agreed to an alliance?'

'Oh, we have made firm our allies there,' said Caradog. 'But Cartimandua is not among them.'

'A divided tribe,' said Prydd, 'does not make a useful ally.'

'I will make use of them,' said Caradog.

'Still,' said Prydd turning to me, 'You must be disappointed that the marriage did not achieve its purpose.'

'Our land has a king,' said Rhain. 'Is that not the marriage's purpose?'

'Of course,' said Prydd.

'So how fares the mare of the Brigantes?' said Hefin, holding out his ale horn for the servant to refill. 'Is she as headstrong as I remember her?'

'More so.' Caradog smiled. He spoke of Cartimandua's refusal and the alliance that had been made with her husband.

'So we lie in her bed skins, but not with her!' said Hefin, delighted. His amusement only increased when Caradog told the story of our encounter with Scapula's soldiers.

'And what is your intention now?' said Prydd to Caradog, when the laughter had subsided.

'Now we make Scapula think that we are planning another attack in the south. We disrupt his supply lines and damage his forts so that he must send more men to rebuild them. Then, when he has drawn his strongest numbers to the south, I will move north to the Brigantes and claim it back.'

'Good,' said Hefin. 'The Silures are ready to fight.'

'As always,' said Caradog.

I stared at him. He had not shared this plan with me. 'What if Scapula moves in the north?'

'Why would he?' said Prydd. 'It is Caradog he seeks. He knows that Caradog is here.'

'But Scapula is a man of harsh retribution,' I persisted. 'We have seen from the disarmaments how swiftly he acts to douse even the possibility of dissent. The Deceangli are the only free tribe on the Brigantes' borders. If he learns that their chiefs have forsworn he will seek to subdue them, and quickly.'

Prydd's eyebrows rose. 'Did you learn augury during your three days in Môn, Kendra? Or was it two?'

The council laughed, but suddenly I was very certain. 'It is not augury. It is merely my sense of this man and this war. Scapula knows we have been in Tir Brigantes. It would be naive to think that he does not suspect we have made ties there. He will want to sever them by claiming the Deceangli. We should act before he does.'

'By sending men?' said Caradog.

'If not men, then metals. And grain so they might spend the spring preparing their defences, instead of their fields.'

Rhain nodded, as he stared at his hands folded in his lap.

'They will not move on the Deceangli.' Prydd's voice was shrill, his humour gone. 'It is remote, difficult terrain, and far from the man who Scapula claims to pursue. Forgive me, Kendra, but your youth betrays you.' He looked to Caradog. 'This is not worthy counsel.'

'Yet the idea is not unimaginable,' said Caradog. 'Scapula has shown himself to be vengeful.'

Prydd's jaw tightened. 'War King, I have served as your first advisor for several years before we were blessed with the arrival of this child of the Mothers.' He glanced at me. 'I am sure you will not forfeit my counsel now. After all,' he paused, 'I cannot continue to represent your campaign to Môn for funding if they do not trust that you follow my guidance.'

I nearly gasped. Surely Caradog would not tolerate such brazen purchase of influence. Cartimandua was right. The journeyman's title was no promise of honour.

Caradog stared at Prydd. 'Then what is your guidance?'

'To send supplies north, with no possible reason for it, will be costly. Môn's grain stores and metal stores are deep but not endless. I have negotiated over many months to direct them here, where they are needed. We must act prudently and where we are certain we will have most effect.'

'A war-cry to raise the blood,' said Hefin gloomily.

Caradog looked at me, at Prydd, and then to the fire. When he looked up, his face betrayed the black sorrow I knew had not left him. 'I know not whose counsel is truest, and it matters not. I will be in Tir Brigantes by the summer. Scapula will not act before then.'

'You showed boldness in the council,' said Rhain as we walked to the cook hut for bread. 'You showed authority.'

'Caradog did not hear it.'

'But I did.'

I looked at him. There was a riddle in his voice. 'Do you say what I hope you say?'

'Certainly, perhaps.'

'Yes, Rhain!' At last he deemed me ready to forge.

He smiled. 'We shall go tomorrow.'

'Can we go today?'

'Are you not tired from travel?'

'I want to begin.'

'Very well. Gather your pouch and staff and meet me at the northern gate.'

We walked the Castroggi to the base of the mountain, where Rhain turned away from the river path we had trodden so often, into thicker woodlands of oak and ash. I knew this route into the bowels of the forest and I knew the destination to which it led.

'Why here?' I asked when we reached the grove.

'Because here you must be strong.'

Even in winter bareness, the grove seemed close, the air unsettled by growth and rot. The bloodied altar seemed alive in this grotto, a beating heart in the forest's breast.

Rhain entered and crouched at the altar. 'Come,' he called.

I took a few steps forward. No birds perched on the branches of this nemeton. No creatures scurried from my step. I felt naked, wary within the ring of oaks. But why should I? It was only the Mothers who prickled my skin.

Rhain finished murmuring a low chant, then called me to his side. His absence of laughter was not helping me to find my ease. I sat beside him on a log and made my own hushed tribute to the bones and dried clots that adorned the altar.

'Are you ready?' he said when my chant had ended.

'Yes.' I had waited four moons for this. Why did I feel so unsure?

'Then summon a battle.'

'Which...battle?' I frowned.

'Your choice. A fearsome battle. One where the Silures knew a mighty victory. '

'The battle of Caerau?' I ventured.

'Good, good, yes,' he said. 'Now recite it to me.'

I turned to the altar, pulled out one of the strings of stones from my pouch, and ran my fingertips over the first smooth bead.

Here is the declamation of a brilliant poem
of immeasurable inspiration,
concerning a brave and authoritative chief,
from the stock of—

It was only the fourth line and I had faltered.

'Again,' said Rhain, without emotion.

I started from the beginning, but the grove had unnerved me. I stumbled again.

'No,' said Rhain. 'You are not with the song. You are elsewhere. Be only with the poem.'

I tried again. The stillness—not even a leaf swayed on this windless eve—the gloom, even Rhain, all seemed to be judging me. I could not speak two lines without an error.

'To which path have you bound this song?' asked Rhain.

'To the river path, as it flattens near the first field.'

'Then take yourself there, Kendra. Pass each rock and bend in your mind to see the places that conjure the memory...'

I closed my eyes and spoke again. But try as I might, I could not summon the poem. My voice grew fainter with each attempt, my mind clouded with my failing.

Rhain stood and picked up the staff he had laid before the altar. 'It is not possible,' he said. 'We cannot heat metal that is unstable...'

'Let me try another...The Song of Wind?'

'Another song will not disguise that you have failed to remember this one. It is my error. I was too hasty. You are not yet ready after all.' He smiled at last.

'Rhain—' I could not bear that I had disappointed him. 'I am sorry.'

'Tell me this, Kendra,' he said, sitting back beside me. 'Do you still wish to become a Songwoman?'

'Above all else!' I startled at my own words. I had not realised, until I said them, that they were true.

'For what purpose?' said Rhain.

'Because...' I hesitated, staring at an oak root that had snaked around the base of the altar-stone. He had asked me this question once before. My answer had hinged on my Kendra's title. But now it meant even more than that. 'Because I...wish to be heard,' I stammered.

As soon as I had uttered it I heard the weakness in it.

Rhain shook his head. 'I do not train you in service of pride, Kendra. We have been five summers at war. The tribes are weary. They need someone to tell them what will come to be.'

I frowned. 'But who can tell them that? No one knows how the war will end.'

'We tell them.' He stared at me. Never had the bones of his face, his brown eyes, seemed so beautiful.

'How?' I whispered.

The very forest seemed to pause for his answer.

'By remembering. Whatever story we remember will determine what endures. This is your purpose. There is no other.'

The boughs stirred as the trees exhaled.

His claim was strong but I knew it was true. I had seen it in his song for Caradog. I had felt it in the scars that marked my chest. 'I understand you, Songman.'

'And yet the smallest drop of my judgement robs you of your memory. How can you give Albion a future, if you cannot be trusted to remember its past?'

I looked to the ground, wincing at his brutality.

'This morning you spoke of the future to the council. I saw your authority. Now it is gone.'

Still I stared at the leaves that covered the grove floor. 'Perhaps I am not strong enough.'

'Self-doubt is a vanity, Kendra, as is pride. Both will erode your authority. Think less of how you are seen and more of what you see.'

I could not speak. Yes, I had been drawn to his craft because of the power I hoped it would give me. There *was* pride in me. And doubt. Each birthed the other.

I looked at my hands, strong-knuckled, pale from the winter, grasping the knotted cord that held my songs.

Rhain was right that I saw myself too readily through the eyes of others, imagining their judgement before I had fully shaped my own. But whose was the approving gaze I sought? Whose was the judgement I held in such deference? It was not only Prydd's. It was not only Caradog's. It was not even Rhain's, although it aligned with all of these men and others.

I lifted my face and looked at my teacher. I saw at last what he must have always seen. The judgement was of my own conjuring. A weapon drawn against myself. Suddenly I saw the impairment it inflicted. As if I cast out an eye to gaze back upon myself, unaware that it left me half blind. Finally I glimpsed the authority of which he spoke.

'Do you understand?' pressed Rhain.

'Yes,' I whispered.

We sat for a moment, unspeaking.

'Rhain,' I said. 'May I try once more?'

'Not yet,' he said. 'Learn your songs. Speak them with authority. Then you will forge a future.'

I returned to my hut by nightfall. Euvrain was waiting at my fire. Her pale eyes lifted to mine. The skin beneath them was shadowed.

'What is wrong?' I asked.

'My husband...'

'Is he taken with illness?'

'Of a kind.' Her forehead was scored with a frown. 'I cannot soothe him...'

I slipped onto the bench beside her. 'You are his greatest comfort, Euvrain. Surely he—'

'He will not speak to me this night.' She stared into the flames. 'He asks for you.'

For a moment I did not speak. 'I am sorry,' I said. 'There was nothing between us, sister...Beyond the ritual, we did not—'

'I know,' she said. 'He kept his promise to me, as I knew he would.' Her fingers tightened around the knot of her shawl. 'But did you, Ailia? Or do you begin to love him?'

Truth would serve no purpose now. Caradog had made his choice and Euvrain deserved no torment. 'I love him as my king. Nothing more. He asks for my herbs, perhaps—'

'Then go to him,' she said, her shoulders softened. 'Heal him if you can. For all our sakes.'

The children had been banished and the room was dim and quiet. Caradog lay alone in his bedskins.

I walked to the edge of his pallet. His shirt was soiled and his eyes were closed. The air around him was thick with his sorrow. What could I offer him? My heart had been all but emptied in the grove and I felt weary of all thought.

I wished I could lay down beside him, but it was only my healing he sought. Not my heart. I sat on the bottom of his bed.

His eyes opened. 'Ailia.'

'What disturbs you, War King?'

I waited for him to answer. His ailment took none of the lustre from his skin nor strength from his shoulders, but it stole his voice. The deep-bellied tone that could win any favour was flattened like a harp stuffed with wool. 'I can do this no longer.'

'Do what?'

Again he lay unspeaking for some time. 'Force this reckless war—'

'It is not reckless.'

'Many call it so.' He paused. 'My father calls it so. He condemns me from the grave. I feel it.'

'He did not face forty thousand men claiming sovereignty of his tribelands. Only you have done this.'

'He would have called me foolish for it. It is the lack of his blessing that weakens me. This is why we cannot gain a foothold in this war. For my every step is in betrayal of my family.'

I had never seen his struggle grip him so tightly. Yet how could I console him? I had known neither father nor mother. I knew nothing of their pull. 'Family is much, but not all. You have not betrayed Albion.'

'Perhaps I have.'

'No,' I said, shaking my head. 'You have kept us free.' I regretted that I had gone with Rhain this day, and not gathered the herbs for the medicine that would bring him relief. 'Tomorrow at dawn I will harvest, and you will have your tincture. It will restore you, I am sure of it.'

He nodded blankly, without faith.

I needed to leave. It was a suffering of my own to be so close to him and yet unable to hold him against my chest.

As I moved to rise, he took hold of my wrist.

'What is it, Caradog?' I asked. 'I do not know how else I can help you.'

'Sing,' he whispered. 'Sing as you sang as we rode from Tir Brigantes.'

Tears threatened to come in place of my words. 'I am not in good voice...'

'Sing that I may know why I must fight.'

I sat back down, drew breath, and began the first line of the battle of Caerau, which I had attempted in the grove. I drew my thoughts away from the quiver of my breath and the question of whether he still esteemed my voice. I gave my thoughts only to the song and what it told of our courage, and the deep roots that held us in this earth.

Every word was perfect.

✣

202

'These leaves are better, Manacca. See how they are newly-opened, and deeper in colour?'

We were harvesting at the shores of the Castroggi, near the lakes, where cattle and washing had not worn the banks. Only the fewest nettles had begun to shoot spring leaves from their wintry stalks, but these frosted buds would be all the more potent for their newness. Mixed with setwall and dried wort, they would make Caradog a powerful tincture.

'Careful!' I told her as she reached her small hand straight for the leaf. 'Use the blade or the plant will sting you.'

'Who is the medicine for?' she asked.

'The war king,' I told her. 'To make him strong.'

'Can I give some to papa?' she asked.

I thought of the man I had glimpsed lying on the floor of their hut as I collected her this morning. His twisted back spoke of a bone ailment that no plant could heal. By the smell from the hut, his skin had become infected from being trapped in his bedskins. The nettle would at least dispel his fear as he passed to Annwyn. 'Of course,' I assured her. 'We'll take him some when it is made.'

Manacca looked up at me, her cheeks red with cold. I was in breach to have brought her here. I had sung to her and told her simple truths. But to teach her the skills to draw medicine from plants was a power to which she held no claim. Yet had I not been given such a chance? And had she not run so joyously into my embrace when I had come to her doorway at this day's first light? The only harm would be in Prydd's discovery.

Dawn mist coiled off the water. I felt unexpectedly peaceful. I thought of the man for whom my basket was filling with stems and leaves. My love for Taliesin had almost drowned me. My love for Caradog was a small, persistent pool of longing that lapped at my edges. But it would not drown me. I could withstand it.

Manacca hummed tunelessly beside me as she picked.

'Shall we try another bush?' I asked, wishing to leave this one a little of its growth. The banks were abundant with nettle and we soon clutched baskets that could hold nothing more.

We took the southern road back to Llanmelin, towards the main entrance. Walking down a hedged lane with a child's hand in my own, it was easy to forget that an enemy watched like an eagle barely three days ride from where we stood.

Manacca stared up toward the walled township as we drew closer. 'You can hardly see Llanmelin from this side,' she said, squinting into the morning sun.

I smiled. She was right. Though it was one of the largest tribal centres of western Albion, it appeared barely more than a hill on the horizon. Its walls were of earth and chalk: a summoning of the land, not a conquering.

'Perhaps Rome will not see it, either,' she said.

'Perhaps not.' I squeezed her fingers. 'They are not good at seeing what is hidden.'

'Then why are you scared of them, Aya?'

I stopped and crouched before her. Her question was honest and she deserved an honest answer. 'Because when they take our towns and forests, they do not know that they also take our song places.'

Her brown eyes suddenly brightened. 'But they cannot take our songs!'

I opened my mouth to correct her, then shut it again and stared at her.

Within her calf-soft gaze was a simple truth I had never seen. *They could not take our songs.*

In those few words, this untaught child showed me, for the first time, what had drawn me to learn Rhain's craft. Not because of its allure, nor for my own standing, but because it held a hope for Albion that neither the warriors, nor even the Kendra, could ensure.

Rhain had said the song's purpose was to shape the future. What if the future to be shaped was far more than a battle outcome, the success of a chieftain or the fate of a township? What if it was the future of Albion itself?

I drew Manacca to my chest and kissed her cold cheek. 'Thank you, pup.'

She giggled and bounced on her bare feet as I let her go.

We walked on. I would push Rhain no further to hasten my training. I would not ask to forge song until he deemed me ready. I would learn with as much diligence as I could summon. For when I was ready, I needed to create a song powerful enough to hold all our land's knowledge, even if the rivers were guarded by Roman gods and the groves were burned to ash.

Was I strong enough to create such a song? I possessed the Kendra's knowledge, the bone-deep memory of our land's forming. If I were not strong enough, no one was.

We brewed plants in my hut, where Manacca might easily scurry behind the blanket box if Prydd called at the door. Once I had returned her to her home, I took the fresh tea to Caradog's house.

'Tidings, Ailia.' Euvrain kissed me at the door. 'I won't ask you inside.' She leaned closer. 'He sleeps...he has barely roused all this day.'

She frowned as I explained what I had made and pressed the clay jar into her hands.

'Has he agreed to take it?' she asked.

'Yes.'

Euvrain looked surprised. 'You have altered him, sister. He has never taken medicine by my counsel.'

'Have him drink half now and half upon waking,' I told her. 'I will bring more when it is made.'

The sense of someone present roused me from sleep the next morning. I opened my eyes to a smirking face not one arm's length from my own.

'Caradog!' I sat up with a jolt. 'What are you doing?'

'I came to thank you,' he said. 'But you were so restful, I did not want to stir you.'

'How long have you been sitting here?'

'Not long. I was watching you in sleep. You are comic. And talkative. I heard several names—' he paused, 'even my own.'

I wriggled to pull my blanket over my under-robe, panicking at what I might have said. 'Why do you thank me?'

'For the river plants. You have worked a magic. There is improvement. '

'There could not be,' I said. 'It takes weeks. It is too soon.'

'And yet,' he said, eyes shining. 'I am released.'

I stared at him in disbelief. His whole being was transformed: brighter, taller, bristling with humour. 'I have never known such a rapid effect.'

'Nor have I.' He laughed, though his eyes were grateful.

I leaned back onto the wall. It was good to have him back.

'You will be my only physician, Kendra. Your arts are Mother-blessed.'

Just as I opened my mouth to protest, he leaned forward, took my face in his hands, and kissed me firmly on both cheeks. Then he jumped to his feet and began pacing a circle around the fire. 'I will call council again today,' he said, 'We need to send scouts to Tir Dobunni immediately...'

He crouched down to my wood basket to take a log for the fire. His unfastened shirt hung loosely from his shoulders.

I felt yesterday's fortitude ebbing away. Somehow it was easier when he was unwell. His struggle had become an intimacy for us. Now, like this, as warm and alive as a roaring fire, he belonged to everyone and no one. 'Caradog, I...'

He looked up.

But my next words, whatever they might have been, were silenced by the clatter of my door bell and Euvrain's face through the doorskins. 'Ailia, I have come to tell you—Oh! Husband, I had not expected to find you here so early...' Her eyes were confused through her smile.

'Come in, sister,' I said as I jumped from my bedskins and pulled on my cloak. 'Join me for some elder tea—your husband is restored...'

The Romans were rebuilding their camps beyond the Habren.

With the first snowmelt of spring, Caradog started initiating skirmishes in Roman territory. The fight bands he sent were small— four or five men who could slip through the forest, hiding in trees then ambushing Scapula's soldiers as they rode between camps. They guarded the banks of the Habren, spearing any soldiers who dared to cross our most sacred boundary.

Soon there were many fresh heads at our gates.

Scapula drew more of his legions to strengthen these camps. His curly-nosed ships glided slowly up and down the channel, keeping close watch on our southern shore. Caradog's plan was working. Scapula was wary of an attack in the south. This was where he was turning his gaze.

While we waited for Caradog's instruction to move to Tir Brigantes, we tended the birthing ewes, sowed the spring crops, and held tight to the observances that bound the Mothers close.

I did not lessen my training in song, yet nor did I attempt to hasten it. If Rhain had noticed a deeper clarity of purpose in my learning, he did not remark on it. I held to my vow to push him no further to teach me to forge, to wait until my readiness was in no doubt.

In turn, I took Manacca out most days to the banks to learn plant-craft. With leather mittens on her determined hands, she dug through still-frozen earth to harvest burdock, setwall and mallow roots, then we spent many hours drying, powdering and preserving the medicine in my hut. I was transgressing Prydd's command, but I hid our movements and carried on. Our knowledge faced a far greater threat than an unskinned child.

When day and night were of equal length, Caradog sent word to Venutius that he would ride north in one month, and the chiefs must prepare themselves to rise. The return message was favourable. It seemed that Caradog's strategy would succeed.

One week later, the Ninth Legion attacked the Deceangli.

8

Duty

The Mothers will perish if we do not sing, over and over,
the stories that attest them.

THE COUNCIL gathered in Hefin's hall, bleary in the early morning.

'Did the chiefs meet them in open battle?' Caradog's face was ashen. 'By Lleu's light, I pray they would not be so stupid.'

'No,' said the rider who had travelled through the night. 'Some have submitted, others have fought by ambush on the paths, but—' he paused, '—it has made no difference to Scapula's strategy.'

'What has been done?' said Caradog slowly.

The rider stared at him. 'The destruction is total. Settlements and grain fields burned, metals taken and cattle slaughtered. Elders are slain and women raped before death. Even babes are not spared...'

Euvrain's moan was stricken.

Caradog met my eye, his face as stone.

I thought of the chiefs whose fires we had shared, who had laid their swords at Caradog's feet.

The rider recounted the names of townships that had been destroyed, their people tortured.

I closed my eyes. The violence he described was known to me. I had seen my own townskin slaughtered in this way. With the rider's every word the memory grew stronger, until I could taste the smoke, hear the hiss of burning hair, and smell the tang of opened flesh.

I leant forward with a wave of dizziness, gripping the bench to keep from falling. I had to leave before I vomited. 'Forgive me...' I gasped, stumbling as I attempted to rise.

Quickly Euvrain was beside me, bidding me sit and giving me sips of her ale. But it was Caradog who crouched before me, forced my eye, and told me, 'Ailia. You are safe.'

I nodded. His voice, its certainty, was a branch I could hold to. My vision cleared, but my heartbeat would not steady.

'What is wrong, Kendra?' said Prydd, watching me. 'So sensitive a soul feels the wounds of war keenly. Do you need rest or can you hold firm through the discussion?'

'I am well,' I said, my breath shaking. I could not allow Prydd to see this weakness, this shame.

The council returned to their places, but Caradog remained at my side.

'Where are they now?' I asked the rider. 'By the settlements you have described, they are heading west...'

'Ay,' he said. 'They are halfway to the ocean of Erin.'

'So far?' I gasped. They had moved like water.

'What does Scapula mean by this?' asked Prydd.

'He seeks to cut off my pathway to the Brigantes,' said Caradog.

The rider nodded. 'He states it is retribution for the chiefs who have sworn allegiance to you. He promises the same for any other tribes who might follow.'

Caradog stared at the fire. 'There is one light within this darkness.' He turned to the rider. 'Return to Venutius. Tell him to command the chiefs to rise now. Quickly. While Scapula is far from Tir Brigantes. Tell him I will come with men to make firm the uprising. This is our chance.'

Prydd frowned. 'What of the Deceangli?'

'When I command the Brigantes, we will claim back the Deceangli.' He looked at me. 'Do you agree, Kendra?'

My heart still pounded with the shock of the attack. But Caradog was right. There was no other way. 'Yes,' I said. 'The Brigantes are our only hope.'

'War King,' said Prydd, 'The girl does not—'

'Silence, journeyman,' said Caradog.

I looked up in surprise.

Caradog had closed his eyes. Only when they opened did I see how angry he was. He turned to Prydd, barely holding his temper firm. 'Ailia predicted this attack, while you called her unworthy. Now her counsel has borne true, and yours false.'

Prydd's face was expressionless. 'My counsel accorded with the wishes of Môn—'

'I do not care!' The room jumped at the roar of the war king's voice. Such anger I had never seen in him. He set his cup on the bench beside him, his hand trembling. I saw how deeply he felt the wounds against his people, how determined he was to gain back the reins of this war. He rose to his feet. 'Prepare the men, Hefin,' he said. 'We leave for Tir Brigantes tomorrow at dawn.'

'What of Llanmelin?' said Hefin. 'We are watched across the Habren as you well know.'

Caradog snorted. 'Do you forget they are Romans?' he said. 'They will not move without their commander. While Scapula is in the north, the Silures are safe.' He strode from the hall and the council followed.

Only Rhain and I remained in the hall.

'It seems the war king begins to warm his hands at the flame of your authority.'

I gave a weak smile. He was right. By the horror of this attack, I had been granted as clear a recognition of my Kendra's knowledge as Caradog had yet given. But now it had come, I could not accept it. Though my heart-pound had calmed, images of my township's attack stained my every thought. It was beyond my endurance that any should suffer as they had suffered. As I had caused them to suffer.

I stood up. Despite my love of him, I could not sit with this man who esteemed me so undeservedly. I had not realised how deep this wound still was. It was not the fire of authority that burned in my chest, it was the hot embers of guilt.

✠

It was a lean war band who rode at dawn the next morning. The strongest fighters, the swiftest horses. No carts, stock, or grain. When we joined the Brigantes chiefs, there would be supplies enough. Rhain came with us for he knew the way-songs. Prydd and Euvrain remained.

We made swift pace through the first hills of Tir Ordovices, gathering warriors as we travelled. On the fifth day a rider bore news that Caradog's instruction had been heeded and the Brigantes chiefs had taken up arms against their queen.

There was a mighty cheer through the war band and no protest when Caradog commanded that we ride longer this day to reach them sooner. Though it had cost the blood of the Deceangli, this was our chance to harness the alliance of one of Albion's strongest tribes. We could not let it pass.'

I rode quietly, battling a fear that had been awoken by the attacks. A fear of what I had done. Of what I may yet do.

After we had set camp that evening, I left the fires while there was still some light, and followed a brook upstream for a few moments' solitude. I came to a pool, part-hidden by ferns. It was black and deep, between shoulders of mossed stone. A stout brown dipper bobbed at its shallows.

Although the air was cold, I hungered to bathe. I shed my cloak, dress and under-robe, and draped them over a low bough. A fistful of leaf-litter would scrub the saddle-dirt from my calves.

Naked, I stood at the water's edge, uncovered to the forest's tingling beauty. I entered the pool, gasping with pleasure as the icy water closed around me. No matter how deeply I plunged, I would never be washed of my actions. Still I drank and ducked until the chill made my temples ache.

'Kendra!' Caradog stood watching from the bank.

'What are you doing?' I called. 'Am I needed at camp?'

'Hefin told me I stink,' he said, pulling off his trousers and shirt. There was little modesty between us. I had seen his nakedness many times as he had dressed in our guest huts.

'Did you follow me here?' I asked, gliding backwards as he entered the water.

He plunged beneath the surface before emerging before me, water streaming from his face. 'Yes.'

'Why?'

'You have barely spoken since we left Llanmelin. I wanted to be sure you were well.'

'Thank you, I am.'

'I saw your distress at the attacks on the Deceangli...'

'Surely any tribesperson would be so distressed.'

'It was more than that.'

'It reminded me of what had happened to my township.'

He slid through the pool and settled against a limestone boulder. 'You have never told me what happened.'

I shivered in the chill water. 'You know they were slain...do not make me describe it.'

He frowned. 'And how were you spared?'

He had asked it. That which I could not answer. My purpose had been pure enough, but poorly, poorly judged. Was that not an equal failing? 'By the Mothers' blessing alone,' I said, staring at my white hands, distorted by the water.

He sought my gaze. 'Then what disturbs you?'

'I wish not...to speak of it.'

'Yet you have forced *me* to speak...and you have helped me,' he said. 'I would help you also.' He stood chest deep in the river, his hair clinging lankly to his neck, his skin pale against the dark water.

My heart lurched with regret and longing. The past felt too heavy to bear. I slipped beneath the surface. When I emerged again, he was beside me.

'Are you going to stay in here all night, little fish?' he murmured.

Water beaded on his chest and shoulders. His body was smooth and solid, as if he were made of pieces of stone that shifted and gleamed with the slightest movement. But he was not stone. A soft heat rose off his skin.

'Husband—?' I had not used the term for so long.

He met my gaze. It should have been torture to stand before him, cold and naked, unspeaking of the love that pressed at my chest. Yet it was not. 'I will tell you my story, when we are free of this war.' I could not tell him now. Failing or none, I still had to stand with the tribes as their Kendra.

'Whatever burdens you, know that I esteem you, Ailia.'

You would not if you knew what I had done, I thought.

He did not look away. In the day's last light, his eyes were many shades of green and grey. For a moment, the war did not exist.

Then he heaved himself from the pool and shook the water from his hair.

The paths grew steep and our horses slowed. For four days we heard no news of the tribelands for which we rode. Then, when we were only days from the border of Tir Brigantes, a rider galloped into our camp, as we were building the evening fires.

'Praise the Mothers I have found you,' she gasped, as she swung from her horse. 'There is trouble in the north. Scapula has learned of the uprising and turned the legion. They march for Tir Brigantes.'

Caradog stood unmoving. 'Do you tell me that the governor has turned five thousand men on their heel and sends them back from where they have come?'

'Yes,' she said. 'This is what he has done.'

'Where are they at this moment?'

'The message is two days old. They will be in Tir Brigantes now.'

Caradog lowered himself to a crouch, then, to my horror, began to laugh. 'By Lleu,' he said, chuckling. 'How this man will dance!'

'War King,' I said, steadying his shoulder.

'Do we ride on?' said Hefin, for once unamused.

'Let me think,' said Caradog, his jaw rigid. He rose slowly. 'What is your council, Kendra? Should we continue?'

I saw in his face that it was no test, no curiosity. He would do as I advised. 'No,' I said quietly. 'We cannot yet meet the legion head to head. We must retreat. And find another way.' I exhaled. It felt much safer withholding the command to war than giving it.

'Tell Venutius that we return to Llanmelin,' said Caradog. 'But

I have not forgotten my pledge. Tell him to keep strong his bonds to Cartimandua so that she does not doubt him. Tell him we *will* fight together—when it is certain to succeed.'

Just like Rome's Ninth Legion, we turned on our heel and rode back from where we had come.

The banks of hawthorn surrounding Llanmelin were heavy with bud. As we approached the gate, children screeched and ran alongside us, newly freed of their winter cloaks. Rome could not halt the seasons.

A rider awaited us at the Great Hall's fire.

Prydd and Euvrain were seated beside him. The news he delivered was worse than we feared. Scapula had borne his legion with an unworldly haste to the Brigantes, where he had swiftly disarmed the rebel bands. Using the Roman tortures that Scapula provided, it had not taken Cartimandua long to identify the chiefs who had incited the rebellion. She had them slaughtered in the town centre of Stenwic, witnessed by their followers, the township, and Scapula himself.

'Did Scapula demand this of her?' Caradog asked the rider. 'Did he order the killings?'

'No. It was by her order. She chose the punishment.'

'Was it a tribesman's death?' said Prydd.

'No,' said the rider. 'It was a Roman death. Forty chiefs were named. They were each scourged to near death, then lashed to a cross of wood and stood upright to bleed out.'

The hall was silent. Only the fire spoke its quiet, crackling comment.

I looked around the faces of Llanmelin's council. Each one appeared lost, struggling, as I was, to understand the shape of these events. 'Were they sung to Annwyn?' I asked, remembering too clearly the anguish that lingers when there is death without rites.

'No, Kendra,' said the rider, with a tone of surprise that I would

216

ask it. 'The journeypeople cannot stand freely before the Romans. It is forbidden for them to ritual with song in any territory allied to Claudius.'

Intuitively, I fingered the stones and feathers of my belt. This was becoming a desperate, unholy battle, its fighters like dogs that no longer knew why they fought, but were driven only to leave each other's necks torn. I had to ensure that the Mothers remained in this war.

Caradog rose and paced the circle around us. 'I knew she held an alliance to Rome. I did not think she would defend it with the blood of her own people.'

'Perhaps she is trapped,' said Euvrain softly. 'You have said many times how valuable the Brigantes are to Rome. It seems that Scapula will go to any lengths to keep it. Maybe she has no choice.'

Caradog shook his head. 'There is always a choice.'

'One thing is certain,' said Hefin. 'Whatever compels her, she stands with the full force of Rome at her flank. We cannot hope for support from Brigantes chiefs any longer.'

Caradog came to a stop. 'And what of Venutius?' he said to the rider. 'Did any of the chiefs betray him to Cartimandua?'

'No,' said the rider. 'He is not suspected. He accepts the affirmation of your bond and returns it. He too awaits the moment when you both will join in arms against Scapula.'

Caradog nodded, but all who were present knew that the chance for this moment had been all but destroyed.

'Has Scapula left the Deceangli guarded?' I asked.

'Heavily,' said the rider. 'It is dangerous to carry messages. There will be few willing to ride those routes now.'

'Yet good reward for those who do.' Caradog smiled, but something had changed in him. He sat back down. The possibility of harnessing the Brigantes to this war had sustained his hope for many moon turns. Now his strongest supporters there were slain, and all others would be weakened by fear. 'The Brigantes are lost to us,' he said.

'The Deceangli also,' said Hefin.

He was right. If Scapula had maimed those settlements as my own township had been maimed, then their tribespeople—what remained of them—would have no more spirit to fight than a speared fawn.

'Perhaps you can explain the Mothers' intention to me, Kendra,' said Caradog. 'For I am unable to see it.'

'As you yourself have said,' I answered, 'they test the strongest of souls.'

There was both stone and liquid in his gaze.

'There is some good news,' said Prydd. 'I have received word from Môn this morning, in response to my request.'

I looked at him in surprise. He had not spoken of any request.

'Speak, journeyman.' Caradog was frowning, clearly also unaware.

Prydd raised his chin. I saw how greatly he savoured the posses-sion of knowledge that others desired. 'I asked my journeybrother Sulien whether I might convene the summer Arbitration here in Llanmelin...'

I straightened my shoulders. It was not well that Prydd had steered such communications with Môn outside the knowledge of both Caradog and myself.

'And what did he say?' said Caradog.

'He honours me with agreement.'

'That means grain!' said Hefin.

'Much grain. Some gold. And weapons. Those who host the Arbitration are given rich reimbursement.' Prydd knew the impor-tance of this yearly gathering of the tribes, where disputes were heard and judgements given.

Caradog laughed, shaking his head in admiration. 'This is welcome news after a long winter.'

'If you fail in this war, Caradog,' said Prydd. 'It will not be because I have not secured you the funds to win it.'

No one spoke further but Prydd's meaning hung clear. Môn was the mother that fed this war, Caradog was her favoured child, and Prydd the bridge between them.

I may have been Kendra, but I had earned my title alone. I had not trained at Môn. I could not influence its journeymen with long-woven ropes of friendship. No matter how greatly Caradog had come to esteem me, he could not afford to put Prydd at a distance.

'So what now, Horse-end?' said Hefin.

Caradog inhaled. 'Now we make them wish they had never started this war.'

After council I walked with Caradog and his wife back to their house.

Euvrain turned to me at the doorway. 'We shall see you on the morrow, Kendra.'

I stopped, shocked at the sudden banishment. I had hoped to take bread and broth at their fire, as I often did after council.

Caradog had gone inside. Euvrain smiled at me with light blue eyes as cold as frost. How foolish I had been to think she did not see me.

⊹

Manacca was poking a dead sparrow around in the embers of a street fire outside her hut. She was still too thin, but I had brought enough bread and soft cheese to feed a farmer. She would eat it. And her hunger would not end with food. She had shown herself to have as great an appetite to learn as I had plantcraft to fill it.

She did not leap up today or call my name. Instead her mother came out of the hut. 'Be gone,' she said, her toothless face full of fear. 'You cannot take the child.'

'Why not?' I asked, pulling bread from my basket to sweeten her temper.

'The journeyman was here this morn. He has forbade it.'

My hands stilled. 'Which journeyman?'

'The hairless one.'

'Do you think you are so different from this child?' I asked Prydd as he questioned me in the Great Hall. I had returned to my hut to find a servant waiting to bear me to my hearing. Now I sat alone on a bench, with Prydd and Caradog opposite me. Rhain sat between us at the north.

I had dreaded this moment, but it was freeing to at last speak my heart. 'We should learn from her,' I said. 'She is one who already lives the anguish that we ourselves face if Rome is successful in cutting us from this land. You know how fiercely Rome forbids the journey-people to ritual in the unfree tribes. If there were to come a time that we cannot honour the skin laws, then we will all need to be as wily as I am with Manacca.'

Caradog scrutinised me as I spoke. 'Perhaps you are right,' he said.

I exhaled with relief.

'She is not,' said Prydd. 'The very opposite is true. It is precisely when we are threatened that we must adhere to our laws. To transgress them will anger the Mothers and weaken our war.' He wore a full wolf-skin cloak and a neckpiece of bone. It was difficult to imagine that he did not speak for our land's spirits.

'Yet Ailia has brought only strength to the war,' said Caradog.

'Certainly,' said Prydd. 'But there have been some disappointments since her arrival. Cartimandua failed to hear us, and now the

Brigantes are lost. Could it be that the Mothers are displeased?' He paused, then looked at me with an expression of concern. 'I seek only the best for the war. I wonder whether your teaching of this skinless child has angered them, and this is their punishment.'

Now my heart took up a harder beat. Prydd's words were not true. Yet doubt had begun to spread across Caradog's face. He sighed. 'Perhaps it would be simplest for us all if you stopped teaching the child, Ailia.'

I shook my head. 'I cannot.' I would not forsake her. But more than this, her brown eyes saw beneath the surface of whatever I showed her. Only such a gaze could see the Mothers. We needed that vision now.

Prydd drew breath. 'I approved Rhain to teach you song because you promised it would improve your judgement. It has done the reverse. Cease teaching this wretch, or your learning with Rhain is forbidden.'

Caradog flinched. 'Are such harsh penalties needed, journeyman?'

'Without doubt,' said Prydd. 'How can I invite Sulien here, where there is such disrespect shown to the laws he honours?'

He positioned us all like the figures of a war game. It drained us for the true fight. He did not love Albion, he loved his own power.

'Did you know of this, Songman?' asked Caradog. He seemed suddenly weary and I hated Prydd more for loading his burden so needlessly.

'No.' Rhain smiled.

'And do you condemn it now?' said Caradog.

He shook his head. 'The war forces our rivers to flow into stranger distributaries.'

'Then answer, Kendra,' said Prydd, impatient with Rhain's riddles. 'Which path will the river now take? Will you cease this wrongdoing?'

I stared back. I would not dance to his drumbeat any longer. 'Manacca will remain my student. I will cease learning song.'

'No,' said Caradog. 'Your singing is—' He turned to the Songman. 'Surely you will not allow this?

'It is the Kendra's judgement, not mine,' he said, though I saw his shock.

I rubbed my eyes. I knew what it was to abandon my people. I would not abandon this little girl. Her strength would have to be my song.

⁜

As the days grew longer, we continued to tear at the periphery of the Roman army, retrieving heads, destroying roads, making scabs on its limbs, whilst avoiding its core.

Caradog voiced a hunger to meet Scapula in open battle, but I argued strongly in the council that he must not. It was better to stab at their edges, bleed them, confuse them, hold our boundary, until they tired of defending against an enemy they could never quite see. In a contest of will and patience, we could win, for we had been with this land since it was sung into form. Time was a weapon we understood.

All—even Prydd—agreed.

Still I wondered, as Caradog rode into Hefin's courtyard with another tribal warrior laid limp across his mare, just how long this resistance could endure.

We sowed the first crops, turned out the cattle, repaired thatch, wove cloth and warmed our hands by the forge fires. But it was a half-life we were living beneath the violet spring skies, neither beaten nor victorious, neither captured nor free.

I kept close watch of Caradog as the days unfolded, to ensure that our loss of the Brigantes had not stolen his hope. But he remained strong, training his fighters through the heaviest spring rains, leading out the attacks whenever council could spare him.

I taught Manacca every day, now openly in the cookhouse, and took joy in the fattening of her legs and knowledge. But the sacrifice of song was a greater cost than I had predicted. Without its daily nourishment, I felt myself weakening, as if it were not just poems that drained from my muscles, but blood.

As I watched Rhain leave for the apple grove each day, to forge new songs under its budding canopy, I ached to go with him. And more than this, I could not silence the soft hum of this threatened earth, which seemed to call for my voice to join it in unison.

I had chosen to betray this call.

I did not betray the child who trusted me.

Within the quietness of my thoughts, as I lay alone in my sleephut each night, I missed Neha, who was still at Môn. I missed Rhain. But mostly I missed the man who slept no more than forty paces from me.

Caradog's respect for my counsel had grown firm, but since our discussion of Manacca, he had avoided both my eye and my company. Was it only my song, I wondered, as I stared sleeplessly at the firelight on my roof beams, that had bidden his affection? Had I relinquished that which he most admired in me?

Sensing my yearning, Euvrain had tightened her hold on her husband. She no longer asked me to her fire for a meal nor invited me to the women's hut to spin or dye. I accepted the walls she erected for she was Caradog's chosen wife.

I was the Kendra, testament and mirror to his kingship, but this was merely a shimmering design on the surface of our true lives. Behind it was a bony-shouldered woman of nineteen summers, with bruised knees from harvesting, fingers that smelled of pig fat and a stupid, guileless dog of a heart, that had fixed to a man who had no want of it.

I bore this truth with silence, as I did the relinquishing of song. I knew it was deserved. For the suffering I had caused.

I had thought the Mothers called for my song. I had thought they called for my joining with the war king. Perhaps I did not hear them as clearly as I thought.

✠

'Soldiers approach!' The watch bell rang through the township as I walked with Manacca in the early morning. It was the first week of summer.

'Run home,' I told her, pushing her toward the northern gate.

I hurried to the main entrance, where I joined Caradog and Hefin on the viewing platform.

Sun glinted on the helmets of two distant soldiers riding towards us. They were brave men to enter enemy territory. By the time they had reached the base of the hill, the full length of the entrance path was flanked with warriors standing in hastily-donned skin cloaks and talismans, their spears poised.

We descended the platform as the soldiers rode past the lines of tribesmen. They wore the uniform of the auxilia, foreign soldiers who had sworn to Rome. But as they dismounted and stood before us, I gasped in disbelief. One of them was not foreign at all.

'Ruther?' I stepped forward, staring in amazement.

He kissed my hand. 'Tidings, journeywoman.'

Caradog put his hand to his sword hilt.

'Hold,' I told him. 'This man is known to me.'

His broad, blond face was of my home. This was a man who had betrayed me. This was Ruther, warrior of Caer Cad, or so he used to be.

'How?' said Caradog.

'He was a tribesman. Once.' I glanced at Ruther's armour and shield. 'He fights for Scapula now.'

'I am Ruther, son of Orgilos, Ninth Auxilia. I fight for what I have always fought for.'

'Payment?' said Hefin.

Ruther ran his gaze over the chieftain whose long moustache was crusted with porridge. 'Albion's future.'

'You are a traitor,' said Caradog.

Ruther stood unflinching. 'If I were, would I have advised Scapula to withhold his attack until diplomacy had been attempted? Would I have offered myself as the envoy, knowing that I, above all others, would understand the will of the tribes?'

Caradog scowled. In his eyes, there could be no greater disloyalty than a warrior donning the enemy's uniform. Even Cartimandua, for all her adherence to Rome, looked and smelled like a woman of the tribes. 'Come to the fire then,' he said. 'Let us see if you can still drink like a tribesman and I will hear your proposition.' He looked at the second soldier. 'Bring your shit-bucket carrier.'

The warriors laughed.

'I will,' said Ruther. 'But first, Ailia—would you take me to offer at your temple? It has been many seasons since I have stood within a journey-shrine and poured ale at its altar.'

I knew Prydd would not want a Roman uniform in the temple. But I wanted the chance to speak to Ruther alone. Traitor or not, he shared my past. 'Follow me.'

We were followed at a distance by several of Caradog's fighters as we walked to the temple. But I knew Ruther would not harm me.

At the temple's threshold, I stopped to chant the skin blessings that would permit my entry. Standing beside me, Ruther took off his helmet and murmured his own greeting to the deer.

'You still honour skin?' I whispered, incredulous, for he had betrayed it so wholly. His companion lurked close behind. Did Ruther not worry what this soldier might report to their Roman command?

He stared at me and shrugged. 'I do not forget my history.'

'You cannot enter,' I called in Latin to the soldier who paced by the outer posts.

'I have no wish to,' he said, staring at the angle of the temple's south corner. 'By Mithras,' I heard him chuckle as I turned to go in, 'can they not even build four walls straight?'

I pushed into the temple with Ruther at my heel.

No sooner had the doorskins closed behind us, than he grabbed both my arms. 'How do you fare, Ailia? There has not been a day that I have not wondered of you.'

'How do you think I fare?' I said, pulling free. 'My land is threatened. My tribeskin are slaughtered for no greater sin than living as they always lived. Should I be well?'

He smiled. 'You are as I remember you.'

I stared at his short blond hair, his shaven jaw, his skin weathered by foreign sun. 'You are not.'

Ruther walked to the shrine and frowned in disgust. 'By Claudius, I'd forgotten the stench of my childhood. Worse than a Roman sewer.' Pungent herb smoke mingled with the thick scent of decaying spring lamb that seeped from the altar.

'Is that where you live?' I asked. 'In Rome?'

'Sometimes,' he said. 'I was stationed for two summers in Anatolia. Then I requested to join Scapula's forces in Albion.'

'To aid our destruction?'

'To help you,' he said. He stood at the altar but had poured no libation from his ale skin.

'I thought you wanted to make an offering,' I said.

'I do. But not to these perished gods.'

I gasped. His skin greeting had been a ruse, but for what? 'Then to whom?' I asked. I had not moved from the doorway.

He walked back and stood before me. 'I am here to offer terms to Caradog. Terms that will prevent further killing.'

'He won't accept.'

'I am sure that he listens to the word of his Kendra. You must tell him to accept.'

'You say I am unchanged. Then you already know that I will never betray the tribes.'

His face softened and he shook his head. 'Perhaps I would esteem you less if you did.'

'We are at war. Your esteem is of no consequence now.'

'It is always of consequence.'

'Are you not yet married?' I asked.

'Yes. To a Cantii woman who waits for me with our first child.' He paused. 'But I would divorce her before Lleu's next rise if you said you would return with me.'

I laughed. 'You are still a faithless dog. As you always were.'

He stiffened. 'Steady, Ailia. You speak to a soldier of Claudius.'

'Do you think I care for your title?'

'You should. Scapula will command these tribelands by the end of the season, and then you will kneel to those of my title.'

Suddenly weary, I lowered myself to a bench before the altar. Ruther sat beside me. Despite all that had passed, there had always been a flow of truth between us. I turned to him. 'Why do you betray us, Ruther?'

'I do not betray you. I want you to taste the wealth and glory of Rome.'

'I am a journeywoman. Wealth and glory are a hindrance to what I seek.'

'Yet no hindrance for Caradog,' said Ruther. 'He is as greedy for power as any emperor.'

'Perhaps he is,' I said. 'But he has what no Roman will ever have.'

'Ale that tastes like piss?' said Ruther.

'No...' I paused. 'Sovereignty.'

His smile dropped away.

Suddenly I no longer saw the short hair, the Roman tunic. I saw the bright blue eyes of a man who had grown on the meat and grain of Albion's earth. He could not have forgotten what made this land ours. 'You were born here,' I continued. 'You know as well as I do that when they mark this ground with their flags, they may have glory, but they do not have sovereignty. They hold no stories, no totems, to tie them to this land. They carry no residue of the Mothers in their blood.'

'Should no man ever stray ten paces from the soil of his birth then? Are we all to be so tethered?'

'No we are not. But if we stand on new land, we must honour its spirits and its laws. The Romans will never be loved by this land, because they do not love its creators.'

'They don't need to.' A frown twitched in his face and I knew I had unsettled him. 'Their strength is not hidden, nor cloaked in riddles that none may learn except by secret rites. Their strength is real. They are free of the curse of journey-law.'

I flinched. 'On this land, none are free of journey-law.' I rose, our discussion over.

'Ailia—' he caught my wrist as I stood. 'I don't know what you have seen since we last met, but I can tell you something about the law to which you are so wedded. The journeymen of Môn are fuelling this war. They are not noble-hearted as you are. They control the chiefs with the cunning of wolves. They incite hatred of Rome, despite that many tribes within the new province are grateful for the peace she has brought.'

I shook free my arm. 'The peace of a caged animal.'

'Do you think they are any less free under the journeymen than under the Roman governors? Do not deceive yourself. Both seek control of the tribes, yet one brings the light of modernity—'

I drew myself tall. 'Ruther, I am not under the command of the journeymen. I am their Kendra.'

'No you are not.' He stood up, his eyes glittering in the half-light. 'You are their trophy, their amulet—' He paused to draw breath, then shot the words like a sharpened spear, '—you have no true power.'

I opened my mouth but could not speak. My voice was empty, soundless. There was something in his certainty that forged its own truth. Any refutation I made would only strengthen his claim.

Ruther walked once more to the altar and gazed at the smoking pots. 'Do your new tribespeople know?' he said, without turning to face me. 'Do they know what you did in Caer Cad?'

'I have kept no secrets,' I murmured.

Still he did not turn. 'But do they understand how grave was your failure?'

The council were gathered at the Great Hall to hear Ruther's proposal to the war king. Silver cups and thick gold arm rings from Ruther's saddlebags were spread on the bench between them.

'Scapula understands that you are a king, and that you must be honoured as a king,' Ruther said, passing Caradog a cylinder of papyrus, sealed with wax. 'He offers a full pardon for your crimes against Claudius. He offers horses, cattle, slaves and your choice of available territory if you choose to commit the Silures to Roman friendship.'

'It is Hefin, not I, who is chief of the Silures,' said Caradog. 'Scapula should learn who commands his enemies.'

'He knows who commands his enemies,' said Ruther. 'Read the treaty.'

Caradog unrolled the document and read it with bemusement.

'If you hunger to fight, Caradog, then you could have the command of forces in Aegypt or Numidia...'

'He wants me at any cost,' said Caradog to his council. 'But no prize will turn a war king to a traitor.'

Ruther's eyes narrowed. 'Do you not already betray your tribesmen by sacrificing them to a war without purpose? Claudius desires only to welcome you into the most powerful empire the world has ever known. It would bring wealth and comfort to the people you claim you protect, and yet you prefer to see them die for your own pride.'

I flinched. The words were shocking in their ignorance of what Albion stood to lose, but even more so for their kernel of truth. I knew how deeply Caradog feared this accusation.

'You are an auxiliary,' said Caradog, staring at Ruther. 'My first encounter with your kind was at the Medway, just after the Romans arrived. The Batvians of Gaul swam upstream to my war camp, emerged from the water in silence, and slashed the hind leg tendons of hundreds of my finest war horses. The air rang with the screeches of horses bleeding to death.'

Ruther held his gaze. 'The Batvians are very skilled in river crossings.'

Caradog stood slowly, held the treaty aloft, then let it fall into the fire, where it flared into white flames. 'Tell your governor that I have not fought the Roman army for six summers in order to make terms. Tell him that he will withdraw from the border of Tir Silures by Winter's Eve, or my warriors will fuck his men till they bleed.'

The second soldier rose, but Ruther waved him still. 'Scapula is the most feared general in the Roman Empire. He was sent here to destroy you.'

Caradog laughed. 'I am honoured by the respect.'

Ruther stood and fastened his cloak. 'This was Scapula's final offer of peaceful terms. The next time he comes will be to claim these miserable bog lands. He hates the Silures with every drop of his blood.'

Hefin rose with his hand at his hilt. 'Tell him we await him.'

'The *chieftain* speaks at last,' said Ruther, smirking.

Hefin stood firm. 'You are mistaken if you think this tribe is merely Horse-end's attack dog. We will never lay down for a Roman, no matter who rides at the head of our war band. We are free people and every one of us will die before we see a Roman flag in this soil.'

'See?' said Caradog, smiling. 'This is why I have found my home here. And that is why Scapula will not destroy me.'

'Oh, he will destroy you. You attack his army by stealth, like a furtive dog, because you do not have the courage to meet him in the light. But he will drive you to battle and he will defeat you.'

'How do you know that...soldier?' Caradog stood in the doorway of my hut after Ruther had gone.

'I told you. He was a warrior from Caer Cad.'

'Is that all? A fellow townsman?'

'No.' I stepped aside that he might enter, then poured two cups of ale and handed him one. 'He ran the fires with me when I came to womanhood.'

'I saw that he desired you.'

'Once,' I said. 'And I was glad of it. He loved me when I was without skin, with none of the Kendra's power.' I picked up my whorl and began to spin.

Caradog sat and watched me. We had not been alone for several weeks. 'Why do you not spin with the women?' he asked.

'I am not asked,' I said. 'Perhaps they do not find the presence of the Kendra restful.' I spun without speaking for a few moments, the whorl turning in the silence.

'Do you admire him?'

I teased out a stream of brown wool that had become too thick.

'He obeys his own conscience,' I said. 'I admire his certainty, but not his purpose.'

Caradog shifted on the bench, his limbs too big for this tiny hut. 'And in me?' he asked. 'Is it certainty or purpose that you admire?'

I set my whorl in my lap and looked at him. 'Is that not better asked of your wife?'

'I ask you.'

'Why?' I whispered. He had not sought my company beyond council since we bathed at the pool. Yet he must have sensed the longing that consumed me. And now he called for my testament as if I were a mirror to be picked up and put down at his whim.

He slipped from his bench and crouched before me. 'Because you see what's true in me. For better or worse.'

I stared at his face, uplifted to mine. The truth was that he was magnificent. I admired all in him and what I did not admire, I loved anyway. My heart yearned to tell him this, but it was not Kendra's business and I was furious that he should ask for my comfort, with no thought of its cost to me. 'No,' I said. 'I will give you my Kendra's council, but I will not flatter your vanity as if I were your dress servant.'

'I do not ask for flattery,' he said.

My gaze was steady. 'Then tell me, War King, what do you ask of me?'

It took a moment before he looked away.

My nostrils twitched at the sudden scent, one I had not smelled for many months, and had almost forgotten, the scent of what was needful in him, what he could not hide, the teeming fragrance of threshed wheat and a tended wound—the smell of his love. But it was meaningless if he could not claim it. 'If it is my affection you seek, then you must offer yours in return.'

He stared at the floor. 'I cannot.'

'Then leave my hut,' I said gently. 'Do not ask me to cut open my heart and show you how full it is of your courage and beauty.'

He looked back to me.

I sat tall. He wished for my appraisal. Seeing Ruther had only made it clearer. I would speak now and let the truth know some air to toughen its edges. 'I love you, Caradog of Cunobelinus, War King of Albion. I love you as I have loved no other. For I love what is weak in you, as well as what is strong. But you will not abandon your marriage and nor must you.' I squeezed the fleece in my lap into a tight ball bound by a length of yarn. 'Unless you are betraying your own heart,' I said, as I broke the yarn and rose, 'and then you are a fool. For if we do not fight for the freedom of our hearts, then why are we fighting?'

I threw my ball of fleece at the ground and left the hut.

Rhain found me in the temple.

He sat beside me as I finished the many-versed chant to the Mothers.

'You did not stand witness to the departure of the soldiers,' he said.

'I could not farewell the knave, Ruther,' I told him. 'To see him so poisoned by Rome was too great a sadness.'

'Perhaps you should have done so, despite your sadness.'

'Why so?' I asked.

'Prydd accompanied them to the outer gateway, so that no tribesmen would attack.' Rhain paused.

I frowned. 'Did they speak.'

'They must have,' said Rhain. 'But only the Mothers know what about.'

I looked away, unsettled.

'Do you miss training?' His whisper was furtive. If Prydd found us here, he would be furious.

'Like breath,' I answered.

'Beware,' he said. 'You are no use to the child, or Albion, without breath.'

✠

We made no more incursions into Roman territory. We were now preparing to meet an attack.

Scapula was amassing a force along the banks of the Habren that was mightier and better guarded than any before it. As midsummer approached, our scouts told us that he had withdrawn all elderly and war-injured men from the front, and sent a vast army of fresh soldiers forward from the east of the province to replace them—Rome's Twentieth Legion—stronger and with a youth's lust for combat. They would move this season. But when and where and how we should meet them were questions we could not answer.

Caradog spoke more insistently about open battle. But all agreed with the messages from Môn that this must be avoided at any cost. We would not defeat them on their terms. Instead they urged him to move his war camp deeper into Silures forests to evade Scapula's grasp.

'Well may they say this...' grumbled Caradog at council. 'They are not fighting this war. They sit safe on their isle and milk feed us weapons...'

'Weapons we need,' said Prydd.

'Scapula has been scorned. He will act rashly,' I said. 'We must forge our strategy of a different metal—more stable, calmer—and we may trip him as he dances.'

'As you wish,' Caradog declared to the council after many moments thought. 'After Arbitration I will ride to determine a new location to settle the camp.'

Although I exhaled with relief that he had seen this wisdom, I understood his desire to fight. We had all grown weary of standing at the brink of war and I knew we could not evade Scapula forever.

When the council had closed, I rushed from the Great Hall before Caradog could speak to me. Since my declaration to him, I had avoided all contact outside the boundaries of war-craft. My heart was grateful for the comfort of distance. And so, I am sure, was Euvrain.

Caradog asked me to make sight of the attack, to predict its time and place. Prydd pushed me to perform this augury by the spilled innards of those who had broken our laws, but I had no patience for this grotesque and showy theatre, designed to silence the township with its slit bellies and thrashing limbs, as much as to reveal what lay ahead.

I preferred to fast and chant day-long in the temple, until my senses slowly altered and opened, and my mind warped towards other places, other moments, sometimes rowdy and vivid with battle scenes, other times filled with fainter, older memories of voices, forests, salmon and deer. Though my visions were alive with the Mothers, I could gain no clarity about how and when Scapula would move.

Prydd was displeased when I told him, yet again, that I had found no certainty. 'A Kendra who cannot augur...' he would murmur, frowning as he left the temple. But it was not a failure of Kendra's knowledge that was blinding me. It was the absence of song.

Day by day soldiers marshalled to the Roman front. By the week of Arbitration, almost half of Scapula's troops were assembled along the Habren. It was the largest Roman force ever gathered on Albion's land.

As I stood on the eastern platform on a warm evening, staring towards the Romans, so close, I remembered when I had last stood on war's threshold—when I had made a mistake.

I had thought, perhaps, that I was pardoned.

But as I felt the weight of our enemy tipping the earth, I knew I was not.

✝

People began to arrive from throughout the free tribes.

There had been discussion within council that it may be unwise to gather at this time, but Prydd convinced us that now, more than ever, our festivals must be maintained. The tribes had a great passion for justice and the judgements of the Arbitration were Albion's most revered pronouncements. Travellers lodged in the township or camped in the pastures at the base of the hill. Llanmelin was alive with the milling, baking and preparing of meat to be served at the festival.

On the day before the hearings, Prydd informed us that Sulien of Môn would sit in attendance at this year's gathering and would arrive that evening.

Curious, I asked him which dispute Môn's highest journeyman was required to arbitrate. (I had walked among the visiting travellers and had heard their complaints; there were few more serious than a contested field boundary, a stolen calf or an unlawful harvest of bog ore.)

'One of the utmost seriousness,' he answered, but said no more.

Despite my ignorance of Sulien's purpose, I felt a great joy when I saw him arrive at the gateway with his two lesser journeymen. I aided him from his mount and embraced him warmly.

'Do you know why Prydd has called for you?' I asked as we walked towards the journey-huts.

'I was expecting you would tell me,' he said, surprised.

I shook my head. 'He has only said that it is a matter of journey-law that has bearing on the war.'

'Then why has he not spoken to you of it?' Sulien asked.

'I don't know,' I said. 'But we shall find out soon enough.'

We walked a few paces in silence, then I asked, 'How fares my dogess?'

He turned to me. 'I do not have good news.'

'By Lleu, has she leapt to Annwyn?' I stopped, my heart thumping.

'I cannot be certain. She disappeared from Cerrig not long before I departed to come here. I called many times as I rode, but I did not sight her.'

Neha's disappearance left me distracted on the morning of Arbitration. I thought only of her as I pulled on my dress, a short mantle of deer-skin, and my sword. She would be twelve summers old now and surely growing frail. I wondered if her coat was still thick enough to endure a forest winter, if there were still enough power in her haunches to make a kill. She was searching for me, I was sure of it. Why had I left her?

The sky was stone grey with summer cloud. A mighty crowd had gathered in the town centre, jostling to gain a better view. Before them, the journeypeople sat on a long bench between two flaming pots. Sulien wore a simple crown of summer oak but Prydd wore the full horn head-dress of the mountain ram and a dark leather cloak that hung to his feet. Silures banners flapped in the wind from the poles behind them.

Two warriors stood guard either side of the judges in case a complainant needed subduing. I sat alone on a carved stool to their west. Without training in law, I would offer no judgements, but my Kendra's presence would lend weight to the decisions.

Caradog sat beside Hefin in the first row. His stare was unfocused and I knew his thoughts were consumed by the war.

'Begin,' called Prydd, when the blessings had been made.

One by one farmers, miners, craftsmen and warriors came forward, spoke their grievances, and nodded in silence as Prydd made his judgements. Where the cases were intricate, Sulien or the other journeymen asked questions and offered counsel on details of law.

'I complain against my neighbour who has felled four trees at the boundary of my pasture,' said a grain farmer with an Ordovices accent.

The accused neighbour made his case for the urgent need of building timber but, when asked by Sulien of the type of trees he had brought down, confessed to there being two young oaks among them. Prydd's punishment for the unsanctioned removal of Albion's most sacred wood was the removal, by axe, of his first finger.

The crowd gasped. This verdict was not in the spirit of restoration that flowed through our laws. The guards had to carry the accused away.

The day stretched on, growing steadily cooler as storm clouds darkened the sky. Several times Prydd's judgements seemed so poorly-made that I wondered whether there were unseen currents directing them, whether the stream of visitors he had taken in his hut over the past few days may have sweetened their cases with coin.

Finally the last of the complainants turned away from the bench. We were all exhausted, eager to break for the meat and ale of festival. One of the lesser journeymen stood and asked if anyone else wished to speak.

A roll of thunder stirred on the western horizon. The air sharpened with charge.

Prydd took off his headdress, laid it on the bench and turned to Sulien. 'I have a case to bring and I have called you here to judge it.'

'Against whom?' asked Sulien.

Another low rumble seemed to rise from the earth. The crowd were restless.

Prydd looked at me. 'Against Ailia of Caer Cad.'

I stilled.

'What is the grievance against our Kendra?' Sulien looked bewildered.

'I contest that she is not the Kendra.'

Now the crowd drew silent.

My heart was thrashing.

'On what grounds?' demanded Caradog.

Prydd lifted his hand to quiet him. None were permitted to speak until the complaint had been made. 'I spoke with Ruther, son of Orgilos, when he came to Llanmelin—'

'The traitor?' Caradog's face was furious.

'Perhaps now,' said Prydd. 'But he was chieftain of Caer Cad when Rome took that township. He told me the story of Ailia's past...It is not as we have thought it.'

My fingers gripped the sides of the stool. My heart beat so violently I could barely hear. The day had come.

Prydd walked forward to speak to the gathering. Now his voice was not thin or shrill. It was as powerful as I had ever heard it. 'Do you know that this woman—whom you call Kendra—decreed that every soul in Caer Cad be slain by Vespasian's soldiers.'

A cold wind began to lash the banners.

'She commanded them to stand against the attack, while she secured herself in a hidden shelter beneath the ground.'

The crowd listened, mute.

'I did not hide,' I whispered. 'I was held against my wishes...'

'She claims she was forcibly hidden,' repeated Prydd to his audience. 'That is one explanation. Another is that she knew Ruther was planning to concede his township to the Romans and that they would kill the journeypeople. She protected herself and let her tribespeople be slain. Once the soldiers were resting from their slaughter, Ruther says, she crept away under cover of secrecy.'

He had opened the belly of my shame.

The crowd chewed the story in frantic whispers.

'It was an error...' I murmured in a voice barely loud enough for Prydd to hear, let alone Caradog or any others who might judge me.

'"*An error*" is her defence!' cried Prydd. 'I ask you, Sulien, would the Mothers permit such a terrible error from their chosen knowledge-bearer?'

The crowd quieted again, awaiting Sulien's answer.

'I wanted to protect them,' I said feebly.

'If you, in truth, wanted to protect them,' answered Prydd, 'then why did the Mothers not stand with you? What should we make of your Kendrahood? Are we to expect the same error, the same misfortune, as you lead *us* into war?'

I had no answer. The error had been made when I was newly made Kendra. The elders of Caer Cad had asked me to vision, to tell them whether to fight or succumb to the approaching army. No vision had come to me, and, terrified of my inadequacy, I pretended it had. I told the townspeople that I had seen them successful and I commanded them to fight. I thought the command would strengthen them. It had caused the death of every man and woman in Caer Cad.

'She does not answer,' said Prydd. 'Because she cannot. She is not the Kendra. She has been falsely placed. I propose we supplant her.'

'Journeyman—' called Caradog. 'She is a valuable advisor. Kendra or not, we cannot lose her.'

'She is almost entirely untrained,' said Prydd. 'Without her title, she has no place to sit at your council.'

'Why do we accept the testimony of a traitor?' It was Rhain who spoke. He had been buried deep in the back of the crowd, always wary of displaying his disfigurement among strangers. Now every face turned to look at him. 'Ruther fights for Rome. But he was born of Albion—he knows where to strike. It is in his interest to weaken our faith in our knowledge-keepers. He has lied.'

'No,' I interrupted, my voice clear at last. 'Ruther has not lied.'

The people turned to me. Slowly I stood to address the men seated on the bench and the crowd before them. 'I did not hide myself, as Ruther claims, but was trapped by him against my will so I could not right my error and call the warriors back.' I saw Caradog slump with relief. 'But the deeper claim he makes is true. I commanded the people of Caer Cad to fight under a false vision. I did not intend harm, but that is of no consequence now. I am responsible for their deaths.'

Sulien and Caradog both stared at me in incomprehension.

How had I ever imagined I was forgiven?

My hair whipped my face in the wind. I turned to Prydd who was smiling in his triumph. 'I am your Kendra. I have known the Mothers. I have heard them sing. Yet you have doubted me and disrespected me. I wish, more than any, that I was not so tarnished a Kendra, but there is no other. Condemn me if you will, but do not say that I am falsely placed.'

'I will say it,' said Prydd. 'No true Kendra would cause her people such harm.'

The wind lulled. The crowd was silent.

Intuitively, my hand rose to my chest and I felt, through my dress, the coiled scars of the Mothers' knife. I could continue to argue. I could show them my wound and hope it might still carry a faint trace of song if it were pressed. But I did not.

For suddenly it barely mattered if I was Kendra or not. Finally I had seen that I had no place here. Caradog did not love me. Prydd did not want me. I had caused Euvrain to suffer, and I could not learn song without abandoning a child who had grown to need me.

I had called on every shred of my strength to convince Caradog that I was more than a figurehead. And now, just as he had begun to esteem me, my failing was exposed. I had no further weapons against his doubt. Nor against my own. Prydd's accusation echoed my own suspicion that there was something askew in me. If I had made such an error once, could I make it again?

I stared at the faces around me, tired and worn by war. They doubted me. But not only this. They doubted my title. They doubted the land. They doubted themselves.

'Ailia?' said Sulien gently. 'Do you refute Prydd's accusation? Do you claim that you are Kendra?'

'I will always claim it,' I said. 'But I cannot prove to you what you no longer have the faith to believe.'

The first fat drops of rain fell from the sky, but no one moved.

I unfastened my Kendra's sword and walked to the bench to stand before Sulien. 'I wish that I could have helped you,' I said as I laid the sword at his feet. 'Strength and courage in the war.'

9

The Shape of All Things

The rise of the sun,
The contour of the oak leaf,
The paths across our land
Are bound by the same angles.
Their pattern is in all things
But not all can see it.

CARADOG CAME to my hut as I was packing a saddle bag. He paced back and forth in agitation. 'Where are you going?'

'North.'

'Where?'

I did not know. I wanted only to be within the forest again. To merge, like a beast, with the mountain and know the simple success of the hunt. To be where I could bring no harm and feel no shame. 'Perhaps, in time, to Môn...'

'But you will return to join me when I leave Llanmelin?'

I looked up from the blanket I was folding. 'No, Caradog. I will not return.'

Now he stood still. 'We may go to war this season. I will need you to stand beside me, to augur the right time and battle place—'

I began to cry. 'I will not tell anyone to fight again.'

'Why not?' he demanded.

'Because I am no longer Kendra. Were you not there at Arbitration? Why do you taunt me?'

'I do not care if you are called Kendra or pig-herd. The soldiers hear you because you are clear-eyed and you understand this war. They trust you.' He paused. 'I trust you.'

'But I do not trust myself. How can I be certain that I would not command them falsely again?' I broke from his gaze and stuffed the blanket into my bag.

'Ailia.'

I looked up. He used my name so infrequently.

'When you came to Llanmelin last autumn, you said you wanted to aid me in war.'

I looked back at the ground.

He crouched before me and took both my shoulders in a firm grip, almost shaking me. 'This is war, Ailia. Many tribespeople have died because of my war calls, many settlements have been burned. Many people will die yet. This is the currency of war. You were not responsible for the deaths at Caer Cad—it was war.'

I stood, pulling free of his grasp, and turned away. If there were any truth in his words I could not acknowledge them. I had lost my township. I had lost Taliesin. I had lost my sister dog. Now I had caused the war king's council to doubt their Kendra. To be in bond to me was to be condemned. I would not subject Rhain or Hefin or Manacca to the risk of it. And especially not Caradog. He, more than any other, needed to be free of me. We had no greater hope against the Romans than him. This was how I would aid his war—by leaving.

I picked up my bag and tied it closed. My eyes were dry now. My endless practice in ignoring the voice of my heart had finally borne fruit. I felt nothing. Just the cold, howling call of the mountains. They would tell me what I was.

Caradog put his hand on my shoulder, more gently, as I went to pass. 'Stay, Kendra.'

'I am not she.'

'Whatever you are, stay.'

'Mothers bless you,' I whispered, as I walked out the door.

'Aya!'

I knew that lilting mispronunciation of my name and I did not turn. I had taken the northern gate because it was less watched, but it required that I walk past the fringe huts.

'Stop, Aya!'

The voice was shrill with panic. I had to turn.

She was running down the path towards me with all the speed her legs would allow. Darkness had almost fallen, but I could see the worry in her face. 'Where are you going?' she gasped when she reached me.

'Walking...harvesting,' I stammered.

'By night?'

'Yes.'

'I will come!'

'No, Manacca.'

'Why not?' She took my hand as if to lead me onwards, but I pulled it away.

'No. You can't come this time.'

Her dark eyes searched my face then dropped to my sack. 'Are you leaving?'

'I have to, my pup.'

She flung her arms around my waist. 'You cannot!' she cried. 'You cannot go!'

I softened at her touch and yearned to embrace her, but I would

245

not. 'Let me go, Manacca,' I said, prising her hands from my waist.

Her desperate grip would not release me.

I cursed the muscles that had served us so well in harvesting and pounding—she had great strength, but mine was greater. With a rough jerk, I pulled her wrist free.

She yelped in pain then fell upon me again, grabbing hold of my thigh. 'Don't leave, Aya.'

'Stop it,' I said, growing angry. We struggled. She would not let go. A fury rose. I took her small shoulders, wrenched her from my leg, and threw her hard to the ground. 'Leave me!' I bellowed.

She looked up at me from the road, her eyes huge with shock. She did not run at me again.

I turned away and began walking. I did not look back.

Her bitter crying followed me deep into the forest.

In all that I had done, I had never known greater shame.

Wet ground. Narrow paths. Dense trunks. The forest by night forced out all other thoughts. The air was livelier, tighter, charged with the spirits that rose off the trees. I sucked deep breaths of the peppery coldness. It was intoxicating, addictive as any mead. I grew drunk on its wildness. My edges softened; I was altered.

I walked through the darkness until my legs felt as though they had been absorbed into the earth and I was gliding, by scent, across the skin of the mountain. The forest would heal me. It would give me my strength.

As the moon set, I stopped at a crevice that was sheltered by a jut of rock in the hillside. By the pungent scent, I knew it had once housed a litter of wolf pups, who would have moved off with the summer, leaving me their hair-lined den. I slipped inside and ran my hands around the walls. There was barely room enough to stand, and I would have to lie curled, but it would keep me dry and protected as I slept.

From the loose stones I felt underfoot I selected one that was flat enough to suffice for an ember-catcher and placed it just within the entrance so the smoke could draw out. I crushed a few dry leaves as tinder, then pulled my fire bow and spindle from my bag. Working by touch, for the darkness was total, I turned the bow steadily, until a small cone of ember began to glow on the stone. My breath and a handful of tinder completed the task. The spider-strewn edges of my chamber were lit.

There was scant dry wood in the sodden forest, but I gathered what I could and propped it around the flames to dry. The fallen branches beneath the lip of shelter outside would be enough for the night.

I had enough smoked mutton and bread to last several days. My sling would feed me after that and here would be burdock and mallow, whose roots would be tender in tomorrow's coals.

When I had eaten, I lay down, curving my body around the fire, the heat from the embers soaking my muscles. Here alone, undistracted, I could hear the Mothers' heartbeat. It was right that I had come. I did not belong to Llanmelin, to the tribes. I belonged to this low and steady pulse.

Rain pattered again outside my nest. The fire spat as droplets flew in on gusts of wind. My face was hot, but my back was cold. I stretched out, then wrapped my body into a circle. Around and around I coiled on myself, until my head lay softly on my full belly and my tail tickled my cheek. I rippled in pleasure and faint surprise. So gently, so tenderly, the Mothers bestowed their grace. Rather than witness me struggle, in my human shape, to hunt and stay warm, they had quietly wrought me to serpent. Here I could be safe from Prydd, from Roman swords, and from the ceaseless enthralment of my own failure.

My eyes closed. My breath slowed. There was just the heat now, sloughing my skin.

Below me, the roots of the forest were listening, thinking, readying their change.

┼

I was grateful to be wild again, to have my every thought consumed by survival.

Each day I arose before dawn and sat on the edges of streams or springs, chanting my devotion to the Mothers, who sang back in the gurgling water. Once Lleu had shown his face in the eastern sky, I hunted and harvested, taking pleasure in a life where the stakes of my labour were a missed meal or a lost sling stone, and not the murder and rape of my townspeople.

After highsun, I walked along the windy crests of the mountains, where paths sheered away to dizzying cliffs, huge hunting birds hovered, and plants grew low and hardy in the cracks of limestone. I spent many hours gathering mossy meadow and roseroot to dry and powder in my shelter, taking comfort in the solitude and wide horizons. I felt a kinship with the stubborn, woody shrubs that grew almost out of bare rock, defiant of the legions bearing down on their home.

At dusk, I sat at my fire, pulled out my song belt, and sang through the poems Rhain had taught me. Though I had gained no more since Prydd's forbidding, I already held more than I could recite in a week of evenings. Through steady declamation, I affirmed my knowledge of measurement, medicine, history and plantcraft, and was surprised how much I held in my memory.

I thought of Manacca, of Rhain, and especially of the war king. I did not think of returning to them. It could serve no purpose. The Kendra's title was a gleaming vessel that Prydd had cracked open. There was nothing within but my error. The only being I wished to be close to was Neha. I longed for her wordless presence.

The weeks carried me to the height of summer. The beech trees, in thick growth, offered bountiful sweet leaves and would yield oily nuts in the autumn. The forest heaved its ancient sigh as Lleu's mighty wheel tilted to begin its slow return towards darkness. Never had I loved this land of Albion so deeply. Never had I feared its loss so greatly.

Every day, I listened to the crumbling soil beneath my fingers. I asked what it needed, what would keep it strong. Despite my mistakes, the memory of the Mothers still glimmered within me—the Kendra's memory. Where could I take it? How could I wield it, that it might protect this land?

But as I laid my head each night on the cave's hard ground, I heard no answer.

My dreams were dark and confusing, full of underground tunnels that never reached light. Had even the Mothers lost faith in me now? Did the land itself renounce its Kendra?

Then slowly, gradually, as I walked the narrow pathways back from the summits with my skirt gathered up and heavy with hawkweed, I came to hear the land's voice.

It did not call for its Kendra. It called for its song.

I walked, I dug, I pounded, I slept. And finally, deep in unaltered forest, I understood. As our land had been changed by invasion, so must our knowledge change if it was to survive. It could no longer remain within the vessel of the Kendra's title, for this was too shining, too easily seen.

In a threatened land, such brightness would reveal us.

In a threatened land, our knowledge must be hidden where no Roman could find it.

As I harvested and hunted, I felt the land's sadness, core-deep, in the marrow of the stone. It was mourning its sovereign people.

And yet its spirits were indestructible.

Then what of me? Whatever I was, I held the voice of the Mothers.

I could not voice it as Kendra. The title belonged to our innocence, when our bonds to this earth were uncontested.

No. If my memory was to endure now, I needed to be stealthy, ever-changing, closer to the earth. Serpent-like.

I needed to be Songwoman.

I understood all this, but I could not return.

For I was still she who was gifted knowledge, and yet had wrought unspeakable destruction. And there was none with the authority to pardon me.

†

At first she could not rouse me.

I was sleeping late, after a windy night had kept me awake.

Her hot breath and rough tongue became part of my dreams, but as she barked and whimpered, I swiftly rose through the waters of sleep and opened my eyes. 'By the Mothers!' I gasped, sitting up. I clutched at her face and forelegs to assure myself she was no conjuring, no vision. 'How have you come here?' I had never felt her back so thin or seen her flanks so wasted. She must have walked the length of Albion to find me. But how? By scent? By magic?

When she had drunk water from my cupped palms and doused me afresh in wet licks, she trotted to the shelter's entrance and barked her announcement that she had found something. But whom was she telling?

'Neha? Hoo!' called a man's voice from a distance and she barked again.

I peered out of the cave and saw a figure approaching through the beech trees.

With a yelp of joy I was beside him, crushing his delicate shoulders in my embrace, breathing the temple smoke that lingered in his robe. 'Teacher,' I murmured into his cheek. 'How have you found me?'

'By your hound,' Rhain answered. 'She came to Llanmelin in search of you. I knew then she would be able to lead me to you in the mountains.' He chuckled. 'It took her barely three days!'

He had brought a cooked lamb's joint and we shared it hungrily until the bones were sucked white and we gave them to Neha.

'You are well,' he said, appraising me. 'Radiant as Lleu.'

'The forest tends me...' I shrugged. 'And what of you? Have you seen my girl, Manacca? How fares Llanmelin?' I had been almost six weeks in the mountains.

'Llanmelin survives,' he said. 'Manacca has taken to visiting the journey-huts since you left, when Prydd does not shoo her away. Euvrain is with child and—'

I could not catch my gasp of shock. Then I forced a smile. Of course she should bear his child. 'She is his wife,' I said with another small shrug.

'You are also his wife.'

I shook my head. 'It is an empty title...'

'But not for Caradog.'

I glanced at him. 'Tell me of the war king. Is he well? To where will he move the war camp?

'He makes no preparations to move the war camp,' said Rhain. 'He intends to stand.'

'In defiance of Môn?' I asked.

'In defiance of all good counsel.'

'He cannot...' I frowned.

'You ask if he is well.' Rhain paused. 'The answer is no. He is dark-tempered and limp.'

My heart sank. 'I know this incarnation of him. It is hard to witness.'

'It puts us in danger,' said Rhain. 'If he is determined to stand, then the warriors must prepare the roadways and banks for attack. But Caradog takes no action.'

'He must,' I said. 'If he will not move the camp, he must at least be preparing the escape paths—'

'So you must tell him.'

I hesitated. 'Others will tell him.'

'He does not listen to others.'

I stared at his face. 'How rude I am! I have offered you no water after your journey.'

'I want no water,' said Rhain as I reached for my bladder. 'I want you to return with me.'

I took a long draught, then held the pouch to Rhain, who shook his head. 'Please,' I said. 'Do not ask this of me. The tribes have made their judgement. I have found a place where I might find some peace.'

'And do you think this place will remain at peace? Do you think that, here, you are shielded from the war?'

I closed my eyes fleetingly. I had thought exactly that.

'If you love this land, you must fight for it.'

'I cannot.'

'Why not?' He stared at me. His face, so warped, was still so familiar to me. I could read its every disappointment and hope.

'Because I am malformed,' I said, feeling shame press in the back of my eyes. 'I cannot serve the tribes, even if it were my dearest wish.'

His words were as certain as a blade. 'You can.'

'Do you forget what was said at the Arbitration—?' My voice was ugly, trapped in my chest. 'I led them falsely, Rhain...I killed them.'

Rhain watched me in silence as I wept.

'Yes, you did,' he said when I had calmed.

I looked up in surprise. Did he, too, condemn me?

'Your actions, your command, caused the deaths of your people. That is your history and no lamentation will change its shape. But ask yourself now—who is aided by your lament? Does your shame serve your people?' He paused. 'Or is it yet another fascination with your own stature, your own presentation? *With how you are seen?*'

'No...' I frowned, confused. Would not anyone lament misdeeds as grave as mine? 'It is not that. It is the fear that I will err again...'

'Who are you that you may never err? Do you deprive your own king of counsel that will strengthen his war because of vanity?'

'*Vanity?*'

'I repeat what I have told you already: self-doubt is a vanity, as is pride. Both will erode your authority.'

'I have no authority!'

'Because you will not claim it!' His voice matched mine. 'You have injured the people of Albion once. But your survival was a chance to serve them again. Your guilt betrays this chance—it injures them a second time.'

I startled with the shock of a newborn lamb and stared at him, my chest pounding, as his words echoed in the quietness of the cave. Gradually I began to sense the shape of something true: my guilt did not serve the land I loved; it served only me.

Rhain must have noticed the softening—the seeing—in my face. 'Relinquish your vanity, Ailia. Take up your authority. Albion requires it.'

I looked at him. 'I cannot be pardoned.'

'I do not pardon you. I do not absolve you. I ask you to bear what you have done and continue.'

I turned to the fire and sipped my water. I had no choice. Whatever I was, I was needed by the tribes. I was needed by the man who could win this war.

'Will you come?' he pressed.

I thought of what the forest had told me. 'Yes,' I whispered. 'But not as the Kendra. I will bear my knowledge only as a learner of song.'

Rhain smiled. 'There is no stronger vessel.'

As we returned to Llanmelin, Rhain told me how close we were to a Roman attack.

'Do we know when?' I asked.

'No. We believe the legion delays because Scapula suffers a weakness of the chest. He is some weeks confined to his barrack with fever.'

My thoughts chewed on the information. A fever of the chest would not lift easily in the damp woodlands and would certainly leave a lasting weakness in his breath. I prayed that his illness would worsen.

Knowing how soon we might need them, Rhain taught me navigation songs that mapped the different routes from Llanmelin to the mountains. As we finally walked up the hill path to the hill town's entrance, my voice was hoarse with the journey we had made, and my muscles were infused with its words and rhythms. I held this tract of country so firmly in my body now, as if you could cut my skin and its river water would pour from my veins, and dark earth would crumble from the hollows of my bones.

✝

I stood before Caradog in the Great Hall. Rhain had sent me in alone.

The war king greeted me with a formal bow. He wore a wolf-skin cloak and his totem feather neckpiece—tribal regalia—as if I were a visiting chief. Were we so distant? He had grown thinner, his cheeks hollowed beneath his stare.

Despite his remoteness, it took all my restraint not to embrace him. His face was impenetrable, yet he looked into me as if I were a pool of water.

'Will you not speak?' I finally asked.

'The words must be yours,' he said.

'I am sorry.'

'Where was your loyalty?'

'It sought retreat. It is returned now.'

'Loyalty is that which does not ebb and flow.'

'I know.'

Our gaze held.

'Rhain has told me you have been unwell.'

'I will grow well now that you are returned.'

'You welcome me then?'

There was no softening in his face. 'You fled like a faithless mongrel, but you bear the spirits of these tribelands and I cannot fight without you.'

'Your wiseman Prydd does not agree—'

'He does not need to.'

'I was deemed to be falsely titled.'

'By his word only. I never doubted it.'

My skin grew warm, infused with his faith. My feelings were unchanged. I still believed in his war. I still believed he should lead it. I still loved him.

I sat on the bench by the fire and he sat beside me.

'Where...is Prydd?' I stammered.

'He left Llanmelin when I refused to heed him. I imagine for Môn. Hefin is not pleased.'

I was relieved Prydd was gone, but aware that any rift between Caradog and Hefin would not be good for the warriors. The weft of war-craft drew taut within me. I was once more of the tribes. 'I hear you will not move the camp,' I said. 'But you must go north.

Scapula comes. You cannot sit in wait for him.'

'It is time to fight them, Ailia.'

I stared at his face, turned to the fire. Within the familiar authority of his voice, I heard something less certain. 'Are you echoed in this belief by Hefin? By the warriors?'

'Yes. They grow weary of waiting. They are ready to stand in battle.'

'It is not our strongest position—to meet them on ground of their choosing.'

'Our numbers are greater now.' He would not look at me.

'But still not great enough. The Mothers can help protect us— they can disguise us in the forests—but they cannot birth warriors from air, to match the numbers of Rome's!'

He exhaled. 'Even if you are right, Ailia, I cannot leave the Silures. Scapula is preparing to move on Llanmelin and I cannot leave Hefin to face an attack unaided. I will not abandon the warrior who has shown me such loyalty.'

'Then bring Hefin with us.'

'He will not come. You know that.'

I nodded. It would be a greater death for Hefin to abandon his homeland than to be slain defending it. 'Then that must be his choice,' I said. 'But it cannot be yours. You are more than a tribal chieftain. You owe a loyalty to Hefin—but a greater one to Albion. You must defeat Scapula. You cannot sacrifice yourself to anything else.'

Caradog laughed. 'Your heart has grown harder in your time at Môn.'

'Not harder,' I said. 'Just stronger, perhaps.'

'Then lend me your strength, Ailia, for I am resolved to settle the question of Albion whenever Scapula is bold enough to ask it.' His gaze remained fixed to the fire. These were warrior words but they lacked the warrior's spirit. He did not want to fight this battle here where it would surely fail. He was not fuelled by strategy in this decision, but by some loss of heart. I had never known his illness to impede his judgement before. Even through his darkest weathers, his sense of war-craft had never faltered. This was a new unease. But what was its source? 'From where does Scapula prepare to launch?' I asked.

'He seeks to confuse us. There are camps along the Habren from Tir Durotriges to Tir Cornovii. He could come from many directions.'

'He will not approach from the west or south because that would leave you easy lines of retreat. Surely he will try to outflank you and come from the north?'

Caradog nodded. 'I have predicted the same. There have been Roman patrols scouting north. The Forest of Dean is rugged marching, but he would be determined enough to attempt it.'

'And how do you propose to meet him?' I asked. 'Rhain told me there has been little preparation of our fortifications.'

'By ambush in those very forests. We will halt them before they reach the hill fort.'

I stared at him. 'But if they breach the forest and make formation in the flatlands, you are trapped with only water at your back. You cannot swim to safety!' This senseless strategy could not be his. He was brave but not foolish. Was he so war-weary that he had lost all judgement? 'What do the elders at Môn command?'

'They desire me to move north, as you have advised. They seek firmer protection of the routes leading to Môn.'

'Then heed them.'

He snorted, 'I am not their hired guard.'

'Yet you must not act against them. One word from the journeymen at Môn and your numbers will be halved—'

At last he turned to me. 'I hear your words. And the words of Môn. But we cannot run forever from this enemy...'

Never had I seen his eyes so heavy. This was a burden beyond even his illness.

'What is within you, War King,' I whispered, 'that you abandon what you have fought for?'

The air in the hall became still.

For the first time, he spoke without shield, without weapon. 'I have been the heart and mind of this war for seven years,' he said. 'I need to finish it. I am tired of bearing it alone.'

'You do not have to bear it alone.'

He stared for a moment longer, then, to my surprise and relief, he moved closer to me and laid his head on my lap.

I put my hand on his shoulder.

'Tell me what to do, Ailia.'

I felt the warmth of his face through my skirt.

We sat in silence. This one man commanded a war against an empire. Now he asked me to command him. My answer held no doubt. 'You must fight them. But not now, not here. Scapula has good knowledge of these lowlands, the river and the coast. His men are strong and long-rested in their forts. We must fight them when they are tired.'

Slowly Caradog lifted his head to look at me.

'Lead him into the mountains, War King, where his army will be clumsy and confused on the narrow paths. Make them march through the valley marshes where they will not know the dry crossings and will exhaust themselves in the mud.'

Caradog frowned. 'I do not know the mountains as well as I know the lowlands—'

'But I do. They will protect us. And they worsen Scapula's health.'

'What do you mean?'

'He has been ill and his chest is weak. The high air of the mountains will irritate him and keep him wakeful at night...'

Something twitched in Caradog's face. 'He will wear down, lose judgement...'

'Yes. We must fight with the Mothers. Let them hold back his arms with their cold, wet air, while we sink a sword in his chest.'

Caradog stared at me, a brightness growing in his eyes. 'I am tempted to heed you, Kendra.'

'Heed me, but not as Kendra'. I paused. 'Heed me as the Songwoman I will become.'

He frowned, then nodded. He trusted me. His gaze locked to mine, bold and seeking.

This was the man I knew. I loved. I saw now what lay between us. I had caused his spirit to weaken by my absence, and I had restored it on my return. This was the truth of us. This was the Mothers' will.

I took his hands. 'Is my disloyalty forgiven?'

'Of course,' he whispered.

'Then yours will be also.'

'What disloyalty?' he asked.

'This.' Gripping his hands for safety, I leaned forward and kissed his mouth.

He tasted of the nettle tea he had drunk at highsun, and beneath that, of the iron and salt of Albion's earth, the pollen of its air. With a groan, he drew me closer, pressing his chest against mine. 'I will deny you no longer,' he said into my skin. 'You are my healing.'

'And you are mine.'

'If you will stay with me, I will pledge you my loyalty above all else.'

I tightened my arms around his neck and repeated the words that had lived true within me since I first spoke them to him on the shores of Môn:

You are blood of my blood.
Bone of my bone.

By the power of the Mothers, may you love me.
As I love you.

With his lips at my temple he spoke them back.

Our love was as unsure and terrifying as the war that was coming, but we clung to each other's strength, our desire the very force of life for which we fought.

⁜

I found Rhain in the temple, clasping a horn of mead. His face lit up with a knowing smile as my flushed cheeks and rapid breath betrayed me. 'Hoo!' he said. 'The dog and the wren!'

I sat beside him, murmuring the briefest blessing to the altar before us. 'How do you see me so well?'

'I am trained to see. And you are a not a dull flame.'

We sat in silence. There was no small cost to the love I had just pledged.

'Am I wrong?' I asked softly.

'Are you?' he answered. 'Who is the authority?'

I felt my heart lurch with the giddiness of freedom. Only I could sanction my actions.

He sipped from his horn.

I reached forward and took it gently from his hand. 'There will be time enough to take the gods' water, for we feast tonight.'

'Have you altered the war plan?'

'Yes,' I nodded. 'We are going north into the mountains and you will need your hard wits to make song of it tonight...unless—' A hope came to me. Was I ready? 'Rhain,' I ventured, 'may I sing at the feast tonight? I learned much on the mountain. I have come to understand something of why we fight.'

He looked at me with the lopsided stare that saw me more clearly than any other. 'Why do you wish to sing?'

It was the third time he had asked the question. This time I did not falter. 'For our sovereignty.'

Rhain's eyebrows lifted. 'How are we sovereign?'

'By the land's desire.'

'Who speaks the land's desire?'

I took a breath. 'I do.'

'Very good!' He laughed.

I waited. 'Well?' I said. 'May I...sing?'

'Soon, soon. Not yet,' he said with his interminable smile. 'Shed one more skin!'

I wanted to tip the horn of ale over his lumpy head. But I trusted him and I nodded my acceptance.

Lleu's shadows were long as I walked to the northern entrance.

Manacca was crouched on the path outside the gates, floating a feather in a puddle, while her mother haggled with the slaughterman over a basket of bones. When she saw me, there was no smile, no yelp of joy at my return.

'Manacca?' I said. 'I am returned...'

She gave no response. Had she lost her wits with an illness or a blow to the head? No. The only blow she had received was mine.

She turned back to her puddle.

I stood unmoving, while she played as if I were not there. Then I handed her mother the basket of silver, salt and a bottle of honey mead that I had brought in the hope of securing Manacca's fosterage. She might as well have it anyway.

The mother's thanks was barely more than a snarl.

Walking back into the township, I clung to my resolve to bear what I had done, reeling at how brutally it could be tested.

As dusk drew near, I prepared in my hut for the evening invocation. I spread a worn pigskin on the floor and began the postures that would settle my mind before prayer. But I could not banish Manacca from my thoughts as I bent and twisted, recalling how she would watch me, enthralled, as I performed this sequence, hopping up to mimic my shapes. I remembered the smell of her skin after a tallow bath and the sound of her giggling at Neha's whimpery dreams. Then I thought of Caradog, and marvelled that the Mothers could take and bestow so much in the gesture of one day.

Neha startled beside me as the door bell was struck.

'Enter,' I called, expecting Rhain.

But it was Euvrain who pushed through the doorskins. By her face, I knew that Caradog had spoken to her.

I invited her to sit and poured her a cup of ale.

She did not lift her gaze as I sat beside her.

'I am sorry, Euvrain.' I said. 'I had dreamt of a friendship between us.'

Her pale hair hung loose, a veil between us, and her eyes remained downcast. 'And I believed there was one.'

We sat in quietness as she rested one hand on her well-swollen belly, only two or three moons from birth. She sipped her ale then began to speak.

'After the Romans first landed and defeated us at the Medway, we could not return to Camulodunum. We took refuge in the forests of Tir Catuvellauni. Caradog asked me if I would leave my tribelands and follow him west to continue the war.'

I waited as she paused.

'When I returned to the township to farewell my mother and father, Plautius himself came to my house.' Now she looked at me. 'He offered me citizenship, gold, guarded protection, servants, a safe home, in return for me telling him where my husband hid.' Her pale eyes darkened. 'I could have been a Roman queen. But instead I have lived in mud and manure and birthed two children in a broken cart as we hid like frightened deer for seven summers. I did not betray him.'

'And now he betrays you,' I whispered, voiceless with shame.

She sipped again. 'I did not come to chastise you.'

'Why then?'

'To give you my blessing.' Her voice was cold. 'I am loyal to my husband and I love him still, but you are the only one who can steer him. For Albion's sake I release him to you. I will not attend the feast tonight. You will take my place at his side.'

'Does he ask this of you?'

She shook her head. 'Your love is Mother-chosen. I will not stand in its path.'

She had the nobility of the moon. How could Caradog have chosen any above her? 'I... I have admired your marriage to the War King.'

'And yet it is yours that will save us.'

I stared at her in awe. 'You are stronger than he or I.'

She laughed. 'I do not feel it. Just promise me that you will guide him well—and ensure that my children's homeland is safe.'

'I promise you this.' My shoulders fell with the weight of my truthfulness.

She rose to leave.

'Euvrain—'

She looked back.

'I am...so wanting of sisterhood. Might we yet spin or weave together when...when all is settled?'

She frowned. 'No. We will not weave or spin together.'

I bowed my head.

✝

After the feast, Caradog came to my bed. Strong as earth, he rocked above me. Fire and water were the sweat that bound us. Our desire for each other was our desire for Albion: a soul's yearning that claimed its object with the imperative of breath.

When we had quieted, he propped himself on his elbow to face me, tracing my scars with the tip of his finger. Were they ugly to him? 'Are you proud that it is you who was chosen?' he asked.

'There is power in it,' I answered, 'but this is not what I am glad of.'

'What then?'

'I am glad of the memory of when they were cut.'

He stared at me, flame light dancing on his face. 'Tell me.'

'It was rapture.' I held his stare. 'I was as the Mothers. I was immortal.'

'I would love to know such a moment.'

'That is my task,' I whispered. 'To know it for you.'

Slowly he moved his mouth to the scars and anointed them with his lips and tongue.

They throbbed and sang between my nipples.

The memory was mine, but he made it stronger.

✠

After three summers in the fields of Llanmelin, it took only four days for Caradog's camp to be struck, the grain barrels filled, the carts loaded, the cattle roped and the warriors weaponed and readied to ride. Caradog was determined that not one of the several thousand should remain behind.

Hefin had resisted all efforts to convince him to ride with us, even bidding his best warriors to ride with Caradog. I knew this was the way of the tribes—a question of honour. Caradog commanded the greater war, but Hefin was chieftain to this tribeland by a long rope of blood. He was ready to give himself as its sacrifice.

I wept as I kissed him farewell on the morning of our departure. 'Show courage,' I whispered into his bristly ear. 'Thank you for your loyalty. The war king would have stood no chance without you.'

We were standing at the edge of the camp field where it met the road, an ocean of people behind us, ready to ride. Caradog and Rhain were tightening the straps on their saddle packs. Euvrain was mounted beside them, wretched with pregnancy, staring, without expression, toward the east. The sky was colourless, the wind sharp on our skin.

Hefin steadied my mare as I mounted. 'Make sure you keep one of Scapula's balls for my trophy shelf,' he said, and I laughed.

While Caradog gave Hefin his final suggestions for ambushes to lay for Scapula, I turned to the war band. They waited, shifting and uneasy. They knew they were moving into more rugged landscapes, where few crops would grow and only strong cattle would survive. They knew that the war was nearing its end.

I had never seen such weariness. Even the Mothers seemed to sigh in the wind's thin wail. I raised my hand before them, and smiled to reassure them that we fought for the Mothers, who needed us all to be strong.

Caradog called, the carnyx was blown, and we surged forward: one great, heaving beast of tribespeople, horses, cattle and carts. The war camp was moving again and I was at its head.

The road circled the township, passing the northern gateway. As we entered the forest, a small figure darted out from behind the trees.

My heart lurched. She had forgiven me and had come to say goodbye. I pulled my mare to the side of the road.

Manacca stepped forward, silent as a sparrow, and held up a small leather parcel, a talisman to ensure a safe reunion. I undid the leather fastening and took a deep breath of the fragrant herbs. Comfrey, nettle, rosemary, properly dried and in beautiful proportions. She had learnt the craft perfectly.

She stared up at me, wide-eyed, in wordless, proud delight. My heart clenched, I could not leave her here. She could ride in the front of my saddle with no strain on my mare.

I called Caradog to halt so I could rearrange my saddle packs, but he could not hear me. When I looked down again, Manacca had disappeared, slipped back into the woodland.

'Move on!' The call came from behind me.

I stuffed the pouch into the bodice of my under-robe and kicked my mare forward.

Four days later, Scapula attacked Llanmelin.

✛

The first message came to us as we were unpacking by the river Usk. Caradog and I were gathering tinder when we heard the rider approach. He wore a Silures tartan, but not that of Llanmelin, and by the pallor of his young face I knew the message was grave. Caradog ushered him to a clearing by the river's edge, where we could listen to his words in privacy. After a long draught of water, the rider spoke.

Scapula had sent two separate legions into Tir Silures within the space of a day. As we had predicted, one—the Fourteenth—had come from the north, marching into the Forest of Dean, then turning south toward Llanmelin.

Hefin had taken his warriors to ambush this northern force before it cleared the forest. A few hours later a second legion had crossed the Habren estuary by boat, to march on the township from the south. They had found it defenceless as a child.

'What of the townspeople?' said Caradog.

The rider paused and blinked. He was scarcely more than a boy. Our messengers were trained to bear news without response, but there were some stories that could leave no soul untouched.

I touched his arm. 'It is not easy to carry the messages of war,' I said. 'Tell us your news.'

Scapula had led the force that had come by boat. Some of the townspeople had fled through the northern gate before he blocked it, but most had not been swift enough.

I gasped. Manacca lived near the northern gate. By the Mothers, let her be safe, I prayed. 'Go on...' I urged.

Scapula had searched the township, settlements and forests for Caradog. When he learned that his prize had evaded him, he was so enraged that he slit the throat of his own soldier who had borne the news of the fruitless search. He then embarked on the most frenzied campaign of killing any Roman general had yet inflicted.

This was their *atrocitas*; the deliberate obliteration of homes, livestock, crops, equipment, temples and life. It was not a strategy designed to meet a threat—Rome was not threatened by children or animals, or the old or ill. It was designed to tell us that we did not exist, that we had no authority over our lives or our land, that we were forsaken and nothing could protect us.

'Who told you all this?' I asked.

'Scapula kept some alive to watch, then cast them free to spread the story to the other townships of the Silures. He means to weaken them with fear before he attacks.'

I stared at the shallow water gliding over pebbles at the river's edge, as the rider recounted the scenes that were described to him: the charred stumps of our dwellings, the smoking grain fields, the ravens that tugged at the bodies growing putrid in the summer sun.

He was igniting my own memories. But this time I could hold myself firm. We were protecting Môn and we were luring Scapula to his defeat. Llanmelin was the price of the greater goal. I was learning the truth of war.

'What of Hefin and his warriors?' said Caradog.

'They did not survive the forest ambush,' said the rider. 'Their bodies swing from the trees in which they had hidden to make their attack.'

Caradog took my hand.

✛

By the next full moon, we were deep enough in the mountains of Tir Ordovices to camp for several days at a time. West ocean winds kept the rounded peaks bare and we needed to nestle in the wooded valleys to ensure we were not seen by Roman scouts. Our own riders traversed the country like darting minnows, bringing us news of the new Roman front.

With his newly-captured territory behind him, Scapula had established a line at the lower Usk, north of Llanmelin. The Twentieth Legion remained in Tir Silures, guarding the townships at sword point to ensure no tribespeople escaped to join the war band. The Fourteenth Legion, with Scapula at its head, had marched into Tir Ordovices in pursuit of Caradog.

We sang no reaping songs and crowned no maiden with a wreath of wheat sheaves when the first harvest moon showed its round white cheek above the mountains. We were far from our crops and we could not afford to addle our minds with feasting and ale. We needed to be ever-watchful for the parties of ten or twelve soldiers that Scapula sent ahead to find us. We needed to kill them before they could betray our location.

On the narrow valley paths, it was not difficult for our warriors to ambush the Roman scouts from well-disguised vantages, our spears shooting from trees, as if the forest itself cast the weapons. Caradog rode with these fight bands, who cloaked themselves in the dawn or dusk, and were not averse to plunging a sword through a soldier's kidney as his morning piss steamed from the cold ground. Each time he would return, flushed, excited, and with a mood of invincibility that worried me almost as much as its opposite, for I knew one preceded the other, and neither were anchored in truth.

'Be careful, my love,' I cautioned one evening as we lay in our tent.

He had not long returned from an ambush on a band of fifteen auxiliaries who had come within half a day's march of our camp.

'Of what?' he said, with a smile that told me he was only partly in earnest.

'Of Scapula, you rooster. It is clear that he grows more determined...' The auxilia had traversed marshlands we had thought unpassable by those without knowledge of where the ground hardened enough to hold hooves.

He kissed my shoulder. Fifteen fresh Roman heads were draining on stakes at the entrance to our camp. He was aroused by the kill. 'But only I have you to advise me...'

'Why must it be you who leads the ambush? It is you Scapula seeks above all others. Why wave his quarry right under his nose?'

He raised his head and looked into my eyes. 'How can I call on the warriors' courage without showing my own?'

And I knew that he was right. His willingness to dance so close to the gates of Annwyn, to dangle himself before the Mothers as sacrifice to their war, was the very reason that the warriors followed him, that we all followed him.

I touched his face. 'Just do not underestimate Scapula.'

Caradog laughed. 'I do not.'

With the Fourteenth Legion edging forward through country we had thought would surely impede it, we needed to focus less on our attacks, and more on remaining hidden. Each week we could keep the soldiers trudging over sodden ground would further exhaust them. If we could elude Scapula until the end of the summer, he would be forced to either retreat or endure a bitter winter in the mountains.

Twice in the next few weeks, we struck camp and moved after only hours, as Scapula's scouts—clumsy and obvious as they crashed through the forest's late summer growth—came too close to our sanctuary. Our watchmen were deft and silent in knitted costumes of browns and greens that rendered them invisible in the foliage. They easily spied the enemy and planted decoys to paths that led scouts in false directions for days.

But to ensure our concealment, Caradog was forced to drive the war camp further north into steeper mountains, where our carts and cattle struggled through pathways barely wide enough for a single horse. He sent messages to Môn from each new location, requesting grain sacks, swords, tents, wheels and new horses when ours had stumbled to their death, or gone lame from too rugged a descent.

The small mountain townships gave us what they could, but if we did not find somewhere to settle soon, somewhere easily defended, where we could lease fields, sow a late summer crop, smoke meat, and aid the cows in birthing their calves, we would soon grow hungry.

It seemed that we had no choice but to move yet further north, back into the mountains of Eryr, where we had been told of a remote valley settlement called Branovi that was prepared to host us.

Caradog was hesitant. 'The walking will be slow,' he said, as the council met at our fire.

'The paths are not easy,' I agreed. 'But what is difficult for us, must surely be impossible for Scapula.'

We left the next day.

I rejoiced in the familiar landscape of Eryr; the towering, treeless slopes and the clefts of dense growth that nestled between them. Deep inland lakes mirrored the mountains, their chill waters flavoured with copper and iron. The forces of Annwyn brimmed beneath us. We would find protection here.

Caradog and I had yet not spoken it, but I knew we were not just looking for sanctuary. We were looking for country where we could stand strong in battle. These mountains were the guardians of Môn, proud, formidable, steeped in the hallucinatory mists of the holy isle. Luring Scapula here to fight would bring him close to our sacred stronghold, but the risk was worth taking. The treacherous peaks unsteadied the eye, the swirling mists deceived the senses. We understood these tricks of the Mothers. The Romans would not.

After five days we reached Branovi, where there was water and paddocks enough to sustain our livestock, and we were protected by escarpments on three sides. There had been no reports of Roman scouts at our heels since we had entered the mountains of Eryr. Caradog said we would stay.

We set about unloading the carts and preparing to slaughter one of our bulls, now that we had time enough to skin and butcher it. It was a relief to fully unpack the baskets, to set up bread ovens and looms.

But no sooner had we licked the roasted bull fat from our fingers one day later, than one of our watchmen cantered into the camp with word that a group of Scapula's scouts had breached the foothills of Eryr's slopes.

'Did you not break their path?' said Caradog, springing to his feet. 'There were nine men at that watch.'

'Of course,' gasped the breathless watchman. 'But all, save I, were slain.'

'Then they still approach—'

'And swiftly.'

Caradog immediately summoned a band of five warriors, who gathered spears, swords and rope, and thundered into the haze of dusk to sever this Roman hand before it felt out our hiding place.

By dawn they had returned, blood-splattered and shadow-eyed, with two of their number hanging limp across their horses' backs. The Roman soldiers were already halfway through the second pass of Eryr, when Caradog's men had found them on a lesser path that led directly to Branovi. They had ambushed the Roman scouts and captured their horses, but two of Scapula's men had escaped on foot.

No fresh-slain beef could disguise the bitter taste of what this meant: when the scouts returned to Scapula, he would learn that these mountains were our haven and come in pursuit. To our north was ocean. To our northwest was Môn. Our east was blocked with captured tribelands.

There was nowhere else to hide.

Caradog and I sat up late that night while the camp lay sleeping.

'I cannot believe he has pursued us so swiftly. It is as if we throw pebbles in his path instead of mountains.'

'You are the Empire's most wanted man. Such a prize will fuel a man.'

'You said he was sick.'

'Determination can cloak even the most painful ailments.'

We sat in silence, listening to the crackling flames. 'I wonder if you and he would enjoy a drink by the fire,' I said, 'if you were not enemies.'

Caradog snorted. 'I do not foresee it. He hates the very air I breathe.'

'Of course he hates you,' I said. 'But beneath that, do you not think he admires you?' I swirled the last of my ale in my cup. 'Just as you admire him.'

'He is a strong commander.'

I stared at his face, lit bronze by the dwindling fire. His hair and beard had grown long and unkempt in the weeks of travelling. He looked almost as a journeyman returned from forest seclusion. But he was not a journeyman. He was a warrior, a weapon-bearer, as I was a knowledge-bearer.

'You want to fight him, don't you?' I asked.

'With all my being.'

10

Some Souls

Some souls are born to a lowland path and walk without effort
over even ground.
Others are born to a precipice and must tread with
constant wariness.
Their path is more difficult,
but they see the world from a dizzying height.

'AILIA, LOOK at this.'

Caradog and I were riding back to Branovi, the river Glaslyn at our side. I stared up to where he was pointing: a slope rose on the other side of the river, as sheer as a wall, thick with bracken and young oaks growing outwards from its face.

'What?' I asked. The scene was no different from any other we had passed in the past few days. We had been riding among the settlements, appraising the mood of the Ordovices chiefs, testing their war vows, searching for a battle site that would favour our weapons and deny Scapula the flatlands he needed to make his formations. The chiefs were ready. They did not wish to remain at the brink of war for another season. They wanted to fight.

The legion was moving slowly. We still had time. But we had

found no strong places, only an abandoned copper mine, where we had sheltered from a violent summer storm this morning. Its entrance was a cleft in a grassy hillside, an hour's walk upstream, and we had spent far too long exploring its earth-scented passages, delighted that so secret an opening had led to such an otherworld of chambers and underground pools, still glinting with pink veins.

Caradog rode to the river's edge. 'Can we cross it here?' he said, staring into the water. 'Ailia, come! I think the horses can get through...'

'What are you doing?' I said as I approached. 'We do not need to cross—'

But his horse was already chest-deep in the gushing river. 'Ha!' He was grinning as I finally caught up to him in the river's belly. 'Look how well the water slows us.'

We emerged wet and bedraggled on the opposite shore. Caradog's face was alive. 'And now we are sodden, and our boots are heavy!'

'And we will be cold as we ride,' I said, wringing my skirt in irritation.

'This slope,' he said, ignoring me. 'See how it is already well-walled?'

I followed his gaze. Between the clumps of oak, bracken and ash were banks of limestone that made natural fortifications along the face of the mountain.

'Scapula will come from the south,' continued Caradog. 'He will need to cross the river. It is too fast upstream and too deep downstream. This is the only crossing point.'

'And we can attack them as they cross,' I said, starting to grasp his vision.

'The river will slow them...We can kill them with stones before they even reach the slope.' He strode to the base of the mountain and craned his neck upwards to study its surface. 'There are many strongholds for the warriors,' he said. 'Scapula's men will need their hands to climb. We will spear them as they ascend...' He turned to me, eyes blazing. 'Ailia, this could be our battle ground.'

'And what of the rear?'

'They can't get there but by crossing this river.'

'But if they did—?'

'There are yet steeper mountains, but I know not their shape.'

'Then let us find out,' I said.

We tethered the horses by the water and began to scramble upwards.

'This is good...' murmured Caradog, as we hauled ourselves up the hill face. The slope was intermittently grassy and rocky, secure enough to stand upon and cast a spear, but steep enough to make climbing slow.

We stopped to catch our breath on a small plateau. The mountain face to either side fell away in sheer drops, topped by ledges of stone that were almost begging for our warriors to stand upon them, in paint and headdress, screaming curses and drawing their arrows.

'It is as though the Mothers have crafted this ground for our purpose,' said Caradog in amazement.

'We are less than halfway,' I cautioned. 'We need to look further.'

We took several hours to explore the jags and crevices of the slope, marvelling at the view as we ascended, but nothing could prepare us for the outlook from the summit.

The mountains lay before us like sleeping giants. No longer dwarfed by their stature, we stood abreast of them, sucking their cold air into our pounding chests. We could see to the distant entranceways of the valley below and every corner of its lakes and flatlands. No matter from which direction it came, no army would be able to approach without being sighted hours before it reached the river crossing.

A long, flat ridge along the mountain's peak would allow our swordsmen to deploy their skills and slay, row by row, any Roman soldiers who might succeed in cresting the ascent. Behind this ridgeline were gentler descents and lush, grassy hollows, well-protected from the wind, perfect for the war band to camp in the days awaiting battle.

Impenetrable mountains formed a bulwark at our rear, but the gorge between them allowed an easy passage to the north, which we could use as a line of retreat if, by some chance, the Roman soldiers gained footing on the front face.

'It is perfect!' shouted Caradog over the howling wind.

We stood before each other as our hair whipped about our faces and our clothing flapped like flags. He reached for my hand and drew me against him. 'Is this where we will claim back our sovereignty?' he whispered into the chill of my upturned cheek.

And there, atop a mountain in the centre of the free tribelands, with my heart beating just a finger's width away from that of Albion's greatest war king, I felt the Mothers' intention surge up from the stone, through my legs and spine and into my chest. I knew that they had wrought this land to strengthen our fight, and that there could be no more powerful place for the warriors of Albion to meet Rome than this.

'Yes,' I said.

But with the utterance came a sadness that I could not fathom.

The mount was called Emrys, meaning immortal. We summoned a measurewoman to test its strength. She came with her plumb stone, wooden pegs and a long coil of horse-hair rope. I accompanied her to Emrys by torchlight an hour before sunrise.

She was old. Perhaps fifty summers, and walked with a hump in her spine that mirrored the mountain. She was scarcely taller than my waist, and her skin was mottled from a lifetime of turning her face to the sky.

She could not climb the mountain. 'Do not worry,' she assured me, tipping her pegs to the ground. 'I can measure from here.'

Under the faint colour of a pre-dawn sky, we walked to an area of flat ground near the mountain-base that permitted a clear view of the eastern horizon. Here, she observed the point at which the sun rose, set an anchor pole, then tracked its shadow throughout the day, marking directions and angles with the pegs and rope, chanting verses under her breath between taking each measure.

I stayed near her side, ready to take a rope end she would hold out or collect a peg that rolled from her reach. Measurement was one of the most sacred branches of journey-craft. Its practitioners positioned our towns, our shrines, our groves and the roads that joined them. Through the reckoning of the sun and the seasons that swayed it, they aligned us to the shape of all things.

The Roman surveyors had no idea of the directions we lived by. It was secret knowledge, passed only by voice and many years of practice. I marvelled at the skill, but my task, I reminded myself, as she called me to attention with a toothless smile, was not to learn it; my task was to protect it.

We returned to Branovi by late afternoon. Caradog strode forth to hear what wisdom the day had yielded. Carefully, he helped the measurewoman from her mount and led her to his fire, where she sipped a cupful of broth before she answered his questions.

'I know why this place called to you,' she finally said, her voice a rasp. 'A serpent lies stretched beneath the earth. At its head is the summer rise, at its tail is Môn. This mountain is its heart.'

'Then it is a strong place to meet an enemy?' pressed Caradog.

'There is no stronger.'

┿

We sent a rider to Môn. Only the journeymen, with their grain and gold and unbreakable ties to all of free Albion, could sanction this battle.

The sun rose and fell six times without a response, and each day saw Caradog pacing around the borders of Branovi while his warriors trained. His agitation was not without reason. Each day that dawned was another opportunity for the legion to move closer. Yet somehow, by the Mothers' grace, our riders informed us that Scapula remained still, as if he too was waiting on the word of Môn to decide the future of these tribelands.

At last a rider came bearing word from Sulien. Caradog and Rhain found me as I draped my washed under-robe over a hazel branch in the late morning sun.

'Ailia—' The war king bowed deeply, kissing my hand. When he lifted his face there was wild excitement in it. 'Cast down your work and go to the groves. See when the Mothers would have us commence battle.'

'They want you to fight?'

He grasped hold of my waist and lifted me high as he had on the first night we had feasted. 'There will be battle!'

'Môn desires it?' I asked, laughing as he set me down.

'Yes, yes, if you can see it...' He waved away the question, smiling at the crowd who were gathering around us.

I stilled. 'What do you mean, Caradog...*if I can see it?*'

Rhain spoke. 'Sulien has asked you to vision for the battle outcome. If you see us victorious, they will approve it. If you don't, we will not fight.'

I stared at him. 'It cannot rest on me.'

'Yet it does,' said Rhain.

'But they know I no longer claim the title of Kendra...'

'It is not your title they value,' said Rhain. 'They are ready to support battle but only if the Mothers command it by your voice.'

'No—' I looked from Rhain to Caradog. 'You know how deep this scar runs in me. Do not make me open it.'

'There is no other way,' said Caradog. 'Go to the forests without delay. Vision for battle. As soon as you have seen our victory, I will speak to the tribes.'

✝

With a thudding chest, I walked through the forest toward the nemeton where I would ritual. I carried what I would need to open my vision: wolfsbane steepings, rods, bells, and a linen sack that quivered with a live hare.

Neha kept pace, whimpering at the twitching sack.

We were deep within spruce forest, dim and moist. Flakes of light fell sparsely through the canopy. Branovi's head journeyman had sung me the twisting route that led to the grove. When I reached it, I would kindle a fire. I would sit day-long in a cycle of breath and song. Then, when the hours of chanting had thinned the boundary between our world and beyond, I would stand at the altar and permit the hare the bliss of my blade. In this small gesture of violence, I would glimpse something of our greater violence. I would peer into Annwyn through death's fissure and see an image of what would befall us in battle.

This time, I would tell no lie.

Neha halted in a convulsion of barking.

There was nothing ahead. I crouched at her bristling shoulder, quieting her. Then I saw it.

The serpent emerged smoothly from the leaf bed onto the path.

'Steady,' I whispered. 'It will pass.'

The adder was long, brilliantly patterned with a black saw-toothed spine against a moon-grey torso. It turned onto the path and rippled onwards in the direction we were heading.

I watched it, unbreathing, as it slid over a rise in the path, then disappeared down the other side. Slowly, keeping Neha to my heel, I edged forwards, hoping the snake would have returned to the undergrowth. When I mounted the crest I stopped in horror.

The pathway fell to a shallow dip. At its base, less than ten paces ahead, was not one, but perhaps twenty, thirty adders entangled in a writhing clump. I lurched backwards, shouting at Neha to stop her lunging.

Never had I known such a thing in flesh—only in song: the adders' nest, the egg of serpents. In the poems it was a manifestation of the Mothers' voice, a strong omen, though dangerous to observe, for the snakes, aroused by their mating frenzy, were easily stirred to attack.

Mesmerised, I watched as the ball of flesh seemed to remake itself in a constantly shifting knot. It was monstrous. And beautiful. I began to feel its pull. Slowly, the forest softened around me as the snakes grew more vivid. This slithering mass felt kin to me, as though my own heart were just as alive, entangled and ever-forming. I wanted to draw closer.

The serpent we had followed circled the pile, sensing where it might penetrate. I could smell the pungent secretions that seeped from its skin. It smelled like my kind.

Neha's bark was faint at the fringes of my awareness. There was only the snakes.

I walked forward.

With the vibration of my footfall, the serpent turned and reared. Its forked tongue flickered, tasting the air between us. The long, muscular rope of its body lifted until it was half off the ground, swaying and lurching through space before me, as if moved by the Mothers.

I knew no fear of it.

With my next step, it reared higher, unhinged its jaws to a yawning cavern, and bared the thin needles of its fangs.

I knew only its beauty. I moved closer again, right before the adder now. Its eyes were red, as if lit by fire.

I reached out my hand.

It hissed, swung backwards, then struck.

The bite pierced the enchantment. I staggered backwards, searing pain in my hand. I gripped my wrist to stem it, but I could not. The poison ran hot up my arm, into my heart. I cried out to the Mothers.

Then, with adder's venom pumping fast through my bloodstream, it came.

The knowing.

Certainty, in every vein.

I sank to my knees with the force of it. My heart pounded with its clarity. I squeezed my eyes shut, but there was no escaping this truth. In all my journeywoman's wisdom, I had never known anything with the sureness that I now knew this.

We would not win this war.

Rome would take Albion.

Neither Caradog nor I could protect these tribelands.

Poison now numbed my body. I could not feel my limbs. Odours of dung and a nearby carcass flooded my mouth. By Mothers, was I taking form? *Please no*, I begged. My spirit reached towards the escape, the rapture, of change, but I fought it back with all my strength.

I needed my human mind. I needed to think. This was a vision from which I must not flee. I braced my hands on the ground, determined to hold my shape. *Stay*, I willed, *stay*. I would not join the adders.

Where was Neha? I knew her presence would bind me. I could smell the oil of her coat and feel the shudder of her barks, but I saw only blurred shapes. With a strangled voice, I called her name and then she was beside me, whimpering, licking the sweat from my face. I laid my arm over her back, drawing her against me so I could lean on her trunk. She bore my weight as I shook and vomited onto the ground.

The change began to lift. I was left panting, my head hanging. Slowly I turned my face, seeing the bark of the spruce trunks with my own eyes and scenting their leaves with my own nostrils. I had held my form. The forces of change had heard my authority. I touched my hand. There was no bite, no pain. Praise the Mothers, it had been a conjuring to awaken my sight.

I stood. In the path's dip there was nothing but a scattering of fallen spruce. I had heard the adders' message. Now they were gone.

The Mothers had spoken. This land would be Rome's.

☩

I sat down on a fallen trunk by the path edge. A pair of warblers perched above me, trilling furiously. A fat, striped slug recoiled from my fingers splayed on the log. The forest seethed with life. I waited, poised for terror or despair. But neither came.

For as I sat, steeped in the vision of our defeat, I began to sense, beneath it, the stirrings of a deeper truth. With each moment of stillness I saw it more clearly.

Could it be that this battle was not a test of war, but of the very laws that our people held most dear? Nothing endured but by death and rebirth: the sun, seasons, crops, our souls. Only in the swirling rhythm of growth and destruction was life sustained. We knew this. Rome, hungry for expansion, did not.

This land was Albion's soul. What if we were not meant to protect it by triumph, but by allowing the Mothers to play out their inevitable poem of death and renewal? Could it be that our land had to fall in order for its soul to live?

I stared at the rotting leaves on the forest floor. If our defeat was necessary, then should we succumb, without battle, to Scapula's army? Should we sign a treaty without having heard the ring of even one sword against another? No. That would be a half-death, an impure sacrifice.

With a wave of horror, I saw what the Mothers asked of me.

Caradog would not fight if I told him the truth. None would ride into a doomed war.

I had to lie. I had to tell Caradog that we would prevail, that he must fight with every shred of his strength. For only such a battle would give us the song. The song of the greatest war king who had ever led the tribes. The song of the most noble battle ever fought on our soil. The song that would preserve the soul of Albion, like a dormant root in our dark earth, until our sovereignty could bloom again.

My task was not to silence this song.

My task was to ensure it would be sung.

Neha flopped at my feet, twitching as she settled, then laid her head on the ground. *Could I do it?* In anguish, I stroked her soft ear. *Could I lie to my people again?*

Then, with the same Mother's grace that had allowed me to see what was yet to befall us, I now peered into my past with a deeper sight. And I saw that even that lie, that failing, was a verse of Albion's story, the fall of her sovereign people, that they may be birthed anew. And I knew, for the first time, some true pardon.

There, in the forest's late light, I wept with the cruelty of what the Mothers asked me: to re-live the very act I had repented since it was done. But now I understood it. We would be this land's sacrifice. We would be its song.

I would tell my lie, but this time I would not allow myself to be hidden from its consequence. I would stand beside my war king in battle and play my part in this poem. I would give myself to this song.

To whomever survived to sing it.

If I sanctioned battle, Caradog would expect me to give him a day. I would choose one that was close. I could not carry the burden of this knowledge for any longer than a mother might be expected to carry the body of her dead child.

My legs were trembling but I knew they would not buckle. They would carry me back to my people and bear the weight of the falsehoods I would tell. I had been gifted a truth that I could not share with another soul.

I reached for my sack. I had forgotten the hare still within it. I loosened the opening. Spared of the sacrifice, it might as well run free. I tipped it onto the ground and watched it bound away.

Only when it had vanished into the undergrowth did I realise that Neha had not even roused at its scent. I nudged her softly with my foot. 'Wake up, dogess.'

Blood smudged my toe. In a flash, I was beside her, searching her pelt for the wound. There was a swelling on her left paw and two bleeding punctures in her skin. A serpent's bite. She must have run among them in the moments I had been gripped by change.

I knew the flowers and the treatments that could remedy an adder's bite. But they were not needed now. Her muscles were limp, her eyes glazed.

Neha was dead.

✝

I returned by late afternoon and spoke to Caradog in his tent. When we emerged, he called for a stump to be rolled up to the fire and set upright to stand on as he spoke.

The camp gathered at his cry.

I stood by his feet, but he hauled me onto the stump beside him.

'My people,' he began. 'The Mothers have spoken through the voice of our journeywoman.' He squeezed my forearm. 'They have seen the Roman soldiers bleeding and weak. They have seen our triumph.' A low murmur rippled through the gathering. 'Prepare to feast and gather for an offering this night,' he commanded, 'tomorrow we will move to the battle camp. And on the seventh day of the next moon—' his fingers tightened, '—we will fight.'

The crowd cheered and surged around Caradog as he leaped from the stump.

I dropped to my haunches and slipped down silently, watching the gathering as if from afar.

I could not see Rhain in the scattering crowd. After searching the journey-tents, I found him among the children, who were milling at the forest's edge, gathering sticks for the feast fire.

'Teacher—' I said to his bent back.

He turned. 'My queen!'

I laughed as we sat down on the grass, a few paces from the children's ears.

'The vision was clear?' he asked with tenderness.

'Yes,' I said. 'Very clear.' This, at least, was not a lie.

He smiled. 'I did not doubt you.'

I had learnt song at his side every day since we had left Tir Silures. Now I wanted to forge under his guidance before it was too late. 'Rhain—' I ventured. 'Might I sing tonight at the feast? I have felt the Mothers' blessing. I want to sing of it.'

He looked at me with one eye half-closed in shrewd appraisal.

I knew his face. I knew its weathers. But this time, I could not read him.

'I will sing tonight,' he said.

For some moments I stared at the ground in front of me, gouging ruts in the grass with a twig. 'Rhain—' I had never challenged him before. '—I want to sing of the power I have felt in the battle site, and the triumph I have seen...'

'No, no,' he said lightly, as if denying a child a second piece of bread.

I felt my breath grow tight. Then I asked what I had never asked. 'Why not?'

Rhain simply smiled. 'Not yet ready.'

Something burst within me. 'By the will of the Mothers, Rhain,' I said, my voice low, so the children would not become curious. 'I am scarred by the Mothers. I am Caradog's first advisor and wife. I bear this authority. What more must I do for you to allow me to sing?'

'Good, good...' he said, nodding. 'You are almost there.'

The speckled mare stood treading and whinnying at the fire's edge. The people of the camp and of greater Branovi had formed a circle to witness the ritual. I stood beside Caradog at the front of the gathering.

A temporary oak altar had been erected behind the fire. Two journeymen stood on each side of it, guarding the gateway to Annwyn so that the dead would not pour forth when it was opened. The mare was tied to the altar, her eyes rolling white, as golden seed oil was poured on her forelock.

The crowd parted to allow one of Branovi's journeywomen to come forward with a knife. She wore a black feather cloak, the costume of all whose task it was to open the gates. I had been asked to wear it this night, but I had declined. I was too weakened by what I had seen to endure the rupture of sacrifice.

The journeywoman positioned herself before the mare, who snorted and strained at the ropes. She raised her knife. Two lesser journeymen mounted the platform and pulled the animal's head back by her leather halter, exposing her tendinous throat. She reared and screamed, shaking the altar with the force of her resistance.

The flames surged as a journeyman fed them with branches. It was the art of the officiant to ensure that the mare's blood would touch, but not douse, the flames.

Everyone stood in silent reverence. This offering was for all of us. To cleanse, to heal, to contain our terror.

I pressed my temple against Caradog's shoulder. Only I knew how important this kill was, how greatly we needed to sense our land's sacredness.

'Mothers of Eryr,' declaimed the journeywoman in the resonant tone of those trained in ceremony. 'We offer you blood, in honour of your power. Let it make a river to Annwyn, by which your song will strengthen our weapons as we fight in your name.'

She brushed her blade across the mare's flesh, opening her skin, her throat. The animal gurgled as the pipes of her neck spurted. Her legs gave way and the weight of her body shook the earth we stood on.

✟

We moved to Emrys.

Caradog set the men to building the fortifications on the southern slope, the battle site. The natural embankments had to be widened with ramparts of tightly-packed stone. Gruelling days were spent carrying rocks and rolling boulders up from the river's edge. Stones inevitably escaped their handler's grasp, crushing feet and snapping spines as they tumbled back down to their watery bed.

Caradog kept our spirits high, lifting the heaviest boulders himself, until the mountain face was an impregnable fortress of walls braced with timber containments, sheer drops, and hidden strongholds.

Behind each walled platform was a waist-high pile of fist-sized river stones, which we would hurl down on the ascending soldiers.

To link the platforms, we built ladders and short bridges that would enable the warriors to move swiftly around the battleground, yet could be quickly withdrawn from an enemy in pursuit.

Caradog sent riders to the Ordovices, to the uncaptured tribes of the Deceangli and the Silures, even to the Demetae in Albion's far west.

Within two dawns, the chiefs and their war bands began trickling into the camp on horses laden with spears, arrows and balls of iron. None brought their war chariots. This was not to be a spectacle, where golden painted war birds thundered over open fields behind sleek black horses. This was to be warriors in kinship with the mountain, killing as quickly as their stones would allow.

First came the Ordovices, many of whom had fought at Tir Dobunni and were eager for another success. Then came the Deceangli, scarred by the *atrocitas*, but no less hungry to kill. The Demetae warriors, small groups of wary-eyed men, were the first of this remote tribe to join the war. Their strange, rolling dialect was hard to decipher, but the clang of their swords against Caradog's in pledge of their loyalty, was as clear as the autumn sky.

Lastly, amid tears of welcome, came the bands from the Silures, seething with hatred for the enemy who had only just entered their tribelands, thinning their numbers, but not their spirit.

'What is known of Llanmelin?' I asked one of the chiefs later, as we drank ale by our fire with these tribesmen whose land we had shared.

'Lost,' he said. 'The Romans are thick as fleas on a dog, guarding it, although it is nothing more than a tomb.'

I sipped my ale and prayed for Manacca.

More arrivals filtered over the borders from the Cornovii and the Dobunni: foolhardy fighters who cared so greatly for Albion's freedom that they risked capture at the enemy line in order to lend their spears to this battle.

Caradog was aflame, sleeping little by night, yet brimming with vigour throughout each day. I saw how he thrived in the task of preparing for battle, how standing proud as war king summoned what was truest in him. The loyalty of the tribes was his milk and he drank thirstily, offering hope in return.

While his spirit grew, my own shrank with every new arrival. Each dawn I sat alone on the cliff edge, asking myself if I acted in truth, holding my knowledge up to Lleu's scrutiny, weighing it, re-living the vision, and enduring the grief of what it meant. Every day I came afresh to the same conviction: Albion would be renewed by this destruction, and I must not stop it.

At last the incoming bands ceased. There were almost twenty thousand warriors camped in the gullies behind the mountain. Môn had sent grain, dried meat, ale and coin for trade with the nearby craftsmen. The weapons were positioned.

We were ready. Now we would cease patrolling the paths and allow the people of the camps to burn large fires and gather openly in the valley. The Roman scouts would soon see the smoke, the weapons, the numbers, and Scapula would not resist the chance to meet his enemy at last.

Standing with Caradog on the bank of the rushing Glaslyn, I stared up at the craggy slopes of our mountain. The Romans would not be able to work their formations, outflank us or make use of their short swords. Their heavy shields would only be a hindrance when both hands would be needed to climb. We, by contrast, would be strong on the steep network of platforms, free to use the spears, arrows and long swords with which our warriors were most skilled.

It was hard to imagine that we would not triumph.

Caradog pulled me against him. He smelled of the mare fat he'd used to oil his leather shield, which now stood gleaming at the foot of the mountain with all the other warriors' shields.

'We have done it,' he said softly.

I nodded, turning my face into his chest so he would not see my tears.

✠

That night, a servant roused me from a restless sleep.

Euvrain's baby was ready to be born. She asked for me.

I attended her in her tent as she howled and writhed with a pain I had not witnessed in a mother that lived. In whispered pleas, she begged to be released of it.

'The child comes,' I assured her, though I knew no certainty. 'Do not abandon it.' Kneeling between her legs, I gasped with relief as a bloodied skull began to bulge at the fleshy brink. With two earth-parting bellows, I grasped a tiny, purple girl in my hands.

I laid her on her mother's breast, but the babe could only stare in round-eyed wonder, too wakeful to suck.

'Look, how curious she is!' I laughed as I severed the cord with my knife. 'And she is fair, like you.'

Euvrain took my wrist. 'Make sure she is safe.'

✠

'Romans to the south!'

I heard the watchman's cry from within my tent. It was mid-morning, four dawns since we had opened the paths to await Scapula, one dawn before my chosen day of war.

Caradog and several other chiefs were already at the viewing platform as I mounted the ladder and looked out. There, blurred by

291

distance yet unmistakeable, were the scarlet-clad figures of Scapula's army, pouring into a clearing about two leagues to our east.

'They are less than a half day's march away,' said one of the chiefs. 'I will tell my men we will fight today.'

'Wait—' Caradog frowned as he watched the army. Smoke rose from their midst. 'They are setting camp. They will move tomorrow.'

'On the very day I chose,' I murmured.

'Do you see, Ailia?' said Caradog. 'The Mothers are telling this story.'

I watched him staring at the enemy from whom he had been hiding for seven summers. He looked at me and smiled. The sunlight caught his eyes, turning them green as young oak leaves.

'Come,' he said to the chiefs. 'Let us send some riders out to reckon their numbers. Then we'll speak to the fighters. Ailia—' he called back from the top of the ladder, 'prepare the plants to ready the warriors.' He jumped off the platform, landing hard on his feet.

In allowing us to see him before he marched on our camp, Scapula had relinquished the advantage of surprise, giving us half a day to prepare. But he had claimed another, perhaps greater, benefit: time for our fear to take hold.

As the warriors paced through their swordcraft, an unease began to spread among them. I could smell it in their sweat as they parried one another. I could see it in the anger that erupted when a poorly-blocked swipe cut too deep into a shoulder or forearm.

With two initiates in assistance, I walked among them for all the hours of the sun's descent, giving them goldenseal to release their fear, and nightshade to numb pain.

Tomorrow they would face an army that had enslaved most of the known world. Of course they were frightened.

The evening brought a second cry from the northern watchmen. Was this to be Scapula's death blow? A late day ambush from the rear? Surely the scouts could not have failed to sight it. I found Caradog at the camp's northern boundary, watching in disbelief as a stream of people emerged from the woodland. One final tribe had come to join the war band.

I gasped, half-laughing, as they walked towards us. Their dark green tartans and horsehair flags belonged to none other than the Brigantes.

Their leader dismounted and stood before Caradog. I recognised the chieftain from our travels through southern Tir Brigantes. He had been one of those who had sheltered us. He unstopped his flask and poured ale on the ground at Caradog's feet. 'We fight beside you, War King of Albion.'

Caradog took the chief's hand and kissed it. 'Has your queen released you to this war task?'

'We are here with no blessing from Cartimandua,' said the chief. 'We must succeed tomorrow. For when she learns we have come, we will find no welcome in Tir Brigantes.'

Caradog nodded. His war band was full of such landless fighters. 'And Venutius?'

'He sent us weapons and scouts to aid our passage.' The chief paused. 'He is still friend to you.'

I brushed my hand over Caradog's back. He had been emboldened by every tribe that had knelt to him, but this—the Brigantes—was the gemstone in his crown. There were at least two thousand men and women gathered in the clearing before us. With this allegiance now given, he stood as Albion's greatest war king.

He threw back his head and let loose a caterwauling war cry, ululating into the crimson sky. The chief laughed then echoed him, as did the Brigantes arrivals and all of Albion's war band, until the entire valley filled with our sound.

Scapula could not have failed to hear it.

As darkness fell, Caradog dressed for ceremony in our tent. It was time to speak to the warriors, to inspirit them for what they must face on Lleu's next rise.

'I want you to come with me,' he said as he fastened his cloak with a thick bronze fibula.

'Of course.' I handed him his chieftain's torc. I had been dreading the request. I had no heart to walk among the men for a second time, to look upon their bodies, knowing that most would lie dead on the earth tomorrow. But I had no claim to the luxury of cowardice.

Grouped in their tribes, the warriors were spread throughout the gullies of the mountain's rear slope. Caradog moved like lightning between them, charging the air with his final battle words, mocking the Romans and proclaiming his certainty that victory was ours. At every hearth he stood with flame light on his face, lit like a god against the mountain darkness, calling on the names of the ancestors who had defended Albion's soil in Rome's first attack.

Rhain stood at his side in bells and feathers, verifying the histories and intoning the bloodlines with rising pitch. He and I followed the War King from camp to camp, as he ensured that every warrior who had pledged to fight heard his call and drank of his spirit. After seven years of crawling in mud, lurking in forests and scrapping like wolves in the cover of darkness, we had reached this moment of light.

'What you hold in your hands,' he told the fighters, 'is nothing less than the future of Albion. Tomorrow you will either win back our freedom or mark the beginning of our eternal slavery. By your swords,

Rome will either claim these lands or be banished forever. Which do you desire?'

Every tribesman was enflamed.

I stood in full journeywoman's regalia, Albion's highest knowledge-bearer beside Albion's highest king. But my knowledge was a wound and my task was to bear it. Across the blazing campfire I met Rhain's eye. How glad I was that he had deemed me unready to sing. What lay within me could not be voiced.

Later, I sat alone in darkness outside my tent. Voices drifted from the war camps, where the men took their last meal before battle.

I could not eat. Tomorrow I would fight and scream the journeywoman's curses. But tonight I was the wife of a man who may not live beyond Lleu's next fall. I had seen Albion defeated. I had not seen what would become of the man I loved.

Beneath his kingship, Caradog was human flesh, a beating heart and a tangled mind that knew me better than any other. Love had made us kin. If he survived our defeat, we might yet live wild, or in the sanctuary of Môn, exiled but together. Even his death in battle I could accept. But for him to be captured, to be carried to Rome, tortured and mocked there as the trophy I knew Scapula so desperately sought, this I could not endure.

I hoped I would be killed and spared any knowledge of it. But I feared the Mothers would not be so kind.

'Ailia?' Caradog had found my refuge. 'Why are you hiding? We are still at the fire...' He crouched before me, then noticed my face. 'My love, what's wrong?'

'I...I do not know what will happen tomorrow.'

'But you do...' He frowned. 'The Mothers have told you we will succeed.'

'Ay,' I said. 'But what if you are lost in the success?'

He laughed. 'Faithless! I have not been war king of Albion for seven years because I cannot swing a sword.'

'And what if the Mothers' prediction was wrong, and it is we who are defeated?' The falsehood, the trickery, sat like iron in my belly. I wanted to vomit it out, yet this was my task, to ensure this cursed battle was fought.

'It may be so,' said Caradog. 'This is why the Mothers have sent the Brigantes to my war.'

'What is your meaning?' I asked, suspicious.

'The Brigantes are ripe to rise,' he said. 'We have already planned paths of retreat that lead to the north. If Scapula's army is stronger tomorrow, I will not push my men into a needless sacrifice. I will pull them back...'

'And then?' I asked, dreading what I knew he would say.

'I will go to Tir Brigantes. I will raise another war band there—'

'No!' I cried. 'Were you deaf to Cartimandua's promise? She will give you to Scapula.'

'I can evade Cartimandua. I will speak to Venutius. For every fighter who came here from the Brigantes today, there will be one hundred more who are hungry to rise. I need only to ignite them.'

I stared at his face, just visible in the moon's glow. When would be enough? 'You have told the men that this is the final battle,' I said. 'But now you say you will go on.'

'Of course I will,' he said, frowning again. 'What warrior am I if I cease to stand against this enemy?'

I fought a swelling anger. 'Is this your concern?' I asked. 'Your warrior's name? What of us? What of the men and women you drag with you through this endless river of war?'

He stared at me, then said slowly, 'You speak as if we were damned. And yet it was you who foresaw our success.'

'Yes...' *Please do not ask me to confirm it*, I begged him silently.

I had no strength to uphold the lie.

He took hold of my fingers. 'Worry not, Ailia. Trust in your vision.'

I pulled my hand free. 'You should sleep,' I said.

'I know.' He looked towards the camps. 'The men have gone quiet. I'll stay here now.'

We sat in the darkness, each with our own thoughts of the morrow.

Beyond the clearing, frogs beat a steady trill, tiny drums of bone and skin, marking the passing of the hours, yet knowing nothing of time's threat. We, in all our learned stupidity, were the only creatures who lived in terror of time.

Inside our tent, I held Caradog's naked warmth against me, sucking his scent into my lungs as if it were my last breath of him.

⁜

By dawn's first light, I prepared to paint the war king's face. He sat on a log before me.

Into a tiny pot of his seed, freshly milked upon waking, I tipped the powdered woad, stirring it quickly to make a binding paste. I dipped a sharpened twig into the colour and brought it to his cheek. 'Look up!'

He turned his face to the sky.

Carefully, I marked a blue line across his cheekbone. The potent colour had only moments to soak into the pores of his skin, before it dried crisp. Working deftly across his nose and brow, I drew the arcs and spirals that would make him seem monstrous and inhuman in battle, terrifying the Romans, while heartening his fighters, who understood the swirling symbols of kinship.

I patterned the translucent skin of his temples, working down to where his beard sprouted in wiry curls. His breath was warm on my cheek. What a privilege it was to know so intimately the furrows and textures of this mighty face.

'Ailia—?' His voice was quiet.

'Yes, my love.'

He hesitated, then said, 'Am I noble? Do I fight for what is true?'

I turned back to him. Never had I loved him more. 'Yes,' I said, with all my heart. 'The fact that you ask it means the answer is yes.'

A soft wind stirred the air around us.

'You have...' he faltered, '... accused me of fighting for my own glory.'

'And so you do.'

Here, between the brightening horizon and the moon sunk low in the western sky, the oppositions were in perfect balance. He was indeed fed by power, enlivened by pride, yet whatever he claimed of Lleu's splendour, he gave back to Albion a hundredfold in the radiance of his vision. His glory was ours.

'In three thousand summers they will tell your story,' I said. 'You are giving Albion her future.' I pressed my lips against his, before taking the twig to his shaven chest.

He was the eye of the animal that would meet sacrifice this day. He did not know how noble he was.

Within an hour of sunrise we were positioned on the mountain. The warriors were shirtless, their skin painted, their wrists wrapped with fur, their hair spiked with limewater. The mountain was strewn with skulls and poles tied with ribbons of fur that flapped in the wind.

I stood at the crest of the hill with a hundred other journeypeople, ready to pour down curses as the soldiers approached. I wore a dog-skull headdress, unbraided hair and ropes of knuckles, bells and feathers around my hips. All our totemic power was invoked to meet this enemy.

Caradog stood midway down the mountain, positioned on a ledge that was visible to the warriors both above and below him.

Please Mothers, I prayed, looking to the empty clearing where Scapula had been camped, *let them come soon. Let our defeat be swift if it cannot be altered*. But I knew, even as I made my silent call, that we must fight as long and hard as we had ever fought. For this would be the strength of the story.

The sun rose higher, yet there was no cry from the watchmen to tell us Scapula approached. He had drawn his army into the thick forests behind our closest hill and appeared to have stopped there.

Lleu reached his peak then began his descent, and still the watchman was silent.

For the full arc of the sun, we stood in wait.

Scapula did not come.

'It is but a strategy,' said Caradog to the warriors as they gathered at the camp after dusk. 'He seeks us to become wearied from our own readiness. They will come tomorrow.'

But they did not come the next day.

Nor the next.

Nor the one after that.

What was their intent? I anguished as we returned from our positions for the fourth time. Were they approaching from another direction? No watchman had seen them cross the river.

'He's not going to march,' said the Brigantes chief as Caradog and I visited his fire. 'He is mocking us as we await him, while he prepares an attack at a ground of his choosing.'

'Do not kindle this falsehood among the men,' said Caradog. 'I know this general's pride. He will not evade battle.'

But it was too late. The war band was hungry from the camp's spare rations and worn from the tension of being four days poised for attack. They were used to stealth fighting: quick, brutal and set to their timing.

The rumbling doubt of the Brigantes spread like fire among the men. Scapula would not come. He would have us wait like hopeful pups, each day belittling us further. Warriors of Albion waited for no one.

Caradog slept fitfully and emerged from his tent in the pre-dawn light to find warriors packing their carts. Some were already departing down the valley pathway.

Caradog strode among them, commanding them to stay, shaming them for their disloyalty, imploring them to honour their oaths.

'We will fight beside you when there is an enemy to fight,' they cried. 'We are no toy for the Romans.' More and more were walking away.

Blood pounded in my head as I walked behind him and watched this unravelling. This could not happen. The battle had to be as the Mothers had foretold it. This was our future.

'Follow me,' I said to Caradog, catching his hand. 'There is a place from where they will hear you.' I began climbing up the rear of the mountain as fast as I could.

Breathless, we reached a vantage that overlooked the northern valley. A narrow ledge of rock jutted over the pathway along which the war band was trailing away.

I waited behind in an open hollow as Caradog walked out to the precipice. Wind flapped his tunic against his torso. It would surely drown his voice.

'War King!' I hissed. 'Call on the ancestors—'

He nodded and, again, called forth the lineages of the warriors that had so heartened the men on the eve of the first day, shouting their names into the skin-coloured sky. But they fell unheard on the backs of the tribespeople.

Our war band was retreating.

I leaned back against the mountain stone. We were destined to lose this mighty place. But if it fell without sacrifice—unbound to us by battle or story—then how could it ever again be ours?

Caradog stood unspeaking.

Suddenly the sun lifted over the eastern ridgeline, casting a flood of light into the valley. I looked down against the brightness, and there—translucent between sandstone pebbles—was the ghost of a snake: a sheath as pale and delicate as river froth. I crouched to look closer. Every contour of its form was intact. Even its eyes had been shed. I touched its brittle surface. How faithfully it evoked the adder, yet it was not the adder. It was skin, emptied of flesh. Against it, my own hands were blood pink—something in their simple, human power, no greater or lesser than any other's, allowed me, at last, to see what I was.

I surged forward, pulling Caradog back and taking his place on the thin lip of rock. The wind threatened to topple me, but I shouted, with all my strength to the warriors below. 'Hear me speak.'

I saw the fighters halt, tribe by tribe, and turn to face me.

Rhain had joined Caradog. 'Ailia!' he hissed from behind me. 'The war king must address them.'

I no longer cared for Rhain's permission. Wind tore through my hair. The Mothers' song flowed up through my feet, anchoring me. 'Hear this,' I commanded, 'that you will return.'

Every face was now uplifted to behold me. 'The Romans will come,' I began. 'The Mothers have foretold it. It may be this day. It may be on the next moon. But whenever they come, they will find us waiting. Because this land, this mountain, has asked for battle. A battle that will decide our sovereignty.'

I did not shout or roar, but my voice seemed to reach every crevice of the landscape.

'This land wants to taste sacrifice,' I continued. 'But whose blood will sate it? The Mothers say Scapula's. I have doubted it, as I know every one of you has doubted it too. This is why you have turned away. And you are right to doubt it. For in truth we may fail—'

'Enough, Ailia!' said Caradog, 'Speak not of failure—'

I glanced back at him. 'Trust me...'

His face was dark with unease.

'Let her speak,' said Rhain, touching his arm.

Caradog paused, then nodded, and I turned back to my people.

'But if we must fail,' I said, 'let us fail because Rome defeated us in a fight to the death, not because we abandoned our Mothers before we even raised a spear.'

The war band listened, unmoving.

I sensed Caradog had moved to my side, though I did not lift my gaze from the tribespeople before me. 'Whether we win or lose, *let us fight!*' I cried. 'For our fight will forge a story that will endure beyond the oldest oak. And all will know, by this song, by this battle, how deeply the Mothers of Albion are loved and will always be loved.'

Caradog reached for my hand. I squeezed it once, then let it go. I was not yet finished. I took a deep breath. 'I am Ailia, witness to the Singing. Voice of the Mothers. I ask you to honour your war king. I ask you to fight.'

The wind had dropped. The entire valley, its trees and the great swell of its mountains, were poised in silence.

'Do not be still!' I called to the warriors. 'Raise your weapons if you have heard me. Sound your voices if you will stay.'

There was a moment as brief as a breath—though it seemed as if it would last forever—and then, by the grace of the Mothers, the tribespeople began to lift their swords.

With a surge, as sure as the tide, a shifting ocean of iron and bronze emerged from the upheld hands of the men and women before me. A sound, first low and growling, then gathering in strength, broke from their throats in an eruption of noise—an animal bellow from the land itself.

Now I sought Caradog's hand. The poem would be told.

Leaving Caradog to command the warriors back to their positions, I staggered, faint with relief, back to the shelter where Rhain steadied me with a draught of ale.

'Now,' he said, smiling. 'Now you have the authority. Now you are ready to forge.'

Just as I opened my mouth to respond, the sharp blast of the watchman's carnyx rang through the valley.

'The enemy is sighted,' called the eastern guard. 'Two leagues to the east.'

My stomach dropped as Rhain and I locked eyes.

Scapula was on his way.

11

Death

Death divides our seasons, our day, our home.
Our rituals enact it. Our gates and lintels wear its skulls.
What are we but that which must die?

W E WERE ready. Our scouts had been tracking Scapula's
approach for the past few hours, galloping back and forth
between Caradog and the watchmen positioned along the ridgelines.

The sky had filled with low, grey cloud that made the mountains
appear to rise without limit. The river Glaslyn was a torrent, coursing
at our feet—the first great warrior of our band.

Again the carnyx blasted. I felt the collective tightening of fists
around spear shafts. They had passed the final watchman. They were
moments away.

All eyes stared at the shivering forest.

I had seen the Roman army at rest after slaughter. I had seen them
in ambush and in twos or fours on the roadway. But nothing could
have prepared me for the sight of Scapula's Fourteenth Legion—twelve

thousand men—flooding forth from the tree line in breathtaking unison, three abreast, they emerged, identical forms in bronze and red, each a sinew, a muscle, of a greater beast.

My belly twisted in terror. It was beauty and power I had not expected.

Behind the legions came the auxilia, more disparate in dress, yet lacking none of the discipline and unity that had carried these men through weeks of marching through mud and marshes.

The warriors stiffened, as though the mountain itself had raised its hackles, and watched, unmoving, as the soldiers made formation on the Glaslyn's south bank. It took a full hour for the force to assemble, the legion in tight rows, the auxilia at their rear and flanks, mostly on foot, perhaps a quarter on horses. Even once they had come to formation, the soldiers did not lift their gaze to look at us, but stared straight ahead, as if we were not there.

A commander, on a chestnut stallion, rode back and forth before them.

'Is it him?' I whispered to Rhain.

'Ay. He wears the governor's plume. That is Scapula.'

He was smaller than I had imagined and I knew his cough-weary chest could not have filled the gilded swell of the breastplate that covered it, but even from this distance, I could see the fury that brimmed in his muscles. And although he was Roman from his costume to his hairless cheeks, I recognised the assurance with which he paced the ground. It was the same as Caradog's.

For several hours he and his scouts rode the bank of the river in both directions, surveying the ground beyond it, looking for other ways to approach the mountain.

But Caradog had chosen well. The sides of the mountain were too steep to ascend and the terrain at the rear was impassable, save for the narrow paths through the gullies, which were heavily guarded.

Scapula had no choice but to approach head on.

He came to stand before his men and, for the first time, faced his enemy. His stare drank in every one of us, lingering on our war king with a twitch of recognition.

Caradog lifted his arm. In a low, steady voice he called, 'Begin the cry!'

With their next breath, the warriors commenced the guttural ululations that preceded battle. The volume rose and echoed off the surrounding cliffs, filling the valley with noise as if the mountains themselves were screaming their protest. As it reached its peak the journeypeople started to curse, screeching one atop another in a deluge of wrath:

The ancestors are with us. Already you have died.
The spirits of the mountain hunger for your souls.
They will dig out your eyes and smash your skulls.
This is the will of the mountain, you are powerless against it.
The land is with us. You will die this day.

The soldiers still did not raise their eyes, but in the almost imperceptible shifting of their weight, I saw that our words found their mark. More than any weapon, the Romans feared the unseen forces that seethed in Albion's mists and rivers. As our cries continued, I saw fear in their faces and the hastening of their breath.

'Do not heed their savagery!' cried Scapula over the din. 'They call on magic because they are too weak to defeat us.'

Against the backdrop of our noise, he had been pacing the river, murmuring to his scouts, searching the brown depths for the easiest crossing. Now he stood at the water's edge and raised his arm. 'Prepare!'

In startling unison, the full Roman force brought their shields to their chests, their staunchness restored. It was its own kind of magic, and I marvelled at this oneness.

The warriors' cries had quieted with Scapula's call.

'Auxilia come forward!' shouted Scapula.

These lesser-valued soldiers moved down each side of the infantry and assembled at their front.

Scapula brought his stallion to the shore. 'Advance!'

When the first soldier's sandal was wet in the river, Caradog shouted for the arrows to fall.

Our screams resumed with our weapon fire.

The water began to run red as bodies eddied downstream. But for each auxiliary we hit, twenty more surged behind them, and no warrior could load fast enough to keep pace with their number.

Swiftly, the auxilia waded through the river, flanked by those on swimming horses. The first to complete the crossing had borne ropes to form hand-holds across the water, which the others now clung to, their shields held aloft, protecting their shoulders and necks from attack.

Still we rained down our arrows, piercing their outstretched hands, their submerged thighs, knocking shields from wet fingers with the force of our slings. By the grace of the Mothers, it was succeeding. They were suffering many hundreds of fatalities as we endured none.

Those who survived the crossing quickly made formation and readied to march on our ramparts. No sooner had the first line reached the base of our defences, than the battle truly began. With carnyxes screeching from every ridgeline, a deluge of spears and stones poured down from the mountain.

For every depleted row of Scapula's men, there was another behind it, each advancing a few steps higher than the one before. But our position was too strong. They could not breach the first embankment.

On and on we cast down our fire, with all our hatred for this enemy and what they had done. I watched the ground turning dark with their blood and the awkward shapes of their fallen men, spasming as fresh soldiers marched over their bodies and slid in the viscera.

Shrieking curses, the warriors fought like gods, plunging their knives into the throats of whichever of Scapula's men managed to raise their head above the lower ramparts, pulping with axes any hands that found purchase over the walls.

The fighters on the upper slope still hurled their missiles, knocking down soldiers as they struggled to scale the fortifications without relinquishing their shields.

Some of our men were now falling. Several naked painted backs lay slumped over the lower ramparts, while others had fallen to the wet mash of bodies below. But our numbers of dead were far fewer than Rome's.

I paused for breath, my throat raw from cursing. We were eagles, feasting on scrabbling mice. In the fire of battle, I lost all thought of the vision. I turned and grabbed a stone for my sling. We would triumph today. We would defeat Rome after all.

A trumpet blasted from the enemy—harsher, more precise than our own wailing carnyxes—and the Roman soldiers halted their advance.

'*Testudo*, front advance!' shouted Scapula, mounted beside the legionaries who had not yet begun the ascent.

Then, like some mystical conjuring, the auxiliaries slipped back like water and the legionaries surged forward into the tightest formation, each raising their shield above their head, locking it firmly against those beside him. It was as if the Mothers had birthed a mythical beast with a shell so unbreachable that our stones merely bounced from its surface.

The tumble of our stones and curses died away as we watched this mighty tortoise stand proud, motionless, gathering itself for what would come. Then, with another shout from Scapula, and a trumpet call to relay it through the men, the immense animal began to move in slow, shuddering steps towards the mountain.

When it reached the embankment it came to a stop. From beneath the shell we heard the sounds of picks clattering against stone. Under the safety of cover they were dismantling the walls.

'Resume!' shouted Caradog and the warriors recommenced their hurling of rocks.

There were dents, small cracks, but the shield-plate held and the tortoise barely flinched as it nosed deeper into the rampart. With the loosening of the stones, the walls were easily lowered and spread in low piles, which now formed footholds up the slope.

Still Scapula's men were being killed, crushed by our boulders, but this was no hindrance to the greater animal for whom the skulls of fallen kin were just pebbles on the path of its steady ascent.

Once the first Romans had found foothold on the narrow platforms, the warriors' long swords were clumsy against the enemy's jabbing gladia, and it was now the tribesmen's blood that seeped down through the stones.

'Mothers stay with us,' I whispered. The battle was turning to fulfil the vision. I gripped the hilt of my sword to stop myself shaking. My pile of sling stones was still high but there was little use in launching missiles that would now just as easily hit our kinsmen as our enemy.

With the first bank defeated, the shelled beast reformed and resumed its path upwards.

All those on the higher defences stared down, realising with horror that our positions would not hold, that the strongest walls had already been overcome and ours would offer no obstacle. Caradog had moved down to fight on the lower banks and was now ascending to rejoin his own band. 'Warriors, move up!' he called to the fighters. 'Move to the plateau and ready your weapons.'

We were to retreat to the hilltop for open battle. Now it was the tribesmen who moved swiftly as water, deftly scaling the mountain, abandoning their defences.

I commanded the unweaponed journeypeople to take shelter, while I tore off my headdress in readiness to fight.

I embraced Caradog briefly as he crested, before he leaped to a platform to speak to the fighters. We had but moments to prepare for the hand-battle.

'He has lost many men,' called Caradog from the crag of rock. 'We exceed him in numbers now. Split their formations! Force them to turn and break! Man on man we are greater. Fight with every shred of your soul—'

His voice was cut off by the wet suck of a spear into flesh and the silent collapse of the tribesman who had stood at his feet.

No longer assailed by our slings and arrows, the soldiers abandoned their *testudo* formation, drawing their shields tight before their chests and commencing the ruthless, thrusting attack that could fell an enemy as a scythe through a field.

I took position beside Caradog.

'Go back!' he hissed. 'Go back to Euvrain and the children and wait for me there.'

'No.' I raised my sword.

We fought together.

Caradog's sword was like fire around him. I slashed and blocked at his side with all my strength. He used a shield and threw me one that had fallen with its owner. Intuitively, we fought back to back, to form a greater creature of our own, two-headed, one-souled, its claws tearing through muscle with furious speed.

The Romans pushed forward, grim-faced, taking no pleasure in the battle they had so long sought. As each line tired, they were called by a lower commander to peel back to the rear, and a vigorous row stepped forth to replace them.

Again and again, I threw my shielded weight against the legionaries, clattering against them, using my woman's voice to curse and disorient them, before hooking my weapon up into their ribs. Between opponents I glanced around me. The Romans had method and unity, but we fought with nobility, lustful and raw. We fought with defiance. We fought for our story.

The air filled with the sounds of killing: grunts, shouts, cries to the gods, the soft splash of entrails released to the ground. The grass was slippery with blood and shit.

But despite our fearlessness, our frenzied pattern was no match for the ordered design of Scapula's army, who were gradually consuming us.

My sword arm was burning; the other throbbed from holding the shield. At the edge of my vision, I saw the fleeting shapes of another force cresting the mount. 'Caradog, look to the north!'

Scapula's strategy was unfolding like cloth. As we had been fighting the legionaries, he had sent the auxilia to climb the flanks of the mountains and gather at our rear, so that we were encircled. Half our numbers turned to engage them. Now we met long swords and pikes, held by men who were not yet exhausted by conflict. Behind us the spears and swords of the legion pressed forward.

Still we fought.

The wailing cries of the journeypeople, sung from vantages of oak branches, grew louder. Caradog screamed desperate commands, trying to steer the warriors into positions that could meet both fronts. But it was no use.

By which weapon would we die? Sword or spear? This was our choice.

Unless we made another.

I pulled Caradog from our war band, seeking the briefest respite within the shelter of our tribeskin. The Romans encroached to the southeast and west of us, but there was still a gap to the north. We had done enough.

He looked at me, his face masked with blood spray, and I answered the question that glowed in his eyes.

'Yes,' I said. 'We must cease this fight.'

'Meet me at the copper mine if we are separated,' he said. 'Wait for me there.'

I nodded.

He turned back to the war band and filled his mighty lungs with breath. 'Retreat!' he bellowed. 'Retreat to the northern paths. Retreat to your safety.'

Then, like a flock of geese lifting from the ground, the warriors fled.

Immediately, the Romans tried to close off the northern retreat, but they were too slow for the tribespeople, who poured between rocks and down cliffs like spilled ale.

Still there was killing, as many warriors remained entrapped by soldiers, but by far the greater number were streaming into the forests that would render them unseen.

Caradog and I ran for the camps, to evacuate the remaining tribespeople before Scapula's men claimed their human bounty. But as we turned a sharp corner on the path, three soldiers split us apart, sending me plunging down a slope of bracken, while Caradog jumped onto higher rocks to evade them.

The slope levelled and I veered westward towards his war camp, passing tents as I ran, screaming to their inhabitants to leave and hide. Tribespeople were frantically untying horses and cattle, stuffing bags with blankets and food, and galloping out through the valley. Caradog was the most fiercely hunted of our warriors. It would be impossible for him to reach the camp uncaptured. He would have to take to the forests, and I prayed to the Mothers that he had. I was headed for the one whom I would not abandon.

It was up to me to protect Euvrain.

She was alone, feeding her infant, when I burst through the flap of the hide. 'Euvrain, make haste.' I could barely speak for the heave of my breath. 'We must away to the forest. They have defeated us and are in pursuit.'

She did not answer, but merely stared down at her suckling babe.

'Euvrain...' I crouched before her. 'Do you not hear me? The Roman soldiers come. You must rise and gather the children.'

Still she gave no response.

'Then I must force you.' I grabbed her wrist, but she pulled away.

Finally she met my eye. 'Hide yourself with my husband, if that is your desire, for he shall surely seek to rebirth this war, if he lives. But I will not run another step from the Romans. If their want for this land is so great, let them have it. I want only a home where my children might live in safety. If I cannot have this, let them have me.'

'They will harm you, sister—'

'They will not harm Caradog's wife. I will be precious to them as a lure.' She gave a quiet laugh. 'They will not know his true wife is another.'

Shouts from outside the tent told us that Scapula's men were drawing close.

I clutched her face, as beautiful to me as Caradog's. 'Please—they will take pleasure in defiling what Caradog has revered, Euvrain. Do not subject yourself to this.'

'This war is over for me.' She leaned forward and pressed her lips against mine, as soft as the air after rain. 'Mothers bless you, Ailia.'

I broke away, and looked back from the tent's opening. 'Caradog will be destroyed by your decision.'

She laughed again. 'If that is what you believe, then perhaps it is still I who know him best.'

I could argue no longer. If I did not leave now, Caradog would lose us both. I pushed through the opening and ran.

Already the soldiers had begun to set fire to the tents and the air was noisy with the screams of rape.

✝

I stood frozen at the mine's entrance. The scent of deep earth drifted from the fissure. The mine was less than an hour's foot journey from Emrys. Unless he had been captured, Caradog would be here by now. Once I entered, I would know if I had lost him. Of all I had faced today, this took the most courage.

I shouldered through the stony crack and into the cavern within. The darkness was cold on my skin. 'War King?'

'I am here.'

✝

When we had held each other for long enough to steady the drum of our hearts, I told him of Euvrain's decision.

'We must go back,' he said. 'I have to find her.'

'You might as well cut your own throat.'

'Would you have us abandon her?'

'It was I who went to her. She would not come.'

'I have to speak to her, Ailia. I cannot leave her.'

I rubbed my eyes. 'Then let me go. If I strip my metals, I will draw no attention. Every Roman soldier will know your face after today.'

Caradog nodded his reluctant acknowledgement.

We emerged from the mine, squinting against the late brightness.

There were only a few hours of daylight remaining. We had determined that Caradog would search for the warriors of his band who might still be hidden nearby, while I would go back to the camp. We would return to the mine before nightfall.

Before we separated, Caradog said, 'Bring her back, Ailia. Tell her the war will not continue unless she comes.'

'I will,' I said. I knew that she no longer cared whether the war continued. But I also knew that the war king would not rest unless she had heard his message.

But when I reached the site of the camp, it mattered not what I might say. For there was not one living soul to hear it. Only the dark shapes of slain bodies among the smoking remnants of tents and carts.

I stared around me. Every tribesperson that lay dead on this ground could have gained a good price at the Roman ports. There were no townships, no settlements nearby to be subdued by the *atrocitas*. This killing bore no purpose. It was the work of a man driven witless by fury.

This was the story. As the Mothers had foretold.

In the falling light, I walked from one slaughtered tribesman to the next, murmuring their rites to Annwyn, checking for Euvrain's pale hair. But I knew I would not find her. Because she was Caradog's wife. And Scapula would know how valuable a prize she was. I felt leaden as I imagined the cruelty with which he would possess her.

I walked to the periphery of the scattered bodies, observing who, among Caradog's closest warriors and their families, was absent, then turned to take my leave of this wasteland.

As I approached the stony pathway that would free me from this horror, a movement caught my eye. I peered into the half-darkness to see a crouched figure against the embankment, rocking beside a smouldering ash pile. I took a few steps forward, for I could not see if it were kin or enemy. 'Who is there?' My voice quavered.

The rocking ceased. Silence, then a thin cry.

Still I could not see a face, but something in the wordless voice was as familiar to me as the taste of water. 'Rhain?'

Again he bleated.

In a heartbeat I was crouched before him. 'Teacher! Where are you harmed?'

His head hung forward. Praise the Mothers, he lived and I could tend him to wellness. But he would not look at me. 'Rhain, can you speak? It is Ailia...'

Slowly he lifted his face to look at mine. Through the day's remnant light, I saw what they had done.

He wore a beard of congealed blood. His eyes were glazed and dull with pain. They had cut out his tongue.

Never had I known such hatred. Every thread of my being was altered by it.

When I could find my words, I drew my sword from its sheath and neared it to his throat. 'I am going to release you, teacher. Is this your wish?'

Rhain gasped through the raw wound of his mouth, then nodded.

'Know this as you ride to the Mothers: every remaining day that I live will be in honour of what you have taught me.'

He reached for my hand.

I returned its grip then released it. 'I need both my hands,' I said with forced lightness. 'I cannot cut quickly without steadying your head.'

Then, after calling forth the Mothers to open the realms and carry this glinting soul to Annwyn, I moved to the back of him, braced his slight body between my spread knees, took hold of his hair, and opened his throat.

When it was done, I sat in silence, taking my first unsteady breaths of the world without him.

✝

Caradog had kindled a fire in the mine and was sitting beside it.

I stood just inside the entrance. 'They have retreated and taken the prisoners. Only the slain remained.'

'Was Euvrain among them?'

'No.' I paused. 'But your Songman was.'

'Is he dead?'

'Yes, Caradog, he is dead! He has fallen to this Mother-forsaken war.'

Caradog stood. 'Do not raise your voice against me. It was you who said the Mothers were with us. It was you who commanded the fight.'

'I know.' I put my face in my hands.

'Perhaps your power is not as strong as I thought.'

'Perhaps it is not.' I walked to the fire and crouched to its warmth. His strike did not wound me. I had heard the voice of the Mothers. I understood the greater sacrifice. But understanding it had not prepared me to live it.

Caradog sat beside me and I flinched from his touch. We sat for several moments unspeaking. Then I saw that he grieved as much as I. He had loved Rhain as I had. I put my hand on his back.

'Where shall we go now?' I asked.

'We have to leave here or Scapula will find us.'

'And what of Euvrain?'

He paused. 'The only way I can retrieve her is to win the war.'

I stared, incredulous. 'We lost the battle, Caradog.'

He frowned. 'Scapula won today, but he will not hold this new front.'

Stunned, I listened as he spoke on, erratic with strategy.

'He is rash...He has no forethought. He has stumbled into these mountains after me, but now he is left with a frontier that he cannot possibly defend. Think of it, Ailia. His line will need to reach from Eryr to Llanmelin, through the most difficult mountains of Albion. He will need to build camps and roads for their supplies. It will take him months and he will stretch his men thin to do it. They will be weak while they are building, and we can inflict much damage.'

'*Who*, Caradog?' I asked, disbelieving. '*Who* will inflict the damage?'

'Do you think it is only I who would fight for this land? While you were at camp I found the men of the Silures. They are not yet tamed. They are ready to continue with the night attacks and hidden strikes that you yourself have always claimed are our greatest power.'

'And what will you do?'

'I have already told you. I will go to the Brigantes.'

'To the southern chiefs?'

'No. To Stenwic.'

'You cannot—Why do you make sport of Cartimandua's warning?'

'Because I need Venutius. Scapula is vulnerable there now that half his forces are here in the western mountains. If I can harness the Brigantes, then we can attack from the east, while the free tribes stand in the west.'

I looked at him, speechless. Before his tribeskin's bodies were cold, he had wrought a strategy to slay yet more. 'And the warriors are in agreement?'

'Those I have spoken to. I have asked them to send messages so that all the western bands know I have not abandoned them.'

I was too exhausted to think further. I tended the fire, then lay on my back while he rested his head on my shoulder.

'Can Venutius be trusted?' I asked.

'I do not know,' said Caradog. 'But we have no other course.'

This was the recklessness of a wild horse, surrounded. I lay unspeaking.

'I will never give up, Ailia,' he said softly. 'While I live, I will fight for our freedom.'

It was his shape and I could not alter it.

The Mothers had told me that Emrys would be our sacrifice. They did not tell me that there would be more.

I had survived the battle. The Mothers had preserved me to protect the song.

No longer Rhain's, but mine.

☩

It took three weeks to reach Stenwic.

News of the defeat at Emrys had travelled before us, and there were fewer chieftains prepared to harbour Rome's most wanted enemy. We were forced onto the least-known woodland paths, for the main roads of Tir Brigantes were crawling with soldiers in search of the war king. Despite his victory, it was clear that Scapula would not rest until he had severed the head from the serpent of resistance.

Caradog grew as bleak as I had ever seen him. He refused to speak of the defeat on the mountain. Each night as we lay in farmers' barns, or wild beneath the northern stars, he would not be drawn by my comfort or counsel. Yet by day he remained bold. 'I will harness the Brigantes,' he told every tribesman who still had heart to hear him. 'Our war chariot will ride again.'

His sadness did not bridle his courage, but birthed it. Perhaps this had always been true. Perhaps only one who knew true despair could find hope in hopelessness.

At last we rode into the moorlands that surrounded Stenwic. Our destination was a farmhouse, half a day's ride from the township. The farmer's eldest son had ridden out to meet us at dusk. This same boy had borne a message to Venutius's private stables this morning as the prince prepared for his daily hunt.

When we walked through the farmhouse doorway, we saw Venutius himself sitting by the fire. He greeted us with nervous gladness, but grew more settled as we drank a thick marrow broth and shared news of the west.

'The men are wounded but still strong,' said Caradog. 'They fought like the hounds of Annwyn. They need only to know that the forces of the Brigantes are prepared to rise and they will take up their swords once more.'

I said little. The warriors of the Deceangli and the Ordovices had been culled to obliteration. Only the Silures and southern Brigantes had retained enough fighters to be called a war band. And of those we had passed in hiding in the forests, shivering in fireless and hungry huddles, few could be described as strong.

Venutius glanced at the farmer and his wife.

'We need wood,' she said rising. 'Husband, help me split it.'

'I have been thinking of nothing else since news of your battle reached our hall,' said Venutius, once they had taken their leave. 'The tribes of the north, especially those of my homeland, are ready to complete what you have begun in the west.'

Caradog smiled. 'Then are you ready to break from your wife and stand beside me?'

I heard the seduction in the word *beside*. Where Hefin had once stood, now there was space for another.

Venutius looked at him. 'I may not have to move against Cartimandua. She has known some kind of alteration since the news of Emrys. In the quietness of our bedchamber, she speaks favourably of the strength of the warriors and questions Scapula's intrusion to the west. I believe she is ripening to another view. Though she cannot say it at council, lest the procurator catches her new scent.'

'What has turned her?' I said.

'I cannot be certain, but I suspect it is the new governor,' said Venutius. 'Plautius understood her power. Scapula shows little respect for the rule of a woman. She is angered by the guards he has placed here since the uprising. The Roman treaty does not taste as sweet to her as it once did.'

The fire crackled as Caradog digested this news. 'Then tell her,' he said, 'that if she desires it, I will come to her and show her the honour she is owed. Tell her I will fight under her command to restore her queendom—to her rule alone.'

I stared at him in shock. Never had I heard him offer to yield to another's command. 'Caradog,' I said, 'do not chance with her warning.'

'It may be too soon.' Venutius cradled his soup cup against his chin.

'Tell her,' said Caradog, ignoring us both. 'Do not reveal where I am. Just make my offer and return with her response.'

After we had watched Venutius ride away, I turned to Caradog in fury outside the farmhouse door. 'Abandon this war if you will, but do not hand yourself to Scapula on a platter.'

'She is my sister, Ailia. We are forged of the same father. She has had two summers under Scapula's whip. She will come back to me.'

'Did you even intend to remain hidden, or were you simply soothing me like a child?'

'You are no child. My intention was to work by stealth, but Venutius's words offer hope that she is not so lost to us as I thought.'

We stood in silence beneath the stars, as I grappled with this new circumstance.

'I could lead the Brigantes against their own queen,' said Caradog. 'But imagine how much stronger our war band would be if she stood beside me at its head.'

Caradog knew Cartimandua better than I did. I had no choice but to honour his judgement. I knew, however, that was she was not a leader who willingly shared her rule.

And nor was her brother.

Venutius returned the next morning. He tethered his hunting horse behind the barn, where it would not be seen from the road, and we gathered again by the hearth.

'She has heard your proposal,' said the prince.

'By your lips?' I asked.

He nodded. 'I told her that your messenger had been sent to me, in respect of the warning she had given.'

'Well designed,' said Caradog. 'And her response?'

'She took some time in her bedchamber and returned to me with this.' From his belt pouch Venutius pulled out a metal ornament and held it out to Caradog. 'She asked that I give it to the messenger to return to you.'

Caradog took the circlet and held it in his open hand.

'She says that she withdraws the threat made against you,' said Venutius. 'She offers you this as a pledge of her loyalty.'

Caradog stared down at the jewel.

'What is it?' I asked.

'Our father made it,' he said. 'I watched him cast it and cut in the design. He said it would adorn the breast of his successor. I was barely five summers old, but I did not forget it. He gave it to Cartimandua when she left his fosterage.'

I leaned forward and picked up the relic from his palm. It was a bronze cloak-pin with a Roman-style fastening, but its tiny swirling face of three interwoven hounds was a design of the tribes. It bore the imperfections of the maker's hand. It spoke of the love of kin.

'She has asked you to come to her hall at your ease. She will receive you.' Venutius laughed softly. 'There was water in her gaze when she gave it to me. I have never seen her weep. It seems the war is not over yet.'

Caradog nodded, strangely quiet. 'I will come tonight.'

'Are you sure?' I said.

'This token was more precious to her than her crown itself. I have no doubt.'

I closed my hand around the jewel. For all her consorting with Rome, Cartimandua was the most forthright creature I had ever encountered. I, too, gave my faith to this metal.

'I will tell her to prepare,' said Venutius.

We waited until darkness, then followed the farmer's son through an unguarded gate in the town's northern wall. Venutius was waiting outside the hall.

'Who attends?' whispered Caradog as he led us through the vestibule.

'Only the queen and her house servants,' Venutius answered.

We pushed through the hides of the inner doorway. The room was as hot as a bread oven.

Cartimandua walked forward to greet us. My memory had done her no justice. She wore a black dress with a hammered gold caplet around her shoulders. Her loosed hair spilled over the metal like dark wine. 'Brother,' she said to Caradog, 'thank you for your trust, even while mine has wavered.'

My muscles began to soften as I watched them hold each other in a long embrace. Despite all that had gone before, there was love between them.

She turned to me. Her face was thinner, but unchanged was her stamen scent as she drew me against her. 'I have hoped for your return.'

I glanced around the hall as we took off our cloaks and handed them to the servant. Torches flamed between the heavy drops of patterned cloth that lined the walls. Unlike most roundhouses, there was no second doorway opposing the first. The fire was built too high for a hall of this size, and I felt a sheen of sweat dampen my temples.

'Eat!' she said, motioning to a table laid with platters of meats, sweetmeats and soft cheeses, abundant enough to feed ten times our number. We each filled a bronze plate then joined her at the fire.

'I mistook you both when we last met,' she said. 'I thought you would be captured before you reached Tir Silures. But you have led our Romans on a lively dance and I have enjoyed the tales of it.'

Caradog laughed. 'You always did.'

She smiled. 'And now, despite Scapula's every attempt, you have evaded him.' Cartimandua looked at me. 'Your Kendra has protected you, after all, brother.'

I took a small bite of a ground nut cake. 'You believed the title to be little more than an ornament.'

'I was wrong. You have kept Caradog safe. You speak the land's will and I no longer wish to act against its command.'

'Then hear my advice,' I said.

'If your advice is to take back the reins of the Brigantes from Rome, then I am well-minded to hear it.'

'What of Scapula?' said Caradog.

'Scapula is a boil of a man. And a fool. He will not meet with me alone, but demands Venutius. He is terrified of speaking with a queen, as if my cunt would swallow him whole. He brings me documents to mark that would hand over half my queendom to the Empire on my death. What does he think I am?'

'I cannot imagine.' Caradog smiled.

'Plautius had foresight and wits. While he kept off my council benches, I enjoyed the fruit of his friendship. But I will tolerate no man claiming what I alone have built. They have had their fun here. Now the feast is over.'

'What of your citizenship to Rome?' I said.

'Bonds to a nation outside your birthplace are earned, not given. How can I value something so easily bestowed?'

She was right, and yet the change seemed too sudden.

Caradog's leg began to tap with excitement. 'What is the mood of your chiefs?'

'You know as well as I do that most of them oppose our treaty. It has been an unending struggle to soothe their disquiet. They will rise in an instant.'

'Are they well-metalled?'

Cartimandua laughed. 'This is the Brigantes. Of course they are well-metalled.'

Caradog took a small chunk of white flesh from a platter that a servant had brought before him. He frowned as he chewed the first bite. 'What is this delicacy, sister?'

'Something I am told is highly-prized in the dining halls of the east—serpent. Adder from the forest floor.'

Blood slowed in my veins.

Caradog laughed and took a second mouthful. 'It is like fish and hare at once,' he said. 'Delicious.'

'What of the adder's poison?' I muttered.

'It is not held in the flesh,' said Cartimandua. 'Surely the Kendra knows such simple truths of animal lore.'

'Eat no more of it,' I said to Caradog.

'Why not?' said the queen, taking a large steak herself. 'It is sweetly flavoured.'

'What is wrong, Ailia?' said Caradog.

He doesn't remember, I thought. The marriage geas. The prohibition. 'Perhaps the heat,' I murmured. My pounding heart was obscuring my senses. I drew a deep breath. I needed to steady.

Cartimandua was staring at me. She drew an iron firestick from the wood basket and prodded the logs into an eruption of sparks. Then she tapped the iron several times on the hearthstones.

One of the curtains rippled with a draft I could not feel.

Caradog fingered the bronze pin, which he had fastened to his tunic. 'Scapula has incurred heavy losses at Emrys,' he said. 'We should strike quickly, before he has a chance to replenish his numbers.'

Suddenly, I smelt the sharp sweat of bodies poised for command.

'Fair counsel,' said Cartimandua. 'We will make our attack after your journey.'

'Caradog...' I murmured.

'What journey?' said Caradog, ignoring me.

Cartimandua looked at him. 'Your journey to Rome.'

I met Caradog's eye. There was one heartbeat of stillness—a flash of understanding between us—before the room came to life and the Roman guards surged forward, conjured from the room's periphery like salmon rising from a river's depths.

'Run, War King!' I screamed, but the door was already blocked.

Caradog jumped to his feet, reaching for his weapon, but fifteen soldiers encircled him, their swords pointed inward like some terrible inversion of Lleu's rays.

'Caradog—' My voice was shrill with panic. This could not be. They could not have him.

'Hush, Ailia,' said Cartimandua, still seated on the bench. 'It is over now.'

'You!' I screamed at her. '*You* are the boil! *You* are the sickness on this soil.'

'Be still,' she said, her eyes flaring. 'I promised you that I would hand him to Scapula if he came here again. Did you think I did not mean it?'

'But your trickery...' I gasped, unbelieving.

'Has he not been breaking his fingers to trick me these past two years? Do you think I don't know half of southern Brigantes joined him at Emrys?' Her voice spat like flames. 'The rulership of my tribe is the most delicate of arts. I can no longer have this man kicking up wasp nests. He is condemning the tribes to war and death. That is no love of Albion.'

Caradog stared, unmoving, at the queen. 'I curse you, sister.'

She nodded. 'Where is the Governor?' she said to the soldier at the door.

'He awaits outside,' he answered.

'Then bring him,' said the queen.

The guards pulled open the doorskins to admit a plain man of middling age and height. He seemed even slighter without his breast-plate, his hair tightly-curled. He walked towards the fire, placed an iron tool into the embers, then commanded the soldiers to part their circle. 'Hold him.'

Two soldiers took Caradog's arms while three others braced their sword tips against his back. He jerked against the restraints, wincing as the swords pricked his skin. Then he was still.

Ostorius Scapula stood before him, drinking in every detail of his Mother-given grandeur: his height, his oxen shoulders, his warrior gaze, unflinching from his enemy's face, his hair and beard that fell in rusted hanks to his chest, but more than this, his sovereignty, his unbreakable certainty that he should stand free on this land.

'Let me grow drunk on this moment,' Scapula said in the castrated sounds of the Latin tongue. He leaned forward and drew a deep breath of Caradog's skin. 'Let me taste the scent of your enslavement.'

Caradog thrashed against the Roman guards, but they held him firm.

I stood, paralysed. I could not make sense of what I saw before me. It was as though the sun itself had been stopped in the sky.

'Was there ever a slave worth more in the Roman markets?' said Scapula to his soldiers. 'I will gain a good price from the Emperor.'

'And will you tell him that you, yourself, were unable to catch me,' said Caradog, 'that you needed a woman of the tribes to do what you could not?'

Scapula darkened. 'Perhaps I will tell him that the payment I desire for your capture is your execution by the torturer's tools.'

'By the Mothers, Caradog,' I whispered. 'Do not speak further.'

'Clever counsel,' said Scapula, still staring at Caradog. 'Though your Mothers will not aid you now. They are Rome's whores and I have fucked them until they are fit for no other.'

Silence spread like blood in water. My heart could not hold the defilement.

'Finish this, Governor,' said Cartimandua.

'I will,' he said. 'But first,' he turned to my husband, 'tell me who you are.'

'I am Caradog, son of Belinus, skin to the wren and War King of Albion.'

Scapula balled his fist, then gave a blow to Caradog's abdomen powerful enough to rupture his stomach. 'Who are you?'

Slowly Caradog lifted his head, spat the vomit from his mouth and repeated his title.

I closed my eyes, bracing for the second blow, but Scapula stood patiently for a few moments, then said, 'We could do this all night, and I would no doubt enjoy it, but I have ridden day-long and I am keen to rest, for we leave at daybreak for Rome. So if you cannot correctly name your position, then I have no further choice but to do it for you.' He turned back the fire and pulled out the iron tool. It had a small square plate at its end, which had heated to a dark orange glow.

With horror, I recognised its purpose.

Scapula said, 'Open his shirt.'

'No!'

'Ailia, be silent,' Cartimandua said, her voice low, her gaze locked to the ground.

'How can you permit this?' I gasped. Did she have no power? No authority? This was her kinsman. He deserved a noble death, not this humiliation.

She sat, unmoving in her seat, and would not meet my eye. She was as toothless as an old woman, her own title merely an ornament on her governor's breast.

'Bring him before Claudius,' I said to Scapula, 'but let him die as the war king.'

Scapula turned, seeing me for the first time. He put the tool back into the fire. 'You are she who consorts with the warrior dog,' he said, 'she who they call the *Kendra*.'

'I am she.'

'Then Mithras has blessed me with a bountiful harvest this day,' he said. 'For I have caught both the swine and his favourite sow.' He ran his eyes over my grey farmer's shawl, my tattered hair. 'And you are she who they revere above all others...' he murmured, shaking his head. 'No wonder you are all still living in mud burrows.'

There was a ripple of laughter among the soldiers.

Scapula glanced back to Caradog. 'I will take you to Claudius as your slut suggests, but her—' he stared at me with the disgust one might show to something wrong-born, '—this demon—I can kill now.'

Caradog bellowed, trying to wrench himself free.

329

'Not her,' said Cartimandua over the scuffle to subdue him. Finally, she had lifted her head.

Scapula turned to her. 'She is too precious to let live.'

Cartimandua stood up. The light from her mantle made a fire of her face. 'You have promised much great favour in exchange for the supply of Caradog. I ask for nothing, but that you release this woman.'

'She will rouse the free tribes.'

'Do not fear it. I will keep her with me.'

They stared at one another until Scapula scoffed and turned away. 'Have her. She'll be useless without her master anyway.'

I did not know if I shook with relief or despair.

'His shirt, I told you!' Scapula was angrier now. Again, he drew out the branding iron from the embers, now even hotter than before.

Clumsily, one of the soldiers cut the ties of Caradog's shirt and pulled its fabric back over his shoulders.

I let my gaze fall on the part-healed grazes and bruises from fighting. The skin was smooth and pale where the war had not reached it. 'Nothing burns you, Caradog,' I said. 'You are as the sun.'

'Silence,' shouted Scapula. He raised the near-molten metal before Caradog's chest.

I willed Caradog to look at me.

He did. He was afraid.

Through my gaze, I held him as Scapula seared the indelible three letters of a Roman slave into his skin.

12

Poetic Land

The warriors determine the fate of our tribes.
But it is the poets who make us immortal.

THE SUN shone through the barred wooden window, falling in crisp stripes on my bed. This was a different light from the soft haze that Lleu cast over the tribelands. It was stronger, prouder, more aware of itself. This was Apollo. The Roman sun.

Despite the brightness, I shivered under the thin woollen blanket. In only four weeks here, the warmth of late autumn had been replaced by a sharp chill. I rolled onto my side and gazed at my now familiar lodgings.

The tiny, white-walled room was furnished only with a narrow bed and a boxwood table, upon which stood a water jug and a scattering of the silver armbands I had carried with me from Albion. An alcove in the wall above the table sheltered a rough plaster statue of the Emperor, but otherwise there was no decoration.

It was a rare private room in one of the thousands of cheap inns that lined the Tiber in the northwest quarter of Rome, a room in which Caradog's wife could easily pass herself as just another in the stream of foreign travellers, labourers and traders who journeyed in and out of Rome seeking their own small slice of its glut. Its lockable door was my room's only testament to the weight of coins I bore in my pouch.

I sat up and peered through the bars to the street beyond. The horse-drawn goods carts that rumbled through the night, while roads were empty enough to allow their passage, were being replaced by the throng of foot traffic and food-sellers, already shouting their trade.

The nutty smell of frying wheat cakes drifting under my doorway told me that the inn's owner had awoken. The day was beginning like every other I had passed within the walls of this city. Yet today was not like any other.

Today Caradog, Euvrain, and all the captured chiefs of Albion would be marched in chains around the stone square of the *castra praetoria*, the largest parade ground in Rome. Today Caradog would face judgement before the Emperor Claudius, a performance purposed only for the amusement of the crowds and the glorification of the Empire, for the war king's execution was certain.

Today I would see him for the last time.

Along with Euvrain and their children, he had been held under close guard within one of the senators' houses.

I had not been permitted to see him. He did not even know that I was here.

I poured a glass of water and drained it in one thirsty draught. Rome's water was never cold and tasted of the leaden pipes that carried it into the city.

I had left for Rome only hours after Caradog had been dragged in leg rings across Cartimandua's floor. She had grasped my arm once we were alone, pressed coins into my hand and whispered, 'There is a horse at the gate. I will give you this night to escape, then I must be seen to hunt you. Be sure you evade me.'

I had ridden nine days to the south-eastern tribelands, sleeping only a few hours each night in the shelter of forests. At the port of Dubris I gained admission to a Roman trade ship by merchants who did not wonder at a woman travelling alone, so long as she had sufficient silver with which to quiet them.

Thus I left the shores of my homeland.

I had travelled with a poor woman's invisibility and a rich woman's purse. Both had been needed. In the port markets of Bononia I had bought a hardy-looking donkey, and had proceeded, by means of firstly farmhouses and, later, inns, through the busy roads of Gaul and onward to the Empire's first city.

I had arrived here in the last moon of autumn. I would leave tomorrow, when I had sung my husband's rites.

I pulled on a woollen tunic and cloak, tied my sandals, and unfastened my door.

The price of my room included a meagre breakfast, but I had grown to prefer the noisy hive of food stalls and taverns—the *thermopolia*—that lined the river round the corner from my inn.

I greeted the house woman as I passed through the kitchen, then stepped onto the street. Immediately I was hit by the stench of people in numbers of thousands of thousands. There were no words in my language to express this number, for we had never had cause to fathom it. Only the Roman language could count numbers without end.

I turned northward on the narrow street, weaving to navigate the out-spilling of wares from the potters, fruit-sellers, cloth merchants and candle stores. A bakery and a flower stall brimming with roses and oleanders offered respite from the reek of rotting food.

Every handspan of this city was sealed by the armour of human life: houses so densely built you could not walk between them, paths paved with flagstones as wide as a bull's rump, and the immense columned monuments—arches and temples—that filled the forum. Nowhere, no time, did this land breathe. Robbed of their porousness, the streets stank of human waste.

I had wanted to hate it. And yet I did not.

It had taken me without question. It did not care that my skin was pale, that my Latin was accented, that I had slain many soldiers of its army. It welcomed any who wished to walk on it.

In only one month I had grown used to what shocked me at first. Rome was a wildness of its own kind. Gone was the steady rhythm of cattle, birdsong, the daily pouring of milk on the earth. This city ran to the drums of trade, the frenzied music of commerce. The hum of the land had been silenced by a human song. It would not last. It could not. It was an illusion, a trance as dazzling and brilliantly fleeting as the fires of Summer's Eve. And yet whole countries had been enslaved in honour of its growth.

I met the river, turning eastward on its bank. Here at least, the earth's breath rose briefly up through the water to kiss my brow. I drank in the fresh coolness. A young girl rolled a spinning wheel past my feet. I watched her as she raced past, shrieking with joy, then disappeared into a dark doorway.

I had reached my favourite *thermopolium*. Small wooden stools stood around a central table, shiny with grease. The cook was smearing spoonfuls of batter across a spitting hotplate and flipping cakes that were ready to turn.

'Two please, Attius,' I ordered, taking a seat beside the hotplate.

Attius, with his keen ear and ready humour, had been a steady supplier of city knowledge for me. 'Sauce?'

'Yes.'

He stacked the cakes on a wooden plate, doused them with thick, black sauce from a spouted jug, and set them before me.

'Where should I stand for the best view today?' I rolled up a cake and took a bite, my mouth flooding with the saltiness of the fish sauce. If there was anything thing I would miss of Rome when I returned to the tribes, it was the bewildering, sun-soaked flavours of its food.

'They muster at the Campus Martius, just up the river,' said Attius. 'Or you can stand anywhere along the Via Triumphalis and you'll see them pass.'

'I'd like to hear the Emperor.'

'You mean watch the strangulation?' He smiled. 'Then you'll need to get inside the barracks. But you'll have to hurry. The ground fills quickly, and the war king from Britannia will draw a mighty crowd.'

Bodies pressed on every side of me. Already my water skin was almost empty, but I would not risk my place in the crowd to go back to the fountain to fill it.

Perhaps because I was a woman alone, or was artful in remaining unnoticed, I had been able to work my way from the entrance of the *castra*, along the northern wall to the eastern side of the parade ground, where I had gradually shouldered forward to a good position beside the stage.

The scene was set for the ritual to follow. Cushioned benches lined each side of the stone platform, and on a marble podium between them stood two carved and gilded thrones. From poles festooned with trails of ivy and white roses, great swathes of white linen billowed above the seating. Many more blooms had been strewn across the stage, threading the air with their innocent fragrance.

It was a stage for the gods, yet its centrepiece was a squat earthen pot, from which emerged a tentative sapling oak. I had not seen one since I had arrived in the city and was not prepared for the blow it would strike. Its scalloped leaves, limp from scant water, awakened every song and poem I had learned at the boughs of its kin. Stunted in its too-small vessel, this was the symbol that proclaimed our subjugation. Our sovereign tree, our deepest wisdom: bound, diminished.

On the ground before the stage stood the full Praetorian cohort, the hand-picked guards of the emperor, a legion of cockerels in their red crested helmets.

For another hour I stood and waited, listening to the murmured stories of the war king that rippled back and forth through the crowd. I smiled to myself. He would enjoy that his fame had spread throughout the Empire.

At last a trumpet cry stilled the crowd. I craned my neck to watch the Emperor and his wife enter. The senators came first, filing through the draped doorway in white robes and laurel head-wreaths. When they were seated, the rear curtains parted. The parade ground hushed.

A narrow-jawed man, dressed in cascading folds of purple, shuffled forth into a deluge of cheers and a shower of thrown flowers. I started at the face beneath the golden head-wreath. He was long-rumoured to be weak and sickly, a puppet emperor, but the man before me looked sharp-witted and thoughtful.

He and his wife took their seats on the thrones, smiling amid the hurled blooms and roars of adulation. Only when one of the senators stood, raising his hand, did the crowd's noise abate. Then whispers swirled through the gathering. The procession was at the gateway. Caradog was here.

My heart pounded for the full hour it took for the head of the parade to reach the stage. First came armed guards to ensure no children or dogs obstructed the parade's path. Behind them came the first of Albion's captured chiefs. The sight of them was a knife through my belly. As well as the leaders captured at Emrys, there were others whom I did not know, defenders of the eastern tribes, who must have been kept years under guard, as the Emperor awaited this day.

Each of my kinsmen was bound in iron leg-rings, chained to each other or to their wives and children. They were not clad in their tribal skins and tartans, but in some mockery of our warrior costume: woad smeared artlessly across their faces, torn strips of fur wrapped around their prisoners' tunics.

They wailed and begged as they staggered, crying for clemency, lamenting the error of their resistance, and appealing to the grace of the Roman Emperor.

The crowds jeered and spat, howling with laughter at their rags and clumsy Latin.

I drew rigid with fury.

Following the chiefs came cart after cart piled high with the spoils of war. These were the metals plundered by *atrocitas*; the swords, shields, knives, torcs, arm-rings, platters and cups wrought from the silver and copper of our soil. Within the deep mists and dark halls of Albion they were luminous, yet their colours paled under this stark light.

Now came the wheeled stages upon which the scenes of the war had been recreated using life-sized models and human tableaux. I saw Claudius riding into Camulodunum on the back of an elephant, several hillforts succumbing to the legions, then lastly, and most spectacularly, a recreation of what could only have been the battle at Emrys.

An enormous model mountain had been constructed on the platform. At its crest were the actors representing the warriors, each naked, but wearing a giant and grotesquely-rendered animal mask over their head. Their arms flailed and their genitals swung beneath the lolling heads of cows, pigs, sheep and geese.

The Roman soldiers climbed the painted mountain, and the hybrid half-creatures began to fight them in plodding, graceless swipes. One of the warriors spun around, enacting a spear fight.

From the cleft of his buttocks sprouted a thick fur tail.

The crowd roared with laughter and disgust. But in their ridicule, they revealed what was strongest in us. We were bound to our animal spirits. Not in the witless, clumsy way the Romans mocked here, but by ways that were potent.

The final cart was much simpler. It did not feature live actors, but giant-sized plaster figures depicting the moment of Caradog's capture. He was easy to identify by the ragged crown they had given him, a jumbled nest of leaves, branches, and animal horns at odd angles. He kneeled before the figures of Scapula (far taller and more muscular than I recalled him) and Cartimandua, who had been fashioned into a yielding posture, her gaze averted, wearing the pale drapery of a Roman noblewoman.

An animal lay prostrate at Caradog's feet. It was at first indecipherable, a hunched beast, with tufts of fur glued randomly across its back. Yet as the cart drew nearer, I saw that the head of the creature was uplifted, and that it was not an animal at all, but a woman, her face crusted with dirt, peering at Caradog with an expression of anguish. At her breast they had rendered a gaping wound from which two serpents emerged, waving and bobbing, by way of some stringed mechanism beneath the cart. It was me.

I touched my scar through my tunic. Again, they had unearthed what was most sacred among the tribes and twisted it into something comic and loathsome.

So shaken was I by the hatefulness of the image that I was not immediately aware of the figure who followed it. He had already reached the ground in front of the stage before I saw him. When I did, my blood stopped.

Amidst the lurid spectacle of the parade, he was pure nobility.

He wore a short, grey tunic and his hair was unbraided. As he walked, his ankles chained to Euvrain's, he did not repent or cry out to the crowd. He stared straight ahead and remained silent.

Some of the audience hissed, but the greater number were quiet as he passed, hushed with respect for this warrior who had defied the most powerful empire in the world.

'Halt, prisoner!' screamed one of the guards.

Caradog stopped and turned. Now I saw the full glory of his face. It was unaltered by bondage. He was a king. All present could sense it.

'Come forth,' said Claudius.

Taking Euvrain's hand so she would not stumble, he slowly ascended the steps, and came to stand before the Emperor of Rome. His ankles were rubbed to bleeding by the rings. Euvrain looked hollow beside him. She and the children beside her would also die this day.

'At last I meet you,' said Claudius.

Caradog stared at his face, unanswering.

Be humble, I willed him, *lest he angers and chooses a crueller death.*

Slowly Caradog bowed to the Emperor and I exhaled with relief. Then he turned and bowed to the Emperor's wife.

The crowd gasped in surprise.

He did not bend to Roman custom, but held to the ways of the tribes honouring queen as equal to king. I ached with love of him.

Agrippina smiled.

'Free his legs,' said Claudius.

The guards released the leg rings and pulled Caradog forward.

Claudius held up a sheet of white vellum and began to read. 'This is the trial of the Briton Caratacus, son of Cunobelinus of Catuvellauni, now the Roman fortress of Camulodunum.' The Emperor's voice halted with the stutter I had heard so often mocked in the *thermopolia*. 'You are accused of waging war against the Empire of Rome, obstructing the advancement of legions in the British province. You are accused of conspiracy against the Governors Aurelius Plautius and

Ostorius Scapula, destruction of forts, property and roads, theft of grain, horses and weapons, and murder of citizen soldiers.' Claudius looked up from the sheet. 'How do you answer these accusations?'

It was a show. Every man and woman present knew that Caradog was to be killed this day. There were no men of law to defend him, no jury to judge him. Foreign insurgents were always killed. There could be no other outcome, especially from an Emperor already fearful of being seen as spineless.

'All you have stated, I have done,' said Caradog clearly.

'By these acts you have defied the natural order of the Empire and the will of the gods who have instated it. The punishment for your crimes is the beheading of your wife and children, then your death by strangulation before the senators and people of Rome.'

Whispers of anticipation rolled through the crowd.

Euvrain stood between her two children, holding her babe. Her tears were soundless.

'Are you prepared to meet this punishment?'

Only now did I see that an executioner stood at the back of the stage, bearing his axe and lengths of chain and rope.

'I am,' said Caradog. 'But first, honoured Emperor, may I speak?'

The crowd murmured.

Claudius raised his brow and turned to the senators, who nodded. 'We will hear you,' he said.

This was mere sport for the crowd's pleasure. Yet the *castra praetoria* was utterly still.

Caradog lowered his head. When he looked up, it was directly towards me.

My heart halted. He saw me. *Mothers be with you,* I silently prayed.

He looked to Claudius, and, in the resonant, perfect Latin he had known since his childhood, he began to speak. 'Noble Emperor and citizens of Rome, before my capture, I was king of western Albion, a territory of great power and wealth.

'If I had been a weaker man, less determined to resist you—if I had loved my tribelands less—I could easily have entered your city as a friend, not as a prisoner. You would not have hesitated to welcome an ally of such noble birth, who bore influence over many tribes.'

Yes, I thought. He was shaping a story that they understood.

He turned to the audience. 'Instead of this, I face death and humiliation, while you are glorious. I had sovereignty, horses, gold and weapons. Whole tribes of warriors knelt down before me. Does it surprise you that I did not wish to lose them? Does it surprise you that I fought for them? *Because you desire empire over the world, does it follow that the world desires to be your slave?'*

My breath held.

A murmur began to swell among the people. It was the sound of agreement, the slow pivot of judgement.

Caradog turned back to the Emperor. 'You would kill me for my resistance, yet if I had been dragged before you as one who surrendered without fighting, what glory would there be in your victory? None would have learned of my fall, nor of your triumph. If you kill me now, both will be forgotten.' He drew a final breath. 'But if you allow me to live, I will stand as eternal testament to your greatness.'

A long silence.

'*Liberato!*' called a lone voice from the audience. 'Free him!'

Claudius's mouth twitched. 'And now,' he said, 'do you honour Rome's sovereignty in Albion?'

Caradog bowed. 'With all my being.'

The chant took hold. '*Liberato! Liberato!* Free him! Free him!'

Euvrain gripped Caradog's hand, rigid with hope.

Claudius shifted and looked at his wife. In the final parry of this war, Caradog had forced him into a room without doors. To execute

Caradog now would seem ignoble, disdainful of the crowd. Finally he lifted his palm to signal that he was about to pronounce judgement. 'Briton, I have heard you speak. You call on my mercy and hope that I will halt your execution. No Emperor has ever shown *clementia* to such an enemy—' He looked out over the sea of people at his feet. 'They did not possess the magnanimity of this Emperor before you—'

My legs were trembling.

'Caratacus of Britannia, you are spared death. You will live out your life on the soil of Rome. And all who pass you shall be reminded of my mercy.'

There was a moment of stillness, then the crowd broke open in an eruption of cheering.

I looked up at Caradog, who met my eye through the milling guards, and smiled.

✛

I followed Euvrain to her courtyard garden. Water trickled from a spout in the wall. The last few crimson grape leaves clung to the vine on the arbour above.

'Wine?' she offered, filling two cups from a jug she had carried out on a tray and set on the table before us.

'Thank you, a little. Is it locally made?'

'Yes. And I believe using some of our fruit.' She handed me a cup, then turned to face me.

I had never her seen her so beautiful. The southern sun had coloured her skin to a wheaten gold that made her eyes an even deeper blue. She had an ease in her bearing that I had not seen before. 'You seem...well,' I said.

'Ailia, I am. I did not foresee it, but, look at this—' She motioned to the courtyard and the fruit groves we could see through its gate.

Rows of apple trees and grapevines stretched over the hills. A child's playful screech rang out from the orchard. 'My children are happy. We have sun, bountiful food, a generous pension. But most of all—' She paused. 'I have a home. One that I won't have to leave with an hour's warning.'

I touched her forearm.

'You will think I have betrayed my tribelands...'

'No,' I said. 'I do not.'

She stared at her cup.

I had not seen her since the judgement. In the tide of dispersing crowds, I had been unable to reach her or Caradog that day. Despite days of asking, I had not found where they had been taken. Only yesterday, two weeks later, had a new crier in the forum told me they had been moved to a country house just north of the city, gifted by one of the senators. It took my last six armbands to persuade him to tell me where it was.

'And what of you?' said Euvrain. 'I still cannot believe that you... that you are here.'

'Who else would have sung your rites?'

She looked at me. 'You strengthened him that day. You have always strengthened him.' She paused. 'I owe you my life.'

'You owe me nothing.'

We sat in silence.

She sipped her wine. 'And now?' she said. 'Have you come for your husband?'

Did she taunt me? 'Is he here?'

'In the stable,' she said. 'I sent the servant to tell him a visitor is here.'

We spoke of Rome's strangeness and wonder. When I asked her whether she had learnt any news of the tribes, or tried to share what I had heard of our homelands in the city, she did not wish to speak of it.

'Not now,' she said, shaking her head. 'I cannot hear it. I must fill my heart with this place now.'

I was astonished. How could she hold such command over her heart?

With a sudden shove, the house door flew open, and a tall, fair-skinned man stood before us. 'By Lleu!' he gasped, his face lighting up. 'Is it you?'

I nodded, too shocked to speak.

I scarcely recognised him. His brown woollen tunic was Roman-style, as were his laced sandals. But strangest of all, he had shaved his face and cut his hair. Short, rust-coloured curls sprung at his temples and around his neck. Without his beard he was utterly altered. It was as if he had lost a limb.

With a glance at Euvrain, he knelt before me, grabbed my hand and kissed it.

Euvrain stood up. 'I will get some more wine.'

We waited until she had disappeared before we spoke.

'I cannot see you...' I said, still staring.

He laughed and swung onto the bench beside me. 'It is I, my love. I am unchanged.'

With his nearness, I began to know him.

'Where have you been?' he said, 'I searched in every city guest house after the tribunal, but none knew you by name or description.'

'I do not speak my name here, of course. I am Cata, war widow from the province state of Trinovantia.'

'See?' He laughed. 'Rome changes you also.'

Our smiles died away.

'You spoke beautifully at the tribunal.'

'I had an audience I wished to impress.'

His hand found mine between us, and our fingers interlaced.

'I thought I would watch you die that day.'

Caradog said, 'I was prepared to die...'

'And yet you did not.'

'No.'

After a few moments I said, 'Is it true that you may never return to Albion?'

'Ay, I am closely watched. I must remain within the borders of greater Rome.'

The trickling fountain was loud in the silence.

'And are you pleased,' I asked, 'at the course of it?'

'I am glad for Euvrain. I am glad for my children to have a father—'

'But for yourself?' Albion was his soul.

'I meant what I said when I spoke before Claudius. I have lost all.'

I gripped his fingers. 'What will you do?'

He shrugged and looked out to the orchards. 'I will eat and shit. I will grow these grapes and make poor wine.'

I paused. 'Why did you speak, Caradog?'

'Because I wanted to live.' He looked at me. 'Should I have done otherwise?'

'No...no.' I drew him to me.

It was his nature, his truth, to endure. How else could he have led our war? Only one with such an instinct for his own survival could have come so close to ensuring that of Albion's tribes.

'And what of you?' he asked, as we pulled apart. 'What will *you* do?'

'I will return to Môn.' The name felt hollow.

'And what of the war?'

I frowned. 'Do you think it will continue?'

'Of course it will. The Silures have already made attacks on Scapula's new camps. The tribes will keep fighting, Ailia, no matter how many times Claudius says Britain is defeated.'

I shook my head. 'I will remain at Môn. My work is there.'

'Have you not thought of staying here?' he said.

'With what purpose?'

'To remain with me.'

'How?' I snorted. 'As concubine? As a house servant?'

'Stop it, Ailia.'

'Then what? You will banish Euvrain and put me in her place?'

He shook his head. 'She has weathered every possible storm with me. I will not abandon her.'

'I would not permit you to.'

A brown wren darted into the vine before us.

Just as Caradog had found new ground in the west, so now he would claim this Roman soil as his own. He was hardy. He would grow in this earth. But I would not.

He said softly, 'What of *our* marriage?'

'Our marriage was between the Kendra and Albion's king. Neither exists now. There is no marriage.'

He winced. 'Then, does anything still bind us?'

'Of course,' I whispered.

'Then stay,' he said. 'There is nothing here for me without you.'

I thought of the long passage back to Albion, the shattered tribes that awaited me there. For a moment, I thought of leaning against his shoulder, succumbing to this comfort. I loved him. I honoured him. But his duty to Albion was finished. And mine was not. 'If I stayed, I would not be what you loved.'

He nodded slowly. 'As I am not what you loved.'

I battled the truth in it. He was strange to me here. I claimed to love him, yet for the first time I wondered if it was him I loved, or his war?

A servant entered with a tray of bread and cheese, but I told Caradog I would not stay any longer. I took his hand and brought it to my lips. It smelt of Roman soil. Though I breathed deeply, I could not smell what lay beneath it. 'What is this?' I fondled the ring on his middle finger. It was thick gold and bore the face of Claudius.

'A gift from the Emperor. I am required to wear it always as a reminder of his mercy.' He laughed weakly. 'They told me it was British gold.'

In that instant, I felt more sadness than I could hold. 'Then treasure it,' I said, fighting tears. I stood to leave, but Caradog kept hold of my hand.

'Please honour me, Ailia,' he said. 'Please honour what I have done.'

'I will.'

'And know that I have loved Albion.'

I met his gaze. 'None have loved it more.'

I lowered my head and kissed him for the last time.

⊹

I turned my mare, gifted by a journeyman at the ports of Dubris, into the final bend of the path that led to Llanmelin. The bare oaks stood witness to my arrival, just as they had one year ago when I had approached this township for the first time, eager to meet the famous Caradog. I kicked the mare forward. This time I had even less idea of what I would find.

Although their camp was half a league south of Llanmelin, Roman soldiers were thick on the township walls.

Caradog's prediction had been correct. The war continued. Scapula had worked day and night to build enough forts to hold the new front, but Silures fighters had attacked them doggedly. The mountainous terrain made it easy for tribal bands to disrupt Roman supply lines and leave the camps hungry.

I had listened with interest to the messengers who rode, unseen, through the captured tribes, but I did not offer my counsel. It was not swords that would preserve us now.

It had been three weeks since I had returned to Albion. At the first touch of its cold earth beneath my bare foot I had wept. I knew then that I was not as Euvrain. I would rather live on this soil in disruption and fear, than anywhere else in peace.

I had ridden the line of the winter solstice, diverting west at the Habren to enter Tir Silures. The Roman-held lands were not safe for a journeywoman, but I knew how to hide within forests and busy markets, and passed through unquestioned. I wanted time enough to compose the poem, but, beyond that, I did not fear my own death. I had known the Mothers. I would know them yet. What harm could be done to me by human hand?

My destination was Môn, where Albion's journeypeople remained safe and free to chant in ritual within the groves. My body hungered to be among them. But I had business in Llanmelin first.

'I am visiting my mother,' I said to the soldier who stopped me at the gate.

'There is no one within,' he said.

'She is among the fringes at the northern wall.'

He stared at me, then laughed with pity and let me through.

The town was a carcass. On both sides of the roadway, the houses sat empty and gaping, their doors and roofs burned away. Blackened fence posts marked the burnt remains of tethered dogs and horses. The forges stood silent and cold.

I rode steadily towards the northern gate, praying there might be some beyond it who survived the *atrocitas*. But when I reached the fringes they, too, were abandoned, their tents charred and strewn on the ground. My heart slowed. She was lost. How could I have expected otherwise?

I rode back into the township and found myself wandering among the remains of the buildings I had known so well: the Great Hall, Caradog's house, the temple, the journey-huts. Within these places I had helped shape the war. Once or twice I passed a house still pouring smoke from its roof, a few livestock penned around it. Llanmelin was not entirely deserted.

I came to my own hut. Its roof and door were intact. The door screen was closed. I looked up. Smoke was rising from the thatch.

I slid off my mare and tied her to the fence.

The doorbell had been taken. My heart thudding, I nudged the screen open.

There, squatting by the fire, stirring a sour-smelling soup, was Manacca. She looked up in fear, then frowned. 'Aya?' Slowly she stood. 'Why are you here?'

She was taller, but very thin. Her voice was strong. I could see her eyes had sharpened. She had seen violence. Would she forgive me mine?

'I have come to take you to Môn.' I paused. 'I want to teach you. Will you come?'

She straightened her shoulders. She was near starving. Ravaged with sores. But I knew I could tend her and nourish her. If she would let me.

'Where is your mother?' I continued.

'Killed.'

'Do any of your fringe-kin live?'

She shook her head.

'And how were you spared, Manacca?'

'I was here,' she said. 'They did not search here.'

I exhaled, closing my eyes in silent thanks to the Mothers. They wished her to survive.

I took a deep breath and asked her again if she would come with me.

'Will you strike me?' she said.

'No.' I stared at her. 'I will never strike you or leave you again.'

She stepped forward hesitantly.

When she allowed herself to be held, her hair smelled of smoke and rain.

We approached a lone farmhouse on the outskirts of Llanmelin. Smoke rose from its roof and its plot was well-tended. An elderly farmer was kneeling in the soil.

'I'll ask for some food for our journey,' I said to Manacca.

We tethered the mare and walked toward the house. 'Tidings!' I called to the man who was absorbed in his sowing. 'Could we trouble you for—'

I stopped still.

The man had looked up. It was no farmer. It was Prydd.

He walked towards us. He wore a farmer's shirt and a peaked woollen hat that covered his mark.

'I thought you were in Môn,' I gasped.

'I was,' he said. 'I returned in the autumn. It seems I would rather live under bondage on my own tribelands, than free anywhere else.'

'But how...' I stammered. 'What is this...house?'

'It was empty after the slaughter. There was no objection to my claiming it. And I tend the orchards.'

I stared at him in disbelief. Manacca cowered at my skirts, still mistrusting. 'But you are a journeyman...'

'On dark moons, perhaps, if I am deep enough in the forest. Otherwise I am a farmer.' He held out his arms with a shrug. 'There was great despair among the tribespeople after the slaughter. It strengthens them that I am here, although I cannot keep their rituals.'

This was not the man who had felled me from my title. War had revealed him. 'You are a true journeyman,' I murmured.

'And what of you?' he asked.

'I came for the child. We are riding to Môn.'

He nodded.

I was about to turn away. I would not ask him for food. He had never wanted to help me.

He grabbed my hand and brought it to his bowed forehead. 'I bless your journey, Ailia. I honour you.'

Was it mockery? A taunt? 'Do not say it,' I said, freeing my hand. 'You claimed I was false.'

'You were not false. You were always true. I feared your voice and I sought to silence it.'

Shock stuck in my throat.

'Now I am sorry.'

Finally, I smiled. 'Can you spare any bread?'

We sat beside a fire in the darkness of the forest.

Manacca was scared. She had never slept in a wild place.

I did not sit close to her at first, but let her feel a little awe, a little of the land's intention, before I reassured her. 'Do not fear this place,' I said. 'It knows a different law from that of the townships, but you will find strength here. This is where you will hear the Mothers.'

She nodded and was quiet.

I breathed the dark, moist air into my chest. No boundary stood between me and the forest. What lay within this dense black earth, this watchful stone, these whispering trees? What was this land? What invisible thread held me to its pulse?

I had been to other places now. I knew that all ground could be dug, sown and stood upon. Only variations of bloom and weather made this land distinct from any other. What was it that I should love it so deeply and need it so utterly, with the steadfast adoration of a babe for its mother?

I moved closer to Manacca and wrapped my arm around her fleshless shoulders. We would take weeks to ride to Môn. Her body was weak and could not sit saddle-bound for long without needing rest. I pulled out some of Prydd's dried pork and wheat cakes from the saddlebag and gave them to her. As she ate, she asked me whether the war was finished now.

'Not yet,' I answered.

'Are you going to keep fighting?'

'No.'

She looked up. 'Why not?'

'Because I'm going to do something more important.'

'What?' Her eyes were round.

'I'm going to teach you to sing.'

I would teach her the songs that Rhain had taught me. She would bind them to the lakes and beaches, as I had to the mountain paths. They would be further adrift of their origin places, and for this they would be altered. But they would endure.

She wrinkled her nose. 'Singing is not more important than fighting a war.'

'Yes it is.'

The fire crackled sweetly in the darkness.

Manacca yawned and sank lower against my chest. 'Sing to me?'

I was tired. It had been a long day. A long year. 'What shall I sing? The battle of the Medway? The story of the river Cam?'

'No,' she said, looking up. 'Sing me a new story.'

I looked at her. I had intended to wait until I reached Môn. I had wanted my first audience to be Sulien and the journeypeople, who knew the craft of song and would best understand the design of my first forging.

But as I met Manacca's gaze, dark as loam, I knew there could be no stronger heart to hear my first song than hers.

I felt a moment of fear. Rhain had said I was ready, but what if I were not?

I had to try. I had to try to sing the song I had been forging in the place beneath thoughts ever since I had met Caradog. Ever since Romans had touched this soil.

Winter stars glowed through drifting cloud.

I took a slow, deep breath and felt it summon, from the grit of my bones, all that I had seen and learnt. There was no other who could tell this story. No other who had known the Mothers, the mountains, the war king, as I had.

The cold air grew warm within my chest.

Then there was sound, a melding of breath and flesh:

I was in many shapes
before I was released.
I was a slender, enchanted sword,
I was a droplet in the air,
I was the radiance of the stars.
I was a word in a poem.

My voice was bright in the silent forest. The words came smoothly, as if yearning to be spoken. This was the proclamation of authority that must precede any new forging:

I was a path, I was an eagle,
I was a bubble in ale,
I was a shield in battle.
I was a string in a harp
I was wood in a fire,
I am not one who does not sing,
I have sung since I was born.

Then I began the story of the Romans at Emrys:

I pierced a great, scaled animal,
With a hundred heads,
A fierce legion beneath the root of his tongue;
Another on each of his necks.
A hundred claws on him.
A crested beast; in whose skin a hundred souls were tortured by their
wrongs.

My heartbeat set a steady pulse. I could do it. The joins were clumsy, the shapes uneven, but the poem was emerging. My memory was the metal, my craft was the tool, and my imagination was the forge fire.

I sang of how the battle had turned, how we called on the Mothers to deliver us. And then, with the fluidity of the smith, and the urgency of the iron's brief softness, I conjured a dream-like tale of the land itself rising to join us:

The Mothers replied:
'By means of language and of the land,
Transform majestic trees into a war band,
And impede the mighty one.'
When the trees were enchanted,
In the hope of our purpose,
They hewed down the enemy
With powerful branches.

Then came a mystical contest, where trees were as warriors defending their soil:

Alder at the head of the line
Struck first;
Willow and Rowan,
Were slow to join,
Spiky blackthorn,
Eager for slaughter.
Raspberry took action:
He did not hide.
And Ivy, despite his beauty,
How fiercely did he go into the fray!

Manacca giggled. I carried on, inspired by her glee, describing every class of plant and shrub, showing her that we and this land were the same.

This part of the song continued for many verses, for I did not wish to reach its end. But I had to tell the ending. That would not come as easily. I took a breath and began:

Black is buried wood,
Heavy is the mountain,
Trees are cut,
I hear no battle cry.

My voice dropped away. Suddenly the truth of what we had lost overwhelmed me. Manacca looked up, her smile gone.

I had to give her hope. If I could not conjure a future in this story for her, then how could I do it for the tribes?

Through spinning words that no Roman would ever unravel, I sang of Caradog, who ruled as the sun, whose story would endure within the earth, until it rose anew. I called him not by his name, for his strength was to remain hidden.

355

Radiant his name, strong his hand,
Like lightning he commanded the war band.
Honoured blood flows
From this king buried in earth
Birch tips sprout
From his vigour,
He is born, re-born, and born again,
He is our language.
Wise people, sing of his return!

Manacca stared up, her face lit bright.

I knew, over time, this song would be embellished, re-shaped and strengthened. It would be sung and heard and repeated by people who would live many thousands of summers from now.

I squeezed Manacca closer against the cold air and finished with the final claim that would give my poem its authority:

Not from a mother and a father was I made,
I was created from the blossoms of trees,
From soil, from the sod
Was I made,
The wisdom of the Mothers shaped me,
As the world was shaped,
Now I hold in song
What the tongue can utter
Now I am Songwoman.

The song was finished.

I rested my chin on Manacca's head.

'Again,' she said.

Author's Note

Songwoman is a work of fiction, although the characters of Caradog (Caratacus), Cartimandua and Scapula, and the military events of their war, are drawn from history. What little we know about Rome's invasion of Britain in the first century CE comes to us primarily through the writing of the Roman historians Tacitus and Cassius Dio.

Caratacus was a prince of the Catuvellauni tribe who fought the Roman army when it first invaded in 43 CE, then went on to lead a nine-year resistance campaign against the colonisers. In the latter years of his guerrilla war, he was based at a stronghold in the tribelands of the Silures, in modern-day Wales. I have sited this township at the Llanmelin Iron-Age fortifications, located near Chepstow, which may have been the tribal capital.

I have adhered to the known sequence of military events. For the purposes of narrative fiction, however, I have compressed time. Events spanning one year in *Songwoman* probably played out over three to four years of protracted fighting.

Tacitus tells us that a final decisive battle was fought on a steep hillside before a river, somewhere north of the Silures tribelands. The specific location of this battle is, however, yet to be determined. When my daughter and I climbed the slopes of Dinas Emrys and stared out at the jagged, mist-crowned peaks of Snowdonia, I felt certain that this was the place.

Cartimandua's final betrayal of Caratacus is drawn directly from the writings of Tacitus, although her motivation remains the subject of speculation.

The mythology and beliefs of native Britain are elusive, as this was a culture that preserved its wisdom via an oral tradition. But the Welsh texts inscribed from the thirteenth century onwards are considered to contain stories that are far, far older. It is from these I have taken my inspiration.

Acknowledgements

This novel would not exist in its current form if it were not for my discovering the extraordinary scholarship of Dr Gwilym Morus-Baird, who runs the online learning portal, whitedeer.earth. Gwilym opened my mind to the ancient stories of Welsh mythology and to the craft of the poet-bards who told them. He was immensely generous and patient with my questions. I hope I have done his work justice.

I am grateful to Dr Lynne Kelly, who conceived an illuminating theory around the memory techniques of oral societies, described in her book *The Memory Code*. Her ideas and research have helped to shape this book.

I drew heavily on the work of Miranda Aldhouse-Green, who writes about the Celtic druids and human sacrifice and was kind enough to answer several email queries. The text preceding chapter six is a reworked quote from *Ardor*, by Roberto Calasso.

For information about the military history of Rome's invasion of Britain and the campaigns of Caratacus, I have drawn on the work of Graham Webster and John Peddie. Caradog's speech before Claudius is taken directly from the *Annals* of Tacitus. Ailia's song at the novel's conclusion is a re-worked version of fragments of the poem 'Kat Godeu', from the *Book of Taliesin*, translated by Marged Haycock. The lines Ailia attempts in her lesson with Rhain are taken from the poem 'Kadeir Teyrnon', from the same source.

Renting & letting

D0317965

"Renting and letting is a fast process that can happen in a few days. Don't let this speedy process take over the need for getting the legal terms and conditions of the rent or let right at the start – or it could cost you dearly in the future."

Kate Faulkner

About the author

Kate Faulkner has been involved in the property market both as a 'consumer' (buying, renovating, renting and letting) and working in the industry, advising on lettings, estate agents, relocating companies and the general public. She runs the website www.designsonproperty.co.uk and is a consultant to residential property companies. The author of three other Which? property books, Kate provides help to people, whatever their property project, throughout the UK.

which?
essential guides

Renting & letting

KATE FAULKNER

This book is for my family and friends, who are always there for me.

Which? Books are commissioned and published by Which? Ltd,
2 Marylebone Road, London NW1 4DF
Email: books@which.co.uk

Distributed by Littlehampton Book Services Ltd, Faraday Close, Durrington, Worthing,
West Sussex BN13 3RB

British Library Cataloguing in Publication Data
A catalogue record for this book is available from the British Library

Copyright ©Which? Ltd 2006.
First edition 2006. Second edition 2008. Third edition 2011.
ISBN: 978 1 84490 116 6

1 3 5 7 9 10 8 6 4 2

Although the author and publisher endeavour to make sure the information
in this book is accurate and up-to-date, it is only a general guide. Before taking action
on financial, legal, or medical matters you should consult a qualified professional adviser,
who can consider your individual circumstances. The author and publisher can not
accordingly accept liability for any loss or damage suffered as a consequence of relying
on the information contained in this guide.

Author's acknowledgements
Big thanks to Sean and Emma Callery for their help, support and continued generosity;
Bob Vickers, Katy Denny and Angela Newton; Sian Evans at Weightmans; Richard Grayson
from Nicholsons; Mark Montgomery from 1st Property Lawyers; Andrew, Mike, Paul and
Terry from Belvoir Lettings; Paul at Lindsays for help with Scotland; Paul Shamplina from
Landlord Action; David from The Letting Network; The Deposit Protection Service, and
Amanda from Designs on Property. The chart on page 23 is published courtesy of
www.belvoirlettings.com.

Additional text by: Sean Callery
Printed and bound by Charterhouse, Hatfield

Essential Velvet is an elemental chlorine-free paper produced at Condat in Périgord,
France, using timber from sustainably managed forests. The mill is ISO14001 and
EMAS certified.

For a full list of Which? Books, please call 01992 822800, access our website at
www.which.co.uk/books, or write to Littlehampton Book Services.

Contents

Introduction

If you are a landlord, the long-term future is bright with an increasing number of people renting instead of buying, but you have to deal with possible stagnating property prices. If you are a tenant, then renting gives you flexibility and often the chance to rent a property in an area you could not otherwise afford to live, but the future holds tightening stock levels and rising rents.

Since the credit crunch, the rental market has boomed, crashed and started to boom again for both tenants and landlords.

From a tenant's perspective, from late 2007 until autumn 2008, rents rose as more people wanted to rent than buy a property. New tenants then benefited from rents crashing by at least 10 per cent due to an oversupply of properties available for rent from 'accidental' landlords who let their properties when they realised they couldn't sell them. From the summer of 2010, however, rents started to rise again as rental stocks reduced and first-time buyers continued to rent rather than buy.

From a landlord's potential perspective, their rental income rose up until October 2008, while their property values fell by at least 20 per cent. Then rental income plummeted and property prices stagnated. For those landlords who had not bought wisely, these falls meant they lost their portfolios and, in some cases, even their own homes.

For landlords that were financially secure and had made good investments, cash rich investors could benefit from low property prices as mortgage lending tightened severely for the buy-to-let sector. As the market stabilised in 2009, finding deals that could stack up was increasingly difficult. In 2010, most landlords started to see their rental income grow and prices started to fall again, creating potentially excellent circumstances for buy-to-let investors.

BE INFORMED

Whether you are a tenant or a landlord, understanding what is happening in the market is crucial so as a tenant you rent at the right time and agree your rent levels for the next 12 months, if you can. Landlords need to understand what is a 'good deal' and whether a property stacks up now and will deliver a good investment return in the future.

What we know is that the private sector rental market is likely to grow. All indications are that, for some

people, renting property is becoming either a necessity or choice in life. For landlords, this is good news as carefully bought properties in good locations and in great condition will be sought after. From the tenant's perspective, this means renting the best properties is likely to be harder, so you have to make sure you are in the best position to be 'chosen' by the landlord.

CHOOSE CAREFULLY

As this market is going to grow, it is vital that landlords and tenants work together as best as possible. To do this, landlords need to understand what tenants want, where they want to live now and in the future and make sure they stay on the right side of the many rules and regulations they must abide by. To survive, they need to carefully choose properties that will always rent well and will grow in value over the average 15 years that a buy-to-let landlord owns a property.

For tenants to survive in an increasingly competitive market, they need to make themselves as appealing to good landlords as possible. However, not every landlord is a good one, so tenants need to appreciate that there are a lot of laws to protect them when they rent. These laws make sure that a property is let legally, in a safe condition and landlords (and letting agents) treat tenants fairly. The laws will only be effective, though, if tenants understand what to look for to

spot a legally let property and what questions to ask landlords and letting agents before agreeing to rent.

Where this often falls down is because properties that are legally and professionally let often cost more than those rented by rogue landlords or those let by private landlords who don't always understand all the rules and regulations they need to abide by. Making sure good properties are rented is as much the responsibility of the tenant as it is the landlord and letting agents.

Tenant's take

Of course, landlords are only half of the equation: many of us will rent property at some time in our lives, and being a tenant isn't always easy. This book offers guidance on choosing the right property (and landlord) and the rights and responsibilities of both tenant and landlord. The legal chapters towards the back of the book are essential reading for both tenant and landlord.

Professional bodies

National Landlords Association: www.landlords.org.uk
Residential Landlords Association: www.rla.org.uk

Letting agents
National Approved Letting Scheme: www.nalscheme.co.uk
Royal Institution of Chartered Surveyors: www.rics.org
The Property Ombudsman: www.tpos.co.uk
Association of Residential Letting Agents: www.arla.co.uk

So tenants need to make essential checks and take time and even some money to check out a property, landlord, letting agent and their tenancy agreement. To help this process, professional landlords and letting agents need to promote the hard work they do to make sure tenants understand it is worth paying a bit extra for a legally and safely let property and to be well looked after through their rental period.

HOW THIS BOOK HELPS

This book explains what tenants and landlords should look for in a rental property and what costs you will incur. As a tenants it explains how to make sure you don't pay too much and as a landlord how you can secure the best income and investment return you can.

Both landlords and tenants can quickly pick up what questions to ask at every stage of the rental or buy-to-let process to make sure that they secure the right properties for them and learn about what makes the 'other' tick. Tenants will learn how to make themselves more attractive to landlords, and landlords will learn how to make their property more attractive to tenants.

Crucially, we cover all the legal aspects of letting and renting a property in easy checklists and table formats. There are also checklists so that both landlords and tenants can assess the legal letting documents.

The book also gives a wealth of information regarding the additional resources you need throughout your letting and renting experience. These include the relevant trade associations and letting organisations that are essential to know about and turn to for help and advice just in case things go wrong.

 If you let property without assistance, you may find it difficult to keep within the law. If you try to let without declaring the extra income and Capital Gains Tax or complying with the rules and regulations, the chances of getting caught are increasing as the Government and local councils are clamping down on rogue landlords.

Letting and renting

There are many reasons why people let out and rent property. This chapter looks at the main ones before delving deeper into the different types of rent that are available to prospective landlord and tenant alike.

Why let?

Approximately 15% of UK housing stock is rented out. Although this is expected to rise to 20 per cent by 2020, it is still far lower than the average of 40 per cent in the rest of Europe. The vast majority of the properties are let by private landlords, and the market is now a national industry that splits into accidental landlords, people who are investing to add to their pension and those that make letting their business.

In a market where the rent is determined by the number of rooms, size matters. Most rented properties are small; a third of privately rented properties are flats and the remainder are mainly terraced or semi-detached houses. Demand is rising, partly due to the property prices over the last 10 years rising more than wages, partly due to a 'lifestyle' choice of our younger generation.

Over 3 million properties are let in the private sector with 47 per cent of 20 to 24-year-olds renting. When asked, 19 out of 20 16 to 19-year-olds expect renting to expand at the expense of home ownership. Many are professional single people or couples who either can't or don't want to buy into the property market and value the sense of freedom that comes with renting: if they want to move on, they can do so quickly and easily. Other factors driving tenant demand are increasing number of students and demand from first-time buyers unable to get a foot on the housing ladder. Increased immigration into the UK following the accession of the eastern European states has also had an impact in certain areas in the UK.

THE PLUSES AND MINUSES

Over many years, property has proved so far to be a sound investment: prices have risen over time, in many cases far out performing what can be earned from a deposit account or equity investment. Letting offers a rental income plus the benefit of any growth in the property value. However, prices can fall as well as rise (as we have seen since 2007) and the landlord is responsible for the maintenance of the property and has to find tenants willing to rent it or pay someone else to do this. It is important to view property investment as a long-term

❝ Rented properties are in high demand: lending restrictions force many buyers to wait longer while they save a deposit. ❞

business investment, not a get-rich-quick scheme. In the main, a higher percentage of the earnings is from the rise in value, as opposed to the profit made on the monthly rent. The introduction of buy-to-let mortgages has encouraged more people into the letting market. These specialist deals are designed for those buying property expressly to let out to tenants (see pages 46–7). There are approximately one and a quarter million buy-to-let mortgages in the UK.

Dreams of yield

The key word for landlords is yield: how much the property is earning for them. Yield can be calculated in lots of different ways, but in its simplest form, it is the total amount of rent, minus running costs, divided by how much the property cost. So a £145,000 property with annual rent of £16,000 that costs £1,500 a year to run will bring in £14,500 income. Divide this figure by the value of the property produces 0.1, which, expressed as a percentage (multiply by 100), is a yield of 10 per cent.

£16,000 – £1,500 = £14,500
£14,500 ÷ £145,000 = 0.1
0.1 x 100 = 10%

The reason it is really important to calculate yield is that you may find your money would give a better return

A property will tie up your money for some period of time, and unlike shares, you can't just decide to sell one day: you will have to consider your agreement with the tenant, and you are likely to need to produce an Energy Performance Certificate and then hope there is a buyer out there willing to pay the price you want!

on investment just left in the bank or in some other investment scheme. Not all properties will deliver a good yield though and yields vary depending on the type of let you invest in.

Make sure that before you commit your hard-earned cash to buy to let you discuss your options with an **independent financial adviser (IFA)** – it may be that you can get better returns from other investments, avoiding the associated administration and risk of buy to let altogether.

❝Work out the potential yield – it might be better to invest your money elsewhere.❞

For more information on yield and how to work out your return on investment, see pages 42–5 and 115–26. Reference: Keynote Research.

In summary, before you jump into buy to let, make sure you plan a realistic figure on the yield you can achieve – for more information, see pages 42–5.

Burst pipes and paperwork

Being a landlord is not easy. There are an enormous number of legal and safety checks to undertake, a lot of administration to keep on top of, and, of course, part of the role involves dealing with people, which brings its own complications. In addition, when a pipe bursts or a boiler goes cold, you get the call and need to sort out the problem fast. You will certainly need to set aside several hours a month to deal with administration and problems: one survey found the average was 12 hours a month – that is a day and a half of working time. Of course, much of this work can be done outside office hours, but that means it will eat into your leisure and family time unless you use a letting agent to do it for you.

Are you right for the role?

Not everyone makes a good landlord. You need to be:

- **Well organised** to deal with all the paperwork.
- **Prepared to get your hands dirty** doing routine maintenance.
- **Fit enough** to shift beds and wardrobes.
- **Good at dealing** with people.
- **Able to handle the responsibility** regarding the legal regulations that come with the role.
- **Equipped** with a cool business head.

If this doesn't sound like you, you probably shouldn't become a landlord, or you need to pay other people to deal with the hassle, which will eat into your income.

WHY BE A LANDLORD?

Most of the time, the answer is very simple: money. Letting to tenants provides a guaranteed regular income while you still benefit from any rise in value of the property itself. It is a form of investment where you have more control than collections of stocks and shares, and can influence the rise in value by modernising and operating efficiently. You can also monitor how well your investment is doing (see page 42).

There are other benefits, too. There is the satisfaction of providing a service to others (how would students manage their accommodation needs without landlords?) and, for some, letting a room at home is a source of companionship. If you are interested in the property market, you can enjoy the stimulation of researching market conditions and viewing properties without the emotional complications that are inevitable when looking for a home for yourself.

Do some research

Talk to as many people as you can to find out if property investment is for you: it's a hard-nosed business that doesn't suit everybody. A good place to start researching life as a landlord is the website of the National Association of Landlords or the Residential Landlords Association (see below). The local authorities may also run local landlord accreditation schemes and events which are worth attending.

A number of companies run courses on property investment. These tend to be over-priced and over-hyped. Much of the information given is widely available elsewhere at a fraction of the cost. If you are interested, sign up for any free courses but don't be sucked into paying over the odds for the follow-ups, and don't take your cheque book or other form of payment so that you can't be hurried into a purchase by a hard sell.

❝ Letting to tenants provides a guaranteed regular income for a landlord, and you can also benefit from any rise in value of the property itself. ❞

For landlord organisations visit www.rla.org.uk and www.landlords.org.uk.

Other ways to make money from property

You may have great faith that property prices will always continue to rise in the long term, but lack the commitment necessary to be a landlord. If so, there are a number of other routes to property investment:

Investing in syndicates

A syndicate is a group of people (it can number up to 15) who own property together while paying a management company to run it and deal with the tenants and maintenance. Syndicates generally operate more than one property, and are often able to negotiate substantial discounts on property purchase by buying in bulk (for example, purchasing a whole block of flats rather than one unit). This allows you to get involved in the property market at relatively low cost, with the risk spread over a number of properties. Syndicates are not regulated by the Financial Services Authority (FSA).

Property funds

These are organisations that buy, sell and manage property, in which you can invest. You have little say in the day-to-day running of the business, which is conducted according to an agreed prospectus. You can join a property fund through an independent financial adviser. Funds are regulated by the FSA.

Renovating for profit

This is hands-on development for those who know the market and have the skills or contacts to improve a property quickly and sell it on. It is a tough route during a recession when property prices don't rise. These investors are often responsible for bringing semi-derelict or uninhabitable properties back into occupation.

Buying and selling property

Again, those who know what they are doing and have the time and expertise will seek out undervalued or unwanted properties, perhaps make a few changes or improvements, such as obtaining planning permission for an extension, then sell on at a profit.

Buying 'off plan'

The buyer purchases unbuilt property from a developer, hoping to sell it on at a profit after it is completed. The investment is highly risky in a static/falling property market.

It's your pension

Some people are concerned that they may not have enough invested to pay a nice bonus for retirement, and decide that by letting out property they can ensure that they receive an income while holding on to the equity of the rising value of their bricks and mortar. Few landlords make a lot of money from rental income: the bulk of their profit is gained through cashing in on the rising value of the properties they let. While property prices went up from the late 1990s to 2007, they fell by 20 per cent or more in the following years, and it is vital to allow for periods for when the property is empty and you are not receiving any income. As always, when making crucial decisions about your future finances, it makes sense to get advice from an IFA.

Room to let

One of the many ways in which people let property is by renting out a room in their own house. There are many reasons why you might choose to do this:

- **To help pay** the mortgage or for extra income.
- **For company,** to combat the loneliness of living on your own, maybe after the children have fled

the nest or after being widowed or divorced.

- **As a way of staying** in a much loved residence that would otherwise be too big.
- **Because you have the space** and feel it is the right thing to do to share it.

You may be able to offer some self-contained accommodation, such as a granny flat with its own bathroom and kitchen. Sometimes the arrangement begins informally as a way of helping out a friend who needs a room for a short time. If you want to try out such an arrangement but do not want to enter into long-term commitments, you could try:

- **Local churches,** which often have links with groups in other parts of the country and may know of someone looking for a local room.
- **English language teaching schools.** There are many of these around the country, mainly based in cities and some towns, where students come from abroad to attend a course for a set period and need somewhere to stay.
- **Local companies** or other large employers, who might be taking on someone based at another location, perhaps as a temporary arrangement.

For more information on the different ways to make money out of property go to www.designsonproperty.co.uk and the Which? Essential Guide: Property Investor's Handbook.

Relocating or can't sell your own home

Another reason you might opt to let out your property is if you need to move or work away, possibly abroad, and do not want to sell your home. Letting out your home allows you to return to it when it is convenient for you to live in it again, while still covering the cost of owning a property. The downside is that, unlike other properties, this is your home and you have emotional ties to it. You may not feel comfortable with the idea of others living in it, and the inevitable wear and tear that goes with occupancy may feel like an intrusion when it is not your children's shoes that scuffed the paintwork.

Working away from home

In today's job market, change happens fast. You might take on a temporary contract for, say, six months in another part of the country, or be offered a job elsewhere with the prospect of changing your conditions of work to do more from home, or from a base nearer to it. You may take a job elsewhere but want to maintain the equity of your current home, or keep your children attending a school where they are happy. There are many circumstances in which it makes sense to take on a flat near work but keep hold of your family home, even if you can only be there at weekends. You might then choose to rent out a spare room in the flat, thus improving its security by having someone living there all the time, and offsetting some of your own costs. The tenant gets a good deal because they will probably have the place to themselves when they most want it, at the weekend.

❝ You might decide to let out your property if you need to move for work and don't want to sell your home. ❞

Your student children need a roof over their heads

One factor that has prompted a number of people to take the plunge into letting is the high costs of student accommodation at a time when further education is already expensive. Buying a property near the university your son or daughter

Case Study — Mr and Mrs James

Mr and Mrs James had just moved up to Lincolnshire having lived and worked around London for ten years. The plan was that Mrs James would buy and renovate property, some to sell and some to let, building up a property portfolio over the years. Unfortunately, the plan went pear-shaped when Mr James landed his dream job – back down south in Reading.

The cost to rent a room in Reading was £400–£500 a month and there were no guarantees that Mrs James could stay whenever she needed to work down south. The cost of property was much more than in Lincolnshire, with the cheapest properties being flats around £140,000 rather than a two-bed property for £70–£80,000!

A compromise was reached when Mrs James found a two-bedroom flat in need of renovation – in a good area in Reading – for sale for £135,000.

The property was part of a housing association block of flats, and so there would always be a limited number of the flats available for private purchase, and therefore likely to always be a high demand for the flat when it came to sell.

However, the flat needed work, with a new bathroom, painting, new carpets and a good clean! To check what other work was required, the Jameses requested a property survey and a gas and electric survey to be done. The cost of the surveys were around £600. However, they found that the property needed a stopcock putting in to allow separation of the water supply from the rest of the block of flats and problems with the electrics that needed doing. The result was that the surveys helped to reduce the cost of the property by several thousand pounds, and offering a quick purchase, the property was actually bought for £125,000.

The work required cost just over £3,000, but the low purchase cost and the renovation to a good standard, fitting the tenant's room with a new desk and bed, trendy curtains and bedding, the room was let within a week of finishing the work for a full 12 months. The low price paid for the property meant that the room rent could always be set at lower than anyone else in the area, ensuring no problems re-letting and no voids. Free broadband was also thrown in as an incentive to secure a 12-month let.

As a result, instead of paying out £400–£500 a month on renting a room during the week, with no flexibility and certainly no chance of capital growth, the flat costs the Jameses much less than this every month as they gain rent from the other room and they have already made a capital gain on the property of over £20,000!

Depending on who you are planning to rent out your property to, you will need to decorate and furnish it appropriately. See pages 22–34 for ideas on what you should be thinking about.

attends means they won't have to pay any rent if you choose not to charge them. You may well be able to let out other rooms in the property, and will be confident that at least one of the tenants has your interests at heart, so the property should be treated fairly well. Of course, you could still be the landlord and will have to shoulder the legal and practical responsibilities that this entails.

❝ You may be able to let out other rooms in the property, and be confident that at least one of the tenants has your interests at heart, so the property should be treated fairly well. ❞

You inherited property

Many people inherit property from their parents. They may choose to move in to it themselves, or to sell it. However, it may not be easy to market or they may be reluctant to let go of what may be a much-loved property that houses many memories, or prefer to see it as an investment. In such cases letting is an option.

You want a holiday home

Buying a second property as a holiday home is a popular choice for many who wish to combine property investment with pleasure. The advantages of this arrangement are that you have ready access to your holiday accommodation, but cover its costs through letting it to other occupants during the holiday season. If you decide not to holiday at it one year, you can rent it out instead. You may decide to limit the renting to friends and family, which may make you very popular within your social circle but won't necessarily earn as much. Buying a holiday home to let out is an excellent way of establishing a foothold in a new area, perhaps with a view to retiring there.

A disadvantage is that the property may only attract interest during the holiday period and could stand empty for half of the year while you still have to pay the mortgage and upkeep. There is also the hassle of advertising for and dealing with holiday renters, although you can pay an agency to do this. Also, the holiday home is likely to be some distance from where you live, so you will not be able to deal with on-site problems quickly or easily. You'll need to do your sums and your business plan carefully if you plan to treat a holiday home as an investment.

 You should consider whether to take on short- or long-term lets for your property. The advantages and disadvantages of both these types of let are described on pages 22–34.

Why rent?

Renters will include prospective first-time buyers trying to save a deposit, but could also include people who have sold a property but have not found the dream home they are seeking.

In such a situation, renting makes a lot of sense: it gives them a chance to see what it is like living in an area where they may buy and to see what facilities and schools are like. They can then make an offer on a property as a cash buyer, rather than someone with a property chain dragging along behind them.

Another trend is for older people who choose to rent in the later part of their lives so that their outgoings are predictable and they can live within a set budget, possibly having sold the house that they owned.

There will, of course, also be some free spirits who choose to rent, preferring the flexibility it offers compared to that or living as an owner-occupier. They benefit from not being responsible for the maintenance of the property, so they can plan their finances very well because all the other costs related to accommodation (rent and bills) are predictable.

❝ Choosing to rent rather than take on a mortgage can provide a flexible lifestyle. ❞

TEMPORARY ACCOMMODATION

Another reason to rent is if your job moves to a different part of the country, perhaps temporarily, or that you are not confident will be a permanent arrangement. It makes sense to take a room or a small flat rather than go through the financial and emotional hassle of buying a property that you may need to sell in the near future. If you are considering moving to a new area, renting for six months to see what it is really like is an investment in your quality of life: if you find out that you don't like the area, you can move to another one far more easily than if you had bought property.

Two other groups of people that require temporary accommodation are students who are unlikely to be able to afford a property to buy, often go to college away from home, returning for holidays.

Many people don't think about taking a holiday cottage as rental accommodation, but it is, in its truest form, going away for a few weeks and staying in a property by the sea or a remote area of the country, or abroad.

The advantage of renting temporarily is that it can be a safer bet in times of economic uncertainty. If you invest in a property when prices were high, a fall in the market – as happened post the credit crunch – can mean you lose money on your investment, whereas rental prices are typically less volatile.

However, the disadvantage of renting in a rising property market is that you are not getting any return for your money apart from a roof over your head. Rent payments are 'dead' money, while the price of the property you might eventually want to buy will go up, possibly out of your range.

Who are you going to live with?

It is important to decide from the start whether you are just looking for accommodation for yourself or with others. Some people thrive on living on their own, others find it lonely. If you don't have a live-in partner, you could still look for two-bedroom properties with a friend or relative.

Advantages	Disadvantages
● Self-contained two-bedroom properties are more cost effective to rent than those with one bedroom. ● You've got someone to share the hassle and the bills with. ● It might be more companionable than living alone.	● Sharing a kitchen or bathroom with others can be tricky if they use your things or don't clean up after themselves. ● It is likely to be noisier – and many flats have poor sound insulation anyway, so someone else's life can intrude on your own. ● If you don't get on well, shared accommodation can be lonely and stressful, emotionally and financially. ● You might not like their friends, and resent the occasions when they visit.

What's your market?

As with any business, if you are planning to let property, it is essential to identify what your target market is, and ensure that your product suits their needs. You will need to do this before you buy, convert or decorate your property.

Short-term lets

Short-term lets are between one week and three months and are furnished. The rent usually includes charges for utilities, with the tenant expected to deal with the cost of the landline telephone (if used). The number of tenants requiring short-term lets is rising as employers increasingly expect their staff to be mobile and to work for short stretches in different locations.

From the landlord's point of view, short-term lets are more work because the property must be in immaculate condition at all times and there is the ongoing need to market it for the next vacant period. In addition to higher set-up and maintenance costs, insurance premiums can be higher. However, rents are significantly higher and in the right location (usually city centres) a short-term let offers a better yield than a long-term one. Typical short-term lets are company and holiday lets.

COMPANY LETS

A company, or corporate, let is when you have a contract with a firm to accommodate their employees as tenants. It can pay very well, but requires properties of a very high (and therefore costly) standard. Senior executives sometimes have a working routine of being in one location for two days then moving to another region, but prefer the familiarity of a house or flat to the anonymity of hotel rooms. Beware that corporations may suddenly decide to relocate and no longer require property: if you go for this market, make sure there is more than one suitably large firm in the area. Hospitals and universities are other organisations that sometimes require short-term, high-quality accommodation.

Typical locations

Obviously, the employee needs to be within easy reach of his or her workplace. Those without families are likely to prefer city-centre locations near shops and leisure facilities. Those with families tend to go for suburban or rural locations with good transport links, preferably near a park.

 If you are a tenant in a short-term let, you have less security that in a long-term let (see pages 28–34). For more information on the legal position of tenants see pages 128–34 and 136–56.

Risk level

This is a general assessment of the level of risk of the buy-to-let market taking into consideration risks such as default on rent, damage to property and the likelihood of taking out legal proceedings.

Type of tenancy	Average yield	Estimated risk level
Company	5%	1–2
Professional	5%	2–3
Social	6%	1–2
Holiday let	5–10%	4–5
Student	9–10%	4
Houses in multiple occupation	9–12%	5

Tenants are likely to be professionals and will have high expectations of local schools if they have a family with them. For those from abroad, an international school within easy reach could be important.

Lets can be long or short term, and often include a charge for water, gas and electricity so that the client does not have to deal with utility bills.

What you need to provide

An executive with no family or one who stays in the accommodation only during the working week is going to want a one- or two-bedroomed property with roomy living space. Families need more bedrooms, bathrooms and living space, a well-equipped utility room, and a garden suitable for children. Secure car parking is essential. The tenants will expect high quality TVs and hi-fi equipment, broadband access and a well-planned kitchen. Furniture should be modern and stylish. At the top end, corporate clients expect luxuries such as Egyptian cotton sheets and limestone bathrooms. Long-term professional tenants may prefer to come with their own furniture, but since they are likely to have vacated their own family home, may also wish you to provide it. Decoration should be elegant (no strong colours) with accessories such as antiques or artwork. Some corporate tenants will expect a maid and a laundry/garden service.

The tenant's take

As a tenant in accommodation recommended by (and possibly paid by) your employer, you'll expect high-standard furnishings and fittings and excellent security to reflect the premium rent being charged. You'll expect to be able to move in straightaway with the minimum of fuss, and know that someone from your firm or relocation agency has vetted the property thoroughly if you can't do so. You may want to arrange for a cleaner to visit regularly.

How to find tenants

- **Letting agents:** You may well have to go through letting agents (see pages 68–71) because companies tend to work with other professionals. However, it might be worth contacting human resource departments of large organisations – you'll save a big fee. They may arrange lettings themselves, especially for staff coming from abroad, or they may provide the employee with a budget and contacts. You may be able to advertise quite cheaply in the company newspaper or intranet.
- **Relocation firms** specialise in helping executives move to new posts. The ideal scenario is when a company takes out a let itself and simply sublets to its staff: you get a guaranteed premium rent without the hassle of finding new tenants or the dreaded void periods. However, try to limit tenant turnover as it can be disruptive, and carry out

You must take out specialist buildings and contents insurance on your holiday home (see pages 75–6): a standard household policy will not be suitable. Your policy should include public liability cover in case someone suffers injury or damage on the property.

Are you sure?

Although holiday lets attract far higher rent than residential lets, especially in high season, there are significant marketing, administration and managing costs. Using the property for your own breaks will reduce the income you receive, and you will probably have to visit regularly to check on its condition, while arranging repairs from a distance can be a nightmare. Finally, you can buy a lot of holidays for the cost of a house or flat! However, you will benefit from any rises in the property market and if you attract a full complement of bookings, you will generate a sizeable income.

an inventory check with each changeover. For a local relocation firm, see www.arp-relocation.com.

SERVICED APARTMENTS AND 'APART HOTEL' LETS

This is where you buy into the ownership of a hotel room or serviced apartment within a hotel or block. Although the rental returns can be good, your ability to sell it on is limited as these are usually for cash buyers only. Typically, these investments are based in international cities, such as London or New York, and you receive a percentage of the income generated from their use. Sometimes you are allocated a set number of days per annum that you can use the room for free.

As the income generated from hotels and serviced apartments is higher than from a standard buy to let, if they are well utilised, your average rental return can be a lot a higher. However, you need ready cash to invest as you can't borrow for these investments. This means that the potential selling market, when you cash in to make profit, is limited.

HOLIDAY LETS

It sounds perfect: buy a property somewhere you enjoy visiting (and perhaps plan to retire to), use it when you like, and get it to pay for itself the rest of the time by running it as a holiday let. In reality, a lot of landlords operating holiday lets are glad to break even in this competitive and labour-intensive market. However, this is an expanding market: more than 4 million people rent cottages and holiday apartments every year, and self-catering holidays are increasingly popular.

Most holiday lets occur during the period of about 20–30 weeks covering late spring, summer and early autumn, but city properties are a likely bet all year round, and there can be high demand at Christmas and New Year. Standard lets are by the week, but weekend and mid-week breaks are popular, again especially in cities.

Typical locations

Obviously there are hotspots such as the Lake District, seaside resorts and major cities, such as London, York and Edinburgh, but the market for holiday lets is wide ranging. Pretty rural or seaside settings are extremely attractive, and a site close to shops and with good transport links is likely to attract valuable repeat bookings.

City properties should be as near the centre as possible, and certainly with good transport links. Elsewhere, the most attractive holiday lets are

---

Can you hear the crowd?

One potentially lucrative sector in the letting market is short-term lets near major events such as sports tournaments. For example, houses located near the annual tennis championship in Wimbledon are much sought after by players and others attending. They expect high quality accommodation and good parking facilities. Privacy is a priority so you would have to move out – but the payback is the very high rent you can charge. Contact the organisers of the event to see what demand is like and to be added to their accommodation list, or seek advice from local letting agencies.

When you are calculating how much income you might earn from holiday lets, don't forget to allow for the potentially longer periods when the property will be empty. For more information on calculations, see pages 42–5.

those that are conveniently situated among the local attractions, rather than on the edge of a popular region. A rural location might look attractive, but it could be vulnerable to burglars because it will be left unattended, and is likely to be equipped with attractive, portable equipment. You need a good burglar alarm.

Holiday lets are a quick turnaround business where the property needs to be freshened up between lets of a week or two, so either you will need to be on hand as a regular commitment, or you will need to find someone to do it for you: you can't run it yourself properly from a distance.

There are strict rules as to what constitutes a holiday let, explained on page 121. A holiday let must be in the UK, furnished, available for letting for at least 140 days a year and commercially let (not at cheap rates to family and friends) for at least 70 days a year, with the lets not exceeding 31 days.

What you need to provide

The biggest market is for two- or three-bedroom properties that can sleep a family of four or five – so one bedroom should have twin beds. Decoration need not be as neutral as for residential properties: visitors will appreciate a cosy, warm atmosphere with plenty of pictures on the walls. The beds in particular should be of high quality – visitors are unlikely to want to return to a property where they slept badly.

The accommodation must be fully furnished, including linen and towels (some landlords charge extra for these). You'll need to provide a television (satellite channels are a bonus), video and DVD. Provide heaters if there is no central heating, and have a cupboard with extra duvets and blankets. Guests will also expect a washing machine. The kitchen should be well equipped with crockery, cooking equipment and utensils, a microwave and a dishwasher. Many people like to have a radio in the kitchen, and possibly a television. Handling furnishings for holiday lets is different to other letting: you'll need to change bedding more often, for example, but general

explained on page 121.

Helpful advice

Put together a handbook about the property with notes on how the hot water system works, when rubbish should be put out, and contact details if there is a problem. Include an inventory of all equipment provided, with a polite request for any broken items to be replaced and any damage or faults notified.

In addition, put together a separate folder containing local information, such as shops, attractions and emergency contacts, such as the doctor. A visitor's book allows guests to leave their own suggestions and may provide you with useful feedback.

---

wear and tear is lower as people tend to be out a lot during their stay.

For changeover day (Friday or Saturday) you will need to undertake or arrange an inventory check, change of linen and towels, renew soap and toilet rolls, plus a clean up. It is kind to provide a welcome tray of tea, coffee, milk and biscuits, plus maybe a bottle of wine.

How to find tenants

- **Independent letting:** Around half of UK rented holiday homes are let independently rather than through agents. Contact the local tourist office and ask what information they need for you to be added to their list of holiday lets. Many people look for holiday lets on the internet and the easiest way to put yourself forward is to add your property to a local or specialist holiday homes directory (the regional tourist board should have a list of properties, or try www.holiday-rentals.co.uk or other commercial operations).
- **Create your own website,** but only try this if you know what you are doing, as it must look professional.
- **Use a letting agent,** for marketing or managing the property. This will take up a sizeable chunk of your income (they'll charge a percentage of income, possibly up to 49 per cent for a full service), but they should be able to fill your bookings list more efficiently than you can. You obviously have the option

of taking a limited number of private (possibly repeat) bookings separately and informing the agent of any weeks that are not available.
- **Let to friends and family.** This is a good option but beware of doing this for long periods at discounted rents as it could affect your tax position (see page 121).

The tenant's take

If you book early (at least six months ahead for the summer), you will be spoilt for choice. Once you have selected your choice of region(s) you can find details of holiday lets via local tourist offices, or via the internet, where you can usually check availability very easily. Smokers and guests with pets will have to shop around as some landlords do not welcome them. Watch out for variations on changeover days, especially if you are transferring from one holiday let to another in a twin location break: some go for Friday, others for Saturday.

Tenants are also becoming a target for criminals. 'Legitimate' properties to let are advertised online with deposits sent electronically. Then, on arrival, there either is no property or it is being rented by someone else! Never send money unless you have an independent reference from a licensing board, tourist bureau. Also, ask to speak to the company's legal representative, tax adviser or accountant.

Long-term lets

Long-term lets are for residential use. The property can be of a lower standard and there will be fewer maintenance costs. Long-term lets are easier to budget for as you can calculate the guaranteed income over a longer period. However, as with any longer-term arrangement, the charge per week or month will be lower than for a short-term let.

STUDENT LETS

The student let market is very active, highly competitive, and growing fast. The number of students has risen dramatically in the last decade, but university and college accommodation provision has not, and about half of all students rent in the private sector. Tenants tend to be aged around 20, so have a young lifestyle that does not always match that of their neighbours – which does not always make them ideal tenants. When marketing to students, remember their parents will be keen that the accommodation meets their needs (and they may well be paying for it) so you are 'selling' to them too.

The bulk of students often only want accommodation during the academic year, which runs from late September to mid June, although some courses run longer than this. Therefore, there will be a void period in July and August for which you may choose to try to charge a holding fee. Many universities and colleges run separate courses during this summer period and the accommodation office should be able to advise you what demand is like during this time. It is also worth knowing that students are exempt from paying council tax.

A high number of students come to study from overseas. They often make very good tenants because they usually behave very responsibly and tend to stay in the property over holiday periods.

A major decision to be made is whether to let your rooms separately or as a multiple tenancy. Letting rooms individually might bring in more rental income, but you will have to deal with more administration as each tenant has a separate

 If you are letting out rooms in a house of three or more bedrooms, then you may need to apply for a licence for a House in Multiple Occupancy (HMO). This type of let is covered on pages 30-3.

agreement. The other issue is whether the tenants get on with each other: domestic tension can result in people moving out or arguing over bills, both of which could have an impact on you.

Typical locations

Accommodation should ideally be within walking distance of the main university buildings, but this is not always possible in cities, in which case good transport links to the campus or other sites are essential.

Students prefer to live near shops for groceries and areas close to the city centre are popular for the nightlife and part-time work, so good locations tend to be in city centres or busy suburbs, near stations and bus routes. Students also like living near fellow undergraduates, so opt for a road or area where there are already student properties rather than branching out somewhere new.

What you need to provide

Students tend to be working to a tight budget and cannot afford high rents, so you need to maximise the number of rooms or beds for your property. Bedrooms can be quite small. Very few students will be willing to share a room unless they are a couple. A real bonus is to be able to offer secure bike storage: many students

cycle, bike theft is endemic and a bike stored in a communal hallway has a lot of nuisance value. Wheelchair access can be valuable and give you an advantage in a sector of the market that requires it. Good security locks on windows and doors will also be a bonus as students are particularly vulnerable to theft. Satellite TV is another popular service, broadband is essential (see box on page 30) but payphones are a thing of the past.

In the kitchen of larger houses, several people may want to cook at the same time, so a microwave as well as a cooker is useful, as is a large fridge and plenty of storage space. Some landlords save expense by not fitting items such as washing machines or dishwashers, which can be hired by the tenant. Put in flooring that is easy to clean, robust or cheap to replace, such as tiling or vinyl.

With kitchens you can invest in a heavy duty kitchen unit carcass, but then ensure that you get cheap doors and a cheap, easy to replace worktop. If you are looking at a shower, make sure you purchase one that manages the temperature of the water, even when others are running taps or a dishwasher in the kitchen. You should also look for one with parts that can be replaced if they go wrong and are

For advice on homes in multiple occupation (HMOs), see pages 30–3. Check with your local council or experienced letting agent if you need a licence and what adjustments you need to make to ensure your buy-to-let property is legal under the new rules.

easy to access – you don't want to have to re-tile after a shower is fixed!

Some rooms offered to students are tiny: this might not be a problem if the tenant is out a lot and the communal living areas are reasonable, but such a room might be annoyingly intimate. A living room is sometimes turned into a bedroom, which can cut the cost for everyone, but reduces the communal living space.

How to find tenants

- **University accommodation agencies.** Many educational establishments operate accreditation schemes listing landlords who fulfil certain criteria such as having current Gas Safe Registered (gas) and NICEIC, ECA or NAPIT (electrical) safety certificates and staff will often act as arbiter if disputes occur. Whether or not they run such a scheme, accommodation offices are

It is common to ask parents to act as guarantors for their child (see page 80). Get contact details for the parents because if there is a dispute, particularly over the tenant's behaviour, you can get them involved: they are likely to have more sway over their child than you have as a landlord.

a valuable route to finding tenants at little cost to you.

- **Advertising in the student newspaper/ internet and on noticeboards** and cards in shop windows in areas frequented by students.
- **Word of mouth** is the best recommendation, and if you have a solid reputation and suitable accommodation, you should be able to find tenants quite easily unless the market becomes saturated.

Broadband briefing

Students use the internet for research and leisure and your property is more attractive to them if it has a broadband connection because it is far faster. Overseas students, in particular, will value this facility. Broadband is offered with 8+MB. For those wishing to download music and videos, unlimited packages are best.

If you sign up for broadband, make a note of when the contract expires so that you can renew, if your tenants require it. If you have enough tenants, it may be worth investing in wireless broadband so that people can use it anywhere in the house.

MULTIPLE OCCUPATION

As a general guide, the definition of a house in multiple occupation (HMO) is that three unrelated people share a property's facilities. In April 2006, however, the Government introduced licensing for some types of properties that are classed as an HMO in England and Wales (see page 32 and pages 179–80 for details of these for Scotland and page 187 for Northern Ireland).

These new licensing rules mean that a property that is on three or

Go pink

You may decide that female students are going to look after your property more carefully than males – or that it is more suited to men, or couples. You can't specify what gender your tenants can be, but you can influence it subtly by, for example, decorating rooms in shades of pink to make it look more feminine, or setting up double rooms to encourage couples.

or with your local authority, to find out whether or not you need a licence.

For example, local authorities can now licence HMOs if there are just three people who are unrelated sharing a three-bedroom home, this is determined by the local authority. Some authorities are also introducing 'additional licensing', which you may need as a landlord. Each local authority can interpret HMO rules differently, so get individual advice from each one. Typical rules for a licensed HMO are:

more habitable storeys (including attics or basements) and is occupied by five or more people (who are not all in the same family) who share some communal rooms is defined as an HMO that requires a licence.

While this is the general guideline, rules around HMOs and licensing are complex and you should work with a lettings' agency specialising in HMOs,

- **A minimum room size** for one individual (6.5 square metres is a typical minimum).
- **Not allowing more than two people** to sleep in each room, including children.
- **Meeting stringent fire regulations,** such as fire doors, fire extinguishers, smoke alarms and fire blankets in all kitchen areas.

The tenant's take

As a student on a budget, price is crucial. You may be able to get better deals by teaming up with friends and renting together, and a group that intends to share accommodation can share the toil of finding it too.

Ask around: if you hear of a room being available before it hits the market, you might get first refusal, and the landlord will be pleased to get a tenant promptly. See page 113 for advice on choosing people to live with.

It is often cheaper to rent a room in a family home. You will benefit from a fairly high standard of accommodation. The downside is you won't be sharing with other students (for some this is an upside!) and you need to get on with the other people in the house (which might include children), who won't share your lifestyle.

Make sure you agree some rules about how you are going to get along together – see also page 113.

- **Having emergency lighting** in areas such as a hallway that would be used to escape fire or flood.
- **Upgrading floors and ceilings** to enhance sound proofing.

Landlords of HMOs must check with their local authority if a licence is needed and how long it will last for. Fees vary widely (from £300 to £1,100), but they are allowed to offer reductions to landlords on their accreditation schemes or to those who pay promptly. It is usually the landlord who is responsible for paying council tax on HMO premises.

Typical locations

These larger properties are usually found in the older parts of cities. A group of people who haven't chosen to live with each other are unlikely to eat together, so it helps to be near grocery shops. You will need plenty of parking spaces near the property.

What you need to provide

Bedrooms are likely to be larger than those you would consider suitable for a student. The kitchen must allow for several tenants to store and cook food, so a cooker, separate hob and a microwave will help. This room will be used a lot, so install units with good carcasses so you can just change the doors every few years. A hard-wearing work surface is important, too. The shower should be easy to repair (with working parts exposed rather than hidden behind tiles) and must maintain water pressure and temperature when other tenants turn on a tap elsewhere in the property. Having en-suite bathrooms for some rooms will help, and, failing that, a sink in the room and a separate toilet helps reduce bathroom queues.

How to find tenants

- **Let to a group of people who know each other.** They can sign one contract – easier to administer.
- **Advertise for individual tenants in local newspapers.** You may get a better return letting but you will need to advertise more, do more paperwork and repeat the process every time one person moves out. Try also advertising on the noticeboards of large institutions, such as hospitals and companies.
- **Employ a letting agency.** More efficient, but you could be faced with fees for placing a succession of tenants.

SOCIAL LET

Social let housing is accommodation provided by councils, housing associations or charities where the tenant has all or part of their rent

For more information on HMOs, visit www.direct.gov.uk, www.communities.gov.uk/publications/housing/licensinghouses, www.landlordzone.co.uk/HMOs1.htm and www.spareroom.co.uk.

The tenant's take

You can check if the property is licensed as an HMO by looking in the register of the local housing authority. Beware! HMOs are often the chosen route of rogue landlords who are more interested in taking your money than providing a decent roof over your head. To avoid rogue landlords:

- Ask which deposit protection scheme your deposit will be looked after by (see pages 83-4).
- Always ask for up-to-date gas and electrical safety certificates.
- If it's not a licensed HMO, ask to see the Energy Performance Certificate on the property.

many undertake maintenance tasks themselves because they want to make the property their home.

If your prospective tenant is applying for Housing Benefit, ask him or her to sign a letter giving permission for the relevant staff to talk to you about the application: then you will know how it is progressing and whether (and when) the tenant is likely to be able to move in. You can ask for an interim payment if you allow the tenant to move in while the application is being processed. Be aware that Local Housing Allowance (LHA – see page 150) payments are now subject to caps by the Government, which could reduce your income. Also, as LHA is paid directly to the tenant, you aren't guaranteed to receive it. So keep on top of payments if you rent to LHA tenants and if there are any problems receiving rent, contact the local authority.

paid as Housing Benefit by the local authority, or the charity pays.

The social let market can be a good first step on the landlord ladder as the costs involved can be lower and if the rent is paid by the state, you are guaranteed regular payments. But it's more difficult to secure a mortgage to fund purchasing property for social lets as lenders are nervous about participating in this sector. However, tenants are often poorly paid or on benefit, and are commonly families so are likely to establish or already have roots in the community, and so are probably going to continue living in the area. If they are happy with your accommodation, a social tenant can therefore provide rent for a long period with no voids, and

Typical locations

One of the most important factors for social lets is that the area has a strong sense of community, probably with a well-run primary school in the vicinity.

Claiming Housing Benefit

Housing Benefit, also referred to as housing rebate or rent allowance, is available for tenants who are on a low income. Although it is paid by your local council, you can download information and a claim form from www.dwp.gov.uk (does not apply to Northern Ireland). There are strict rules on who can claim it, depending on your age, income and savings. The benefit will not necessarily cover the full rent of a property.

Small pockets of houses where people tend to look after each other – such as cul-de-sacs – are popular. Transport links are very important but car parking less so as social tenants are less likely to own a vehicle. For similar reasons, a local shop is a must.

What you need to provide

As the tenants often have children, they are likely to want a garden and at least two bedrooms. The property must be furnished to legal standards and decoration needs to be clean. Bedsits, studio flats and flats above shops are generally not accepted by housing associations.

How to find tenants

- **The local council.** Many councils keep a list of registered providers of social housing and will allocate tenants to properties. They may also run an accreditation scheme for private landlords.
- **Housing associations** usually own the properties they let out, but it is sometimes possible to lease property to a housing association for a specified period: they will then handle letting, rent collection and day-to-day running. Such schemes typically run for two-year stretches and have the particular benefit that

the landlord's rental income is guaranteed for all of that period.

- **Charities.** Some charities secure rental accommodation from the private sector for the people they are supporting. They will usually engage a local letting agent to look after the property on their behalf, so speak to agents to see if they work with any charities you might like to help to support.

The tenant's take

Council housing departments allocate social housing in their district according to a points system or banding scheme, which assesses need. However, you can also use 'choice-based letting' (CBL). This allows approved tenants regarded as a high priority to apply for specific properties that are advertised in the neighbourhood. You still need to apply for Housing Benefit well before your planned moving date as the process is not always fast. Be realistic: the benefit is designed to cover your needs, not necessarily your wants, so don't expect a three-bedroom property if you only need two. Stay within the terms of the benefit – you can't allow other people to live in the property and must inform the claims department if you start working.

For more information on social lets, see pages 150-6. For more information about CBL, contact your local council and visit webarchive.nationalarchives.gov.uk/+/communities.gov.uk/housing/housingmanagementcare/choicebasedlettings. To find places to rent, go to www.council-exchange.org and www.tenantservicesauthority.org.

Buying property to let

If you have already bought and sold property for yourself and your family, forget everything you did before! Buying property to let to someone else requires a business plan, an understanding of what income and capital growth your buy to let will deliver.

Looking at the local market

It is important to have read the previous chapter to ensure that you make a decision on which is the best market to aim for before you buy a property to let out.

You also need a good grasp of the market in your target area:

- What types of let are required?
- Are there any gaps in the market? Why has no one else met them?
- Can you afford to purchase a property of the right type?
- How will you target the right tenants in this market?

Critical to the process is to understand how the market differs now and in the future. For example, if you want to buy in a rural area, it is unlikely there is much demand for student lets. In the future, though, a new rural college may open and change this situation. On the other hand, this type of property may appeal to a family with children if the local school has a good reputation and the property is not far from a major town (see the chart opposite). However, if the school closes, this may put families off renting there in the future.

BACKGROUND INFO

There are a number of very useful things that you can do to find out about the best market to let to in an area you are interested in.

Visit letting 'only' agents

These tend to be first port of call for anyone looking to let, so it is worth popping in, particularly during quieter times, such as a Monday or Wednesday.

Ideally, start with a lettings specialist as those that also sell property may be keener to sell to you. A good lettings only agent will be happy to brief you on the market as they will only want you to buy properties they can let easily – especially if they don't earn money from selling property.

Questions to ask a lettings specialist include:

- **What types of properties** are easy to let?
- **Are there any types of let** that are short in availability locally?
- **What is the variation in rent** for the different types of let?
- **Are there any types of let** that have noticeably long or short periods of being empty?
- **Where are the best areas** to look for property to suit the different target letting markets?

Summary of the key differences when buying a property to let

Buying process	Buying a property for you	Buying a property to let
Looking for property	• Choose the best location you can afford	• Choose a location that gives you the highest yield (return) (see page 43)
Choosing a property	• Find a property that suits your own requirements, needs and wants	• Choose a property that suits the needs and wants of the market you have chosen to let to
Financing a property	• Gain the best rate from a lender • Put down the highest deposit that you are able to	• Often have to pay a higher rate if borrowing money to buy to let • Will have to put down a minimum deposit, but don't always put down the highest deposit you can
The legals of buying a property	• Look for information that affects how you live in the property	• Look for information that affects how or if you can let it out
Surveying a property	• Currently a survey is optional, although you should always have the minimum of a HomeBuyer Report	• A survey not just of the structure, but of the gas and electrics, too. Safety is essential as you may be liable for any damage the property may inflict on tenants. You will also require an energy performance certificate (EPC) to understand how the EPC affects rental potential
Preparing a property	• Choose décor, fixtures and fittings to suit your taste and lifestyle	• Choose décor, fixture and fittings that will stand the test of tenants and suit the lifestyle you are aiming to let to. If renting as an HMO, check with an experienced letting agent and local council that it meets legal requirements
Furnishing a property	• As above, you would choose furnishings that would suit your lifestyle	• Choose whether you are going to offer furnishings or not, and if you do, make sure they adhere to the regulations (see pages 74–5)
Repairing a property	• Repair as soon as you can and to the standard that you want	• Repair to legal requirements to match national and local regulations
Household bills	• Choose which utilities you would want	• Choose the best deals for tenants, consider energy saving measures

If a couple or more agents give you the same information, then you can be fairly sure that it is accurate. You can also 'watch the market' to help verify the information you have received about letting potential.

Watch the market

Unlike the buying and selling market, watching the letting market is a little more difficult as the process of putting a property up for let and then letting it can happen in less than 24 hours. However, it is an important part of researching what sort of let you will go for. The best way is to track a few properties of each type, checking how long it takes for them to be let. Look through the paper, or ask letting/estate agents. To help choose between different types of let, use the table, below.

You might find that the same types of let vary in how long it takes to let them and this type of research helps you to find out why. For example, it might be that the letting price is much higher, or that people prefer a top-

Small is big

The majority of rented properties have only one to three bedrooms. More people are living on their own than ever before, or as single parent families. In general:

- Studio and one-bedroom flats are less popular than two-bedroom flats.
- Smaller properties are typically cheaper. If you have a lot of money to invest, consider buying two or three small, two-bedroom properties rather than a large property that could prove much harder to rent to a more limited market unless you are considering HMOs (see pages 31-2).

floor flat, rather than a ground-floor flat, or indeed that one has parking and the other doesn't. All of these aspects are important to understand so that you can work out what property specifications you need to look for when going out to buy.

Examples of different times it might take to let a property				
Property	Date on market	Rental price per week	Date let	Time on market
Company let to a professional	1 September	£150	15 September	15 days
Student let (per room)	1 September	£85	10 September	10 days
Private professional let	1 September	£125	5 September	5 days
Social let	1 September	£80	2 September	2 days

Check on local authority research

This is a great resource for anyone looking to buy to let as a local authority plan gives you information, such as population trends, for example, are people moving into the area, maybe for temporary jobs? Perhaps there is growth in a young or old population that creates a need for smaller properties near shops, hospitals and public transport.

Looking at the local plan can also give you an indication of what is happening to local transport. For example, there may be a new bus route, or train/tram terminal being built, or indeed a new road network that would speed up someone's journey to work and back. This could mean an increase in the potential population and therefore an increase in demand for properties to let.

Talk to local landlord groups and associations

These organisations may well be able to help. Although in theory you are 'in competition' with everyone, there are usually people who are willing to help and give you advice. Some may have been caught out on particular types of properties and may be happy for you to learn from their mistakes. However, always verify any advice you gain from people you don't know.

Approach other relevant organisations

If you are looking to research a particular type of let, such as company, student or social let, you could approach the local organisations that are likely to help the tenants find accommodation in the first place. For example, if you are looking at the market for company lets, then talk to some of the major organisations in the area – try their human resources, personnel or accommodation departments, if they have one.

For students (or indeed academics, who tend to move fairly frequently), talk to the local university or college accommodation department. The department will be able to tell you if you are better off finding a property to let to undergraduates, mature students or, better still, one of the visiting lecturers or professors.

If you are considering a social let, then chat to your local housing authority. Many run accreditation schemes, which are well worth joining. You should try your local housing association, too, as they are likely to know what is required in the area and what type of rent you could expect in return.

Local plans are available online through the website of your local council. To Find your local authority housing contacts, visit your local authority website or local council office, or look in your local phone book.

Finding the perfect location

The next step to buying a property is to establish what are the letting growth areas now and in the future. For example, you might find currently there is a shortage of student rents, but in two years' time this shortage will reduce due to a planned new development.

THE INTERNET

Unlike with buying and selling property, the internet does not help you research huge amounts of information about the letting market because it is fast moving and the information available tends to be out of date. It is useful, however, for finding average rental values in the markets you are interested in. There are various sites that concentrate on certain types of let (see below), which will help you find what is already available in your chosen area, and suggest areas to start looking.

For example, in Reading, Berkshire, there are known areas for student lets. These are typically the older, Victorian-style houses on the west side of the town. The rents in this region tend to be cheaper than the north, south or east and it's easy to get to college/university and the town centre – both major benefits to the student community!

If, however, you want to target the professional in Reading, then you are more likely to be looking at apartments around the centre, which make it easy to get to the large companies that are located in the town centre.

On the other hand, if you are looking more at families, then you are likely to need to target two- to three-bedroom houses, in good condition, with a garden, away from a main road and within easy reach of schools and local transport. An area that fits this description well is Lower Earley, just southeast of Reading, near Winnersh Triangle, a big area for offices and industrial companies. This example shows the value of local knowledge in deciding what sector of the required market to aim for.

Useful websites to look at when considering different areas in which to buy are www.findaproperty.com's area guides; www.zoopla.co.uk's rental rental and price estimate information and for renting rooms, http://uk.easyroommate.com/RC/flatshareindex/map.

Local authority websites

These are extremely useful in identifying local areas that are likely to change. The changes to search for are:

● What regeneration and transport changes are there that might enhance an area's desirability?

● What new properties are being built and where, which might increase or decrease the value of future properties?

IN NEWSPAPERS

Another good place to look is the local property paper, *Loot* or *Daltons Weekly*. This will give you an idea of postcode areas to concentrate on for different types of let. Usually properties are listed by area and price, so some areas are quoted in 'price per week' and could be anything from £100 to over £500 a week, depending on the type of property, its location and who it is aimed at.

This research will also help you later on when you are looking for tenants/letting agents to help let your chosen property (see pages 66–73) as you will begin to get an idea of which agent or advertising route is likely to be the one to work with to reach your target market.

LOCAL LETTING AGENTS

As with who to look for, when researching the market, it is worth getting the 'lists' that the local agents produce on a weekly and sometimes daily basis to get an idea of where properties are for different markets. These lists are helpful as they:

● **Tend to be given** in price order.
● **Often have the date** the property becomes available to let – allowing you to gain some idea of how far in advance you may need to start marketing the property to gain a tenant.
● **Give an indication** of the prices you gain for the different postcodes.
● **Allow you to research the prices** that the properties available to let have sold for.

Letting agents (especially those that only let) can also assess property opportunities for you and may have ready made buy to let properties that other landlords want to sell. If they know the area really well, call them with the postcode of a property you are interested in and they should be able to give an indication of what its rental value might be worth and whether it is the right investment for you.

To find local papers in an area, go to the website www.newspapersoc.org.uk (the Newspaper Society) where you can search for daily and weekly local papers both paid for and free. Try also www.loot.com, the online version of Loot, and www. daltonsproperty.com.

Value versus rental income

Assessing a property's value as opposed to its rental income is probably one of the biggest differences between buying a property for yourself or to let out. The calculations that you should do are completely different as there are more factors to consider.

When buying, you are likely to have salary constraints and be limited by how much of a deposit you can afford. When buying to let, there are far more important things that the lender will want to know before they will be happy to lend on a property for you to let.

THE RETURN ON LETTING

Think of buying to let as running a business. You basically need to make sure that your turnover (that is, your rent) is in excess of the costs of buying/funding and maintaining the property. As a guide, look for a property where the rent will exceed your running costs of the property by 20–30 per cent.

For an example, see the box below left. In this case, the profit means that the rent (that is, the income) is 20 per cent more than the costs, which is likely to cover the owner for times when the property is not rented out, any large investment such as a broken boiler, and any tax he or she may have to pay on the rental income. It also gives an opportunity to reduce the rent should prices drop locally, and all without causing financial trouble that could mean having to sell the property.

Establishing the profit

Income	
Rent:	£600 per month
Costs	
Mortgage cost	£425 per month
Insurance	£15 per month
Maintenance	£50 per month
Household bills	£10 per month
Total costs:	**£500 per month**
Monthly gross profit therefore = £600 – £500 = £100	

Jargon buster

Rental yield The annual rent of a property as a percentage of its capital value or acquisition price

Return on investment A more detailed analysis of income versus expenditure to establish a long-term view of earnings on a let property

Turnover The amount you earn from rent

RENTAL YIELD AND RETURN ON INVESTMENT

If you are going to make it as a property entrepreneur through letting property, terms such as **rental yield** and **return on investment** will become part of your daily vocabulary. They are no different to any term used in business to assess how profitable a venture is, and are used by companies to sell you property to let out and by letting agents to help you work out what is a good investment of your money – or not.

They are a good way to assess which type of rent and which type of property to purchase to help you make the most of your money. Don't forget there are lots of ways of making money and buying property to let can be a high risk strategy if you borrow too much. As you are investing for a return, you must compare returns to other investment methods, such as shares or a pension scheme.

Rental yield

This is calculated from everything that you spend on buying a property, from expenses such as petrol to drive around and look for property to the cost of any money that you borrow to fund the let, and then takes into consideration the amount of money you earn over and above the costs/

investment. As a guide, the table on page 44 shows some of the costs that you need to consider.

The simplest way to establish your rental yield is to subtract running costs from the amount of rent earned and divide that figure by how much the property cost. Multiply your answer by 100, to express your rental yield as a percentage (see opposite for an example and also the table on page 45). This allows you to compare different investment decisions. There are many different ways that yield and return on investment are measured.

Return on investment

As an example of how to work this slightly more complicated calculation, see the table on page 45. By working out some sample calculations, you will help yourself to choose which type of property you want to let out.

Usually Homes in Multiple Occupation yield higher returns as you rent each room rather than a whole house. You have to spend more to legally let them though.

On the other hand, better-paying company lets can be volatile depending on the economy and you may face higher levels of competition, causing your property to lie empty or get lower returns from decreasing rent in order to compete.

 For help assessing rental yields and return on investment, visit www.designsonproperty.co.uk and www.paragon-mortgages.co.uk and for affordability calculators also go to the paragon website.

Costs to consider when establishing your rental yield

One-off costs of buying

Research costs

Subscriptions to websites

Books that you purchase to research the let

Any professional fees incurred

Costs of finding a property

Petrol/travel costs

Food out on full days

Overnight stays

Cost of financing the property

Mortgage fees (administration, arrangement and broker fees)

Deposit monies

Cost of buying the property

Survey

Legal fees

Stamp duty land tax

Any removals fees

Gas/electricity safety checks

Ongoing costs

Costs of preparing/keeping the property ready for rent

New carpets/curtains/kitchen/bathroom

Maintenance, for example, painting or fixing the roof

Any appliances

Gas/electricity safety checks

Finance costs

Mortgage interest/repayment costs

Buildings/contents insurance

Professional insurance/protecting your let

Letting costs

Finding a tenant

Contracts

Letting agent fees

Inventory costs

Energy performance certificate (see page 54)

Deposit protection fee, which may be included in your letting fee (see pages 83–6)

Optional extra cost of becoming a member of one of the landlord associations (see pages 67 and 103)

Exit fees (when you sell the property)

Estate agent fees

Energy Performance Certificate

Legal fees

Removal fees

❝ Use these lists as the basis for working out your potential rental yield. You may have other costs to add as well. ❞

Examples of establishing the return on your investment

There are lots of methods to calculate yield and return on your investment. Here is one example, worked out before tax, that helps to compare different buy-to-let opportunities.

	Student let	Company let
Property purchase	£120,000	£250,000
Costs of buying	£2,500	£10,000
Home improvement	£0	£ 5,000
Total investment:	£122,500	£265,000
Expected monthly rent	£775	£1,750
Annual rental income	£9,300	£21,000
Likely amount of time empty (voids)	15%	10%
Annual rental income after voids	£7,905	£18,900
Deduct expected annual expenses	£1,080	£3,000
Income after expenses and voids	£6,825	£15,900
Gross income yield per annum♦	5.57%	6%
Mortgage loan	£90,000	£175,000
Annual mortgage costs▲	£5,400	£10,500
Annual income (after expenses and voids less mortgage costs)	£1,425	£5,400
Initial investment for purchase (capital investment)●	£32,500	£90,000
Net income yield per annum■	4.38%	6%
Capital growth after 5 years:		
Estimate future property value at 3%	£139,100	£290,000
Deduct outstanding mortgage	£90,000	£175,000
Deduct selling costs	£3,300	£6,800
Future value of investment	£45,800	£108,200
Growth of initial investment	£13,300	£18,200
Capital return on investment	8.18% per annum	4.04% per annum (RoI)♦

♦ Gross income yield = Income after expenses and voids ÷ property value x 100

▲ An annual mortgage cost is that of financing the loan and you will have to get this from a buy-to-let mortgage calculator

● The initial investment = purchase price + costs of buying – mortgage loan

■ Net income yield = income after expenses and voids – mortgage costs ÷ initial investment x 100

♦ RoI = Growth of initial investment/initial investment x 100/number of years (in this case, five)

Financing your buy to let

Approach financing a property as if you were funding a new business, which is effectively what you are doing. Be aware, too, that gaining a mortgage for a buy to let is different to gaining one for your own home. There are two types of financing to consider.

LETTING A PROPERTY YOU HAVE LIVED IN

If you are already living in a property and are moving out, the first thing you need to do is to inform your lender and let them know you are planning to let your property to tenants.

Depending on the reason why – for example, company relocation, moving abroad – your lender may let you continue with your current mortgage or request that you move to a buy-to-let mortgage instead, or just charge a slightly higher interest rate. It is important to check out alternative offers from other companies at this point as they may well be more competitive than your own lender.

They will be likely to want to assess your property for rental value to ensure that it meets their lending criteria as a property being let rather than lived in.

BUYING A PROPERTY SPECIFICALLY TO LET

For most buy to lets, the mortgage company will require that the gross rent you receive from letting the property is 125–130 per cent of the

Differences between mortgage for your home and buying to let		
Mortgage	Buying for yourself	Buying to let
Deposit	Require 10%+	Usually 25–40% required
How much you can borrow	Earnings related	Related to your financial security and the rental income versus costs
Survey	Requires value of the property	Requires a value of the property, plus independent verification of the rental income
Fees	Tend to be fairly competitive	Often pay more as a business venture and can be off-set against income

mortgage costs you will incur before they will consider lending to you.

The lender will also assess the value of the property, and whatever their valuation gives (which may be lower than what you are offering to pay for the property), they will then offer you 60–75 per cent of that value – leaving you to put down the rest of the money in the form of a deposit.

Over and above the rental income and the property value, the lender will also take into consideration your income to check that you can afford the property should there be a downturn in the lettings market.

If you already have some properties you are letting out, the lender is likely to check your current borrowing versus current rental income. If you are too much of a risk – for example, if your gearing is above 75 per cent – they are unlikely to lend.

THE CREDIT CRUNCH

This has caused lenders to offer money more cautiously with a view that property prices might fall or buyers might default. As a result, flexible lending for buy-to-let investors, which was outside the normal 85 per cent lending, has stopped and on new build flats, some lenders have reduced their loan-to-value lending to 60 per cent. Anyone with a history of bad debts,

Jargon buster

Gearing How much you borrow versus an independent valuation of the property/property portfolio

however small, may not be able to secure money. The second effect is the cost of the mortgage. Some lenders are increasing the costs of organising a mortgage and the ongoing interest rates have risen to an average of 6 per cent. In addition, you may have to pay significant arrangement fees. More now than ever, you need to source a good mortgage deal by consulting IFAs mortgage brokers and lenders directly.

Lenders' fees

Lenders that offer buy-to-let mortgages often charge a higher rate of interest (around 1-2 per cent more) than if you were buying a home for yourself. They also typically charge more in fees to get the mortgage. The types of charges you are likely to pay will vary by mortgage broker or lender, but will be anything from a fixed fee of £200 to up to 3 per cent of the mortgage value, and you will need to fork out for a valuation fee by the mortgage lender, which could be anything from £200.

 For more information on buying a property, see the Which? Essential Guide: Buy, Sell & Move House.

What to look for in a property

Although there are different things that you would look out for to meet the needs of specific types of let (see pages 22-34), there are many things that you should check for, whatever type of property let you are thinking about.

SPECIFIC PROPERTY LETS

If you are looking for a property to let, bear in mind the likely individual requirements of the type of rental market you are going to aim your property to – see the table, opposite.

Unless you are planning to renovate a property to let, check you are purchasing a structurally sound property before you make an offer. So if you are viewing properties, follow the checklists on pages 50-2 and then ensure you have the correct surveys so you know you have purchased a sound investment, rather than one that eats up any profit you may make.

The surveys you need to have done include a surveyor, gas engineer and electrician, but a good look around a property can save you thousands of pounds of wasted money on making an offer for a property you can't legally let and have to pull out of. Alternatively, it might mean you can make a lower offer to cover the cost of updating it to legal standards.

A few tips on location

The truism that location is crucial when choosing property is just as applicable when buying to let for your chosen market:

- Tenants may not have cars, so local transport links are essential.
- Concentrate on streets that are popular to live on and have shops nearby.
- View at different times of day to check on traffic conditions and noise levels.
- Upmarket company lets often go to managers on secondment from abroad who will have families, so a location near an international school is a big bonus.
- Buying property near where you live allows you to draw on your knowledge of the area and be on hand to deal with problems. However, it is more important to identify where the properties that serve your chosen market and give the best yield are located.

Choosing a property to match your let of choice

Type of Let	Number of bedrooms	Internal décor	Furnishings	Parking space	Garden
Student	3+	• Blank canvas, easy to re-decorate between tenancies	• Meeting legal and safety requirements, but cheap and easy to replace	• One or two ideal, but not a necessity	• Ideal if more than three people renting
Social	2+	• Welcoming but easy to decorate	• Meeting legal and safety requirements, but cheap and easy to replace • May have own furniture to bring	• One ideally	• Yes if renting to a family with children
Company	1+	• Follows current trends, chic	• Up to date and good quality, such as leather sofas	• Two, ideally secured	• Not required
Young professional	1+	• Follows current trends, or blank canvas	• Mid range quality, but follows current fashion, may want to furnish themselves	• At least one, ideally two	• Some will require a garden, especially with an eating out area, others not interested
Family	2+	• Blank canvas, easy to maintain and decorate after tenants have left	• Likely to have own furnishings, otherwise easy to clean such as imitation leather	• At least one	• Yes, grassed for children to play in

VIEWING CHECKLIST

Roof and chimney

Look at these from the front, back and side of the property (if possible). The key things to look out for are any obviously missing tiles or parts of the roof; ensuring that the chimneys are straight; and that there are no cracks or heavy wear and tear on the bricks.

If you don't, this could end up in the roof/chimney leaking over time, rotting the timbers underneath and causing thousands of pounds worth of damage. It is also a very good idea to go up into the loft and check that the roof felt is intact and there is the legal level of required insulation (270mm thick). Look for any holes that might show light, any decay on the timbers suggesting an infestation of some kind and any leaks – usually shown by stains or wet/damp patches.

Flat roofs are a must to check out. Take a ladder and look at any flat roofs as the life of these range from a few years to 15 years plus. Knowing how sound a flat roof can be could save you thousands of pounds in fixing one.

Viewing during or just after a bout of rain is ideal for these checks, so don't be put off viewing properties during an inconvenient storm: it could be a blessing.

Guttering and drainage

This is as important as the roof structure as poor guttering and drainage can cause horrendous damage to a home, resulting in the worst cases in subsidence of the property – which is very expensive to fix. The key here is to catch the property when it is wet and check that all the joints are healthy, with no bits of guttering 'hanging down' or not properly linked to the next piece.

Check, too, where all the water drains out. It should go into proper drains, and the area around the drains (such as nearby walls) should not be unduly soaking wet.

Concrete around a house can cause the build-up of water and therefore damp in the walls – especially when

Case Study Nadine

On one property, Nadine's survey showed up damp in the front room. The surveyor looked outside only to find that around the bay window, the previous owner had dug a hole below ground level, filled it with concrete at the bottom and then built a brick wall around the window bay. This was effectively creating a well when it rained as the water coming down had nowhere to drain to! Nadine fixed the problem by having the concrete at the bottom taken out and replaced with gravel, allowing the water to drain away and the wall to dry – and all for a few hundred pounds investment. This piece of creative thinking avoided thousands of pounds of re-plastering and damp proofing at a later date as it was caught early enough.

the property is on a slope. So if you see any concrete around the walls, find out from the surveyor if it is likely to cause any problems, and cost out having the concrete taken away and replacing it with gravel, which allows water to soak away.

External walls

Check for cracks in a property. Most are likely to turn out to be harmless and on older properties they tend to exist as land has settled over time or, indeed, on new properties, they form a few years after a property has been built and there is some settlement onto the land. The main cracks to worry about are large ones with no obvious cause. For example, cracks below a window may mean that solid wooden windows were taken out and replaced with plastic ones without adding a lintel to hold the weight of the bricks. At worst, it could mean subsidence. This can be caused by damp, or by movement below the house, which is more serious and would need costly investigation.

Some external rendering has a minimum life, such as 25 years. Some of these coverings can damage a property by not allowing the walls to 'breathe', so letting out the moisture created inside the property. Some renders provide additional protection

to the property, but if cracks appear, check what damage this is causing as rain may be able to get in, creating further problems, such as introducing damp, or freezing and expanding, which will enlarge the crack.

Ask your surveyor to comment on this type of covering if you have it on the property you are looking at.

Windows and doors

There are two key issues here: maintenance and security. A rented property needs to be low maintenance, as making repairs can be expensive, disrupt life for the tenant and could even require the property to be vacated. In particular, what you don't want is wooden windows that are rotting and require lots of attention, particularly if they are of a 'non-standard' size as they will have to be made specially and be repainted every two years. Security is often an important issue for tenants, so good security locks on windows and five-lever, two-bolt mortice locks are an asset. The ideal property for rent has easy-to-maintain UPVC windows and doors offering excellent security.

Internally

As a landlord, look for a property that seems to require minimum investment in terms of time and money. You

 For a free viewing checklist that you can download, go to www.which.co.uk/money/mortgages-and-property/guides/viewing-a-house/viewing-checklist.

want easy-to-maintain floors, such as those covered with laminate, stone or vinyl rather than carpets, which can stain easily, require regular cleaning and will probably need to be replaced every 2–3 years.

Walls are easier to maintain when painted rather than wallpapered, and look for areas of condensation or damp, particularly in the kitchen and bathroom or an en suite, as this can be expensive to sort out too.

In the kitchen and bathroom, there is often a choice between having long-lasting items that you invest in and hope the tenant appreciates and looks after or a cheap but 'stylish' kitchen, which can be replaced every 2–3 years, giving the property a 'fresh' appeal and helping to let it more regularly. It is relatively easy and cheap to replace cupboard doors, which is a good option every few years, provided the basic carcass is of good quality. Check how smoothly the drawers open and how sturdy the carcasses are.

Tenants will want at least a shower – and a clean one at that – and ideally a bath with a shower above. If more than two people will be occupying the property, you need washing facilities for more than one person at a time: no one likes to queue for the shower!

OTHER CHECKS

A frightening number of people still do not have a proper, independent survey carried out on a property before they buy. Even if you follow the viewing advice on pages 50–2, that does not mean you have checked everything you need. An independent surveyor will:

- Check the condition of the structure of the property.
- Check the condition of the internal walls and floors where they can be accessed.
- Advise on immediate, short-term and long-term repairs that the property needs.

This will give you a good idea of the likely maintenance costs of the property. If they are more than you expected, then you could use this to negotiate down the value of the

What to look for, what to ignore

Look at any potential letting property you are considering with a tenant's eyes. Tenants are most attracted to properties that are clean, easy to maintain, offering plenty of space for the money, and in a convenient location. Try not to be put off if your reaction is, 'Wow, the wallpaper is horrible!' Although grim décor can make a property look terrible, it is easy to correct with a pot of white paint. You can transform the look of a room quickly and cheaply by re-decorating. Badly decorated properties can be bargains because buyers are often put off.

property – hence reducing your costs and increasing the potential of your financial return.

It is important to ensure that you have a minimum of a HomeBuyer Report or a building survey if the property is pre-World War Two or in a poor state of repair or of an unusual construction. Or if you have a new build, make sure it's in top condition with a snagging survey. This gives you some protection should things go wrong that the surveyor hasn't picked up, or indeed show that the property has too much wrong with it to bring it up to letting standards.

The costs vary across the country for surveys and are between £300 and £1,000. You can deduct the cost from your income, so it is 'tax deductible' (see pages 116–17).

However, the survey that is done on the property is not the only one you will need when you buy looking to let. It is also crucial that you check the gas and electrics and any appliances that the vendor is leaving behind.

Gas and electric survey

As Energy Performance Certificates are now supplied with a property for sale, you will gain some information about the property's electrics and/or gas. This will include the likely costs of gas and electricity bills and how energy efficient the property is.

However, it is essential as a potential future landlord of the property you are buying, that you have various surveys done to ensure it can be let legally

and, from a landlord's perspective, in as stress-free a way as possible. These surveys include the plumbing system, gas installation and appliances, central heating and electrical installation.

The surveys report on the condition of the items above that are easy to access and say if they need to be replaced or are within the law. Without this, no agent or tenant should accept to let or rent your property. The exception is for people who are renting out a room in their own property when you may not have to have the gas and electric safety certificate as it is your own home. However, anyone buying a property or looking to rent out to others should really have this survey done too, for yourself as much as your potential new tenant.

There are several companies that have been created especially to help with this type of survey. The charges are not cheap, and vary according to the size of the company. They range from £150 upwards. However, it is a legal requirement for the gas to be safe and all costs are tax deductible (see page 116).

Alternatively, a qualified electrician and Gas Safety Registered engineer will be able to check the property and

 When letting a property, the landlord is liable to the tenant(s) for anything that goes wrong with the gas and electrics and to legally let a property, you must have a certificate to confirm it is all safe.

Energy performance certificates (EPCs)

From 14 December 2007, the Government introduced the compulsory use of HIPs when selling a property. Although HIPs have now been scrapped, you still need an energy performance certificate (EPC) showing the energy efficiency of each home.

Any property you buy should have an EPC and ideally with the highest rating. New builds should have an 'A' rating and the worst properties will be those with no loft insulation, double glazing or cavity walls. If you are marketing your property to rent from 1 October 2008, you will, by law, have to have an EPC available for prospective tenants. If you have a good EPC rating (within A–C), this should appeal to prospective tenants as it means lower heating bills.

An EPC costs from £50 and you can organise your EPC by choosing an energy assessor from www.epcregister.com or your letting agent should be able to do this for you.

give you the certificates, or advise on how much it will cost to bring the property up to legal letting standards.

TENANTS IN COMMON OR JOINT TENANTS?

When you buy a home with a spouse or partner, you usually buy it as 'joint tenants'. If you are buying a property for investment purposes, consider buying as 'tenants in common' as it can be more tax efficient and you can decide who your part ownership of a home can be left to in your will.

LEGAL CHECKS

When buying a property to let, make sure that you understand exactly what you are buying and what costs you are liable for. This is particularly relevant if you are purchasing a flat and/or leasehold property. If you are unsure of any legal clause, ask a solicitor to advise you. Here are some legal phrases to look out for.

Rights of way

This is simply what right people may have to walk across your garden, or how costs are shared for a jointly accessed driveway or area where the rubbish bins are kept. If you are buying to let, you want as few problems as possible with the neighbours as disputes are much harder to resolve if you are not on

Useful websites to check out for the gas and electrics survey are www.gassaferegister.co.uk, www.competentpersonsscheme.co.uk and www.niceic.org.uk. For more information about EPCs, go to http://epc.direct.gov.uk/index.html.

the spot. So make sure that you are clear about what the rights of way are and build into any contract with the tenant that they respect these.

Restrictions of use or change of use

This is particularly relevant when buying to let as there may be something in the contract that suggests you cannot turn a house you are planning to buy into two flats to let out. It may be that you plan to have an office in part of the property and let the rest. Check that there are no restrictions of this kind with your legal company.

Covenants

Some properties are sold with a covenant. For example, a property with a large garden that looks ripe for development may have a covenant that stops anyone from building on the land unless they pay a premium to a previous owner, or maybe you just aren't allowed to build anything else or even extend the building until the end of the covenant.

Property boundaries

It is important, too, to check where your property starts and finishes and exactly what you are buying. You don't want a boundary dispute while you

---

Case Study | Mr Grabel

Mr Grabel wanted to start buying flats to let out in a small town near the sea on the south coast. He went to an auction to see how much properties were and happened to see a property that seemed really cheap and in a good location. It should have struck Mr Grabel that caution was a good idea at this point, but instead he went ahead, started bidding and then secured the property.

Unfortunately, as Mr Grabel had bought at auction, he was committed to completing on the flat within 28 days. This was despite the fact that he

hadn't checked the property's condition or, more importantly, the legal expenses associated with owning the flat, and as it was a flat, that meant the lease.

Once bought, Mr Grabel went into the flat and found it in quite good condition and indeed in a good location. He went about spending money smartening up the flat, with fresh paint, new carpets, a new kitchen and even a new shower. At this point, he then sat down to read the lease agreement. What a shock!

Mr Grabel found a clause that prevented any owners of the

flats renting out the property to a tenant.

The result was that Mr Grabel then had to put the property back on the market, for not much more money, and lose a substantial amount of money as well as time in the process. The purchasing costs would have included the legal advice and stamp duty land tax and then on top of this there were the selling fees via an estate agent and yet more legal advice.

All in all, this turned out to be a very expensive mistake for Mr Grabel, which he could easily have avoided!

are trying to rent out the property and need to be clear as to what to put in the contract with the tenant to ensure they understand what they are renting and what belongs to the neighbours.

LEASEHOLD PROPERTIES

It is essential that you check the rules and regulations within the leasehold, particularly in a leasehold flat, as some do not allow you to sublet a room, or the property itself. Many people have made this mistake, not read the agreement in detail and then found that after to purchasing they can't then let out the property.

You must also ensure that the legal company/letting agent that prepares the contract with your tenant incorporates any 'noise' and 'communal use' into it.

The lease agreement will also lay out the costs of **ground rent** and **service charges** and it is important that you understand how these are worked out and what you are liable for. For example, it may be that the whole block needs new water tanks or windows and your share of this cost is £5,000. This could be a nasty shock if you didn't realise you were liable.

It is also important to establish how any repairs (together with the service charge and ground rent) are paid for – by you or the tenant. Bear in mind

that no tenant is likely to sign up for a 6–12-month contract if they know they will have to fork out £5,000 for repairs on a building they do not own even part of!

LENDER RESTRICTIONS

Your lender may impose some restrictions on you and how you run your lettings business and your legal representative needs to ensure that you are aware of all of these before making the purchase. For example, some lenders will insist that you let only on an 'assured shorthold tenancy' basis (see pages 128–32), and many lenders will not lend on properties that are intended to be let to social tenants, which is important if this is the market you have chosen to target.

Jargon buster

Ground rent Payment by the leaseholder to the freeholder. Low sums are sometimes referred to as a peppercorn rent

Leasehold Ownership for a set period, most commonly applied to flats and other shared buildings

Service charges Payment for maintenance of shared areas, such as communal hallways, the roof and drains

 See pages 125–6 for more information on running a letting business, on both a small- and large-scale basis. See also www.holidayletmortgages.co.uk/ for specialist lettings finance.

Buying property already let

One way of buying a property and ensuring instant income is to buy one that is already let. This will need an assured shorthold tenancy agreement and you will have to find a lender that will be prepared to lend under these circumstances.

If you are buying with a sitting tenant, make sure the legal company has plenty of experience in this field: even if it costs you slightly more, this is definitely not a time to 'save money' when buying – it could cost you a fortune later on if you don't use the right person.

FINDING A PROPERTY TO PURCHASE

Most properties that are already let and are up for sale are sold via auction houses or directly from one investor to another. The auction house will typically advertise the property in its catalogue with these details:

- Guide price for the property (remember this means it may sell for less or much more).
- Number of tenants in the property.
- Rental income generated.
- Annual yield/return.

You can also talk to local estate agents and check local property papers to see if anyone is advertising a property for sale with tenants. Talk to local letting agents, too, and ask

them if they know of any landlords who are likely to want to sell their property and investigate purchasing prior to it being put on the market.

WHAT TO LOOK FOR

Unlike buying property for yourself or buying a property to let out, there are many more things that you need to investigate – preferably before you make an offer.

Why is the landlord selling?

It may be for good reasons in that they just want to cash in on the capital growth of the property, or are moving abroad and want to sell off all their UK investments. However, there may be hidden factors, for example, the property is in desperate need of repairs or the tenants are complaining about things not working, or are not paying! Worse still, the landlord may be about to go bankrupt.

Alternatively, perhaps the landlord is getting daily complaints from unhappy neighbours – so make sure you pop by and ask the neighbours how they get on with the tenants before making an offer.

What is the general condition of the property?

Again, it might be that someone just hasn't the money, time or inclination to keep maintaining the property in good condition. They may not want the hassle of sourcing new boilers, bathrooms and kitchens and if these all need replacing, you need to be aware of the costs involved. It may be the case that the repairs are severe enough for the tenants to have to move out for a while and you will need to work out what happens if they do. Do you offer reduced rent or are they really happy to stay/move out to friends knowing that they will benefit from the upgrade?

Contracts with the tenants

This is the crux of whether the purchase is a sound investment or not. Basically, the agreements that you take over with incumbent tenants will determine:

- What your rights are as a landlord.
- What their rights as tenants are.
- What likely running/on-going costs you may have.
- Whether you can purchase the property and the tenants 'as a going concern'.

As far as the agreements are concerned, you will need to gain a copy of the first AND current tenancy agreements. Your legal representative may ask for these anyway, but the sooner you can read them – preferably

before you make an offer and incur any expense – then the faster the purchase process will be too. You should also establish:

- The date the tenant first moved in.
- The payment record of the tenant(s).
- What level of deposit the landlord has taken and that this is transferable.
- If there are any possession notices that have been served.
- If there are any Section 21 notices (see page 163) as this is what the current landlord would send to advise a tenant that their agreement is coming to an end.

Ideally, you will want the agreements to be assured shorthold

Jargon buster

Assured shorthold tenancy A form of tenancy that assures the landlord has a right to repossess the property at the end of the term specified in the tenancy agreement, which can be for any length of time

Ordinary assured tenancy (also shortened to 'assured tenancy') A form of tenancy introduced where a property is let out as a separate dwelling and used as the tenant's only or main home. The tenant can stay in occupation until either he or she decides to leave or the landlord obtains a possession order

(see page 131) as these give you, as landlord, the most rights to your property and are the agreements most lenders will request anyway.

However, if it isn't an assured shorthold tenancy, you and your legal company will need to do further checks, such as whether you control the rent levels or have to refer them to a 'rent officer' as the tenants are covered by a protected, statutory or ordinary assured tenancy (see page 128).

Final checks include the landlord having no arrears on their mortgage payments and hasn't been issued with any notices from the lender. You also need confirmation that the local authority hasn't served any notices to upgrade the property in any way.

Case Study Mrs Elmer

Mrs Elmer decided that she wanted to expand her property portfolio. She was an experienced buy-to-let investor and was used to dealing with the legal aspects, money and the tenants. However, she had seen that some properties she would quite like to add to her portfolio were already let. She investigated buying a property with sitting tenants and found that if she could ensure there was an assured shorthold tenancy in place at the time of exchange, then finding finance would not be too difficult. On the other hand, buying a property with assured tenancy agreements could be much cheaper, but lending would be harder, or more expensive to obtain.

After going to estate agents and looking in the newspaper, the auction houses seemed to be the best bet. Before every auction, Mrs Elmer purchased the catalogue well in advance of the auction and then did a drive-by visit of the ones that she was interested in. Once she'd found several properties she liked, Mrs Elmer checked with one of the mortgage lenders that they would be happy to lend on a tenanted property.

For each property, she found out why the landlord was selling, spoke to neighbours to ask about the tenants and obtained a copy of the latest agreement, information about the tenant and asked a surveyor to check each property within a day and advise on any serious conditions.

Finally, on auction day, Mrs Elmer had identified the maximum she was going to bid for the properties that she had investigated. On the day, Mrs Elmer managed to secure another buy-to-let property and has now been managing the property for some years, along with the same tenant, who was happy to stay.

Furnished versus unfurnished

One of the main decisions you need to make when you are buying to let is whether you are going to let a property furnished or unfurnished. There are advantages in both, the first being that if you let unfurnished, you don't have to go to the expense of buying furniture for the property in the first place!

However, you are still likely to have to provide carpets and appliances, such as a cooker and washing machine (see also the table, opposite below).

66 You have the choice of letting unfurnished, part-furnished or fully furnished, depending on what market you are aiming at. **99**

In the main, whether you choose to let property with or without furniture is really down to what type of market you are aiming to target. If it is the higher value, shorter-term market, such as company lets, then you are likely to be expected to let the property furnished. However, if it is a family home, tenants may prefer to bring their own furniture for familiarity and potentially to save on storing it.

You can part furnish so you provide the basics such as beds, wardrobes, a settee, etc., and leave the tenants to provide whatever else they wish within the home.

Alternatively, you could give tenants the choice, they could pay a higher rent and deposit for a fully furnished property versus a property where they have to provide the furnishings for themselves.

With the growth in buy to let over the last ten years in the UK, there are alternatives to buying furniture.

- **For example, you can rent** furniture from companies on a short- or long-term basis.
- **Even furnishings stores** like Ikea or some of your local shops might be happy to give you a 'package' deal to regularly furnish your property.

See below for some useful websites.

Useful websites for funishing a property include www.buytolet-furnishings.co.uk and www.roomservicebycort.com. For a quick calculator to help you cost the items listed opposite, out go to www.designsonproperty.co.uk.

Pros and cons of letting property furnished versus unfurnished

	Furnished	Unfurnished
Property rent	• Typically earn up to 5% more rent	• Typically gain less rent, but depends on furnishing
Property insurance	• Higher as you will need to insure the items within contents insurance	• May only need to take out building insurance as opposed to contents insurance
Rentability	• Often required with some lets and may mean the difference between someone taking the property or not	• Can be an advantage for some who intend to buy a property later, or are renting temporarily so that they can fit in their own furniture and don't have to pay any storage costs
Expense	• Costs around £1,500 to furnish a one-bed, £2,500 for a two-bed and £5,000 or more if it is a premium let • Benefit from a wear and tear allowance of 10% of the 'net rent'	• Save on this investment, but need to weigh up the lower rent received and whether your target market will be happy furnishing themselves or buying their own furniture to fit

Checklist for furnishing a property

	Essential	Recommended
Kitchen*	Cooker Washing machine Kettle Fridge/freezer	Microwave Dishwasher Toaster/coffee maker
Also choose whether you provide crockery such as plates, cups, bowls, cutlery, cooking utensils, pots and pans		
Lounge	Settee Chairs	Coffee/side table TV cabinet
Dining room	Dining table Dining chairs	Sideboard/dresser
Bedroom	Bed Wardrobe	Bedside table Chest of drawers Desk
Bathroom	Cabinet Toilet holder/brush	
Within some of the rooms you may also need to provide additional lighting, such as lamps.		

* Make sure all appliances meet safety rules and regulations, for example are Portable Appliance Tested (PAT).

Renovating or building to let

To try to gain a better return on investment, some people are now looking at building or renovating to let. Essentially, you will need to do everything that you would when building or purchasing for yourself, but you still need to follow the suggestions on pages 36-9 to ensure that you can let the property once finished.

RENOVATING TO LET

The key difference in renovating to let is that you will have to check out what building regulations will apply to the property and carefully check the cost of renovating the property before you make your offer. In the main, if the property requires just doing up – for example, new windows or doors – then few regulations will apply. However, if you are planning major alterations to the structure of the building or the drainage – such as removing a load-bearing wall – then you will need to check the specific building regulations that apply to you.

You will also need to ensure that the changes you make include any legal requirements for letting to the market that you have chosen.

With regard to your choice of fixtures and fittings, invest heavily where it saves you long term on maintenance and invest only to a required level where you are likely to have to replace or repair on a regular basis. Bear in mind the 'What you need to provide' information for different types of let on pages 22-34.

Don't forget that any increase in the cost of the renovation will affect your final yield (see pages 42-5), so it really does pay to make sure that the cost of the renovation adds enough to the property value. Even better would be if the renovation improves the property value sufficiently to ensure you gain a return.

BUILDING TO LET

The first thing that you need to do is to find a plot of land to build on or a plot with a property that you can pull down. Ideally, you should find land that already has outline or detailed planning permission, unless you are prepared to take some months or years to get planning permission and for your invested money to give you a good return.

Where to look

This partly depends on where you are planning to build. There are certain areas that are more likely to have plots than others. For example, there is not much for sale in central London but areas such as Yorkshire and

Lincolnshire have relatively plentiful plots available.

Wherever you decide to locate your build to let, then you will need to spend as much time as possible looking for a plot and ideally have your finances in order before you make an offer as competition for good plots tends to be high.

- **Auction houses:** It is worth checking out the local auctions to see what is available over, say, three months. This will give you an idea about how competitive a market you will be working in as well as where the plots are typically coming up. Perhaps you can get hold of some 'back catalogues' from the auction house, or if they are an estate agent, too (as is often the case), then you could ask them what land has become available and the average price per square metre and get an idea of how much it will cost you to buy your ideal plot. To find out more, visit www.eigroup.co.uk.
- **Internet searches:** There are some good database online search engines, such as: www.plotsearch.co.uk, which you can subscribe to. They cost around £50 to £100 to register but are good for researching across a range of areas. It can also save you lots of time driving around as some have aerial photographs that allow you to get a good view of the plots and their surroundings.

With any database make sure:

- **They show you** how many plots are available in each area before you buy so that you do not waste your money.
- **They are clear** about what planning permission has been given or what is required.
- **They update and validate** the plots regularly, so that they are truly available, rather than having been sold months ago.
- **They list what services** are available on the land as this can be expensive to provide if not already there.

Finally, search the local newspapers, trawl the estate agents, and drive around looking for potential plots. It is always worth talking to friends and family, too, as someone may have a large back garden they are willing to part with, or know someone who is looking to sell off some land, or has seen some land where you want to build.

If you are building on a plot, then you need to make sure it fits your target market – see pages 22–34 – and you need to measure the potential returns to ensure that you are making the right decision. For example, there may be more money to be made by building small two-bedroom properties for young professionals or newly weds than building a larger house with a student let in mind.

The land

Check there is already outline or detailed planning permission. Even if you don't own the land, you can contact the local planning office to ask them for their view. Study the plans that have been submitted. You can't assume that the planning office will accept plans for apartments when they have given permission for a five-bedroomed house. Check with them first if you are looking to change the plans in any way. If necessary, you may need to get some help from a planning consultant to ensure:

- **There are no restrictions** on the land, such as preservation orders on trees or indeed on a building that is on the plot.
- **Whether the ground is sound** to build on. For example, you will need to know if the land is within 250m of a landfill site as this will require a special membrane before you build on it.

Check out the local environment

Check that this is suitable for your target market. If the area is a village, for example, and you are looking to build to rent to a family check that they can get into the local school, dentist or doctor's surgery, otherwise

this may affect your ability to rent. Make sure, too, that there are good transport links for road, rail or airports.

How to assess the return

It is likely that if you go to the trouble of purchasing land and then building a property and renting it out, you are likely to gain a capital return as well as monies from rental income. In the past, building a home on a plot versus buying one 'already built' typically saved people around 30 per cent. Since the credit crunch, plots of land, for the short term, have become quite good value for money. If you are to make a good return out of building a property rather than buying and renting out, you need to be careful of the following figures before you make any offers:

- What price per square metre to pay for the land.
- Any costs to get services to the plot.
- Labour and material costs.
- Likely rental income.

Getting it right from the start is important as your build is likely to take a year or so before you can start earning money from letting the property, so you have to play 'catch up' versus buying a property already built, which you could have let straightaway.

 Use the yield and return calculation on page 45 to assess whether it is worth buying a property to rent versus the one you are looking to build. For more information see the Which? Essential Guide: Property Investor's Handbook.

Letting a property

This chapter deals with the practicalities of letting, from managing it yourself to using an agent, dealing with tenants, and deciding when and how to upgrade your property.

Who will run the let?

Whether you choose to run the let yourself or through a letting agent (see pages 68-73), there are advantages and disadvantages. Read these pages and then make up your mind as to which you would prefer.

DOING IT YOURSELF

There are a number of good reasons for managing the let yourself rather than going straight to an agent, particularly if you are just starting out as a landlord. However, make sure you know what the disadvantages are before rushing in and then finding yourself on the wrong side of the law.

Advantages of self-managing

- **Saving money:** In the early days of any venture, money is often tight, and if you've just invested tens of thousands of pounds in a property, you want to start getting a decent return as soon as you can. You will be more motivated to keep costs to a minimum rather than use an agency, because it is your money you are saving. Managing it yourself will save you money because you won't have to pay a 'finder's fee' or an on-going management fee (see pages 68–73).
- **Learning the business:** There is no better way of learning how a business operates than by doing every job involved in it. You will learn what the most common

problems are, how to deal with them, and what they cost. This will be valuable if you choose to bring in a manager or agent, because you will know as much as they do about your properties – and possibly more.
- **Making contacts:** Having people that you trust on hand to deal with the things you can't is invaluable. This might be a reliable plumber, a cheap, efficient handyman, or someone to hand over to when you have a holiday or your business expands.
- **Learning new skills:** Fixing things yourself is far cheaper than paying someone else to do it, and it can be interesting improving your DIY skills or facing new challenges. However, make sure you are aware of what repairs you can and can't make. For example, you now can't do major electrical work, nor can you do anything with regard to gas unless the gas engineer is on the Gas Safety Register.

Disadvantages of self-managing

- **Acting illegally:** There are so many new and changing laws in letting,

66

from deposit protection and energy performance certificates to running HMOs (see pages 30–3), that you need to make sure you know what is required for your type of let. Join a landlord's association or consider using a letting specialist to let the property so you can benefit from their knowledge.

- **Time:** Dealing with the day-to-day running of a tenancy takes time. There is paperwork to keep on top of, much of it a legal requirement, and you will want to keep an eye on the property and deal with maintenance issues quickly to avoid antagonising your tenant. A useful calculation is to assess your time at the rate of pay and compare it to an estimate of how much time you will spend on landlord duties (including travel). You can then work out the cost of doing the job.
- **Location:** You can't manage a rental property from a distance, because you have to be on hand: it should preferably be fairly close to where you live and work.
- **Stress:** Tenants expect any problems to be dealt with fast and arranging that can involve a lot of hassle. You are on call at all times and you can, through no fault of you own, be put into stressful situations where there is conflict with the tenant; for example, if there are problems with their behaviour or if they don't pay the rent.
- **Lack of expertise:** If you don't know much about letting a property, it can

be a steep and expensive learning curve. For example, repairing a leaking roof is an expensive job and if it isn't done right, you will be faced with an irate tenant and a damaged, damp property. Good landlords need to know quite a bit about repairs, and a lot about handling relationships with tenants and workmen. There are also legal issues on types of tenancy on which you should get professional advice. Finally, you'll have to deal with marketing the property, another drain on time and resources.

Helpful contacts

These organisations offer advice on being a landlord. Many are trade organisations that offer extra benefits and information to their members:
Association of Residential Letting Agents: www.arla.co.uk
National Landlords Association: www.landlords.org.uk, www.landlordzone.co.uk
Residential Landlords Association: www.rla.org.uk
Residential Landlord: www.residentiallandlord.co.uk
The Property Ombudsman: www.tpos.co.uk
National Approved Letting Scheme: www.nalscheme.co.uk
Royal Institution of Chartered Surveyors (RICS): www.rics.org
UK Association of Letting Agents (UKALA): www.ukala.org.uk

LETTING THROUGH AN AGENT

Using a good agent will cost you a proportion of your rental income in return for saving you a lot of trouble. A bad one will take the money but not provide the service. Most agents offer a range of services from 'letting only' (which costs about 10 per cent of the rent) and letting and rent collection (12–15 per cent) to 'full management' – which can be 15 per cent or more.

- **The letting-only service** should include suggesting a rental value, introducing and vetting tenants, taking a deposit, checking tenants in and out of the property. They may also collect rent and chase arrears, prepare inventories and ensure that bills are put in the tenant's name.
- **The full management service** should deal with urgent tenant enquiries and with routine repairs and maintenance. Agents may also make other charges (see box below).

On top of the commission on rent, agencies may also charge landlords:
- An administration fee at the start of the tenancy.
- A renewal fee every time a tenant renews their contract.
- A fee for carrying out an inventory.
- Some agents charge advertising costs.

Advantages of letting through an agent

- **They know the market:** A good agent can advise you on preparing your property for the right market so that you have the best chance of letting it. A good agent will also be able to advise on what rent you can charge.
- **Legal responsibilities:** If you have a good letting agent, they should know the legal rules and regulations, keeping you and your property up to date and fully within the law. They can also keep your costs down if they negotiate favourable rates for insurance and maintenance issues.
- **They take care of marketing:** Finding reliable tenants is the trickiest aspect of the rental market and a good agent will save you the trouble of doing it. Their expertise should also help you to minimise the dreaded void periods when you have no tenant and therefore no income. Tenants looking for larger properties, and corporate clients, tend to expect to deal with professional agents.
- **They have the expertise:** If you are starting out as a landlord, you can learn a lot through employing a good agent so that if you choose to go it alone or save outgoings by taking on some of the responsibilities, you will have a better grasp of what to do.
- **You don't have to deal with tenants:** An agent can be a very

useful buffer between you and
your tenants. This is particularly
helpful if you get one who is
difficult to deal with, or if you do
not relish handling dealing directly
with tenants.

- **They will deal with repairs:** Stuck for
a plumber or a roofing contractor?
A good agent won't be.
- **They will deal with the money:**
Having an agent handle money
is simpler and takes away the
responsibility of dealing with the
deposit (see box on page 73).

Disadvantages of letting through an agent

- **Money:** Fees vary, but they will
charge a percentage of your rent
plus other fees for renewing
contracts or finding new tenants
(see opposite). Agents can also deal
with sorting out repairs, but while
some will have negotiated discounts
to give you a good deal, others will
make additional charges, including
their own fees.

Read the contract

You must always read the contract
and make sure that you understand
the small print before signing it.
Terms to check on include:

- **The length of notice to cancel.** One
to three months for either side is
typical, but some agents will ask
for more.
- **Any fees that will be charged** by the
agent in addition to the commission
on rents.
- **Exactly what the agent will deal with,**
for example, chasing arrears and
handling repairs.
- **Charging for periods** when there are
no tenants – this is acceptable only
if you are on a full management
contract.
- **A 'sold fee'** if you put the house up
for sale and the tenant buys it.

For more details on these points and
additional information on a terms of
business agreement with an agent,
see pages 200–5.

Scrutinise agent charges

There are many fees that letting agents
charge and they also vary depending
on where you live. Some offer great
'headline' fees, but then you find you
are paying for everything else on top,
so to help compare agents' charges and
understand what costs you will incur see
the points outlined to the right.

- Ask for a single page document that
highlights all the charges made.
- Request a cost per hour if you want
help with things not included on the
list, like going to court on your behalf.
- Always compare agent fees over a 12
month period, including a tenancy
renewal.

Key questions to ask a letting agent

- Will you give a valuation and advice on a property before purchase? ✓
- Are you a member of a trade body? ✓
- If not, why not? ✓
- If you are, can I see the code of conduct and what happens in case of a dispute? ✓
- How do you keep up with the legal rules and regulations of letting? ✓
- How many properties similar to mine do you have available for rent? ✓
- How many are currently NOT being let – and for how long? ✓
- How long does it usually take from advertising to gaining a tenant? ✓
- How many viewings normally need to take place – and do you do this as part of your fee or not? ✓
- Have you anyone currently looking for my type of property? ✓
- Will you advertise the property in the local paper and in your window – using pictures or just text? ✓
- What online websites do you advertise on? ✓
- What qualifications have you/your staff got in letting? ✓
- Can you provide a copy of your fees, charges and services and your terms and conditions of business? ✓
- Can you give me a copy of your contract between a tenant and your agency (you should then check this with your own lawyer)? ✓
- If there are issues raised by the tenant, how would you deal with them? (Would they just pass the problem to you or try to resolve it first?) ✓
- What happens if the tenant leaves before the end of their agreement? ✓
- What happens if the tenant doesn't pay up? ✓
- What happens over repairs to the home? ✓
- What tenant checks are carried out? ✓
- How long does it take from the tenant paying to it appearing in my bank account? ✓
- If you go bust, will I get any outstanding rent back? ✓
- If you do the repairs, am I charged at cost? If there's a mark-up, how much is it? ✓
- If there is a discrepancy over the inventory report between you and the inventory company, how will this be handled by the letting agent? ✓

Choosing an agent

The good news is that there are about 8,000 letting agents in the UK who are members of trade bodies, which offer some kind of protection. The bad news is that that leaves possibly as many as 9,000 agents who are not regulated at all, working in a growing market with high demand in which people are likely to enthusiastically sign up to let their new home without checking the small print, which sometimes has outrageous clauses hidden away.

Always go for an agent who is a member of the National Approved Letting Scheme (NALS) or belongs to one of the professional bodies who support it: the Association of Residential Letting Agents (ARLA), the Royal Institution of Chartered Surveyors (RICS) or the Property Ombudsman (TPOS) and the UK Association of Letting Agents (UKALA) (see box on page 67). Also make sure you opt for an agent who deals with the market you want to serve as they will have the expertise you need.

The reason this is so important is that there is a clear course of action if you have difficulties and can't come to a conclusion yourselves. This can be an invaluable time and money saver, just when you will need support and help if things are not working out.

NALS or ARLA please

Members of the National Approved Letting Scheme (NALS) (which is government financed) have to abide by a code of conduct and must:

- Have a client's money protection scheme covering any landlord or tenant's monies misappropriated or lost by the agent.
- Be a member of ARLA, RICS or TPOS.
- Operate an internal complaints procedure.
- Be linked to a legally binding arbitration service.
- Maintain professional indemnity insurance.

The UK Association of Letting Agents has its own code of practice and also supports the NALS scheme.

Many estate agents are now operating lettings divisions due to a lack of sales. Be warned that they may well not be as up-to-date with letting legals and regulations or as good at essential lettings administration.

The relevant websites for the professional letting agency bodies are: www.arla.co.uk (ARLA); www.tpos.co.uk; www.nalscheme.co.uk and www.rics.org.

LETTING THROUGH AN ACCOMMODATION AGENCY

Accommodation agencies mainly aim at the student market, nursing, police and fire services, working in many cases in markets where price is all important. Some large companies with a big workforce also run what are, in effect, accommodation offices. Many higher educational establishments operate their own agency on-site. They often vet their landlords so that they meet certain minimum requirements, and can act as mediators in disputes.

Advantages of accommodation agencies

These agencies frequently make no charge to landlords at all, as they are paid by the tenant when they take on a property. Because they are often part of large organisations with many potential tenants, they are a major player in their local markets.

Disadvantages of accommodation agencies

These agencies do not usually provide the fuller service a letting agent offers: they are really simply filters for information on what is available. University accommodation offices will list the accommodation offered by and through the university, including halls of residence and other properties owned by the university, and the recent trend for high quality dedicated student blocks available for quite reasonable rents, such as those offered by Unite (see www.unite-students.com). So they are marketing a range of competing properties. This is good for the tenant, who gets a wide choice of property, but makes the market more competitive for the landlord.

LETTING VIA SOCIAL RENT

The market for social letting is described on pages 33–4. Social lets are for people on low income or Housing Benefit, and are provided by local authorities or housing associations, who also usually own the properties. However, such is the demand that private landlords can enter this market. Local authorities vet private landlords carefully and can decide and cap the rent they charge. Housing associations also have clear requirements, but will often manage the property themselves for a very reasonable fee.

Social tenants

Tenants claiming Housing Benefit are often referred to as social tenants, because payment ultimately came from the Department of Social Security, which is now part of the Department for Work and Pensions.

66 Accommodation agencies filter information on what is available, mainly for students. 99

Advantages of social lets

For a landlord, a social let has a number of benefits:

- **Guaranteed rental income** on long leases if the LHA (see page 150) is paid directly to the landlord.
- **Low fees** for what is, in effect, often a full management service.
- **Often there is an optional repairs** and maintenance service.
- **Cheaper insurance** through the organisation.
- **The satisfaction of making an ethical investment** in social housing, which helps the disadvantaged.

Disadvantages of social lets

- **Some lenders forbid landlords from letting** to these groups (and some landlords choose not to), partly because Housing Benefit regulations can result in the landlord being held responsible for

---

Local housing allowance

Housing Benefit is no longer typically paid directly to the landlord and some tenants don't pass the allowance monies onto the landlord. This has led to an estimated £4,000+ arrears for some landlords. Some local authorities help resolve the situation, some don't. Find out more about your local housing officer's attitude towards private sector rentals/landlords.

---

large financial liabilities incurred by the tenant if, for example, they are found to have been claiming benefit fraudulently or have been overpaid by the local authority.

- **Council rent officers have powers** to limit the amount of rent charged to ensure tenants are treated fairly.
- **Move to LHA,** which means Housing Benefit is paid directly to the tenant, not the landlord.

An alternative to a deposit

Because people on benefits often cannot afford to pay a deposit, some councils make a one-off, non-returnable fee to landlords who start letting to tenants on benefit. The fee is typically £1,000–£1,750, depending on the size of the property.

The local authority will vet the property to ensure it is of a reasonable standard and set a reasonable rent. They will then introduce potential tenants to the landlord, who can vet and choose them in the usual way.

The authority does not manage the property or act as guarantor for the tenant, but it will provide a shorthold tenancy agreement. Essentially, this fee is a down payment on any damage or loss the landlord may incur when letting to tenants on benefit.

Preparing the property

As a landlord you are bound by the law to ensure that the property you let is safe for people to live in. There are many laws that you need to abide by and these cover anything from gas and electricity safety through to the Data Protection Act (see pages 76-7).

SAFETY FIRST

Gas

The Gas Safety (Installation and Use) Regulations 1998 require landlords to ensure that all gas appliances are maintained in good order and that an annual safety check is carried out by a tradesman who is registered with the Gas Safe Register. You must keep a record of the safety checks and issue it to the tenant within 28 days of each annual check. Although not a legal requirement, you may also choose to install carbon monoxide detectors. Some student accommodation offices have a stock of detectors so tenants can check levels of this invisible and odourless gas.

Electricity

You are legally obliged to ensure the electrical system and any electrical appliances you supply, such as cookers, kettles, washing machines and immersion heaters, are safe to use. While it is not a legal requirement, a check on electrical equipment prior to the start of the tenancy, and annually thereafter, will reassure you and your tenant. Use a member of the National Inspection Council for Electrical Installation Contracting (NICEIC), National Association for Professional Inspectors and Testers (NAPIT) or the Electrical Contractor Association (ECA). It is a legal requirement to employ only qualified people to carry out major electrical work, such as installing an electric shower.

Fire safety

Any furniture and furnishings you supply must meet the fire resistance requirements in the Furniture and Furnishings (Fire) (Safety) Regulations 1988. These set levels of fire resistance for domestic upholstered furniture. All new and second-hand

 For safety advice, go to www.gassaferegister.co.uk, www.carbonmonoxidekills.com, http://firekills.direct.gov.uk/index.html and www.shelter.org.uk. ARLA (www.arla.co.uk) supplies a leaflet for landlords on safety.

A booklet called **A Guide to the Furniture and Furnishings (Fire) (Safety) Regulations** can be downloaded from www. communities.gov.uk.

furniture provided in accommodation that is let for the first time, or replacement furniture in existing let accommodation, must meet the fire resistance requirements unless it was made before 1950. Most furniture will have a manufacturer's label on it saying if it meets the requirements.

Smoke alarms

All properties built after June 1992 must have a mains-operated, inter-connected smoke alarm fitted on every level of the property. Older properties do not meet this requirement, but you should provide battery-operated smoke alarms in suitable locations for your and your tenants' peace of mind. It is reasonable to ask the tenant to check these regularly and inform you of any

problems. A good tip is to put new batteries in the smoke alarms when the tenant moves in or ideally have them connected to the mains.

OTHER RESPONSIBILITIES

The landlord is responsible for the structure and exterior of the property and must also ensure that all hot and cold water supplies, and the drains, are properly maintained.

Insurance

Landlords cannot rely on standard household insurance policies, which can be invalidated if the property is let out. Insurers regard rental property as a greater risk than other residences, especially those that are HMOs or occupied by students or Housing Benefit tenants, and consequently charge higher premiums for it. Your policy should include:

- **Property owner's liability,** which covers for death, injury or damage to anyone on the property, including tenants, their guests and other visitors. If your tenants are students or on Housing Benefit,

Appliances

Because of the safety regulations on appliances supplied by landlords, keep the number of appliances you provide for tenants to a minimum. If they really want a dishwasher or washing machine, they can hire one (unless, of course,

you are seeking a corporate let). Leave written instructions on how to operate any appliances you provide: what may seem obvious to you may not be so clear to someone else. All appliances should ideally be portable appliance tested (PAT).

the university or local authority will specify a minimum amount of cover. This 'third party' cover is often overlooked by landlords, at potentially great cost.

- **Cover for employers' liability** for a handyman, decorator or gardener who is injured on the property.
- **Insure only the property** that belongs to you, either the cheaper 'limited contents cover' or 'full contents cover', which is generally worthwhile if the contents are valued at more than £5,000.

 Some companies offer cheap insurance for landlords which, when push comes to shove, you find doesn't really cover you for anything at all. Make sure you have good insurance cover or it could cost you thousands. If you are letting through an agency, you may be able to secure a comprehensive insurance policy more cheaply. Buying this makes your life easier as you then know you are covered for most problems that might occur.

- **Also consider paying for emergency assistance insurance** to cover urgent repairs – this is particularly valuable if you live a long way from the property you are letting out.
- **Cover for damage caused by the tenants** accidentally or maliciously.
- **Other possible elements of cover** are for rent guarantee (which reduces the risk of losing money through bad payers and is more attractive to small-scale landlords) and legal expenses insurance, because solicitors are not cheap.

You should also protect your investment by taking out buildings insurance in case the property is damaged. This covers you for the cost of re-building the property. Specialist landlord's policies will also cover you for loss of rent while re-building work is in progress. Some policies have the option of cover for malicious damage caused by the tenants.

Data protection

Landlords often hold private information about their tenants, such as references, a list of who is claiming benefit, and if they are not paying their rent. The Data Protection Act 1998 sets out who they can pass this information on to.

 More information about data protection can be found from the Information Commissioner's Office at www.ico.gov.uk or tel 0303 123 1113. Click on the relevant tab where there are several links to different parts of the website.

- **A landlord can pass on** the names of new tenants to utility companies, and should tell individuals this may happen when they agree the tenancy.
- **Landlords are entitled to see tenant references** given to their letting agent, provided the agent made it clear to tenant and referee that this would happen.
- **Landlords cannot display** a list of tenants in arrears.
- **If a tenant does not pay the rent,** the landlord can pass on their details to a tracing agent or debt collection company. It is good practice to include this information in the tenancy agreement.

General good practice is to consider:

- Whether the information in question is personal.
- Whether you have told the tenants you may give out the information.
- Who wants the information and why it is wanted.
- Whether you are legally obliged to give it.
- Whether it is necessary to give it.

Who else needs to know?

When letting a property, it is important to inform these organisations:

- **Your lender.** If the rental property is mortgaged, you must get the lender's consent to let it. Without this consent, the lender has the right to demand full repayment of the loan and ultimately to take possession of the property and sell it to recover its money. Request consent in writing. Lenders normally agree as long as the tenant is to have no **security of tenure**. Some lenders charge a fee for considering the application and giving consent. Others give consent subject to a 0.25 or 0.5 per cent increase on

Identity theft

Landlords are particularly vulnerable to identity fraud because their tenants will have access to their personal details and may well have opportunities to intercept mail, especially if the landlord once lived at the property now being let. Measures that will reduce the risk to landlords are:

- When you move out, have your post re-directed by Royal Mail, rather than returning to pick it up.
- Remove yourself from direct mail listings at the rental address through the Mailing Preference Service (www.mpsonline.org.uk).
- Provide individual mail boxes for tenants who are sharing a property.
- Check your financial statements and credit reference regularly.

 Trade bodies such as the National Landlords Association (www.landlords.org. uk) offer special insurance for landlords and www.landlordzone.co.uk has links to many insurers. Try also the Association of British Insurers at www.abi.org.uk, www. homelet.co.uk and local lettings specialists may have good value, bespoke insurance.

Housing Health and Safety Rating System

Local authorities have the right to inspect any residential property to check on its safety. The Housing Health and Safety Rating System (HHSRS), introduced in England and Wales in 2006, applies a hazard rating to private and public sector dwellings. The most common hazards are cold, fire, falls, lead in drinking water pipes and old paintwork, and hot surfaces that could scald. Inspectors can visit any property, most probably prompted by the concerns of a tenant, and can insist on repairs being carried out, backed by the threat of a £5,000 fine for non-compliance. This system replaces the Housing Fitness Standard, set out in the Housing Act 1985. Further guidance is available from www.communities.gov.uk/documents/housing/pdf/150940.pdf. HHSRS can be interpreted differently at a local level, so make sure you understand what is required by your local authority.

the loan rate. In this case, it may be worth seeking independent financial advice to make sure that staying with your current lender is viable.

- **The local authority finance department,** which deals with Council Tax.
- **If the property is a house in multiple occupation (HMO),** your local authority may have an HMO Registration Scheme with which you have to register (see page 31).
- **The neighbours.** They may need to contact you about the tenants, and, if you have a good relationship, may let you know if they spot a maintenance problem.

VIEWINGS

It is particularly important that you prepare the property carefully for viewing. Check it is clean and tidy, making sure all the lights work and there are no obvious flaws like a dripping tap.

- **Have someone with you for security,** or at least tell a friend or colleague the time of the visit and when you will be back.
- **Tidy the garden/exterior.**
- **Wash the front door.**
- **Tidy any communal areas,** such as a hallway.
- **Check the kitchen** for cleanliness and smells, including hidden parts, such as grills and microwave interiors.
- **If you are furnishing the property,** cover bare mattresses with a throw or blanket – it gives a much more homely impression. It may even be worth dressing the rooms with, say, some pictures and a vase of flowers for a better 'homely' feel.
- **Air the property** thoroughly, and sort out any sources of smells, such as a blocked drain.
- **Have all relevant information handy,** including estimated running costs.
- **Check you've got keys** to all areas/rooms.

78

Entering into a contract

Before entering into the contract, it is important you do some basic tenancy checks to establish that your potential tenant is who he says he is and also has a good credit record. You don't want to be left with a non-payer on your hands.

TENANCY CHECKS

When you have a vacant property, you naturally want to let it as soon as possible. However, it is vital to carry out checks on every tenant before offering them a tenancy: an empty property is less hassle than a problem tenant, and you can lose more money through having a bad tenant than a void period. The ideal tenant will:

- Pay their rent on time.
- Respect and look after the property.
- Be a good neighbour.
- Probably want to renew the lease.

Someone like this is unlikely to cause you financial and emotional stress, so it is worth investing some time in screening out the tenants who don't match these criteria. Part of this will be gut instinct: do you want to deal with this person and have them living in your property? You can start to do this over the phone – the most likely first point of contact. Have a checklist prepared for each conversation, covering the items listed to the right.

- Name.
- Address (and if they are currently renting, contact number for the landlord or agent).
- Landline and mobile numbers.
- Reason for moving.
- Job (including name of employer) or course (if in higher education).
- Date accommodation required, and preferred length of lease.
- Number of people who will be living in the property and whether this includes children.
- Do they smoke?
- Do they have pets?
- Can they supply a reference?

Tenants with children and pets

There are many horror stories of dogs, cats and, unfortunately, children causing untold damage to carpets, curtains, paintwork, the garden and other fixtures and fittings. This can cause issues as it may take a few weeks for you to repair the damage to the property and you may lose the income rather than let straightaway. However, some landlords are happy to let to tenants with pets and children and allow smoking in their property. Visit Lets with Pets to find out about letting safely to pet owners: www.letswithpets.org.uk.

This will give you a good start in assessing how trustworthy the person is. If they view the property and are interested, ask them to fill in an application form, which gathers more information on their background (see below).

Identity check

When you meet the tenant, ask to see their passport or other proof of identity, and note down its details.

Credit check

A credit check will identify people with a bad credit record or with County Court Judgements against them. The main credit reference agencies are Experian (www.experian. co.uk), Equifax (www.equifax.co.uk) and Callcredit (www.callcredit.co.uk). There is a charge per check, so you will want to keep these to a minimum, and may, with their agreement, pass the cost on to the tenant.

Financial and/or character reference

If the person has a job, a reference from their employer will confirm their financial stability and give you some idea of their character. Write to the employer yourself rather than accept a letter handed over by the tenant (they are easy to forge). Otherwise their bank should be able to provide a reference. For those with jobs, the three most recent salary slips will show how much salary is being paid in each month.

No record

Remember that not everyone has a credit record: many students, for example, have not built one up by the time they need accommodation. In these cases, it makes sense to ensure they can provide a reliable guarantor, who will need to be vetted in the same way as the tenant. Credit checking is also tricky for people from overseas, and it would be very difficult to pursue an overseas guarantor. However, if they have a job, their employer may be prepared to do it. An alternative is to ask for the rent to be paid for the length of the contract in advance.

66 When it comes to making all these checks you can't be too careful – make them all just to be on the safe side. 99

You can download an application form free from www.landlordzone.co.uk, or members of the Residential Landlords Association can go to www.rla.org.uk.

Rental history

If they have rented before, ask for details of their previous landlord or letting agency. A phone call will establish if they paid regularly and what condition they kept and left the property in.

Your decision

A landlord has the legal right to choose which tenant to let to, provided the decision is based on legitimate business criteria and complies with anti-discrimination laws. If you are accepting the tenant, wait until the checks are complete and inform them promptly. If you are rejecting them, do so promptly and politely explain the reason. Keep a record of your evidence in case you are accused of discrimination.

Screen test

Specialist tenant screening companies (see box below) will carry out a number of checks on potential tenants. This can save a lot of time and effort, but, of course, they will charge for their service.

THE CONTRACT

You must have a proper legal agreement with the tenant. If you fail to do this, there is enormous potential for confusion and conflict later on, even if you are only renting a room out to a friend. Never hand over the keys before this agreement is signed.

All agreements post 1997 are known as assured shorthold tenancies (see pages 131) unless otherwise specified. They should be signed by you, as landlord, the tenant(s) and, if there is one, a present guarantor, plus an independent witness (see page 200).

If you are using a letting agency, they'll have a standard contract – but make sure any special clauses you

Sadly there are bad tenants who are practised in obtaining accommodation when they have no intention of paying rent regularly. They know how the letting process works and tend to avoid large, professional letting companies in preference for small-scale landlords. This is because such landlords don't necessarily have the experience or the resources to vet their tenants thoroughly.

Specialist tenant screening companies can be found at www.tenantverify.co.uk and www.rentchecks.com. For more information about contracts, see pages 190–204.

need have been correctly added – even a tiny mistake can invalidate a clause.

You can ask a solicitor to draw up the contract (choose one who has experience in this area), but you can also buy standard contracts from legal stationers or order online from suppliers, such as www.legalhelpers.co.uk, www.clickdocs.co.uk or www.letlink.co.uk. There are also sample clauses given on pages 190–204. Either the landlord pays for the contract, or you share the cost of preparing the tenancy agreement. Of course, once you have bought one agreement you can use it for all your subsequent tenants. But just make sure it is up to date with the latest legal changes.

If your tenant has children or pets or they smoke, you might want to ensure that you (or your legal representative) has put clauses in the contract regarding any damage to the property caused by the pet/child/smoking. These may include 'making good' the damage to your satisfaction prior to leaving or to the satisfaction of an independent inventory check. Perhaps a higher deposit would be advisable, just in case.

How will you be paid?

Clarify at the outset how the rent will be paid. If you are using an agent, they'll handle this. If not, a standing order to your bank account is the most reliable. Try to avoid regular visits to collect cash, for security reasons, and because there is always the danger the tenant will try to delay payment or say they can't pay in full this time. If the tenant writes you a cheque, allow time for it to be cleared by their bank – usually three working days. If you agree to be paid weekly, by law, you must provide the tenant with a rent book and fill this in every week when the money is sent or collected.

Setting the rent

The key when setting a rent for new or existing tenants is to be realistic and follow the market rate: a month's void while you are marketing the property at a higher rent will cost more than the increased income you are trying to bring in. Social lets tend to be set at a lower level and will be capped from April 2011, but the landlord can benefit from a guaranteed long-term income. See page 154 for legal obligations when setting the rent.

For more information on the background to different agreements, see pages 128–34. The chapter on assured shorthold tenancies is on pages 136–48.

THE DEPOSIT

The deposit, or rather its return, is the source of more conflict than anything else in the letting process. One survey suggests that a quarter of tenants lose part of their deposit, and only one in seven thought it was done fairly.

It is essential to take a deposit to cover the cost of any damage to the property or its furniture found at the end of the let. It is usually equivalent to four to six weeks' rent (the average is just over £750) and must be paid before the tenant moves in. A deposit can cause problems because:

- **Tenants feel deductions** have been made unfairly, when the property has not been left in poor condition.
- **Tenants withhold payment of rent** at the end of the tenancy on the assumption that the deposit covers their rental payments.

So with this in mind, the Government introduced new legislation affecting any deposit paid after April 2007. It applies to properties rented under an assured shorthold tenancy agreement (AST) in England and Wales and when rent is less than £100,000 per annum. It deems that any landlord taking a deposit must safeguard it with a tenancy deposit protection scheme.

Any tenant must be notified via the tenancy agreement or by a letter within 14 days of the tenancy to confirm the deposit is protected and by which company and the type of scheme. If this isn't done, a landlord may not be able to serve a Section 21 possession notice (see page 163), and may be penalised with a fine of three times the deposit. The tenant should also get the contact details of the scheme and guidance on what to do if there is a disagreement.

About the schemes

- **Custodial scheme.** This is where the tenant pays the deposit money to the landlord/agent and it is then passed to the scheme itself. It is free for landlords/agents to use as the interest generated by the deposits pays for the scheme.
- **Insurance-based scheme.** In this instance, the tenant pays the deposit to the landlord or agent, who keeps the deposit (and any interest payable) and pays a premium to the insurer.

There is one custodial scheme, The Deposit Protection Service (The DPS), and there are two insurance-based schemes, My Deposits (formerly the Tenancy Deposit Solutions Ltd) and the Tenancy Deposit Scheme (TDS).

To find out more about the tenancy deposit protection schemes, go to www. depositprotection.com/ (The Deposit Protection Service), www.mydeposits. co.uk/ (mydeposits) and www.thedisputeservice.co.uk/ (the Tenancy Deposit Scheme).

If things go wrong

If all parties agree, information concerning the dispute is collated by the scheme. This information is then typically considered by an independent case adjudicator.

Are the schemes working?

The schemes have received mixed reviews since they started. On the one hand, they have built enormous costs into the system and the expected number of disputes has been far less than originally predicted. On the other hand, the organisations that back the schemes suggest that low dispute numbers mean the system is working! Figures from The DPS from October 2010 suggest that the dispute levels are reasonably even, with around 1 per cent of their 651,000 deposits going to dispute. Of the 6,660 disputes, 18 per cent of claimants were awarded 100 per cent in favour of the landlord, 37 per cent in favour of the tenants and 45 per cent were split between the landlord and tenant.

Top tips for avoiding disputes

As a landlord, you can never rule out a potential dispute, but follow these tips and help yourself to avoid them:

- Ensure there is a thorough check in and out of reports, which is signed by both parties.
- Use photos as evidence of the property, both before and after.

- Send or request instructions of what the tenant should do/leave at the property.
- Make sure all communication, particularly deposit related, is in writing.
- Include everything required by the schemes when disputing a deposit.

THE INVENTORY

It is in the interest of both landlord and tenant to agree exactly what is in the property at the start of the tenancy and, crucially, its condition, so that you will both know if anything is missing or damaged. Sometimes known as a schedule of condition, the inventory should list items (including the carpets, fixtures and fittings) room by room. This document is as vital as the tenancy agreement: it will provide evidence to indicate whether or not money should be deducted from the deposit, and it is valuable as a record of contents for insurance purposes.

If you carry out the inventory (it can be time-consuming), create a document with four columns: item, condition, comments and final inspection.

- Note the make, model and serial number of any electrical goods (this is also useful for insurance purposes).

- **Be specific about any faults:** for example, note 'fridge light not working' rather than 'fridge faulty'.
- **Make sure you write legibly** (not always easy when you are moving from room to room, but use a clipboard and take your time).

For an idea of the sort of items that will be included in each room, see page 86.

If you let the property via an agent and use their inventory company to carry out the checks, make sure you know which party is responsible for any errors. For example, if the inventory company ticks to say something is there and you then find it isn't, check that the letting agent/inventory association will sort the dispute out for you and don't sign the inventory until you are happy it is correct. If it requires legal action, know before you agree to use them whether you would take action against the inventory company or the agent that employs them.

Using an independent company shows you value your property and its contents. The Association of Independent Inventory Clerks (AIIC) is a trade body specialising in inventories: www.theaiic.co.uk. See www.theinventorymanager.co.uk for online inventories. If a dispute arises, go to www.depositprotection.com.

Inventory table for each room

Choose the appropriate items from these suggestions to make your own inventory. Once created, the inventory can be adapted and reused for each tenant.

Kitchen

- Door
- Windows/locks
- Lighting
- Flooring
- Curtains/blinds
- Oven/hob
- Microwave
- Kettle
- Toaster
- Fridge and/or fridge freezer
- Washing machine
- Dishwasher
- Sink and taps
- Iron/ironing board
- Crockery
- Cutlery

Living room

- Door
- Windows/locks
- Lighting
- Flooring
- Curtains/blinds
- Sofa
- Chairs
- Table(s)
- Shelves
- Cupboards
- Fireplace

Bathroom

- Door
- Windows/locks
- Lighting
- Flooring
- Curtains/blinds
- Bathtub
- Shower/shower curtain
- Toilet
- Sink
- Cabinet
- Mirror
- Toilet roll holder
- Towel rail
- Other fittings
- Extractor fan

Bedroom

- Door
- Windows/locks
- Lighting
- Flooring
- Curtains/blinds
- Bed
- Table
- Wardrobe
- Chest of drawers

Hallway/stairs

- Door
- Windows/locks
- Lighting
- Flooring
- Curtains/blinds
- Fire extinguisher
- Thermostat
- Boiler

Floor flaws

One of the most common reasons for dispute is when a landlord says the carpets or other floor coverings have been left in such a bad state they need replacing. This is particularly frequent if the tenant kept a pet in the house. Always check flooring in hidden areas, such as under sofas and, if possible, take photographs or video of existing wear or damage.

Ideally, the tenant should be present when the inventory is checked, and in any case they should make sure they agree with all the information in the document before signing it. Date it and give a copy to the tenant.

You or your agent may choose to use an inventory company, in which case ensure the company is a member of the Association of Independent Inventory Clerks (www.theaiic.co.uk) as they offer third party resolution for any disputes that can't be settled.

Who pays?

Inventory costs can be borne by the landlord or shared by the tenant and landlord, so landlord and tenant pay half each, or sometimes landlords pay for the initial inventory and charge the tenant for the one conducted at the end of the tenancy.

KEY POINT

Before you hand over the keys (and make sure you've got a set for each tenant), take the tenant on a detailed tour of the property, showing him or her where to find: the meters, the fuse box, the water stopcock, the boiler, central heating controls, smoke detectors and window lock keys.

Put all this in a folder with a copy of the agreement, contact details in emergencies, utility company information, guidance on how to operate the appliances and information on how and when the bins are emptied. Add to this a list of contacts for:

- **You:** landline and mobile numbers.
- **The agent,** if you have one.
- **A contact** if you are unavailable in an emergency.
- **A trusted plumber, gas fitter and electrician** in the event of an emergency when you cannot be reached. In the eventuality of the tenant paying for the work to be done, you would normally reimburse your tenant. Ideally, leave your insurance details with the tenant so it is all sorted properly.
- **It is a nice gesture** to give them a list of other useful contacts, such as the nearest doctor and details of bus and train services – much appreciated if the tenant is new to the area.

Before you leave, note down and even photograph all meter readings as paying these bills is the tenant's responsibility (unless you are operating a short-term let). You will then have relevant information to hand if there is a problem and the utility company contacts you.

Managing the let

Contented tenants pay the rent and are more likely to want to renew their agreement. This is a winning formula for landlords as they get a nice regular income with very low marketing costs.

There are a number of golden rules on being a good landlord:

- **Be available.** Either you or your agent must be ready to communicate. Some tenants won't want to pay for the extra expense of ringing a mobile number, so check your landline message system regularly. There is generally a four-to-six week teething period at the start of a tenancy after which things settle down.
- **Deal with repairs quickly.** Living with a leaking ceiling or a dodgy boiler is no fun, and tenants can become frustrated if repairs take a long time – giving them an incentive and a reason to withhold part of the rent in compensation for the inconvenience. Using the same reliable workmen all the time builds trust and commitment with them, too.
- **Respect the privacy of the tenant.** Don't 'pop in' on them: always give at least 24 hours' notice that you need to enter the property, and always use the doorbell, not your own key. See page 114 for guidance on when you are allowed to enter the property.
- **In all your dealings,** stay businesslike but friendly.
- **Visit fairly regularly,** by appointment. While the tenant will tell you if there is water coming through the roof, he might not notice a slow build-up of damp in a corner. Try to visit your property every three months, in daylight, and check it thoroughly as if you were looking to buy it. You (or if necessary, an experienced colleague) should spot any developing problems before they become serious. If you can see that problems are arising from the tenant's conduct, write to them with a warning that additional costs may be being incurred for damage or cleaning beyond normal wear and tear.

 Despite best intentions, the time can come when a landlord needs to turn to the law for support. See pages 160-7 for how to take legal action. Grounds for possession are also included in that chapter on pages 168-71.

- **Stay organised** with ongoing maintenance, such as getting the boiler serviced and the gas fittings checked. Write the due dates well ahead in your diary.
- **Keep notes of communication** either way: in a dispute over repairs it may be helpful to know the exact date or even time you were contacted.
- **Check your bank account** regularly and if the rent has not been paid, act immediately. It can take a few months to move out a tenant who turns out to be a bad payer (see pages 160–76) and the earlier you spot a problem and do something about it, the better.
- **Small kindnesses** can be worth a fortune in goodwill. Some landlords reward good tenants with gestures, such as paying their TV licence, for example: it is much harder to fall out with people with whom you are on good terms, and the benefits work both ways (provided they pay the rent!).

RAISING THE RENT

The cost of the rent will be set out in the contract and cannot be changed until it is time to negotiate a renewal. Be careful not to agree a long-term let of, say, two or three years without allowing for a rent review as the rent could stop bringing a good return and you won't be able to fund maintenance. Some agreements set out how any rent rise will be calculated, usually linked to changes in the retail prices index.

RENEWING THE CONTRACT

Tenants who renew their contracts are by far the easiest to manage: both parties know each other, and, provided the tenant is behaving within the terms of the agreement, there is every reason for you to renew the let and avoid a costly void and the trouble of finding and vetting a new occupant. If you are employing a letting agent, they are likely to charge a renewal fee.

Watch out for agents charging you to renew your agreement with a tenant to give you, in theory, two rather than one month's notice. Once a periodic agreement is in place, notice can be served at any time with two months' notice from the landlord and one month from the tenant (the notice period must start from the date the tenancy started).

ENDING THE TENANCY

For advice on how to evict a tenant who has broken the terms of their contract, see pages 160–76. However, most tenancies end happily and the tenant just decides to move on. Nevertheless, this is the point where conflict can develop over any deductions that are made from the deposit, and it is in both your interests to follow the termination process fairly.

- **The tenant should ensure the property** is as clean and tidy as when they moved in.
- **On an agreed date,** check the inventory together (you may ask your agent to do this), checking for

damage. If professional cleaning or repairs are necessary, obtain two estimates and show them to the tenant to prove you are handling the matter fairly. Check small details that can end up costing a lot in money or time, such as the vacuum cleaner still has all its attachments, that no fittings have been knocked loose, and that the oven is clean.

- **Check the tenant** has removed all their belongings. If he hasn't, remind him, pointing out that he will be charged for their removal and storage or disposal otherwise.
- **Take meter readings.**
- **The tenant should return all sets of keys.**
- **The tenant should provide a forwarding address.**

If there is a dispute and you are a landlord or tenant, make sure you include the following in your complaint to the deposit scheme:

- **A signed and dated** Tenancy Agreement.
- **The signed and dated** check-in and check-out reports.
- **A collection of signed** and dated photographs.
- **All correspondence** relating to the claim.
- **Each invoice** that relates to the claim.

If you haven't done so already, meet the tenant to discuss and agree any repair bills. This is also a chance for you to get feedback on your property:

there may be a noise problem, for example, or the tenant may feel the kitchen fittings have reached the end of their useful life.

UPGRADING

The end of a tenancy is a good time to reassess the property and decide if anything needs replacing or improving. Keep an eye on the local market and see if your competitors are ahead of you in offering, say, broadband access or power showers.

The (hopefully) short period between lets is the ideal time to spruce up the property with some fresh decoration and possibly new furniture. Check how tired the sofa, mattresses and shower curtains are if you are offering a furnished let. You may already know that the kitchen will need updating – kitchens take a real beating when there are a lot of tenants in a house. However, it may be that you only need to change the worktop and, at worst, the doors in the kitchen if you have invested in good solid kitchen units initially. Your upgrade may enable you to charge a higher rent, or stay competitive with local landlords.

❝ The end of a tenancy is a good time to decide if anything needs replacing or upgrading. This may enable you to charge a higher rent. ❞

Renting a property

Research suggests that more people are considering renting as a long-term option than ever before. This might be due to the costs of buying a home, to survive today's requirement to be 'mobile' for the job market or purely through lifestyle choice.

First decisions

Nothing focuses the mind like paying out your own money on a monthly basis, and since rental costs are based pretty much on the number of rooms, it is worth renting the smallest space that meets your needs.

If you are renting somewhere near work and only need the accommodation during the working week as you will live elsewhere at weekends, you'll probably be better off looking for a room in a house, rather than a more expensive self-contained property. You may also have other priorities, such as security (particularly important in properties that share an entrance) or easy parking.

You'll also need to decide if you want a furnished or unfurnished property. If you are renting with a view to moving into the area, you may want to use your own furniture, as putting it into storage is very expensive. If you are thinking of buying a property in the future, you may be happy to start purchasing items such as beds and wardrobes as you'll need them in your new home and you won't need to go on a shopping spree at that stage. The equipment in furnished flats varies

greatly in quality from the stylish and durable to cheap and tacky oddments that the landlord has acquired over the years, probably as cheaply as possible.

&& Research the local property market to get a feel for the prices that are charged for what you have in mind. ,,

Landlords too!

This chapter benefits landlords as well as tenants because it gives a customer's perspective on renting property. It will help guide good landlords to do a better job, which will hopefully make it more profitable in the long term.

 With the exponential development of the internet, there has been a huge growth in 'online letting' for finding a property in which to live. To find out more, go to www. which.co.uk/money/mortgages-and-property.

WHAT'S THE MARKET LIKE?

It is worth researching the local market before getting in property details. You will get a feel for the maximum and minimum prices charged for the type of property you are interested in, and whether there are variations according to location. Look at advertisements in local newspapers and have a word with local letting agents (see pages 101–3), asking to see their current rental list. This will also tell you how active the market is and whether demand matches supply – information that may help you negotiate the price down when the time comes. The rental list will also give you an idea of what is coming up in the future, as well as what is available now.

❝ If you rent, you can probably live in an area that you might otherwise not be able to afford. ❞

Check that the rents quoted are weekly or monthly – it makes a big difference! And find out what terms you have to take properties on for, whether it's just for six months, or more.

WHERE TO LOOK

One major plus about renting property is that it allows you to live in areas where you might not be able to afford to buy: you can go for the most convenient or pleasing location and see what it costs. Some properties are excellent for renting even if you would not want to buy them. For example, living above a shop can be peaceful and convenient – unless it's one that serves kebabs until two in the morning.

For a private let

To find private property to rent, go to:

- **Local newspaper advertisements,** including *Loot* and *Daltons Weekly*. There are usually plenty of advertisements in newspapers, but attractive properties get snapped up quickly, so get the paper as early as you can and start phoning as soon as office hours commence.
- **Internet sites,** like www.findaproperty. com, www.rentright.co.uk, www. rightmove.co.uk, www.zoopla.co.uk, www.easyroommate.co.uk and many more. As with local newspapers, it takes time for properties to be loaded up to the net, so you still need to contact letting agents directly.
- **Advertisements** in post offices and other shops. These are an excellent source of local information, which is particularly good if you already live where you want to rent. This cheap form of marketing is very popular with small-scale landlords with one or two rooms to let.

- **Work.** Human resources departments may be able to advise on local accommodation, and there may be a noticeboard with advertisements. It isn't always easy living and working in the same place, so try to make sure that you really do get on with the person you are looking to rent with.
- **Talking to friends** and contacts is useful if they can recommend a good landlord or warn you off a dodgy one. You may find out which properties are likely to be available before they hit the high street, so you can get in early.
- **Letting agents.** All the above search methods can be time consuming, and you might find it easier to let an agent do the work and provide you with a list of suitable properties. Usually they produce a free list on a daily/weekly basis, or some agents will charge an arrangement fee for finding a specific property, which is usually somewhere between £25 and £150. For advice on choosing a letting agent, see pages 101–3.
- **Accommodation agencies.** If you are a student, start with the university accommodation office for information and advice, and then perhaps tour the local accommodation agencies because they work in this market sector. For

more information on accommodation agencies, see page 103.

For a public sector tenancy

Local councils usually allocate their accommodation on a points system or a banding system in which priority is given to people who have lived in the area for a certain length of time but other factors relating to specific needs are also considered. Your council should be able to provide a leaflet explaining how their system works. There is often a long waiting list.

You could also try a **housing association**, also sometimes known as **registered providers of social housing**. These are non-profit-making bodies that aim to provide affordable accommodation and are one of the major providers of state-funded housing. In many cases they have taken over what was council housing stock. There is a central waiting list for all council and housing association homes in most areas, but some housing associations also run their own separate waiting lists.

WHAT TO LOOK FOR

The most important question is what can you afford? Most rents are charged by the calendar month and you will pay utility bills and council tax on top of this. Look through your

If you have a postcode of the area you are in, www.direct.gov.uk will give you information on the local council and also provide a link to their website.

Key questions to ask yourself

What are my needs? Do they include:

- Number of rooms, especially bedrooms, and whether they need to be double or single? ✓
- Parking space required? ✓
- Furnished or unfurnished? ✓
- Close to local transport or shops? ✓
- Storage space? ✓
- Telephone points (including broadband)? ✓

Add to this your preferences:

- Bath or shower? ✓
- Do you want an open-plan kitchen? ✓
- Do you want a garden? ✓

Other questions worth considering are:

- Would you be prepared to share the accommodation, or part of it, with other people? ✓
- Would you share with a live-in landlord? ✓
- Do you want or need to be on the ground floor? ✓
- Do you feel you will have enough privacy? ✓
- Will you be sharing with anyone else? If so, meet them to see how you get on. ✓

Have you got children or pets?

If you have children or pets you obviously need space for them, including a garden, and will want to know the accommodation is suitable and safe for them. Some landlords will let to tenants with children or pets, but they are few and far between, so start looking in plenty of time before you need to rent somewhere. Check the place before you view and the contract terms and conditions. Visit www.letswithpets.org.uk for more help.

last three months' bank statements and work out what you can afford to pay from your income.

Also consider how long you are likely to want the accommodation for (most lets are for a fixed term of six months that is renewable), and whether you are likely to want to extend this. Some lets are short-term only, and there may be a definite ending time if, for example, the owner is working abroad for a set period.

Location

As always with property, location is the key. If you prefer to use public transport, you need to be near a train or bus route. You may want to live near family, friends, work or a certain school, or like the look of an area. However, as when buying a property, do visit at least twice, at different times of day, to investigate noise levels and traffic conditions, or neighbours! Work out practicalities, such as where you will do grocery shopping and how safe you feel on your route to the bus stop, college or your work.

What do you need?

You need to be clear about what you need. For example, it is not worth renting a property with a spare room if it is not going to be used frequently: it is cheaper to put guests (or yourself!) up in a local hotel or B & B for the night, or buy a sofa bed. Quality, size and price vary enormously. Write a list of your needs, such as those listed on page 95.

 When you phone to check the property is still available, get as much information as possible to save wasted visits. Take basic safety precautions, such as telling someone else where you are going. Get the landline and mobile number of the person you are meeting. If possible, go along with someone else for security and a second opinion.

❝ Most lets are for a six-month term that is renewable, but others are short term. Check that the property you want to rent has an appropriate letting period for what you want. **❞**

The cost of renting

The nearer a city centre and the more luxurious the property, the higher the price will be. Suburban and rural properties tend to be cheaper per room - but your transport costs are likely to be higher.

It can be tricky assessing the merits of prices between properties because you are not necessarily comparing like with like. To make an assessment of the value for money (as opposed to aesthetic considerations, such as the décor or how nice the view is), try the following process:

- **Make sure you are comparing** the price per calendar month (pcm). Charges per week will seem lower when multiplied by four but this is not the monthly charge, as most months are longer than 28 days. If the price given is per week, multiply it by 52 and divide by 12 for a true monthly comparison.
- **Consider the price per room.**
- **Calculate the price per square foot.** The agent or landlord should be able to tell you the area of the accommodation. Divide this number into the monthly rent to find the cost per square foot. This allows you to make a rational comparison of how much space you are getting for your money. For example, a one-bedroom flat covering 100 sq m and costing £569 per month costs £5.69 per sq m (569 divided by 100 = £5.69). The cost for a two-bedroom flat the same size with a monthly rent of £704 would be £7.04 per sq m (704 divided by 100). Obviously this would become more attractive if two tenants shared the rent.
- **Consider other factors,** such as location, fittings, furnishings and décor. Obviously the better these are, the higher the premium.
- **Take into account terms and conditions,** such as how much deposit is required, and particularly what bills are included - or are they extra?

As a guideline, the table overleaf shows some average cost of accommodation per calendar month. They illustrate that prices in London are more than double the average for the rest of Great Britain.

“When comparing prices, make sure you are comparing like for like. ”

Average cost of accommodation per calendar month (2008)

How the average cost of a flat in London compares with the rest of Great Britain.

	1-bed flat	2-bed flat	2-bed terrace	3-bed semi-detached	4-bed detached
London	£1,275	£1,700	£1,800	£2,500	£3,500
Great Britain	£570	£700	£740	£850	£1,250

Other costs to be aware of
There are other costs to take into account:

Deposit (returnable)	equivalent of 4–6 weeks' rent
EITHER: Reservation deposit	up to £200 or the equivalent of the first month's rent, usually refundable
OR: Administration fee	£100 plus
Tenancy reference	£30
Agreement fee	£25
Inventory fee	£50–£100
Renewal fee	£25 plus

Jargon buster

Deposit A sum of money that is paid in advance to cover any potential costs of damage to the rented property or should you fail to pay the rent. If there is no damage when you leave the property, all the deposit should be returned to you

Guarantor Someone, often a parent, who agrees to pay the rent for the tenant in case of default

Inventory A list of items that are in the rented property on your arrival

Reservation fee A sum of money that may be payable to a letting agency to keep a property on hold while you get hold of a deposit and/or references

Not all letting agents charge fees, and they vary from firm to firm, so it shop around and find the right letting agent for the type of property you want and fees that seem to be fair.

Cheques and references

Some landlords and agencies won't accept personal cheques as deposits or rent in advance, so you might have to pay in cash or organise a banker's draft.

- **When paying cash,** get another person to go with you and always ask for a written receipt.

 There are different types of tenant agreements, although most of them are what is called an 'assured shorthold tenancy', which gives the landlord more rights than an 'assured tenancy'. The chapter Tenancy Law on pages 127–48 explains further.

If you are paying your rent weekly, the landlord must provide you with a rent book, which is filled in each week.

- **Some landlords want rent to be paid by standing order** so you may need a bank account.
- **You may also be asked to provide a reference:** bank details or a letter from your employer confirming your employment are usually sufficient, but you may be asked for a character reference or a reference from a previous landlord. It will save time if you arrange these in advance and take copies with you when you view. For first-time tenants a letter from a parent or guardian should be enough.
- **Some landlords ask for a guarantor** to pay the rent if you don't (see pages 30 and 200). Check what the guarantor is agreeing to: in some cases they are held to be liable for costs, which include rent owed, damage to the property and any costs of evicting you, the tenant, from the property.

Whatever you are renting, find out why the property or room is available, it will give you an idea of how long the property might be yours for, or if there is a set time. The longer you agree to rent a property for, the better rate you may be able to negotiate.

What the tenant pays for

One of the critical things that you need to understand is what charges you will be responsible for. For short-term lets, these are often included in the rent, whereas for longer-term rents, you are likely to have to pay for:

- Electricity, gas and water.
- Council tax.
- TV licence.
- Telephone.
- Any broadband charges.

Make sure that these bills are either in your name, or, if renting with others, in everyone's name as then the responsibility is spread, just in case someone decides not to pay. If you leave, make sure that you check the readings and advise and obtain acceptance letters of the day you are moving out. Most utility companies will accept about ten days' notice for change of address.

If you are taking on these bills, make sure you see how much it costs and if you can reduce the monthly price by paying by direct debit – or indeed changing the supplier. Note that you will also be responsible for insurance cover on your own possessions (see pages 75–6).

❝ Put all amenities in your name or, if renting with others, in everyone's names so the responsibility is evenly spread. ❞

Letting agents and landlords

A good letting agent will find you a suitable property, negotiate the tenancy, and only charge you when you pick up the keys. It can be well worth the money for the saved hassle, time and foot slog.

A dodgy letting agent might find you decent accommodation, but they'll charge (and overcharge) for minor administrative tasks and get you to sign agreements with small print that commits you to pay them for doing almost anything except blowing your nose. You don't have to use a letting agent to find property (see the list of other routes on pages 93–4), but your choice may be restricted if you do not.

The property letting market is unregulated and it is growing fast, creating conditions where there are many opportunities for unscrupulous agents to make a quick buck. They can do this because people looking for accommodation are often in a hurry and are understandably keener to discuss the size of the kitchen and how many bedrooms a property has than whether they'll be expected to pay for repairing rotten windows or to be charged £30 for letters telling them the rent is going up.

There are about 17,000 letting agents in the UK. About 8,000 are members of trade bodies (see box, right) and if at all possible you should stick with them because then you'll have some comeback if there's a dispute, as they will have a code of conduct that they have to stick to. It is wise to check if a firm is a member of one of these bodies (it's easy to do this through their websites) rather than just take their word for it.

Letting trade bodies

Sadly the new government decided not to regulate letting agents so choose ones which offer you and your money some protection. The best protection on offer is the National Approved Letting Scheme (NALS): www.nalscheme.co.uk, The Association of Residential Letting Agents (ARLA): www.arla.co.uk, The Property Ombudsman: www.tpos.co.uk and The Royal Institution of Chartered Surveyors (RICS): www.rics.org.
A letting and management service is also sometimes offered by these bodies. Each runs its own code of practice, but NALS and The Property Ombudsman offer further security with an internal complaints procedure, a legally binding arbitration service and a scheme to protect money if it is lost or misappropriated.

FINDING A LETTING AGENT

There are different types of letting agency:

- **Some find tenants for properties** and are also known as accommodation agencies (see page 103).
- **Others manage the property as well** so the tenant deals with them, rather than the landlord.
- **Many estate agents** offer a lettings service as well as selling property, so they may belong to several of the schemes in the box, opposite.

Legally, agents represent landlords but they can charge fees to both landlords and tenants. Some don't charge tenants at all, but others have fees for drawing up tenancy agreements, providing inventories and administrative costs, such as phone calls and postage.

Letting agents advertise in local papers and there is also often a list in housing advice offices and branches of the Citizens Advice Bureau (www.adviceguide.org.uk). Because registration is free, it makes sense to sign up with any that you feel you can

trust (see box, on page 100). They'll ask you about your needs (see page 95) and how much you want to pay. If they supply details of suitable properties, follow it up straightaway as good accommodation gets snapped up quickly. They may invite you to contact the landlord or, if they are offering a fuller service, show you round it themselves.

Once you decide to rent a property, the agency may ask for a holding deposit to remove the property from the market while they take up your references – another reason to take copies of references with you when viewing. This is not the same as a deposit on the tenancy, and you could lose it if you pull out of the rental process.

Identifying a good agent

The best recommendation is word of mouth, so ask friends and local contacts if they know an agent with a good record. They will be members of a recognised trade association (see box, opposite) or at least follow the NALS scheme or are ARLA registered: look for the logo, and ask if they are still members. Check the local paper and relevant website (some firms fraudulently claim to be members, or have left but still display its signage). These websites are also good for finding agents in the area if you lack local information.

Some agents don't charge tenants at all. Others do, which is quite reasonable given the amount of

It is against the law for a letting agent to charge a registration fee for property details: if you are asked to do this, head straight for the door.

Although you pay a fee to an agent, their main income is from their client, the landlord, so bear in mind they are likely to give the landlord's needs more priority than yours. That also means that the legal agreement is likely to be in the landlord's favour, so make sure you get an independent person to check any legal documents before you sign.

work involved in managing a rented property well, but good agents will tell you early on what you are expected to pay for and will provide a receipt for it. Ask for a list of likely charges when you first meet them; see the box on page 98 for a list of likely costs.

Sign up with as many reputable agents as you can (this is free) and continue to look for accommodation by other routes as suggested on pages 93–4, as many are still likely to be cheaper than going through an agent. You will then cover all possibilities and are less likely to miss out on a good property at a reasonable rent.

Are you receiving Housing Benefit?

Since benefit is paid four weeks in arrears, you'll need to pay the first month's rent yourself, and Housing Benefit will not cover deposits or agency fees. Some agencies and landlords will not accept tenants on Housing Benefit. This may be because the lender on the property won't allow them to, so it is not always prejudice on their part.

Unfair fees

Some letting agents sneak all sorts of extra charges into their contracts, so it is really important to read the small print before you sign an agreement with them. Don't just sign up in the office without reading the document, however desperate you are for accommodation.

Ask for a copy in advance, or take it away with you. Examples of unfair fees used by some unscrupulous agents include the following:

- A fee for information on rental properties
- A charge for sending letters, even ones telling you the rent is going up
- A penalty payment if you don't pay the rent by standing order
- A charge for moving out as well as one for moving in
- A charge for re-let even when the landlord agrees to re-let the property early.

Spotting a bad agent

Naturally your mind will be focused on the accommodation you want, not spotting deficiencies in the agency. However, there are things to watch out for that could save you money and hassle. A letting agent who is unprofessional in their dealings with you is likely to be just as unfair with the landlord, which is a recipe for disaster. Here are some indicators that an agent could be dodgy.

- **Not a member** of one of the trade associations listed on page 100.
- **Poorly organised,** so you always get the answerphone, the office is untidy, and they miss appointments.
- **Asks for money** up front.
- **Doesn't offer receipts.**
- **Doesn't give you time** to check agreements.
- **Doesn't do an inventory.**
- **Doesn't explain arrangements** clearly.
- **Include a plethora of financial penalties** in tenancy agreements.

 Under the Accommodation Agencies Act of 1953, an agency cannot charge for registering your details and/or supplying addresses. However, some agencies try to do this, dressing them up as registration or administration fees. If they try this, walk away: the only payment they are entitled to is for providing details of accommodation that you subsequently rent. You can safely register with as many agencies as you like at no cost.

Accommodation agencies

These are more specialised letting agents and if you are a student, you are more likely to come across them. They charge tenants who take up accommodation a small fee (typically a week or two's rent, but sometimes less – and see Unfair fees, opposite). Some student accommodation offices allow you to search for property online, which is very useful if you do not yet live in the area.

They tend not to be able to offer services, such as showing you round the property: rather they are a contact point between student and landlord. If you are interested in a property, you'll probably be asked for a holding deposit, which you would lose if you

change your mind. Finally, demand can outstrip supply in this market: if this is the case in your local market, you may need to start your search early to find rooms for the new academic year. In others, you will have more choice and can take your time.

FINDING A LANDLORD

There are several ways to locate landlords apart from relying on who is advertising at the moment. There are two trade bodies, the NLA and the RLA (see box, page 100), and local councils, colleges and landlords associations run accreditation schemes that set minimum requirements for landlords. Details on this can be found from Accreditation Network UK (ANUK) (see overleaf). Ask the landlord

 University websites have links to their accommodation office so are the best starting point. Also try www.accommodationforstudents.com and www.homesforstudents. co.uk, www.studentaccommodation.org and www.studentpad.co.uk. There is more advice available from www.shelter.org.uk and www.designsonproperty.co.uk.

to show you their accreditation scheme membership card or certificate. The landlord is responsible for:

- **Repairs and maintenance** to the structure and exterior.
- **All sanitary installations.**
- **Heating and hot water** installations.
- **The safety** of gas, electrics and electrical appliances (see page 53).
- **The fire safety** of furniture and furnishings supplied by the landlord.
- **In a flat or maisonette,** other parts of the building the landlord owns or controls and whose condition would affect the tenant.
- **Complying with the legal regulations** of owning and letting out a property.

The landlord can claim against tenants who cause damage to their property.

Avoid rogue landlords/letting agents!

Many people complain about being badly treated by landlords/agents. If you ask these three questions, though, you can avoid most rogue ones.

1 Will my deposit be protected in a tenancy deposit protection scheme? If yes, which one?
2 Can you bring a copy of a current gas and electrical safety certificate with you on visits?
3 Can I have a copy of the EPC (see page 54)?
If a landlord or letting agent says no or can't provide any of these, walk away.

Meeting a landlord

For your own security, always get a landline phone number as well as any mobile numbers offered, plus an address. The landlord is likely to ask you for references and it is reasonable for you to do the same: is he a member of a trade body such as the NLA or RLA? Can he supply contact details of other tenants who can vouch for him? If possible, visit other properties let by the landlord (he may have several in the same block or nearby).

The encounter won't necessarily feel very comfortable: after all, you are both in the process of checking the other one out, and the landlord will want to make sure his new tenant is going to look after the property, which he may have sunk his life savings into buying. The landlord will probably also have been through this process many times before, so his responses may be trotted out quite fast.

As with agents, be suspicious of anybody who appears disorganised or is not forthcoming with information. and do not pay any money before checking out the contract. This person will have access to your temporary home, and you need to feel you can trust them. Ask at your local Citizens Advice Bureau or other housing advice office if any landlords in the area have caused concern in the past.

 Some useful contacts are: the National Landlord's Association (NLA) (www.landlords. org.uk); the Residential Landlords Association (RLA) (www.rla.org.uk) and the Accreditation Network UK (www.anuk.org.uk).

Viewing a property

When people are looking for a property to buy, they view it at least twice so that they can get a feel for what it is like to live in and its surrounding area. If at all possible, you should do the same if you are intending to rent. After all, you might end up spending longer living there than a person who purchased the property next door!

Always view properties during daylight hours as that is when flaws show up best. Follow the suggested list of vital checks that follows on this page and on page 107 and also bear in mind the 'key questions' given on page 106.

ʿʿThe exterior of a rented property is just as important as the interior. A well-maintained building shows that the landlord cares about it. ʾʾ

VITAL CHECKS

Make a list of the priorities of what you want from the property and score each one as you view properties to help you come to a decision.

If you will be sharing the tenancy, agree this list in advance, and if at all possible, view the potential properties together.

- **Study the exterior** and judge if it is well maintained. If the outside is badly maintained, the interior is likely to be in a poor state of repair, too. Are the windows in good condition? Do the gutters leak? The landlord or agent won't tell you if the neighbours are noisy, but the current tenants might if you get a chance to talk to them, or you may know someone who lives in the road and so be able to check with them directly.

A landlord has legal responsibilities, ranging from fire safety and smoke alarms to various types of insurance. If you want to find out more, see the advice for landlords given on pages 74–7.

Key questions to ask the landlord

Key questions to ask when you are interested in renting a property include:

- Why is the property or room available? ✓
- What is the rent (as a monthly or weekly figure)? ✓
- Does the rent include any costs such as water and electricity? ✓
- Is a deposit required? And, if so, how much is it and which company is it protected by? ✓
- When is the property available from and to? ✓
- How much notice do I need to give to leave? How should this notice be given? ✓
- What council tax is payable? ✓
- How is the property heated (even if you're viewing in the summer!)? ✓
- How much are the heating and electricity bills? ✓
- If I'm responsible for their payment, can I change the supplier if I choose? ✓
- Can I please see the EPC and Gas and Electrical Safety Certificate? ✓
- Who do I contact if repairs are necessary? (This must be a UK address.) ✓
- Are there any special clauses in the contract that I should be told about? ✓
- Are children and/or pets allowed (if relevant)? ✓

Is the rent reasonable?

Draw on the research you did at the start of the process to answer the question 'Is this property worth the rent being asked?' If it isn't, you may be able to negotiate the price down and you stand a better chance of success if you can explain why your price is more reasonable than theirs. Before you agree to rent a property, double check that you can afford it, factoring in the estimated amounts for utilities, Council Tax and other bills.

- **When you get inside,** do check that lights work, taps produce water and windows open. Every property has its own atmosphere and you get a gut feeling for places you feel comfortable in. Unlike a buyer, you won't be able to change the décor or, if provided, furnishings. If you hate them, don't condemn yourself to the torture of living with them. If, however, you are renting for a while, the landlord may be OK with you changing it. It's always worth asking!
- **If the property you're looking at was built after June 1992,** it must have smoke alarms on every floor. All electrical equipment must be safe to use, including the power sockets.
- **If the property is occupied,** check to see if the tenants are using extension cables to run appliances, which would suggest there are not enough sockets for everyday use.
- **Any property rented out** should have a gas and electric safety certificate and all furnishings must meet the fire safety regulations (see page 74–5).
- **An Energy Performance Certificate** (see page 54) should also be supplied for all properties marketed for rent.

If at all possible, ask if you can view again at another time of day. This will allow you to check for noise levels, see how much light enters the rooms. Visiting during rush hour allows you to judge traffic noise and ease of

Safety first

You should be given a copy of the official safety record for the furniture, furnishings, gas appliances and recent electrical work.
- Furniture and furnishings must meet fire safety regulations unless they were made before 1950.
- The gas appliances and supply should be checked once a year by someone on the Gas Safety Register. There should be a record of inspection dates, defects identified and action taken.
- Although there is no legal requirement for landlords to install carbon monoxide detectors, it is worth asking about this valuable safety equipment. They are available from hardware stores.

parking. Even if you can't get in, you can get a fair idea of this from outside the property. In the meantime, ask for a copy of an example tenancy agreement.

"Every property has its own atmosphere and you get a gut feeling for places that you feel comfortable in."

107

Entering into a contract

As well as understanding the contract, you need to ensure the deposit, inventory and insurance are handled well. The deposit and inventory, in particular, are the most frequent areas of disagreement, but if dealt with efficiently, this need not be the case.

THE CONTRACT

Never sign a contract without reading and understanding it, however desperate you are to get hold of the keys to the property. There is advice on all aspects of contracts on pages 79–82, 128–34 and 190–204.

Deposit know how

- Some landlords may claim that they are not taking a deposit, but then take two months' rent in advance. As a deposit is largely defined as any money that is held in any way, shape or form to guarantee the tenant abides by the agreement, then any monies that are over and above normal rent payments can be considered as a deposit.
- Even before you have a written agreement, any verbal understanding counts as a legal agreement – although they are harder to enforce. It is in both your interests to understand your rights and responsibilities. Get anything you agree in writing.

THE DEPOSIT

You will be asked to pay a deposit to cover any damage you cause to the property and as insurance in case you default on the rent. The deposit is usually to the value of 4–6 weeks' rent. This is perfectly fair, but getting the deposit back after moving out causes more problems than any other aspect of renting property. Here are some ways you can help yourself:

- **Make a dated note** if any items are removed from the property by the landlord or agent in order to avoid misunderstandings at a later date about where they have got to.
- **Make sure you get a receipt** for the deposit.

Since April 2007, there are strict rules for where landlords bank deposit money – for more information, see page 83.

 Since April 2007, legislation (the tenancy deposit scheme) has come into effect to help overcome the conflict that surrounds the subject of deposits (see pages 60-2 for more information).

If you are paying your deposit by cheque, you'll have to wait until it clears before you can move in. If it is urgent, you could pay with a banker's draft, a building society cheque or cash. The simplest way to ensure you pay the rent on time is to set up a standing order. Landlords do not take kindly to late payment. See also the advice on guarantors on page 84.

At the end of the tenancy, do not withhold the last month's rent on the assumption that the deposit more than covers the amount: the landlord or their agent will want to assess the state of the property at the end of the let, so cannot make deductions from the deposit before then.

THE INVENTORY

It is in your and the landlord's interest to make a full inventory of what is in the property (see pages 85–6). This is a list of everything you could be held responsible for damaging or losing, including furniture and other items such as kitchen equipment. It is by far the best option to be present when the landlord or agent makes this list, as you can agree on what is present. Be thorough about this. For example, look at the carpet under beds and sofas to see if they are stained: you do not want to be held responsible for damage that is already there.

If you cannot be present at the inspection, or are simply issued with a list, check it thoroughly with another person and get them to witness it. If something is missing or damaged, inform the landlord in writing immediately. Take photographs of any damage present before you began living there, and date them. If no one provides you with an inventory (a major warning sign of a dodgy landlord), make one yourself, take a copy, and send it to the landlord together with any photographs, if relevant. You should also consider why a landlord would not undertake this basic procedure and keep a careful eye on his dealings during your residency.

If anything is removed during your tenure, make a dated note and, if possible, take a photograph. Evidence

While there are plenty of stories of landlords from hell, there are many of tenants who have behaved irresponsibly too. You might want a reference from your landlord in the future or need to negotiate with her: if you've been fair with them, they are more likely to be fair with you.

You can find more advice on an independent inventory at www.theaiic.co.uk. There is more information on contracts, the deposit and inventory on pages 79–87.

could be invaluable if there is a dispute about items in the property in the future.

If you can, repair any damage you have caused, or replace items that cannot be made good. If you can't do this, you must expect to be charged for repairs. Make sure the property is clean at the end of the let – you could have the carpets professionally cleaned or hire a carpet cleaner and your contract may require you to do this anyway. Take photographs of the property on the day you leave, showing its condition (this is most useful if you photographed any damaged items at the start of the tenancy).

If the inventory is carried out by the letting agent, there is usually a charge (see page 87). Typically the landlord and tenant share the cost – one paying for moving in and one moving out – but better agents and landlords don't charge the tenants at all. If you are paying a high deposit, it may be worth investing in an independent inventory if the letting agent or landlord are not intending to do so.

INSURANCE

While you are listing the items in the inventory, make a separate list of your own possessions, if you have not done so already. This will help you decide the value of the insurance cover you should now take out. To ease any claims you may have to make, ensure you have photos of costly items, any serial numbers on equipment and always keep your receipts somewhere safe. The landlord's insurance policy only covers the buildings and his possessions. Sadly, rented properties are often targeted by burglars, especially in areas where students live, as they know there are likely to be portable and valuable items such as hi-fis and computers in many of the rooms. Some insurance brokers have special policies for people who rent rooms or whole properties.

Policies in high-risk inner city postcodes sometimes carry a requirement to have minimum-security locks on doors and accessible windows/locks, which may require negotiation with the landlord. If you are in social housing, your local authority may run an insurance scheme for the tenants. As always with insurance, it pays to shop around, provided you are confident you are comparing like with like.

Policies can be bedroom-rated (based on the number of bedrooms) or sum-insured (based on the cost of your belongings) and it is worth getting quotes based on both methods.

 Companies who specialise in flat-share insurance include Endsleigh (www.endsleigh.co.uk), Entertainment and Leisure Insurance (www.eandl.co.uk), Harrison Beaumont (www.hbinsurance.co.uk) and Leisure Insure (www.leisureinsure.co.uk).

A tenant's obligations

It's worth being a good tenant because you might want to rent from the landlord or agent again, or need a reference from them. Although being a tenant does not carry the responsibilities of home ownership (which is one of its joys), it does come with certain expectations of behaviour and basic maintenance.

As a tenant you are also expected to:

- **Pay your rent on time,** usually a month in advance.
- **Live in the property** and not leave it empty. If you go on holiday, tell your landlord. Otherwise they might think you have left and are trying to avoid paying rent. Also an inhabited property is less likely to be burgled than one that is standing empty.
- **Keep the property secure,** which means locking doors and, if possible, windows when you go out and not giving the keys to non-tenants.
- **Have a general responsibility** to look after the property reasonably and inform the landlord of any repairs required. A good landlord will appreciate being told of such maintenance needs as promptly as possible, because it could prevent a worse problem developing and it is likely to be a condition of your tenancy agreement. For example, a leaking pipe left to drip could damage flooring or bring down a neighbour's ceiling. Minor maintenance such as replacing light bulbs is down to you.
- **Undertake basic maintenance,** such as changing light bulbs, tightening loose screws and replacing smoke alarm batteries. If you need to contact the landlord, try to do so at sociable hours unless it is a genuine emergency.
- **Respect your neighbours** by keeping the place reasonably tidy, clearing rubbish, not playing loud music late at night. That doesn't mean you have to live like a monk, but anti-social behaviour can be grounds for eviction. Remember that you can also be held responsible for the behaviour of guests.
- **Use it as a home,** not a base for a business, unless agreed with the landlord/agency.

❝ Look after the property reasonably and tell your landlord of any necessary repairs as soon as possible. ❞

Moving In

- Before you physically move in make sure you have checked the inventory.
- Read and make sure you understand the contract before moving in.
- Check you have been given a copy of the gas safety certificate.
- Know where any fire exits are, and check you can get to them.
- Contact the utility companies and take meter readings on the day you move in.
- Set up your standing order so that the rent is paid on time. Keep track of your finances so that you know you can afford to pay the rent (sometimes bills can be higher than you thought, or unexpected events affect your finances).

&& Always try to be professional in your dealings with the landlord. &&

Be professional in your dealings with the landlord or agent. They are running the property as a business and you are their client. Make notes of conversations where appropriate (for example, if the landlord says he'll fix a broken toilet before the weekend) and confirm any important details in writing. Keep a copy of all communications, including emails and notes of telephone calls. If you are sharing the property, it makes sense to keep all this paperwork in one well-organised file so that everybody knows what is going on. Include all contact details in the file so that everyone has access to them. Treat the tenancy as a job of work that you need to stay on top of.

Don't let yourself be treated as if you are some kind of paying guest: for the duration of your tenancy this is your home where you have a right to feel safe and happy. Some

Tips for a trouble-free tenancy

- Read, understand and follow the terms of the tenancy. If the landlord does not do the same, point this out politely.
- Pay the rent on time.
- Pay other bills on time.
- Communicate promptly when necessary.
- Ask permission if you want to do things such as sublet, take in a lodger, pass the tenancy to someone else, or make improvements to the property.
- Treat the property with respect.
- Try not to antagonise the neighbours - if you are having a party, tell them (you don't have to invite them!).
- End the tenancy properly (see pages 89-90).

Beware of being charged a renewal fee by a letting agent: they are employed by the landlord, not you, and you should not have to make any payments that are not specified in your original agreement.

landlords can be over-zealous in their understandable wish to protect their property, but all have to give you a right to enjoy the property quietly and an amount of notice if they want access to the property. That said, if you annoy the neighbours, they are likely to complain to the landlord, who is likely to want to keep relations amicable: he'll probably know the neighbours for longer than he'll have contact with you.

Sharing a house with others

Living with other people, especially if they are strangers and/or you are sharing communal areas, isn't always easy. To help make the tenancy work out well, follow this advice.

- **Try to meet all the tenants** before you move in, and find out what the other people do for a living (early or late working patterns will mean people entering and leaving at unsocial hours, for example). Ask if they tend to socialise together or lead separate lives.

- **Agree how bills will be shared out.** It clearly makes sense to divide council tax and utility bills by the number of people sharing, but if one person uses significantly more than the others – perhaps by excessive use of an electric heater – there is likely to be conflict.

- **Establish what the agreed system is for paying shared bills** and cleaning communal areas. If there aren't any house rules, there is a lot of scope for conflict so perhaps you could suggest some. House rules should be in writing and include:
  - Agreeing which parts of the property are communal, and which rooms no one can enter without permission.
  - A cleaning rota.
  - Is smoking allowed, and if so, where in the property?
  - Can tenants have guests to stay over regularly?

❝One of the most important things when sharing a house with others is to communicate.❞

For more information on letting agents, see pages 68-71. Although much of that information is aimed at the landlord, there is useful advice there that applies just as well to the tenant. For help moving all your addresses, visit www.iammoving.com.

Renting a property

DISPUTES

Most disputes begin with small incidents that could have been avoided with decent communication, and then the problem escalates. It is easy to feel vulnerable when you are a tenant. A landlord or their representative who is responsible for unpleasant or abusive phone calls, unexpected visits, interference in the supply of utilities or other forms of intimidation, which make your life at home difficult, may well be guilty of harassment, which is a criminal offence.

Who can help when you are in dispute?

You may be able to get advice from:

- A tenancy relations officer or specialist in harassment issues in the local housing or environmental health departments.
- A housing aid centre.
- The Citizens Advice Bureau (www.adviceguide.org.uk).
- A law centre.
- A solicitor.

“ Harassment from a landlord or his or her representative can be intimidating and most unpleasant. It is a criminal offence and, as such, you have rights for dealing with it. ”

The accredited tenant scheme

Landlords who are members of an accredited landlord scheme (see box, page 104) should know if it includes an accredited tenant scheme. These recognise good tenants and provide a reference that is useful when moving within the rented sector or as a general character reference.

If you are involved in a dispute with your landlord, get advice early as someone may be able to intervene and mediate. If all else fails, see pages 160-73 for dealing with legal action. Pages 174-6 specifically covers harassment from a landlord.

Money matters

This chapter looks at small-scale and larger-scale letting businesses. Among other things, it describes how to keep on top of records and how to calculate your profit and pay your tax. The benefits of setting up a limited company and planning for capital gains are also looked at.

Rent as 'extra income'

Rent money is income, so you will have to pay tax on the profit you make on it. Before becoming a landlord, it is therefore important to have a clear understanding of how the system works, and how much you are likely to be liable to have to pay to Her Majesty's Revenue & Customs (HMRC): it might change how you do things, or whether you decide it is worth letting property at all.

KEEPING RECORDS

Profit is what is left once you have deducted the allowable expenses from the rental income. This will, of course, be mainly rent, but other sums you may receive can be included, such as a charge for use of furniture, or for cleaning or providing heat. It is taxed at the same rates as income from business or employment, 20–50 per cent in 2011–12, depending on the income band you fall into. If you let more than one property, all the income is grouped together – so you can offset a loss on one property against a profit from another.

Deductible (or 'allowable') expenses

The expenses you can deduct from letting income include:

- Letting agent fees.
- Legal fees for lets of a year or less, or for renewing a lease for less than 50 years.

- Accountancy fees.
- Insurance.
- Interest on property loans.
- Maintenance and repairs (but not improvements).
- Utility bills if you are responsible for them.
- Ground rent and service charges.
- Council tax.
- Services you pay for, such as cleaning or gardening.
- Other costs of letting the property, such as advertising, phone calls, and travel to and from it.
- Professional fees, such as belonging to a landlord's association.
- Energy performance certificates.
- Tenancy deposit protection.
- Legal fees (for advice on letting issues, but not for buying or selling the property or for planning applications).
- Bad debts.
- Capital allowances for office equipment involved in running the business (see page 118).

You can only deduct expenses directly related to letting the property. If the expense is partly for another business, or if you use the property yourself, you can only claim for part of it. For example, if you go to a town and stay overnight partly for leisure, partly for business, you can only claim a proportion of the expense, not all.

What you can't claim

You can't deduct:

- Capital costs, such as the property itself, or the furniture.
- Personal expenses unrelated to your business.
- Any loss from selling the property.

Go to the experts

Property tax is incredibly complex and it is difficult to generalise as it is bespoke to your – and your family's – individual circumstances.

It is therefore essential that you seek advice from a property tax specialist as well as check any

advice with Her Majesty's Revenue & Customs (HMRC) before you even think about buying a property, let alone start receiving rent. With buy to let you are likely to be classed as a 'property investor' – someone who invests in property for ongoing income. Professional advice can cost around £200 per hour, which may seem a lot of money, but it can save you thousands.

When considering what tax you will pay, you need to take into consideration your earnings. Think, too, about what your reasons are for investing in buy to let; for example, is it to boost your pension or pass capital on to your children? A specialist tax advisor will need to know your intentions from the outset so that he or she can advise you how best to invest your money and to help you know the tax implications and when you will be billed. Top tips to make your tax returns easier include:

- **Seek help from a tax specialist,** at least in your first year.
- **Keep your records for six years** after the tax year to which they apply.
- **Don't forget to sign and date your tax return** – it's one of the most common mistakes.
- **Speak to the tax office** if you have any queries.

 If you are using the Rent-a-Room Scheme (see page 120), the rules are different, so discuss this with your financial adviser.

 For more information on running a small business and the associated tax implications, go to the HMRC website: www.hmrc.gov.uk, and also www.direct.gov.uk, where there are lots of leaflets and booklets designed to help you.

- **Keep up to date with changes to tax** via a landlord association, your property tax specialist, or specialist landlord magazines.

Capital cost allowances

Capital costs are expenditure on assets, such as the property itself, furniture and machinery. You can claim for some of these. A distinction is made between repairs (fixing or replacing a leaking gutter), which are running costs and therefore deductible, and improvements (refurbishing a kitchen), which are capital expenditure. Replacing traditional materials with modern ones is usually classified as a repair: so, for example, you can replace a single-glazed wooden window frame with a double-glazed PVC sealed unit and set the cost against tax.

Other examples of capital costs you can claim include: office, cleaning and gardening equipment, or a boiler.

Furnishings and equipment

You have a choice on how you claim for furnishings and equipment including small items like cutlery: either 'wear and tear' or 'cost and replacement'. 'Wear and tear' is 10 per cent of the rent less amounts paid

Once you've chosen which of these allowances to claim, you can't switch between them from year to year.

Go green!

There has been talk of a green landlord scheme since 2004 to explore ways to encourage landlords to 'go green'. Most landlords must have an EPC (see page 54) when marketing properties. Landlords and tenants are entitled to a government grant (known as CERT funding), which encourages insulating properties. If the tenant is on qualifying benefits, for example LHA or over 70 years old, then the grant may cover the full cost of loft and cavity wall insulation. If the tenant doesn't qualify, it can cost less than £150 to insulate a property.

by the landlord, which would usually be paid by the tenant (such as council tax). See the table, below, for a typical calculation. You can't claim 'wear and tear' on furnished holiday lettings in the UK (see opposite).

Rent	£7,400
Less Council Tax paid by landlord	£400
Net rent	£7,000
Wear and tear allowance (10 per cent)	£700

The alternative to 'wear and tear' is for you to claim the cost of replacing old items with a new equivalent (that is, not an improvement), minus any money you receive for selling the old one.

Furnished holiday lets in the UK and other EEA countries

Here you can claim a 'capital allowance' for the cost of each item of furniture and equipment you provide with the property, or you can claim a repairs allowance, as explained in Capital cost allowances, opposite. You can't claim wear and tear allowances.

How much can you claim?

Capital allowances vary depending on the item. You can now claim 100 per cent on the first £100,000 of expenditure in a year and 20 per cent on the remainder. From 6 April 2011, this changes to 100 per cent on the first £25,000 and 18 per cent on the rest.

Remember that you can only claim for items legitimately used in the business, or a fair proportion. For example, if you also live in the property, you can only claim half the capital allowance.

CALCULATING PROFIT

Your net profit is the figure remaining once you have deducted all allowable expenses from your rental income. Your taxable profit is this sum less your allowances. This is added to your overall income and used to assess your total Income Tax. Income from more than one property is grouped together, but you have to work out holiday letting and overseas letting profits separately.

Paperwork

Keep receipts and invoices for six years after the tax year they are for, so that you can substantiate any figures you put in your tax return. You'll need:

- Rent books.
- Receipts.
- Invoices.
- Bank statements (make sure you can separate your business and personal expenses).
- Details of dates when the property was let out.
- Details of other income for services provided to tenants.
- Details of your allowable expenses.
- Details of your capital costs.

Paperwork

During 2010, the Government reviewed holiday let taxation and are due to make changes. To keep up to date visit www.hmrc.gov.uk and http://fhlcampaign.co.uk/.

 For advice on working out your yield and return on investment see pages 43-5, which provide you with a detailed cost analysis and all the necessary calculations to work out these important figures.

Case Study Bill

Bill charges his lodger, Ben, £450 a month rent to share his house. As the annual rent of £5,400 is more than the Rent-a-Room allowance (£4,250), Bill has to decide how to deal with the income.

If he stays in the Rent-a-Room Scheme, over a year £4,250 of Ben's rent will be tax free. That leaves £1,150 to be taxed at Bill's top rate of tax, which is 20 per cent. So he pays tax of £230 on Ben's rent for the year.

He could, however, opt out of the Rent-a-Room Scheme and have the whole lot treated as ordinary rental income, which means he can deduct relevant expenses and have only the 'profit' taxed. The expenses Bill could claim against the rent come to about £2,500 for the year. When deducted from the total rent received, this would leave him with a profit of just £2,900 and a larger tax bill of £580 (20 per cent of £2,900).

Rent-a-Room Scheme

Rental income	£5,400
Rent-a-Room allowance	-£4,250
Profit	£1,150

Tax payable* = £1,150 x 20% = £230

Rental income

Rental income	£5,400
Expenses	-£2,500
Profit	£2,900

Tax payable* = £2,900 x 20% = £580

*If you are a 20% tax payer

What if you make a loss?

You can carry a loss forward to the next year and offset it against future profits as long as they are in the same property business. Losses on UK holiday lettings can be set against any other income.

THE RENT-A-ROOM SCHEME

If you let a furnished room or rooms in your only or main home, you can choose to join the Rent-a-Room Scheme. This allows you to receive the first £4,250 a year free of tax, or £2,125 if you are letting jointly, but you cannot claim expenses on running the property or any capital allowances.

- **Your lodger can occupy** a single room or even a whole floor of your home, but it cannot be a separate flat.
- **You can join the Rent-a-Room Scheme** even if you are renting the property yourself: you do not have to own it, but you do need to operate within the terms of the lease (which may specify that you cannot have a lodger).
- **If you have a mortgage,** check whether renting out a room is within your lender's and insurer's terms and conditions.
- **You have to include any extra sums,** such as charges for meals, cleaning

 More details about the Rent-a-Room Scheme are available from www.hmrc.gov.uk/manuals/pimmanual/PIM4030.htm and www.direct.gov.uk.

or laundry to give a total figure for receipts from your lodger.

- **If you don't normally receive a tax return** and your receipts are below the tax-free thresholds, you don't have to do anything. If your receipts go above the thresholds, you must tell your tax office.

You can choose year by year whether to use this scheme, according to whether it is to your advantage.

TAX ON HOLIDAY LETS

Rules on tax for holiday lets are slightly different to those for residential lettings.

A holiday let must be:

- In the UK or other EEA country.
- Furnished.
- Available for letting for at least 140 days a year.
- Commercially let (not at cheap rates to family and friends) for at least 70 days a year, with each let not exceeding 31 days.

These rules for holiday lets apply for a seven-month period each year, meaning that you can let out the property on different terms, not as a holiday let, for the other five months if you wish. If you meet these criteria, you claim capital allowances rather

On the sale of a property, furnished holiday lets may be able to benefit from the new CGT entrepreneurs' relief, which could be up to £5 million in a person's lifetime, depending on how long you have owned the property/business. Seek specialist property tax advice so you can take advantage of any reliefs available.

than 'wear and tear'. This covers items such as:

- Furniture and furnishings.
- Equipment, such as refrigerators and washing machines.
- Machinery and plant used outside the property (such as vans and tools).

Any loss can be offset against your other income (reducing your overall tax bill) or carried forward.

LIVING ABROAD

If you move outside the UK for at least six months and let out your house, you must pay income tax on the rent, and can claim reliefs and allowances in much the same way as

If you live abroad, you can obtain further information from the Centre for non-residents at www.hmrc.gov.uk/cnr.

if you lived in the UK. You can choose which way to pay the tax:

- **Your letting agent or tenant** deducts tax from the rent at the basic rate each quarter and pays it direct to HMRC. You then set off the tax paid against your personal tax bill. Or:
- **You apply to HMRC** to receive rent

with no tax deducted and include it in your self-assessment form.

WHEN, HOW AND WHERE TO PAY

If you are employed or receiving a PAYE pension and your taxable income from letting is under £2,500, your tax code can be adjusted to

Case Study Jack and Joanne

Jack is a bachelor and earns £90,000 in a well-paid city job, so is a 40 per cent tax payer. He met Joanne, the girl of his dreams, and soon they were married. Joanne gave up work shortly afterwards (she is therefore a 20 per cent tax payer) and they decided they could no longer live in Jack's one-bedroom city apartment, so they bought a new house and decided to rent out the existing apartment.

Jack transferred the apartment into joint ownership with Joanne, as 'tenants in common in unequal shares', with Joanne owning 90 per cent of the property. They filed a form 17 with their tax office, asking to be taxed on these proportions of the rental profit. Jack did this before they moved out of the flat to live in the new house.

The annual rental profit on the apartment was £4,000 per annum. This meant that Jack was taxed on £400 (10 per cent), and Joanne was taxed on £3,600 (90 per cent). Joanne had no tax

liability as her £3,600 profit was covered by her personal tax allowance (£7,475 for 2011–12), whereas Jack had a £160 tax liability on his share of the profits. This meant that by transferring the property into unequal joint ownership, they would have an annual tax saving of £1,440 per annum. Over a ten-year period, this means a tax savings of £14,400!

NOTE: If there had been a mortgage on the flat, it is possible that there would be a liability to stamp duty land tax (SDLT) (see page 146) when Jack transferred a 90 per cent share in the property to Joanne. Joanne would be treated as taking over 90 per cent of the mortgage, and thus 'paying' Jack that amount for her share of the property. If this deemed payment was over the SDLT threshold (£125,000), then SDLT would be payable. Even if the amount of the mortgage was less than £125,000, the transfer would have to be notified to HMRC on Form SDLT 1.

collect the tax payable. To do this, you will need to complete form P180 from your tax office.

You also don't need to tell the taxman about your rental income if you have opted for the Rent-a-Room Scheme (see page 120).

If your letting income is more than £2,500 and you are not on PAYE, you must fill in a self-assessment tax return. If the taxable income is less than £15,000 you can fill in a shorter, four-page return, otherwise you must declare it on the land and property pages of the full self-assessment tax return, which requires a breakdown of costs. The quickest and easiest way to do this is online, because calculations are done for you and the filing deadlines are more generous than by post.

LETTING JOINTLY

When letting jointly, both parties must show their share of income and expenses, and the profit or loss.

Her Majesty's Revenue & Customs' booklet IR150, *Taxation of Rent. A Guide to Property Income*, provides more information. If you are planning to live abroad for more than a few months while letting your home, you may need to read IR140, *Non-resident landlords, their agents and tenants.*

Income tax savings can occur by letting property jointly. This is particularly the case if you pay tax at 40 per cent and your spouse (or civil partner) pays no tax, or tax at 20 per cent. In this scenario, it really does make sense to own the property jointly. This is because you will be passing on a portion of the rental profit to your spouse, who will be able to use his/her annual income tax personal allowance (see the case study opposite).

A married couple (or civil partnership) are deemed to receive equal shares of income from jointly owned property, unless they in fact own it in a different proportion, and elect (using form 17) to be taxed in that proportion.

Tenants in common

Many people don't realise that, in most cases, when buying with a partner or spouse, your property should be bought as tenants in common, not joint tenants. This is especially significant if you are business partners and if you are married and want to pass your properties onto your children. Seek professional wealth and tax advice to best mitigate your property tax bill.

 For more information on property tax go to: www.direct.gov.uk (search for 'Tax on property'), www.hmrc.gov.uk, www.property-tax-portal.co.uk and www.nicholsonsca.co.uk.

Money matters

CAPITAL GAINS TAX (CGT) PLANNING

A property investor is likely to incur a Capital Gains Tax (CGT) liability in the following two situations:

- When a property is sold at a higher price than that for which it was purchased.
- When a property, or part of a property, is transferred to anyone other than a spouse or civil partner – in such a case the person making the gift will be treated as if he had sold the property (or part of the property) for its market value on the date of the transfer.

" There are two reliefs that can be used to reduce the amount of CGT: only or main residence relief and letting relief. "

The tax is paid on the gain made and can be as high as 28 per cent of that gain. This means that on a £100,000 gain, the CGT payable could be up to £28,000.

This does depend on whether you are a higher or lower rate tax payer and there are two reliefs that can reduce the amount of tax you owe.

Only or Main Residence (OMR) Relief

This tax relief is available if the property was used as your main residence. This relief is calculated based on how long the property was your OMR. The longer the property was your OMR, the greater the relief will be. Ultimately, if the property was your OMR for the whole period of ownership, then all the gain made on the property will be exempt from tax.

If a property has ever been your OMR, then it is deemed to be so for the last three years of your ownership

Strategies for reducing Capital Gains Tax

- Use the '36 Month Rule': Provided that a house has at some time been your main residence, the last three years of ownership are deemed to be a period when it was your main residence, regardless of where you actually lived during that period. If you purchased a property in January 2003 and lived in it as your main residence until the end of December 2005, when you moved out and let the property, then provided you sold the property before the end of December 2008, there will be no CGT liability.
- Use joint ownership: If a property is jointly owned, then each person will be able to use the annual CGT allowance, which is £10,100 for the 2010-11 tax year.
- Benefit from living in and letting a property: If you have lived in and also let a property, then you can benefit from letting relief, which can be as much as £40,000.

Personal CGT allowance

Every individual has an annual CGT allowance. For the tax year 2010-11 this is £10,100. This can be deducted from the total gains you make in the tax year. Over this amount, the tax is a flat rate of 18 per cent.

Comparing a company versus an individual let

	Company	Individual
Rental profit	50,000	50,000
Company admin	(1,000)	NIL
Taxable profit	49,000	50,000
Tax at 21%*/40%	(10,290)	(20,000)
Cash after tax	38,710	30,000
Tax on dividend	(9,677)	N/A
Cash in hand	29,033	30,000

of it, whether or not you actually live there during that period.

Letting relief

This relief is available if the property satisfies the following two conditions:

- **The property was your OMR** at some time during your ownership of it.
- **The property has been let out** as residential accommodation when it was not your OMR.

The calculation of this relief is quite complicated, but essentially up to £40,000 (or, in the case of a jointly owned house, £40,000 for each owner) of gains can be treated as exempt from tax. To check if this relief applies to you, see document HS283 'Private residence relief' on www.hmrc.gov.uk/helpsheets/hs283.pdf.

FORMING A PROPERTY COMPANY

If you intend to build up a significant portfolio of let properties by ploughing the rental profits back into buying other properties, then you may wish

to consider setting up a limited company to hold the properties. The information given here can only be a brief outline of what this entails. If you are thinking of making this change, consult your accountant and property tax specialist for more information.

Using a limited company

Deciding to add buy to let to your current income and tax circumstances or to create a company is a major and complicated decision. Part of that decision depends on how and why you are investing in property and, as each set of circumstances is individual, it is essential that from the start you consult a property tax expert or two to ensure you are making the right decision.

Limited companies pay corporation tax (CT) on their profits (both income and capital gains). The rate of CT depends on the level of profits for the

year, but for profits up to £300,000, the rate is 21 per cent in 2010–11. If you are a 40 per cent taxpayer, then by owning your property through a company, the tax payable on the rental profits will be 19 per cent lower. This is not the whole story, however.

After the company has paid CT on its profits, the remaining cash is still in the company. Generally, the most tax-efficient way to extract this cash is by the company paying dividends to its shareholders. The additional income tax on a dividend for a 40 per cent taxpayer is 25 per cent. However, in any company, the circumstances of the directors and shareholders need to be considered fully in determining the most tax-efficient strategy.

You must also remember that a company is a more formal structure, and that there will be costs associated with running it – these are likely to be around £1,000 per year for even the simplest company.

If you are going to draw all the cash out of the company by way of dividends, it is likely that you will make little or no savings (see the table, page 125).

If, however, you intend to reinvest the profits rather than extract them from the company, you will see from the same table that after paying its CT, the company has £8,710 more available to reinvest than the individual does. This means that a company can provide a good vehicle for growing your portfolio of properties, because you have more cash left to reinvest. But if you intend to draw out your profits for other expenditure, there is little or no saving to be made by using a company.

&& A company has a more formal structure and there are costs associated with running it, which will amount to around £1,000 per year for even the simplest one. 99

Tenancy law

Before looking at specific types of tenancy in greater detail, it is important to understand the definitions of key legal words and phrases and know something about the history of tenancy Acts in both the private and public sectors. When considering the legal aspects of tenancy law, it is important to seek independent, legal advice from a tenancy law expert.

Private-sector tenancies

The law is different according to when the tenancy began – see the chart below, which sets out the differences.

RENT ACT TENANCIES

Residential tenancies that began before 15 January 1989 are governed by the Rent Act 1977, which gave most tenants very good security of tenure. Thousands of Rent Act tenancies originally entered into prior to 15 January 1989 are still running.

Their terms stay in force even if, as a tenant, you were granted a new tenancy by your landlord after this date and if you have since moved to another property owned by the same landlord. This rule also applies if a new landlord buys the property, provided there is no gap between the end of the original Rent Act tenancy and the granting of a new one.

If you are buying a property, particularly at auction, you must make sure you fully investigate the type of tenancy as it may well have this type of arrangement in place.

Tenant Acts since 1977

Act	Implementation	Type of tenancy	Other information
Rent Act 1977	Until 15 January 1989	Protected or statutory tenancies	Tenant has full security of tenure and can control the amount of rent paid
Housing Act 1988	15 January 1989 to 28 February 1997	Either ordinary assured tenancy or assured shorthold tenancy (also known as 'old' shortholds) with a minimum fixed term of six months	Tenant has full security of tenure with the ordinary assured tenancy, but no security after fixed term has elapsed on the assured shorthold tenancy; there is some protection for the tenant against excessive rent
Housing Act 1996	On or after 28 February 1997	Assured shorthold tenancy	There is no security of tenure after the fixed term has expired

Some legal definitions

Fixed or ascertainable period

The period of a tenancy or lease must be defined from the outset, stipulating when it is to begin and when or how it is to end. Although the tenancy of a periodic letting can go on indefinitely, either party can terminate it by giving notice to quit, which expires at the end of a relevant week or month, meeting the requirement of certainty that the arrangement will end at some point.

Grounds for possession

Grounds for possession may be cited in possession proceedings against a tenant when a landlord wants to regain possession of his or her property. There are separate grounds for possession relating to assured tenancies and public-sector tenancies. They were laid down in the Housing Act 1988, as amended by the Housing Act 1996. Landlords may also seek possession when it can be demonstrated that a tenant is no longer using the accommodation as his or her principal home.

Lease

The same as a tenancy, but the term is usually used to indicate that the property is let for a fixed term, such as six months or a certain number of years, while the word 'tenancy' suggests periodic letting from week to week or month to month.

Licence

If the occupier is only given the right to share the property (for example, with the owner) rather than have exclusive use of a specific part of it, the arrangement would be a licence, not a lease or a tenancy. This is an important point because tenants have far greater statutory legal protection than licensees.

Security of tenure

Gives the tenant an indefinite right to stay, unless the landlord has specific grounds for eviction.

Tenancy

An arrangement with two key requirements: the letting is for a 'fixed or ascertainable period of time' and it grants 'exclusive possession' of the property. Although this is usually in return for rent, such a charge is not legally part of the tenancy.

Among the terms to watch out for are:

- **The landlord cannot take possession** of the property without providing a 'ground' or 'grounds' for doing so.
- **If the tenant dies,** their tenancy could be passed on to their relatives if they lived in the property for a certain period before the death. There are a number of restrictions in place and the tenancy usually becomes an assured, rather than statutory one.
- **The amount of rent is controlled by rent officers,** who generally set a 'fair rent' below the market level, which cannot then be changed for two years.

Protection is given to 'protected tenancies', which subsequently become 'statutory tenancies'.

A protected tenancy exists where a house was 'let as a separate dwelling', which does not have to be the tenant's only home, while the tenant does not have to be an individual: it could be a limited company. Protected tenants have rent control and succession rights, but not necessarily security of tenure (see page 129), and would require them to be a statutory tenant.

At the end of a protected tenancy, the tenant will become a statutory tenant with security of tenure only 'if and so long as he occupies the dwelling house as his residence'. Now he can only be evicted once the landlord has been to court and established one of the grounds for possession (see pages 160–2). Statutory tenants must be individuals.

Certain tenancies are excluded from this legislation. For example, if the landlord is a resident landlord living in another part of the same building

Tenant's take

While it was deeply unpopular with landlords, the Rent Act offered admirable protection for tenants. If you are still covered by it, you have security of tenure and your rent is likely to be set below the market rate. These terms are likely to be handed on to your spouse when you die, and other relatives can still benefit from them, although they are likely to be entitled only to an assured, rather than protected tenancy. However, you should always seek professional advice if you have any queries or need to confirm your situation for any reason. As for landlords, this is a complex legal area and if you feel your rights are being affected, consult the Citizens Advice Bureau or a solicitor.

 If you have any legal problems or queries, the Citizens Advice Bureau (CAB) are there to help. To find your nearest branch, go to www.adviceguide.org.uk or your local phone book. Alternatively, use your legal representative.

containing the rented accommodation, subject to certain conditions, the tenant will have none of the rights granted to Rent Act or Housing Act tenants. See pages 138–9 for more information.

The Rent Act protected tenants but made it almost impossible for landlords to operate profitably, many of whom stopped letting altogether. As a result, new legislation was passed in 1988 that radically changed the law regarding tenancy to encourage more private landlords.

HOUSING ACT 1988 TENANCIES

The Housing Act 1988 came into force on 15 January 1989 and remained so until 28 February 1997. This legislation covers assured tenancies and assured shorthold tenancies and gives landlords a choice on how much security of tenure they give. There are still many tenancies in existence that began during this period.

Ordinary assured tenancy

An ordinary assured tenancy (so-called to distinguish it from an assured shorthold tenancy), gives tenants some security of tenure because the landlord has to cite a ground for possession before taking back the property, even if the term agreed between both parties has expired. It does not restrict how much rent can be charged. Any new letting to an existing ordinary assured tenant will remain an ordinary assured tenancy whenever it was granted, even if it was after 28 February 1997 when the legislation was changed.

However, the tenant can serve a notice on the landlord that he wants the new tenancy to be a shorthold. This rule was introduced to allow a compromise when a landlord had a ground for possession (see page 168), and would discontinue the action in return for giving the tenant a new, shorthold letting (see below), thus ensuring the tenant still had accommodation, albeit with less secure tenancy.

Although this is possible, it is questionable that it would be in the tenant's best interests to do so as it is sometimes difficult to obtain a final possession order relying on a discretionary possession ground, and therefore the tenant may be best taking their chances at a possession hearing.

❝ It pays to understand the difference between types of tenancy regardless of whether you are a landlord or tenant. ❞

Assured shorthold tenancy

An assured shorthold tenancy has to be for at least six months (but could have a fixed term of many years despite its name), after which the landlord is entitled to claim possession through a court order, should the need arise.

Periodic tenancy

A periodic tenancy comes into being when a landlord doesn't reclaim possession at the end of an original assured shorthold tenancy nor does he issue a new tenancy agreement. The terms and conditions of the original assured shorthold tenancy agreement remain in place, as does the landlord's right to bring the tenancy to an end by service of the required two months from the date the rent started.

If the tenancy is granted after 28 February 1997, a landlord cannot obtain an order for possession which takes effect until at least six months after the tenancy started. There is some protection for tenants against excessive rent.

To regain possession, the landlord was required to serve the tenant with a prescribed form of notice informing them of the consequences of the tenancy being shorthold at the commencement of the tenancy.

If they didn't do this, the tenancy was regarded as an ordinary (or fully) assured tenancy, which offers full security of tenure. Many landlords who did not comply properly with this rule found they were unable to evict tenants even when the six-month term expired.

If the parties are the same, a new tenancy of the same (or almost the same) property will be deemed to be shorthold unless the landlord informs the tenant in writing that it is not. In such cases, as no shorthold notices have to be served, the letting need not be for a fixed term, and if it is, the term can be less than six months.

HOUSING ACT 1996 TENANCIES

The Housing Act was amended in 1996. After 28 February 1997, most private tenancies have been assured shorthold unless the landlord opts for an ordinary assured tenancy (see page 131).

If a landlord lets a property on an assured tenancy, the tenant has the right to remain in the property unless the landlord can prove there are grounds for possession. The landlord does not have the right to just repossess the property when the tenancy comes to an end.

❝If a tenancy was granted after 28 February 1997, a landlord cannot obtain an order for possession until at least six months after its start. ❞

Public-sector tenancies

The Housing Act 1988 brought registered social landlord tenancies into the private sector on or after 15 January 1989, and these tenants have either (mostly) an assured tenancy or (sometimes) an assured shorthold tenancy.

Assured tenants have security of tenure as the landlord must provide a statutory ground for possession under the 1988 Act if he or she wishes to evict a tenant. There is no legal control over rent increases, even though one of the aims of housing associations is to let at affordable rents. Registered providers of social housing should provide their tenants with a written agreement specifying the level of rents to be charged and the conditions of the tenancy. The Tenant Services Authority (TSA) has produced a set of standards that specify the delivery requirements by social housing landlords. Broadly speaking these are created in conjunction with the priorities of the local tenant communities they serve.

Other public-sector landlords include housing action trusts, which aim to improve and modernise council housing prior to transferring or selling it. Many local authorities have transferred some or all of their housing stock to registered providers of social housing.

Housing associations are non-profit-making bodies that provide affordable accommodation and these organisations are one of the major providers of state-funded housing.

- **Some are registered with the Tenant Services Authority (TSA)** or with the Welsh Assembly.
- **Some (but not all) are registered charities** and have their own charitable rules as well.
- **Others are run on a co-operative basis** where tenants themselves own and manage the properties.

❝ Assured tenants have security of tenure as the tenancy relates to the 1988 Act. ❞

The website for the Tenant Services Authority is www.tenantservicesauthority.org and that for the Welsh Assembly is www.wales.gov.uk. The grounds for possession for an assured tenancy are on pages 168-9 and those for possession for a public-sector tenancy are on pages 170-1.

The law relating to security of tenure and rent control will depend on the type of housing association and the date when tenancy was granted. Those begun before 15 January 1989 are dealt with differently to those commencing on or after that date. If you want to compare how your current registered provider of social housing performs, visit www.tenantservicesauthority.org to find out how tenants rate their service.

Some housing associations choose not to register and retain their independence so that they can set up shared-ownership schemes. This means they do not qualify for state funding and are not supervised by a government body. After 15 January 1989, they are governed by the same rules as registered providers of social housing (see above), except they do not have the benefits of a 'tenant's guarantee'. These come under the protection of the Rent Act 1977.

❝Some housing associations aren't registered, which means they aren't supervised by a government body.❞

 The chapter on social lets (see pages 149–56) answers the most frequently asked questions by landlords and tenants on the subject of social (or public-sector) lets.

Assured shorthold tenancies

Nearly every letting begun on or after 28 February 1997 will be an assured shorthold tenancy, which gives no security of tenure when the contractual letting term ends. The landlord can also obtain possession without having to give a reason, provided he follows the correct procedure (see pages 160–71).

The landlord's viewpoint

Assured shorthold tenancies suit landlords because they have the absolute right to possession, which can be obtained using the accelerated possession procedure (see pages 164–5). This means that possession can be obtained faster and cheaper than under normal court procedures.

 Are you a prospective tenant rather than landlord? Read this section, too, as there is useful advice here for both sides of the tenancy agreement.

In addition, the landlord can get his property back during the tenancy under certain circumstances, such as if the rent is not being paid, as long as a special term has been incorporated into the letting agreement.

How does a tenancy qualify as a shorthold?

Various conditions have to be fulfilled for a tenancy to qualify as a shorthold in a house let as a separate dwelling:

- The tenant or each of the joint tenants is an individual.
- The tenant, or at least one of the joint tenants, occupies the house as his only or principal home.
- The tenancy is not specifically excluded by other provisions of the Housing Act 1988.

Jargon buster

Tenancy The letting must be a tenancy, not simply a licence to occupy the property

House This is any building designed or adapted for living in, so the term includes flats, barns, etc.

Let as a separate dwelling The property cannot be let for business purposes, and must be 'a' single dwelling (not, for example, a house converted into several flats – although each of these separate flats could fall within the definition). It must be 'separate', which boils down to whether the tenant regards and treats it as 'home'. For example, a single room could qualify as a dwelling even if the tenant has the right to share other rooms, such as a kitchen or a bathroom. If the facilities are shared with the landlord, the tenancy would not be seen as an assured or shorthold tenancy because it has a 'resident landlord' (see pages 138–9)

The key point is that the tenant must have the right to exclusive possession of one part of the house. If the property is simply shared by the occupiers who are left to decide between themselves who has which bedroom, they are licensees rather than tenants.

Can any property be used for an assured shorthold tenancy?

There are a number of exceptions that are excluded from the definition of an assured tenancy:

- **Tenancies entered into before 15 January 1989.**
- **High value properties:** for tenancies granted before 1 April 1990, the cut-off point is a rateable value of more than £750 (£1,500 in Greater London). After that date, the tenancy is excluded if the rent payable is £100,000 or more per annum.
- **Low rent:** on lettings made before 1 April 1990, if the annual rent is less than two-thirds of the rateable value. Since that date, the exclusion applies if the rent does not exceed £250 per annum (£1,000 in Greater London).

- **Business tenancies:** if the premises are occupied for the purpose of business. So a traditional corner shop with living accommodation for staff over it would be excluded.
- **Tenancies of agricultural land,** although such tenants will probably have other statutory rights under legislation on agricultural holdings.
- **Lettings to students:** lettings to students by educational bodies, such as universities and colleges. This exception does not apply to lettings by landlords other than the institutions themselves.
- **Holiday lettings:** a holiday let cannot be an assured tenancy.
- **Lettings by resident landlords,** when the landlord lives in another part of the building occupied by the tenant.
- **Crown, local authority and housing association lettings:** although they may have other protections (see the next chapter on pages 149–56).

❝For an assured shorthold tenancy to conform, the tenant must have exclusive possession of one part of the house.❞

If you are a tenant, and your needs aren't met on these pages, turn to pages 145–8, where frequently asked questions by tenants are answered. For social lets, see pages 149–56.

Do I need to get planning permission to alter a property?

If you are converting a house into several flats, planning permission will be required for change of use from occupation by one family to occupation by tenants, and it will probably be needed for the building works, too. If you are not converting a house, but are letting it to a group of people (such as students), rather than as a family home, this could also represent a material change of use. Ask for advice from your local planning office. See also the advice on HMOs on page 31.

Which would be better – an assured shorthold tenancy or an ordinary assured tenancy?

Most landlords let on a shorthold basis because they can regain possession of the property more easily when they want to, and because, if they are borrowing money to purchase the property, the lender will insist on it. However, if you are letting the house in which you have lived at some time in the past (not necessarily recently), you may want to consider an ordinary assured tenancy. These normally give the tenant full security of tenure, but if you previously lived in the property, there is a mandatory ground for possession so you could still get your property back.

Offering permanent security to a tenant through an assured tenancy can tie up your assets in a property you cannot gain possession of, and so there is a danger that you cannot realise your investment.

I've heard mention of the 'resident landlord exception'. What is this?

The majority of lettings by resident landlords occupying another part of the same building are not assured or shorthold tenancies and their tenants have no security and few rights under the legislation protecting them from eviction. This is known as the 'resident landlord exception'.

The main significance for this is with regard to lettings entered into before 28 February 1997, after which all tenancies are shortholds with no security of tenure anyway. In the case of these later lettings, the effect of the resident landlord rule will be that:

- The tenant cannot refer the rent to the rent assessment committee (RAC) (see below).
- The tenant is not entitled to two months' notice terminating the shorthold.

 The RAC is a local panel with the power to set a maximum rent on a property on behalf of the council. For more information, see page 145.

- The tenant may not benefit from protection-from-eviction legislation.
- Statutory succession provisions do not apply.
- Statutory rules on increasing the rent and not assigning will not apply.

For the letting to be excluded from the definition of an assured or shorthold tenancy all of these conditions must apply:

- The house that is let must form only part of the building.
- The building must not be a purpose-built block of flats.
- The tenancy must have been granted by an individual (that is, not a limited company) who at the time of the grant occupied another part of the same building as his only or principal home.
- At all times since the tenancy was granted, the interest of the landlord has continued to belong to an individual who continued so to reside.

So the resident landlord exception applies when the tenant lives in a part of the same building as you, the landlord, provided it is not a purpose-built block of flats. A landlord living in a large house that is partly let out, or converted into several flats, is outside the definition.

You must be in occupation throughout the tenancy and if you move out, the exception no longer applies. If you are letting jointly, only one needs to be in residence at any time. Absences for holidays or illness, or at times of change or death of the landlord or change of ownership, are permitted. If the tenant has an assured tenancy during which the landlord moves in and subsequently grants a further tenancy, the exception does not apply.

❝Offering permanent security to a tenant by an assured tenancy can tie up your assets for years. ❞

How should I confirm a tenancy?

It makes enormous sense to arrange the tenancy using a written tenancy agreement – there are examples of clauses at the back of this book. This will help avoid disputes over the terms of the let. Perhaps surprisingly, such a deed is not legally essential in most cases (a tenancy can be granted orally in many typical circumstances) and many residential lettings are entered into quite informally, but it is highly advisable to put the arrangement in writing in the form of a deed.

The agreement must be signed and the signatures witnessed, and it should end 'signed as a deed'. It is best if two identical copies of the tenancy agreement are drawn up and signed, one for the tenant, the other for you. Your copy is the actual lease, and the tenant's copy is called the counterpart.

Should the agreement be for a fixed term?

Most shorthold tenancies are for a fixed term of either six or 12 months. If it is longer, the tenant can get the rent checked by the legally binding decision of the rent assessment committee and you could be stuck with a tenant paying a rent which inflation has seriously eroded in value.

If you wish to let for a shorter period, such as three months, remember that under a shorthold, the courts cannot order possession before six months have passed since the tenancy began.

You may intend to sell or occupy the house yourself by a particular date, but bear in mind that although a shorthold tenancy has no security of tenure, not all tenants leave voluntarily at the end of a letting. If this were the case, you would have to obtain a court order for possession. Although this is a formality, it will take two or more months and you may want to allow for this when you decide the length of the tenancy.

If you don't have a fixed date for when you want the property back, you can let on a periodic tenancy, which can be either weekly or monthly. This allows you to continue the letting for several years, changing the rental charge when you wish if you choose to.

With a fixed-term tenancy you will only be able to charge the agreed rent at the end of the term.

What terms should be included in a shorthold tenancy agreement?

The agreement should include:

- **A description of the property,** clearly indicating the number or precise location of a flat, for example.
- **Details of how the rent is to be paid:** The common law implication is that rent is payable in arrears, unless the contract expressly says it should be paid in advance. If weekly intervals are chosen, you must provide a rent book. Intervals should be weekly, fortnightly, monthly, quarterly or yearly.
- **Interest on arrears:** If the rent falls into arrears, you cannot claim interest on it until you start court proceedings. This problem can be overcome by including a term that allows you to add interest to any arrears at a specified, reasonable rate.
- **Council Tax:** The tenant is liable for Council Tax unless the property is an HMO (see page 31), in which case you must pay, adding a figure to cover it to the rental charge. In such a case, the agreement should include provision to increase the rent to take into account any rise in Council Tax. Otherwise, the agreement should stipulate that the rent is exclusive of Council Tax and requiring the tenant to pay it or reimburse you should you become responsible for its payment.

- **Water charges:** In the absence of a clause to the contrary, it is assumed that the tenant pays these, although the landlord often pays on short-term lettings. If so, there should be some provision allowing for a rent increase should the water charges go up.
- **Repairs and decoration:** The Landlord and Tenant Act 1985 imposes an obligation on you to repair, for example, the structure and exterior of the property where the tenancy is for a term less than seven years. However, a provision should be included allocating responsibility for non-structural internal repairs and decoration. Without this, neither party would have any obligation to do this. It is reasonable to impose the liability for these matters on the tenant if the term is for more than 12 months, but not if the let is shorter than that, unless the repairs are necessary because of the tenant's acts or neglect. If the property has a garden, it is worth including an obligation on the tenant to maintain it or at least cut any grass.
- **Alterations:** It is essential to prohibit the tenant from making alterations to the house, even if he considers them to be improvements, unless approved by you.

- **Use:** It is standard to restrict the use of the property to that of a single private dwelling and impose obligations not to cause nuisance or annoyance to the neighbours or to damage the house or its contents.
- **Assignment and subletting:** See page 143 for guidance on these points.
- **Address for service:** Section 48 of the Landlord and Tenant Act 1987 states that no rent is lawfully due from a tenant unless and until you give the tenant in writing an address in England or Wales at which notices can be served upon him. It makes sense to include this address in the agreement. It can be your solicitor's or the letting agent's.
- **Deposit:** Within 14 days of when the tenant paid the deposit, your agent or you should supply:
  – Your or your agent's contact details.
  – Which tenancy deposit scheme is being used (see pages 83–6) and the contact details for the scheme.
  – Information about the purpose of a tenancy deposit.
  – Information about how the tenant can apply to get the deposit back at the end of the tenancy.
  – What the tenant can do if there is a dispute about the deposit.

 Use the explanation of these terms in conjunction with the examples of clauses given on pages 190–204.

All this information can either be within the agreement or provided in a separate document or letter.

- **Rent increases:** See page 82.
- **Break clauses:** This is a term allowing the party specified to bring the lease to an end before it has run its full length and may be appropriate in a fixed-term tenancy. The break clause allows you to terminate the tenancy if you, or a member of your family:
  - Wish to occupy the house or you want to sell with vacant possession.
  - If you die and your personal representatives need to obtain possession.

  If this clause is included, there should be a tenant's break clause too, or the agreement is likely to fall foul of the Unfair Terms Regulations (see page 158).

- **Children and pets:** If you want to prohibit these, it must be expressly stated in the agreement and ideally when you advertise the property at the start. However, you will want to avoid breaking the Unfair Terms Regulations (see also page 158). Unattended pets left to roam the property during the day can cause damage, so dogs and cats are often not allowed without consent – which can also be offered for pets kept in secure cages. It would be unlawful to prevent a blind or deaf person from keeping their guide or hearing dog in the house.

- **Forfeiture:** A forfeiture clause is essential in any fixed-term assured tenancy of any length, including a shorthold (it would not apply to an assured tenancy). The clause

Get it in writing

'Get it in writing' is the golden rule with many dealings, none more so than letting, yet many tenancies are still granted orally, and this often leads to disputes when the two parties differ about what was agreed. The Housing Act 1996 places an obligation on the landlord of a new shorthold tenancy to provide the tenant with a statement of at least the more important terms of the tenancy, which include:

- The tenancy commencement date.
- The rent payable and the due dates.
- Any terms providing for rent review.
- The length of a fixed-term tenancy.

If these are not provided, the tenant should request them in writing. It is then a criminal offence for you to fail to give the information within 28 days without a reasonable excuse. The Act makes it clear that the statement by you is not to be regarded as conclusive evidence of what was agreed, and your version can be challenged by the tenant.

“ The golden rule with many dealings, especially tenancies, is to get it down in writing. ”

permits you to end a fixed-term lease before it ends if the tenant fails to comply with agreed obligations, such as paying the rent. Some of the assured tenancy grounds for possession can be used to end a fixed-term tenancy provided the tenancy agreement makes clear provision for this, stating which grounds are considered to apply. As always, it is important that these clauses are written in clear plain English: many traditionally worded forfeiture clauses could be declared void because they are incomprehensible to all but lawyers.

Can a tenant transfer or sublet the tenancy?

The 1988 Act suggests that the tenant shall not assign or sublet any part of the property without your consent. This statutory prohibition does not apply if a premium was paid on the grant or renewal of the tenancy. A premium is any money payments in addition to rent or a returnable deposit worth more than one-sixth of the annual rent. Statutory prohibition does not prevent taking in lodgers or sharing with another person. You have no obligation to be reasonable in deciding if you will give consent.

Because these statutory restrictions do not apply to fixed-term tenancies, there is a potential problem for landlords granting assured shortholds. While the assured

shorthold tenant has no security of tenure, the person he sublets to could arguably have an assured tenancy with full security of tenure and this security could be binding on the landlord. To avoid the problem, make sure the tenancy agreement contains an express provision prohibiting subletting, while allowing assignment of the lease with the landlord's consent.

What happens if the tenant dies?

In the case of a fixed-term tenancy, since the tenant owns the tenancy, it can be passed on in the same way as the deceased's other property. If he or she is a joint tenant, the other

---

Periodic tenancies

There are specific provisions in the Housing Act 1988 regarding succession of periodic tenancies on the death of a sole tenant and these override other inheritance laws. The tenancy passes to the tenant's spouse provided they have been occupying the property as their principal home immediately prior to the death. The couple do not have to have been married and can be of the same sex.

These succession rights do not apply if the deceased tenant was a successor themselves – through this rule, by inheritance, as the sole survivor of joint tenants, or under the provisions of the Rent Act 1977. Therefore, only one statutory succession is possible. If there is no qualifying 'spouse' or if the tenancy has already succeeded one, the tenancy passes on under the will or intestacy of the deceased as already explained.

becomes the sole tenant, but on the death of a sole tenant, the right to live in the property goes to the person nominated in the will. If the tenant dies without a will, ownership is decided by the laws of inheritance.

How do I obtain possession?

The court must order possession on or after the ending of a shorthold, provided you follow the correct procedure, serving a Section 21 notice and giving at least two months' notice that you require possession.

What are the grounds for possession?

As a shorthold is a type of assured tenancy, the mandatory and discretionary grounds that apply to ordinary assured tenancies also apply. But as you have right to possession under a shorthold, you would not normally need to use these grounds.

However, the normal shorthold procedure to obtain possession can be used only after the expiry of any fixed-term granted. So if a 12-month fixed term was granted, possession under the shorthold procedure can only be obtained at its end. This could pose a serious problem if a tenant is not paying the rent.

A solution here is offered by the fact that some of the ordinary assured tenancy grounds can be used during a fixed term, including mandatory ground 8 and discretionary grounds 10 and 11 (see pages 168–9). All of these deal with rent arrears. As with other assured tenancies, these grounds can be used during the fixed term only if the tenancy agreement contains provision for their use. Without such provision, you cannot obtain possession from a defaulting tenant until the end of the fixed term: you could sue the tenant for arrears, but with no guarantee of payment.

Faced with a periodic shorthold tenant who won't pay the rent, you can use the normal shorthold procedure for obtaining possession and immediately serve the usual two months' notice (see pages 160–1). As stated, possession can still not be ordered until the tenancy has run for six months.

Chapter 10, Legal action, beginning on page 157, explains the procedure for taking possession of a property. The grounds for possession are also listed in this chapter, on pages 168-9.

The tenant's take

If you are a landlord, you will find there is information in this section that is every bit as useful for you as for the tenant. Rent levels, stamp duty land tax and ending an agreement are the main subjects that are discussed here.

How much rent can I be charged?

Under a shorthold tenancy, there is no restriction on how much rent can be charged, so market forces will prevail. You may have the right to challenge the amount originally agreed by referring it to the Rent Assessment Committee (RAC) – a local panel with the power to set a maximum rent on a property on behalf of the council. You can do this at any time during your first shorthold term. The landlord can only raise the rent if he follows the right procedure. He cannot do this without your consent, unless the terms of the tenancy include a provision for rent increase.

In a fixed-term tenancy, there are also no statutory provisions for setting a rent increase, so a landlords might well include provision for it if your tenancy lasts longer than, say, 12 months. Even then, you can still refer the original rent to the RAC.

At the end of the fixed term, you continue in possession as a statutory periodic tenant and the landlord can follow the procedure outlined above. Alternatively, at the end of the shorthold the landlord can take up his or her absolute right to possession and grant a new tenancy at a higher rent. You would then have an unenviable choice of agreeing a higher rent or losing your home. See www.rpts.gov.uk for more information.

Call out the RAC

If you feel you have signed up to pay an over-the-odds rent, you can go to arbitration from the local Rent Assessment Committee (RAC). You can only do this once and it must be during the first six months of the tenancy. The committee then compares rents being charged for similar properties and sets the tariff at what it considers the market rate. A lower rent is fixed only if it is felt the landlord is charging 'significantly' more than he should.

If it is a fixed-term tenancy, the rent becomes the maximum chargeable for the remainder of the term, however long it is – a good reason for landlords not to agree to five-year shortholds.

In the case of a periodic tenancy, the rent is fixed and the landlord must wait 12 months after the assessment before he can increase it using the statutory procedure (see page 89). However, as he has an absolute right to possession, he could give two months' notice and start a new tenancy at whatever rate he desires.

In the case of periodic (that is, weekly or monthly) tenancies, there is, however, provision for the landlord to raise the rent even when not permitted to do so by the tenancy agreement. It is a complex procedure requiring the landlord to serve a notice on you in a prescribed form stating a new rental figure. If you don't agree the figure, you can take it to arbitration with the local RAC.

"Under a shorthold tenancy, there is no restriction on how much rent can be charged. "

Do I have to pay stamp duty land tax (SDLT)?

Stamp Duty has changed its name to Stamp Duty Land Tax (SDLT). In the past it was a voluntary tax for the landlord, but is now a compulsory tax to be paid by you, the tenant.

SDLT becomes liable when you take a lease that exceeds £125,000. As a result, unless you take a particularly long lease, or are renting at extremely high costs, it is unlikely that you will have to pay it.

Below are two examples of how the tax might be levied. However, the rules are complicated, so seek independent advice from an experienced letting agent, Her Majesty's Revenue & Customs (HMRC) or a property tax specialist. Even if it appears you are likely to need to pay SDLT, it may be possible to reduce the amount owed.

Example 1

Mr Pragel rents a property for 12 months at a monthly rent of £1,000. The rental value over the period of the lease is £12,000. The rental value is less than £125,000, so no SDLT is payable by the tenant.

Example 2

Mr Locum rents a property for £4,000 per month for a three-year period. The amount of the lease is therefore 12 months x £4,000 = £48,000 per year. Over the three-year period of the lease, this would mean the value of the lease is £48,000 x 3 years = £144,000. This would exceed the SDLT threshold and trigger a payment, which would be calculated as follows: £144,000 – £125,000 = £19,000.

SDLT is charged at 1 per cent of the amount of the lease in excess of £125,000, so would be calculated: £19,000 x 1% = £190.

 For more information on SDLT, visit www.hmrc.gov.uk/so/sdlt/index.htm or you can call 0845 603 0135 for advice.

Is there any regulation for the way a contract is written?

The Unfair Terms in Consumer Contracts Regulations cover all consumer contracts, including tenancy agreements, but not company lets, and declare that any terms that have not been individually negotiated and which can be considered unfair to the tenant would be void. A term is unfair if it tips the contract against the consumer (you, the tenant) in favour of the business (the landlord).

Examples of clauses that would be open to challenge include:

- A requirement to pay an excessive deposit.
- Penalty clauses for the late payment of rent.
- Clauses giving the landlord the right to enter the premises without reasonable notice.
- Provisions allowing for arbitrary increases in rent.
- Clauses making you pay unreasonable costs.
- Total prohibitions on assigning and subletting.

In addition, the agreement should be in clear language without the use of legal jargon or words with special meanings that you don't know. See also 'What terms should be included in a shorthold tenancy agreement?' on pages 140–2.

Can I transfer or sublet the tenancy?

In theory, a tenancy belongs to its signatory like any other possession and can be 'assigned' (sold or given away) to anyone you choose, or you can grant a lease shorter than your own (sublet) or take in lodgers. Not surprisingly, a landlord who has carefully vetted you will not be best pleased to find his property sublet to someone he has never even met, so most tenancy agreements expressly forbid assignment and/or subletting.

Trying to prohibit both risks contravening the Unfair Terms in Consumer Contracts Regulations, so landlords tend to allow assigning or subletting on the condition that it is with their consent. This allows the landlord to check up on a potential new tenant in the normal way. Consent cannot be unreasonably withheld and he must respond to your request within a reasonable period. If there is nothing prohibiting assigning or subletting in the agreement, the landlord can use the statutory prohibition included in the Housing Act 1988.

The Office of Fair Trading (OFT) has a consumer helpline (tel: 08457 224499) and the website is at www.oft.gov.uk. The OFT also produces leaflet OFT356 on tenancy agreements, which is downloadable from its website.

What happens at the end of the fixed term?

At the end of a fixed term, you can remain in possession as a statutory periodic tenant, but with no security of tenure, the landlord can evict you through possession proceedings (see pages 160–5). A shorthold that is a periodic tenancy can be terminated in the same way.

However, in both cases, the court cannot order the tenant out before six months have started since the grant of the tenancy, even if the fixed-term letting was for a shorter period, such as three months. A landlord who wants to let for a period of less than six months and be sure of obtaining possession can only do so by granting an ordinary assured tenancy and using one of the ordinary assured mandatory grounds for possession (see pages 160–1).

❝If you move out of a rented property before the end of the fixed term, the landlord can claim the full amount of rent that is due until the end of the period. ❞

Can I do whatever I like once the tenancy has been agreed?

Once a property is let, the law allows you to do more of less what you like with the premises. If the landlord wants to prevent a particular activity, it must be written into the agreement (see the sample clauses on pages 190–204).

Can I terminate a fixed-term agreement early?

The tenancy is a contract with obligations on both sides, so you can't sign a 12-month fixed-term agreement and expect to terminate it early without the landlord's consent. If you move out, the landlord can claim the full amount of rent due until the end of the fixed period.

You can terminate a periodic tenancy by serving notice in writing (a month for a monthly tenancy, four weeks for a weekly tenancy) unless the landlord agrees otherwise.

To complete a period of tenancy, under the 'corresponding day rule' the notice must expire on the same day of the week or month. So a weekly tenancy beginning on a Monday must terminate on a Monday (or technically midnight on Sunday), and a monthly tenancy commencing on the 23rd must expire on the 22nd or 23rd.

Social lets

Social lettings are those made by local authorities and some housing associations to tenants on Housing Benefit. As a private landlord you can apply to be a registered provider of social housing (see page 72).

The landlord's viewpoint

The questions in this section cover such subjects as means testing, the security of a local authority tenancy and the main responsibilities of a landlord with public-sector lets. If you are a tenant, this material may be of interest to you, too.

Is Housing Benefit means tested?

Housing Benefit, also known as rent rebate or rent allowance, is a means-tested payment to tenants who cannot pay their rent because they have no or a low income. It is administered by the relevant local authority, which is then reimbursed by central government. Payment of benefit is governed by the Housing Benefit Regulations. Over four and a half million households in England and Wales claim Housing Benefit.

If you rent from a private landlord, you may be able to claim means-tested Local Housing Allowance (LHA), which is a new way of calculating Housing Benefit as it takes into account the different rental costs by area. Payment is normally made to the tenant who should then pass it onto the landlord. Check the LHA by visiting the local authority website or the Rent Service's website (see below).

Are you affected by LHA caps?

The Coalition Government have announced caps on the amount of LHA, which can be claimed from April 2011. If you are worried how this will affect you, speak to your local housing office or Citizens Advice Bureau.

For the latest information on LHAs in your area visit www.voa.gov.uk/LHADirect/lha-rates-england.htm.

What is a secure tenancy?

Properties let by local authorities and some housing associations have their own system of protection under the Housing Act 1985. If a tenancy is defined as a 'secure tenancy', the tenant has extensive security of tenure. There are also succession rights on their death and a 'right to buy' at a discount (see page 155–6).

A secure tenancy is a tenancy or licence of a house let as a separate dwelling at any time when both the

To get information on Housing Benefit, go to www.direct.gov.uk, www.dwp.gov.uk and from your local council. See also www.shelter.org.uk and www.adviceguide.org.uk. The Rent Service website is https://lha-direct.voa.gov.uk/Secure/Default.aspx.

'landlord condition' and the 'tenant condition' are satisfied.

The landlord condition denotes that the interest of the landlord belongs to one of a specified list of bodies, including a local authority, a new town corporation, and an urban development corporation. A secure tenant is most likely to be a tenant of a district council.

The tenant condition denotes that the tenant is an individual occupying the house as his only or principal home. With joint tenants, only one needs to meet this requirement.

Unlike the definition of assured and protected tenancies, a social let expressly includes a licence to occupy. The licence can only amount to a secure tenancy if it confers the right to exclusive possession on the occupier; without it the tenant has no protection.

Even when these two conditions are satisfied, there are exceptions where there will not be a secure tenancy. Consult your legal representative before entering into an agreement.

Can a secure tenancy be assigned?

Secure tenancies cannot usually be passed to a new tenant and if a supposed assignment takes place, the tenancy is no longer secure. The exceptions are: as an exchange with another secure tenant; as part of a property adjustment order made in matrimonial proceedings, and to a person who, if the tenant died, would be entitled to succeed to the tenancy.

Can I end a security of tenure?

A landlord can only end a secure tenancy with a court order for possession. A notice to quit has no effect and when a fixed-term secure tenancy ends, it becomes a periodic secure tenancy. To obtain the court order for possession, the judge must follow a procedure and establish at least one of the grounds for possession laid down by the Act (see pages 170–1). There are no mandatory grounds, so there is no guarantee that possession will be ordered even if the ground is established.

Am I responsible for repairs to the property?

In the vast majority of cases, you are responsible for repairs to the structure and interior of the property and for keeping the facilities for the supply of gas and electricity, space and water heating and sanitation in repair and proper working order. The Secure Tenants of Local Housing Authorities (Right to Repair) Regulations 1994 give secure tenants the right to up to £50 in compensation if certain types of repair, to a maximum cost of £250, are not carried out within a prescribed period.

What happens on the death of a tenant?

The tenancy does not currently end with the death of a secure tenant: their spouse succeeds to it, subject to government changes provided they

were still occupying the house as their only or principal home at the time of the death. The spouse is a person living with the tenant as husband or wife, including the survivor of an unmarried heterosexual couple.

If there is no 'spouse', a member of the tenant's family who has resided in the house with the tenant for at least 12 months prior to the death will succeed to the tenancy.

Only one succession is permitted, so there is no further succession after the death of a secure tenant who himself succeeded to it. In cases where there is no succession, the tenancy will pass on in the same way as the rest of the deceased's property, that is, either by their will or according to the rules of intestacy. However, it will no longer be a secure tenancy and you can take possession when it is terminated. This will take place under normal common law rules, for example, by notice to quit in the case of a periodic tenancy, and a court order will still be required.

How do I obtain a court order?

You must first give notice to the tenant in accordance with Section 83 of the Housing Act 1985 in the form laid down by the legislation, stating the particulars of the ground for possession with absolute clarity. If you fail to do the correct procedure, the tenant can claim that the notice is invalid.

If it is a periodic tenancy, as most council tenancies are, the notice must specify the earliest date on which possession proceedings can start, which cannot be earlier than the date on which you could have brought the tenancy to an end with a notice to quit. For a notice to be valid, as well as being of the correct length, it must expire on the day of the week or month corresponding to the one on which the tenancy began. So for a weekly tenancy commencing on Monday, the notice must expire on a Monday or a Sunday. With a monthly tenancy commencing on the 10th of the month, the notice must expire on the 9th or 10th of a subsequent month.

How do I set about obtaining possession?

Provided you follow the correct procedure (see page 160), the court must order possession. The notice must tell the tenant of his right to request a review challenging the landlord's decision to apply, which must be sought within 14 days of service of the notice. If requested, this review must be carried out and the tenant notified of the result before the date specified as the earliest on which the landlord could apply to the court. There is no further right of appeal.

Can anti-social behaviour be prohibited?

Under the Housing Act 1996, persons in secure or introductory tenancies can be prohibited from:

- **Engaging or threatening to engage** in conduct causing or likely to cause a

nuisance or annoyance to a person residing in or visiting or nearby the premises.

- **Using or threatening to use** the premises for immoral or illegal purposes.
- **Entering such premises** or being found in the vicinity of such premises.

The local authority and registered providers of social housing can apply to the county court for an order only if the person in question has used or threatened violence and there is a significant risk of harm if the injunction is not granted. If the order is obtained, the person can be arrested if they breach the injunction.

Does a demoted tenancy relate to anti-social behaviour too?

The demoted tenancy is a one-year council probationary tenancy introduced as a means to help prevent anti-social behaviour. Local authorities and registered social landlords can apply to the county court to ask for a secure or assured tenancy to be amended to a demoted tenancy for a period of 12 months. If a demotion order is made, then during the 12-month period the landlord may obtain an order for possession without establishing a ground for possession. If the demoted tenant doesn't break their tenancy agreement, they should become secure tenants again after 12 months.

The effect on the tenant depends on whether the tenant is a secure or assured tenant. If the court decides to grant a demotion order, this will end the secure tenancy and be replaced by a demoted tenancy. An assured tenant of a registered provider of social housing will find their tenancy is relegated to a demoted assured shorthold tenancy. Any tenant who comes within either a demoted tenancy or demoted assured shorthold tenancy will lose a number of rights enjoyed under their previous tenancy, for example, the right to buy their home (see pages 155–6).

If you want to seek a demotion order, you must serve a notice and then proceedings for the court. Check the type of tenancy agreement your tenant may have, whether it is secure or assured, as there are different requirements when serving the notice. If you have a secure tenant, you must serve a notice that is in a prescribed form giving particulars of the grounds that you are relying on. If the tenancy is assured, the notice is not prescribed so there is no standard form for it.

The grounds for possession are limited to anti-social behaviour grounds. The court will only make an order if the tenant, someone else living in the property or a visitor to the tenant's home has behaved or threatened to behave in a way which is capable of causing nuisance or annoyance. The court must also be satisfied that it is reasonable to make the order. If you want to pursue this step, take advice from your legal representative.

The tenant's take

The questions in this section cover key areas that you, as a tenant, should know the answers to. It answers questions about tenancy agreements and rent levels through to problems with the property you live in and rights that you may have to buy your own home one day.

Is there anything I should be aware of in the agreement?

The use of the phrase 'at any time when' indicates that the status of the tenancy can change during its term, depending on whether the landlord condition and the tenant condition (see page 150) are satisfied. Security is lost if either condition ceases to apply. There is no requirement for rent to be paid, nor exemption for low-rental tenancies. If you are ever in doubt about your agreement or have any queries, consult a legal representative before signing it.

I've heard about an introductory tenancy. What is this?

The Housing Act 1996 allowed local housing authorities to elect to set up an introductory tenancy scheme. When such an election is in place, any periodic tenancy or licence that would

otherwise be a secure tenancy will instead be an introductory tenancy: a one-year trial period before being given security of tenure. This cannot be applied to a tenant who already has a secure tenancy, even if it was for a different house or not granted by the local authority.

If you then prove suitable, your tenancy automatically becomes a secure one. If you don't, the local authority can obtain possession without having to prove the usual secure tenancy grounds. A court order will still be required and proceedings must be commenced during the trial period.

What rent control is there?

For secure tenancies, rents are fixed by the local authority, so you can't control the amount of rent paid, but you can claim Housing Benefit to help. However, if you have a tenancy that started before 15 January 1989

 The website for the Housing Ombudsman Service (HOS) is at www.housing-ombudsman.org.uk. Although the service is mainly aimed at landlords, there is nevertheless plenty of advice for tenants, too. Read also pages 150-3.

and you are a housing association or housing co-operative tenant, your rent is likely to have been registered and assessed by the rent officer. This means the rent won't be changed for two years from the start of the tenancy.

Can I make improvements to the property?

An implied term of every secure tenancy is that you can't undertake any improvement, alteration or addition to the property without the landlord's consent. This cannot be unreasonably withheld and if it is, you can proceed anyway. Technically, consent is required for installing a satellite dish or TV aerial, although such an act is unlikely to be accepted as grounds for possession.

Can I complain about my accommodation?

Tenants of registered social landlords can complain direct to the Housing Ombudsman Service. The ombudsman has wide powers to order the landlord to pay compensation, to alter contracts and to publicise poor practice.

Local authority tenants who are unhappy with the service they receive can complain to the authority's housing department or talk to their local councillor. They can also go to the local government ombudsman.

Can I sublet or take in a lodger?

A secure tenant can indeed take in lodgers but cannot part with possession or sublet without the written consent of the landlord – which cannot be unreasonably withheld. If you part with possession or sublet the whole house, the tenancy is no longer secure and the landlord will be entitled to possession on the termination of the tenancy.

Can I end a security of tenure?

Yes, a tenant can end a periodic tenancy with the usual notice to quit – see page 151.

Might I have a right to buy?

The right to buy gives secure tenants the option to buy the freehold of a house or a 125-year lease on a flat, and has proved very popular since its introduction in 1980. You or your spouse must have resided in public-sector accommodation for at least five years post January 2005, not necessarily all in the same property or as a secure tenant.

The discount depends on how long you have been a public-sector tenant, whether the property is a house or a flat (which get a higher discount), and the age and condition of the property. It is calculated as a percentage of the value of the property but there is a maximum discount for properties in different areas of the country. In parts of London and the southeast, for example, the maximum discount is £16,000, regardless of how much the property is worth.

Suspension of right to buy

A local authority landlord is entitled to apply to court for a suspension order providing that a right to buy may not be exercised in relation to a property. A court will not make a suspension order unless it is satisfied that the tenant or a person living or visiting the premises, engaged or threatened to engage in anti-social behaviour or used the premises for unlawful purposes. The court must also consider that it is reasonable to make an order.

You have the right to buy if you live in a housing association property and, under the Housing Act 1996, most tenants of registered provider of social housing have the right to buy their homes on the same terms as council tenants, provided the property was built or purchased with public money and has remained in the social rented sector. Secure tenants with a local authority may have the right to buy their own home, too. In the case of demoted tenancies (see page 153), different rules apply – seek advice.

How do I apply for the right to buy?

Contact your local council and request the right-to-buy claim form (RTB1). Complete and return the form, keeping a copy. The council has to provide a decision within four to eight weeks. It must give a reason for any refusal, and you can ask for a more detailed explanation. Contact a local advice centre if you are in this situation.

What should I do if I receive a court order?

If you receive a notice of intention to start possession proceedings, you will not get a notice to quit as well: the next step the landlord can take is to begin court proceedings. These must commence within 12 months, but if ground 2 (see page 170) is being alleged, the landlord can start possession proceedings as soon as the notice has been served.

If you decide to sell your home within the first five years, or it is repossessed by your mortgage lender during that time, you will have to repay some or all of the right-to-buy discount.

The grounds for possession relating to a public-sector tenancy are given on pages 170-1. Taking legal action is described on pages 160-1 and 167.

Legal action

Letting is a business, and disputes can occur, as in any other trade. This chapter explains the rights and responsibilities that tenants and landlords need to respect, and describes what you need to do if you have to start legal proceedings. In all cases, it is important to seek professional legal advice prior to taking any action.

10

Avoiding legal action

Start out on the right track and you are less likely to reach the position where legal action has to be taken. It is important that the rights and obligations of the landlord and tenant are clear in the tenancy agreement.

In the main, most tenants have a good renting experience and most landlords enjoy letting their properties. There are times, though, when things just go wrong. Sometimes these are due to human error or just bad luck and in these cases, the best thing to do as a landlord or tenant is find a compromise that you can both live with that brings any disagreements to a swift close.

There are times too when as a landlord or as a tenant you are deliberately targeted and have to take legal action to put the situation right, but this should always be a last resort.

To help avoid legal action on both sides and find ways of swiftly resolving situations, both landlords and tenants need to understand what their individual responsibilties are.

AS A LANDLORD

A landlord is generally responsible for the following:

- Providing an EPC when marketing the property.
- Any obligations that are agreed within the terms of the tenancy agreement.
- General property repairs.

 When creating a contract, you need to be aware of the Office of Fair Trading (OFT) guidance on unfair terms in tenancy agreements. This states that landlords and agents deal fairly with tenants and not balance tenancy terms so much in the landlord's favour that it affects the tenant's legal rights.

- Fire safety.
- Fixtures and fittings, such as baths, sinks, basins and other sanitaryware.
- Heating and hot water installations.
- The structure and exterior of the property (if the property is a flat, then other parts of the building or installations that the landlord owns and/or controls).
- Complying with legal regulations, such as gas and electrical safety regulations.
- Protecting the tenant's deposit in an independent scheme.
- Securing any licences required by the local authority, for example for licensed HMOs.

The landlord can also expect to have the the property handed back in the same condition and with the same items in it as at the start of the let.

See also 'Entering into a contract' on pages 79–87 and 'Managing the let' on pages 88–90 for more advice.

AS A TENANT

A tenant has the following rights:

- To understand when searching for a property how much it would cost to heat the home and how energy efficient it is via an EPC.
- To rent a property that is safe to live in with tried and tested utilities.
- To be allowed to live in the property without being harassed by the landlord who is not able to enter the premises without the tenant's permission unless in an emergency.
- To have things repaired in a reasonable time frame.

See also 'Entering into a contract' on pages 108–10 and 'A tenant's obligations' on pages 111–14 for more advice.

WHAT IF THE AGREEMENT ISN'T BEING FOLLOWED?

There are various ways of dealing with disputes, which are covered by the tenancy agreement.

First, whether you are a landlord or a tenant, you need to understand what it is that the other party is doing, has done or hasn't done and whether this had broken the agreement in some way. Ideally, if you have a good relationship with the each other, or indeed with the agent, it is worth making a phone call or meeting them to talk through the problem and what you would like to happen next. Make a note of the date, time and detail of the discussion, what was agreed and when things were agreed to be done by. If you can, also discuss what happens if the matter is not resolved as agreed.

If it's not possible to meet or nothing happens after the meeting or call, then you need to write to the other party, explaining what has happened (or not) and what needs to happen next. If you have to post a letter, do it via recorded delivery or if it's by email, ask for a 'read receipt'.

If there continues to be a problem, then you need to seek some specialist advice from someone like the Citizens Advice Bureau or a legal company and then write again (as above) and explain what will happen if nothing is done.

This process should solve the problem, but if not, as a landlord you need to decide whether the problem warrants taking steps towards eviction. If you are a tenant, you need to consider (and seek legal advice) as to whether you withhold some or part of your rent, or take steps to report the landlord/letting agent to a trade association or ombudsman.

If you rented/let the property through a council scheme or accommodation office, it might be worth approaching them to discuss what else you can do to resolve the problem.

Obtaining a court order

In most cases, a landlord needs to obtain a court order for regaining possession. The way to set about doing this varies, depending on your agreement.

To obtain a court order, you need to:

- Show that the tenancy has ended and that you have issued the appropriate termination notices.
- Prove there are grounds for possession.
- Show it is reasonable for the court to grant possession if the ground is discretionary rather than mandatory.

Following the grounds for possession (see right), information for each type of tenancy is given on pages 163–7.

If the landlord resorts to obtaining possession without a court order, this will normally amount to unlawful eviction, for which an injunction may be taken out against the landlord. If this is successful, he may be ordered to pay substantial damages, a fine or, in extreme cases, may even be sent to prison.

GROUNDS FOR POSSESSION

There are 17 grounds for possession relating to assured tenancies, all discretionary to some degree – they are described on pages 168–9. In addition, there are grounds for possession relating to public-sector tenancies, which are described on pages 170–1. At any time, it is important to gain independent legal advice for possession as it is a complicated matter and the legals may have changed once this book has been published.

Notice periods

You must serve a notice seeking possession of the property on the tenant before you start court proceedings. You must give the following amount of notice:

- For grounds 3, 4, 8, 10, 11, 12, 13, 15 or 17: at least two weeks.
- For grounds 1, 2, 5, 6, 7, 9, and 16: at least two months. If the tenancy is on a contractual periodic or statutory periodic basis, the notice period must end on the last day of a tenancy period. The notice period must also be at least as long as the

160

period of the tenancy, so that three months' notice must be given if it is a quarterly tenancy.

- **For ground 14:** you can start proceedings as soon as you have served a notice.

Grounds 1 to 5 (see page 168): These are grounds where you have to provide prior notice, which means these can usually only be used once you have notified the tenants in writing before the tenancy started that you always intended to ask for the property back on one of those grounds.

The court may give possession on grounds 1 or 2 if prior notice has not been given if the court considers there are reasons for not serving the notice. If you also have grounds for possession, then you have to give written notice to the tenant that you intend to go to court to seek possession. The period of the notice can be between two weeks and two months, depending on the ground that has been used. The notice must be given on a form (see box, right) required under Section 8 of the Housing Act 1988. This is called a 'notice seeking possession for property let under an assured tenancy or an assured agricultural occupancy'. This notice is available from law stationers and rent assessment panel offices.

 The forms for court orders are described in the Housing Act 1988. If you deviate from the format, you run the risk that the notice will be found to be defective. Although rare, there is provision for the court to suspend service of the notice if it is unreasonable. So check these forms with a specialist legal adviser.

The tenant should leave the property on the date specified in the court order. If this doesn't happen and the tenant refuses to leave, you cannot evict the tenant yourself as a claim could be made against you for unlawful harassment. You must apply for a warrant for possession from the court. The court will arrange for bailiffs to evict the tenant.

If a mandatory ground is used and the court orders possession, the tenant will have to leave on the date specified in the court order.

If a discretionary ground is used, the court has the discretion to either grant a final possession order or may allow the tenant to stay on at the property with a suspended possession order. The terms for allowance of the tenant

 Companies that will help you evict tenants either by yourself or do the work for you include www.landlordaction.co.uk, www.landlordlaw.co.uk or www.landlordzone.co.uk/rent_arrears_evictions.htm.

Occasions when you do not need a court order to obtain possession

The exceptional cases in which a court order is not needed are called 'excluded licences or tenancies'. These include resident landlords where the following conditions exist:

- The landlord/licensor occupied the property as his only or main residence before the tenancy/licence began, and under its terms the occupier now shares accommodation with them; or

- The occupier shares accommodation with one or more of the landlord's family and the following conditions also apply:
  a) The landlord/licensor's main home is in the same building (unless it is a purpose-built block of flats)
  b) A member of the landlord/licensor's family shares accommodation with the tenant-licensee.

Other excluded tenancies/licenses are:

- Holiday lets, where the occupier fails to vacate

- Gratuitous lettings, where the accommodation is made available rent-free

- Squatters and trespassers, where the agreement was given as a temporary measure

- Hostels, where the accommodation is a residential hostel.

In all other cases a court order is essential

- In any of these cases, you may still need to gain possession by obtaining a court order but a notice to quit may not need to be served under the Protection From Eviction Act 1977 and the occupant will not have any defence to a possession claim.
- No unreasonable force can be used to evict an occupant.

162

to stay on in the property would be to pay back an amount of rent arrears each week or to abide by the terms of the tenancy if possession was sought on anti-social behaviour. If a suspended possession order is made, the tenant cannot be evicted, provided the tenant meets the conditions.

If a tenant breaches the terms of a suspended possession order, then you are able to apply to the court for a final possession order. Which step you take depends on the terms of the order that was made by the court.

ASSURED SHORTHOLD TENANCIES

If the tenancy has expired and you do not wish to renew it, or if it is a periodic assured shorthold tenancy and you wish to terminate it and not grant a new tenancy to the same tenant, the procedure is:

- **Give at least two months' notice** under Section 21 of the 1988 Act (known as 'Section 21 notice' – see box, right) requiring possession when the notice expires.

 Sometimes a tenant will not answer the door and so cannot have notice served on them. Take a witness and put the notice through the letterbox before 5pm. It is then deemed to have been served on the following day.

- **If the tenant does not move out** as a result of the notification, you will have to go to court to seek a possession order. The court cannot make a possession order in the first six months of the tenancy. You must take legal advice at this point.
- **You do not need to issue a ground for possession** for an assured shorthold tenancy and there is an 'accelerated possession action' (see overleaf).
- **You also do not need to show** that granting possession is reasonable.

Section 21 notice

The precise form of this notice can vary, but it must be in writing and must specify the date of required possession, which cannot be sooner than two months after notice is served. You can obtain printed forms from law stationers or (in some cases free) from www.rla.org.uk, www.clickdocs.co.uk, www.landlordlaw.co.uk and www.landlordzone.co.uk.

The specified date cannot be earlier than the end of the fixed term, and if the fixed term has expired or tenancy was periodic, the date specified must be the last day of a rental period. So for a monthly tenancy with a rent day on the 15th of the month, the date specified will be the 14th of a month at least two months after the date of service. As the two-month notice period is a minimum, there is nothing to stop you issuing a Section 21 notice early in the tenancy, to take effect at the end of that six months' let.

If the tenancy was granted initially for more than six months, the notice cannot take effect before the fixed term expires. So if the tenancy was granted for 12 months, the notice is not effective until the end of that period. If you seek possession before it expires or during the first six months, it must be based on a ground for possession (see pages 168–9).

Accelerated possession

This is a quicker way to gain possession as there is no court hearing. However, take independent legal advice on any type of possession.

- **Find the county court for the area** where the property is situated, then fill in form N5B claim for possession (accelerated procedure), obtainable from Her Majesty's Courts Service.
- **You will also need to supply:**
  - A copy of the tenancy agreement.

- If the tenancy began before 28 February 1997, the notice stating that the tenancy would be an assured shorthold.
- The notice requiring possession served under Section 21 of the Housing Act 1988.
- A copy of the form and witness statement for each defendant.
- **You will need to pay a fee** before the action can commence.

The court posts the papers to the tenants with a form of reply allowing them to lodge an objection within 14 days if they wish to. The district judge checks the papers and any reply from the tenants and orders possession or, if the paperwork is not in order or the tenant has raised a legitimate issue, refers the matter for a hearing. If the court is satisfied that all is in order and there is no defence, it notifies tenant and landlord of the order for possession.

ORDINARY ASSURED TENANCIES

If you are trying to get possession on grounds 1, 3, 4 or 5 (see page 168), you can use the accelerated possession

This procedure only deals with possession claims and for the costs of making the application. Claims for rent arrears are covered by an ordinary possession action (see page 160).

164

action (see left) but otherwise (for instance, if you are also claiming for rent arrears), use the ordinary possession action on page 163.

Ending the tenancy

First, issue a 'claim form for possession of property' and a 'particulars of claim (rented residential premises)' form, both downloadable from www.hmcourts-service.gov.uk.

The completed form is filed at the local county court for the area where the property is situated, together with a copy for each tenant and the court fee. The court serves these forms and notifies both parties of the hearing date. The tenant can file a defence or reply if he or she is going to dispute the claim for possession.

The matter is listed before either a district judge or a circuit judge and both parties can give evidence. The judge must be satisfied that you have made your case, that the tenant has no defence and, if you are relying on a discretionary ground for possession, that a possession order is reasonable.

The standard procedure

This is slow but effective. If you are lucky, the defaulting tenant will move on receipt of a court summons, but he or she may wait until a judgement is given or for the bailiffs to arrive. The

process can take three to five months. The speed with which a case is heard is decided by factors such as the amount of arrears and the importance given to the defendant or the landlord keeping or regaining possession. Be aware that the Government spending cuts may mean there are a reduced number of courts, so cases may take longer.

- **Notice of proceedings** takes at least two weeks.
- **It takes an average two months** to get a hearing date.
- **A possession order** can be up to six weeks from the date of the hearing.

If the tenant doesn't leave, apply for an eviction appointment with a county court bailiff. It could take up to six weeks to get an appointment. Given this timescale, some landlords offer the tenant a month's free rent on condition that they move out. The loss of rental income is balanced by the opportunity to start re-letting the property when the month is over.

Online procedure

Rent possession proceedings can be issued online. The court issue fee is £50 cheaper than for a paper application and the progress of the case can be tracked online. The final hearing takes place at the county court.

To find the nearest county court, go to www.hmcourts-service.gov.uk or telephone 020 7189 2000 or 0845 456 8770. For more information on the online possession procedure, go to www.possessionclaim.gov.uk.

Legal action

ASSURED TENANCIES

Fully assured tenancies give the tenant full security of tenure under the Housing Act 1988. This section also applies to assured shorthold tenancies where the landlord is seeking possession before the end of the fixed term.

Ending the tenancy

- **You must serve notice under Section 8 of the Housing Act.** There is a set format for this form, which can be bought at law stationers or downloaded for a fee from sites, such as www.rla.org.uk, and other sites including www.clickdocs.co.uk and www.landlordlaw.co.uk.

PROTECTED AND STATUTORY TENANCIES

These tenancies created by the Rent Act 1977 offer great security to tenants, making it very hard for the landlord to get vacant possession.

Ending the tenancy

- **If the tenancy is periodic, you must serve a notice to quit,** properly known as notice requiring repossession, containing the information stipulated by the Protection from Eviction Act 1977 and the regulations made under that Act.
- **The eviction date** must be at least four weeks after the notice and must bring the tenancy to an end at the close of a complete period of the tenancy (for example, at the end of a month, if the tenancy is by the month).

- **It must also include the information that** if the tenant or licensee does not leave the dwelling, the landlord or licensor must get an order for possession from the court before the tenant or licensee can lawfully be evicted. The landlord or licensor cannot apply for such an order before the notice to quit or notice to determine has run out.

The form will be provided by your legal company or can be purchased from a law stationer or downloaded from www.clickdocs.co.uk and www.letlink.co.uk.

Grounds for possession

The landlord has to prove a ground for possession, which does not have to be specified in the notice to quit but will be pleaded in the court action. Some grounds are mandatory, others are not, but it is worth pointing out that rent arrears are always discretionary grounds in Rent Act cases, however large the sum, in contrast to those in assured and assured shorthold tenancies where serious arrears are mandatory grounds. The grounds are described on pages 168–9.

Reasonableness

If the ground stated is discretionary, the court will decide if it is reasonable to grant the order for possession. In rent arrears cases, it is common for the order to be suspended if the tenant pays the correct rent and an agreed amount with each payment to cover the arrears.

PUBLIC-SECTOR TENANCIES

If the landlord is a local authority, the Housing Act 1985 applies, but if it is a housing association and the tenancy was granted on or after 15 January 1989, the rules on assured and assured shorthold tenancies normally apply. So this advice relates only to council houses and flats.

Ending the tenancy

- The authority or landlord must serve a notice seeking possession in a prescribed form, giving at least four weeks' notice of intention to commence proceedings. The actual notice period is decided by when the rent is payable. For example, if it is a monthly rent, one calendar month's notice is needed. Notice is valid for 12 months, during which period the landlord can start proceedings at any time.

Grounds for possession

Unless it is an 'introductory tenancy' (see page 154), you will have to specify and prove a ground for possession (see pages 170–1). The court cannot make an order for possession on grounds 1–8 unless it considers it reasonable to do so. It can only agree to possession on grounds 9–11 if it is satisfied that suitable alternative accommodation will be available to the tenant when the order takes effect. Grounds 12–16 must be considered reasonable and, again, only if alternative accommodation is available.

Reasonableness

If the ground is discretionary (which includes rent arrears), the court decides if it is reasonable to grant possession.

In cases of rent arrears, the court often suspends the order if the tenant pays the correct rent and an agreed amount with each payment to cover the arrears.

OTHER TENANCIES

Some tenancies, such as where the landlord is resident, are not covered by the rules explained in this chapter, and offer no security of tenure. However, you, as landlord, will still need to show the tenancy has come to an end, or the licence to occupy has been terminated. An ordinary possession action in the local county court is subsequently required, with a hearing before a judge.

Ending the tenancy

- **If the tenancy/licence was for a fixed term,** no notice is required and possession proceedings can start as soon as the term ends.
- **If it is periodic,** you must give 'reasonable notice', which may be specified in the agreement or is otherwise generally agreed to be four weeks.

Grounds for possession

None are required.

Reasonableness

Not required.

Grounds for possession: assured tenancy

A tenant has to break one of these grounds before a court order can be obtained, as described on pages 160-1.

Mandatory grounds on which the court must order possession

Ground 1:
A prior notice ground
You used to live in the property as your main home. Or, so long as you or someone before you did when the tenancy started, you or your spouse require it to be lived in as your main home.

Ground 2:
A prior notice ground
The property is subject to a mortgage which was granted before the tenancy started and the lender, usually a bank or building society, wants to sell it, normally to pay off arrears.

Ground 3:
A prior notice ground
The tenancy is for a fixed term of not more than eight months and at some time during the 12 months before the tenancy started, the property was let for a holiday.

Ground 4:
A prior notice ground
The tenancy is for a fixed term of not more than 12 months and at some time during the 12 months before the tenancy started, the property was let to students by an educational establishment, such as a university or college.

Ground 5:
A prior notice ground
The property is held for use for a minister of religion and is now needed for that purpose.

Ground 6
You intend to substantially redevelop the property and cannot do so with the tenant there. The ground cannot be used where you, or someone before you, bought the property with an existing tenant, or where the work could be carried out without the tenant having to move. The tenant's removal expenses will have to be paid.

Ground 7
The former tenant, who must have had a contractual periodic tenancy or statutory periodic tenancy, has died in the 12 months before possession proceedings started and there is no one living there who has a right to succeed to the tenancy.

Ground 8
The tenant owed at lease two months' rent if the tenancy is on a monthly basis or eight weeks' rent if it is on a weekly basis, both when you gave notice seeking possession and at the date of the court hearing.

Note: This ground was amended by the Housing Act 1996 and applied from 28 February 1997.

Discretionary grounds on which the court may order possession

Ground 9
Suitable alternative accommodation is available for the tenant, or will be when the court order takes effect. The tenant's removal expenses will have to be paid.

Ground 10
The tenant was behind with his or her rent both when you served the notice seeking possession and when you began court proceedings.

Ground 11
Even if the tenant was not behind with his or her rent when you started possession proceedings, he or she has been persistently late paying the rent.

Ground 12
The tenant has broken one or more of the terms of the tenancy agreement, except the obligation to pay rent.

Ground 13
The condition of the property has got worse because of the behaviour of the tenant or any other person living there.

Ground 14
The tenant or someone living in or visiting the property who:
- Has caused, or is likely to cause, a nuisance or annoyance to someone living in or visiting the locality; or
- Has been convicted of using the property, or allowing it to be used, for immoral or illegal purposes, or an arrestable offence committed in the property or in the locality.

  Note: This ground was amended by the Housing Act 1996 and applies from 28 February 1997.

Ground 15
The condition of the furniture in the property has got worse because it has been ill treated by the tenant or any other person living there.

Ground 16
The tenancy was granted because the tenant was employed by you, or a former landlord, but he or she is no longer employed by you.

Ground 17
You were persuaded to grant the tenancy on the basis of a false statement knowingly or recklessly made by the tenant, or a person acting at the tenant's instigation.

  Note: This is a new ground added by the Housing Act 1996 and applies from 28 February 1997.

Grounds for possession: a public-sector tenancy

Ground 1
Rent lawfully due has not been paid or some other obligation under the tenancy has not been complied with. There is no minimum amount of rent which must be due before this ground is used, but the court takes into account the amount and frequency of the arrears in deciding if it is reasonable. Landlords, including those who are local authorities, must provide their tenants with an address in England or Wales at which documents can be served on them in order for the rent to be lawfully due.

Ground 2
The behaviour of the tenant or someone at the house (even a visitor) is or is likely to cause annoyance or nuisance to others in the neighbourhood, or they have been convicted of using the house for an illegal or immoral purpose or of an arrestable offence committed in the locality. This ground is identical to assured tenancy ground 14 and has been used by some authorities to 'clean up' housing estates.

Ground 2A
Intended to provide help to victims of domestic violence, this ground applies where the house was occupied by a couple (not necessarily married or of different sex) but the tenancy was in only one of their names. It allows for possession if one of the occupants has had to leave the house due to violence or the threat of it by the other and it is unlikely that they will return. It does not matter if they are not the tenant: the landlord can gain possession against the violent partner and thus provide a safe home for the victim.

Ground 3
The condition of the house has deteriorated due to the acts or neglect of the tenant or another resident. If it was the latter, it must be shown that the tenant has not taken reasonable steps to try to remove the other person.

Ground 4
The same as ground 3, but relating to the condition of the furniture provided by the landlord.

Ground 5
The landlord granted the tenancy due to a false statement by the tenant or their representative. This is the same as assured tenancy ground 17.

Ground 6
The tenancy was assigned to the tenant and a premium was paid in connection with this assignment. Secure tenancies cannot usually be assigned at all. If an unlawful assignment is made, the tenancy is no longer secure and the landlord can take possession without proving a ground.

Ground 7

The house is part of a building that is used mainly for non-housing purposes and the house was let to the tenant by reason of his employment and the tenant or a co-resident has behaved in a way that it would not be right for him to stay in the house, given the purpose for which the building is used.

Ground 8

The house was made available while the tenant's previous property was being repaired and this house is now ready.

Ground 9

The house is so overcrowded it is an offence under the Housing Act 1985. The definition of overcrowding is complex, but includes situations such as two or more people of different sexes over the age of 10 sharing a room, unless they are living together as man and wife.

Ground 10

The landlords intend to demolish or reconstruct the house and cannot reasonably do so without having obtained possession.

Ground 10A

The house is within the area of a redevelopment scheme approved by the Secretary of State or the Housing Corporation and the landlord intends to dispose of it in accordance with the scheme.

Ground 11

The landlord is a charity and the tenant's continued occupation of the house would conflict with the aims and objectives of the charity.

Ground 12

The house forms part of a building that is used mainly for non-housing purposes, was let to the tenant by reason of his employment, and is now required for occupation by another person in the landlord's employment.

Ground 13

The house has features designed to make it suitable for physically disabled persons, is no longer occupied by such a person, and the landlord requires possession to allow a disabled person to live in it.

Ground 14

The landlord is a housing association or trust which lets property to persons whose circumstances (other than financial) make it difficult for them to get housing, is no longer occupied by such a person, and possession is required for occupation by such a person.

Ground 15

The house is one of a group of houses let for occupation by persons with special needs, is no longer occupied by such a person, and possession is required for occupation by such a person.

Ground 16

The accommodation is more extensive than is reasonably required by the tenant and the tenancy vested in the tenant on the death of the previous tenant, who was not his spouse, and the notice of proceedings for possession was served between 6 and 12 months after the date of the previous tenant's death.

Hearing a possession action

The hearing of a possession action is normally held before a district judge, and you should attend to give evidence and the tenant is also obviously entitled to attend as well. If you are relying on discretionary grounds (see pages 161 and 169), the judge will decide if they are sufficient to make an order of possession.

The types of order are:

- **Absolute order for possession.** This specifies a date 14 days (for possession on mandatory grounds) after the hearing when the tenant must leave the property, unless they will suffer exceptional hardship, in which case the date is postponed by up to 42 days. When grounds are discretionary, the normal period is 28 days.

Order against the landlord

If you fail to make out a claim for possession, perhaps by not serving the appropriate notices properly, your proceedings may be dismissed. The tenant can then apply for an order for costs against you, and if the tenant succeeds in a counterclaim against you, he can claim damages.

- **Postponed order for possession.** These are used frequently in rent arrears cases. The court may decide to suspend the order if the tenant complies with obligations, typically paying off the arrears by instalments. If the tenant defaults on these terms, you can return to court to make the postponed order final.

Adjournment

When you are relying on discretionary grounds, the court may decide not to make a possession order at all, but adjourn to a later date or indefinitely subject to certain terms and conditions. Typical terms would be for the tenant to pay off the arrears by a certain amount each week or month. An adjournment is rather like a postponed order, except

See pages 169 to remind yourself of which grounds are more discretionary than others! There are strict laws laid down for which grounds the court has more leeway on than others.

that the landlord has to re-apply for a possession order if the tenant breaks the set terms.

Legal costs

The court decides who should pay the legal costs incurred. The successful party can make an application for costs as appropriate, and the court will decide how much the losing party should pay.

Enforcement of possession orders

If the tenant does not vacate by the date specified, the order must be enforced by the court bailiff. The landlord must apply for a 'warrant for possession' and the bailiff will carry out the eviction.

❝ The court can hand down an absolute order for possession or a suspended order for possession, depending on the circumstances. ❞

Harassment

Sadly, some landlords resort to making life hell for their tenants by disrupting their lives, making threats or using violence as a cheaper, easier, quicker method of eviction. This is traumatic for the tenant, but it is against the law and there are remedies they can pursue.

Here are some examples of unacceptable behaviour by landlords:

- Locking the tenant out, or preventing them from getting into part of the accommodation.
- Interfering with the gas, electricity or water supplies.
- Interfering with or confiscating tenant's possessions.
- Removing doors or windows.
- Persistently disturbing the tenant.
- Refusing to allow friends to visit.
- Moving in to part of the accommodation.
- Insisting that you hand over the keys.
- Using threats.
- Making abusive phone calls.
- Throwing out the tenant.

It is also possible for a tenant to harass a landlord and a landlord then has the right to go to law, too.

Dealing with harassment

As a tenant, never respond physically or abusively or withhold rent: tell your landlord in person or (better) in writing that they are disturbing your peaceful occupation of the property. If possible, have someone with you as a witness whenever you are speaking with the landlord. Keep dated notes of any relevant incidents.

The landlord should give 'reasonable' notice (which is generally 24 hours) if he or she wants to visit the property, and you are entitled to refuse entry if this is not given – this also gives you time to ensure a witness will be present. A landlord should never let himself into the

---

Get advice

People who may be able to help mediate or advise in disputes include:

- Most councils have a tenancy relations service or other staff who work in this field.
- Large institutions with accommodation offices usually have staff trained to help in this field.
- Students can consult their Student Union.
- Your local Citizens Advice office.
- If you believe an offence is being committed, call the police.

If a dispute is developing, get advice as soon as you can to try to stop the conflict escalating.

property, and entering it without permission is trespassing. If you feel threatened, you could add a security chain to the front door or change the locks, and you can also inform the police. If you are locked out, keep any keys you have as evidence.

Most disputes originate from simple misunderstandings that are allowed to escalate, and the majority of disputes can be settled early on through improved communication, sometimes with the help of a mediator. However, if things do get out of hand, tenants who receive poor treatment from their landlords may have civil remedies as well as criminal sanctions available to them. The basic remedies are damages, either compensation for loss suffered, or an injunction ordering the landlord to stop the behaviour.

CRIMINAL SANCTIONS

If you are dealing with harrassment, there are various legal sanctions designed to help you.

The Protection from Eviction Act 1977

This Act imposes criminal penalties for harassment and unlawful eviction, and proceedings are normally brought by the local authority (although private prosecutions are possible).

Protection from eviction

A residential occupier (which includes all tenants and licensees, whatever their statutory protection) cannot be evicted without a court order unless

Contact the landlord

It is usually preferable to settle a matter out of court and it is possible the landlord did not realise his actions were unlawful. If at all possible, you or your solicitor should contact the landlord or letting agent, even if only by telephone, and explain the problem. The matter may be resolved at this stage, and if not, the record of this contact can form part of the evidence on the landlord's conduct.

the landlord reasonably believes he no longer lives on the premises.

Protection from harassment

There are two offences of harassment:

- **Section 1(3) harassment** is an act likely to interfere with the peace or comfort of a residential occupier or to withhold services reasonably required for occupation with intent to cause the occupier to leave. Proving 'intent' may be difficult, but it can be presumed if the actions had a foreseeable result: removing the doors makes it very difficult for the occupier to remain on the property!
- **Section 1(3A) harassment** covers similarly defined acts that the landlord knows or has reasonable cause to believe will cause the occupier to leave. Because of the absence of the need to show 'intent' this offence is easier to prove.

The Criminal Law Act 1977

The police are responsible for prosecutions under this Act in which

Section 6(2) states it is an offence for anyone 'without lawful authority' to use or threaten to use violence to enter premises if there is someone there at the time who is opposed to the entry. Again, it is possible to prosecute privately.

Compensation in criminal proceedings

Section 35 of the Powers of the Criminal Courts Act 1973 gives magistrates the power to order compensation for personal injury, loss or damage resulting from an offence. This provides an easy, cost-free method for a tenant to obtain compensation, but magistrates' courts tend to award less than civil courts would, and are not empowered to order a landlord to restore a dispossessed tenant to a property.

CIVIL PROCEEDINGS

Criminal proceedings punish bad behaviour but are not always the best option for a dispossessed or threatened occupier who is more likely to want to claim for damages or obtain an injunction to stop the landlord's behaviour or to regain possession of the property. You have to go through civil proceedings in the county court.

Get a solicitor

It is possible to bring proceedings for harassment or unlawful eviction on a 'self-help' basis, but speed and accuracy are essential and, if possible, it makes sense to get professional help from a solicitor who has experience in landlord/tenant litigation. If you qualify for public funding, a solicitor can be instructed at little or no cost. If not, you can get assistance from law centres, housing advice centres, the local authority tenancy relations office and the Citizens Advice Bureau.

Injunctions

Injunctions aim to prevent the problem recurring. An occupier who has been awarded damages will still want protection and reassurance that the harassment won't happen again. Injunctions are discretionary. The court will try to hear both sides of the case before ordering an injunction unless it is clearly an emergency.

The proceedings

Proceedings take place in the county court for the area in which the premises are located or where the landlord lives.

Complete the claim form N1, available from www.justice.gov.uk/civil/procrules_fin/menus/forms.htm together with a statement of case, listing the cause of action, the relief or remedy sought and the material facts. An application notice should also be completed. Serve the relevant documents on the landlord at least two days before the hearing.

The hearing will be heard by a single judge, possibly in chambers. Often the judge accepts an undertaking from the landlord about future conduct without making a formal order – failing to comply would be contempt of court.

Scotland and Northern Ireland

The laws in Scotland and Northern Ireland differ in places from those in England and Wales. It is these differences that this chapter is concerned with.

Scotland

Housing law in Scotland differs in a variety of ways from the legislation for England and Wales and, on the whole, is more demanding of the landlord. This is a summary of the major differences, and as such is not exhaustive. From a legal perspective, please seek independent legal advice.

Unlike England and Wales, where a change of government has led to a halt in activity to increase regulation in the private rental sector, Scotland continues to legislate to improve the sector. This is despite the fact that their own research shows landlords and tenants in Scotland get on very well – according to the Scottish Government, '85 per cent of tenants were either "very or fairly satisfied".' This research also shows that the majority of landlords are individuals who own one or more properties. Most appear to invest for capital growth as opposed to income.

> **"There is a gap in landlord and tenant understanding of their legal obligations. "**

The research does, however, highlight the fact that there is a gap in landlord and tenant understanding of the rules and regulations they need to abide by. As a result, two very useful websites have been set up to help communicate the information that you need (see below).

LANDLORD RULES, REGULATIONS AND ACCREDITATION

As a landlord of Scottish properties (whether you live in Scotland or not) it is important to understand and abide by the rules and regulations, especially as the new Bill (see page 183), if passed, could impose £50,000 fines on you if you don't!

The Scottish Register

Since April 2006, private landlords of residential properties in Scotland have been required to register with the

 The websites set up to explain regulations for landlords and tenants are: www.betterrentingscotland.com and www.landlordregistrationscotland.gov.uk.

local authority the property is let in to ensure they are a 'fit and proper person' to let property. The scheme aims to take disreputable landlords out of the market and ensure that landlords co-operate with councils to try to reduce anti-social behaviour by tenants. At the time of going to print, six landlords have had their licence revoked.

If you are a landlord, you must register with every local authority where you let property (most agents also register). The registration fee is £55 per landlord plus £11 per property registered. If you own a property jointly, such as husband and wife, then you nominate one 'lead owner'. If you are unrelated, both owners need to be registered.

If you are letting out a house in multiple occupancy (HMO), you do not need to register (see right and pages 31–3), as you are covered by your HMO licence.

You can receive a 10 per cent discount on these fees if you apply online and if you work with multiple authorities.

As in England and Wales, you must also have an Energy Performance Certificate if you market properties for rent, and abide by the gas, electric, furniture and furnishings safety regulations (see pages 74–8).

In addition, any tenancy agreements must be fair, as regulated by the Office of Fair Trading.

House in Multiple Occupation (HMOs) Licence

In Scotland there is a specific definition of an HMO. The requirements to obtain an HMO licence may differ though from one local authority to another. The Government definition of an HMO is 'A house is an HMO if it is the only or principal residence of three or more qualifying persons from three or more families.' A 'house' is 'any building, or any part of a building occupied as a separate dwelling', so, really, all residential property. HMOs typically refer to lets such as student or anyone else that shares a property.

If you let a property as an HMO, you will need to make sure you have a licence or you can be fined up to £5,000 (or more if the Bill is passed, see page 183). You need to apply to the local authority for an HMO licence. To be accepted, both you and the property are vetted by the local authority and your application is sent to the police and fire authorities. In order to process your application, the property is normally inspected by the local authority and you will have to supply all the relevant safety certificates.

Details for the Scottish register are on www.landlordregistrationscotland.gov.uk. The accreditation scheme is on www.landlordaccreditationscotland.com. The grounds for possession in Scotland can be seen in full at www.scotland.gov.uk.

Licence fees vary depending on the local authority and the number of properties. They can be from £400 up to £1,800 initially and can be valid for up to three years when renewal fees are likely to apply.

Landlord (and letting agent) accreditation

In an effort to improve the knowledge of letting rules and regulations, landlords and letting agents can also join a voluntary accreditation scheme. This helps to reassure tenants that you are a good landlord or agent to rent from.

The accreditation scheme is free to individual landlords and for letting agents this varies from £50 to £350 depending on the number of properties managed. To be accredited you need to ensure you meet the Scottish Core Standards for Accredited Landlords and there is a two page summary checklist that you can view. To find out more and apply, visit www.landlordaccreditationscotland.com.

The Private Rented Housing (Scotland) Bill

This was laid before Parliament on 4 October 2010 and, if passed, the legislation is likely to come into effect from 31 August 2011.

Below is a summary of the proposed changes and new legislation that is currently included in the Bill. However, this may change as the Bill goes through Parliament, so please check for updates via the Landlord Accreditation Scheme (see page 103).

The key proposed changes to the Bill are:

- **Landlord Registration numbers** to be given legal status.
- **Definition of a 'fit and proper' person** will be expanded including allowing local authorities to obtain a criminal record check.
- **Increase the fine** for unregistered landlords and non-licensed HMOs to £50,000.
- **Include the power** to disqualify a landlord for up to five years.
- **Unregistered agents** can be charged a fee for any checks.
- **All property renting adverts** need to include the Landlord Registration Number (except 'to let' boards).
- **The Private Rented Housing Panel** is required to pass on any details to the local authority that are requested by them.
- **Allow Ministers** to increase the categories for HMO licensing.
- **Give the local authority powers** to address problems of overcrowding in privately rented homes.

 To find a solicitor in Scotland, look at www.lawscot.org.uk and for an HMO guide for landlords, go to www.scotland.gov.uk. The Private Rented Housing Panel is at www.prhpscotland.gov.uk. For legal housing advice, go to www.lawscot.org.uk.

- **Landlords and agents** must provide specified information to the tenant at the start of a tenancy.

TENANTS

It is important for anyone renting in Scotland to know that most legal protection only applies to tenancies, which in addition to the requirement for exclusive occupation (as in England) and payment of rent in money or in kind, should set the

❝ The good news for tenants in Scotland is that you only need to ensure your landlord is registered and, ideally, belongs to the Landlord Accreditation Scheme. ❞

Tenant's take

If you are renting in the private sector, then you have lots of ways to ensure you don't rent from a rogue landlord or rent a property that is unsafe – even more so than in England and Wales. Unfortunately, according to research from the Scottish Government, most tenants don't understand them. For example, 3 per cent of households don't have a tenancy agreement, 7 per cent agreed they don't understand their tenant rights and 2 per cent said they have never had their gas serviced.

The good news for Scottish tenants is that you just need to make sure that your landlord (or letting agent) is registered (see pages 181-2) and, ideally, belongs to the Landlord Accreditation Scheme. Other memberships that landlords or letting agents may belong to include:

- Scottish Association of Landlords
- National Landlords Association
- Scottish Rural Property and Business Association
- National Federation of Residential Landlords

For letting agents they should be members of ARLA and the Property Ombudsman Scheme and/or Royal Institution of Chartered Surveyors, Scotland.

Some rogue landlords might say they are registered and members of organisations. However, this might not be the case so it is important to check their registration online via www.landlordregistrationscotland.gov.uk and with the associations above.

For more help renting a property in Scotland, use our 'Viewing a property' help on page 105 and checklist on page 106 and if you have any problems with your landlord or letting agent during the tenancy, visit www.prhpscotland.gov.uk, who will help with disputes.

length of the rental period. If none is agreed, common law may imply a period of one year where the circumstances of the case allow such an implication to made. At the end of that period, unless the parties have contracted otherwise or any lesser period as the lease provides for under common law, the tenancy automatically renews for the same period unless the landlord or tenant has formally terminated the tenancy at the termination date. This is called 'tacit relocation'.

The agreement must be in writing if the tenancy is to last for more than a year. Licences are rarely used in Scotland: the courts have a wide definition of 'tenancy' and what is accepted as a licence in England might be classified as a tenancy north of the border. Licensees have fewer rights than tenants, especially regarding security of tenure.

PRIVATE-SECTOR TENANCIES

Tenants in the private sector are still small – accounting for approximately 7 per cent of housing stock – and they have different rights to those in the public sector.

❝Assured tenancy agreements must be in writing and the tenant must be given a copy free of charge. ❞

Assured tenancies

These were introduced to revitalise the Scottish private rented sector from 2 January 1989. An assured tenancy is essentially a tenancy at a market rent with a reduced degree of security. Assured tenancy agreements must be in writing and the tenant must be given a copy free of charge. If the tenancy has been terminated by a notice to quit or if it was inherited, the landlord can still increase the rent provided there is provision to do so in the tenancy agreement in the form of a formula or a specified rise. If there is no such provision, the rent can only be raised by a more complicated procedure and the tenant has the right to go to the Private Rented Housing Panel.

- **Succession:** An assured tenancy can be inherited by a spouse provided the house was his only or principal home at the time of death. The tenancy is called a statutory assured tenancy and can only be inherited once.
- **Security of tenure:** The general principal of security of tenure applies, so even after the contractual tenancy has been ended (for example, by a notice to quit), the tenant can stay under a statutory assured tenancy until the landlord recovers possession through a court order.
- **Obtaining possession:** To obtain an order for recovery of possession the landlord must do the following things

- Serve notice on the tenant, specifying the grounds.
- Terminate the contractual assured tenancy at its 'ish' (termination date or lease expiry) with notice to quit of at least 28 days.
- Raise an 'action for recovery for possession of heritable property' in the sheriff court for the area where the house is located. If the sheriff accepts one of grounds 1-8 of schedule 5 to the Housing (Scotland) Act 1988 are established, he must grant decree. If only one of grounds 9-17 are established, he may grant decree. The decree is issued two weeks later. The grounds for recovery are similar to those under English legislation (see pages 168–9).

Short assured tenancies

Introduced by the Housing (Scotland) Act 1988, these give little security of tenure. They are created when the landlord gives, prior to the creation of the tenancy, the proposed tenant a formal notice (the AT5) stating it will be a short assured tenancy. The term must be for a fixed period of not less than six months, which automatically renews unless either party gives formal notice otherwise. Although after the initial six-month period ends, the tenancy tends to roll on a month-on-month basis. A form of wording in the tenancy is required to cover this practice to ensure 'tacit relocation' doesn't happen.

In the past, a tenant could go to the Rent Assessment Committee (RAC) if the rent was thought to be too high. However, the RAC was absorbed into the Private Rented Housing Panel in September 2007 and now a rent can only be lowered if it is set significantly higher than the market rate.

- **Recovering possession:** No reason need be given when requesting an order for possession, and the sheriff must grant it if:
  - The tenancy has reached termination.
  - A valid Notice to Quit is served timeously (that is, in time which would be 40 clear days before the ish) and competently (in accordance with legislative requirements) preventing tacit relocation and terminating the tenancy at its ish.
  - No further contractual tenancy is in existence.
  - At least two months' notice has been given, followed by an AT6 (if the owner is repossessing) and a Section 33 notice.

Better repairs

The Scottish Government intend to make changes to the rules on repairing property which if passed will include an increase in the landlord's right to access the property to make the repairs. If they do not comply with repairing obligations, tenants can report them to the PRHP.

Protected tenancies

Very few of these tenancies remain as none have been created since 1989. For advice on a protected tenancy, consult a solicitor with experience in this area.

Statutory tenancies

A statutory tenancy offers similar rights to a protected or Assured or Short Assured tenancy and arises when a tenant remains in possession of a house after the contractual tenancy has been terminated (that is, by a notice to quit) or a tenant succeeded to the tenancy before 1990.

No repair, no rent

On 3 September 2007, Scotland introduced the Repairing Standard in Terms of the Housing (Scotland) Act 2006. It was introduced to ensure that private landlords keep a let home suitable for 'human habitation' and to bring into line the regulations in the private rental sector so they are similar to those in the social sector. Work on the property must be carried out to meet the repairing standards set out in this Act. The landlord is responsible for keeping the property and fixtures and fittings in a reasonable state of repair and in proper working order, for example:

- Making the property wind and watertight.
- The structure and exterior, including drains, gutters and pipes.
- Water and gas piping and electric wiring.
- Basins, sinks, baths and toilets.
- Any fixtures and fittings, such as gas fires and water heaters.
- The house needs to have satisfactory provision for detecting fires and for giving warning in the event of a fire or suspected fire.

If the landlord does not do this, sometimes the tenant withholds (but does not spend) rent equivalent to the amount owed for the service or problem. However, if a tenant, you must follow the procedure set out in your contract to the letter, or you risk the landlord taking action against you for non-payment of rent. If you are considering this, do not do so until you have obtained guidance from Citizens Advice or a solicitor.

Assigning and subletting

Assured tenants cannot assign, sublet or part with possession of any part of the property without the landlord's consent – and this can be refused without giving reasons. A permitted sub-tenant becomes a tenant of the landlord if the other tenancy ends for any reason.

"Common law tenants can stop other people entering without permission."

184

Harassment and eviction

Provision to prevent harassment and illegal eviction is similar to that of English law although it is essential to seek specialist legal advice.

Common law tenancies

If your tenancy is not regulated by any other laws, you still have rights under common law, which may apply if:

- **The landlord is also resident in the house,** using the property as their only or main home. A separate flat in the property does not meet this definition, and the landlord needn't own the house – he could be a tenant who is subletting.
- **The tenant is a student** in university-owned accommodation.
- **The landlord is in the police** or fire service.
- **The tenant is homeless,** living in temporary accommodation provided by the council.

Common law tenants have the right to possession, meaning they should be able to stop other people entering without permission.

- **Other people can only move** in to share the property with the consent of the landlord.
- **The agreement will automatically repeat** ('tacit relocation') unless either party gives notice otherwise.
- **Either party can give notice to quit** in writing at any time (although such notice may only apply at the termination date), giving four weeks' notice on a six-month let or 40 days on a year's lease. However, if the tenancy is not due to expire, the landlord can only ask the tenant to leave if they have broken a condition of the tenancy agreement and under specific grounds, getting an order from a sheriff.

PUBLIC-SECTOR TENANCIES

Most public-sector tenancies granted since 30 September 2002 are Scottish secure tenancies. These were created in the Housing (Scotland) Act 2001 and mean that virtually all tenants of local authorities and registered social landlords have the same terms of a single, common tenancy. Prior to this, council tenancies were termed 'secure tenancies', governed by the Housing (Scotland) Act 1987, while most housing association tenancies were assured tenancies governed by the Housing (Scotland) Act 1988. Exceptions to this change are:

- 'Short assured tenants' of registered social landlords remain short assured tenants.
- Some tenants will be given 'short Scottish secure tenancies' instead of 'Scottish secure tenancies'.

Scottish secure tenancies (SSTs) and short SSTs are complicated and if you have any issues, it is important to consult a legal specialist for your specific circumstances.

Northern Ireland

Much of the legislation covering letting and renting is the same as for England and Wales. However, it does appear that Northern Ireland is working more towards the Scottish model, so expect increased regulation for landlords and better protection for tenants.

THE PRIVATE SECTOR

In April 2007, new legislation was introduced that substantially changed the way the private rental sector operates. This new system, together with investor landlords buying and renting new, high quality properties, appears to have made good improvements to the private rental sector.

New strategy for private rentals

At the time of going to print, the Northern Ireland Housing Executive produced a new strategy for the private rental sector: Building Sound Foundations. This strategy suggests that the following new rules and regulations may be introduced in Northern Ireland in the future:

- Mandatory landlord registration.
- Increased notice to quit for tenants that live in the property for five or more years.
- Introduction of a tenancy deposit scheme (see below).

In the past, there were two types of tenancy agreement: controlled or uncontrolled. The main changes affect the controlled tenancy agreements, but also impact on the uncontrolled tenancies, because if they don't pass a fitness inspection, they will become 'interim controlled' until they do.

Controlled tenancy

A tenancy that is controlled is one that hasn't passed a fitness inspection report (see box, opposite) and used to include restricted and regulated tenancies and protected shorthold tenancies.

- **Restricted tenancies and regulated tenancies.** Restricted tenancies are usually old, small terraced houses in poor repair. The rent was set at its 1978 level of around £1 per week. A landlord can modernise the property and apply for it to

For more information on the possible introduction of a tenancy deposit scheme, visit www.dsdni.gov.uk/index/hsdiv-housing/private_rented_sector.htm and look out for free landlord seminars provided by your local authority.

The fitness inspection report

Once a tenancy is ready for renewal, or a landlord wishes to increase the rent, a fitness inspection report is carried out. This is a report made by the local district council, which assesses the fitness of a property for someone to live in. It is normally made at the request of the landlord but sometimes it can be at the request of a tenant if the property has fallen into disrepair.

The inspection costs £50 and, should it be passed, the landlord is then free to charge any rent.

However, if the fitness inspection report highlights any repairs that are required, the rent will then be controlled by the rent officer for Northern Ireland until the work has been done and a second – successful – inspection (costing £100) is made. This will check and assess factors that affect the property's condition such as:

- Structural stability.
- Any levels of damp (which could cause health problems).
- Provision for heating, lighting and ventilation.
- Adequate supply of water.
- Bathroom and waste water facilities.
- Kitchen and cooking facilities.

become a regulated tenancy. Under a controlled tenancy, restricted and regulated tenancies essentially stay the same, but tenants who have succession rights (see page 143) will now only be allowed one succession right.

- **Protected shorthold tenancies.** New legislation abolishes these types of tenancies and they will become uncontrolled tenancies.

If a landlord wishes to increase the rent on a restricted or regulated tenancy agreement, he or she has to apply to the rent officer and must have passed a fitness inspection report unless the property meets any of the following criteria:

- **Was built post 1945;** or
- **Had a regulated rent certificate** in the last ten years.
- **Was given a renovation grant** by the Housing Executive in the last ten years.
- **Was granted an HMO** within the last ten years.

If the fitness inspection report has not been carried out, the rent officer will set the rent on the assumption

For more details of the changes in legislation, visit www.nidirect.gov.uk/rent-control.htm information_leaflet_on_rent_controlled_tenancies.pdf. For information about HMOs (see pages 30–1) in Northern Ireland, go to www.housingadviceni.org/migrant-workers-sharing-accommodation.html.

that the property does not meet the standards.

Uncontrolled tenancy

Tenants in uncontrolled properties have increased rights. Before the new legislation, they would be entitled to a rent book, freedom from harassment and illegal eviction, a notice to quit period of 28 days, due process of law and the right to claim Housing Benefit.

Now, the tenant must also be given a copy of the tenancy agreement, or at least a statement in writing of the terms of their tenancy.

PUBLIC SECTOR TENANCIES

Social housing is regulated by the Northern Ireland Housing Executive (NIHE), and application forms for accommodation can be downloaded from its website. Tenants' rights are similar to those offered in social housing in England and Wales.

The NIHE operates a rent scheme to calculate the rent on most of its properties, based on points given according to fitness, age, design and amenities. A rent calculator (see below) allows tenants to estimate the rent payable on the type of house they need, and to see if their current rent is correct.

For more information about uncontrolled tenancies, go to www.nihe.gov.uk/publications/leaflets/Renting_Privately_HB_rent_etc.pdf. To calculate the rent due on NIHE housing, go to www.nihe.gov.uk.

Checking your agreement

Most of the time people rent and let out property without any problems. It's only when they do occur that we realise how important contractual agreements are. Rather than wait until then, whether you are a landlord or a tenant, make sure you get an independent legal lettings expert to check the contract and recommend changes.

12

Assured shorthold agreements

Most private tenancies between a landlord and tenant are assured shorthold tenancies (ASTs). This agreement lasts for at least six months (but could have a fixed term of many years) after which the landlord can claim possession through a court order, should the need arise. However, there is some protection for tenants against excessive rent.

The clauses highlighted on pages 191–9 are the main ones that you will see in an agreement. Although they run consecutively throughout this chapter, they may appear in a different order in the agreement you see.

The sample clauses covered in this section relate only to assured shorthold tenancies, so are not necessarily relevant to a company let.

 All guidance notes and clauses in this chapter are examples only and need to be used in conjunction with chapters 7 and 8. All explanations and notes are given in square brackets.

Help is at hand!

The Office of Fair Trading (OFT) produce a document that can be viewed online called 'Guidance on unfair terms in tenancy agreements'. It lays out what should be included in a tenancy agreement and what might be considered to be unfair (see pages 76 onwards).

If in doubt about signing a contract, either as a tenant or a landlord, for a view on whether the agreement is fair, you can visit your local:

- Trading standards office: go to www.tradingstandards.gov.uk to find your nearest office.
- Citizens Advice Bureau (CAB): go to www.adviceguide.org.uk to find your nearest CAB.
- Lettings specialist legal company.

 To download a checklist for an agreement, see www.which.co.uk/ rentingandletting. To download 'Guidance on unfair terms in tenancy agreements', go to www.which. co.uk/money/mortgages-and-property/guides/checking-a-letting-agreement/.

Top 10 dos and don'ts for ASTs

1 Don't sign a tenancy agreement unless it is easy to read and you have read every clause. If in any doubt, get it checked out by a legal expert.

2 Do ensure you take time (two days or more is acceptable) to check the agreement.

3 Don't sign an agreement that clearly includes clauses that don't apply, such as an agreement given to you by a landlord that is renting to you privately, but frequently mentions or refers to 'letting agent', or keeping a garden tidy when there isn't one!

4 Make sure that you have read and understood every clause in the tenancy agreement – if in doubt, ask an independent party BEFORE you sign.

5 Check that along with the agreement you have information about the tenancy deposit protection scheme (see pages 83–4).

6 As a tenant or landlord, query any clauses that are too 'onerous', such as 'no pets allowed' (see page 142).

7 If you are a landlord accepting a guarantor, make sure that the guarantor is present during the signing of the agreement to ensure they agree and understand the responsibility they are taking on. If this isn't possible, make sure you speak to them and they fully understand what they are signing.

8 Get a legal lettings specialist to check any additions or alterations to an agreement (otherwise changes you make could invalidate the agreement).

9 If you are a landlord, make sure you have met all the tenants that will be renting your property and check they have all signed the agreement.

10 Do ensure any new letting agreements are up to date with the latest legal changes.

DEFINITIONS

Some legal agreements are very confusing as they use a lot of legal terminology as opposed to 'plain English'. Here are the most used legal terms in a lettings contract:

- **'Agreement':** meaning, the tenancy agreement you sign. It usually states 'including any variation or amendment of it', which allows for specific changes to be made that could be requested by the tenant or the landlord or to adapt to changes in the law.

- **'Contents':** the landlord's fixtures, fittings, furniture and contents that belong to the landlord, listed in an attached inventory.

- **'Deposit':** the amount that a tenant normally pays to cover the landlord for rent arrears and if the tenant fails to fulfil his or her obligations.

- **'Term':** the amount of time agreed for the tenancy (normally a fixed term of six months for an AST

agreement). Some agents insist on a 12-month agreement, which ties you into a minimum of a six-month let, and then offers one to two months' notice (for both the landlord and tenant) to end the agreement. However, watch out – some agreements may not give you this six-month break clause, and it is vital to make sure you have an agreement checked with an independent legal lettings expert.

Some agreements may also give a summary of the 'key parts of the agreements' or these may be included in other clauses.

- **'the Term':** '...... months from and including ...... [specify commencement date], including any extension or holding over whether under the Housing Act 1988 or otherwise'.
- **'the Property':** [insert full postal address of property to be let].
- **'the Deposit':** '£..... pounds' [stating the amount in figures].
- **'the Rent':** '£....... pounds each month/week, payable in advance on the ... day of each month/week, the first payment payable .... and the method of payment [for example, direct debit].
- **'the Interest Rate':** '4 per cent [ranges from 4 to 6 per cent] per year above the base lending rate of .... Bank plc [should state the name of the bank]'.

PARTICULARS OF PARTIES INVOLVED

This typically refers to contact details of all those involved in the let. It may include reference to a 'guarantor' or 'relevant party', should a third party be supporting the tenant (see pages 200–01).

Date of contract

This is typically the day that the contract becomes binding and is therefore likely to be the start of the tenancy.

Parties involved in the agreement

As a landlord, try to ensure the address given by the tenant isn't just the property he or she is currently letting, but also an address where you can contact the tenant after the tenancy has ended.

As a tenant, ask for it to be clear how and who you contact if there is an emergency.

To aid communication, it is also advisable to have other ways to contact the parties concerned, such as an email and telephone number (preferably a landline and mobile).

❝ The date of the contract will be the start of the tenancy . ❞

Data protection

An additional clause that should be included is to cover circumstances where the landlord/agent can share the tenant's details with required third parties, such as the inventory clerk or utility companies, should there be any problems after the tenancy.

THE PROPERTY

These clauses usually define what constitutes 'The Property' and should include the property's address and the terms:

- **'fixtures and fittings':** for example, light fittings, fireplace, kitchen and bathroom fittings.

- **'effects set out in the inventory':** for example, a phone, washing machine, cleaning bucket.
- **'outside space' or 'garden':** for example, a garden, driveway, walls or fencing owned by the landlord.

THE DEPOSIT

This is one of the most important clauses to look for in an agreement – especially if you are the tenant. It is covered in more detail earlier in the book (see pages 83–4). The types of clauses that will apply may include those shown in the box on page 194.

Clauses relating to interest on the deposit

One of the questions often asked is who keeps the interest from the deposit monies held? Tenants often think it should be paid to them, but this may not be the case if the agreement says otherwise. Indeed, The DPS (see page 83) scheme is free because part of its costs are paid for by the interest generated from the

❝ Make sure there's a data protection clause to protect yourself. ❞

Clause examples: the deposit

1. The Landlord holds the deposit as security for:
   a. unpaid Rent or other money lawfully due to the Landlord; and
      unpaid accounts for gas, electricity, telephone, television licence, council tax, water and environmental and sewage charges;
   b. any other breach of the Tenant's Obligations; and
   c. any other claims made against the Landlord because of any acts or omissions of the Tenant.
2. The Landlord may, where it is reasonable to do so, take money from the Deposit:
   a. to cover the matters listed in Clause 1 above; and
   b. to pay on the Tenant's behalf the charges mentioned in the rest of the agreement; and
   c. to pay for gas, electricity, telephone and water services to be reconnected, if disconnected due to the Tenant's default.

The return of the tenant's deposit

1. Subject to clauses [which would result in the landlord keeping all or part of the deposit] set out in the Tenancy Deposit Protection Scheme rules, if the Tenant:
   a. complies with the Tenant's Obligations; and
   b. vacates the Property; and
   c. returns all the Property keys; and
   d. both the tenant and the landlord agree on any deductions then the Deposit (or the balance of it, if any), without interest, will be refunded to the Tenant, or where the Tenant is more than one person, to any of them, within 10 days of the Tenant and Landlord/Letting agent agreeing on the amount to be repaid.
2. If the amount lawfully due at the end of tenancy is more than the amount of the Deposit, the Tenant must reimburse the Landlord/Agent the excess within 14 days of the money being requested.

deposit with the rest being refunded to either the tenant or landlord. In other cases it may be the landlord or the letting agent that keeps the interest. For example:

'the Deposit (or the balance of it, if any) will be repaid without interest to the tenant', OR it may state who keeps the interest, for example: ' the Landlord or the Letting Agent'.

A further clause that may be added explains what happens if the landlord sells the property on, with the tenant still within the property (see the clause example, top box on page 195).

❝Tenancy deposit protection schemes have streamlined who holds what money and where. ❞

Clause example: the deposit if the property is sold

If the Landlord:

          sells his interest in the Property; and

          pays the Deposit (or balance of it, if any) to his buyer,

the Tenant shall release the previous owner from all claims and liabilities in respect of the Deposit.

RENT CLAUSES

These clauses cover everything that is relevant to paying rent, including how much, payment method, rental increases and what happens if the rent isn't paid (see the clause examples, box below). In some agreements, these clauses may come under the tenant and landlord obligations (see pages 197–9) or in the summary information at the start.

There are two ways of dealing with rent in an agreement.

- Rent information can be mentioned specifically in the AST (as below) OR
- The agreement may refer to a 'Section 13 notice', which advises that a tenant's rent is going to be increased (see page 145).

(see pages 197–9)
(see page 145)

❝ Rent clauses tell you how much to pay, when, increases and what happens if it's not paid. ❞

Clause examples: the rent

1. 'the Rent': £... (.......pounds) each month/week, payable in advance on the ... day of each month/week, the first payment payable .... and the method of payment [for example, direct debit].
2. To pay to the Landlord/Agent the Rent by [direct debit or other payment method] into the Landlord's/Agent's Bank Account according to the terms of the Agreement.
3. To pay to the Landlord on demand:
   a. interest at the following Interest Rate (......) on the Rent if the Rent or other money is not paid on time; and
   b. sufficient money to make up the deposit to its original amount; and
4. Unless a court orders otherwise, the tenant will pay Landlord's reasonable legal costs and expenses (including VAT), properly incurred, in:
   a. recovering Rent or other money from the Tenant; and
   b. enforcing the Agreement; and
   c. serving any notice on the Tenant in connection with the enforcement of the Tenant's Obligations; and
   d. recovering possession from the Tenant.

Clause examples: rent increases

1. The Landlord may increase the rent by giving Tenant .... months' notice in writing prior to a rent payment day specifying the amount of the new rent.
2. The Tenant will then pay the increased amount as the Rent on and from that rent payment day.
3. If the Tenant does not agree to the amount specified, he may give the Landlord not less than one month's notice in writing, expiring on any day [if the tenancy is periodic, then the notice should expire at the end of the period of the tenancy], terminating the tenancy from that day.

Rent increases for an AST are allowed if the agreement says so and via Section 13 of the Housing Act 1988, which provides a statutory procedure for rent increases. Rent increases are sensitive to introduce to tenants so it is essential either to have the clauses on rental agreements clearly in the tenancy agreement or seek specialist lettings legal advice if you apply to increase the rent under Section 13 of the Housing Act 1988.

POSSESSION AND NOTICES

These clauses explain how you need to give notice that as a tenant you

Clause examples: notices

1. Under section 48 of the Landlord and Tenant Act 1987 notices by the Tenant are to be left at, sent via ordinary post or sent by recorded delivery post to, the Landlord's/Agent's address as set out as below.
2. In the case of notices to be served on the Tenant, unless the Tenant has notified the Landlord of another address, they will be sent to the Property or the last known address of the Tenant.
3. If anyone is lawfully residing at the Property or if the tenancy is an assured shorthold tenancy, the Landlord must obtain a court order for possession of the Property before re-entering it.
4. If at any time the Landlord:
    a. requires the Property for occupation by himself or any member of his family; or
    b. wishes to sell the Property with vacant possession; or
    c. has died and the Landlord's personal representatives require vacant possession either to sell the Property or so that it can be occupied by a beneficiary under the Landlord's will or intestacy then, in any such case, the Landlord may terminate the tenancy by serving not less than two months' notice in writing.

want to quit the tenancy or as a landlord, take the property back into your possession. It is a complex area and, as such, is described in detail on pages 160–71.

TENANT'S OBLIGATIONS

Whether you are a tenant or a landlord, it is really important to read these clauses carefully so you understand what is expected. Clauses that explain the tenant's obligations are extensive. They can appear in a list or in a series of separate clauses (as on pages 198–9).

LANDLORD'S OBLIGATIONS

Some agreements don't have a separate section covering a landlord's obligations, as they are defined by law, so you may find that the clauses listed in the box below are specifically referred to in the agreement under headings such as 'Quiet Enjoyment'; 'Notices' or 'Insurance'.

As with tenant's obligations, it is imperative that both landlord and tenant understand these obligations. If you are a landlord and outsource the let to a letting agent, then it is crucial that you are clear – and have in writing (see pages 200–4) – which parts of the letting agreement you are responsible for and which the letting agent is responsible for.

FAIR WEAR AND TEAR

The fair wear and tear clause is often an area for confusion, and it is important for both the landlord

Clause examples: landlord's obligations

1. Quiet enjoyment
   The Landlord may keep keys to the Property, but during the Term may only enter the Property at reasonable times and on reasonable written notice [being at least 24 hours] having been given [except in cases of emergency].
2. Insurance
   The Landlord will supply a copy of the insurance policy and must purchase suitable insurance cover for the property which covers the property's fixtures and fittings; anything owned by the Landlord such as appliances and standard risks such as loss or damage from flooding, fire, storms, burst pipes. The Tenant must insure their own belongings under a separate insurance policy and can have the option to insure the Landlord's items against accidental damage caused by themselves.
3. Repair and Maintenance
   Under the Landlord & Tenant Act 1985 (as amended) the Landlord must keep good repair the structure and exterior of the Property and keep in repair and proper working order the installations in the Property for the supply of water, gas, electricity, sanitation and for space and water heating.

Clause examples: tenant's obligations

1. Replacing locks and keys if the Tenant loses any keys or breaches other security clauses; and
2. To pay during the Term a proportionate part of:
   a. the Council Tax for the Property; and
   b. of the water, sewerage and environmental charges for the Property; and
   c. the television licence fee for the Property.
   d. to use the Property as a home for one family only. [Note this is to avoid it being an HMO that might need to be licensed.]
3. Keep the Property and Contents clean and in good decorative repair, and in particular to:
   a. remove rubbish from the Property regularly; and
   b. protect the Property from frost damage; and
   c. ensure rooms are properly ventilated; and
   d. clean the inside of all windows regularly; and
   e. vacuum-clean all carpets regularly; and
   f. not to block any drains, pipes, sinks, basins or baths; and
   g. keep the garden tidy; and
   h. cut the grass regularly during the growing season; and
   i. not to allow the Property to become infested with vermin of any kind.
4. To comply with notices from the Landlord to remedy breaches of other clauses within a reasonable time. Not to, or allow anyone else to:
   a. Do anything that would cause the Landlord's insurance policy to become ineffective; or
   b. damage the Property or Contents; or
   c. remove the Contents from the Property; or
   d. change the locks at the Property; or
   e. alter, add or attach anything to the Property; or
   f. tamper with the water, telephone, gas or electricity systems and installations serving the Property; or
   q. overload, block up or damage any drains, pipes, wires or cables serving the Property; or
   h. assault or abuse the Landlord, the Landlord's agents or any members of the Landlord's family.
5. To notify the Landlord promptly of:
   a. any vermin, defects or disrepair in the Property or Contents; and
   b. any notices or mail addressed to the Landlord delivered to the Property.
6. To permit the Landlord and/or his Agent(s) to enter the Property at all reasonable times and on reasonable written notice [being at least 24 hours] having been given [except in cases of emergency] to:
   a. inspect the Property and Contents; or
   b. repair the Property; or
   c. repair or replace any of the Contents; or
   d. replace the locks at the Property; or
   e. comply with any legal obligations; or
   f. show prospective buyers or tenants around the Property.

7. Not to do or allow at the Property anything which:
   a. might cause a nuisance or annoyance to others; or
   b. is dangerous; or
   c. is illegal or immoral.
8. Not to, or allow others to keep any birds and animals at the Property (other than in secure cages or containers) without the consent of the Landlord, such consent not to be unreasonably withheld or delayed.
9. To ensure that all windows and doors are properly secured when the property is unattended.
10. Not to:
    a. assign; or
    b. underlet; or
    c. part with; or
    d. share possession
    of the Property or any part of it without the Landlord's consent, such consent not to be unreasonably withheld or delayed.
11. On the termination of the tenancy to return to the Landlord:
    a. the Property and the Contents in a clean and tidy condition in accordance with the Tenant's Obligations; and
    b. all keys to the Property.

and the tenant to understand what is considered to be fair wear and tear, and what is 'damage' to the property. Typical wording for this clause would be:

'The Tenant is not liable for fair wear and tear to the Property or Contents and is not liable to put the Property or Contents into a better condition than they were in at the commencement date of the Term.'

An example of fair wear and tear would be a carpet that becomes threadbare as opposed to a carpet that has been damaged in a way that wouldn't be classed as 'reasonable', such as holes caused by cigarettes. An inventory is essential to help with this issue.

To help avoid disputes over fair wear and tear versus damage, a qualified inventory clerk should be employed (see page 86).

SIGNING THE AGREEMENT

Finally, once you are happy with all the clauses in the agreement, the relevant parties will need to sign it. The witnesses should ideally be someone independent of the landlord and tenant – so not necessarily a relative.

OTHER CLAUSES

Agreements vary dramatically so you may find clauses other than the ones highlighted here. Some of these clauses are specific to certain circumstances, such as when a third party (for example, a parent) pays the deposit.

199

Other forms of agreement

There are two other forms of agreement that are used regularly: a guarantee agreement, where someone other than the tenant acts as a guarantor should the tenant default, and a terms of business letter, between a landlord and letting agent.

GUARANTEE AGREEMENT

The guarantee agreement is where someone (other than the tenant) agrees to 'insure' the landlord for the tenant's deposit value. The relevant clauses for the guarantor can either be added into the AST agreement or offered as a separate agreement with the particulars of parties involved (with the addition of the guarantor's details) and the property information at the start of the agreement and the signing details at the end.

The guarantor

As a guarantor is agreeing to pay the rent should the tenant default, it is usually a parent who signs the agreement, but it could be anyone or more than one person (for example, mother and father) if required. The guarantor can also agree to pay the deposit on the tenant's behalf.

There is no legal requirement for who can be a guarantor, but check and double check that they know what they have signed and are happy to be a guarantor and, most especially, have the money available!

TERMS OF BUSINESS AGREEMENT

This is an agreement that a landlord has to sign when handing over the full or part responsibility for letting a property to a letting agent. The most important details in a terms of business agreement are outlined on pages 202–4.

❝Always read a terms of business agreement before signing it.❞

Many landlords sign a terms of business agreement without even reading through it. It can be anything from a few pages to more than fifty, but however long it is, it is essential that as a landlord when you are considering an agent, this is one of the first things you read. Don't leave it until you have chosen your agent.

Clause examples: the guarantor

It is agreed as follows:

1. In consideration of the Landlord granting the Tenant a tenancy of the Property upon the terms of the Agreement, the Guarantor guarantees:
   a. the payment by the Tenant of the rent and any other monies lawfully due to the Landlord under the Agreement; and
   b. the performance and observance by the Tenant of all the other terms contained or implied in the Agreement.
2. The Guarantor covenants with the Landlord as follows:
   a. If the Tenant defaults in the payment of the rent or any other monies lawfully due to the Landlord under the Agreement, I will promptly upon written demand by the Landlord pay to the Landlord the full amount owing from the Tenant.
   b. If the Tenant defaults in the performance or observance of any of the terms contained or implied in the Agreement, I will promptly upon written demand by the Landlord pay to the Landlord all reasonable losses, damages, expenses and costs which the Landlord has reasonably incurred because of the Tenant's breaches.
3. It is agreed that this Guarantee cannot be revoked by the Guarantor:
   a. for so long as the tenancy created by the Agreement continues;
4. This Guarantee is not to be revoked by:
   a. the death of the Guarantor [or any of the Guarantors]; or
   b. the death of the Tenant [or any of the Tenants]; or
   c. the bankruptcy of the Tenant [or any of the Tenants].
5. This Guarantee continues in operation:
   a. notwithstanding any alteration of the terms of the Agreement including any increase in the amount of the rent payable for the Property; and
   b. in relation to any new or further tenancy entered into between the Tenant and the Landlord; and
   c. in relation to any statutory periodic tenancy which may arise in the Tenant's favour under the Housing Act 1988; and
   d. notwithstanding that the Agreement may be terminated during the term by agreement, court order, notice, re-entry, forfeiture or otherwise; and
   e. notwithstanding any arrangement made between the Landlord and the Tenant (whether or not with the Guarantor's consent) nor by any indulgence or forbearance shown by the Landlord to the Tenant.
6. This Guarantee constitutes the Guarantor as principal debtor.
7. Any demand by the Landlord under the terms of this Guarantee shall be validly made if sent by registered or recorded delivery post or left at the address(es) specified above as the Guarantor's address or such other address(es) as the Guarantor may notify to the Landlord.
8. Where there is more than one Guarantor, the Guarantor's Obligations will be joint and individual.
9. Where there is more than one Tenant, references in this Guarantee to 'the Tenant' shall be construed as referring to all or both or either or any of the persons so named.

Services on offer

These are likely to include:

- Tenant find, which is where the landlord only pays the agent to find a tenant and thereafter the landlord is responsible for the let while the tenant is in the property.
- Let only.
- Let with rent collection.
- Full management.

Pre-instruction

These clauses include information such as:

- **The landlord appoints the agent** to act on their behalf.
- **The landlord must comply** with the following regulations:
  - Gas Safety (Installation and Use) Regulations 1998.
  - Plugs and Sockets Etc (Safety) Regulations 1994 and Electrical Equipment (Safety) Regulations 1994.
  - Furniture and Furnishings (Fire) (Safety) Regulations 1988.
  - Usually a minimum of one smoke alarm per floor (although this is not a legal requirement, it is a good idea to do this as a landlord).
  - Building regulations.
- **The landlord must give the following information** and confirmation:
  - That the property is clean and fit to rent out.
  - If a leasehold property, that the landlord has permission to rent out the property.
  - If the property is mortgaged, that the landlord has permission from the lender to rent out the property.
  - If the agent doesn't handle the deposit, it is the landlord's responsibility to protect it via one of the three protection schemes (see page 83).
- **The landlord must confirm there is adequate insurance cover** for the property or purchase it from the letting agent. Most agents will charge a 10 per cent fee (excluding VAT) for handling insurance claims. If an agent is either directly selling or offering to handle claims insurance for you, they MUST be registered with the Financial Services Authority (FSA) and must be on their letterhead. To find a registered IFA, go to www.fsa.gov.uk.

Fees

These can vary dramatically and make the difference between what is a competitive full management fee and one where you are being stung with charges you thought were included. It is important, therefore, that at the outset you establish if the agent:

- **Is entitled to commission** earned as set out in the scale of charges.
- **Will make any additional charges** (this may be set out in the scale of charges only).
- **Is required to give notice** to the landlord for increasing their charges (usually two months).

- **Can keep the interest** earned on the rental income from their account to when it is deposited in the landlord's account and, in some cases, that they can keep interest on deposits held too.
- **Can claim back any costs incurred** due to errors made by the landlord or the agent spending money to comply with the letting's contract.
- **Can impose additional charges** for looking after any insurance claims.
- **Can charge for statements** given to third parties, such as accountants.
- **Is duty bound to release information** on monies the landlord earns to the HMRC if requested.
- **Will add a commission charge** for introducing a buyer for the landlord's property.

If letting property to a tenant on Housing Benefit, there will also be a clause that ensures any money collected in rent by the agent classed as an overpayment will have to be reimbursed to the local authority. The landlord will then have to pay back the agent the monies previously received.

Scale of charges

A good agent will give a landlord one sheet of paper explaining all the charges the landlord will incur during the tenancy. It should also outline any 'additional' work and how much it will cost on an hourly rate so you know in advance how much you would pay before you sign up with the agent.

The scale of charges should include the following items.

- **An amount that the letting agent may hold back** for emergencies in your account, for example £250.
- **What is and isn't included** in each of the services provided, such as:
  - Visits to the property are sometimes included in full management charges, other times they are additional.
  - Set-up fees may include the cost of an inventory (for checking in and out), or they may charge extra.
  - Tenancy agreements may be included in letting the property or they may be charged extra.
  - Notification of whether the agent charges a percentage fee for organising tradesmen into the landlord's property.

Normally agents will charge for repairs:

- No additional fee; or
- 10 per cent over a fixed cost of works, for example £250 or £500; or
- 10 per cent on all works organised by the agent.

Typical costs to be aware of include:

- **Costs of different services:**
  - Tenant Find.
  - Let only.
  - Let with rent collection.

- Full management. Some agents charge a lower full management fee the more years that you let the property through them, so check whether the charges are the same ongoing or if you can negotiate lower fees after the first year.
- **There may be clauses that charge other fees,** such as:
  - Professional hourly rate for additional work.
  - Property visits to empty properties.
  - Re-signing fee for the tenant.
  - Costs of inventory, energy performance certificates (see page 54), gas and electrical safety certificates.
- **Whether the costs quoted include VAT or not,** which is 20 per cent, so for every £100 costs incurred, this is actually £20. By law, the OFT require all consumer contracts to include VAT.
- **Handling deposit disputes,** such as preparation work for dispute resolution.

- **Some agents may charge you banking transfer fees** – these can add up, so check whether this is free or not when comparing the cost of different letting agents.

Exclusion of liability or indemnity clause

This is a clause that protects the agent from any claims made against them that are due to the landlord's errors.

Termination of agreement

This can vary dramatically from one agent to another but typically will state that you have to give one to two months' notice to the agent that you wish to end your arrangement. If you pull out of the letting agreement once a tenant has been found but not yet moved in, there may be a charge that you have to pay for pulling out at this late stage.

 Do not sign a terms of business agreement that states 'other charges are available on request' without getting a full list of charges and checking the agreement with an independent legal lettings expert.

Glossary

Accelerated possession procedure (APP): A way for landlords to gain possession of their property quickly and cheaply, without a court hearing.

Accreditation scheme: A voluntary system for checking that landlords offer a reasonable service, often run by local authorities or other interested parties.

Assured shorthold tenancy (AST): Now the most common form of tenancy, at the end of which the landlord can repossess the property.

Assured tenancy: A type of tenancy which offers the tenant good security of tenure.

Buy to let: Buying a property in order to let it to a paying tenant.

Buying off plan: Purchasing un-built new property from the plans.

County court judgement (CCJ): A judgement for debt recorded at a county court, which will show up in a credit check.

Credit check: Check on a person's credit rating which will show if they pay their bills. Usually carried out by a credit reference agency.

Deposit: A sum of money that is paid in advance to cover any potential costs of damage to the rented property or should you fail to pay the rent. If there is no damage when you leave the property, all the deposit should be returned to you.

DSS: Department for Social Security, now part of the Department of Work and Pensions. DSS is still used as a term describing tenants who receive Housing Benefit.

Energy Performance Certificate (EPC): This rates your home on how much energy it takes to keep it warm and lit. It gives information on how much it costs and what you can do to make your home more energy efficient and reduce carbon dioxide emissions.

Eviction: Forced, legal removal of a tenant.

Fair rent: The rent determined by a rent officer (or a rent assessment committee) under a regulated tenancy.

Financial Services Authority (FSA): www.fsa.gov.uk.

Fixed or ascertainable period: The period of a tenancy or lease must be defined from the outset, stipulating when it is to begin and when or how it is to end. Although the tenancy of a periodic letting can go on indefinitely, either party can terminate it by giving notice to quit, which expires at the end of a relevant week or month, meeting the requirement of certainty that the arrangement will end at some point.

Gearing: How much you borrow versus an independent valuation of the property/property portfolio.

Ground rent: Payment by the leaseholder to the freeholder. Low sums are sometimes referred to as a peppercorn rent.

Grounds for possession: Grounds for possession may be cited in possession proceedings against a tenant when a landlord wants to regain possession of his or her property. There are separate grounds for possession relating to assured tenancies and public-sector tenancies. They were laid down in the Housing Act 1988, as amended by the Housing Act 1996. Landlords may also seek possession when it can be demonstrated that a tenant is no longer using the accommodation as his or her principal home.

Guarantor: Someone, often a parent, who agrees to pay the rent for the tenant in case of default.

Harassment: Actions which interfere with the peace or comfort of the tenant, such as violence, threats, or removing access to services. Harassment is a criminal offence under the Protection from Eviction Act 1977.

House in multiple occupation (HMO): Three unrelated people sharing a property's facilities and some communal rooms. Some HMOs must be licensed. The definition of an HMO is different in Scotland.

Housing Benefit: State support covering part or all of the rent payable by someone on a low income. Likely to be replaced eventually by the local housing allowance.

Housing Health and Safety Rating System (HHSRS): Scheme which provides a hazard rating for all residential property. It requires the structures, means of access, outbuildings, gardens and other spaces to be safe and healthy environments for occupants and visitors.

Independent financial adviser (IFA): Someone trained in the complexities of financial management. Always check that anyone you speak to is regulated by the FSA.

Inventory: A list of items that are in the rented property on your arrival.

Lease: The same as a tenancy, but the term is usually used to indicate that the property is let for a fixed term, such as six months or a certain number of years, while the

word 'tenancy' suggests periodic letting from week to week or month to month.

Leasehold: Ownership for a set period, most commonly applied to flats and other shared buildings.

Let as a separate dwelling: The property cannot be let for business purposes, and must be a 'single dwelling' (not, for example, a house converted into several flats – although each of these separate flats could fall within the definition). It must be 'separate', which boils down to whether the tenant regards and treats it as 'home'. For example, a single room could qualify as a dwelling even if the tenant has the right to share other rooms, such as a kitchen or a bathroom. If the facilities are shared with the landlord, the tenancy would then not be seen as an assured or shorthold tenancy because it has a 'resident landlord'.

Licence: If the occupier is only given the right to share the property (for example, with the owner) rather than have exclusive use of a specific part of it, the arrangement would be a licence, not a lease or a tenancy. This is an important point because tenants have far greater statutory legal protection than licensees.

Long-term let: A fixed-term let (usually of six months) that is for residential use.

National Approved Letting Scheme (NALS): Government backed accreditation scheme for letting and letting management agents.

National Inspection Council for Electrical Installation Contracting (NICEIC): Independent consumer safety organisation for the electrical contracting industry.

Non-resident landlords scheme: A scheme for taxing the UK rental income of non-resident landlords in which the tax is deducted by the letting agent or the tenant.

Notice to quit: Properly known as notice requiring repossession but also known as a Section 21 notice as it is issued under Section 21 of the Housing Act 1989, this is notice to a tenant that they must vacate a property at the end of an assured shorthold tenancy agreement.

Ordinary assured tenancy: See Assured tenancy.

Registered rent: A maximum rent on a property set by the Rent Service or Rent Assessment Committee (RAC), publicly available on the Rent Register. Registered rents (often known as Fair Rents) apply to regulated tenancies.

Regulated tenancy: A type of tenancy created by the Rent Act 1977 and ended from 15 January 1989 which offers excellent security of tenure and a regulated rent.

Rent-a-Room Scheme: System offering tax relief when you rent out a room in your own house.

Rent Assessment Committee (RAC): Two- or three-strong panel of people with expertise in the property field who can set a legal maximum rent on a property. There are 14 RACs in England and Wales.

Rent officer: Local authority official who deals with Housing Benefit and liaises with the rent service.

Rent Service: Agency which carries out rental valuations, sets fair rent levels and provides other information to local authorities. The Rent Service is part of the Department for Work and Pensions.

Rental yield: The annual rent of a property as a percentage of its capital value or acquisition price.

Reservation fee: A sum of money that may be payable to a letting agency to keep a property on hold while you get hold of a deposit and/or references.

Resident landlord: Landlord living on the same premises as a tenant.

Return on investment: A more detailed analysis of income versus expenditure in order to establish a long-term view of profit on a let property.

Security of tenure: Gives the tenant an indefinite right to stay, unless the landlord has specific grounds for eviction.

Service charges: Payment for maintenance of shared areas, such as hallways, the roof and drains.

Shorthold tenancy: See Assured shorthold tenancy.

Short-term let: A furnished let of between one week and three months.

Stamp duty land tax (SDLT): Tax payable on property purchases and on the notification of tenancy agreements.

Subletting: When a tenant lets part of all of a property to another party.

Tenancy: An arrangement with two key requirements: the letting is for a 'fixed or ascertainable period of time' and it grants 'exclusive possession' of the property. Although this is usually in return for rent, such a charge is not legally part of the tenancy.

Tenancy deposit protection schemes: Schemes aiming to keep tenants' deposits safe and to solve disputes over how much the landlord is allowed to keep to cover damage caused during the tenancy.

Turnover: The amount that you earn from rent.

Void: Period when a property is unlet.

Yield: How much money your property is earning.

Useful addresses

Accreditation Network UK
155/157 Woodhouse Lane
Leeds LS2 3ED
Tel: 0113 205 3404
www.anuk.org.uk

Association of British Insurers
51 Gresham Street
London EC2V 7HQ
Tel: 020 7600 3333
www.abi.org.uk

The Association of Independent Inventory Clerks (AIIC)
PO Box 1288
West End
Woking
Surrey GU24 9WE
www.theaiic.co.uk

Association of Residential Letting Agents (ARLA)
Arbon House
6 Tournament Court
Edgehill Drive
Warwick CV34 6LG
Tel: 0844 387 0555
www.arla.co.uk

Citizens Advice Bureau
Myddelton House
115–123 Pentonville Road
London N1 9LZ
Tel: see your local phone book
www.citizensadvice.org.uk (England and Wales)
www.citizensadvice.co.uk (NI)
www.cas.org.uk (Scotland)

Council for Licensed Conveyancers (CLC)
16 Glebe Road
Chelmsford
Essex CM1 1QG
Tel: 01245 349599
www.conveyancer.org.uk

Council of Mortgage Lenders (CML)
Bush House
North West Wing
Aldwych
London WC2B 4PJ
Tel: 0845 373 6771
www.cml.org.uk

The Council for Registered Gas Installers (CORGI)
1 Elmwood
Chineham Park
Crockford Lane
Basingstoke
Hants RG24 8WG
Tel: 0870 4012200
www.trustcorgi.com

Department for Business Innovation & Skills
Response Centre
1 Victoria Street
London SW1H 0ET
Tel: 020 7215 5000
www.bis.gov.uk

Department for Work and Pensions (DWP)
Room 112
The Adelphi
1–11 John Adam Street
London WC2N 6HT
Tel: 020 7712 2171
www.dwp.gov.uk

The Deposit Protection Service (DPS)
The Pavilions
Bridgwater Road
Bristol BS99 6AA
Tel: 0844 4727 000
www.depositprotection.com

Designs on Property Ltd
Newland House
The Point
Weaver Road
Lincoln LN6 3QN
Tel: 0845 838 1763
www.designsonproperty.co.uk

Financial Ombudsman Service (FOS)
South Quay Plaza
183 Marsh Wall
London E14 9SR
Tel: 020 7964 1000
www.financialombudsman.org.uk

Financial Services Authority (FSA)
25 The North Colonnade
Canary Wharf
London E14 5HS
Tel: 020 7066 1000
www.fsa.gov.uk

Her Majesty's Courts Service (HMCS)
102 Petty France
London SW1H 9HD
Tel: 0845 601 5935
www.hmcourts-service.gov.uk

Her Majesty's Revenue & Customs (HMRC)
Stamp Office helpline: 0845 603 0135
www.hmrc.gov.uk

Homecheck
Landmark Information Group
The Smith Centre
The Fairmile
Henley-on-Thames RG9 6AB
Tel: 0844 844 9966
www.homecheck.co.uk

The Housing Rights Service
Middleton Buildings
10-12 High Street
Belfast BT1 2BA
Tel: 028 90245640
www.housingrights.org.uk

The Inventory Manager
Tel: 0844 725 2000
www.theinventorymanager.co.uk

Land and Property Services
1st Floor
Lincoln Building
27-45 Great Victoria Street
Malone Lower
Belfast BT2 7SL
Tel: 028 9025 1515
www.lpsni.gov.uk

Landlordzone
Parkmatic Publications Limited
2 Moor Way
Hawkshaw
Lancashire BL8 4LF
Tel: 0845 260 4420
www.landlordzone.co.uk

Law Society of England and Wales
113 Chancery Lane
London WC2A 1PL
Tel: 020 7242 1222
www.lawsociety.org.uk

Law Society of Ireland
Blackhall Place
Dublin 7
Tel: 0353 1672 4800
www.lawsociety.ie

Law Society of Northern Ireland
Law Society House
98 Victoria Street
Belfast BT1 3GN
Tel: 028 90 231614
www.lawsoc-ni.org

Law Society of Scotland
26 Drumsheugh Gardens
Edinburgh EH3 7YR
Tel: 0131 226 7411
www.lawscot.org.uk

Legal Services Ombudsman
3rd Floor, Sunlight House
Quay Street
Manchester M33JZ
Tel: 0845 601 0794
www.olso.org

mydeposits
Ground Floor, Kingmaker House
Station Road
New Barnet
Hertfordshire EN5 1NZ
Tel: 0844 980 0290
www.mydeposits.co.uk

National Approved Letting Scheme
Tavistock House
5 Rodney Road
Cheltenham GL50 1HX
Tel: 01242 581712
www.nalscheme.co.uk

National Association of Estate Agents (NAEA)
Arbon House
6 Tournament Court
Edgehill Drive
Warwick CV34 6LG
Tel: 0844 387 0555
www.naea.co.uk

National Inspection Council for Electrical Installation Contracting (NICEIC)
Warwick House
Houghton Hall Park
Houghton Regis
Dunstable
Bedfordshire LU5 5ZX
Tel: 0870 013 0382
www.niceic.org.uk

National Landlords Association (NLA)
22–26 Albert Embankment
London SE1 7TJ
Tel: 020 7840 8900
www.landlords.org.uk

Northern Ireland Federation of Housing Associations
6c Citylink Business Park
Albert Street
Belfast BT12 4HB
Tel: 028 9023 0446
www.nifha.org

Northern Ireland Ombudsman
Freepost BEL 1478
Belfast BT1 6BR
Tel: 0800 34 34 24
www.ni-ombudsman.org.uk

The Office of Fair Trading (OFT)
Fleetbank House
2–6 Salisbury Square
London EC4Y 8JX
Tel: 020 7211 8000
Consumer helpline: 0845 7224499
www.oft.gov.uk

OneSearch
1st Floor, Skypark SP1
8 Elliot Place
Glasgow G3 8EP
Tel: 0800 052 0117
www.surveysonline.co.uk

Rentchecks.com
Creditas Ltd
Church House
102 Pendlebury Road
Swinton M27 4BF
Tel: 0844 412 7752
www.rentchecks.com

Residential Landlords Association (RLA)
1 Roebuck Lane
Sale
Manchester M33 7SY
Tel: 0161 962 0010 or
0845 666 5000
www.rla.org.uk

Royal Institution of Chartered Surveyors (RICS)
Parliament Square
London SW1P 3AD
Tel: 0870 333 1600
www.rics.org

Scottish Association of Landlords
20 Forth Street
Edinburgh EH1 3LH
Tel: 0131 270 4774
www.scottishlandlords.com

Scottish Federation of Housing Associations
Pegasus House
375 West George Street
Glasgow G2 4LW
Tel: 0141 332 8113
www.sfha.co.uk

Scottish Legal Services Ombudsman
Scottish Legal Complaints Commission
The Stamp Office
10–14 Waterloo Place
Edinburgh EH1 3EG
Tel: 0131 528 5111
www.slso.org.uk

Shelter
88 Old Street
London EC1V 9HU
Tel: 0808 800 4444
http://england.shelter.org.uk

The Tenancy Deposit Scheme
The Dispute Service Ltd
PO Box 1255
Hemel Hempstead
Herts HP1 9GN
Tel: 0845 226 7837
www.thedisputeservice.co.uk

Tenant Services Authority (TSA)
Maple House
149 Tottenham Court Road
London W1T 7BN
Tel: 0845 230 7000
www.tenantservicesauthority.org

Tenant Verify
Parkmatic Publications Limited
2 Moor Way
Hawkshaw
Lancashire BL8 4LF
Tel: 0845 260 4421
www.tenantverify.co.uk

UK Association of Letting Agents (UKALA)
PO Box 10582
Colchester
CO1 9JD
Tel: 01206 765456
www.ukala.org.uk

UpMyStreet
111 Buckingham Palace Road
London SW1W 0SR
www.upmystreet.com

Property websites

www.eigroup.co.uk

www.findaproperty.com

www.fish4.co.uk/homes

www.heritage.co.uk

www.houseprices.co.uk

www.houseweb.co.uk

www.myhouseprice.com

www.ourproperty.co.uk

www.periodproperty.co.uk

www.primelocation.com

www.propertybroker.co.uk

www.propertynews.com (for Northern Ireland and Ireland)

www.rightmove.co.uk

www.ruralpropertyindex.co.uk

www.ruralscene.co.uk

Websites dealing with property-related money and legal issues

http://wales.gov.uk/topics/housingandcommunity/housing/ (housing news in Wales)

www.betterrentingscotland.com (general advice on renting in Scotland)

www.communitylegaladvice.org.uk (Community Legal Advice)

www.direct.gov.uk (directory of public services)

www.housingcorp.co.uk (portal for social housing)

www.landlordlaw.co.uk (legal documents online shop)

www.landlordregistrationscotland.gov.uk (information on the Landlord Register in Scotland)

www.landreg.gov.uk (registers title to land in England and Wales)

www.lawscot.org.uk (details of local solicitors in Scotland)

www.lease-advice.org (Leasehold Advisory Service)

www.letsure.co.uk (has links to specialist insurers)

www.lloydsbankinggroup.com/media1/research/house_price_calculator_page.asp (Halifax/Lloyds House Price Index)

www.moneynet.co.uk (finance comparisons)

www.nationwide.co.uk/hpi (Nationwide house price index)

www.rooms.co.uk (shared ownership information in Scotland and England)

www.scotland.gov.uk/Topics/Housing/Housing (all aspects of housing in Scotland)

www.tradingstandards.gov.uk (consumer protection information)

Index

Index

Which? is the leading independent consumer champion in the UK. A not-for-profit organisation, we exist to make individuals as powerful as the organisations they deal with in everyday life. The next few pages give you a taster of our many products and services. For more information, log on to www.which.co.uk or call 01992 822800.

Which? Online

www.which.co.uk gives you access to all Which? content online and much, much more. It's updated regularly, so you can read hundreds of product reports and Best Buy recommendations, keep up to date with Which? campaigns, compare products, use our financial planning tools and search for the best cars on the market. You can also register for email updates and browse our online shop – so what are you waiting for? To subscribe, go to www.which.co.uk.

Which? Legal Service

Which? Legal Service offers immediate access to first-class legal advice at unrivalled value. Members can enjoy unlimited legal advice by telephone on a wide variety of legal topics, including consumer law – problems with goods and services – employment law, holiday problems, neighbour disputes, parking, speeding and clamping fines and tenancy advice for private residential tenants in England and Wales. To subscribe, call the membership hotline: 01992 822800 or go to www.whichlegalservice.co.uk.

Which? Money

Whether you want to boost your pension, make your savings work harder or simply need to find the best credit card, *Which? Money* has the information you need. *Which? Money* offers you honest, unbiased reviews of the best (and worst) new personal finance deals, from bank accounts to loans, credit cards to savings accounts. Throughout the magazine you will find tips and ideas to make your budget go further plus dozens of Best Buys. To subscribe, go to www.which.co.uk.

www.which.co.uk/books

Other books available from Which? Books

NEW EDITION Buy, Sell & Move House

Kate Faulkner
ISBN: 978 1 84490 108 1
Price £10.99

Navigating the property market is difficult, whether you are a first-time buyer or trying to climb the property ladder. *Buy, Sell & Move House* makes the process as smooth as possible, explaining how to avoid being gazumped, gazundered or getting stuck in a chain. This new edition of the bestselling guide also contains valuable information on dealing with changing housing markets.

Property Investor's Handbook

Kate Faulkner
ISBN: 978 1 84490 051 0
Price £10.99

Property Investor's Handbook is the essential read for both the would-be and the more experienced investor. From buy to let and off-plan to new-build and buying overseas, this book is packed with practical advice and tips on how to plan and research your investment, plus the latest information on renovation, property funds and syndicates.

Hiring Builders and Professionals

ISBN: 978 1 84490 076 3
Price £9.99

An indispensable guide to hiring contractors and ensuring your project is completed on time and within budget, and how to complain if it's not. *Hiring Builders and Professionals* covers estate agents and gardeners as well as builders and lawyers, looking at the legal qualifications and paperwork contractors should have, as well as how to plan timescales and schedules, and keeping costs under control.

NEW EDITION Tax Handbook 2011/12 – Available Spring 2011

Tony Levene
ISBN: 978 1 84490 119 7
Price £10.99

Tax Handbook 2011/12 is essential reading for all UK taxpayers, from employees and freelancers to retirees planning to give money to loved ones. Cut through the red tape and easily navigate the current tax system using the no-nonsense advice and practical tips featured in this book. Tony Levene, award-winning consumer champion, demystifies tax and explains the essentials, including how to avoid making those common mistakes when filling in a self-assessment form online.

NEW EDITION Pensions Explained

Jonquil Lowe
ISBN: 978 1 84490 110 4
Price £10.99

Gone are the days when you could rely on the state pension to provide a comfortable retirement. Fully revised and updated, *Pensions Explained* offers a complete guide to saving for your retirement, covering all the options available, and issues such as how much to put aside and pension investments. This practical and accessible handbook takes a realistic look at how you can safeguard your future, whether you're setting up a pension for the first time or approaching retirement age, moving company pensions or setting up a private scheme.

Making a Civil Claim

Melanie McDonald
ISBN: 978 1 84490 037 4
Price £10.99

Making a Civil Claim is essential reading for anyone involved in a dispute and/or potentially facing court or even a trial. It covers small claims as well as fast-track and multi-track cases and explains everything from mediation and legal aid to finding the right solicitor or barrister for your case.

Which? Books

Which? Books provide impartial, expert advice on everyday matters from finance to law, property to major life events. We also publish the UK's bestselling restaurant guide, *The Good Food Guide*. To find out more about Which? Books, log on to www.which.co.uk/books or call 01992 822800.

❝ Which? tackles the issues that really matter to consumers and gives you the advice and active support you need to buy the right products. ❞

I wish to thank everyone at Text Publishing, especially my editor, Penny Hueston, for her artistry and care. Emily Kitchin, at Hodder & Stoughton UK, was a joy from beginning to end.

I thank my fellow writers who assisted with the novel at various stages: Suzy Zail, Richard Holt, Carla Fedi, Brooke Maggs, Michelle Deans, Melinda Dundas, Ann Bolch, Rebecca Colless, Mary Delahunty, Vivienne Ullman and Nghiem Tran.

I am grateful to my mother, Jane Mills, for understanding the process.

Most importantly, loving thanks to Adam, Amaya and Toby.